MONOCHROMICON

THE COMPLETE MONOCHROME TRILOGY

ALSO BY TODD KEISLING

MONOCHROMICON

THE COMPLETE MONOCHROME TRILOGY

TODD
KEISLING

PRECIPICE

— 2025 —

PRECIPICE

www.toddkeisling.com

This book is dedicated to my longtime editor and dear friend, Amelia Bennett. You were right. It really was a trilogy.

TABLE OF
CONTENTS

FOREWORD

by Amelia Bennett

I t was the fall of 1998, and I was in the basement of a picturesque suburban home about 30 minutes from Chicago the first time it happened. The boy I'd been spending time with when I had a chance to get off campus had just given me a tour of his family home, and now he was telling me more about the band he played drums for.

"We did a little time in the studio. Do you wanna hear the rough tracks?" They weren't mastered yet, but I would get the gist of their sound. We talked about music a lot when we'd hang out, had even caught a couple shows in the city at the Metro or Fireside Bowl.

"Yeah, let's hear it."

The recording was, as promised, unpolished. Naïve, even. None of the band members were old enough to buy liquor, but their talent was as clear as their lack of experience. The singer was a baby, just fifteen. He lived here, too—my charming host's younger brother.

And when I heard his voice, I knew I was hearing Somebody.

Before I graduated from college, the group would get a mention in Rolling Stone and be plucked from the Chicago scene for a mentorship with one of the greats of grunge. Odds are good you've heard this same voice if you've caught the Superbowl, or watched TV, or seen the occasional big Hollywood film.

Experiences like that, where you run across Somebody before anybody else really does, are rare. People trot out the clichés about lightning in a bottle, but the truth is that being around Somebody really is electric.

It happened to me again in the first half of 2005. I had joined an online forum, of sorts, where creatives of all kinds gathered to share their work, provide feedback to each other, or—in the case of at least one couple—fall in love. Maybe I shouldn't have been surprised, but I was.

This time, I was in an IRC chat room. Todd and I had been running in the same circles, and had interacted with each other's writing a bit, but we hadn't yet met in the virtual sense. And the moment we did is just as clear in my memory, twenty years later, as that day in a basement outside Chicago.

"Omg, it's THE Todd."

Did you know you could meet your brother that way, two thousand miles apart and with next to nothing in common? I counted myself a poet back then, and made fun of the way Todd's writing rambled and meandered and spent words generously, while my own style was more terse. Either way, I knew he was Somebody.

"You don't know when to shut up," I taunted.

"You haven't got anything to say," he shot back.

He designed a pair of mugs with these jokes on them, and we sold a smattering of them to our friends and erstwhile fans. I still have one above my precious espresso machine.

Years later, I would tell him about a continuity error I found in his novel, in which the protagonist picks up his mug twice in the span of about as many pages, without having put it down. When he decided to clean up the manuscript in order to re-publish it, he asked me to edit it for him.

"You probably want to hire an editor, Todd. Someone who knows what they're doing."

"Yes. You're my editor."

At the time, I was close to flickering out of existence myself, but Todd saw me and told me who I was. Stubborn and insightful as always, Todd gently insisted that I was wrong about myself, and his project wouldn't be the same with another editor. Over the next decade, we'd take turns being right about Donovan's journey through the Monochrome. We met in person, got to know and love each other's families, and proved the old adage about the blood of battle being thicker than the water of the womb. Sure, the battle wasn't literal, but we fought it together anyhow.

I balked again when Todd asked me to write the foreword to the omnibus. I don't have an audience with the potential to goose his sales. He should ask a writer. Someone whose words will add something to his story.

"Yes. You are a writer."

It remains to be seen who's right this time, but once again, Todd has insisted and I have relented. This is the nature of our back-and-forth.

But it's not that he's always right. In fact, if he were, the book you're holding would be much shorter: a diptych. After *A Life Transparent*, Todd and I agreed that Donovan's story wasn't over. So Todd ventured back into the Monochrome to bring back *The Liminal Man*, I learned to use Tracked Changes to bring the editing process out of the stone age, and this time at the end of the book it was my turn to be right. He wasn't done.

It was a trilogy.

It took ten more years and a lot of spent ink to bring about *Nonentity*. Every couple of years, between other projects or when the internal pressure built up some steam, Todd and I would have a strategy call to bounce plot elements back and forth. There were some false starts, lots of rewrites, and even a few discussions about quietly closing out the project without the final installment, but I had a feeling Todd couldn't leave Donovan and Donna forever, not without the ending they fought so hard for.

So whether you're about to visit the Candles for the first time, or a struggle with your own Flickering is bringing you back for an injection of motivation, welcome to the Monochrome.

Keep your eyes peeled for Cretins.

Amelia Bennett
Chandler, Arizona
April 2025

BOOK I
A LIFE TRANSPARENT

THIS BANAL COIL
1986 CE

Albert Sparrow didn't know the man all that well, which made him easier to kill. Smith huddled near the mouth of the alley, his dirty paws reaching out in supplication to the people passing by. Sparrow admired Smith's humility even though it would profit him nothing. No one ever saw them, and if their master was to be believed, no one ever would.

"Spare some change?"

Smith's pleas fell on deaf ears. Lunchtime crowds raced down the sidewalks, busy with daily tasks and self-importance. The smell from a pizzeria across the street carried over, displacing the funk of garbage and exhaust fumes.

Sparrow looked into the sunlight, basking in its simple radiance. He licked the air, tasting its intricacies. Every moment of freedom from the gray was a cherished blessing. He couldn't remember how long he'd been trapped there, or what today's date was. Fortunately, it wouldn't matter for much longer, not after he'd done what he had to do. He'd had an idea, a flash of brilliance in the gloom, and it would lead him to salvation.

"Anyone? Change for food? Haven't eaten for days."

Sparrow tried to ignore Smith's grating pleas, busying himself with the task at hand. He knelt beside the dumpster and shoved his arm into the dark gap underneath. His fingers blindly searched through the grime that blanketed the alley floor. Where was it? Sparrow sucked in his breath, stemming the panic rising in his gut. After years locked away in a drab prison, the idea struck him suddenly, violently, and he'd spent weeks planning for this moment. He only had this one chance to follow through. Their warden would not allow him another opportunity.

His heart raced with adrenaline. He wouldn't go back. Not to the fate that awaited him. The master had plans for him. Grand plans. He heard that monotone voice in his head, booming: *We will shuffle you off your banal coil, Mr. Sparrow, and it will be glorious. The Ungod will unmake you in its unlight, and then you will be perfect.*

Sparrow's searching fingers finally skated over the blade. He smiled, pulling the knife from its hiding place and caressing it in his hand. A day's food rations, a mugging, a liquor store robbery. Who knew such a simple object would carry such a high price? Contraband, he supposed, had a steep cost—but here in this colorful void, their warden had little control.

"Mister? Coins for a sorry soul?"

Albert Sparrow climbed to his feet. He took a breath, listened to his heartbeat, and tasted copper on his tongue. Smith continued his futile begging, oblivious to Sparrow's slow advance toward the mouth of the alley.

Overhead, the sky dimmed. Cars crowding the street faded from view. The occupants of the busy sidewalks dissipated into transparent outlines, ghosts wandering a desolate painting of civilization. Sparrow gripped the rusty blade by its hilt and stood behind Smith.

"They can't hear you," Sparrow said.

"I can try." Smith offered his companion a fleeting glance. The world lightened, flooding with color once more. Cars and people returned in full form. "There's always hope I can change things."

Sparrow raised the blade but hesitated. He almost pitied the man. "We made our choices. Some of us belong here."

Smith scoffed. "Easy for you to say. You've got his favor. The rest of us are going to rot." He pulled back his sleeve, revealing pale flesh marked with clusters of gray pox. "Bastard's sucking us dry."

Nothing ventured, Sparrow thought. He sliced the air in a short arc, plunging the rusted blade deep into the man's neck. *Nothing gained.*

Smith convulsed in shock, clutching for his throat as blood spurted into the air. He turned, eyes wide in shock, one hand grasping for the weapon. In an act of twisted benevolence Sparrow yanked the blade free, gritting his teeth as a gout of blood shot from the wound.

"Sorry, friend. You're my ticket out."

Smith sank to his knees, gurgling in agony as he struggled to breathe. A moment later, Smith's body crumpled in a bloody heap. Sparrow watched as life left the man's eyes.

He dropped the knife and stumbled backward. The sky dimmed and the world flashed gray, erasing all features and life in an instant. A force clutched at his stomach, threatening to tear it from him, but after a moment it relented. Crowds and traffic reappeared.

Sparrow sucked in the air, calming himself as he wiped Smith's blood on his pant leg. Smiling into the sunlight, he walked out of the alleyway toward traffic.

His master spoke in a whisper, tickling at the back of his neck. In the gray world beyond, his master's voice would've boomed across the heavens, through the very fibers of his being. Here in the glorious sunlight, the old monk's words were no more threatening than the soft kiss of the wind.

You are breaking the rules, Mr. Sparrow.

But Sparrow was running, and he would not look back.

1

A LIFE ORDINARY

Present Day

Donovan Candle stirred in his sleep, eyes fluttering behind their lids as the alarm blared. He struggled to keep himself wrapped in the warmth of sleep, treading the peaceful waters of an otherwise vivid dream.

Donna's elbow promptly jabbed his ribs. His eyes snapped open, and after silencing the alarm, Donovan sat up. He stared at the clock and frowned. He'd already lost two minutes of his morning.

He was careful not to disturb Donna, whose alarm was set to wake her fifteen minutes later. She justified those fifteen minutes, saying she needed them on account of beauty rest, and he didn't argue. Donovan paused at the door and looked over at her sleeping face. He smiled and made his way to the bathroom.

An unsteady feeling rose in his gut, a sensation like fingers curling around his insides, tugging. He put a hand to his belly, steadied himself, and waited for it to pass.

What the hell was that?

The feeling relented, giving way to a low rumble of hunger. He shrugged it off and busied himself with a shower and shave.

Donna was awake when he finished. The coffee maker gurgled downstairs, and a scent of frying eggs made his stomach growl. He went to the bedroom and dressed. smiled when his watch struck 7:00. *Right on schedule*, he thought, and wandered downstairs for breakfast. Donna greeted him with bleary eyes, a tender smile, and a kiss. He poured himself a cup of coffee and winced when the pull in his stomach resurfaced.

"You okay?"

"Yeah," he said, rubbing his gut. "It's a stomach thing."

"I hope you're not getting sick." Donna brought over the frying pan and served his eggs.

"Thanks, hon. How are you feeling today?"

"Not too bad. The pain in my hip has dulled. There's bacon on the stove, too." She returned to the counter and placed the pan in the sink. Donovan watched her move slowly, carefully, with purpose. Her fibro flares were bad as of late, often leaving her semi-crippled half the day until her medication kicked in. *One day at a time,* he thought.

"Aren't you going to eat?"

Two pieces of toast popped out of the toaster. Donna tossed them onto a plate and returned to the table. "I'm starting a diet today."

"A diet?" He took a bite of eggs and dabbed his chin with his napkin. Donna nibbled her toast.

"Yeah," she said. "I want to lose a few pounds."

"I think you look great, honey."

"But *I* don't." She took another bite of toast. They finished breakfast in silence. When he was done, Donovan took his plate to the sink, poured himself a second cup of coffee, and went for the newspaper. He checked his watch again. 7:22.

When he returned to the kitchen, he kissed Donna once more.

She blushed. "What was that for?"

"Nothing. I can tell today's going to be a good day."

"Yeah?"

He nodded. "It's just a feeling, I guess. Besides, everything's still on schedule, so that always makes for a good day."

Donna chuckled. He delighted in her laughter. The sound of it made his heart skip a beat, and always brought a smile to his face. A good morning indeed. Still grinning, Donovan sat and unfolded his newspaper. There wasn't much worth reading—mostly articles about local politics, the announcement of a new reality television show's premiere, rising taxes, falling stocks, and so on. He beamed when he saw a familiar advertisement: *"Has your identity been compromised? We can help! Contact Identinel, your security sentinel."*

He'd worked for the company going on nine years, although it had been a bumpy road at first. Fresh out of college, he'd quickly learned that an English degree was useless. The liberal arts were sinking fast, and needing something to make ends meet, Donovan had finally taken a low-end position in the sales department of Identinel.

Nine years later, he'd managed to work his way up the corporate ladder rung by agonizing rung, and now he was a team leader in his department. Sometime soon, hopefully tomorrow, he would receive another promotion. Spotting the company's latest ad in the paper was a good omen. He skimmed the rest of the paper and finished off his coffee.

"Anything good?"

He passed the newspaper down to her and shook his head. "Same 'ol, same 'ol."

The microwave clock read 7:39, which Donovan confirmed with his watch. If he left now, he'd make it to the office with a good twenty minutes or so to spare. His punctuality could earn him a few points when it came time for his review.

"I think I'm going to leave early today, hon."

"What's the rush?"

"No rush," he said, rising from the table. "That review's tomorrow. I want to impress Butler."

She snorted. "I hope he paid attention this time."

Donovan shared his wife's disdain. Impressing Butler was no easy task, given his inflated sense of self-accomplishment, but Donovan had proven himself reliable and earned the highest sales record for four years in a row. How could he *not* have earned this promotion?

"I'd better be going," he said.

"Don't forget to charge your phone."

He double-checked his pocket, nodding as the phone knocked against his car keys. Donovan had resisted acquiring one for as long as he could, but Donna wore down his arguments, and they'd settled on a pre-paid model. A new addition to his morning routine, he still struggled to remember charging it. The damn thing drained its battery every day.

"Got it."

Donna's attention remained with the newspaper. "Have a good day, dear."

"What, no kiss?"

She looked up at him, arching an eyebrow. "You'll get more than that tonight, Donnie."

Donovan grinned, leaning over to kiss her. He felt a flush of heat in his cheeks. He loved it when she called him Donnie.

"Hold that thought," he told her, and opened the door. Mr. Precious Paws, their brown-haired Persian housecat, scampered out past him, furry head and tail held high. *Excuse me, your highness.*

He stood on the porch and breathed in the crisp, morning air. That phantom hand tugged at his gut for only a moment and then it was gone. Donovan steadied himself. He looked up. The sky was clear. Birds chirped overhead.

He slowly exhaled and smiled.

A good day, he thought. *A very, very good day.*

The morning commute was bumper to bumper for most of the way, as it was on every weekday, but nothing could dampen his spirits. He wasn't about to give up his good mood for a few angry drivers. The heavy traffic let up after ten minutes, and soon Donovan was speeding down the freeway listening to a morning radio host welcome a guest on the air.

Bits and pieces of the show worked their way into his thoughts as he navigated the car. The guest was an author promoting his latest book.

"—itle of the book is *A Life Ordinary: A Comprehensive Study in Human Mediocrity.*"

Donovan frowned. A life ordinary? What was wrong with being ordinary? He was content with his life. Sure, he didn't have the best job in the world—not the kind he'd imagined having during those dreamy days of college—but for now he had to give up that youthful idealism and work nine-to-five like every other John. Q. Taxpayer. Paying those dues, they called it.

Though Donovan still dreamed of writing the Great American Novel, the demands of work and marriage limited his writing time. One day, Donovan mused, he would be the one on the radio promoting his latest work.

An image floated in the back of his mind. He saw himself seated in his home office, fingers poised over a computer keyboard, while the joyful sound of his wife playing games with their children carried down the hall.

That fantasy took him away from the radio program and back to Donna's pleasant face. The two of them had wanted a baby for so long, and now, after several years of saving and planning, they were finally giving things a try. Donna insisted her health wouldn't be a problem, and their doctor agreed, but her irregular flare-ups were always cause for concern. He couldn't stand to see her in constant pain, but he also wanted her to be happy. Sometimes he wondered if the two could ever be reconciled.

The radio program cut to a commercial as Donovan took his exit. He looked at the console clock: 8:38. The lights at each intersection turned green upon his approach, and he sped through them without interruption. When he reached the Identinel parking lot, he pulled into a space near those reserved for upper management.

The odd tugging sensation intensified as he walked across the lot toward the building. He paused at the door, took a breath, and put his hand on his belly. *What did I eat last night?*

Donovan shook off the discomfort, promising himself antacids for lunch, and pushed his way into the building.

———————————•———————————

*C*lick.

Donovan removed his headset and sighed. Another sale lost. He tapped a few keys on the keyboard, adding another phone number to the growing "no call" list. The old tricks to save that sale just weren't working anymore, and people did not want to guard their identities as much as they should.

From somewhere beyond his cubicle, he heard the screeching call of the Two Tammys, Identinel's dual Human Resources Coordinators. Tammy Perpa and Tammy Quilago formed an unholy union of professionalism, leaving most employees trembling in their wake. Their voices stirred the acid in his stomach.

Around the office, many called them "The Terrible Tammys." Tomorrow, along with Butler, they would preside over Donovan's review. Understandably, this did little to ease the discomfort slowly climbing into his chest.

He stood, peeked over the wall of his cube, and watched the two women make their way down the main aisle of the call center. After an unproductive morning, the last thing he wanted was a conversation with them about performance.

Donovan ducked back into his cube to check the time again: 10:30. He reached for his coffee cup—a custom-made mug featuring a photo of Mr. Precious Paws—and made his way to the employee lounge. The Terrible Tammys were no longer in sight.

The lounge was furnished with two refrigerators, three microwaves, and four coffeepots. A lonely water cooler sat in a corner. A few of Donovan's coworkers loitered around the tables in the room, chatting about their weekend exploits. Donovan wasn't there to make small talk. He just needed coffee.

"Hey, Candle!"

Timothy Butler entered the room, his bright face split with a smug grin. The other employees scattered. Donovan shot a quick glance over his shoulder, muttered "Shit" under his breath, and poured his coffee.

Just smile, he told himself, but it wasn't that simple. When Donovan did not respond, Butler repeated himself. Donovan closed his eyes for a moment. Butler's insistence on dropping a person's first name was grating on even the best of days. Donovan tried to maintain his composure.

"Morning," he said. He poured cream and sugar into his coffee.

"How was your weekend, Candle? Mine was great…"

Oh really? How great was it?

Timothy Butler yammered on, and the discomfort in Donovan's gut returned with force, startling him so badly that he almost dropped his mug. A few drops of coffee spilled onto the counter. Butler's words—something about a weekend, a lake, time on a boat with his wife—ran together, and for a few agonizing seconds, all Donovan heard was a low, metallic drone.

What the hell is happening to me?

The feeling ceased. Butler was still talking. Donovan put a hand to his forehead, and it came away slick with sweat.

"—played eighteen holes after we got home from the beach on Sund—"

Donovan knew this conversation, had heard it a thousand times before. He'd seen others caught in this same corner, forced to listen to Butler's monologue about weekend excursions, and now it was his turn again. After nine years Donovan had learned to tune him out.

He stirred his coffee. The sensation swelled in the pit of his stomach once more, but only for an instant. *Maybe Butler's sucking the life out of me,* he mused. The thought made him smile.

"So, yeah, how was your weekend, Candle?" Butler clapped a hand on Donovan's back, causing him to spill a few more drops of coffee on his shoes. He looked into his Butler's cold blue eyes and forced a smile.

"It was a weekend."

Staring into his superior's face, Donovan was reminded of how little he'd accomplished—how, after nine years, he'd advanced only one or two rungs up the corporate ladder. Timothy Butler, only a few years older, had a much higher salary and a more fulfilling life.

Your time will come, he told himself. He wanted the extravagant stories and financial freedom. He wanted that new TV, he wanted to buy Donna that jewelry she'd had her eye on, he wanted to finish that novel. He wanted to remodel the guest room, to have a child, to build a legacy and pass it on.

He wanted life with all its trimmings. Staring into Butler's eyes, he realized he'd have to work harder, to toil and reach for that goal. He'd have to want it more than anything else.

"Mr. Butler."

"What's up, Candle?"

"I wanted to remind you about my review tomorrow."

Butler's expression faded, and for a moment Donovan feared the man had forgotten about his review, but then his face lit up and he said, "Don't worry, amigo! It's all taken care of!"

Relief came over him, but it was short-lived. As Timothy Butler walked away, Donovan saw the man's reassuring facade fall away for an instant. He stood there, not quite sure whether it was his imagination or something more sinister. Butler's conniving expression made him uneasy, a feeling that followed him back to his desk.

There he finished his coffee and continued working through his lunch hour, making cold calls to customers to sell them a service they did not want. As the hours crawled by, he found he was unable to escape the black cloud of Butler's troubling expression.

Was it that he did not trust his own boss? Was it the insincerity in Butler's eyes that put him on edge? He thought about asking around the office, but that would only lead to gossip, and this would be better played close to the chest. Even so, uncertainty nagged him. It encompassed his mind so completely that he almost missed the clock striking 5:00 P.M. The entire day was lost to an odd hint of suspicion.

He felt like a failure when he left the office. His sales for the day were the lowest in months. People under his wing—even new hires still in training—made more sales that day. Donovan had no one to blame but himself. He wanted to blame Timothy Butler, but his rational conscience spoke too loudly to be ignored. *It's all you*, it told him. *Quit worrying and get on with it.*

Donovan sat in his car for a few minutes, waiting for the emptiness to subside. When it did, he felt the first pangs of hunger rumbling in his stomach, accenting that deeper, more troubling sensation. He tried to ignore it.

Traffic was less agreeable that evening. Shortly after taking the highway entrance ramp, Donovan found himself sitting bumper-to-bumper with other lost souls trying to get home. He switched on the radio to help pass the time. A recap of the morning's interview was playing, and this time Donovan caught the name of the book's author.

"Please welcome Dr. Albert Sparrow—"

Outside, an SUV blared its horn and sped around Donovan's car. He gripped the steering wheel and tried to focus on the road.

"Thank you," said Dr. Sparrow.

"I understand you've got a new book available?"

"Yes, the title is—"

Donovan chimed in, "*A Life Ordinary: A Comprehensive Study in Human Mediocrity.*" He snorted. *So pretentious.*

"Care to give us the gist, Doc?"

"Through my studies, I've found that most people live painfully boring lives. We get up, we go to work, we slave away for eight, ten, even twelve hours a day, only to go home and meander for a few more before sleep."

"Yep," the host quipped. "Sounds about right."

"Over the last five years I've studied this phenomenal tendency toward the ordinary life. While some of my contemporaries refute my argument, I believe atypical activity is essential for our species to survive."

"So, what, we should go camping or something every other weekend?"

"Not exactly, for even in such an escape we may confine ourselves to routine. Our failure to recognize these patterns leads to a kind of ennui which—"

"On-what?"

"*Ennui.* It's—"

Donovan changed the station, replacing Dr. Sparrow with the screeching singer of AC/DC.

As he listened, the faint metallic buzzing filled his ears. He grimaced at the sound and switched off the radio to help clear his head. The droning stopped. By the time he pulled into his driveway, he'd forgotten all about the good Dr. Sparrow, AC/DC, and Timothy Butler. For a day begun with such high hopes, it had fallen far below the mark.

"So, I was wondering…"

Donna dabbed the corners of her mouth with a napkin. Steam from a platter of broiled chicken rose between them.

"Uh huh?"

"I was wondering if we could, you know, maybe take a vacation?"

"A vacation?"

"Not for a week or anything. Just, I don't know, a long weekend?"

He swallowed his chicken, cut another piece, and asked, "When? To where?"

"I don't know, Don. I thought we could go to the shore. It would be nice."

Donovan finished his chicken, washed it down with a glass of iced tea, and released a low belch. He excused himself, then stood and walked to the fridge to examine their cat-themed calendar. A kitten-shaped magnet held it to the refrigerator door.

"We could go early next month," she offered, "before the tourists arrive."

He flipped back and forth between the current month and the next, frowning. "Honey, I—" he began, but then interrupted himself. "Oh hell."

"What?"

He held out the calendar page and pointed to a circled date. "Today's the 16th."

Donna shrugged. "So?"

"It's Michael's birthday."

Before she could say anything else, he reaffixed the calendar to the fridge door and reached for the wall-mounted phone. He lifted the receiver from its cradle and dialed. Donna sighed and mumbled something. He turned away just as she rose from her seat to begin clearing the table. By the time his brother answered the phone, she was already running water in the sink.

"Hello?"

"Mike! Happy birthday, man."

Michael Candle chuckled. "Oh. Damn, already?"

"Wasn't sure I'd catch you at home. Figured you'd be out chasing crooks and the like."

"Ah well, you know me. Always busy somehow."

Although Donovan grew up reading the work of Raymond Chandler, he never fashioned himself as much of a detective. His brother, on the other hand, eschewed the fiction of their youth and chose to make detective work his career. Donovan admired Michael's dedication to hard-boiled facts, so it didn't surprise him when Michael struck out on his own as a licensed private investigator. Whenever Donovan spoke about his brother, he was always sure to mention Michael's career as a Private Eye.

Donna turned off the faucet. Dishes clanked together in the sink.

"Yeah, I actually just got back from vacation this weekend. Went down to the shore. You know how it is. I like to get out of town this time of year. You know…"

"Yeah, I know." Donovan closed his eyes, listening to the hesitation in his brother's voice. Their parents had died in a car accident seven years ago, the anniversary just a week prior. They'd both taken the loss hard, but between the two of them, only Mike had the means to get out of town. Donovan buried himself in his work to make himself forget. Donna took care of the annual floral arrangement. "I'd do the same thing if I could."

The silence on the line unnerved Donovan, and he knew what came next. The same thing as last time. "So, little brother…what's up? How long's it been now? A few months at least. How's life?"

There it is. He sucked in his breath. He pictured his brother on the other end of the line, arms crossed. After the loss of their parents, Michael took it upon himself to act as the concerned father figure. Their conversations, however innocent, always shifted focus to Donovan's quality of life and what he was doing to improve it. They'd drifted apart over the years since their parents had passed, and if pressed, Donovan would say Mike's need to play Dad was part of the reason. He cleared his throat and tried to redirect the conversation's flow.

"Same as usual. You know how it goes…"

He glanced over at Donna, and his face fell when he remembered their conversation. Maybe they could drive down to the shore, but not soon. A list of financial reasons raced through his mind. They had to save up money for the baby, there was Donna's upcoming appointment with her doctor, and the interest rate on his student loan had spiked again. The job at Identinel kept them afloat, but barely.

"Don? You there?"

"Huh? Yeah. Sorry, just spaced out for a sec."

"I asked how Donna's doing? Is she still having those flares?"

"Donna's doing all right. She still has flares, but not as often. She's happy."

Donna paused for a moment, shot him a quick glance, then splashed her hands back into the dishwater.

"How's—how's *your* girl? Jennifer, right? Any kids yet?"

It was laughable, the thought of Michael having children. He was too wrapped up in his own life to focus on kids. It was astounding that he even had time to date. Donovan hadn't met Michael's new girlfriend, but he hoped to soon. From what his brother told him, she seemed lovely, a perfect match.

Michael said, "No, no kids yet. We're not that serious."

"You know, Donna and I are trying—"

"You still a phone jockey?"

Donovan closed his mouth. Thick pockets of heat collected around his face, accenting his shame. The phone's plastic casing popped, and he realized he was gripping it too hard. That invisible hand pulled at his gut again, working its nonexistent fingers around his spine and threatening to pluck him away. Donovan heard a hiss of static, and then it was gone.

He collected himself, measured his words. "Yes. I still work for Identinel. Just like the last time we talked."

Michael chuckled. Donovan imagined his brother's smug grin. It was an expression he knew well. While growing up, his brother picked on him for burying himself in his books, mocking his choice to view life through imaginary eyes rather than living in reality. Even now, well into the age of thirty-three, Michael's condescension still pulled at Donovan's strings. Michael knew this, and that made it even worse.

"You need to live a little, Don."

"I'm happy with the way things are, Mike."

It was the same conversation as always. Why did it always come to this?

"No, Donovan," his brother said, "I don't think you are. I really don't. And you want to know why?"

I'm sure you'll tell me anyway, Donovan thought, biting his lip in silence.

"It's because you have no life. Not really. You only think you're happy because that phone jockey job—"

"I'm one of the top salesmen—"

"—Whatever. That job is all you know. You've worked there, what, ten years? Twelve?"

"Nine," Donovan muttered. The phone's casing popped again. He relaxed his fingers.

"Nine years and you're a top salesman. Congrats. Four years of college, tens of thousands in debt, and you're a fucking salesman. I thought you wanted to write, Don. What happened to that book you were working on?"

He sighed. *Every damn time.* It always turned into a bickering contest, revolving around how his older brother thought he should live his life. There was always that air of elitism hanging over every conversation, about how Donovan wasn't living up to his expectations, how he was letting himself and his wife down by not reaching his potential.

Donovan frowned. *Somehow Michael's always been happier. Always more successful.* Once Michael knew what he wanted, he went after it, not stopping until it was his. On the other hand, Donovan meandered in indecision. He wasn't sure what he wanted. As the years slipped by, he chose the path of least resistance, and now he was frowned upon for swimming with the current. He didn't understand how someone who went against the grain could be so successful, while he—the more compliant of the two—remained static.

"Go out, Don. Take Donna and just go somewhere. Do something, don't just plan it. Pick up your shit and go, man. Otherwise you're just living in a box while the world moves on without you."

"I can't afford to," he snapped. His voice was shaky, eyes watering, and a lump had lodged itself in his throat. Worse, the weird indigestion kept coming back. Sweat dotted his forehead. In the span of the last five minutes he was reduced to a bullied ten-year-old all over again.

"And that's because—"

"Look," he said, "I'm sorry I didn't live up to your expectations. I'm sorry I don't live the glamorous lifestyle, Mr. Private *Dick.* I'm sorry I don't make as much money as you do, or that I'm not as successful, or that I took the wrong path according to you. I'm doing the best with what I can, Mike. My job is my job and it pays my bills."

"It pays your bills," Michael countered, "and that's all. To top it off, your job is sucking the life out of you one day at a time."

"No." He slammed one hand against the refrigerator door and startled Donna. She dropped a plate into the sink. "It's just a job. I'm still working on that novel. One day soon—"

Michael sighed. "Y'know what I want for my birthday, little brother?"

"What?"

"For you to get a fucking life."

He scrambled for a retort, could even feel one climbing up the back of his throat, warm and boiling with venom. *Thanks, Dad.*

But the line was dead. The dial tone hummed in his ear. He hung up the phone and turned. Donna leaned against the counter with her arms folded across her chest and a damp dish towel hanging over shoulder.

"How's your brother?"

Donovan stared at her, noting the slant of her lips and the glint in her eyes. He knew that look. He knew he should choose his words carefully, with little hesitation.

"He's an asshole."

"What did he say?"

"Same old crap about how I should find another job, how I'm not really living, blah, blah, blah."

He twirled one finger in the air. Mr. Precious Paws pranced into the room and rubbed against his leg. He knelt, picked up the cat, and scratched between his ears.

Donna frowned. She turned back to the sink, reached into its murky water, and pulled the plug.

Donovan said nothing, kept scratching the cat's ears. The dishwater gurgled as it went down the drain, and he cleared his throat when it finished.

"So, about that vacation."

"Just forget I said anything, Don."

There it was. The tone. It grated down his spine.

"Honey, you know we can't—"

"And why not?"

"We can't afford it."

"We *can* afford it." She turned to face him. "I'm not sure what your brother said to you, but I've got a pretty good idea."

She counted off details of their conversation with her fingers. "He probably asked you about your job. He asked how long you've worked there—"

He smirked. "You're pretty good at this."

"—and how you've not done anything with your life because you don't have one. Am I right? Am I in the ballpark, Donovan?" His face fell. Donna shook her head. "If you don't want to go, just tell me. Don't give me the same excuse as everything else. We can afford it, Don. I can check the savings account too, you know."

He chewed his lower lip. "But we have to save for the baby, Donna. With you out of work, we have to watch every penny. You know that."

"I just—" She stammered. "I just want to do something with our lives, Don. It's always save, save, save, and for what?" She paused, held back a sob, and said, "It's not about the money. You know that. We don't have to stay at a five-star resort. I would be happy just driving to the shore for a day, but you won't let me finish. You've already made up your mind."

The first tears streamed down her cheeks.

"Face it," she went on, "your brother's right. You live for that job, and nothing else. Money, time, routine—it's all that's important to you, and what you earn is never enough for you."

He squeezed Mr. Precious Paws tightly enough to elicit a low growl from the feline.

"That's not true."

Donna wiped the tears from her face. "Then take a day off."

"To do what?"

"Nothing! Absolutely nothing! Not a goddamn thing!"

"But—"

"But what?"

He searched for an answer. A plausible answer. One that would make sense to her in this state. He scratched away at the interior of his mind looking for the perfect thing to say, and still he came up with the very excuse he'd tried to avoid.

"But...we have to save."

Donna forced a smile, shook her head, and made her way out of the room. His words hung in the air, thickening, weighing down upon him.

He *had* a life, dammit. He had a wife, a job, a house, and maybe a child soon—what more to life could there be? Had he missed some vital detail about growing up, something explaining the process of "having a life?"

Mr. Precious Paws yowled and scratched at his cheek. He yelped in pain and watched as the feline ran for the stairs. He stood there for only a moment longer, rubbing the scratch and nursing a battered ego. He looked at his watch: 6:49. Within the span of twenty minutes, he'd managed to alienate every member of his family. It was a personal record.

D onovan retreated to his office and turned on his computer. He tried to escape into the world of his novel, hoping he could salvage the day with something productive. On the page, a disillusioned private eye named Joe Hopper and the often philosophical, often dangerous Mistress Colby experienced their plight as two people trying to survive in the decline of Western culture.

He pecked at the keyboard for an hour, listening to the dry Southern drawl of Hopper in his own head. When he typed a thousand words, he stopped to read over them.

Ain't no good, hoss. Donovan frowned and deleted them all. He started again.

He'd been stuck on this scene for over a year. Every evening he would sit down to work out the details of the plot's climax, and no matter how much he wrote, no matter the quality, it would always end in deletion. The story was frozen on page 299.

After a second attempt and another deleted set of words, he sat back in his chair and shook his head. The cursor blinked.

He leaned forward, buried his head in his hands. "I don't know anymore."

He looked back at the stack of pages on his desk. The first 298 pages of his magnum opus stared back, waiting for completion, but he couldn't find the narrative. His head was too clouded by conversations with his brother and his wife. Memories of Timothy Butler's smug grin only served to drive the feeling home. And there was that damn indigestion, too.

Perhaps Identinel *was* sucking the life from him. Had he made the right choice by staying with the company for so long, rather than working for a few years before moving on to greener pastures? *Of course*, he told himself. *I did what I had to do, especially when Donna couldn't work anymore. I've kept us afloat. I've made enough money to sustain the both of us for years.*

Donna's voice chimed in his head, *It's not about the money.*

And it wasn't. He knew that. Turning in his seat, Donovan stared at the document on his screen. He frowned. *Should've finished this damn thing by now*, he thought. *I could've pumped out five novels in the time I've spent on this one.*

He thought about Joe Hopper, and wished life could truly imitate art. He wished he had the guts to face an uncertain future, walk into work tomorrow, and tell Butler to cram the review up his ass. It was something Hopper would do with Southern grace and style. It was something Michael Candle might do, too.

Staring at the great white nothing beneath page 299, Donovan suddenly saw the story's faults. Page 300 would never be realized, because nothing had really happened in the previous 299. He'd fallen into complacency with the story, certain that this was the best it could be. In that security, he'd resigned his characters to the same fate.

He'd lost his drive, his vision. To fix the story, he realized, he would have to start over from the beginning. A fresh perspective might change things. Going this far only to throw it all away wouldn't be a total loss. Knowledge of the journey would allow him to fix past mistakes.

Satisfied with his intentions, Donovan closed the document and deleted the file. The indigestion, which had grown from an occasional discomfort to a constant annoying sensation, relented for a moment.

Maybe I'm getting an ulcer.

He looked at the blank page and was just about to type the first sentence when he glanced at the clock. He smiled, closed the document, and turned off the computer.

"Almost forgot," he muttered, "it's time for *CSI*."

———————•———————

The discomfort in his stomach grew worse as the minutes passed. It wasn't pain, so much as uneasiness building up within him. A sharp droning chime filled his head, making concentration difficult, and he gave up halfway through the TV show.

Donovan tiptoed into the bedroom half an hour after Donna retired. He thought about waking her to tell her about the strange sensation he felt, but that would make him even more of a jerk. The pain was negligible, so he decided to take it like a man.

Donna stirred as he crawled into bed. She rolled to her side, facing him. He pulled the blanket over himself and stared at the ceiling.

Her fingertips brushed his arm, and when he looked over, he saw her eyes were open.

"Hi," he said. She smiled, leaned forward, and kissed him. That kiss led to another. He began to say something, but she pressed her finger against his lips. She sat up and climbed on top of him. He gasped when she took him in her hand and slid him into her.

They made love for what seemed like an hour, their bodies entwined in a chaos of sheets and blankets, until they collapsed into one another with one, climactic shiver. Sweaty, dizzy, Donovan leaned back against the headboard and sighed. He closed his eyes. Donna raised up, kissed his forehead, and said, "I love you, Donnie."

"I love you too." He opened his eyes and expected to see her there, but she wasn't. She'd rolled away from him.

"I'm still mad at you, though," she said. He remained there for a moment longer before uttering a long sigh. The room suddenly felt cold, gray. The weird pull in his gut strengthened. He closed his eyes and rolled over, trying his best to ignore the feeling. For now, Donovan was just happy to go to sleep.

———————•———————

His night was filled with odd, troubling dreams. The alarm woke him, and he silenced its blaring call on his way to the bathroom.

He yawned, flipped on the light. Phantom shapes of static faded in and out of view, and Donovan dismissed them as a figment of his lingering dream state. *Wake up*, he told himself. *Early bird and all that crap.*

Something tugged at his guts, threatening to disembowel him. He almost didn't mind the sensation, would've preferred it to what he saw happening before his eyes.

The world around him dimmed, lost its detail and texture, the colors slowly draining from his sight. He held out his hand, staring in slack-jawed terror as his skin—flesh, meat, bone, *all* of him—flickered in and out of existence. For a fleeting moment, Donovan Candle disappeared, and the only thing rooting him to that waking reality was the sound of his horrified scream.

2

THE FLICKERING

He silenced himself and watched his reflection fade in and out. *I'm dreaming. Gotta be.* He ran water over his hands, expecting the stream to pass through his palms, but instead it pooled and spilled over into the sink. Certain that he was truly awake, Donovan stared at his hands once more. They were solid, opaque.

Get a grip, hoss.

Donovan pushed the thought aside, leaned forward, and took a long look at his reflection.

"Just a dream," he muttered to himself. "That's all."

The uncomfortable force wrenched at his gut so hard that he doubled over in pain. He fought off nausea and a surging drone in his head. *Keep it together,* he thought. *Just getting sick, is all. Take a shower.*

The warm water delivered him from the sickening feeling, and he let his mind wander. Perhaps he was sleepwalking? He'd read about it happening to people of all ages. It was a sound conclusion, one that put him at ease. He chuckled about it, his voice a hollow echo in the shower stall. *What a strange dream,* he thought. *Almost like I wasn't there—like a projection.*

He burst into laughter and reached down to turn off the water. His hands faded in unison, followed by his arms. His laughter twisted into a hollow sob. He ran his hands over himself, down his torso, hips, manhood, and buttocks. All of him seemed to fade in and out like static, his skin first growing transparent, then vanishing entirely for an instant before reappearing as solid matter.

Donovan pushed open the shower door and returned to the mirror, staring in abject horror as his own reflection dimmed and faded.

"Donna," he muttered. It was low at first, then grew to a trembling plea. "*Donna!*"

He staggered down the hall, leaving a trail of damp carpet in his wake. The alarm clock on the nightstand read 6:40, five minutes shy of Donna's alarm.

"Honey."

She stirred beneath the blankets. Frightened, Donovan's eyes darted between his fading self and his sleeping wife. Beads of water rolled down his forehead and fell to the floor.

"Donna?" He nudged one of her exposed feet.

She grunted. "What, Don?"

"Honey, there's something wrong. I—"

Donna sat up, squinting. "Where're your clothes?"

Her question seemed strange to him. What did it matter where his clothes were? He stared at her, held out his flickering hands and frowned. Water dripped onto the bed.

"I was in the shower, and—"

"And you're still wet. You're dripping all over the floor, Don. Go get a towel. Jeez."

Donna pulled back the blankets and gasped when her feet met damp carpet. She glared at him. He stood there, naked and soaked, with both hands held out in a gesture of confused apology. His stomach lurched again as his skin flickered into a transparent state.

"Don't you see this?"

She looked at him, groggy-eyed and puzzled. "See what?"

"*This!*" He held out his arms. The tug in his abdomen settled down. His skin returned to normal as if to mock him.

Donna covered a yawn, and he watched her in disbelief. How could she not see? Was this some sort of weird head game, retaliation for their argument yesterday? No, they'd known each other for too long to sink to such petty levels. Besides, he knew she loved him too much to ignore something as serious as this.

"I *see* you making a mess I'll have to clean up. And," she fought back another yawn, "I *see* that if I don't get some coffee soon, I'm going to bite off your head."

Donna pushed past him, uttered a small sigh when she saw the soaked trail to the bathroom, and went downstairs to the kitchen. Donovan stared at his hands again and flinched as his flesh began to deteriorate once more.

I must be dreaming, he thought. *I have to be—*

The second alarm startled him. He reached over, turned it off, and fanned out his fingers. They were there, and yet they weren't, fading from opaque to translucent, from flesh to nothing and back again.

You ain't dreamin, hoss. Hopper again. He cursed his imagination for breeding a Southern detective.

More water dripped from his arm. He regarded his hands once more with caution before retreating to the bathroom for a towel.

———————•———————

D onovan skipped shaving. His flesh vanished every time he drew the blade across his face. The last thing he wanted was to misjudge and slit his own throat. Getting dressed was just as difficult. His leg would dim and vanish each time he tried to put on his trousers. Once clothed, he found his shirt and pants flickered along with the rest of him.

When he finally journeyed downstairs, Donna watched him with mild irritation. An empty bowl sat before his place at the table along with a box of cereal. He took the hint. She was still angry, but for God's sake, couldn't she see what was happening to him?

Donovan ate his cereal in silence. Mr. Precious Paws traveled into the kitchen and sat at his feet. The cat looked up at him with wide eyes, ears perked with attentive curiosity. When Donovan lifted a spoonful, his hand dimmed and flashed out of reality. A quick jerk in his gut startled him. He dropped the spoon, startling Mr. Precious Paws out of his reverent stare, and frowned as the cat scampered away.

For a moment the room drained of color, and the sensation in his stomach tugged with such force that he cried out in pain. He wiped tears from his eyes and stared about the room. Its warmth was gone, replaced with a stagnant gray tone covering every surface. Donna was cast in its hue as she poured herself a bowl of cereal.

He blinked. Color returned to the room.

"Donna," he whispered, "there is something wrong here. With me."

She flipped through the morning newspaper, seemingly oblivious to his statement. He reached down, picked up his spoon, then leaned forward to stare at his wife.

"Donna."

Nothing. Not so much as a raised eyebrow.

Mr. Precious Paws wandered over, stood on his hind legs, and scratched at Donovan's knee. He yelped, startled by the prickle of the cat's claws, and kicked his leg. The cat yowled and slid across the kitchen floor, colliding against the cabinetry with a soft thump.

"Don't kick the cat."

He looked back at his wife. She glared at him, frowning. He held up his trembling hands and twiddled his fingers.

"Look at this," he said flatly. All ten digits vacillated between solidity and transparency.

She strained to look at him. After a moment of eye contact, Donna put a hand to her temple and rubbed.

"What, Don?"

"This," he said, and recoiled as his hands flashed in and out of existence.

"Sorry." She rubbed her temple and winced. "I have a headache, and you aren't helping."

His heart dropped into his stomach. *She can't see it.* He placed both hands on his knees and frowned. Had he finally snapped? Was this hallucinatory transparency just the first step? He wondered if other strange mental anomalies would follow.

He tried to work out what was happening to him, but all he could do was stare at his skin, at the way it faded and filled with a flesh-colored static. His vision danced from a full spectrum of color to cold gray tones. Color-blindness along with insanity? He grew so distracted by these disturbing possibilities that time slipped by him. Donna snapped him out of these troubled musings.

"Don," she said, "you're going to be late."

"Late?" He scrambled to his feet. "What time—"

His eyes fell upon the microwave clock. It read 8:05 in large, digital numbers.

"Oh hell."

Donovan quickly kissed his wife's cheek, grabbed his keys, and darted out the door.

Donna sat back in her seat and rubbed at her temples once more. It was an ungodly headache, slicing through her thoughts with measured, low throbs.

Her husband's behavior meandered on the strange side of things. *It's just stress,* she told herself. *Just stress over his review—*

A drone of noise surged through her head, filling it with an interminable buzzing. She lost her concentration. For a moment she stared off into space, lost in a white, agonizing static. Finally, after a few seconds, the buzzing stopped. Donna looked about the room, then down at her feet. Mr. Precious Paws stared up at her.

"What's up, Paws?"

The cat blinked. Donna reached down and scratched between his ears. "Good kitty."

She went back to her reading. The headache did not return.

———•———

D riving on Tuesdays was no different than on Mondays. The same traffic, the same commute, the same moronic drivers. Now he was one of those morons, leaving too late and driving too fast to make up for lost time. He honked the horn and screamed as another driver cut him off.

"It's okay," he told himself. His voice was distant and empty in the absence of the usual radio banter, but he couldn't bear listening to morning radio personalities go on about inane garbage. His mind was elsewhere. "There's an explanation. Always an explanation."

His hands flickered, disappeared, and reappeared on the wheel. Though he still maintained the sensation of touch, he could not see his own flesh, and the very idea horrified him. He wondered if he should go see a doctor. *And just what the hell would you tell 'em, hoss?*

Donovan didn't have an answer to that. A red Suburban came to a stop ahead of him, and he slammed on the brakes just in time.

A logical explanation. There had to be one. He retraced his steps in hope that somewhere along the way his memory might creep upon an answer. Perhaps he'd inhaled a toxic fume of some kind, or maybe—

There ain't a logical explanation, hoss, 'cause what's happening ain't logical at all.

Joe Hopper's drawling wisdom wasn't helping, but Donovan knew there was truth in those words. There was no logical explanation for this, other than a loss of his sanity. His hands flickered again, and he saw the steering wheel through them.

I'm crazy, he thought. *Certifiably insane.*

The explanation made his stomach lurch. The world faded gray for a blink before shifting back to a vibrant sunny morning. The most damning piece of evidence to support his newfound insanity was Donna's inability to see the phenomenon. He considered the possibility that she was angry enough to ignore his malady, but even that did not make sense. *Pissed or not, she wouldn't do that to me.*

Traffic lurched forward once more. Donovan took his exit. The dashboard clock read 8:49. He tried to ignore it and pressed his foot on the gas.

"Come on," he said, smiling at the purr of the engine. He shot off the exit ramp and sped through the intersection just as the traffic light turned red.

He was two blocks from the office when he spotted red and blue flashing lights in the rearview mirror. As the police cruiser neared, he caught a glimpse of his own reflection. His face, eyes, forehead—all disappeared before his eyes. The world went gray again, turning the cruiser's red and blues into meaningless shades.

"No," he moaned. "*No.*"

The officer flipped on the siren. Donovan frowned, signaled, and pulled the car into an empty gas station parking lot. The clock read 8:56. In four minutes, he would be late for the first time in nine years.

He shoved the ticket in his pocket and sat down at his desk. His watch read 9:22. He checked his phone and discovered three missed calls—one from Tammy Quilago, Tammy Perpa, and Timothy Butler.

His legs turned to limp noodles, his arms and stomach to jelly, and he felt his pulse on the back of his tongue. For the first time since waking, Donovan did not mind that he was disappearing. At that moment, he wanted nothing more than to vanish from the face of the planet.

According to the messages, his superiors were waiting for him in the conference room. On any other day he would have walked into the conference room calm and collected. Today he had a five o'clock shadow at nine in the morning, a speeding ticket, and an order of invisibility with a side of colorblindness. His plate was full.

"Oh hell." He leaned over to pull up both pant legs. His left sock was blue; the right was brown. His hairy shins flickered as if to mock him.

A young woman walked past his cubicle just as he dimmed. She said nothing. He sighed, rose from his seat, and made his way down the aisle toward the conference room.

One of his coworkers, Phillip, got up from his seat as he passed.

"Good morning, Don."

"Morning, Phil."

The young man recoiled at the sound of his voice. He pinched the space between his eyes. The room went gray, and Donovan thought he saw movement over Phil's shoulder. He blinked. Everything was back to normal—except for Phil. He was pale.

"You all right?"

Phil said nothing. He pushed past Donovan and hurried to the restroom.

Work carried on around him, and no one else gave notice his strange affliction. Their attentions were focused on their monitors while they spoke into headsets, performing monotone sales pitches about a full range of Identinel's services. He passed a trainee on her way to the employee lounge and felt himself flicker as he opened his mouth to say hello. She simply smiled and went on her way.

A gut-wrenching thought occurred to him: his symptoms really were figments of his imagination. It explained everything, including Donna's apathy. *I've truly lost my mind*, he thought. He reconsidered going to see a doctor. *You best stop that*, Hopper scolded. *You got other things to be done 'sides bellyachin'.*

Donovan obeyed his creation and made his way to the conference room. He stood outside for a moment, sucked in his breath, and waited for his pounding heart to calm itself. When he was finished, he entered the room.

———————•———————

The conference room was sterile, its white walls accented by a pair of large potted plants which sat in opposite corners at the far end. In the center was a long table, around which sat Timothy Butler, Tammy Quilago, and Tammy Perpa.

Donovan stood with his hands clasped behind his back, trying to smile while the icy fingers of the phantom hand yanked at his insides. He strained to conceal his discomfort.

They paid him a series of short glances before returning their attention to the pages of Donovan's file. The Tammys put their hands to their heads almost in unison, squinting as they tried to read the words on the page. Butler dug a finger into his ear.

Can they even see me? His fear grew with each passing second. Finally, after a full minute of waiting, Butler spoke.

"Have a seat, Don." Butler motioned to the table.

He sat. Tammy Quilago smiled coldly before looking away. He realized none of them would make eye contact.

"Let's get started, shall we?"

Donovan nodded. He wiped his sweaty palms on his trousers. Yesterday, he was prepared for this. He knew what he would say in response to their questions. Today he found the words weren't there. They were stolen from him by an apparent lapse of sanity.

"Mr. Candle," Tammy Quilago said, "we commend you for nine whole years of service."

Tammy Perpa chimed in. "That's quite a feat!"

"Indeed." Tammy Q. nodded. "Turn-over rates in this business are embarrassingly high. It's employees like yourself who keep Identinel ahead of the game."

She looked down at a sheet of paper. Her script. Donovan wondered how many other employees had heard this spiel. She began to speak again, but he could not hear her. A series of chimes rose in his ears, filling his head with the drone of distant bells, signaling his further descent into madness. His skin prickled, blinked out, and reappeared. He held his breath, expecting one of them to say something, but he was met with a silence that confirmed his suspicions. He was on his own.

The chimes slowed just as Tammy Q. finished her part of the script. Tammy P. took her turn to go over the review's structure. When she was done, Butler cleared his throat and flashed Donovan that award-winning smile. Sweat beaded on his forehead.

"Got any questions for us so far, Candle?"

"No."

"Good. First off, let's discuss your punctuality."

Donovan slumped back in his seat. He put a hand to his forehead. That prickly feeling crept up again, like thousands of insects crawling across his skin. Butler spoke, but Donovan could not understand him. He tried focusing on the man's words, but the more he tried, the more incomprehensible they became.

His vision turned gray once again. It lingered this time, and he watched in panic as objects lost their color and texture. His coworkers were dark gray ghosts, silhouetted against planar walls absent of texture. The furniture lost its features, appearing as simple geometric shapes. The air had no warmth, and it was possessed of an unsettling gravity pushing against him. He felt its familiar grip down in the center of his gut.

What the hell is happening to me?

Even Joe Hopper was silent in his mind. There were no answers for this. He wanted to flee the room, race back to his car, and check himself into hospital before something worse happened. Instead he remained frozen in place, unable to make out Butler's words as the world around him was systematically drained of color.

That's when he saw the shape—a long slender figure standing almost as tall as the ceiling. It had long white limbs, and through the gray haze he saw the faint indentations of a face. The giant figure had eyes and a mouth, lingering in the gray gloom, watching them from its corner.

He realized he could no longer see Butler's features, nor could he understand anything the man said. His voice was a garbled mess. The same was true of the two Tammys, who made various quips and asides throughout Butler's conversation, but Donovan could not understand a damn word of it.

The lanky albino thing swayed lazily in the corner, shifting its weight from one foot to the other. Its knuckles brushed the slate floor with slow strokes. Donovan watched in confusion, fear.

I'm insane. He admitted it to himself. His heart beat a heavy tattoo in his chest and sweat ran from his pores. *I've lost my mind.* In that moment he realized how limitless the depths of his insanity truly were.

The pale thing noticed him. Its swaying ceased as it planted its full weight on both feet. The creature cocked its head in his direction, raised a spindly arm, and beckoned to him with a loud forlorn moan.

-3-
GRAY SIGHT

The creature squinted empty black eyes and pointed at him with a single spindly finger. Another guttural cry escaped its maw, and a tremor rippled across its pallid flesh.

Donovan's heart raced. The pale thing's presence defied his grasp of logic, tickling a place down in his brain, a place he used to call his imagination. This was a figment of his own creation, a repressed idea manifesting in the form of a waking nightmare. He'd lost his mind after all, and this was his body's way of telling him.

He blinked. The room flooded with color, texture. Butler and the Tammys were still in their seats, each one sounding off a number which did not make any sense to him. He was still distracted by what had just happened. It was a hallucination. Had to be. It was a chemical imbalance in his brain, maybe, or perhaps a side effect of head trauma he could not remember. These possibilities plagued him so much that Butler's voice startled him.

"Whoa, easy there. Are you okay, Candle?"

Donovan stared at his superiors, then back to the corner of the room. The lanky creature was gone. He slumped in his chair, and the tension slowly leaked from the room, replaced with a wave of dread.

"I'm sorry, what were you saying?"

Timothy Butler chuckled. "Overall we gave you a score of 3.8."

Donovan's eye twitched. He forgot about his bizarre hallucinations. A 3.8? What kind of number was 3.8? Never in his nine years had they given him anything but a whole number, which was usually a four. But

3.8? He repeated it to himself. Three. Point. Eight. It implied he'd done worse this year than the last, which made no sense to him—after all, he'd worked harder this year than any other. He could understand receiving a 4.8, but this?

"A three-point-eight?"

"Yeah." Butler shuffled his files together. He stood and finished off a cup of coffee. "New ranking system. Nifty, huh?"

"But a 3.8?"

Tammy Q. frowned. "Is there a problem with your score, Mr. Candle?"

He shook his head, ignoring the flashes of gray before him. "No, not a problem. I was just…"

Tammy P. strained to look at him, wincing as she forced a smile. "Yes?"

"The score seems a little low, that's all. I thought I worked very hard this year. Harder than last year."

"And you have, Candle! We just see it as a means of incentivizing you to achieve even better results. Am I right, Tammy and Tammy?"

The Tammys nodded, spoke in unison. "That's right, Mr. Butler."

Donovan chewed his lip and studied their smiles. "Incentivizing me to achieve better results? But my results were better—"

"That's right. For you to work harder and strive for even more excellence." Butler stood and opened the door. He wore that same smug grin from the day before. Donovan's blood pressure spiked. "Besides, there's always room for improvement!"

Timothy Butler didn't wait for a reply. He turned and left the room. The Tammys whispered among themselves. Tammy P. giggled at something Tammy Q. said, but Donovan could not hear what passed between them. After a moment, he cleared his throat and spoke.

"Was there something else?" They looked up, startled by the sound of his voice, and stared in his direction. Tammy Q. strained her eyes as though he were a mile away instead of sitting across the table.

The room shifted gray for an instant, allowing Donovan a glimpse of a second lanky figure standing behind the two women. A moment later they were gone, replaced by a world in full color, and Tammy P was speaking.

"—a teensy-tiny thing," she said.

"Your salary increase," Tammy Q. added.

Donovan nodded. "Which is?"

"Since your performance score falls into the median bracket, you're eligible for the standard half-percent increase."

His stomach lurched once again, and he tried to ignore the feeling as he rolled their words in his head. Half a percent. Not even enough to cover the cost of living. After taxes and the annual insurance premium increase, Donovan stood to earn less than last year. Kissing ass and working self-imposed double-time was only worth half a percent?

Donovan opened his mouth to speak, but a flash of gray silenced him. A sharp jolt shot through his gut, and his skin crawled with the prickly sensation of needles like physical static. One of the Tammys spoke, but her voice was slow and garbled.

He forgot about the measly raise and focused his attention on the pair of tall albino figures in the room. They stood in place, swaying in tandem as their spindly arms scraped the ground. Their black eyes looked upon him with unflinching apathy. He was but an insect to them, a passing curiosity.

The second figure stepped toward the table. Donovan recoiled, listening to his heart race. What were these things? And why did he see them? His imagination filled in the gaps. *Ghosts*, he thought, *or demons—*

"—any questions, Mr. Candle?"

Color bled into the room, and he found himself staring at Tammy Perpa. He couldn't bring himself to speak. His mind raced with impossibilities, all of which seemed alien. Spirits? Invisibility? These things weren't possible. This was reality, and—

"Mr. Candle?"

"Y-Yes?"

"Do you have any questions?"

He shook his head without thinking.

"Good!" The Tammys stood and collected their things, giggling at their sickening uniformity. Donovan watched them leave the room. When they were gone, he closed his eyes and buried his face in his hands.

My God, what next?

Tuesday morning's confusion spread through the rest of the week, and Donovan struggled to rationalize the strange transparent disease afflicting his body. He spent the next few days in a state of disbelief and horror. There was no pattern to the flashes of gray sight, nothing to prepare him for the fleeting glimpses of a world bled of life. A world inhabited by impossible monstrosities.

Donna ignored his distress. His attempts to communicate with her were met with silence. The few times she did acknowledge his presence was to reciprocate the staples "I love you" and "Good night." Even then, he saw the confusion on her face, as though she hadn't noticed his presence until those precise moments.

He wanted to believe it was a dream, that he would wake up Wednesday morning and discover it was still Tuesday. He imagined waking to find his life the same as before, full of hope and color. Maybe Donna wouldn't give him the cold shoulder, would make him a nice breakfast, would kiss him on the cheek again when he came home.

But when he woke the next morning, nothing had changed. He rose at the same time and found himself cloaked with a curtain of gray static. The room shifted back to normal as he rubbed the sleep from his eyes. He got up, frowned at himself in the mirror, and went about his morning ritual.

Downstairs, he watched in silence as Donna made herself some toast and took a seat at the table. He sat across from her, watching her mannerisms, waiting for her to acknowledge his presence. She did not look up from her breakfast.

Frustrated, Donovan flipped through the morning newspaper. He stopped when a photograph caught his eye. A young woman stared back. Below the photo, a caption read HAVE YOU SEEN ME? He considered how easy it was for someone to vanish without a trace. *Maybe I'm going to disappear*, he thought, and shook off a chill.

The young woman's dark eyes rendered grainy and pale by the newsprint filled him with anxiety. A deep hum rose up from within his head, causing a slow throb at his temples. He looked away from the photograph. The hum stopped, and the room around him shifted, losing its color. The kitchen's gray tones deepened, the cabinetry and appliances losing their texture, becoming nothing more than blank slates of empty geometry. Donna became a silhouette, and that's when he saw the tiny creature on her shoulder.

A white figure emerged from behind Donna's head. It was small, no taller than a few inches, its rubbery flesh glistening in the dim un-light of the room. The tiny creature stood on two stubby legs, its hands settled on what might have been its hips.

He stared at it, unblinking, unable to move—not out of fear, but out of shock. Just when Donovan thought he'd reached the bottom of his sanity, the floor dropped out from underneath, spilling him further into an abyss.

The white thing sat next to Donna's ear, put its head against her earlobe, and spoke in a droning language he could not understand. The voice sounded like a record played in reverse, tinged with the electronic interference of a bad phone connection.

Kitchen walls flickered and slowly lost their gray hue as the world returned to normal. Donna's features regained their definition. For a few seconds both realities overlapped, and Donovan saw the white thing sitting beside her head. She chewed on her toast, unaware of its presence.

"What the hell is this?"

The white thing looked at him with two black beady eyes and said something else into Donna's ear. She didn't notice, stared at the table.

"Get off her." Donovan reached forward to knock the pale thing from her shoulder, but his fingers passed through it. Donna did not move. The white thing grinned at him, extended its white hand and gave him the finger.

He scoffed. *Fuck you too.*

The overlap of color and gray subsided with another flash. Donovan ignored the prickling of his skin as the kitchen returned to normal. He watched the creature fade from view, and though it was gone, he still felt its eyes upon him.

For the first time since the affliction began, Donovan considered the possibility that he wasn't imagining these horrific creatures. *No, things like this don't happen. They're impossible, unnatural.* He'd written about things like this in his youth, long before he traded supernatural stories for hard-boiled crime, but for the precise reason that they *didn't* exist.

Donovan stood and he looked down at Donna, unsure of himself and his sanity. He reached out, expecting to feel the form of that creature rendered invisible by the kitchen's lively color. Instead, his hand fell upon her shoulder.

Donna looked up at him and smiled. "I love you, too. Have a nice day at work, dear."

"I didn't—" he began, then remembered the thing on her shoulder. He remembered the way it whispered its backward language into her ear. Was it filling in the blanks? Was it the reason she couldn't understand him?

He glanced at the clock, saw he was running late, and made his way to the door. He stopped short, looked back at Donna. She flipped through the newspaper.

"Love you," he said, and closed the door behind him.

He agonized over the morning's incident for the rest of the day. At work, even as he read the sales prompt to a stranger on the line, his mind wandered back to Donna. He saw the white thing on her shoulder every time he closed his eyes. When a potential customer hung up on him, he removed his headset and retreated to the men's room.

Donovan closed the stall and sat on the toilet. He ran his hands over his face, through his hair.

You can figure this out. There's a logical, reasonable explanation. There gotta be. To this argument, Joe Hopper replied, *Only logic I see in this is that you're crazy, hoss. How's that sound?*

He didn't like it one bit. The alternative prospect was also one that filled him with dread. What if he were truly disappearing? What if these creatures were real? The little thing on Donna's shoulder was bad enough, but the tall ones lurking in the corners of the office conference room terrified him. A chill slowly worked its way down his back.

When he returned to his cubicle, he discovered he'd been gone for almost a full hour. There were no messages waiting for him in his inbox or on his phone. Given all that had happened—and all that *was* happening—he was not surprised. First his wife ignored him, and now his coworkers. With enough time, everyone just might forget he existed.

Donovan studied the sales floor. His stomach twisted into itself as the room overlapped its gray counterpart. Other salespeople darkened into silhouettes, and he saw more of the little white things sitting on their shoulders. They turned their bulbous heads in a single uniform motion. Their dark eyes looked through him.

Donovan flickered back into reality. The office returned to its normal state. He sat and put on his headset, determined to ignore the impossible things he'd witnessed. Unlike those in his immediate presence, the strangers to whom he spoke over the phone always heard his voice.

"Seriously, man, don't you ever get bored?"

"Sometimes."

"I'd say all the time, from the sound of it. Do you always call customers sounding like this?"

"Like what?"

"Like you've had the shit kicked out of you six ways to Sunday. Seriously, you sound like you're completely drained. How long have you been doing this?"

"Nine years."

"Wow. I dunno, dude. That's a long time to be making calls to strangers. Did you go to college?"

"I did. Haven't thought about that in a long time, though."

"Didn't you have any goals? Any dreams?"

"Yeah. I wanted to be a writer."

"I can dig that, man. Well hey, I gotta go, but look, dude, don't waste your life there, okay? Go write something. Realize your dream."

"Yeah," Donovan sighed, "I'll get right on that."

"Cool, cool. Oh, and thanks for the introductory offer, but I don't think I need to protect my identity right now. Peace."

Click. Beep.

The script for saving a sale lingered on his tongue. *No one ever wants to protect their identity until it's taken from them.* Donovan cancelled the automated dialer and sighed. Dozens of calls, not a single sale, and he did not care.

What could he do about the gray visions and his own disappearance? To whom could he turn?

Michael crossed his mind. He imagined working with his brother to track down the cause of the phenomenon. Twin detectives. The notion stirred a dying ember of creativity in his mind.

Whatever. Michael may have been his inspiration for Joe Hopper, but he was hardly empathetic. Michael Candle was more likely to laugh at his plight than help him. That was assuming his brother could even see or hear him.

Donovan pushed the thought away. He was desperate, but not *that* desperate. Not yet.

He flickered and colors drained from his vision. He caught a glimpse of the lanky white figure standing between two cubicles along the far wall. It saw him, took a few shuffling steps down the aisle, and was gone in a blink. The office bustled around him. He checked his watch, gathered his things, and made his way out of the building.

By the time he got to his car he'd forgotten all about his brother. Whatever was happening to him, he understood he would have to handle it on his own—and that, above everything else, frightened him most.

-4-
THE OMITTED

Donovan saw more of the tall white things and their Lilliputian counterparts over the next few days. On Wednesday night he happened to look outside and spot a lanky one on the sidewalk. He turned away from the bedroom window and looked at Donna, but she was rendered a dark specter in the gray gloom.

When he turned back, the creature beckoned to him with a spindly finger. Its mouth shivered open as it uttered a low moan. A moment later, the creature vanished as color returned to the world.

Donna was already fast asleep, wrapped in a tangle of blankets. He tried to snuggle next to her, but she rolled away from him. Defeated, Donovan turned on his side and fell into a troubling sleep in which he was haunted by nightmares of the white creatures.

Donovan woke Thursday morning drenched in sweat and twenty minutes late. Donna was already downstairs, and like the day before, she did not acknowledge his presence. When the gray sight overcame his vision, he saw the tiny white bastard sitting atop Donna's shoulder. It pressed against her ear, whispering with backward chatter.

"Stop it." He wished his voice didn't sound so weak. The creature's head twisted in place. It grinned, revealing a set of prickly teeth, and winked at him.

The kitchen returned to normal. Donna did not look up at him. She ate her breakfast and read the newspaper in silence. He left that morning without saying goodbye, and found that things at work hadn't changed, either.

At lunch time, he spent an hour in the men's room trying to sort out his troubled life. *What if this is permanent?* Joe Hopper spoke up in his head: *What makes you think it ain't, hoss?*

The symptoms were getting worse. He was isolated now, living among the rest of the world while slowly being omitted from it. Logic and reason had failed him, left in the past with Monday and some semblance of reality. He wondered if his soul would fade away with the rest of him. He wondered if Donna would remember him once he was gone.

Until this bizarre malady, Donovan thought he had his life under control, and the hard times were behind he and Donna. He considered his life after college, when they'd moved in together. Tiny apartment, tiny paychecks, massive bills. They'd lain awake at night, stressing over the next due date, the next loan payment, how they would afford to replace the brakes on their only car.

Life pulled no punches for young Donnie Candle, but he'd learned to get back on his feet, swallow the pain and his pride, and push back. Bills came and went, money came and went, and the hardships only strengthened his resolved.

He wasn't alone in his endeavor. The day after he proposed to Donna, she'd received her medical diagnosis. Fibromyalgia, chronic flare-ups which varied in severity, treatable but incurable, and though Donna wore a brave face, he saw the pain she dealt with every day. Long afternoons on her feet at a retail job left her in agony every night.

Holding her while she sobbed from the pain wasn't enough. He loved her, needed to help her however he could. He'd heard Identinel was hiring for a new sales office, heard they paid well and offered decent insurance plans, and applied. Never mind the hours, the commute, or the loss of flexibility. Donna was his best friend, and he'd do anything for her.

The day he accepted the job offer, Donna sat with him in their tiny apartment kitchenette—the "shoebox," they called it—and asked him if he was sure about his decision.

"*It's an hour each way to work, hon.*"

"*I know, love.*"

"*But we only have one car. You know we can't afford another one. Not if we want to move out of this place.*"

"*I know that too. That's why you're going to stay home.*"

"*Don—*"

"*You know your job isn't helping your pain, and we can't afford the medication without better insurance.*"

"But what about you? It's not fair to you. You won't have as much time to write, or much else…"

"I don't care. This isn't about me. It's about you. Putting my goals on hold isn't going to kill me. And if giving up the writing is what I have to do to get you the care you need, well, I would for you. Besides, this is just until we get on our feet. It isn't forever."

That was nine years ago. In the time since, Donovan rolled with life's punches, working his ass off to keep the seams of his world from tearing. At the center was Donna, and if he could overcome those early years of hardship, he could overcome this—whatever it was.

I would for you, he thought. *I'll find a way through this.*

He left the restroom strengthened by his determination, but as the day wore on, he wasn't entirely sure he believed it.

———————•———————

A five-car pileup on the highway made him late for dinner, and Donna was finished with her meal by the time he arrived home. He tried to apologize and explain himself, but his efforts were in vain. She could neither hear him or see him; worse, she didn't seem to miss him, either.

He thought of the crude thing on her shoulder, of the way it whispered its strange language into her ear. Was it the reason she didn't notice him? Donovan struggled against a tide of hopelessness washing over him. How could he stand to confront these strange circumstances when he didn't understand its nature? The tide was strong, and he feared he might drown in the current.

Donovan locked himself away in his office, busying himself with his novel while trying to put the troubling thoughts out of his head. He struggled for half an hour as he tried to begin again, but his mind kept wandering back to the matters at hand. *How would Joe Hopper solve this? Or Michael Candle, for that matter?*

He looked at the phone, contemplated picking it up and calling his brother, but feared he would be met with more silence. Just because the unwitting customers at work could hear him did not mean anyone else could.

Instead, Donovan retired early and tried to sleep away his trouble. His thoughts kept him awake, and he laid there for an hour before Donna crawled into bed beside him. She usually kissed him goodnight, but for the last two nights she hadn't, and tonight was no different. If his suspicions were correct, he couldn't blame her, but the lack of affection still hurt.

He reached over to give her a kiss and she rolled away. The move was sudden and cold, and watched her in stunned silence. *I would for her,* he reminded himself, *but sometimes it's so hard.*

"I love you, Donna."

She said nothing, and he lay there for a time, fighting back tears until sleep finally claimed him.

───────────·───────────

Friday morning began with more of the same. He woke, experienced the gut-pulling transition between color and gray realities, and saw creatures that should not be. Donna ignored him, as did his co-workers. By eleven o'clock he'd progressed through a block of automated calls, and the strangers on the phone were the only ones who paid him any attention.

He didn't understand how they could hear him when those around him could not, but Donovan was so starved for interaction that he didn't care. Many shouted and screamed at his intrusion, but even in their hatred for an annoying sales rep, Donovan found hope in their frustrations.

To better connect with his temporary audience, Donovan abandoned the standard Identinel sales script. Instead he interacted with his potential customers, engaging them in all manner of conversation. What else did he have to lose?

All topics were fair game. If he connected with the right person, the conversation could last up to an hour. One call went to a woman in Iowa named Eileen Carmike. For forty-seven minutes and fifty-three seconds, she and Donovan held a conversation about philosophy and the proper way to bake a turkey. Another call went to an elderly gentleman in Oregon named Zachary Rosen who had a passion for old cars and The Grateful Dead.

Though he enjoyed these conversations, Donovan grew increasingly depressed as he realized what he was missing from life. Here were people living their lives, with their own quirks and faults, and yet they were still somehow perfectly content. After a call with young Jimmy Frank, and their strange conversation about the nature of first and last names, Donovan removed the headset and checked his watch.

He had time for one more call before braving traffic for another silent night at home. He rubbed his eyes, yawned, and put on the headset. The automated dialer generated a new phone number with a single keystroke.

Click. Beep.

Static surged through the earphone, punctuated with the screech of an old dial-up modem before devolving into a regular series of rings. Donovan cringed from the abrupt noise, was about cancel the call when a connection was made.

The monitor revealed no name or address. All information fields were blank.

"Hello? Anyone there?"

More electronic interference shot through the line and took shape as a man's voice, steady and confident and cold. A whine of digital noise hung in the background.

"Hello."

Donovan cleared his throat. "My name is...you know, it's not important. I'm just a sales rep for Identinel Security Services. We offer identity theft protection. Do you mind if I give you a sales pitch?"

"I find it ironic that a man of little identity is offering to protect the identity of others. How noble."

Donovan held his breath, unsure of how to respond.

"In lieu of a sales pitch, I would not mind hearing a life pitch from you."

"I'm sorry, but I'm not sure I understand what you mean."

"You sound like a man who is not getting all he wants out of life. Perhaps you are stagnating in your current station. Tell me, Mr. Candle, what do you want out of your life?"

The stranger's words hung in the air, and Donovan froze up trying to think of a reply. Customers rarely turned the tables on him so effectively, and he found he lacked the desire to redirect the conversation. The cold tension in the stranger's voice unnerved him, but Donovan's curiosity pushed him to answer.

"It's not every day I'm asked that question. Let's see..."

"You do not have to answer that now, Mr. Candle. It was rhetorical."

"No, sir, it's perfectly fine. My life has taken a strange turn these last few days. To be honest, I'm not sure what I want out of life anymore. Today, after talking to other folks like yourself, I've realized just how much I'm missing."

"Missing?"

"In life. There's not much that defines me anymore. I guess if something interesting doesn't happen to me, or if I don't do something soon, I may disappear for good." An uncomfortable silence followed his words. The static on the line rose and fell, accenting a low chuckle from the strange man beyond it.

"Do you truly think so?"

"Yeah, I do. Just a feeling, really."

"Actions birth definition, Mr. Candle. Good luck finding your way."

The noise ceased with a faint click and the line went dead. Donovan stared at the screen, puzzled by the lack of information, and canceled the auto-dialer. Before he packed up his things to leave, a quiet thought wriggled to the front of his mind. *I never told him my name.*

"So how are things?"

Donna Candle juggled the phone and a mixing bowl. Her sister, Amanda, waited on the other end of the line for a response.

"That's a loaded question and you know it."

"Oh, please. It is *not*. You've bitched about Don all week."

She reached into the cupboard and retrieved a bag of flour. "I haven't *bitched*. I'm just concerned, that's all. He's never behaved like this."

"I don't know, Donna. From what you've told me, it seems pretty damn suspicious."

Donna sighed. She regretted mentioning Donovan's odd behavior. "I trust my husband, Amanda, so don't go putting any ideas in my head. There's something going on, but I doubt it's what you think it is."

"If you say so. You know the man better than anyone."

"I do," Donna said, and trailed off. *I thought I did.* She'd run the gamut of emotion and suspicion in response to Donovan's silence. At first, she wondered if there was someone else, but he wouldn't do something like that. Not the man she knew, anyway.

"Donnie's no cheat. He knows what I'd do to him if he ever did."

Amanda laughed. "Oh, hey—I should get going. Quinn just got home."

"Give my love to my favorite nephew"

"I will. Hang in there, okay? Call if you need me."

They said their goodbyes. Donna hung up the phone and looked at the mixing bowl. After spending most of the day in a restless fervor, she'd decided to bake a chocolate cake from scratch, with peanut butter icing. Donovan's favorite. She'd gone over every plausible reason as to why he would act in such a manner toward her, and their argument was the only logical solution. The cake would be her olive branch.

Her discomfort and irritability hadn't helped matters. Along with the usual fibro pain in her hip, Donna spent the last few days suffering from a series of strange migraines. The headaches came out of nowhere, in buzzing surges filling her head with blinding static. They made concentration so difficult, erupting at the most inopportune moments.

She'd tried explaining them to Donovan, but he was distant and quiet. Some nights, she thought he was with her in the living room, but when she looked over, his chair was empty. Sometimes, when he was there, he said strange things that didn't make sense, but she couldn't remember what they were. She went to bed alone, and her concerns grew as the days went by.

Had she gone too far? The more she strained to remember the details of their argument, the more they slipped from her grasp. She remembered her tone and regretted it. She remembered the gist of what she'd said, and that it was honest. She was tired of always saving, always scrimping for a goal that he kept pushing farther back. He'd promised her the job wouldn't be forever. Just a few years until they got on their feet, but they'd been standing for nearly a decade now, and she wished Donnie would take some time to sit down. It disappointed her, seeing her husband slowly transform into the man he was, when she remembered how vibrant and lively he was in college.

Donna smiled. Those were better days. She loved Donovan with all her heart—always would—but she admitted to herself that this week tested her resolve. It simply wasn't like him to ignore her. That morning he hadn't even said goodbye. She'd called her sister to vent, and now suspected Amanda was already on the phone with their mother, spilling the latest gossip.

One of the headaches crept into her forehead. She winced, steadied herself against the kitchen counter, and waited for it to subside.

When the migraine passed, she looked at the clock. Donovan would be home in an hour. She turned on the radio and went about preparing his cake.

The doorbell rang. Donna turned down the radio, listening. A series of knocks followed in quick succession.

She wiped flour from her hands and left the kitchen. There was a man at the door, his features distorted by its segmented windows.

Great, a salesman. Donna opened the door. When she saw the look in his eye, she caught the door with her foot, wishing she'd not opened it.

Smudged glasses clouded his bloodshot eyes, his irises painted gray with flecks yellow. Burst capillaries marred his nose, and a smudge of dirt clung to his chin. He wore a bulky green coat over a tattered suit. His tie was torn in half and flapped limply in the breeze, its threaded entrails stretching the length of his stained white shirt. Slick silver strands of matted hair were tucked behind his ears, and a rank smell of musty earth and old sweat haunted his presence.

Donna wrinkled her nose and held her breath. The man looked beyond her, into the kitchen. She tightened her grip on the doorknob.

"Afternoon, ma'am."

She offered the stranger a smile, but inside her alarms were sounding. *Close the door,* she told herself. *God, that smell.*

"Are you Donna Candle?"

"Yes, I am." His eyes darted back and forth, focusing on her and something behind her. "Can I help you?"

His lips curved into a nervous smile as his greasy hand shot to the door. He shoved his weight against it with such force that Donna lost her balance, sprawling backward. She landed hard on the kitchen floor and cried out in pain.

The dirty stranger stepped over the threshold and laughed.

Donovan caught the middle of another interview with Dr. Albert Sparrow while inching along the highway. He turned up the volume to drown out the noise of idling engines and blaring horns.

"—sometimes, when we're at our very limit, we may find ourselves in what I have labeled a *state of liminality.*"

The line of cars lurched forward a few more inches. Donovan flickered gray, and for a span of seconds he saw the white figures wandering between the rows of traffic.

"A state of transition. Think of it as if you were standing in a doorway, with one foot inside and one foot out."

"So, you're saying mediocrity places us 'in the doorway,' so to speak?"

"Something like that, yes. In this so-called doorway, a person stands on the threshold of two states—one of complete and dissolute anonymity, and one of profound activity. In my book, I—"

He switched off the radio. Traffic finally eased up, and ten minutes later he parked in his driveway. He took a breath as he approached the door, preparing himself for another evening of solitude. On a whim, he called out to Donna as he stepped inside.

"Honey, I'm—"

His voice faltered, and his brain refused to accept the message relayed by his eyes. Every mental function shut down and he forgot to breathe. His aborted greeting echoed across the entrance and into the kitchen. He had an unobstructed view of the disarray.

The garbage can was on its side, its contents strewn across the tile floor. Package wrappers, soda cans, and potato peels mingled with an overturned canister of flour and a puddle of milk. Some eggs remained on the counter, while others were crushed into a runny, yellow amalgam on the floor. Donna's mixing bowl sat on the counter next to a jar of peanut butter.

What the hell happened?

He stepped forward, saw the scattered cutlery and pattern of footprints in the dusting of flour. The wooden knife block was overturned in front of the refrigerator door. One of its knives was missing. Donna's name repeated in his head, a constant mantra of panic and fear urging him to move.

"Honey?"

His voice rang hollow in the empty room, too small, too weak. The clock in the dining room ticked off the seconds *Might be best shut your mouth, hoss. S'pose you ain't alone?*

If he wasn't alone, then who might still be in the house? His imagination built the scenario. Donna was preparing to bake a cake when someone— man or woman, it didn't matter—burst into the room, catching her off guard, and—

He looked at the knife block again. The scene played on in the back of his head. He saw a person in a black ski mask lurking in their bedroom closet, Donna bound, and gagged on the bed—

Donovan blinked, tried to calm his racing heart. He knelt, plucked a steak knife from the floor, and followed the trail of violence into the dining room.

Blood dotted the table cloth. He moved along the edge of the table, whispering a silent prayer that the blood didn't belong to his wife. A lump rose in his throat when he saw the furry shape in a dark pool of scarlet.

Mr. Precious Paws lay sprawled on the floor, the largest of Donna's butcher knives buried in his back. Another blade jutted from the cat's neck. A dark trail of arterial spray trailed between the poor animal and the wall. The cat's eyes were relaxed, staring on a point in space beyond the room.

Donovan chewed his lower lip and grimaced at the taste of bile at the back of his throat. His efforts couldn't last, and he retched.

"Mr. Precious Paws," he whimpered, and the reality of the situation struck him. "Oh God, Donna!"

Blinded by panic, Donovan dropped the knife and scrambled up the stairs.

"Donna!"

He threw open the bedroom door, ready to tackle any intruder he might find there, but the room was empty.

"Donna!" He screamed until his throat burned, the words scratching their way out of him like a frightened animal. The bathroom was empty, as were the office and spare bedroom at the end of the hall. *Donna,* his mind raced. *Donna, Donna, Donna.* Spots of black and purple blossomed across his vision, and he teetered on his feet.

When the splotches of color dimmed, Donovan found himself filled with a new urgency. The cops. He had to call the cops.

On his way into the office, he realized he'd trampled right through the crime scene. *They'll get over it, hoss.* He sucked in his breath to calm himself, reached for the phone, and nearly dropped the receiving when it rang in his hand.

The screen lit up to say UNKNOWN CALLER. Donovan pressed TALK. He lifted the receiver to his ear and tried to speak.

"H-Hello?"

A hiss of electronic noise filled his ears, and the drone took shape as a man's voice.

"Hello, Mr. Candle."

Realization spread through him in a series of chills. The hairs on his arms and neck stood at attention. He shook so badly that he almost dropped the phone. *How could that man get my number?* He had to hang up and call the police. He didn't have time for this, he had to—

"Focus, Mr. Candle. I require your full attention."

Donovan closed his eyes. "I'm here."

"Good."

Electronic noise filled the line, ghostly banshees shrieking and distorting in his ear. Donovan replayed their conversation in his racing mind, desperately attempting to make sense of what was happening. *No information on the screen, no phone number on the auto-dialer, so much interference—and he knew my name. He knew my name.*

A cold weight settled in the bottom of his gut as the digital noise unmasked the mysterious caller's baritone laughter. The erratic chirr was unlike anything Donovan had heard before.

Cold and deep, the sound of glaciers shredding the earth over eons, sheathed in a layer of gray static. A pulsing voice spoke in tandem, swollen with waves of white noise, undulating above and below the laughter before forming a single tone.

Donovan trembled, remembered to breathe.

"Is this interesting enough for you now, Mr. Candle?"

-5-
PUPPETS

Donovan gaped into the phone, confused and horrified by the stranger's revelation. Numerous replies came to mind, but all words failed him in that moment. *Can't be. Impossible. How?*

Electronic noise surged through the line, erratic glitches of audio compiled from a dozen other voices. A legion of identities masking the stranger's ominous persona. Donovan swallowed his fear and gripped the phone. "Who the hell are you? What have you done with my wife?"

"Please answer my question, Mr. Candle."

Donna. Oh God, Donna, what has he done to you? A suffocating cloud of anxiety surrounded his face, cutting off his air and making his head swim. His knees buckled, and he sank into his office chair.

"Mr. Candle."

"What question? Look, I—"

"Is this interesting enough for you?"

He tried swallowing the lump in his throat. "Yes."

"Good." The stranger's tone lightened, now almost jovial. "Allow me to introduce myself. My name is Aleister Dullington."

Donovan closed his eyes. "Mr. Dullington, did you take my wife? Did you hurt her?"

"Do not despair, Mr. Candle. I assure you that your wife is quite safe for now."

For now. The bottom dropped out of Donovan's gut. *Keep it together, hoss.*

"Where is she?"

"In due time."

Donovan shot out of his seat. "You tell me where she is, you son of a bitch. You tell me *now*."

"Now, now, Mr. Candle. It is not wise to curse the one who determines whether your precious Donna lives or dies."

The last of his adrenaline drained away, leaving him weak, feeble. He sank back into his chair and closed his eyes. *Whether your precious Donna lives or dies.* The words tumbled and spun in his head, bouncing off images of the kitchen and dead cat. *He's hurt her, oh God, he's hurt her or he's going to hurt her, or—*

"Calm yourself and focus, Mr. Candle. What I have to tell you will be most displeasing."

Sweat dotted his brow. The air in the room was hot and stale, and Donovan took it all in with one prolonged breath. He held it in until his lungs were on fire and his heart calmed, his head cleared. "I'm listening."

"You are a boring man, Mr. Candle."

Donovan scoffed. His wife was missing, and this bastard had the gall to criticize him? "Where is Donna? I want to talk to her right *now*—"

"I ask for your patience, Mr. Candle." Dullington spoke in measured syllables, with a flat intensity which ran beneath every vowel and consonant. "Do not push me. Or else."

Donovan shut his mouth. He tried to ignore the thoughts racing through his head and took another deep breath.

"You have spent the last nine years of your life in a job that stifles you. You slave toward empty goals, making empty promises to yourself and your wife."

"Mister, I don't need your insults."

"These are not insults. These are truths. If you find them insulting, I implore you to consider why that might be."

Donovan choked back a bitter reply.

"The transparency afflicting you is what I refer to as the 'flickering.' It is the result of your supersaturation with mediocrity."

"What? Listen, asshole—"

"Mr. Candle, if you interrupt me again, I will have your wife's non-vital organs separated from her body." His voice darkened, tinged with electronic resonance hiss through the phone. "We will begin with her ovaries."

Donovan fought back tears. His mounting frustration broke and withered under the man's threat.

"Do I have your undivided attention, Mr. Candle?"

"Yes."

"Good. You are experiencing odd things, seeing things that should not be, and your eyes reveal a world in gray."

"Yeah."

"Indeed. You are seeing the Monochrome, the world behind the world. This place will become your prison should you fail to cure your banality."

The strange man's words tumbled through Donovan's mind as he tried to process everything. Monochrome? A world behind the world? The words sounded ridiculous when spoken aloud, and Donovan would have discounted them as the ramblings of a mad man had he not experienced things exactly as Dullington described them.

But there was something else, something far worse than his own absurd affliction. Donna was gone, and Dullington was behind it. That was all Donovan needed to forget himself. Donna was his priority now, flickering be damned.

"Are you listening, Mr. Candle?"

"I am."

"You may speak. I am eager to hear your response." Aleister Dullington spoke with authority, his inflection cold, proper, almost courteous.

"What have you done with my wife?"

"Mrs. Candle is well."

"Answer my question." Donovan clenched his teeth, desperate to keep his temper under control. The situation demonstrated the sort of man he was dealing with, and he knew igniting Dullington's fuse would be a grave mistake—not just for Donna, but for himself.

"Your ire is encouraging." Dullington's rise in pitch gave Donovan the impression of a smile on an otherwise expressionless face. "I like a good show, Mr. Candle, and you seem like a man with the potential to deliver." He paused. Static filled the line like crashing waves. "Forgive me. You asked a question, and I will answer. Your wife is bound ankle and wrist. A bag covers her head. Before you ask, Mr. Candle, no. No one has had their way with her. Yet."

Picturing Donna in such a predicament made him nauseous. "Go on," Donovan said.

"As to where she is, I am afraid I cannot tell you now. She is safe, as comfortable as her situation allows. On this you have my word."

"Why are you doing this?" Donovan's voice was dry, weak. Distant bells rang in his ears and cold sweat blanketed the back of his neck. He fought against the nausea stirring in his stomach.

"We all serve a purpose, Mr. Candle. I am a reaper of mediocrity and a keeper of the Monochrome. The flickering delivers you to me."

Donovan thought of the visions, the white creatures lurking in the gray haze. Was this what he had to look forward to? Was this Monochrome his destination?

"Are there others?"

"You are one drop in a vast ocean, Mr. Candle. Your purpose is like so many before you: to sustain a balance."

Sustain a balance. The implication drove a chill down Donovan's spine.

"If you do not change your course, you will flicker out entirely. Most will not miss you, many will not remember you existed. But all is not lost, Mr. Candle. I am willing to offer you a rare chance at redemption in exchange for something I have lost."

"What do you want from me?"

"One of my prisoners escaped some time ago. Find him, return him to me, and I will return Mrs. Candle to you unharmed. Agreed?"

"But—" He paused, considered hanging up the phone and dialing 911, but what would he say? And what could the police do? He feared that doing so would only bring harm to Donna. The ball was in Dullington's court, and Donovan would have to play by his rules or forfeit.

"Before I leave you, Mr. Candle, I will tell you the man who kidnapped your wife is at a place called Rossetti's. His name is George Guffin. I have instructed him to guide you onward. Do you understand?"

Donovan's heart sank, and he once again fought the urge to vomit. The taste of bile filled his mouth and his stomach burned. Rossetti's, where he and Donna had their first date. He felt a deep hatred for the man on the phone. Though he'd never considered himself a violent person, he wanted nothing more than to wrap his fingers around Dullington's throat and squeeze.

"Time is running out, Mr. Candle. What you do next is your choice alone. Deliver what is mine, or your wife will die, and you will be forgotten. I look forward to your decision either way."

"Yes, but—" Donovan began, cut off by a pulsing drone surging through the line, a rhythmic noise like heavy digital breathing. "—but who *are* you?"

Dullington spoke through the drone, his voice one with the noise. "Who are *you*, Mr. Candle?"

Donovan wasn't sure how to respond. The question probed far deeper than he cared to explore. There were more pressing matters at hand.

"You do not have to answer now, Mr. Candle, but you will before our business has concluded. On your plane of reality, or mine."

A crush of static swept over the line before the deafening silence of a disconnect. In the solitude of his office, Donovan Candle hung up the phone, buried his face in his hands, and cried.

———————————•———————————

*T*hink, Don.

The cops. Should he call them? Logic dictated he should, but his gut said otherwise. After everything he'd experienced over the last week, Donovan was hesitant to dismiss the stranger's warning. Reporting Donna's abduction made sense in a logical world, but Donovan's world had dismissed logic days ago. What would he tell the cops? What *could* he say?

In the time it would take for the cops to arrive, investigate the scene, and question him, he could be well on his way to meeting George Guffin at Rossetti's. Even then, Donovan knew he would be the police department's prime suspect. His wild story would be laughed at by the entire police force.

He looked back at the phone. Aleister Dullington's demands flashed through his mind. *The world behind the world.* His stomach churned. He flickered, his office suddenly cast in a gray tone. After four days of seeing and experiencing the impossible, Donovan still found himself in disbelief. He struggled to reconcile the apparent cause of these bizarre symptoms. A boring existence? Mediocrity?

Many will not miss you.

When the flickering stopped, Donovan realized he had no choice but to accept his predicament. Dullington had him whether he liked it or not.

He thought of Donna, imagined her curled up in some dark room, the restraints cutting into her skin. Was she in pain? Had she taken her medication before her abduction? And how long before it wore off? Could she move, keep her muscles from getting stiff?

The dangers of a fibro flare-up weren't his only cause for concern. What lurked in the darkness beyond? Though he believed Dullington's statement that no one had touched her, he was certain this was merely circumstantial, and that if he didn't act soon her situation might change.

Donovan rubbed his eyes. *Get it together. You can do this. She's okay.*

He picked up the phone and listened to the dial tone. *What would Joe Hopper do?*

He wouldn't call the cops. Too much red tape, and he hated the cops.

But who, then? The answer came immediately, blurted out by the frantic voice of his conscience: *Call the* real *Joe Hopper.*

Michael was born to be a hero—from their childhood days in the backyard to his current career in private investigation, he always had to be the good guy. It was this trait upon which Donovan drew much of Joe Hopper's character, and one that hadn't diminished in its significance to him despite all the years of suppressed sibling rivalry.

He dialed Michael's number, preparing himself for assault with the press of each button. What if Michael couldn't hear him? Worse, what if he didn't believe Donovan's story? He hoped the news of Donna's abduction would be enough to erase any doubts his brother might have. For once, the issue at hand was not Donovan's inability to live up to his older brother's expectations.

As the phone rang a third time, Donovan realized he didn't care what Michael thought of him, so long as he got Donna back safe and sound. After a fifth ring, Michael's voicemail answered. Donovan waited for the beep, then cleared his throat.

"Mike, it's Don. Listen, I need your help. I really don't know how to say this, but—Mike, she's missing. Someone broke in and took Donna while I was at work. *Please* call me back as soon as you get this. Thanks."

Minutes later, Donovan stepped outside into the cool evening air. He shivered in the breeze as he locked the front door, zipped up his jacket, and went to his car.

The dashboard clock read 6:37, but he tried not to think about what he would have normally been doing on a Friday evening. Right now, he had only one thing on his mind: George Guffin.

A jolt of pain ripped Donna from a troubled slumber. Her head swam and her hip ached. The world was dark, the air hot and stale, and her exhalations clouded her face.

I can't breathe. The words surfaced from a murky pool of thoughts, and she panicked. She moved her head, desperate for fresh air, only the warm cloud of breath remained. She realized there was something coarse pressed against her face.

Confused, Donna tried to sit up. She wanted to pull the material from her face, only her hands were tied behind her back. Her heart raced, hammering nails into her chest. She tried to roll on her side and gasped from a jab of pain shooting through her hip. Her meds. How long had it been since she'd taken her last dose?

Too long. Hours, maybe. She had to take her meds, or the pain would only get worse. Donna tried to climb to her feet and realized her feet were tied as well.

What the hell is this?

She tried to sit up once more and winced from a stabbing pain in her temple. What did she do to her head?

Wait. My head.

Memories of what happened rushed back to her in a heap of broken images—

The man smiles and quickly shoves his weight against the door. It catches against her foot with such force that she loses her balance. The world spins, and for a moment she is falling. The floor catches her, and she cries out in agony upon impact. Her hip screams louder as red-hot fire surged through her body.

Dazed, her head fills with sparkles of light, and she looks up to find the dirty man standing over her. She sees him reach into his pocket and pull free two items. One is a black cloth. The other is a handgun.

She panics at sight of the weapon. Her heart races, and she reacts instinctively, scrambling onto her back and aiming a forceful kick at the intruder's groin. He yelps in pain and lurches over in agony. She struggles away from the door and back into the kitchen as he falls to his knees.

Donna's next impulse is to find a weapon of her own. She thinks of taking his but realizes she hasn't the slightest idea how to use a gun, nor how to retrieve it without putting herself within his reach. He could easily grab her, wrestle her to the ground, and choke her to death. Instead she crawls to the kitchen. Her foot ignites with pain when she tries to put her weight on it, and she thinks she may have twisted it when he forced open the door.

She crawls to the kitchen counter, reaches for a knife from the wooden block. She doesn't care what kind, so long as it has a blade, but before she can find one—

"You sneaky bitch."

There is pain in his voice, but worse, there is anger. She feels his hands on her legs, and she cries out when he squeezes her bad ankle. Desperate, she clings to a drawer, and it gives way as he pulls her from the counter. The drawer's contents spill to the floor. She spots a steak knife and strains to reach it, but the man is one step ahead of her. He kicks it away and forces her onto her back.

He's going to rape me, she thinks. *Then he's going to kill me. A dozen images flash before her in light of this realization—things she always wanted to do, a baby she wants to have but never will, Donovan's smiling face—and regrets that she will die with him angry at her.*

Donna fights. She kicks at the man, her foot connecting with his stomach, and he yowls like an animal. Seizing the opportunity, she scrambles for the dining room, unsure of where to go but not caring so long as it's away from this lunatic. Mr. Precious Paws is underneath a chair, watching. The man mumbles something that sounds like, "I won't let you down," and he's upon her before she can climb to her feet. She rolls on her back in time to see him standing over her, a butcher knife in each hand.

He moves toward her and the cat yowls. He's stepped on the animal's tail.

"I won't let you down," the man screams. He drops to his knees, catching the cat as it tries to escape. He holds the animal steady with one hand, swipes the blade, and exterminates Mr. Precious Paws in a single violent stroke.

Donna watches the feline's eyes, sensing its terror as the pitiful thing utters a final gurgling cry. Blood pours from its gut and its legs twitch.

"I. Won't. Let. You. Down."

He spears the second knife through Mr. Precious Paws's neck. Blood spurts onto the wall and dribbles across the floor.

"No," Donna gasps. She cannot muster a scream. The man turns to her, shaking his head, his eyes wide with rage.

"I killed the cat," he whispered, looking at the blood on his hands. He set his murderous gaze upon her. "You made me kill your fucking cat."

He pounces on her, and she does not have time to react. The man pins her to the floor. She thrashes against him, but he's too heavy. His entire weight immobilizes her. She watches his arm block out the light on the ceiling. His hand is balled into a fist, and it drops in a swift arc.

She feels it strike her temple, but there is no pain. There are only stars and the dark.

Donna found the darkness lingered and reasoned her head was now covered by the intruder's black cloth. She held in her breath to slow her heart. When the echo of its frantic pounding finally subsided, she discovered the sounds of movement, voices.

"Hello? I-I need help. Somebody?"

"She's awake."

"What do we do?"

"Shut her up."

Two men, somewhere in the darkness.

"Help me," she croaked. "I'm hurting—"

Donna tried to move closer toward the sounds, and pain shot through her hip. She uttered a sharp cry. One of the men laughed.

"Damn right you are. Now you shut your mouth, lady, or I'll—"

"What the hell do you think you're doing?" A new voice. A woman's voice. "Get away from her."

"I don't have to take orders from you, Alice."

A loud smack echoed across the darkness. One of the men gasped. "Maybe not, but I'll be damned if I'll sit here and watch you torment her. *He* didn't tell you to do that, did he?"

"No. He didn't."

"Now get out of here. *I'll* watch her." Another beat of silence filled the dark. "Go on. Fuck off, you two."

Donna chewed her lip, unsure whether this Alice person was any better than the two men. And who was this "he" she referred to? Donna wondered if he was the man who abducted her.

She gasped as the bag's coarse surface tore away from her skin. Dim light faded into view, and she had to squint to see it. An orange glow, licking the air like a serpent's tongue.

A shape drifted into view. Donna blinked, waiting for the blurriness to abate, and she saw the face of the woman who'd come to her rescue. She was young, barely thirty, her face spotted with dark grime. Her dark hair hung over her shoulders in knots.

"Here," Alice said. Hints of a smile teased the edges of her lips. "Drink."

She slipped her hand behind Donna's head, helped lift her up, and put a mug to her mouth. Donna sipped, grimacing from the water's bitter taste, but she forced herself to drink. When she was done, Donna pulled away from the mug and looked into the hardened eyes of the woman called Alice.

"Please let me go." Tears filled her eyes. "Please, I won't tell anyone. Just let me go. Let me go back to my husband."

Alice frowned. For a moment Donna feared Alice would put the bag over her head again. She watched the young woman rise to her feet. The fire beyond the room turned Alice into a silhouette.

Beyond the doorway, Donna saw columns of some kind, and benches. Trash bags piled atop one another, a rusty shopping cart tipped on its side.

"Where are we?"

The young woman turned and shook her head. "Just be quiet and lie still. It'll be over when he gets what he wants."

"Let me go. *Please—*"

Alice left the room, pulling the door closed behind her. The darkness returned, washing over Donna's body in a cold wave.

Rossetti's parking lot was filled with Friday night patrons, and the memory of his first date here with Donna twisted Donovan's stomach in knots. He parked the car and sat for a moment.

What would he say to this man? He'd thought about it during the drive. Playing the tough guy wouldn't go over well—after all, he didn't know how closely tied this George Guffin was to Mr. Dullington. He wished his brother was home to answer his—

Phone.

Donovan remembered the cell phone. He reached into his jacket pocket and retrieved it. His heart sank. *Don't forget to charge the phone,* Donna's voice echoed in his head. He unlocked the device. There was one bar of juice left.

He thumbed across the screen, selected his brother's number. Three rings followed by an error tone. He tried a second time only to be met with the same result. Donovan pulled the phone from his ear and looked at the screen: CALL FAILED.

"No shit." He looked out the window at the restaurant. "Just get it over with, Don."

His voice sounded tiny, lost. He flickered and caught a glimpse of five white figures loitering along the sidewalk before the world resumed in color. He shook off the sensation in his stomach, slid out of the car, and made his way across the parking lot.

When he reached the diner entrance Donovan realized he didn't know what the man looked like. He imagined someone physically intimidating enough to subdue another person.

He stepped inside, saw no such figure. To his left and right were booths filled with teenagers, adults near his age, and even a few elderly couples. Straight ahead was a bar lined with stools and a pair of cash registers. Vintage photographs of diner promo ads from the 1950s adorned the walls, and even the wait staff were dressed in pastel colors reminiscent of the era.

Donovan stood against a sweeping tide of nostalgia. He remembered vividly the details of his and Donna's first date, the way she smiled when he opened the door for her, the scent of her perfume. The atmosphere was inviting, comforting, and made him forget about the drab alternative he'd come to know so well.

As he stood in the doorway, Donovan realized just how alone he truly was. No one—not even the nearest waitress—looked up in his direction. *They can't see me,* he thought. The flickering overcame him, painting the café in shades of gunmetal. The diner's patrons darkened, their features obscured in a cloudy gray haze.

Except for one.

When his gray sight relented, Donovan spotted a small man picking at a plate of greasy fries. He wore a green coat that swallowed him in its folds. Buried underneath were the tattered remains of an expensive suit. Thick glasses gave him a wide-eyed paranoid look, his face cast in permanent shock.

George Guffin watched Donovan approach, a skittish animal ready to dart for an exit at the first sign of danger. He took a handful of fries and stuffed them into his coat pocket. Donovan noted the man's gaunt features, the way his face hollowed under the diner's unforgiving fluorescent lights, and the knotted strands of hair hanging over his shoulders. Dried blood on Guffin's hands gave Donovan pause, and he fought back a rising tide of nausea.

"George Guffin?"

The man in the green coat nodded. "Sit down. Candle, right?"

"That's right." Donovan took a seat across from the filthy man. George Guffin pushed the plate of fries toward him in offering, but Donovan's attention was undistracted, staring hard into Guffin's wild eyes. He realized he was squeezing his hands into fists, and tried to relax, but how could he? He wanted to be angry and violent, to smash Guffin's plate, to use its shards in torturing the truth out of him.

That's how Joe Hopper did business. The barbaric nature of his thoughts troubled Donovan. He swept them to the back of his mind.

George Guffin licked his lips. "Do you smoke?"

Donovan shook his head.

"Too bad." Guffin dropped a wad of crumpled bills on the table. "Let's move this party outside, shall we?"

"Listen, mister, I—"

Guffin slammed his fist on the table. "No, *you* fucking listen—" He pulled a handgun from his coat. "—Yeah, that's right. Now I've got your attention."

Donovan froze. "My undivided attention."

"Good. Now, you do what I say you do, and we'll get through this nice and quick-like. Do you understand that, Candle-man?"

Guffin tipped the gun barrel toward the door. Donovan left the booth with his hands held out to his sides while Guffin followed behind. No one in the diner noticed their exit.

Donovan thought about turning on the man. He saw himself pinning Guffin to the wall and wrestling the gun from his grip.

Stay put, hoss. You're no good to Donna with a hole in your head.

"Where's your car?"

"Over there." Donovan swallowed back all the nasty things he wanted to say. He calmed himself before speaking. "Mr. Guffin, I'll take you where you want to go, but just—just meet me halfway, all right? Where is my wife?"

George Guffin breathed deep and smiled. "I've missed this air. So alive."

Donovan ignored him. "I asked you a question."

"And I heard you, Candle-man." Guffin met Donovan's stare. "Your wife's fine."

"That doesn't answer my question."

"I know, but I've got rules to follow, just like you do." Guffin frowned. "Now I suggest you take me where I need to go."

A young couple walked past them toward the diner. They ignored the weapon in Guffin's hand. The world flashed gray, and Donovan saw the white creatures on their shoulders. "Can you can see them?"

Guffin nodded. "Of course I can. Dullington gave me a free pass tonight to do what I need to do, and—" His face flushed. He jammed the gun barrel into Donovan's gut. "Quit stalling."

Free pass? Donovan filed it away for later. He did as he was told and led Guffin to his car.

"You know the parking garage at 8th and Dwyer?"

Donovan nodded. "Other side of town, across from the courthouse?"

"You got it, Candle-man. And no funny stuff, or I'll blow your fucking head off."

Friday night traffic was slow-moving as they crossed into the city. What should've taken twenty minutes took close to an hour, and by the time they turned onto Dwyer Street, Donovan's nerves were shot. Guffin leaned forward in his seat and placed the handgun on the dash. Donovan glimpsed the weapon and wondered if it was real. He decided he did not want to find out.

"Three more blocks. It's on your left."

"Mr. Guffin, are you going to tell me what this is about? I mean, really?"

"You know what it's about."

Donovan braked at a red light and looked at his captor. "I know what's happening to me, but I don't understand it."

"Trust me, Candle-man, you don't want to."

"You understand it?"

"I understand you need to shut your fucking mouth." Guffin took hold of the handgun. "This is about what *he* wants, and I should know. I've seen others play his games. This is my turn. We're all his puppets. He makes the rules, and we move when he says to."

"We?"

Guffin ignored him. The light turned green, and they sped through the intersection. The garage at the corner of 8th and Dwyer covered more than half a city block like a concrete fortress. Donovan guided the sedan through the entrance and pulled a ticket from the gate. The crossbar rose, and he tapped the gas.

"Top floor, Candle-man."

They ascended slowly. Guffin didn't object to their speed. Donovan took the opportunity to scout the surrounding levels in hopes that someone—anyone—might be parked there for the evening, but the garage was empty except for a few cars on the lower levels. He parked alongside the edge of the roof overlooking the entrance.

When Donovan shut off the engine, Guffin raised the gun and shook his head.

"Leave the keys."

Donovan slowly raised his hands. "Okay, no keys."

"Get out, Candle-man."

Donovan did as he was told, fighting to stop himself from shaking, but his body refused to obey.

Outside, clouds rolled overhead, and thunder clapped in the distance. From this height he saw the twinkling lights of the lower city, as well as some of the taller skyscrapers. Across the street, the courthouse shone bright with orange halogen lights, illuminating the statue in the courtyard. Donovan cracked a smile, remembering a time when he and some college friends toilet-papered the old statue while Donna and the rest of their girlfriends watched with feigned amusement.

That memory stirred the chunk of ice in Donovan's gut, and he turned to face Guffin. "Where is she?"

"She's not here."

"*Where is she?*" Donovan took a step around the car. Guffin raised the gun.

"You stay right there, Candle-man. Hands on your head."

Donovan hesitated and did as he was told. A cold breeze swept over them. Lightning flashed, followed closely by a crash of thunder. A few drops of rain pelted his head and hands.

"What are you getting out of this?"

He saw the man's trembling hands in the glow of the garage lights. Frowning, Guffin approached him with terror in his wide eyes. Droplets of rain pattered and rolled off his coat.

Donovan glanced at his feet, measuring the space between himself and his captor. *Two steps, maybe three.* His heart thudded a cacophonous rhythm in his ribcage. Was he really going to do this? Could he? He thought of Donna tied up somewhere at the mercy of a lunatic and decided he would damn well try.

"Answer my question, Guffin."

"A permanent free pass. He lets me out of his hell. I do this, and he'll let me go. That's the plan. That's our agreement. I bring you here, he takes you, and I stay. Goddammit, that's how it's supposed to go. *Where are you, Dullington?*"

Guffin trembled as he screeched into the wind. He lowered the weapon, and Donovan made his move. His hands took on a life of their own, moving against his better judgment, and they connected with the muzzle.

Startled, Guffin jerked his hand away, but lost his grip. The gun hit the ground and skidded across the pavement.

Donovan met the eyes of his adversary. In that moment he saw only Donna, her hands bound, a bag over her head. He saw the lifeless eyes of Mr. Precious Paws.

Get 'em, hoss.

He charged forward and tackled George Guffin. The collision sent both sprawling to the ground. Donovan's hands found their way to Guffin's throat.

"You bastard, yo—*urch.*"

Donovan squeezed as hard as he could, concentrating the pressure of his fingers into the tender flesh of Guffin's neck. He was so intent on crushing the man's trachea that he didn't see Guffin's fist until it was too late.

Colored lights exploded before Donovan's eyes, followed by a searing white pain across his jaw. The force flung him back onto the cold concrete. He tried shaking off the splotches of purple and black.

Guffin climbed to his feet. He hacked and coughed, rubbing at his throat.

"You motherfuckin' asshole." He stumbled, regained his footing, and planted a swift kick into Donovan's ribs. The blow cleared all the misshapen forms from Donovan's eyes, and he managed to catch Guffin's foot before a second kick.

He sank his teeth into Guffin's ankle, biting down as hard and far as he could go, tearing through the man's flesh and stopping only when he reached bone. The coppery taste of blood filled his mouth, but he dared not stop.

This is for Donna, he thought, and bit down even harder. Guffin screamed into the night. He fell backward, kicking his foot free of Donovan's mouth.

Donovan realized he held a piece of Guffin's flesh between his teeth. He spat out the chunk and retched. Guffin cried in agony as he scrambled to put pressure on the wound.

Lightning split the sky, followed by another heavy crash of thunder. Sheets of rain fell upon them, limiting visibility, but Donovan found what he was looking for in the pale light. The gun lay just beside the car's rear tire. He crawled across the pavement to claim it, braced himself against the back of the car, and watched Guffin writhe in pain.

"You...you *bit* me."

"You kidnapped my wife." Donovan climbed to his feet, wincing from the sharp pain stabbing into his ribs, and approached his wife's assailant. He leveled the gun to Guffin's head. "Start talking, Mr. Guffin."

Blood gushed from the wound in the man's ankle, forming a dark pool around his leg. Watching the pitiful man struggling in pain, Donovan realized Guffin was far smaller than he thought. Buried within the bulk of the coat and draped in the remains of a suit was a small-framed man suffering from starvation.

Guffin spat at his feet. "Fuck you, Candle-man."

Donovan squeezed the trigger. The recoil sent the bullet off course, barely missing Guffin's head. The shot startled Donovan so badly that he dropped the gun. It clattered on the pavement at his feet.

"He played me," Guffin groaned. "He'll play you, too. Dullington's sadistic. He's using us, feeding on us."

Feeding on us. Donovan shivered.

"There are others like you 'n me. He lets us out sometimes, only lets people see us when he wants them to. Some forget about us and others don't. We're just his pupp—" Guffin's eyes widened. He screamed. "Oh God, please no, not now—"

At first Donovan did not understand what was happening, or to whom Guffin was speaking. The hiss of rain grew muffled, and when he blinked, he found himself amid the gray sight. Sensations of rain and damp air were displaced by an unsettling emptiness. The sprawling cityscape beyond was but a lifeless outline on the horizon.

Donovan blinked a second time, and the gray sight remained. He looked down just in time to watch his body flicker and solidify.

George Guffin moaned. Donovan looked up and saw the man flickering as well. The pool of blood around his ankle now appeared as a black puddle.

"—no, please no, please, please! What did I do wrong?"

A mournful sob erupted from behind them. Donovan turned, and watched in frightened awe as one of the albino figures approached. His whole body went cold. The world was soundless but for his heart, pounding with a fury all its own.

"Not the Yawning! ALEISTER! PLEASE!"

As the albino thing neared, Donovan realized just how large the creature was. Seven, maybe eight feet tall. Its hulking arms reached the ground, dragging lazily behind as it took one determined step after another. The lanky thing paused, regarding Donovan with its empty eyes, then uttered a deep sound that could only be described as a lazy yawn.

Yawning.

Guffin beckoned to Donovan. "Help me! Candle-man, I-I'm sorry, just—*fuck, just HELP ME—*"

The Yawning stood over Guffin and leered, swaying on spindly legs. Its mouth shivered and twitched. Donovan watched, helpless, frozen in place by his terror. The Yawning's mouth opened wide, forming a gaping maw that appeared bottomless.

And still its mouth opened, stretching until its jaw touched the ground.

Guffin screamed. *"NO! ALEISTER, I'M SORRY! I'M SO SORR—"* The otherwise sluggish creature moved with sudden agility, engulfing the screeching man into its blackened hole of a mouth. A sickening crunch of bone issued from the monster as its jaw closed.

Donovan gasped, felt his stomach lurch.

The albino thing turned and faced him. A ring of scarlet circled its thin lips. George Guffin was no more.

Now there was only Donovan and the Yawning.

-6-
MONOCHROME

The Yawning lurched forward, raised its massive arm, and beckoned to him. Its quivering jaw relaxed as its mouth opened, and from it came that same low-pitched howl. It echoed in the empty air and carried across the lifeless cityscape, inciting answers to its solitary call from other Yawning somewhere below.

Chills raced across Donovan's arms, snapping him from his frozen state and urging his feet to move. On the far side of the rooftop, just beyond the creature, was an access door to the garage stairwell. The Yawning took a long stride toward him, and Donovan reacted without thought, bolting for the door.

He charged forward, past the hulking beast, feeling its coarse flesh scrape his arm as he went by. The sensation reminded him of rubber. *This isn't happening. This can't be happening. He—it just gobbled him up.*

Donovan ran. He knew that if he stopped, he would scrutinize and postulate, and now wasn't the time. The last thing he wanted was to be consumed like Mr. Guffin.

As he raced across the garage rooftop, Donovan realized just how empty everything was. He saw faint droplets of rain falling all around him, but he could not feel their touch. There was no breeze, no violent storm gusts, and crashes of thunder were absent. Lightning in this realm flash a brighter gray, barely noticeable among the other shades. A mechanized drone hummed in his ears, emanating from every corner and every street, the sound of tinnitus manifest in the physical world and given voice.

Donovan pushed himself forward, told himself to ignore the bizarre intricacies surrounding him. He ran as fast and as hard as his body allowed. His chest heaved, lungs ablaze with a fire urging him forward, every breath a violent combustion of fear and resolve.

He looked back only once, and that was all the motivation he needed: The Yawning lumbered after him. Despite its sluggish pace, its long scrawny legs carried it a great distance with each stride. When Donovan reached the door, the albino monstrosity was perhaps three strides away.

Donovan stumbled down the stairs, shoes slapping loudly against concrete in the empty space. He cleared the last four steps with a single leap, pausing long enough to get his bearings. The door opened above, and a guttural sob filled the stairwell with vicious melancholy.

He looked up. The Yawning glared down at him and uttered another moan.

"Oh shit."

He willed his legs to move. They carried him out the door and into the empty street. There were no cars, no silhouettes of life elsewhere. For the first time since the flickering began, Donovan saw the Monochrome in full clarity. It was an image of the regular world, bled of color and wiped of all texture. In this guise, the city at ground level appeared as a series of jutting structures composed of planar geometry, each surface cast in gray tones. Featureless, erased of texture, the city was draped in a sheet of monochromacy, and he was lost somewhere beneath its folds.

Another moan echoed from down the street. A second Yawning rounded the corner of what once was the courthouse. More appeared from behind an object Donovan recognized as the courthouse statue. Beyond the courthouse, three more emerged from another structure's entrance.

His heart sank. He might outrun them now, but his legs would give out sooner or later.

A door slammed open from behind. The first Yawning shouldered itself through the exit.

He sprinted away from the garage and the courthouse, diverging from the path he and Guffin had taken to get there. After crossing a nearby bridge, he realized he was lost. Without definition, all the city's buildings looked the same, and Donovan had no reliable landmarks. For all he knew, the Yawning were still on his trail, but he allowed himself enough time to think.

Okay. You can do this. For Donna. Think, Don. North side of the city. Courthouse, garage—

He looked back, tracing a mental map from where he was to the to the highway.

The highway itself, he realized, probably wasn't a great idea. He remembered his commutes earlier that week, when random bouts of gray sight revealed hundreds of the lurking monstrosities standing between rows of traffic.

If one spotted him, it would call out to its friends, and he'd soon have an entire population of them breathing down his neck.

George Guffin's screaming face flashed before his eyes, and Donovan shook his head in disgust. He thought of Guffin's weapon, felt foolish for dropping it, and laughed at himself. Would a gun cross over into this horrible place? And would a bullet even be useful? Even if it were, he doubted a handgun would be enough to drop one of those hulking beasts. He'd never fired a gun before tonight, and that had been an accident. All he had to go by was what he'd seen in movies. His brother was the real gun expert—

Michael Candle's face popped into his head. He turned in the opposite direction, gambling that the street to his back was Poplar. If his mental compass was accurate, this street would take him right to Michael's neighborhood. Getting back to the real world was a mystery he'd have to solve when he arrived. Walking to Michael's home would take hours, and there was no telling how many of those things stalked the streets. He needed his car.

Get moving, hoss.

Donovan jogged toward the street corner and froze when he heard the sob of a nearby Yawning. It turned the corner ahead of him and stopped alongside the adjacent building.

Silence seeped into the gap between them, broken only by the rapid thump-thump-thump of Donovan's pounding heart. It sounded like a marching band warming up in his head.

The Yawning opened its quivering maw when it saw him, and Donovan was already running when the white thing took its first steps toward him. His aching rubbery legs carried him through an intersection he thought to be Poplar and Rose. There he paused just long enough to look back and watch the Yawning bellow one of its angry communicative calls. A chorus of responses rose from deep within the labyrinthine city, heightening his terror and urging him to move. *Don't stop, don't look back, just go! Go, go!*

When he turned the corner, he caught sight of a row of gray trees. *The city park.*

He raced ahead, feet clattering across the pavement as the Yawning closed in on him. Their cries echoed from beyond, but all Donovan heard was the frantic pacing of his heart. He darted into the grove of trees and hid behind one of the trunks until the moaning call of the creatures grew distant.

When he was sure they were gone, Donovan stepped away from the tree and wandered into the park. The sameness of his surroundings was disorienting. Flat palettes of gray provided little depth, and the shadows were indiscernible from their sources.

The park covered a city block, and he had no way of knowing which side he was on. He wandered through the trees, terrified of what he might find lurking just out of sight, and desperate to find a way out of this gray labyrinth. And if he made his way out of the city, Michael's neighborhood was still an hour's walk from the park, maybe a little more. Getting there wouldn't matter if he couldn't find his way out of this prison.

Frustrated and exhausted, Donovan climbed a knoll and dropped to his knees beneath a nearby tree. He brushed his hair back and focused on his breathing, tried to calm his heart and stop the panic from rising.

"Think, Don. Where are you? There's gotta be a landmark or something…" A round object caught his eye just beyond the tree line. He stared at it for a moment, trying to make out its features against the muted tones, and realized where he was.

The fountain.

He and Donna had spent the latter half of their third date here, huddled together on the grass, watching the water spout from the fountain's center. Donovan remembered that night clearly because it was a night of firsts. Their first concert together, the first time Donna said she loved him. The first time he saw her cry.

————————◆————————

Donna Kemper was a lithe phantom on campus, inhabiting the commons with her easel or sketchbook, devouring the world around her with the stroke of a brush or pen. Curly red hair pulled back into a bun, mismatched socks, paint-spattered jeans, a T-shirt for a band he'd never heard of—everything about her screamed "punk artist," long before the world smoothed out her rough edges, and the first time Donovan saw her he couldn't stop staring at her almond eyes.

They shared the same circle of friends, fellow inhabitants of the campus liberal arts department, amassing a mountain of student loan debt on the promise of making it big someday. Donovan had delusions of grandeur, fancied himself the next Dashiell Hammett; Donna kept her dreams in check, was far more grounded in the reality of the art world, and hoped for a steady graphic design gig.

A mutual friend introduced them on a whim during a university art showing—Donna had three pieces on display in the gallery, one of which now hung in their house—and by the end of the night, he'd worked up the courage to ask her out.

Two months later they were a solid couple, inseparable except for their classes and part-time jobs, and when Donovan won tickets to see his favorite band at a club downtown, Donna agreed to go. She wasn't a fan, found the music far too electronic and abrasive, but she respected Donovan's passion for the art.

He should've known the danger, should've noticed the logistics of so many people crammed into a tiny club. The band had just come out of a lengthy hiatus, its reclusive front man a tortured artist just like everyone else they knew, and the show was sold out within minutes. That Donovan won tickets through a radio giveaway was a miracle—spare tickets were going for hundreds of dollars online.

When the lights went down and the music began, every person in the club pushed forward toward the stage barrier, and Donovan nearly lost Donna in the undertow. He gripped her wrist, digging his fingers into her skin as the crowd tried to tear her away. One song faded into the next, angry guitar chords and violent drums working the crowd into a frenzy, and the surge continued. Donovan struggled for air as the bodies of a dozen others pushed forward.

He nearly lost his grip on Donna's wrist as a crowd surfer's boot kicked him squarely in the back. Stars exploded before his eyes, the whole world dimming as the pain shot through his body, and the music grew fuzzy, muted in his ears.

Donnie.

Her voice. A scream from somewhere far away and yet right there in his ear.

Donnie, don't let me go. Don't—

He lost his grip. Donovan clenched his teeth, pushed against the guy in front of him, and managed to turn himself around. The crowd was a turbulent sea, churning to the beat of the band, the bodies moving in singular waves. He spotted Donna's panicked face just as she dipped below the surface, and he dove forward after her.

Donovan didn't remember much of what happened after. He clocked someone in the jaw on his way through the crowd, evidenced by his swollen knuckles afterward, and someone stepped on his calf as he reached down to pull Donna to the surface. Just as he wrapped his arm around her waist, a concertgoer's knee connected with his nose, and blood gushed from the wound as stars danced before him.

Someone—security, maybe, or possibly just a Good Samaritan—eventually noticed their struggle and forced a path through the crowd for them to escape. Trembling, Donna clung to him as they limped toward the venue's entrance.

"Oh God, Don, you're bleeding."

She went to the bar for some water, and when she returned, Donovan noticed the marks on her wrist. Four red welts in the shape of his fingers.

"I'm not the only one with a war wound." He watched her smile as she wet a cocktail napkin and cleaned the blood from his face. Pain shot through his nose. "How bad is it?"

"It's not crooked."

"I guess I can live with that."

Two more concertgoers, a man and a woman, were escorted from the crowd with similar wounds. Donovan leaned against a wall, closed his eyes and listened to the throbbing in his head drown out the music.

"I'm sorry," Donna began. "It's your favorite band, I didn't mean—"

"Do you want to get out of here?"

"I—" She searched his face, blinked back tears. "Yes. Can we?"

"Let's go."

They left the venue, walking hand in hand for a block until they reached the park. The night was clear, the air cool, and he relished the feel of the breeze on his face. After the violence of the last ten minutes, the normal bustle of the city seemed almost peaceful.

He led her to the park, toward the fountain square. There they sat beneath a tree and counted their wounds. Donna's wrist would bruise, and she had some scratches on her shins. Donovan was worse off, with a broken nose, swollen knuckles, and scrape on his calf. His back ached from the crowd surfer's boot.

Donna put her head on his shoulder. "I'm so sorry, Donnie. You're missing your band, and it's my fault."

"It's not your fault, Donna. I promise." He looked at her, wiped a tear from her cheek. "You were going to drown. I had to do something to keep from losing you in there." He paused, recounting his words, and relishing the sudden warmth in his chest, the flutter in his belly. "I'll miss out on a dozen shows if it means being with you. I would for you, Donna."

They sat together in silence for a time, watching as couples strolled by, tossing coins into the fountain. Listening as the world moved on around them.

"I have a secret to tell you," she whispered. She nuzzled his neck and kissed his cheek. "I think I'm falling in love with you, Donnie Candle."

He rested his head against hers and took her hand, threading their fingers together. "That's okay, Donna Kemper." He closed his eyes. "I fell for you a while ago."

———————•———————

Donovan resisted the tears elicited by the tender memory. He pushed away from the tree and passed the fountain, following a walkway to the park's plaza. A pair of vendor shacks, once decorated with menus and graffiti, stood out like two gray monoliths. He stopped beside the nearest one and rubbed his eyes.

How could he let this happen? He'd been careless with his own life, and now Donna suffered for his mistakes. He regretted not conceding to her wishes Monday night. All she wanted was to get away for the weekend. She was right—it wouldn't break their bank account. He knew that. Even a full week away wouldn't do them in. Years ago he would've agreed to it without a moment's hesitation.

Donovan shivered. When had he grown so selfish and boring? Perhaps Aleister Dullington was right. He *was* saturated with mediocrity.

Chin up, hoss. This ain't over yet.

He took a breath, made a silent vow to take Donna on a real vacation if they made it through this, whatever *this* was.

"Okay." His voice was tiny, insignificant amidst the droning noise of the world. "Get a grip on yourself, Don. Keep moving. Kee—"

Movement stole his attention. It was nearby, a subtle scuttling like a small mass of insects.

Donovan peered around the corner of the shack toward the tree line. His heart stopped, and the world sank into the pit of his gut.

The tiny white things marched across the grass, a veritable army of them numbering in the thousands. They looked harmless while standing on the shoulders of others; now he found their mass intimidating.

More movement in his peripheral vision. A small wave of the little bastards crashed over the fountain, their pudgy bodies sprawling across the walkway, backward voices meshed together in a singular hum. One of the creatures saw him. It screeched and pointed. The others cheered.

"I'm not seeing this." His declaration fell flat against their wall of reversed language.

The throng of miniature albino soldiers marched onward. When they reached the plaza's perimeter, Donovan turned and ran, managing only a few strides before realizing he was surrounded. The Lilliputian monsters streamed from all corners, over the grass, the benches, even on the limbs of trees. He was lost in the Monochrome wilderness and had stumbled into a hive.

Donovan flattened against the wall of the shack. *I'm going to die here. They're going to drag me down and tear me to pieces.*

The creatures stopped a few feet away. They chattered in unison, looking up at him from a sea of black eyes.

"Such a shame Mr. Guffin could not follow instructions." Aleister Dullington's voice boomed overhead, and the ground trembled with each syllable. His words thundered with authority, asserting one immutable fact: this was his kingdom, and here he was God. "But you, Mr. Candle, have proven most obedient. Most entertaining."

Donovan turned, frantically searching for his enemy, but the voice echoed from every surface and every corner, from the very air itself. The army of creatures condensed into itself, each creature scrambling over the next, forming a mound of pale flesh writhing like maggots on a corpse.

Extensions took shape as limbs. A stump became a hand, fingers carved out of the air by an unseen knife, and the figure of a man slowly took shape from the squirming mass. Two arms connected to a torso, the torso to a head, and the black eyes of the white creatures came together, forming a pair of bulbous obsidian orbs.

The white flesh dimmed, outlining the features of a robe. Aleister Dullington stepped away from the pale mass, walking atop their writhing bodies as if on water. His ashen robe draped from his shoulders to the mass of creatures at his feet, and Donovan could not tell where one ended and the other began.

Parts of a whole. He sees what they see, and they speak for him. Everything he knew of the creatures made sense now. They were Dullington's sentinels, their language his own.

He looked upon the pale man before him. The robe's cowl obscured a face of porcelain, featureless except for the pair of black eyes, unremarkable except for the lack of eyelids. No hair, no eyebrows, sallow cheeks, and thin lips. Aleister Dullington was nothing like Donovan had pictured in his mind, a far cry from a cartoonish villain or embodiment of evil. This was a solitary figure of secrets, a tortured shade among the shadows, and for a moment, Donovan wondered if the warden was also a prisoner in this place.

"My sincerest apologies, Mr. Candle. I did not instruct him to murder your feline pet. Perhaps I waited too long to grant Mr. Guffin his opportunity for redemption. He was overzealous."

Dullington pushed back his cowl as he approached, and Donovan discovered he was too frightened to move. "You continue to surprise me, Mr. Candle. The way you handled Mr. Guffin was most unexpected. I am glad I chose you." The creatures beneath his feet whispered in reverse. Dullington looked down at them, listening. "The Cretins say you have spirit. I am apt to agree. We haven't witnessed spirit like yours in some time."

Donovan choked back his fear and met the pale monk's bulging eyes. "Where's my wife?" The frailty in his voice disturbed him, like he'd aged forty years in the last two hours.

"In due time, Mr. Candle."

"No. You fucking tell me where she is right now."

Dullington remained unfazed, expressionless. His dark eyes offered no emotion. "Do not misunderstand your position here, Mr. Candle."

"Guffin said you played him. How do I know you won't do the same to me?"

"I gave Mr. Guffin rules he chose not to follow."

"What rules?"

"Simple rules, Mr. Candle. I gave him the opportunity to redeem himself by doing what I cannot. I told him to take your wife without doing harm. I did not tell him to take a life as well."

"Would you have let him go?" Donovan watched his enemy bow his head in thought. He realized the man looked like a demonic monk.

"I would. There will always be others." A thin smile spread across Dullington's pallid face. "Always people like you."

Chills crept down Donovan's spine. *People like you.*

"You are my puppet, Mr. Candle. Make no mistake of that. I am using you, just as I used Guffin, and just as I have used countless others."

"This person you want me to find, is he one of your puppets, too?"

Aleister Dullington frowned. For a moment Donovan feared he'd touched a nerve, but the hints of emotion on his adversary's face were short-lived.

"A puppet, yes. One who must have his strings cut. But that is not for discussion at this time. Tonight was a test to see if you truly are the right man for the job. You performed well, and as a reward, I will allow you to speak with your wife." He reached into his robe and retrieved a cell phone. The device was ancient by tech standards, a plastic brick with an antenna. Donovan hadn't seen one like it since the 90s. "Consider this a gesture of good will."

Speak with your wife. Donovan's heart sang. He reached for the phone, but Dullington snatched it away.

"Listen to me, Mr. Candle. You will return to your reality when you are finished."

"And then what?"

"And then you will await further instructions. My Cretins will not inhibit your progress, so do not fear speaking to your brother. He will see you."

Donovan stared into Dullington's dark eyes and realized there was nothing he could hide. The ruler of this world saw everything, inside and out, and the suggestion filled his gut with lead.

"Call your wife."

Dullington held out the phone. Donovan hesitated a moment before taking it. He put it to his ear, recoiling from a sharp hiss of electronic interference. The dissonant noise converged into a series of clicks.

Voices of men and women filled the background. He heard someone say "Speak."

"Donna?"

Heavy breathing filled the line, inhaling and exhaling in quick gasps. Haggard, dry, weak. "Don? Donnie, is that you?"

He closed his eyes, turned away from his captor. "Honey, are you okay? Has he hurt you?"

"My head hurts, but I'm all right. Where are you, Don? God, you sound a thousand miles away."

The sound of suppressed sobs in her throat forced tears from his eyes. "I-I'm in the city, near the park. Our place in the park. Listen, I can't talk for long, honey. I'm coming for you. I promise, I—"

"I love you so much, Donovan, I lov—"

The line went dead, and Dullington plucked the phone from his ear. He was still forming the words to reciprocate his love when he met Aleister's lidless gaze. He forced himself to stare deep into those glassy black orbs with a newfound ferocity.

"That is enough for now, Mr. Candle. You will return to the Spectrum. Expect to hear from me on the morrow." Aleister Dullington offered Donovan a stoic nod as he pulled the cowl over his head. Below him, the Cretins chuckled backward in mockery.

Their laughter grew dim as the flickering overtook Donovan, their bodies fading out of existence as the world came to life. Texture and color returned, the steady rainfall once again pelting his head, the cool breeze driving a chill down to his toes.

He blinked a few times, trying to accommodate the onslaught of color and depth. Friday night sounds met his ears. The park was empty. Crowds of people huddled beneath umbrellas as they rushed by on the sidewalk ahead of the park plaza. Cars honked and came to a full stop as traffic lights changed.

The cold air was refreshing, nothing stale like that of the Monochrome. What had Dullington called this side of reality? The Spectrum?

Fitting.

Donovan surveyed the park to get his bearings. He zipped up his jacket, shoved his hands into his pockets, and began the walk back to his car. Along the way, he tried to work out the situation with Aleister Dullington and this mystery man he was supposed to find, but Donna dominated his thoughts most of all. She'd sounded so scared, so tired.

He forged into the downpour, his wife at the forefront of his mind. Her image kept him warm in the night air.

I'm coming, honey. I'll find you. I promise.

-7-
THE MISSING

One moment her husband was there, a panicked voice out of the dark, and then he was gone again. Donna fought to keep her tears at bay.

The haggard thing in tattered clothes pulled the phone from Donna's ear and frowned. A sour stench of old sweat lingered in the air, curdling Donna's stomach. She wondered how long it had been since the poor girl had bathed last. Months, maybe.

The flames of a barrel burning just beyond the doorway licked the air, casting wicked shadows over the area. The heat stung her eyes, and she had to look away. The young woman sat beside her for a moment, staring at the floor, whispering to herself.

"Alice? That's your name, isn't it?" She looked down at Donna and slowly nodded. Their eyes met, but only just, and Alice soon looked away. "Please talk to me."

"I'm not supposed to."

"Can you tell me where my husband is?"

Alice looked away. "He's in the Monochrome. Aleister has him now."

Donna opened her mouth to inquire but stopped short when Alice produced a roll of duct tape. She tore off a small strip.

"Sweetheart, you don't have to do that. I'll be quiet if that's what you need me to do."

Alice paused. She stared hard at Donna, her eyes aglow in the firelight, her face shifting in the dancing shadows.

"Not a word?"

"Not a word. Cross my heart." Donna offered a smile, thought she saw the faint traces of one reciprocated on Alice's face, but the light was too dim to know for sure.

"I always liked you, Donna, and I want to see you through this. If anyone comes near you, you scream, okay? You scream, and I'll come running. Not all of us are good. Some of us deserve to be here."

I always liked you. Her words stole the breath from Donna's lungs. Did they know each other? And then the weight of Alice's words pressed down, made Donna's heart race, forced her to focus on more urgent matters. *You scream. Not all of us are good.*

Alice stood and left the room. Darkness filled the enclosure, punctuated by a sliver of flickering light seeping through a crack beneath the door. Voices spoke in muffled whispers from beyond her prison, but she couldn't make them out.

Donna rolled herself onto her side, wincing as her muscles and joints cried out in protest, wiggling her fingers and toes to keep the blood flowing. Her head still ached from the blow. She feared she might have a concussion, but the agony in her hips was a greater concern.

Breathe in. Count to ten. Exhale.

She guided herself through the steps of pain management as her therapist taught her, but the throbbing ache was still there, deep in her bones. Instead, she thought of Donovan, tried to picture his face, tried to imagine him in the park.

Why was he there? It didn't make sense, but given all that had happened, not much else did either. There was someone else with him, but the voice was obscured with electronic noise. She'd heard the others outside her cell mention two names: Dullington and Sparrow.

The latter was a name spoken with disdain and mockery; the former was barely spoken at all, and when it was, the fear in their voices told her everything she needed to know. Who he was, and why he was doing all of this, was beyond her scope of understanding. She could think of nothing she and Donovan had done to offend anyone. They weren't rich, so that left out ransom as a motive. What, then? Donna sighed, thinking back to the phone call. Donovan sounded so far away.

She tried not to think about that. Hearing his voice in this murky place was dream-like. It was the last thing she expected would happen, but when she saw the phone in Alice's hand, her heart leapt up with the hope that it would be her love on the other side. There was something in his voice, though. Something that had been there for the past week, something she couldn't put her finger on.

"Distant" came to mind, and she realized that was a perfect way to describe his behavior. There were times when she felt he wasn't there at all, as if he was just a ghost haunting their home as she went about her day. Sometimes she'd hear him speak, only to look up and find she was alone in the room. And the headaches—God, the headaches were unbearable.

It was stress. Had to be. Donovan's stress became her stress, and that gave her the migraines. And his stress was that job. Always *that job*. She knew it wasn't good for him. He was meant for something more than that, but—

His voice spoke up in her head before she could finish the thought: *But we needed the money*. That disturbed her. Fresh out of college, they had their share of debts, and those first few years were tough. They shared financial duties with a number of part-time jobs, until the pain in her joints grew too much to bear and Donovan made her go see a doctor. The medical diagnosis changed everything, changed their goals, their lifetime plans. And then Donovan decided to go work for Identinel so she could stay home and recover—

God, she wanted to hate him for that, even if it was a selfish impulse. He did what he did for her, but the guilt she felt was more than she could bear some days. She wanted to scream and rant like the caged animal she'd become, but at the end of every panicked episode and every fury of expletives to an empty house, there was Donovan's innocent intention to help her. She wanted to hate him for it and would if she didn't love him so goddamn much.

If only he hadn't taken that damn job.

But where would they be if he hadn't? She needed the insurance. Their part-time jobs alone couldn't afford the premiums alone. And his salary had enabled them to move out of their tiny apartment and into a tiny house. But to every minor luxury was a price, one which Donovan paid with his soul one piece at a time. He allowed them to mold him into what they wanted him to be: a company man. They led him along with a carrot on a string, promising more and more, but in the end it never amounted to as much as they took away.

She saw him slaving over his writing, watched him put it off to work overtime at the office. In college, he lived for his writing. He had big dreams. Watching him slowly walk away from those dreams depressed her. She wanted the best for her husband, and she wanted him to be happy.

But what of her own happiness? She thought of their argument Monday night. She was so unhappy and fed up—not with him, but the way he'd allowed the job to ruin his life. He was stuck there, the company knew it, and Donna was terrified he would blame her.

She feared she might grow to resent his selflessness; worse, she feared he would grow to resent her for putting him in such a position. His distance over the last week triggered such fears, and over the last couple of days, she'd wrestled with how to bring it up to him. Now she might not get the chance.

Stop it. You're going to drive yourself crazy.

Donna twiddled her fingers to keep the blood flowing. Ghostly pins prickled her fingertips. Her hip sang when she tried to get comfortable, and the movement called the pressure in her bladder to her attention. Would they let her out to pee?

She wanted to call out, tell them she had to go to the bathroom, but remembered her promise to Alice. The thought of duct tape wrapped around her mouth kept her quiet.

She squeezed her thighs together to hold back the sudden ache in her bladder.

He'll come. He'll get us out of this mess.

If they came out of this in one piece, she would make him quit that horrid job.

But what about the baby? she heard him ask. If they wanted a baby, they had to save and save and save—

What about living? They'd barely lived their own lives—what made them think they could foster another life into being?

Stop it. Just stop it. Keep it together, or there will be no baby.

Donna blinked her tears away.

You'll see him again. He's going to figure this out. He always finds a way.

The ache in her bladder prompted a round of shivers. She tried to squeeze her legs tighter but gasped softly when the sensation of warmth washed over her. Warm urine gushed, then trickled between her legs, soaking her clothes, forming a puddle around her waist. The heat of shame overcame her, and she reminded herself that it didn't matter anymore.

She shivered, yearning for freedom from her dark prison. Her head swam, and she closed her eyes, eager to be rid of the chills and the throbbing pain in her hips, free of the frustration and loss in her heart.

Oh Don, where are you?

———————•———————

"**W**as that good for you?"

She rolled off him, perching herself on the edge of the bed in a single fluid motion. He was impressed, but figured she'd had plenty of opportunities to perfect her craft. *Maybe*, he thought, *or maybe she's just a good actress.*

Albert Sparrow sat up flipped on the hotel lamp. "It certainly was." He gestured to his shriveling cock. "I'd say he enjoyed it too."

The prostitute looked over her shoulder. The way her black hair spilled down her naked back roused his interest. Maybe he'd have another go with her before sending her back where she came from.

Her coquettish smile was infectious. He leered at her, excited by the taboo of their copulation. He was old enough to be her father.

"So, my dear—" He climbed out of bed and walked across the suite. He put on a white robe. "—how, exactly, does one become a woman of your *profession?*"

She looked away, embarrassed.

"Forgive me," he said. "Drink?" Sparrow gestured to the minibar. The woman—he thought her name was Lindsay—offered a sheepish smile and nodded. Sparrow opened the door, plucked two single-serving bottles of whiskey from the top shelf, and poured them into a pair of tumblers.

She took the glass and drank the whiskey in one gulp. "Thanks, mister—"

"*Doctor.*"

"Oh." Lindsay—or was it Linda?—brushed the hair from her eyes. Sparrow pulled his own silvery hair back into a ponytail. "What sort of doctor?"

"The scholarly kind. *Philosophiae doctor.*" He made a theatrical bow. "Dr. Albert Sparrow, at your service."

"Wow. Aren't you the author of that book—" She snapped her fingers, searching for the title. "A Life—something."

"*A Life Ordinary: A Comprehensive Study in Human Mediocrity.*"

"That's the one! I heard you on the radio."

"Indeed."

He strolled over to the dresser and slowly opened the top drawer. He saw what he was looking for, smiled, and put his hand on it.

"Tell me, Lindsay—"

"Lanna."

"Apologies, *Lanna*. What did you want to do in life? Surely this wasn't it."

Her face darkened, cheeks flushing a deep red. Lanna looked toward the window with its drawn curtains, then back toward the door. Sparrow stood between her and the exit.

"Lanna?"

"Huh? Oh—a dancer. I wanted to be a dancer, but—I dropped out of school because I needed the money, yeah, and then I fell on bad times, my mother got sick and I had to help her out, so—"

Sparrow let his smile fall. He stared hard at the woman, right in the eye, so she would know he *knew*.

"—I think I should be going." Lanna lunged for her purse. Sparrow lifted the gun from the drawer, pointed it at her pretty face. She froze in mid-step.

"The first thing I learned about lying was to keep it simple. Never embellish more than you have to." He motioned to the bed. "Have a seat. You're going to tell me everything."

Lanna glanced back at her purse. It didn't match her thousand-dollar price tag. It was stained, dirty, like she'd found it at the bottom of a dumpster. Sparrow closed the gap between them and pressed the gun barrel against her forehead.

"Sit down."

She did as he bade her. Sparrow looked over at her handbag. He went through its contents: a revolver, a couple of spare bullets, a pack of smokes, a lighter, and a photograph. Sparrow smirked, held up the photo and showed it to her.

"Do you think the photographer got my best side?" Lanna turned away, her head down like a scolded child. A tear dripped from her chin. Sparrow looked at the photo. "I still can't believe they picked this one for the book jacket. Such a shame." He shook his head.

"Look, mister—"

"Doctor."

"*Dr.* Sparrow—we don't have to do this. He just wanted me to find you, and—"

He lifted the weapon from her purse. "Coerce me? Allow me a moment, dear, and tell you what *I* know. *I* know you aren't the first. *I* know you won't be the last. He's had Missing just like you on my trail since the day I escaped, and I've got news for you, bitch—"

Sparrow thrust himself upon her. She tried to scream, but he was too fast for her. His hands found her throat. Lanna slapped his head, his shoulders, trying to beat him back, but Sparrow would not be denied his freedom. He dug his fingers into her flesh, grimacing like a rabid dog as he watched the life drain from her eyes.

"I'm not going back. Not for him, *never in a million—fucking—years—* and *certainly* not because of a whore like you."

Spittle flew from his lips, splattering against her cheek. Lanna held his gaze as the life slipped from her in a hushed whimper. He gave her throat one more squeeze to be sure. She did not move.

Dr. Sparrow climbed off her body, wiped the sweat from his forehead and spittle from his chin. He stepped away from the bed. The room flickered for a moment, as did Lanna's body.

"Take her back. Go on, take her back, you sadistic bastard. Come collect your whore."

Lanna's body dimmed, flickered, and vanished from the bed. An imprint of her body remained in the sheets. His former master's words echoed in his head: *Once a part of the Monochrome, always part of the Monochrome. It is the sum of its parts.*

Sparrow opened the minibar and took out a tiny bottle of vodka. He unscrewed the cap and drank it in one gulp.

Dullington would never let go of him. Never. His plans for Sparrow were too grand, too selfish to abandon. The vodka burned all the way down his throat, setting fire to his stomach. He grimaced, waiting for it to go to his head.

He spent the night on the floor, his feet facing the wall. He'd slept in the bed for two nights in a row. A third time might establish a routine, and he could not be too cautious. It was this caution which kept him out of the gray world, away from Dullington's reach. So far it worked, but he had to remain on his toes. He had to be ready. The whore was obvious, singling him out at the bar, her advances too strong. He'd had his share of whores, and Lanna wasn't one of them.

Nice try, Al. You'll have to try harder.

An image of Aleister Dullington sprang to mind. It prompted a chill that lingered in his old bones for hours. Dr. Albert Sparrow curled up in the coarse blankets, closed his eyes, and tried to sleep away waking memories of his years lost in the gray maze.

They were nightmares on tiny white legs, and they followed him down into the depths of sleep.

-8-
CANDLES

The storm let up as Donovan neared his brother's neighborhood. Remnants of thunder boomed in the distance, but the rain fell elsewhere, and he was grateful for its passing.

The flickering lingered after leaving the Monochrome. He hoped it would stop, as he'd found more excitement in the last several hours than he'd had in his whole life, but the brief glimpses of a gray world did not relent. Phantom hands wrenched at his guts while the world bled color in moments of fractured reality, the veil pulled back to reveal the impossible nightmares beyond. Dozens of Yawning stood along the sidewalks and streets, lurking in the corners of buildings and in the shadows of tall trees. They were everywhere and they were nowhere, an army of white sentinels guarding the maze of gray.

Donovan tried to put the abominations out of his mind and focus on the task at hand. He wondered if Michael was even home. He'd tried calling again after returning to the car, but the phone's battery was dead. Not that it mattered. Michael turned off his phone, especially on Friday evenings; however, he also knew Michael had to come home sometime, and decided he would wait his brother out.

When Donovan turned onto Michael's street, he was relieved to see he wouldn't be reduced to shivering on the curb. Lights glowed warmly from the windows of Michael's house. Donovan parked along the curb and sat for a minute.

What if he doesn't believe me?

He looked down at Guffin's weapon on the passenger seat. Recovering the gun from the garage rooftop seemed like a good idea at the time, but now he questioned his intentions. Joe Hopper's reassuring drawl piped up in his head: *Won't come to that, hoss.*

They spoke different languages, he and Michael, but Donovan had learned to adapt over the years. Michael Candle might not buy into the more sensational aspects of Donovan's story, but he would respond to Donna's abduction.

Donovan took the gun and got out of the car just as a strong gale swept down the center of the street. Thunder hammered farther out over the city. He shoved the weapon in his jacket pocket and hurried up the sidewalk.

A glow of shifting light from the television lit up the picture window in front of the house. Donovan took a breath before ringing the bell, embarrassed to be crawling to his brother for help, relieved to be seeking his brother's help.

A full minute passed before the door swung open. Michael Candle stood before him in a green bathrobe sporting several days' growth of facial hair, clutching a bottle of beer in one hand.

"Don? What—"

But Donovan's mouth was dry, and words he'd imagined saying to his brother faltered on his tongue. His legs turned to jelly, and he all but collapsed at Michael's feet. The sobs came in long whiny gusts. Michael stood over him, shocked, unsure of what to do or say. Finally he knelt and put a hand on Donovan's shoulder.

"Talk to me, man. I tried to call, but I couldn't get through on either line. What's going on?"

After a few seconds, Donovan collected himself, and met Michael's concerned stare.

"I need your help."

"**D**rink this." Michael handed him a tumbler of scotch. "It'll warm you up."

Donovan sipped the drink, feeling its slow burn all the way down to his belly. Michael perched on the edge of his recliner and picked up Guffin's weapon from the coffee table. He ejected the magazine and examined it.

He grunted. "No registration number. You realize how much trouble you'd be in if you were caught with this?"

"It doesn't matter. No one can see me, anyway" Michael returned the gun and stared at him. Donovan put down his drink. "It's complicated."

"Try me."

"Fine."

Donovan told his story, starting with Monday's argument and finishing with his drive from the parking garage. Michael sat back, swallowed by the armchair's upholstery, and gave his brother a hard look.

"You...do understand how insane all of this sounds, right?"

Donovan nodded. He understood all too well. A shiver ripped its way through him, and he took another sip of the scotch, relishing its fire on his tongue.

"Of course I know how it sounds, but if you go to my house, you'll find that my wife isn't there. The kitchen is a disaster. And Mr. Precious Paws—" He paused, recalling the cat's lifeless eyes. He took another drink. "My cat's dead."

"And you didn't call the cops?"

"No, I didn't call the cops. What the hell would I say to them? Honestly, Mike, if I called the damn cops—even your friend, the old guy—"

"Detective Brock."

"—Right, Nathan Brock. Even if I called him, do you think they'd be hot on the case?" He waited. Michael didn't answer. "Exactly. I'd be sitting at the station, regurgitating my story over and over while they decide whether or not I'm out of my fucking mind."

"Don, I can't decide if you're crazy or not."

"Funny."

Michael smirked. "Y'know, I thought you were joking when I got your message earlier."

"Joking?" Donovan set down his glass with a loud clank. "Donna is fucking gone, Mike. My wife is—" He bit his lip. He couldn't bring himself to finish the sentence and wasn't certain he wanted to.

Michael frowned. "I'm sorry, okay? I didn't mean it like that. All I meant was, nothing unexpected ever happens to you."

Donovan opened his mouth to speak but paused. His brother was right, nothing unexpected ever happened to him. He'd lived his life in a safety net of his own construction, going about his days without so much as a variation in routine or structure. It had led him down this path, and now Donna's life was at stake because of it.

"Anyway, you've got a point about the cops. They'd have you detained under suspicion while they search your house."

"That's why I called you instead. At least you'd hear me out before calling the men in white coats to carry me away."

"Jury's still out on calling the men in white coats; your story's logic doesn't add up."

"My story's logic?"

"Yeah." Michael poured himself a glass of whiskey. "If you're flickering out, how come I can see and hear you? You said no one else could."

Always looking for the con. Donovan had to smile, but it quickly faded when he remembered Dullington's words. *My Cretins will not inhibit your progress.*

"I had reservations about coming here, about calling you, but Dullington knew that. The best I can figure is, you can see me because he wants you to see me." Donovan shrugged. "Otherwise, I haven't the slightest idea."

Michael leaned forward, tumbler in hand, his eyes alight like a child waiting for a magic trick. "Are you doing it now? The flickering?"

"Not right now. It's random. Sometimes it will be hours, and it will start up out of nowhere. Just like—"

Hiccups, he wanted to say, but the sensation silenced him in mid-sentence. His stomach knotted as color drained from the room. Michael lost detail and form, reduced to a shadow, and no Cretin stood on his shoulder. This observation confirmed Donovan's suspicions: The Cretins made people oblivious.

When he flickered back, Donovan found his brother staring in shock. Michael's hands trembled.

"Mike?"

"You vanished. How did you do that?"

Donovan shrugged. "I told you, it's random. I can't shut it off."

Michael sat back in his chair. He drank his scotch in a single gulp, grimacing as it burned its way down. He scrutinized Donovan, his eyes narrowing to an intense gaze. *He doesn't believe it,* Donovan realized. Even after seeing it happen, he still doesn't believe it. For a moment he was angry, but when he put himself in Michael's place, he realized he couldn't blame him.

"Mike, I know this might be difficult to believe—"

"Do you remember when we were in high school, and you had a hell of a time with calculus? You couldn't wrap your brain around it, no matter which way it was explained to you."

He did. Simple arithmetic was one thing, but math with numbers and letters still perplexed him.

"What's your point?"

"Whatever just happened to you," Michael went on, filling his glass, "well, I saw it. And I'll be damned if I understand it. Like it doesn't compute."

"Maybe you're not supposed to understand it."

"Maybe not, but it does tell me one thing about all of this." Michael took another drink. "It means you're not nearly as batshit crazy as I thought you were. Or if you are, it's contagious."

Donovan smiled. "Or genetic."

"That too."

Donovan wanted to believe he was crazy, that this situation was a delusion concocted by his sick mind. That meant everything was fine, Donna was still home, safe and sound, their cat was still alive—

But that ain't the way it's goin', hoss. You know it, 'n I know it.

Donovan did know, and the knowledge left a bitter taste in his mouth. He reached for the bottle and poured himself another drink.

"So let's say you're not crazy, and I'm not crazy." Michael paused, grinning while Donovan tipped back the glass. He drained it in two swallows. "Go easy on that."

Donovan wiped his mouth. "I'm fine. You were saying?"

"Right. If we're not losing our minds, then it means what's happening is really happening. That means you're not bullshitting me."

Donovan nodded. "I wouldn't make this up."

"I know. That's what scares me." Michael paused, thinking. "This guy who took Donna, what did you say his name was?"

"George Guffin."

Michael rose from his armchair and left the room. He returned a minute later with a notepad and pen. He sat, scribbling across the top page.

"This Dullington guy—" Michael kept writing. "—did he give any indication as to who he's looking for?"

Donovan shook his head. "His protégé. No name. I think we'll find out tomorrow."

He watched Michael write, filling the page with a quick scrawl, pausing every few words to check the previous lines. His eyes darted up and down, double-checking himself. Donovan found it fascinating, watching his brother work, and he felt comforted by it. He recalled writing scenes with Joe Hopper, wondering how Michael might go about his work. He'd been too timid to ask, and he was happy to see that he got it right.

A few minutes and a full page later, Michael paused, looking up at his brother.

"Anything else?"

"No." Donovan gestured to the notepad. "What's all that?"

"My curiosity."

"What the hell does that mean?" Donovan watched Michael rise from his seat. He capped the bottle and returned it to the kitchen.

"It means I've got work to do. Have you eaten anything?"

Donovan realized he hadn't since lunchtime, but all the panic had ruined any sort of appetite he might have had. The scotch burned in his empty stomach. His head swam.

"No, but I'm not hungry."

"Well, there's food in the fridge if you do get hungry." Michael motioned to the stairs. "Come on."

"Where are we going?"

"You're going to bed. I'm going to check on some things."

"I can't—"

Michael smiled. "You need to sleep, Don. I don't know what you went through to get here, but you look like hell now. Go sleep. You need it."

Donovan fought back a yawn. He didn't like the prospect of sleep—not with Donna in captivity—but his brother had a point.

"Go to bed. I'll wake you first thing in the morning."

He followed Michael upstairs to the guest room. They stood in the doorway for a moment, unsure of what to say to one another. Donovan wanted to thank his brother, and the words were on his lips to do so, but Michael silenced him with a simple gesture. He put his hand on Donovan's shoulder.

"She's going to be okay, Don. We'll find her."

Donovan tried to smile. "I hope so, Mike."

He turned away before his brother could see the tears in his eyes. He closed the door, choking back the sadness and the sobs, and waited to hear his brother's descent before letting it out.

Michael stood over the coffee table, staring at his page of notes. George Guffin. The name had a familiar ring to it that wouldn't relent. It was somewhere in his head, buried deep enough that he couldn't quite retrieve it, but its presence nagged enough to let him know it was there.

The other name, however—Aleister Dullington—raised no flags. It was an odd name, almost too self-aware to believe given what his brother told him tonight. He still had a hard time buying it, but then he'd seen his brother disappear before his own eyes.

I'm just tired. Or maybe it's the booze.

Michael ran his hands through his hair, staring at his notes. He kept thinking about the way Donovan faded, the way he could see the sofa's texture through his brother's body. A chill crawled up his spine.

He took the tablet and went into his home office. Each wall was lined with filing cabinets packed with stacks of files representing years of work. At the opposite end was his desk, heaped with files piled as tall as his computer monitor. He'd long thought about expanding the business and renting office space but had been too busy to follow through. Not that he minded. The money made being busy worth the lack of free time.

"Guffin, Guffin…" He opened the cabinet drawer labeled "G," rifled through the mess of folders until he came upon the name. "There you are."

The folder's contents were scant. It contained the requisite paperwork—filled out by Darlene Guffin, the man's sister—a few handwritten notes, a copy of the final invoice, and a single photograph clipped to the inside of the file. He moved into the light, stared at the man's pallid face, and thought about what Donovan told him. This Guffin fellow didn't even look capable of doing such things. He looked like a sneeze might knock him over, but then again, acts of coercion could change a man.

Michael sat at his desk and switched on the computer. He chewed his lip. *Donovan, what the hell have you gotten yourself into?*

He was used to his brother's fantastic stories. As children, Donovan used to tell Michael the wildest tales after bedtime. They were stories of superheroes, vigilantes, and inhuman creatures.

Monsters.

Descriptions of this "Monochrome" reality seemed like something his brother might concoct from his imagination. Donovan's insistence on speculation, despite simpler logical explanations, did not help matters. These Cretins, the Yawning, even Aleister Dullington—were all too far-fetched, and yet—

He just vanished in front of me. In and out, completely transparent.

Michael had read about tricks of light, even scientific experiments to bend it, but such things were the stuff of illusions and laboratories. So, what was it, then? Not a trick, certainly. And, he figured, it didn't matter.

Regardless of this thing he'd witnessed—for which there had to be a logical explanation—the life of his sister-in-law was at stake. *That* much he did believe. He'd never seen Donovan so troubled. His brother was the most devoted person Michael knew, and his love for Donna was sacred. This wasn't something he would joke about.

Michael leaned back in his chair, staring at the ceiling. He yawned. The liquor was getting to his brain, making things fuzzy around the edges. *Change tracks,* he thought, putting his hand on the mouse. He opened his web browser and searched for "Aleister Dullington."

Zero hits. He looked down at his notes, then tried another: "Monochrome."

There were too many entries to sort through.

What did Donovan call it? Right, the "flickering."

Michael searched for the term. Again, it yielded too many results. The hour was late, and the scotch was pulling at his eyes. He tried one more phrase: "Monochrome + Flickering."

Another grouping of results popped up. Halfway down the page, one entry caught his eye: "It is the point at which a man throws off his shackles and declares 'No more.' He must justify himself in the face of flickering anonymity, lest he be subjugated to an eternity of monochrome oblivion."

Michael clicked the link, which directed him to an online retailer offering a discount on the book *A Life Ordinary: A Comprehensive Study in Human Mediocrity.* The same quote was farther down the page, along with a photo of its author. He was an older man with salt-and-pepper hair tied back into a ponytail. His eyes were a cool blue, and he wore a smirk like an old hippie who'd finally sold out and cashed in.

Michael scribbled some more notes on his tablet. "Now we're getting somewhere."

———————•———————

Sleep found Donovan quickly, but so did the nightmares, and they made short work of the day's remains. He saw Aleister Dullington's grinning face, two lidless eyes peering out from a shroud of blackness. At first, his dream-self thought the face was just an image, a tapestry hung upon some vast wall. Then the eyes moved and the mouth opened, bellowing laughter both mechanical and human. It was the sound of the Cretins, their voices like records played backwards, coupled with the grinding of rusted metal against metal. A low electronic drone filled the spaces in between, twisting together, culminating into an ominous wave. The noise thickened the air, and Donovan felt himself swallowing quicksand he could not see.

Dullington opened his mouth, spilling out a seemingly endless sea of Cretins and Yawning like gobs of mucus. Donovan stood, rooted in place by an invisible hand which squeezed him, expelling the air from his lungs. He found he couldn't blink, and his heart pounded with fury, threatening to burst from his chest.

Looking down, Donovan saw his skin bulge. There was no pain. He watched in silence as his chest cracked, splintering into thin red lines that crawled outward. Each breath spread them wider, allowing his heart to beat its way out of captivity. The bloody organ flopped down onto the black floor below.

The wound sealed itself, and Donovan's heart kept its rhythm, beating a counterpoint to the terror coursing through his mind. He tried to speak but found his voice was gone. Dullington leered at him, a disembodied face against the darkened shroud. Donovan wanted to look away, but no matter where he looked Dullington was there, grinning.

Who are you, Mr. Candle? I will tell you. A nothing-man, with a nothing-face and a nothing-life. A liar unto yourself; you are a great deceiver.

No, Donovan thought, *I'm not a liar.*

Dullington's face bulged and broke, seams splitting around his eyes, down the sides of his nose, and into his mouth. A pale gray sludge gushed from the seams as his skin peeled back, revealing the meat and muscle underneath.

You are, Mr. Candle. There are no greater lies than those you tell yourself.

His black eyes fell from their sockets and rolled over a throng of Cretins. Donovan watched as one of the eyeballs moved past and into the darkness. *I see you,* it whispered, *and you see me, see you, see me, see you...*

Donovan felt a sharp tug at his face, followed by a wet tearing sound. A piece of his skin fell from his cheek, landing with a sickening plop. He wanted to scream, but his mouth wouldn't move. His lips detached from his skull to join the pile of flesh at his feet.

I will show you, Mr. Candle. You will see there is nothing underneath you but a waste of flesh and a wealth of lies.

I'm not a liar, Donovan wanted to cry, but his body's actions were no longer his own. He stepped outside of himself, becoming an observer as his body tore itself apart one piece at a time. The visage was one of meat and bone, devoid of flesh, eyes inset in a state of constant shock.

A voice spoke from these ghoulish remains: "I am perfectly content."

Each of his eyes plopped from his head and dangled just below his nose.

Don, a voice said. *Donovan*.

He tried to scream as his former self decayed, but he found himself unable to make utterance. There existed only the hushed sound of movement, of little legs scampering across the black divide.

"Donovan, wake up."

The Cretins swarmed the pile of flesh at his feet, consuming his remains. The last thing he heard before consciousness pulled him from that black abyss was the sound of Dullington laughing—not from somewhere else, somewhere above or around—but from within.

———————◆———————

Donovan squinted, rubbed his eyes, and looked up. Michael stared down at him, a mug in his hand.

"You okay?"

Pale light filtered through the window. He looked around the room, confused about how he got there. Fragments of the dream clung to his conscious mind, taunting him with flashes of Aleister Dullington and his monochromatic minions. Donovan ran a hand across his face, feeling for scars left by his nightmare, but it just came away wet with perspiration.

"Don?"

The previous day rushed back to him. He frowned, shook off the dream, and yawned.

"You were struggling in your sleep. I heard you talking."

Donovan thought of the nightmare, fighting back a chill. "I'm okay. What time is it?"

Michael sat on the edge of the bed. "It's almost ten."

"Did anyone—"

"No one's called. I made you some coffee. I hope you like it black."

Donovan took the mug and drank. The coffee was bitter and burned his tongue, but he didn't mind. When he was finished, he gave his brother a once-over. "You look like shit."

"Thanks. I'm usually not up this early on a Saturday."

"Still a night owl?"

"Always." Michael went to the door. "I did a little digging last night, found some things. It's downstairs, for when you're ready."

Donovan took another sip of the coffee. He climbed out of bed and stood at the window, gazing out at the overcast morning. A neighborhood of cookie-cutter homes lined the block, the driveways occupied with new SUVs and sports cars. He remembered his dream—*I am perfectly content*—and frowned, thinking about how he used to pine to live in such a place.

But that's not you, hoss. Never was.

It wasn't. He wasn't sure who he was anymore, but he knew who he'd become was not the man he wanted to be.

A bird cawed overhead. Across the street, one of Michael's neighbors got in a car and backed out of their driveway. Life went about its business, oblivious to the gray layer underneath.

He thought of Donna, cursing himself for bringing all this upon her.

"I'm sorry." Tears welled up in his eyes, but he wouldn't let them come. He'd done his share of crying. No more.

He stepped into the bathroom to refresh, then went downstairs where he found Michael in his his office, surrounded by filing cabinets and stacks of files. Donovan surveyed the room, recalling how messy his brother had always been, and smiling at how things never seemed to change. There were stalagmites of paper rising from the floor of the office cave, mute testaments to Michael's years spent as a private investigator.

"You've been busy."

Michael followed his brother's gaze, surveying the surrounding disorganization. He shrugged. "It's a living."

"What did you find?" He peered over Michael's shoulder at the open file in his hand. There was a photo clipped to the inside, and he recognized Guffin's face immediately. He doubted he would ever forget. "You had a file on him?"

Michael handed him the folder. "Missing Persons case from a few years ago." He motioned to the stacks. "Most of these are Missing Persons cases. Been my bread 'n butter for a long time, especially these last few years."

Donovan forgot about Guffin's file for a moment, looking at the folders stacked upon one another. Something stuck in his brain, tickling the same place where he'd constructed Joe Hopper.

"All of these people are missing?"

"I usually get five or six calls a day. A kid who's run away, or a spouse who's fled town. Sometimes it's an estranged family member who fell out of the picture."

"Do you ever find them?"

"Sometimes." Michael separated a stack of papers into smaller, manageable portions. "Other times, it's like they just vanished—"

They shared an unsettling glance for a moment before Donovan cleared his throat and looked down at Guffin's photo. It was a professional portrait, revealing a well-groomed man with thick glasses. He wore a gray suit and red tie. It was the kind of photo that might hang in a corporate lobby, and Donovan had seen his share hanging in the entrance to the Identinel offices. Staring at the photo reminded Donovan that Guffin was once a normal man—not a wife-abducting cat-killer.

In this snapshot, Guffin feigned pride and happiness with a thin smile. It was a smile Donovan knew. He'd worn it himself on many occasions, the false smile of a man lying to himself. A smile that said *I am perfectly content.*

He opened the folder and read over the report. Guffin was last seen four years ago on his way to work for Brooks & Foster, a local accounting firm. Unmarried, no friends, with no discernable hobbies—George Guffin was an empty silhouette of a man.

Donovan looked at his brother. "Do you remember anything about this?"

"Vaguely. There wasn't much to work with. He left for work one day and never got there. Never returned home. Poof. Gone."

Donovan remembered the desperate look in Guffin's eye, the way he screamed in fear as the world changed around them. *There are others like you 'n me. He lets us out sometimes, only lets people see us when he wants them to.*

He went to the nearest stack and opened one folder after another. Each contained the same forms—invoices, expense sheets, photographs, testimonials—filed by family or friends desperate to find their missing loved ones. He looked at each photo. Most were adults, men and women from all corners of life, possessed of a smile that betrayed them. *None of them are happy,* he thought. *Not really.*

And now he's got 'em, hoss.

Donovan flickered without realizing it. The stack of papers dimmed, and when color returned to the room, he found Michael staring at him.

"I see it happen, but it still doesn't compute."

"Sorry." Donovan returned the stack of folders. "It's not easy for me, either." He noticed a few sheets of paper in Michael's hand. "What's that?"

"Something else I think you need to see. Decided to search a bit online, and—" The phone startled them. Their eyes met. "Hang on." Michael turned in his chair, found the cell phone under a pile of junk mail, and silenced it. He turned back to his brother. "Anyway—"

Donovan's pocket vibrated, catching him off guard. He'd forgotten about his own phone. However, when he retrieved it, he found the screen was blank. The battery had been almost dead the day before and leaving it on overnight had surely drained it. Still, the phone vibrated, sounding its polyphonic tones in rising scale.

Michael's cell phone rang again, joining the chorus. For a moment, Donovan was overcome with panic. Should he answer? Should Michael answer? The ringing continued, and finally the brothers answered their phones in tandem.

Static greeted Donovan's ear. He heard the same echoing from his brother's phone. Michael heard it, too, and mouthed *What the hell?* Donovan shrugged.

A familiar voice formed out of the static, and a lump rose in Donovan's throat.

"Brothers Candle," said Aleister Dullington. "Good morning to you both."

"Did you sleep well, Mr. Candle?" His voice crackled through both phones, creating a reverb effect that mimicked the odd language of the Cretins.

"Well enough."

"I am disappointed, Mr. Candle. You have not yet introduced me to your brother. But that is no matter, I am all too familiar with him." The brothers looked at one another. "Yes, Michael Candle, I know all about you." Static seeped through the line, accenting Dullington's voice, distorting it into a mechanized growl. "You and I are natural enemies."

Michael cleared his throat. "That so?"

"Quite. You seek those who are missed, while I facilitate the missing." Dullington chuckled. "In some ways, we perpetuate a cycle. You may consider it good business."

Donovan cut in. "Get to the point, Mr. Dullington. Who do you need me to find?"

Michael snapped. "Why don't you do it yourself, Al?"

Shut up, Mike, keep your damn mouth shut for once. He thought about knocking the phone from Michael's hand. His brother's smartass tone had landed him in plenty of trouble over the years, mostly with their parents, but this time it was for keeps.

"Shall I make your brother a bargaining chip in this affair?" Dullington's voice was solemn, resigned. "It can be arranged."

"No," Donovan said, glaring at his brother. "That won't be necessary."

"Good. I seek a man named Albert Sparrow. You are to find him and bring him to me."

Michael looked down at the pages in his hand. The name rang a bell, but he couldn't place it. It was there in the back of his brain, swimming around, avoiding his grasp.

"Who is he?"

"That is no concern of yours, Mr. Candle. You are to simply find him and deliver him unto me."

"But where—"

"There is a reason I freed your brother from the grip of the Cretins, Mr. Candle. He is a detective, is he not? A good one, by my understanding. After all, isn't that why you modeled your own character after him?"

Donovan's face flushed with embarrassment. The secret of Joe Hopper was something he'd never told his brother, but now that game was up. He turned from his brother, desperate to shrink away and hide.

"Where do we take this guy once we find him?" Michael asked. "And what if he doesn't want to join us?"

Static hissed through the line once more, distorting Dullington's voice.

"I guarantee he will not go with you willingly. He knows what awaits him on the other side. It is why he ran, and that is your problem to solve. Mr. Candle—"

Donovan closed his eyes. "Yes?"

"Have you given any more thought to my question?"

For a moment Donovan wasn't sure what he was talking about, but then he remembered the dream, and the long day preceding it. He hesitated, unsure of how to respond.

"It is no matter, Mr. Candle. You still have time to answer—and you *will* have to answer. For now I leave you brothers to your task. Good day."

The resounding surge of digital noise made both men pull away from their phones. Michael sat back in his chair and stared down at the floor.

"What did he mean? What question?"

Donovan leaned against one of the cabinets and shook his head. "It's nothing." He pointed to the pages in Michael's hand. "You were going to show me something else?"

"I was, but your friend beat me to it." Michael handed him the papers.

They were print-outs about Dr. Sparrow's book, his photograph, and a list of tour dates. "Seems we have a common interest."

He scanned the itinerary, pausing at the current date. Sparrow was in town. Donovan looked up at his brother. Michael grinned.

"Want to go meet a celebrity?"

———————◆———————

M ichael took a bite of his breakfast sandwich. They had an hour to kill before Sparrow's event, and their growling stomachs mandated a stop for food. They sat in the car on the second level of a parking garage a block from the bookstore.

"What's this about 'modeling your character' after me?"

The question took Donovan by surprise. His mind was elsewhere, away from the demands of his ravenous body and the imminent confrontation with Dr. Sparrow. He was focused on his wife, all the things he feared he'd never get to say to her.

"Modeling my character?" He thought for a moment. "Oh. That."

A cloud of heat covered his face. He'd expected the conversation, but not so soon. He pictured Dullington somewhere in the Monochrome, grinning.

"Well?" Michael jabbed Donovan's arm. "Come on, out with it."

"All right. The book's about a detective."

A thin smile spread across Michael's face. "Go on."

Donovan imagined Joe Hopper, his face cast in a permanent five o'clock shadow, cigarette hanging limp from the corner of his mouth. He thought about Hopper's early life, the life written nowhere else but in Donovan's own mind. *Might as well go 'n tell 'em, hoss.*

"His name is Joe Hopper. He's a gruff son of a bitch. Southern stock. Tough guy. He's searching for someone."

"Who?"

Donovan smiled, feeling excited about his story for the first time in weeks. "For a woman. A lady by the name of Mistress Colby."

"Her first name is Mistress?"

"Sort of. Haven't worked that bit out just yet."

"When were you going to tell me about this?"

He sighed. "I don't know, Mike. The novel's been in and out of the works for years now. I guess I didn't want you to know until it was done."

Michael finished his sandwich and wiped his chin. "Are you going to try and get it published? That's still your dream, isn't it?"

Here we go. It always comes back to this.

"Yeah," he said. "Someday."

"How long have you been working on it?"

"About seven years, I think."

"So why not finish it?"

"Real-life matters. Work, sleep, that sort of thing. Necessary distractions, I guess. And—" He stopped to think. What was it that he'd found so wrong with the novel almost a week ago? It was too predictable, too bland. He realized that it was nothing more than a reflection of his own life. Joe Hopper was based on his brother, but on another level, he was based on Donovan's own yearning for the things he lacked: something different, something adventurous, something more fulfilling than the nine-to-five grind he had lived every single day for the last nine years. In the face of his desire he'd deleted the document, frustrated with its lack of direction.

Only now did he realize that frustration stemmed from something far more prevalent than a collection of words. It sickened him when he realized this terrible incident had been necessary to understanding his own pathology.

"And?"

Donovan looked up from his breakfast. He'd lost his appetite. "And the story was just empty, anyway. Dull. Kind of like me."

"You really think so?"

He nodded. "I do. Took me too long to figure that out."

"Well, aren't you supposed to write what you know? Don't take this the wrong way, but you're not exactly the most exciting person in the world, Don."

Michael's words stung, but Donovan didn't try to defend himself. He knew his brother was right. It was a harsh truth he had to face. He returned to a fact that haunted him: his delusion of happiness and contentment was the cause of Donna's abduction. His stomach tied itself into knots.

"You always nagged me for not taking more chances. I always wanted to play it safe, and now it's come back to bite me on the ass. This is all my fault."

"I nagged you because I wanted to see you do better. Our folks were always at work, slaving away at their jobs to make it better for us, and I didn't want us to resign ourselves to that kind of life. I expected more from you because I knew you could do more."

Donovan turned away, staring out the window at empty rows and concrete columns.

"I won't bullshit you, Don. If what you told me is real, then yeah, this is nothing else but your own fault for being a boring guy. But—" Michael drummed his fingers along the steering wheel. "—self-pity isn't going to help you. It's going to drive you deeper into the hole you're already in. You need to focus. For Donna, and for yourself. Got it?" He reached out and put his hand on Donovan's shoulder. "And for what it's worth, I really dig your story idea. I'd like to read it someday."

"Thanks, Mike. For everything."

"Don't mention it."

The brothers shared a smile. Afterward, Michael started the car. Donovan reached over and turned on the radio. A blast of rock music startled him, the industrial noise of Nine Inch Nails making his head hurt. He cringed at the synthetic drones. They reminded him too much of the Monochrome, and he quickly changed the station.

"—is 5'9", roughly 150 lbs, and has long, black hair. If you or anyone you know has information of her whereabouts—"

The grainy photo from the newspaper sprang to mind. He used to ignore the Missing Persons reports, but in light of his new suspicions, it chilled him to think about how many reports he'd seen and heard over the years. *How many people disappear every day? How many end up with Dullington?*

His gut clenched, accenting his thought with a brief shift of the world's color. The interior of Michael's car vanished for a moment, leaving Donovan hovering between Spectrum and Monochrome. There were Cretins standing watch along the garage floor.

When he flickered back, he found Michael changing the station. He hadn't noticed Donovan's brief disappearance. Donovan leaned his head against the window and stared out, his thoughts drifting back to the task at hand.

Fear inched its way into his gut. What if Dullington was lying and all this was just a game? He remembered the way Dullington frowned when he asked about Sparrow. Anger was one of the few emotions he'd witnessed splashed across the pale canvas of Dullington's face.

No. Dullington's not lying. He's too particular, a devil for the details. Manipulative, yes, but not a liar.

His thoughts turned to Sparrow. He wondered what a man could possibly do to inspire such resentment and determination from a being like Aleister Dullington? Furthermore, what kind of man was capable of such a thing?

Donovan looked at the dashboard clock. He would find out in fewer than twenty minutes.

9

THE GOOD DOCTOR

The door was open when Donna awoke. She tried to roll on her side and whimpered from the rush of pain through her joints. The air was freezing and damp, and her whole body sang a chorus of aches when she tried to move. Outside, the orange glow of firelight was absent.

Voices spoke from somewhere beyond the doorway. Hushed tones, the syllables muted and hissed through clenched teeth. She strained to listen.

Two men. She didn't recognize them.

"—supposed to happen today."

"You sure?"

"Yeah, that's the word. Old Dull's got a lot of faith in this Candle guy."

"What's so special about Sparrow, anyway?"

"The ones who've been here the longest—

"The ones who haven't wasted away to nothing?"

"—right, them. They say Sparrow used to be one of us, but he found a way to escape."

"Jeez...I didn't think that was possible, you know? Dullington told me I was shackled here forever."

"Me too, but Sparrow broke free. Dullington had plans for him, something different than the rest of us, and he's been after him ever since."

"How long?"

"Who knows. Years, probably."

"Jesus."

She'd heard Dullington and Sparrow whispered about in the dark, through the closed door, and she wondered how her husband was mixed up in their affairs. Donna closed her eyes and tried to ignore the ache resonating through her hip and legs, the rising pangs of hunger, the sting of her bladder. She thought of Donovan. She feared for him, feared what might happen if he couldn't do whatever was expected of him.

He'll find his way. He *always does.*

Donna found warmth in the thought. She clung to it in the bitter dark, cherishing the fading. It was all she had left.

The brothers waited for the crosswalk light to change. Across the street, a line of patrons stretched beyond the doors of Harrison & Main Booksellers and wound its way around the corner. Michael nudged Donovan and pointed toward the crowd.

"Do you think your book could sell this much?"

Donovan shrugged. "No way. This self-help crap always sells more."

"Sounds like you're in the wrong business."

"Maybe I am." He observed another large group join the line from an adjacent street as traffic inched through the intersections. A breeze picked up around them, and the city's colors shifted, losing depth and focus, allowing Donovan to see a different sort of crowd gathering outside the building. A few Yawning loitered in the middle of the street, towering over a churning sea of Cretins.

Looks like the whole fan club's here.

They vanished and were replaced by two lanes of traffic. The crosswalk signal changed. Donovan took a breath, fixed his eyes on the bookstore, and made his way to the other side. Michael followed.

"Have you thought about what you're going to say to this guy?"

Donovan shook his head. "It's not every day I have to tell a man I've been sent to kidnap him, y'know?"

"Well, you'd better think on your feet. This thing's supposed to start soon, and the line's not getting any shorter."

Michael was right. Donovan couldn't see the end of the line, and he knew the bookstore wasn't very large. He looked to the entrance and smiled.

"I think I have an idea." He walked away from his brother, toward the front of the line.

"Well? Are you going to share?"

Donovan looked back. "Go get in line, Mike. I'll see you inside."

A force swelled within him as the invisible hand clutched at his stomach, pulling him out of the Spectrum.

Michael watched his brother vanish and shook his head. He shoved his hands in his pockets and walked to the back of the line. "I hope you know what you're doing."

The street squirmed with pale creatures, a river of thick white insects crawling over a corpse. Yawning staggered over their tiny counterparts. Caught between both realities, Donovan heard their chattering cacophony with frightening clarity.

They're waiting.

Ahead, two Yawning stood guard at the entrance. Donovan held his breath as he hurried between them. Inside, he positioned himself between the outlines of two figures, each with a Cretin on their shoulder. The tiny white bastards looked up and grinned.

Donovan winced. The foyer sprang to life as he flickered back into reality. He stood between two women, neither of whom paid him any notice. They each held a copy of Sparrow's book. Donovan scrutinized the cover.

A *Life Ordinary: A Comprehensive Study in Human Mediocrity.* The title bled pretension, printed in bold letters across a sketched outline of a light bulb, with Sparrow's name aligned at the top. A blurb read, "A revolution in human progression." Donovan doubted that was the case, but the turnout for the day's event proved he was one of a small minority.

Twenty minutes passed, and the line didn't move. Outside, police waved people through the intersections, the streets now at a standstill. Donovan watched the chaos unfolding outside. *I want this guy's publicist.*

He wondered what he would say to Dr. Sparrow. What *could* he say? *Hi, I'm Donovan Candle, and Aleister Dullington sent me to find you because, if I don't, he's going to kill my wife.* It was to the point but sounded ridiculous in his head. He didn't know if Sparrow would even see him.

Doubt you'd be invisible to him, hoss. He's public enemy numero uno in Monochrome land.

His mind raced with possibilities—what might happen if Sparrow didn't cooperate—but a push from behind displaced such thoughts. A woman bumped into him, confused, and her eyes glazed over when he tried to apologize. She squinted, straining to see him. Donovan shut his mouth and started walking.

He moved through the foyer, past a counter of cash registers, and worked his way through the crowd. Rows of bookshelves had been rearranged for the event, and in the center of the clearing was a lectern. A small group of chairs were claimed by those at the front of the line, leaving the rest to stand and fill out the store to its capacity. Donovan found a spot close to the lectern, just behind the last row of seats.

Then he saw the doctor, and his heart inched its way into his throat.

Dr. Albert Sparrow was a tall man. He wore a three-piece suit, colored gray to match silver hair pulled back into a ponytail. A thick mustache adorned his upper lip, accenting a grin which now spread across his face.

Sparrow swaggered to the lectern, taking the microphone in hand with the confidence of a rock star. The audience erupted with applause. Sparrow basked in it, listening to the cheers. He leaned into the microphone and said, "I'm sorry, I didn't catch that. Come again?" The crowd ate it up, cheering and whistling.

He reached into his suit coat and pulled out a pair of glasses. As he did, a woman in a black dress walked to the lectern and whispered in his ear. He nodded, leaned toward the microphone.

"Excuse me. I need your attention for a moment." Sparrow's voice boomed over the sound system. Most of the crowd's cheers slowly died down. "I'm sorry to be the bearer of bad news, but it appears the store is at capacity. I'm afraid if we let anyone else in here, we'll be in violation of the fire code."

Donovan turned and saw the entrance doors were closed, an angry mob of readers peering inside. A scan of those who got through revealed Michael was not among them.

Looks like I'm on my own.

"I'd like to welcome you, and to thank you for coming out and joining me today. As most of you probably know, my name is Dr. Albert Sparrow." More cheers erupted from the audience. Sparrow wore a smile of confidence, a greedy expression yearning for the attention, lusting for the power he held with mere words. Donovan knew the type. He worked for people just like this. "First, I will read from our favorite book for thirty minutes, after which I'll take a few questions. Then we'll move on to the signing. And if you didn't bring your copy, don't worry—the store has plenty in stock."

Sparrow held up a hardcover copy of the book. He adjusted his glasses, cleared his throat once more, and opened to a bookmarked page.

As the good doctor began his reading, the gray sight overcame Donovan. Sparrow remained in full clarity, standing like a Technicolor beacon in a silent film. All around him, Cretins cringed as he spoke. The man's voice was garbled in the droning language of the Monochrome.

Hints of the Spectrum bled through the gray haze, and Sparrow's voice became clear as Donovan's gray sight relented.

"'—apter one: The Disease. There are two sides to every coin: light and dark, day and night, good and evil if one is inclined to take it that far. As human beings, we restrict ourselves to one side at a time. We wake up in the morning, we have breakfast, we kiss our spouses goodbye, and we travel off to work. At the end of the day, we come home, we have dinner, we relax, we sleep. Over the course of time, however, the human mind begins to fit this self-imposed mold—an act which it is not meant to perform, as this routine causes a state of banal atrophy.

"'Unfortunately, this is a common side-effect of the nine-to-five grind. The human existence isn't meant to be confined to a box, a computer screen, a telephone, or any other device for a large amount of time. We begin to lose touch with reality, with our loved ones, with our own lives. Mediocrity is a disease of our society, and unlike diseases of the natural world, this one is entirely man-made. Affliction is a choice.

"'Over the course of this study, three distinct 'life' dichotomies will be discussed in further detail, but for the purposes of this introduction, each will be broached so as to set the proverbial stage.'"

Sparrow paused, turning the page. Someone behind Donovan coughed. The rest of the audience was silent, hanging on the doctor's every word.

"'A life ordinary is the setting in which most of us live our lives. It is not aware of the layers underneath or above; rather, it is merely aware of itself and its own formulaic devices. A life ordinary plots itself from point A to B to C and beyond, until it reaches a point at which the obvious choice is to return to A, and so the poisonous cycle repeats until death. Over the course of this life, offspring are taught to live the same lifestyle, propagating yet another ordinary, banal existence.

"'However, there are grave consequences for some of those who choose to follow this bleak path.'"

Donovan listened, understanding creeping into his mind. He saw the road Sparrow traveled, and it looked very familiar.

"'Some of us bury ourselves in our jobs, becoming machines of a sort, built with only one purpose—to do more work. Others may devote their lives to one thing, shutting out all of life's delights and interesting quirks. Some choose to convolute the very essence of humanity by saturating themselves with mediocrity. At this point, a life ordinary deteriorates into a life transparent.

"'A life transparent is a life in flux and transition. It is a liminal state, fraught with confusion and despair, attributed to a constant feeling of ennui. Most times, however, when one enters this stage it is too late for recourse. A person living a life transparent stands upon the threshold of decision: to vanish into obscurity, continuing on their self-destructive journey into a monochromatic version of the world devoid of life and warmth, ignored by those around them; alternatively, a person living a life transparent may take a road less traveled, if they recognize the symptoms early on.

"'A drastic change in lifestyle is necessary. This requires identifying the source of mediocrity and expelling it from daily life. It could mean changing one's job, finding a new hobby, or eliminating any other malignant preoccupation. Only then can one find the means with which to breach the veil and reenter the world's spectrum. It is through this 'life pitch,' so to speak, that one may leap from the precipice of virtual anonymity, transcending through a subset of dichotomies—hesitation, penitence, liminality, definition—and land safely in the shoes of a life random.'"

Dr. Sparrow looked up for a moment, adjusted his glasses, and locked eyes with Donovan. Sparrow's face reddened. Donovan might as well have been the only person in the room. He felt exposed. The doctor's sharp glare left little room for denial: he could see Donovan just fine.

⁕

The man in the crowd caught Sparrow off guard, threw him off his game. He always prepared for the worst, expecting that Dullington might send an army to any one of the stops on his publicity tour. There were others, of course, but they always came before or after his public appearances, turning up in airport bars or at restaurants, trying to pass themselves off as fans. Last night's whore was one such attempt. After all these years, Al was finally getting creative.

There were always the tell-tale signs of dirt under the nails, hair that hadn't been washed in weeks or months, a foul stench. Lately, Dullington had taken to giving them the means to disguise themselves—even the whore had dressed her part—but this man in the crowd was different.

He didn't look like one of Dullington's puppets. At a glance, he looked like a normal fellow, but the longer Sparrow stared, the more he recognized the quiet desperation in the man's eyes.

For a moment, Sparrow faltered at the lectern. A cold sweat broke out on his forehead, and the gun holstered inside his coat pulled at him. Paranoia swept over him in a heated wave.

He felt the room shift around him, felt the wrenching pull in his torso. It was a cold reminder of what awaited him if he let it catch up. *I won't go back. Never.* He locked eyes once more with the stranger, trying his best to transmit a warning across the space between them.

Do not fuck with me.

Sparrow returned to the book and read to the end of the chapter.

The audience applauded as Dr. Sparrow finished the reading. Donovan had observed a change in the doctor's demeanor since they locked eyes: he was less boisterous than when he'd first approached the lectern, and when the crowd saw fit to give him a standing ovation, he had merely thanked them. A moment later he excused himself, motioning to the woman in the black dress. She took his place at the microphone.

"It will be just a few minutes before we conclude with the Q&A."

The old man walked along the back wall toward a short hallway. A sign hung above the opening that read "Restrooms."

Better now than never.

Donovan pushed his way through the crowd, circumventing the lectern and following his target. He jogged through a maze of bookshelves, past a group of store clerks, and into the hall. Entrances to both restrooms stood opposite one another. A third door, labeled "Employees Only," stood at the end of the hall.

The door to the men's room swung to a close. Donovan pushed it open and stepped inside. Dr. Albert Sparrow ran water in the sink. He let it pool in his hands before wiping down his face and forehead. He looked sallow under the fluorescent lights. They aged him twenty years.

He dabbed his face with a handkerchief, pausing long enough to regard Donovan in the mirror. "Can I help you?"

Donovan blinked, searching for the right words. "Aleister Dullington sent me."

"Of course he did." Sparrow looked down at the sink, then into the mirror. He smiled and shook his head. "This will never end, will it?"

Donovan wasn't sure what to say. He shifted his weight from one foot to the other, uncomfortable with the situation. Dr. Sparrow now appeared old, feeble, far from the smug bastard he'd made himself out to be.

"I'm so tired of this." He looked up at Donovan and put on his glasses. "Would you mind accompanying an old man to his car? I need my medication. This old heart isn't what it used to be."

Donovan agreed, following the doctor out into the hallway. They turned left through the Employees Only area, passing a small lounge and entering a loading zone filled with boxes of books. Donovan paid little attention to anything but the old man, the way his silver ponytail swished back and forth as he walked. He feared that if he took his eyes off the man, Sparrow would disappear.

They exited the building at the far side, stepping out into a wide alley. There was a silver BMW parked alongside the loading dock, marked with out-of-state plates and flagged with a rental company's logo. Donovan wasn't surprised by the car's elegance; it was just what he imagined a man like Sparrow might drive.

"Dr. Sparrow," Donovan began, "listen. I need—"

"Please, son. Spare me. I'm sure whatever story he's given you to justify your actions helps you sleep at night, but it won't work with me. Just let me have my medicine before you do what it is you've come to do."

"You know why I'm here?"

Dr. Sparrow reached into his pocket and pulled out a set of keys. He disengaged the lock, prompting the car to chirp in agreement, and walked around to the passenger side door. Donovan wanted to plead with the man, explain the situation. Together, maybe they could find some sort of solution. Something that would work in their favor.

"Been after me for years," Sparrow mumbled. The old man turned, looking first to the alley's entrance, then back at its exit. "I've learned a thing or two along the way."

Donovan said nothing. He approached the side of the car. "Look, Dr. Sparrow, this is about my w—"

Sparrow leveled the gun barrel at Donovan's forehead. "Like how to deal with people like you."

Stunned, Donovan slowly raised his hands in a gesture of intent. He'd misjudged this old man, figured him for someone of reason, but when Donovan traded focus from the barrel to the wide-eyed desperation in Sparrow's eyes, he understood what sort of mean he was dealing with. This was Guffin all over again; worse, this was Guffin with resources, the means and the will to evade capture no matter the cost.

"Listen," Donovan began. He spoke evenly, slowly, trying to hide the mounting terror in his voice. "I'm sure we can work this out. I understand where you're—"

Sparrow pressed the barrel against Donovan's skull. "I've learned not to trust a single fucking thing any of you rubes say. I don't care why you're here, or what he's promised you in return—I'm *not* going back, and I'll do whatever I have to do to keep it that way. Do you understand *that*, son?" Spittle flew from his quivering lips like a rabid dog. His trigger finger twitched. "I'm going to remove you from this equation just like the rest of them."

10

NEGATIVE SPACES

"Put it down, old man."

Sparrow's eyes widened at the sound of a cocked hammer. Michael Candle pressed the revolver into the back of Sparrow's silver mane.

Donovan's legs nearly gave out as the adrenaline slowed. "Mike, thank God."

"I said put it down."

Sparrow stared ahead, possessed with a hatred more vicious than Donovan had ever seen. He almost wanted to apologize to the man, but the look in Sparrow's eyes made him hold his tongue.

The old man licked his lips and spoke through clenched teeth. "Well played." He lowered the weapon.

Michael reached over, plucked it from Sparrow's hand, and shoved it into his jacket pocket.

"Got anything else up your sleeve, old man?"

"No, I don't."

"Then you won't mind if I pat you down." Michael was quick about it. He came up empty handed. "Get in the car."

Sparrow's face darkened. He didn't look back at Michael, but forward, glaring into Donovan's eyes. "I didn't catch your name, son."

"Name's Donovan Candle."

A thin smile cut across Sparrow's face. "Mr. Candle, I'm going to remember you. For the rest of my days. That's a promise."

Likewise, Donovan thought. Michael opened the door and shoved the doctor inside. He looked up at his brother. "You okay?"

"Yeah." Donovan motioned to Michael's revolver. "Do you normally do this?"

Michael flashed a smile. "Do what, break the law? Only when my brother and his wife are in danger." He leaned into the car and held out his hand. "Keys."

Dr. Sparrow tossed the keys outside. He spat. "Fuck you."

Michael slammed the door and picked the keys off the ground. "Get in. I'm driving."

"Where are we going?"

"Away from here. Now get in before someone sees us."

———————•———————

*M*ichael Candle, you are one crazy son of a bitch. The words repeated in the detective's head as he guided the car out of the alley and into traffic. Everything caught up to him in those moments, the sequence of events replaying in a constant blur behind his eyes, and he realized the gravity of what they'd done.

Armed kidnapping. Hostage-taking.

He looked in the rearview mirror at Dr. Sparrow. The old man glared at Michael's reflection, his cheeks stained a dark shade of red, his whole face like a giant bruise.

What are you doing, Michael? He faced the road, struggling against the urge to turn the car around, or to sucker-punch his brother for dragging him into this mess. Maybe both. *Take the old man back to the bookstore. Drop him off. Apologize for the bad prank and get the hell out of there.*

Even with his brother's inexplicable vanishing acts, he still resisted belief in what he'd witnessed. He'd relied on an inherent need for logic over the years, a cognitive requirement that ran deep in his veins. This logic dictated they *would* be caught, they *would* go to jail, and his brother *would* end up in a hospital for psychiatric evaluation.

However, there was more to all this than he understood, something more which undermined his rationale and stirred deeper fears. What if there *was* something greater at stake, something rooted in the world which they took for granted. This vague notion, this terrifying speculation, filled him with certainty he would never fully understand that *something* between the lines, woven between the threads. And his immediate and irrational fear of the unknown, however absurd, overpowered his fear of breaking the law.

For the moment, all he understood was that his sister-in-law was in trouble, and he'd do whatever was necessary to help his brother get her back.

Michael drove, following a straight line from downtown toward the outskirts of the city, eventually headed toward the countryside beyond. His mind raced, replaying the image of his brother in the path of a stranger's bullet, processing the possibilities of what might have happened otherwise.

Providence led him to that alleyway. The store was at capacity, and he was one of the many who were denied entrance. He watched from the window, and when the old man retreated to the back, something—a stir in his gut, a prickle at the back of his neck—spurred his feet to action.

The gut feeling. Every gumshoe had one.

Now his gut told him the old man was bad news, and not just because of the gun. There was a cold intensity Sparrow's tired eyes: murderous, calculating, desperate. And when he looked up in the rearview again, he was relieved to find the good doctor staring out the window.

Donovan spoke up. "How did you know—"

"I didn't. Just a hunch, is all."

"Well, I'm glad."

Michael glanced over at his brother, then back at the rearview reflection. Dr. Sparrow stared back.

"Are you two fags or something?"

Michael signaled a turn, guiding the car to the far end of a vacant parking lot. He parked and shut off the engine. "We're going to sort all of this shit out." He pointed to Sparrow. "Starting with you, Dr. Dickhead."

"Don't patronize me," Sparrow said. "I may be old, but I've killed punks like you for less."

"Right." Michael pulled Sparrow's gun from his pocket. He set it beside his own revolver on the dashboard. "Is that why you carry this thing? To threaten your fans?"

"I carry it to keep shits like you from doing what he wants."

Michael shot a glance to his brother. Donovan said nothing, his furrowed brow reminding Michael of their youth. It was "the Donovan look," a sure sign that something was brewing somewhere in that rich expanse of brain matter.

"Dr. Sparrow," Donovan said. He spoke slowly, careful with his words. "Mr. Dullington has my wife."

"I want to be clear with you, young man. How can I say this and avoid euphemism?" Dr. Sparrow reclined in the backseat and chuckled dryly. "You're fucked."

D onovan glared at the old man, sizing him up. He'd hoped this man might have some answers, that Sparrow might work to help him recover Donna in one piece, but after looking into the man's eyes, he realized it would be a waste of time.

He thought of Donna, her smile engraved in his memory, over a decade of shared moments rushing forward in a tidal wave.

Donovan plucked Sparrow's gun from the dashboard. He put his finger on the trigger and leveled the barrel to the old man's forehead.

"You *will* help me, Dr. Sparrow."

"Or what? You'll kill me?" Sparrow rolled his eyes. "Your master wouldn't like that very much, would he?"

Joe Hopper's words bubbled out of a red haze and found their way to Donovan's lips. "One way or another, you're going back. Donna's life is worth ten of yours."

Sparrow ground his teeth together, baring them like a rabid animal. "Do you really think he'll let you go?"

"He's kept his word so far."

"So far," Sparrow scoffed. "But Dullington always has an angle. He might let your wife go, but he'll still have you. One way or another, *he'll still have you.*"

Michael shook his head. "This guy's so full of shit."

"Full of shit? You don't even know what you're talking about. You're not exactly Dullington's type. You haven't been there. You haven't seen the things—" Sparrow locked eyes with Donovan. He slowly nodded. "But *you* know what I'm talking about. You *have* been there."

Donovan looked away. He tried not to think about the Monochrome, its emptiness, the lifeless drone humming through the very air, or the pale things inhabiting it. Sparrow propped his elbow against the window. "You aren't the first. You won't be the last. His game's been going on for a very long time."

"Why does he want you?"

Sparrow twirled his fingers. "Because I'm the one who got away. The rest of them, they're just there in the 'chrome to be sucked dry. You, your brother, everyone on this planet—you're all cattle. Once you go over for good, you belong to him." The old man paused, thinking. "What do you do for a living?"

Donovan lowered the weapon. "I work in a call center. Sales department."

"So you're a salesman? Oh my." Sparrow put his head back and let out a hearty laugh. "I can't imagine a more mediocre job. No wonder you're flickering. Frankly, I'm surprised everyone in your workplace hasn't vanished."

"That's beside the point."

"Ah, so it is." Sparrow removed his glasses and cleaned them with his handkerchief. "Dullington wanted me to take his place. I used to be just like you, living an empty life. Then one day I woke up and found I was disappearing. And I let it happen, too. I started seeing little things on people's shoulders, whispering for them to forget me, and then I started seeing the bigger ones—the Yawning, he calls them. Not long after that, I found myself lost in a gray haze. Aleister Dullington made himself known to me. He said, 'I will set you apart from the others, Mr. Sparrow. I will deliver you unto banality itself, and you will reign in the light of the Ungod.'"

"Light of the Ungod?"

Sparrow ignored him, continued cleaning his glasses. He squeezed so hard the lenses cracked. One of them fell from its frame. "I didn't like the prospect of an eternity in that gray hell, so I found a way out."

Donovan leaned forward, caught up in the doctor's reverie. "How?"

"Mediocrity is a fickle thing. Anything can be mediocre. I surmised that whatever boring thing led me to the Monochrome could be counteracted by an equal and opposite excitement. It was quite a brilliant epiphany. A true eureka moment."

Michael muttered under his breath and shook his head. Donovan shot him an annoyed glance but said nothing. Sparrow went on:

"Being one of the Missing means being on the brink of starvation. There's nothing tangible in the Monochrome. No food, no water. Dullington let us into the Spectrum once a day to feed, and our time there was limited to scrounging for table scraps, rummaging through dumpsters, living like transients." Sparrow put down his broken glasses. He picked up the cracked lens and examined it. "I figured an event of drastic proportions could propel me out of the Monochrome just long enough to weaken its pull. I needed to reach a kind of escape velocity, if you will."

"What did you do?"

Sparrow held up the lens with both hands. "He let us into the Spectrum in pairs, one to watch the other. If one misbehaved, both would suffer punishment. My partner was a man called Smith, a sad sack of shit who clung to some perverse hope that things might change one day. I knew better. I knew change wouldn't come; it had to be pursued and taken with force." He snapped the lens in half. It broke in two jagged pieces. "So, I took matters into my hands. I murdered the poor bastard. It was enough to get me out of there."

The doctor's macabre confession didn't surprise Donovan. He'd already witnessed more than enough of the man's true character to be anything other than sickened. Phantom fingers curled around his stomach and pulled, causing him to flicker for a moment. Sparrow remained in full clarity as the car faded and colors bled from the world.

When it stopped, Donovan caught the old man's eye. "But you're still flickering. If you're flickering, how come people can see you?"

"It's all a matter of negative space."

Michael grunted. "Negative space?"

Sparrow sighed. "It's a matter of perception. The odds are you've seen one of the other Missing without even knowing it." He traced his finger along the edge of the lens shard. "Imagine a painting of a vase. At a glance, you see the vase, but if you were to look closer, you might see a face on either side. Both images are visible, but you only see one at a time."

"But what about those—" Michael snapped his fingers, searching for the right word. Sparrow finished for him.

"Cretins. They act as a veil, covering up the faces. They exist so you only see the vase. And in the odd chance you're lucky enough to perceive the faces, they ensure you won't remember it."

"That doesn't answer my question," Donovan said.

Sparrow grinned. "A person can weaken their chain to the Monochrome, but they can't break it. Once it's in place, it's there to stay. The weaker it is, the more others are able to see. Even his Cretins can't interfere. In my case, the chain is weak enough that others can see the faces for the vase."

Donovan smirked. "Sounds like you're living on borrowed time."

The sly humor drained from Sparrow's face. He looked away. "I've taken great pains to keep myself at a distance, correcting where I went wrong. I went back to school and finished my doctorate. I wrote my book and found success, fame. Constantly changing, keeping track of any possible routines, sleeping on the floor once or twice to break the cycle of sleeping in a bed—you'll do anything to keep your head above water when you're drowning." Sparrow looked back at Donovan for a moment, sizing him up. "You're going to wind up just as I did if you don't change your ways. Everyone does."

"Everyone?"

"Poor saps who are tethered to the other side. He's used some of them, sending them after me to do exactly what you're doing now. All of them have something to lose, all are given the promise of freedom if they succeed." A wry grin split his face. "You're no different. You're just sinking to new lows to save your own skin."

"All you had to do was talk to me," Donovan whispered. "I didn't want to force you."

"Oh, please." Sparrow rolled his eyes. "You know damn well I wouldn't have come with you, regardless of whatever sob story you tried to sell me."

Donovan closed his eyes and took a breath. Joe Hopper's voice spoke up within the darkness of his head, and Donovan didn't like what he had to say. *Up against a wall, hoss, and you're damned either way. But the old codger's got a point—sometimes you can't wait for change to come. You have to make it yourself.* He thought of Donna again, and he realized he'd already made up his mind long before encountering this vile excuse of a man.

"I told Dullington I'd bring you to him, and that's what I intend to do."

"Your weakness is beneath you. Even if you get her back, it won't change the fact that you'll soon be his. Too many people refuse to change, and you're just like them, another tick on Dullington's fucking chalkboard." His words ran together in a guttural deluge of rage. *"You'll end up right back there with me in the end, and I'll make sure you regret it every fucking day."*

Sparrow took the broken lens and lunged forward. Donovan reacted without thinking, lifting his hand to block the attack, crying out as the lens cut a gash across his palm. Sparrow recoiled, growling incomprehensible words as he pulled back for another slash—

Michael struck Sparrow with the butt of the revolver. Donovan watched the lights go out in the old man's eyes. The glass shard slipped from his fingers and fell to the floor. Sparrow slumped back into the seat with a faint groan. A thin line of blood trickled from his silver temple.

"You okay?"

Donovan put pressure on his wound to slow the bleeding. "Yeah."

He was distant, his mind lost in a mental replay of the doctor's words. He wondered if he would be stuck living a life transparent forever, flickering in and out of existence while fading into complete obscurity. Thinking back, he realized it was all he'd done for the last nine years. Working at Identinel had drained the last ounce of life from his body. Now he was just a drone, and he had nothing to show for his life because he hadn't done anything with it.

"So what now?"

"Now I guess we—"

Donovan's cell phone vibrated in his pocket. A moment later, Michael's cell phone rang. Outside, a row of old pay phones rang in succession, forming a melody of buzzing notes.

Michael shook his head, amazed. "I think it's for you."

"I think you might be right." Donovan pulled the dead cell phone from his pocket, flipped it open, and answered.

———————◆———————

"You impress me more with each passing moment, Mr. Candle. I applaud you."

"I have him. What do you want me to do with him?"

The static in the line rose and fell, echoing laughter. "Listen to yourself. You kidnap one man, and now you are ready to take on the world."

Donovan clenched his teeth. "I'm not proud of what I had to do."

"Do not pity him, Mr. Candle. He is not as innocent as he makes himself out to be. I assure you, given the opportunity he would do the same to you without a second thought."

He looked back at the unconscious man, remembering the hatred in Sparrow's eyes. "I just want my wife back, Dullington."

"And so you shall have her, in time."

Donovan shook so hard he almost dropped the phone. He balled his free hand into a tight fist. The anger came from a deep place, fueled by his fatigue and heartache.

"I have your goddamn puppet," he growled. "Now just give her back. She's all I want. I've done what you've asked."

"Calm yourself, Mr. Candle. You are correct in your statement—you have done everything I have asked of you, and you will be rewarded."

He closed his eyes for a moment and cleared his head. He told himself to focus, to suck it up and suffer the last few strides to the finish line. An image of Donna's smiling face rekindled the dying fire within. Donovan opened his eyes and looked outside.

"Where do you want us to take him?"

"Are you familiar with the Yellow Line?"

Donovan thought for a moment. "The subway?"

"Correct. It is not in use anymore. I prefer it due to its level of discretion." Dullington paused, allowing a hiss of static to fill the space. "You might say it also possesses a certain liminal quality. Appropriate, I think."

"Anything else?"

"I believe that is all, Mr. Candle. My associates will be waiting for you at the entrance."

A rush of white noise filled his ear before the click. Donovan stared at the phone's blank screen. Dead again.

"Well?"

He looked up at his brother. "She's at the subway."

"The subway?" Michael frowned. "Which one?"

"The Yellow Line."

"Christ. It's been out of service for years."

"I know. Can you get us there?"

Michael started the car and let its engine answer for him. He turned around in the parking lot and entered traffic.

"Why the subway? Of all the places…"

Donovan shrugged, watching as they returned to the city. *A subway is in a constant state of transition. It's always between two points. Always liminal.*

Liminal. That word again. He decided he would be happy if he could live the rest of his life without hearing that word.

Dr. Sparrow stirred, whimpering quietly to himself. Donovan looked back at the old man and thought about his words. *You'll end up right back there with me in the end. Too many people refuse to change.* Getting Donna back from Dullington was his priority, but he'd let her down if he didn't make it through this, too. He'd cheated her enough over the years. He needed to atone and make things up to her.

Michael was about to turn onto the bypass and take the shorter route when Donovan asked him not to.

"Why? This is faster."

"Trust me."

"All right." Michael shrugged. He guided the car out of the turn-lane and moved on toward the city. Taking the long way was the opposite of what Donovan would've done. For the first time since the flickering began, he felt a strange sense of peace come over him. It felt right, doing what he was doing, even if it scared him to death.

Fear of the unknown and the unplanned had held him at bay for so long. Now, for the first time in his life, Donovan Candle chose to accept that fear and embrace it.

As they drove on through the city, Donovan made a silent commitment to Donna, to himself. From now on, he would choose to take the path less traveled. A life transparent was not one he wanted to live, and he would do everything he could to prove Dr. Sparrow wrong.

11

THE PALE MONK

A leister Dullington watched the strings vibrate and stir, the fragile threads of lives intertwined, lives severed. They crisscrossed and wove together across the gray sky, threaded by the benign slumber of the Great Weaver, the center of all dreams and nightmares.

He stood on the edge of a nearby rooftop, watching the essence of Donovan Candle travel once more into the city. A desperate man in a desperate situation, for certain; but a man who had also excelled where others before him had failed. So random, this twisting of threads, and yet…

Something had happened which Dullington hadn't foreseen. The entwining of strings which were otherwise independent of one another, two paths with no reason to cross. Candle's voice was no different than the others. Another lost soul pleading to the infinite whether he knew it or not. Another wretch who'd given up on his place in the scheme of things. A future prisoner for Dullington's monochrome cage.

And yet—

Dullington turned away from the city, directing his darkened gaze toward the horizon. Beyond the edge of the dead city, where the mediocrity faded and gave way to the true desert of the Monochrome, stood a distant structure aglow in pale light. The Needle, as his former master once told him, where the Great Weaver slumbers.

The Ungod.

Oh, how he yearned to close his eyes and forget. Such was his curse in this place, such was his duty. A Keeper must see all—even the memories of what came before—and that entailed his own transformation. The loss of those he loved, the loss of his soul, the loss of his brothers of the Order. All were echoes in the great tapestry woven into both realities, constant reminders of what made him and what he must do.

Somewhere inside the massive column, beyond the scope of Dullington's vision, his adversary pulled strings independent of the Ungod's slumber. Changing course. Distorting the flow and narrative.

Those strings led back to Sparrow. Dullington didn't know why or how. His adversary had weakened the Monochrome's grip on Sparrow somehow, pulled back the gate long enough for the prisoner to slip free of his cage. Whatever his adversary had planned, Sparrow was at the center of it, and Dullington would do his duty to uncover the truth.

Candle's wife was a means to an end. Another piece in a long game. But the longer he observed Candle, the more Dullington suspected the man was more than a simple pawn. No, there was something more to him, more than any other flickering fool who'd come before.

A slow ache climbed through Dullington's chest. The sensation took him by surprise. It was a phantom of human emotion, something he'd not felt since his disincorporation in the Ungod's light, and he relished the uneasiness.

Sadness, he realized. Sadness through kinship. Even a Keeper such as himself wasn't free of the strings. He had his own, and when he turned skyward, he saw the projection of pale light entwine with that of Candle's lost soul.

The great human tapestry was woven in moments, displaying the lives, dreams, and failures of all who'd come before and all who would end. Aleister Dullington could see the strings as they entered the cosmic loom, and he could predict how they may weave together, but he could not foresee the final picture.

His adversary had Dullington at a disadvantage. Did he anticipate this sudden rise of emotion? Did he see the apparent link between Dullington and his manikin? Perhaps he had. And perhaps he hadn't. This was a gamble Dullington was willing to make, if only to force his adversary's hand.

"So be it."

Aleister Dullington summoned forth his Cretins to carry him toward the city. On the horizon, a halo of pale light encircled the Column, and just before Dullington departed, he heard the crash and boom of what might have been thunder.

But he knew better.

It was laughter. Cold, bitter laughter.

12

A STATE OF LOVE AND LIMINALITY

Movement and footsteps. Donna opened her eyes just as a dark shape knelt beside her.

"Mrs. Candle?"

She exhaled, relieved it was Alice and not anyone else. Donna tried to make out her face in the gloom. Firelight cast dancing shadows upon the wall of the room, painting the young woman's cheeks a faint orange outline that traced a smile in the dark.

Donna tried to sit up, wincing as her muscles woke in agony. Alice put a hand behind Donna's neck to help.

"He's coming," Alice said, and for the first time in a day, Donna broke her vow of silence.

"Donnie?"

There was a quick tearing sound, and Donna discovered she could move her legs again. Alice helped her to her feet.

"We're moving you to the meeting place. You'll see him very soon."

———•———

"**I**s that it?"

Michael stopped the car alongside an abandoned department store. Its display windows were shattered and boarded up. Graffiti artists had claimed those boards as their own, marking them with bright neon colors and insignias. "HE'S WATCHING," one of them read. "GRAY

MAN TELLS NO LIES," read another, along with a few odd symbols Donovan didn't recognize.

Across the street was an entrance ramp. A sign stood beside it, its letters faded, featuring a yellow circle in its center. Donovan surveyed their bleak surroundings. "I think so. Looks like the place."

Since construction of the highway bypass over thirty years ago, this previously bustling portion of town had dwindled, dried up, and finally died. Most of the city's crimes were committed in the South district, and even the cops were hesitant to venture its cracked, transient-ridden streets after dark. Donovan and Michael had the advantage of an overcast afternoon sky, but not much else.

Michael shut off the engine. "Do we know what we're doing?"

A cold tendril snaked its way around Donovan's gut. "No, Mike, I don't think we do."

Michael checked both guns, then handed his brother the revolver. Donovan took it with reservation, afraid to put his finger anywhere near the trigger. He'd decided in the last 24 hours that he didn't like guns very much.

"When did you get this thing?"

Michael shrugged. "A few years ago. Figured it might come in handy."

"Has it?"

"You tell me." They exchanged nervous smiles. Dr. Sparrow mumbled in his sleep.

Donovan looked back at the old man. A trickle of dried blood decorated Sparrow's forehead, charting a course between an array of age spots and wrinkles. Bile rose in the back of Donovan's throat. *Can I do this?* The answer came, as it always did, from Joe Hopper: *Sure you can, hoss. What other choice do you have? Now get to it.*

"I guess we should wake up Sleeping Beauty."

They got out of the car. Michael opened the passenger door. "Hey, doc." He tapped Sparrow's cheek. "Rise and shine."

Dr. Sparrow stirred in the backseat, a low groan escaping his thin lips as consciousness found him. He opened his eyes and winced when he tried to sit up. "You hit me," he whispered, searching his forehead with a trembling hand, slowly rubbing the small lump and feeling the tackiness of blood.

"I did." Michael took him by the arm. "Get out of the car."

Donovan turned to the subway entrance across the street. The flickering overcame him, revealing a street teeming with Cretins and Yawning. The creatures separated, forming a path toward the stairs.

When the Spectrum's colors bled their way into reality, Donovan turned to find Dr. Sparrow staring at him.

"It won't be long. You're going to fade right into oblivion. You and me, we'll be in prison together. Won't have your big brother to protect you then."

Donovan gripped the revolver and gestured to the subway entrance. "We'll see about that."

They crossed the street in a single-file line. Michael led the way, while Donovan took up the rear. He pushed the gun barrel into the small of Dr. Sparrow's back.

A gate barred their entrance at the bottom of the stairs. Donovan pulled on it, but it did not budge. A padlock was affixed to the handle from the inside.

No. He gripped the bars and pulled as hard as he could. *Not now. I'm so close.*

He cursed as he shook the bars, the rattling metal echoing down into the darkness beyond.

Sparrow laughed. The hoarse noise rose slowly within his tiny frame, transforming into a cruel, maniacal cackling. The old doctor's face reddened, his cold eyes alight with triumphant fury.

Donovan glared at him. A new strength found its way to his legs. He was on his feet and at the old man's throat within seconds, but Michael was faster. He held his brother back.

"Don't."

Donovan clutched at Sparrow's collar. For a moment there was fear in the old man's eyes, but it quickly faded. Sparrow smiled.

"Listen to him, Donovan. If Dullington wants me alive, you'd do well to mind him."

Donovan stepped back. He leaned against the concrete wall, took a breath, and ran his hands through his hair. *What would Joe Hopper do? What would I do?*

He looked at the gate and its padlock, then remembered his weapon. Michael connected the dots just as Donovan moved toward the bars.

"If you're thinking about shooting the lock, I wouldn't do it."

Donovan looked back at his brother. "Why not? I've seen it—"

"In movies. So have I. But if you shoot that lock, all you'll do is damage it, and then no one's getting it open."

"Do you know how to pick locks?"

Michael shook his head. "Maybe there's another entrance. Keep an eye on him—I'll be right back."

"Mike—"

But Michael was already halfway up the steps. When he reached street level, he looked down at Donovan and winked, though the gesture did little to alleviate the panic welling up inside him. After all he'd gone through to get to this point, Donovan couldn't help but feel the cold sting of defeat, the anxious heat of doubt. Had Dullington set him up to fail? Did he even intend to follow through with his part of the deal?

The gray sight returned, painting the world in Monochrome shades. Dr. Sparrow shone through, a malignant beacon in an otherwise unremarkable landscape. When he flickered back, Donovan found the good doctor watching him.

Donovan sat on the steps. He kept the revolver in plain sight to ensure there were no illusions between them. He might not be able to kill Sparrow, but he realized he would have no problem putting a bullet in the man's leg.

"It's happening," Sparrow said, "and it's only going to get worse." He nodded to the gate. "And do you think he'll really give back your wife? Once he gets what he wants, he'll fuck you over just like the rest of them."

The rest of them. Donovan let the doctor's words sink in. He remembered Sparrow's analogy about negative spaces. How many times had he given a homeless person more than a hurried glance? There were invisible men and women inhabiting every part of the city, in every part of the country, and no one acknowledged them. How many of them were Dullington's slaves?

The prospect of millions lost in the Monochrome terrified him.

"Are there really others?"

Sparrow rested his head against the wall and closed his eyes. "More than you could ever imagine. People like you, with meaningless lives, born with no real purpose, and obscured by their own mediocrity."

"Is that why you wrote your book?"

Dr. Sparrow looked down at him. He seemed genuinely surprised. "Why do *you* think I wrote my book?"

"I'd like to believe you wanted to help people. To warn them."

Sparrow scoffed. "I don't *care* about people. I don't *care* about you. The book is eighty thousand words of bullshit wrapped in a neat package and marketed to people who think they want to better their lives. *Help* people? Please." He shook his head. "People are insects. They don't give a shit.

They don't want to better themselves. They only want to eat, fuck, and watch reality television."

Donovan frowned. "I'm not like that."

"And I don't believe you. You wouldn't be here if that were true."

He thought about this. *I just want to support myself and my wife. Maybe a child some day, too.* Days before, if asked, Donovan would have said he wanted life with all its material perks. He would've wanted that promotion at his job, which in the scheme of things meant only a few more pennies on the hour. And what good would that do? He would just use it as a reason to strive for even more he couldn't have. Donna was right: it was never enough for him.

Donovan realized these things weren't all he wanted out of life. Not really. A flash of Donna's smiling face in his mind confirmed what he already knew.

"I just want to be happy," he whispered.

"Ah, happiness. Society raises you to believe it's attainable. They show you their view of what happiness is, and then they set you free to find your own. 'Go, find happiness.' It's the greatest con of all."

"Con?"

"Of course. I figured a man of your apparent intelligence would recognize that. It's a rigged game, kid. The happiness we're taught to buy doesn't exist. We're all running in place trying to snatch the carrot dangling out of reach. People sacrifice their lives for something they can never have. Some of them—the worst of them—end up like us." He rubbed absently at the wound on his forehead. "Tell me, how long have you been a salesman?"

Donovan's face flushed with the heat of embarrassment but found no reason to run from the truth any longer. "Nine years. Nine long, fruitless years."

"And here you are. I saw you flickering. It's how you're going to pay for your greatest crime."

"What are you talking about? What crime?"

"A crime against your own humanity. You've squandered your life by not reaching your own potential as a human being. That's what brought me to the Monochrome, and that's what will inevitably happen to you. Yours has become a life transparent."

Footsteps above broke the tension between them. Michael Candle jogged down the steps and caught his breath. "I found another entrance, but it was locked up, too."

Donovan's heart sank. He looked back at the gate, wishing he had a crowbar or—

A beam of light traced across the wall, revealing markings of graffiti and cracks in the concrete. The light bobbed up and down, growing brighter as it neared. Donovan rose to his feet and took a step toward the gate. He peered into the darkness beyond the bars. A pale circle of light drifted into view, bobbing its way toward them.

"Donovan Candle?"

The voice was weak, quiet. At first Donovan wasn't sure if he should answer. When the voice called out to him again, he walked to the gate and spoke.

"Yes, I'm here."

A mousy young man stepped forward, squinting into the daylight. A tattered button-down dress shirt and torn khakis clung to his emaciated body. Half of a ripped tie hung from his neck like a noose. He held a flashlight in his hand.

Donovan took a good look at the pale thing beyond the gate, realizing he was staring at his future. Another one of Dullington's prisoners.

"Who are you?"

"Name's Joel."

"Joel. Do you know why we're here?"

"Oh yes. Mr. Dullington told us to expect you. He said you'd be nearby, and here you are." Joel shifted his gaze over Donovan's shoulder, toward the old man. "Mr. Sparrow. Welcome home."

Sparrow glared and spat at Joel's feet. "I haven't been Mister for years. You'll call me Doctor Sparrow or nothing at all."

Joel smiled. "Nothing at all, then." He produced a key from his pocket. "I'll let you through."

He opened the padlock and pushed open the gate. It swung back with a shrill cry of agony that echoed down into the dark. He looked back at the trio and pointed his flashlight at the shadows.

"This way."

Donovan hesitated, then took a breath and entered. The air was stale, musty. *This must be what a tomb smells like*, he thought, turning back to face the opening. Michael lowered the handgun and pushed it against Sparrow's back.

"Easy does it, old timer."

Sparrow waited at the threshold, glaring into the darkness. Beads of sweat dotted his forehead, and there was a slight tremble in his chin. He caught Donovan's eye just before stepping into the darkness.

"This is going to haunt you, Donovan Candle. *I'm* going to haunt you." Sparrow's words echoed down the stairwell. Donovan thought about responding, but the words faltered on his tongue.

Once Michael was inside, Joel closed the gate and engaged the padlock. He pointed the flashlight at Sparrow, forcing the old man to back away and squint.

"I've heard much about you, Sparrow. Heard you defied our master. He said you might try to run."

Sparrow grinned, baring his teeth like a wild animal. "Your master was right."

He moved fast, shoving his elbow into Michael's gut. Donovan was still looking down into the darkened stairwell, and when he looked back at the commotion, he was blinded by daylight pouring across the threshold.

The gun clattered on the floor. Sparrow snatched it up, spun on his heels, and aimed for Joel's head. *"I won't go back!"*

But Michael was faster. He growled, gripping the old man's arm just as the gun went off. The shot lit up the concrete cavern with blinding light, echoing a small explosion that filled Donovan's ears with hundreds of ringing bells.

Sparrow used his free arm to claw at Michael's face as the two men struggled into the shadows.

Reeling, half-blind and half-deaf, Donovan lifted the revolver, but he couldn't find a clean shot. Not that it would have made a difference— his hands trembled with the jackhammer pounding away in his heart. A moment later, he lost the two men altogether, their silhouettes devoured by the darkness below.

Joel pointed the light, searching for the two men, but the beam failed to reveal them. Donovan muttered under his breath and stepped into the dark. Joel followed, lighting the way.

They found Michael at the next landing. He knelt on the ground, a hand to his jaw.

"The son of a bitch clocked me. Old bastard's got a hell of a punch."

Donovan snatched the flashlight from Joel's hands and descended the steps two at a time. Michael called out to him, but he dared not stop. Not now. His body moved with a will all its own.

The beam danced across the walls, compounding his confusion and panic. *Find him*, his mind screamed. *His life for Donna's.* That thought raced laps across his brain as he moved down to the subway terminal.

The stairwell opened into a larger terminal littered with garbage and other human detritus: broken furniture, bags of trash, food wrappers, discarded cans. A fire in an old refuse barrel illuminated the room, casting dancing shadows across its walls. Donovan concentrated his flashlight along the floor, following the beam of light to a token booth, its windows shattered and door smeared with years of grime. The stench of dried waste made his head swim. How long it had been since the transients—the Missing—had made this place their home? Years, maybe. Decades.

A gunshot from the dark broke his mind free of contemplation. The scream which followed filled his heart with ice. *Was that a woman's scream? Oh God, no.* A lump formed in his throat. He fought back a bout of nausea.

Keep your head straight, hoss. You don't know if it's her.

More shouts now, some of them belonging to his brother and the young man he'd left in the stairway. Others echoed from somewhere further ahead, distorted and impossible to decipher.

She's here. She's close. And she'll be dead if you don't find that old bastard.

He sucked in his breath and leapt over the turnstiles.

———————•———————

M ore barrels illuminated the boarding platform with dancing shadows. The walls moved and shimmered with varying shapes, the room aglow a sinister hue like a Halloween bonfire. A crowd of people dressed in old clothes and tattered rags stood in the center between two support columns. Donovan couldn't tell how many there were.

They waited, focused on something at the edge of the platform. Some of the people, he saw, were covered in grime, their skin mottled with an ashy-colored pox. The smell here was even worse, and Donovan had to suppress the urge to vomit.

"*Put it down,*" a young woman screamed. Mumbles of concern and dissent spread among the group. Off in the corner, Donovan spotted a pair of men kneeling over a woman's body. He panicked for a moment, fearing it might be his wife, but her voice over the crowd caught his attention.

"Mister, please, you don't have to do this—"

"Shut up, bitch."

Donovan gripped the revolver and cocked back the hammer like he'd seen on TV. It clicked. A woman in the crowd turned, saw him standing there, then pointed him out to the man next to her. They watched Donovan force his way through the crowd toward the pair at the edge of the platform.

Sparrow stood with an arm wrapped around Donna's neck. She was frozen with fear, her arms limp at her sides like a ragdoll. Tears streamed down her face. She winced when her captor pressed the gun barrel into her temple.

"I'm not going back." He saw Donovan working his way through the crowd and growled. "I don't know if I made that clear enough yet, but I think I've got your fucking attention now. Drop the gun, Donnie."

"You don't have to do this." Donovan struggled with the words, forcing them through a mouth of cotton and sand. The revolver was a lead weight in his hand.

Donovan looked into his wife's eyes. He wanted to cross the gap, take her in his arms, and hold her. He wanted to tell her how sorry he was—not just for her abduction, but for everything. For not being the man he'd promised to be. For not taking her to the shore. For everything and more, but now he'd never get the chance. After all he'd done to get this far, this petulant old man was going to put an end to the tiny life they'd built for themselves. Worse, he was going to punish Donna for her husband's inaction.

"Drop the gun or I swear I'll fucking put a bullet in her right goddamn now, Candle."

He glared at Sparrow as knelt, placing the gun on the dirty floor. Joe Hopper's words came to him, except they weren't really Hopper's at all. They were Donovan's, and the sound of them on his lips filled him with an unsteady terror.

"If you hurt her," he said, "*I* will haunt you."

Sparrow flashed a grim smile. "Your wife and I are going to walk out of here, and we're going to take the car. You'll find her dumped on the side of the road somewhere. What you do now determines whether or not she'll still be breathing when you do."

Anger welled up within Donovan, climbing from his gut all the way to his head. His vision reddened. For a moment, he forgot about everything else. He forgot about the flickering, about his brother and the others, about his own measly existence. In that quiet span of seconds, Donovan saw only the old man and his wife. A cold weight coiled around his stomach, transforming into fingers gripping his torso, lightly pulling him out of the Spectrum. He met Donna's terrified stare. "I love you, honey."

Donovan breathed deeply and took a step toward them. The old man pointed the gun at him just as the world shifted. Shadows gave way to a graying haze that filled the room like thick smoke. The cracked, grimy tile floor vanished, revealing a blank slate beneath. The others shone through in clarity. He saw their features. *Liminal people*, he thought.

Sparrow was there, too, holding Donna's darkened silhouette.

Donovan crossed the gap and charged into the doctor. The grays faded, filling in the blanks of the room with the spotted orange glow of fire in the shadows. Donna fell free of Sparrow's grasp as the two men tumbled off the platform and onto the old tracks.

The impact drove the air from Donovan's lungs, but the fire burning within raged on. He drove his knee into Sparrow's groin, eliciting a hoarse cry from the old man. His gnarled fingers searched the ground around them, fumbling for the gun, but it was just out of reach.

Donovan clutched Sparrow's throat. He balled his other hand into a fist and let his rage take over. All Donovan heard was the smack of his knuckles against the old man's face. All he saw was the image of Sparrow's gun to Donna's head. After coming all this way and compromising his values, Donovan would not let anything happen to her, and certainly not at the hands of this selfish monster.

The room shifted again, colors bleeding into gray. The empty drone of the Monochrome took over. Donovan thrust himself off the doctor, panting. Blood oozed from his swollen knuckles, spotting the floor beneath him. The dark splotches vanished moments later, absorbed by this pale reality.

He looked up. The Missing stood at the edge of the platform, watching. *Is this it? Have I flickered out?*

"Not quite, Mr. Candle."

Dullington's voice shook the world around them, each syllable accompanied by a tremor running through the threads of reality. Cretins emerged from the tunnels, spilling over one another, chattering incessantly. They stopped short of Donovan and Sparrow, climbing atop one another to form a column of white squirming bodies. Aleister Dullington's features took shape from the writhing mass.

The pale monk looked down upon Sparrow's bloody face and smiled. "Contrary to what Albert Sparrow told you, Mr. Candle, I am a being of my word."

"No…" Sparrow groaned. "Not like this…"

Dullington ignored him. He set his black eyes upon Donovan. "I am in your debt. You have done what no one else could do, and all in the name of love."

"So that's it, then?" Donovan crawled backward, resting against the side of the platform. "You'll let my wife go?"

"Indeed, I will, Mr. Candle. I must confess, under normal circumstances I would keep you here, and I still may." The smile slipped away from Dullington's face. "But that is up to you."

"What do you mean?"

"Your second chance, Mr. Candle. It *is* a second chance, and it *is* yours. Not many are granted one, but when they do it is earned." Dullington's voice degraded into a slow growl. "Albert Sparrow cheated his way to it." He looked up at the others standing on the edge of the platform. "Take him away. He will flicker out in time."

Albert Sparrow groaned, his voice distorted by the gravity of the Monochrome. Donovan watched the good doctor flicker back to the Spectrum.

"What's going to happen to him?"

"I have plans for him, but he is no longer your concern, Mr. Candle. Do you remember what I asked you yesterday?"

"I do."

"Good. Therein lies the way to your second chance. Consider it a life pitch."

"A life pitch?"

Dullington nodded. "Define yourself, Mr. Candle. It is the only way you will truly stop the flickering. If you do not do this, you *will* see me again, and I am not in the business of granting third chances."

The room shifted before Donovan had a chance to respond. He found himself sitting in the darkness of the subway tunnel. Dr. Albert Sparrow was gone.

———————•———————

"Donnie?"

Donna's voice gifted him newfound strength. Donovan pulled himself onto the platform where the group of Missing watched him in quiet awe. Donna pushed her way through the crowd and threw her arms around him. He held her tight, eyes closed, relishing the moment, then pulled back and kissed her. It was a kiss of desperation and love, a reconciliation of their worst fears and greatest hopes.

Tears welled up in Donna's eyes as he pulled away. "I'm so sorry, Don. I—"

"This isn't your fault." He swallowed back his own tears. "Not at all."

A young woman approached them. Donovan gave her a curious glance as recognition teased his mind. He'd seen her before, somewhere. Donna offering the woman a weak smile.

"Mrs. Candle, I'm sorry all of this happened to you. And you, too, Don."

"Do I know you?"

Alice nodded. He couldn't tell if she was smiling or frowning—the shifting shadows cast by the firelight obscured her features. "You did, once. We worked in the same department at Identinel."

"What's your name?"

"Alice Walenta."

The name rushed out of the depths of his mind with the velocity of a bullet. He knew her face, and he knew her name, but he wasn't sure how. The name stirred something deep inside, a long-buried spirit now restless from the disturbance of its grave, but recollection slipped between his fingers like smoke. She belonged to Dullington now, another casualty of the flickering. George Guffin's panicked words came rushing back: *"Some forget about us and others don't."*

"The last time I saw you, Don Candle, you had a Cretin on your shoulder. You never even knew I was gone. Do you still work for that hideous company?"

He didn't know what to say to her. For the life of him, he couldn't remember her at all from the workplace. There was a hazy spot in his memory, like a square cut away from canvas. How many others had he known and forgotten? The implications of the question chilled him.

Michael Candle approached them, a mix of confusion and relief painted in shadows across his face. "Are you two okay?"

"Yeah," Donovan said, giving Donna a squeeze. "I think so."

"Good." Michael nodded. "Now can we get the hell out of here?"

Alice turned away, led them back the way they came, through the suffocating darkness, up the stairs toward the locked gate. The daylight stung their eyes. Alice kept her head down while she opened the lock.

Michael bounded up the steps to the sidewalk. As Donovan helped his wife across the threshold, he took a breath, relishing the fresh air. Alice waited at the gate, squinting up to the sky. She breathed in the air and smiled.

Donna paused to look back.

"Alice. Come with us. I don't know what's happened, but maybe we can help you? Surely you have family. They'd be looking for you."

Alice stepped back into the shadows. She offered them a passing glance but lingered a moment longer on Michael's silhouette atop the stairs. Then she closed the gate, engaged the padlock. "I'm sorry, Mrs. Candle. It doesn't work like that." There were tears in the young woman's eyes. She blinked them away. "This is my place now, and it wouldn't matter if I went with you. Sooner or later, you're going to forget about me. I don't think I could go through that a second time..." Alice wiped her eyes. "Besides, once a part of the Monochrome—"

"Always a part of the Monochrome," Donovan whispered. He met the young woman's stare and offered a solemn nod. Donna beckoned to the woman beyond the gate, but Alice slipped into the shadows and was gone. Donna looked at her husband, confused, and took her first reluctant step toward freedom.

When they reached the top, Donovan stopped to look down at the gate. He thought about what Alice said, measuring the weight of her words. He understood them and their heavy implications, and when he looked back at his wife, he realized what he had to do.

Donovan put his back to the threshold and wrapped an arm around Donna. "Come on. Let's go home."

-EPILOGUE-
LIFE PITCH

The alarm clock sounded at 6:30 Monday morning, stirring Donovan from a troubled slumber. He opened his eyes and stared at the sunlight streaked across the ceiling. Memories of the weekend tumbled upward from a shallow grave, threatening to drag him down into its hole.

Donna rolled over and nudged him. He reached for the clock and silenced the blaring alarm. "Thank you," she mumbled, and slipped once more into a peaceful sleep. Donovan thought about doing the same, but his dreams troubled him, as did the prospect of the day.

Monday morning. The start of another week at Identinel. Worse than the denizens of the Monochrome were the prospects of returning to an empty job, an empty routine. An empty life. Timothy Butler and the Tammys didn't help matters, either.

Staring at the ceiling, listening to Donna's slow breathing, Donovan replayed Saturday night in his head, after they retrieved his car and left Sparrow's rental in the parking garage. They stayed at Michael's place that night, mindful enough not to wake him as they made love well into the dawn.

When they arrived home Sunday morning, Donovan made his wife wait in the car while he collected the remains of Mr. Precious Paws. He buried the feline in the backyard, marking the grave with a ceramic food dish. They spent the rest of the day cleaning the kitchen together, careful not to dwell on what had happened, afraid to mention it to one another.

Donovan saw the Monochrome side of his own home three times that day. Seeing Donna reduced to a dark transparent ghost left him with a chill that would not relent. After all he'd gone through, the flickering almost didn't seem real, like a bad dream from which he'd yet to awaken.

As he stared toward the ceiling, the room's color drained away. The effect lasted only a few seconds, but it was enough to reassure him Dullington wasn't bluffing about there being no third chances.

Sooner or later he would have to confront the demons that had condemned him for so many years. He'd spent so long running from the unknown, scraping and saving for a comfortable life of conformity and societal expectation, that he'd never considered what might happen if he turned around to look the other way.

Donovan rolled on his side and faced Donna. He brushed the hair from her face. She was so beautiful. He'd gone through hell to get her back, digging to depths of himself he didn't care to know, and it had been worth every moment—but there was still one more life that needed saving.

Ain't no better time than today, hoss. Get to it.

Her eyes fluttered open. She smiled. "Morning."

"Hi." He tucked a strand of hair behind her ear. "I need to talk to you about something."

"Mmm, about what?"

The words were there on his tongue. They'd been there ever since Tuesday morning, but other matters had stolen his attention. Even then, he realized, he wouldn't have meant them. Not like now. Now he knew the error of his ways, and he owed her an apology.

Donovan leaned over and kissed her forehead. "I'm sorry about our fight Monday evening. It was stupid, and you were right all along. It's not about the money." He felt the heat of tears in his eyes and tried to hold them back. "When I came home on Friday and you weren't there, I thought I'd lost you forever. That I'd driven you away, and in some ways, I think I did. But I want you to know that I'm going to change all that. Today. Because I love you, because I owe it to you, and because…" *Because if I don't, I'll disappear forever.* The words hung on his lips, and he wanted to voice them, but he couldn't bring himself to do so. "Just because."

Donna smiled, wiping a tear from his cheek.

"We'll be okay, Donnie. We've seen worse before, and we survived. And if we can survive this, I'd say we're damn near invincible."

"I love you."

"And I love you."

They kissed. He'd spent over twenty-four hours without her, and it caused him more agony than he'd ever known before. In some ways, losing her proved his love for her, and now that she was back, he intended to embrace her company for as long as he could. The thought of spending the day away from her while he toiled for nine hours in his cubicle sickened him.

"So, Mrs. Candle," he said. "Would you like to accompany me on a trip to the shore?"

Donna smiled, opened her mouth to speak, but recoiled with a jolt. She cringed for a moment, putting her fingers to her temples. "Sorry. It's this damn headache. It's bothered me since last week. What were you saying, honey?"

But Donovan didn't respond. He saw all he needed to see in a brief flash of gray. There was a Cretin on her shoulder, its head pointed toward her ear. Alice Walenta's words echoed in his head: *Sooner or later, you're going to forget about me.*

Color seeped back into the world, filling in the detail of Donna's concerned face. "Honey, are you okay?"

"Yeah, I'm fine."

"You're very pale." She put her hand to his forehead. "Doesn't feel like you're running a fever, though. What were you going to say a few seconds ago?"

He looked at her for a moment, contemplating what to say. What could he say? And would it even matter? She could still see him, but what about that evening after work? These questions raced through his head. He had to confront Dullington's challenge, and soon, or else all he'd done would be for nothing. *Define yourself, Mr. Candle.* It was a simple imperative, and yet so daunting. Where could he possibly begin?

Donna looked at the clock, wincing as she sat up. "You're going to be late for work."

The answer came to him. He smiled, kissed her, and scrambled out of bed.

———•———

He skipped the bypass and took side-streets across the city. Along the way he listened to the local rock station instead of his usual talk radio, cranking it as loud as the car's tiny stereo could manage. His windows and rearview mirror rattled with the beat, and whenever he came to a stop, pedestrians turned and stared. He imagined he looked goofy, blaring this raucous music from the meager speakers of his four-door sedan, but he didn't care.

The gray sight happened only once during his drive, just as he neared his destination. He saw specters walking along the sidewalks. Some of them had Cretins on their shoulders. Others didn't, and he took comfort in that.

When he neared his office building, he felt that unsteady pull at his stomach. The sensation was fleeting but served as the warning he'd expected. He drove past the Identinel offices and further into the city.

After half an hour, he found himself back at the city park. He parked along the curb and took a stroll. It was mostly empty at that hour, with only the occasional jogger or elderly person out for their morning walk. Donovan found a quiet spot near the fountain and took a seat.

He thought about Donna, about his job. He'd practically had an affair with Identinel for nine years, yet nothing good had come of it. Donovan's commitment to the company had put a strain on his life, his relationship with Donna and with his brother. For that he could not forgive his employers, and he certainly could not forgive himself. Not only had he let Donna down, he'd let himself down as well.

Who are you, Mr. Candle?

Donovan wanted to believe he knew the answer to that question, maybe when he was younger, before he'd learned the hostile truths of the real world. *Always wanted to be a writer. Wanted to make a living with my art. Wanted to be someone who'd mattered in the grand scheme. Who was that guy? Where did I lose him? Where did our paths diverge?*

He idly plucked blades of grass from the earth, rolling them between his fingers before letting them fall.

Back in college, he'd had a plan. He'd get his degree, go to graduate school, marry Donna, write a bestseller, and support a family with his earnings. It wasn't until the end of school that he realized how fantastic it all seemed, and the bitter reality was that this lifestyle he dreamed of living was experienced by so very few.

He never expected to grow complacent. Twenty-year-old Donovan wouldn't believe the man he'd become. Another cog in the corporate machine. Another company man in slacks and a dress shirt, eager to please his masters, desperate for another dime on the hour. What happened to the kid with all that fire in his heart, the one who wanted to conquer the world?

Life and bills. Donna's fibro diagnosis. Insurance premiums. Safety. Two weeks of vacation a year. Weekends off work.

What price comfort but a mere piece of his soul and pay it he did.

Donovan remembered something else Dullington told him. He'd said it on Friday, when they first spoke on the phone at Identinel. *Actions birth definition.*

He thought about what he'd done to Sparrow, thought of the old man's accusing glare, and felt a twinge of guilt. The old man awakened something within Donovan, a primal and violent urge to protect what he cared about, and the means to make a difficult decision when it had to be made. Knowing the kind of person Sparrow was made it easier to make some sort of peace with himself, though he feared what he'd done would come back to haunt him, that he would have to answer for it.

He had it comin' to him, hoss. You did the right thing. It's the rest of your life you should be concerned about.

Donovan could almost smell Hopper's cigarette smoke on his breath. He closed his eyes. What had he done to define himself?

As the world bustled on around him, Donovan realized he'd traded his dreams for dull reality that first day at Identinel. *It's only temporary*, he'd said to himself as days turned to weeks, and so on. Time eroded, and soon he found himself ten pounds heavier. His hair was streaked with gray. The creativity upon which he'd once prided himself was all but gone. Joe Hopper was born out of a last-ditch effort to prove to himself that he still had the chops to create something.

And now that effort had died, was just as empty as his own life.

Is this how I want to be remembered?

Donovan stood and brushed grass from his trousers. He stared up at the sky and the surrounding skyscrapers, then back down at the row of trees. The flickering reminded him of his brief chase through the Monochrome. As he walked to his car, he realized that Aleister Dullington's intervention in his life was, in some ways, a good thing. It was the wake-up call to his future happiness.

His father once told him that to betray oneself was the greatest sin of all, and to forgive oneself was the hardest thing to do. Donovan understood that now.

He started his car and pulled away from the curb. The dashboard clock read 10:05, and the morning was beautiful.

So this is what Mondays are really like.

He turned a corner onto another side-street and stepped on the gas. It was time to make his life pitch.

He drove back to Identinel, took the parking space closest to the building, and ran inside. Some of his coworkers acknowledged him, stopping to stare as he jogged across the foyer and swiped his badge. He took their notice as a good sign, wearing a stupid grin on his face as he marched through the cubicle farm toward Timothy Butler's office.

The Tammys sat across from Butler's desk, their mouths framed wide as they bickered to each other. Butler sat in his executive leather chair with his hands behind his head. All three were startled to see him. Donovan stared at each one, focusing on their faces.

"Candle," Butler began, "what is—"

"My name is Donovan. If you call me Candle one more time, so help me, I'll cram a headset up your ass."

Fire and smoke spewed from his mouth. He tasted venom on his lips. It made him ravenous for more.

"No one gives a shit about your stories, Butler. We don't care. Pay attention the next time you walk into the lounge. Everyone becomes suddenly occupied with other things for a reason, Tim. Think about that."

"*Mr. Candle,*" Tammy Quilago snapped, "I think you're out of line—"

"Tammy, please shut your mouth."

Red splotches blossomed across her neck and cheeks. Tammy Perpa started to chime in, but he held up a hand to silence her. He hesitated, the smile pulling at his face. Two words perched at the tip of his tongue, where they'd been for the last nine years aching and waiting for their turn to be spoken. That time had finally come.

"I quit."

He turned and left the office. Outside, his coworkers peeked over their cubicles, headsets around their necks and eyes wide. *Now they can see me*, he thought.

He was halfway to his desk when Butler and the Tammys emerged from the office. As they passed by, Donovan experienced the gray sight for a brief interval. What he saw both frightened and filled him with sick satisfaction. Timothy Butler and the two Tammys were fully visible, shimmering with the same sickening glow as Dr. Sparrow. He saw their wrinkles and graying hairs, their bad taste in clothing, and the frowns on their faces. Other people in the office appeared as dark phantoms with Cretins on their shoulders, and Donovan knew those creatures were not there for him. Not today. The Tammys and Timothy Butler would soon have their turn in the Monochrome.

The office's color returned. Donovan boxed up what little belongings he had and left Identinel a free man.

He did not look back.

————————————•————————————

Donovan made one stop before returning home. The local animal shelter, where years before they'd adopted Mr. Precious Paws, was located not far from his neighborhood. He wandered between the rows of kennels and cages until his eye fell upon a tiny orange ball of fur. When he leaned closer to the cage, two ears perked up, followed by a pair of big green eyes. The tabby kitten purred.

A tag hanging from the wire mesh gave the feline's information. The owner had vanished, leaving behind a pregnant cat. This kitten was the only one of the litter to survive.

He smiled and poked his finger through the cage. The kitten pawed at it.

"I think I'll call you *Mrs.* Precious Paws."

————————————•————————————

A few days later, Donovan received a phone call from his brother in the middle of dinner.

"Please don't answer that," Donna said. "Finish your meal."

He looked over, saw it was Michael's number on the ID, and winked at Donna. Any other time he would've let it ring, but he and his brother had grown close following their adventure.

"Hey, Don. What's going on?"

"Not much. Just having some dinner. You?"

"Ah, nothing really. Just finished up for the day." Michael paused for a moment, then lowered his voice. "Listen, I keep trying to remember what happened. And I know something happened, I know we saved Donna, but every time I try to remember why, it just isn't there."

Donovan closed his eyes. He'd experienced the same thing with Donna. Some details of the weekend remained, but others were lost to her, and Donovan didn't have the heart to fill them in. He preferred to be the only one to remember it all. For his wife and brother, some things were better left forgotten.

"It isn't important," he said, changing the subject. "Did you hear? I quit my job."

Michael's mood lightened. "I did. Proud of you."

"Thanks."

"No, I mean it. I know I don't say things like that very much, but yeah, I really mean it, Don. You really surprised me. I didn't think you would. Mom and Dad would be proud of you too."

Donna finished her dinner, walked over, and kissed him on the cheek. Mrs. Precious Paws scampered after her, pawing at her ankles.

"And," Michael went on, "I'd like to offer you a job."

"A job? Doing what?"

"Being my partner." An uncomfortable silence drifted across the line. Michael cleared his throat. "I mean, you've seen all the paperwork I have to deal with—"

Donovan laughed. "Me, a private investigator? You're serious?"

"Well, you'll have to be licensed first, but yeah, I'm serious. I figure it'll give you something to write about. And it's good job security, too, what with people disappearing left and right all the time."

The laugh they shared was a nervous one, but both knew the other meant well. Donovan accepted, and though the rest of the conversation whirled around the usual trivialities, he did not lose focus of his new prospect. Working with his brother seemed exciting, even validating, and when Donna later asked why he wore such a goofy smile, he could only say, "I'm going to work with my brother."

———————•———————

Two weeks after the incident which nearly cost Donna her life, Donovan Candle experienced the flickering for the last time at 11:33 PM on a Saturday night. The instances of gray sight had become less frequent in the following days. The violent tugs at his stomach were reduced to vague tickling sensations, more uncomfortable than painful, and were so faint that he barely noticed them anymore.

He sat in his office staring at the blank computer screen. Over the last two weeks, he'd grown more as a person than at any other point in his life. If he'd done enough to remain in this reality, he and Donna would finally make their trip down to the shore for a weekend.

"Things," she'd told him, "always have a way of working out." He knew she was right. And somehow, as the days went on and the flickering diminished, he knew this was the case with his fate.

Tonight, he sat down to begin the novel he'd put off for so long. It was his brother's encouragement that finally spurred him to action. Michael's job offer had started the wheels in his mind. *Together, we'll be Candle and Candle. Just like Spade and Archer.*

He'd never seen himself as a detective, but after all that had happened, he realized it was just the kind of excitement he craved, even if reality couldn't match what he put to paper.

And so he'd wandered into the office after psyching himself up to face the interminable white space of his word processor. He sat down, pecked at the keys, and opened up the file for *The Great American Novel*.

He stared at the title and deleted it. In its place he typed MONOCHROME DREAM.

Just as he was about to jump to the next page, his vision went gray, and he felt the tickle of a hand around his gut. In the liminal space of his office, he saw the figure of Albert Sparrow standing in the corner of the room. The old man glared through the haze, his teeth bared and hands shaking.

Donovan met the old man's stare and shook his head. "I proved you wrong."

Sparrow raised his fists and let loose a silent scream. The gray sight faded for the last time, the shimmering curtain of reality pulled once more into place, and the tickle in Donovan's stomach ceased. For first time since that fateful Tuesday morning, he felt whole. But he didn't dwell on his victory over Sparrow and the Monochrome. Instead, he turned his attention back to the title.

Monochrome Dream. A novel by Donovan Candle.

On the next line, he typed a dedication. "For Donna, I would for you." Her love was all the meaning he would ever need, and it marked the perfect place to begin. Joe Hopper admonished him from somewhere beyond the white space, in the depths of his head.

Get to it, hoss.

He scrolled to the next page, a great white nothing daring him to act. Donovan smiled, put his fingers on the keys, and began to write.

THE TRAVELERS

S parrow screamed as the shade of Donovan Candle slipped away like smoke. He screamed so hard and for so long he saw spots of color burst before him. Weakened, he fell to his knees in the empty box of Donovan's office, the once-fiery rage within now nothing more than a pile of charred embers. After all this time, all this effort, Dullington had finally won.

Come, Albert Sparrow. Your time is done. We must be on our way.

The world trembled from Dullington's words. Resigned and hopeless, Dr. Albert Sparrow climbed to his feet and left the planar structure of Candle's house in the Monochrome. Aleister Dullington waited outside among a pale river of scuttling, chattering creatures. A trio of Yawning lingered on the fringe, guarding their master, waiting for his command to feast.

"No tears, Mr. Sparrow. We both know your path always leads you here."

The old man wiped his face, straining to keep his emotions in check and failing horribly. He'd not felt this hopeless since the days before his final flickering. That was a lifetime ago, when he was still a lowly adjunct at a community college, in a town he'd all but forgotten. Surely the town had forgotten him as well. His old friends, distant relatives in a family he despised—all gone. He was alone now and forever.

"I was meant for more than this..."

"For once, Mr. Sparrow, you and I are in complete agreement." Aleister Dullington motioned toward the horizon, where the skeletal shapes of

Spectrum structures dissipated into a seamless haze. "But I do not think it is what you hope it will be."

Sparrow followed his master's gaze and stared. "You're taking me there, aren't you? What is it, Dullington? What the fuck are you going to do to me?"

The pale monk nodded, walking along the river of Cretins. Sparrow took a few defiant steps toward his master but stopped short when the trio of Yawning turned in his direction and growled.

"Answer me, Aleister. You owe me that much."

In the distance, beyond the demarcation between remnants of the Spectrum and the true barren wastes of the Monochrome, a tall spire pulsed with light. A beacon to travelers across the gray desert of nothing. A haven and a warning. Aleister Dullington looked over his shoulder and offered his prisoner a thin smile.

"I am taking you to meet an old friend."

BOOK II
THE LIMINAL MAN

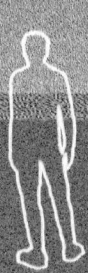

THE THIRTEENTH MAN

18 months later

Joe Hopper shoved the gun into the assassin's temple. The beaten man winced, struggling against the cuffs.

"I got your number," Hopper growled. "You and the rest of 'em. Now you tell me something, hoss. How many are there? Who else was behind this?"

The assassin looked up at him with blood and hate in his eyes.

"Twelve plus one, amigo. And the thirteenth, good 'ol Butcher Pete, he's the one you should be afraid of. He's gonna gut you and your whole goddamn family."

—Donovan Candle
Monochrome Dream

Richard Henza awoke in a haze of blood and liquor. His head throbbed, rusty nails shooting behind his eyes and down his neck. Dark maroon splotches burst and trailed like fireworks across the black expanse of his vision.

His thoughts swam fuzzily through his head. Where was he? Was he still at home? Sounds drifted in and out around him, accompanied by a dull ache pulsing to a beat.

The Talking Heads. Of course.

He *was* still at home. His stereo was still on.

And there was something wet on his face. Warm.

He tried to wipe it away, but his hands would not cooperate, and forcing them to action made his joints sing. He gasped, suddenly aware that his wrists were bound to the arms of his chair.

A deep, grating chuckle issued from somewhere across the darkness, startling him. *The man with the beard.* The sound of his throaty voice called forth a memory of grizzly features: tall, big, a surly son of a bitch with gnarled hair and dirt caked into his wrinkled face.

Remnants of the evening swam into focus. Richard recalled an empty glass, his hand reaching for the bottle, turning to find a huge grimy intruder standing in his den. The last thing he saw was the bastard swinging the bottle, a burst of stars, then nothing.

Richard winced as he tried to move again. His head throbbed as a fresh stream of blood coursed down his face. When he opened his eyes, he felt his eyelids brush against something rough.

Blindfolded. He relaxed, fighting the hazy cloud smothering his thoughts. The evening played back in the darkness like a silent film, and he was its captive audience. He'd been drinking, brooding over his meeting with the heads of the network—and one new face he did not recognize. *Bastard thinks he can take my show away from me? Not without a fight. He hasn't met my attorney yet.*

More laughter. Richard Henza cleared his throat.

"Look, you can have anything you want. Anything. Want a check? I'll write you a check for a hundred grand right now. I'll give you my car. Brand new, less than two thousand miles on it. I'll give you anything, just please, please don't—"

The air in the room swelled, growing heavier between syllables. Henza sucked in his breath. He was wrong—there *was* more than one person in the room with him.

"Everything is in place," said another man. His imperious voice raised the hairs on Richard's neck. "You can remove the blindfold now, Mr. Abrams."

The first man hacked out what must have been a laugh, but which to Richard sounded like the choked cry of a wild beast.

"Sorry, Dick. You'll have to pardon my associate." The blindfold came away from his face, and the onrush of light blurred his vision. Cloudy shapes swirled into focus, revealing the bearded man's hulking form. "I hope Kale didn't hurt you too badly. I need you to be lucid. You're no good to me with a concussion—not that it will matter for much longer."

Richard squinted at the other figure. His blood pressure spiked, amplifying the throbbing in his head. Even though the man lacked definition in the haze, Richard knew him, knew his voice.

Yesterday afternoon's events rushed back in a furious reverie. There were twelve directors for the WBS television network. Richard Henza had sparred with them all for the sake of maintaining creative control over his show, but this man had changed everything in the span of one meeting.

This smug asshole had remained in the shadows, barking directives and ultimatums, and the rest of the board cowered in his presence. Richard didn't know his name, and he didn't care to know. This thirteenth man was an interloper, an enemy, and he wouldn't allow one smug son of a bitch in a suit to take away the success he'd worked so hard to achieve.

Richard looked up at the thirteenth man. His fear vanished. In its place was pure unbridled anger. He wanted to tear himself from his restraints and choke this man. How *dare* he enter Richard's home. Henza was not one to be coerced, and he'd show the bastard—

"Dick, please. Don't scowl at me like that. You brought this on yourself."

"I'm going to have your head on a plate for this, I swear to Christ."

"Christ? Oh come now. You're not a man of God any more than I'm a man at all."

Richard fell silent and stared. "What?"

The thirteenth man grinned at his prisoner, revealing two rows of perfectly aligned teeth. His eyes lost their sheen, darkening for an instant before returning to normal. Richard wanted to believe the odd effect was just the result of bourbon on an empty stomach, even a possible concussion, but lingering doubts suggested otherwise. He searched for something witty to say, some statement sharp enough to hurt this impenetrable figure, but nothing came to mind. He glared at his captor.

"Dick, you and I need to come to terms with something." The thirteenth man knelt before him. He put his hands on Richard's knees. His fingers were cold. "*Fading Out* isn't yours. It never was."

"The hell it isn't." He'd nurtured that show from the ground up, crafting the pitch, seeking investors, and giving his all to sway the opinions of anyone who would listen. Hell, he'd been in the production van during the first week of filming. That show was his baby, and damn anyone who told him otherwise.

"I know you think it is, Dick. I can appreciate that fact. After all, you've helped make the show a success." The man walked to the bar and poured a shot of bourbon. "But did you ever stop and think about why that board of geriatrics agreed to carry the show? Or why they let you have complete autonomy?" He returned, pushing the shot glass against his prisoner's chin but Richard turned away, spilling bourbon on his shirt. "I mean, you seem like a thorough guy, am I right? Surely you would've wondered why a TV network saturated with other reality TV shows would pick up yours. What good could they possibly see in a show all about following around dipshit millenials struggling to make ends meet?"

Richard didn't want to admit it, but he had a point. Sometimes he *did* wonder why the WBS boys offered him a contract at all. The right place, the right time, the right idea—everything was in the cards, as he'd heard so many times before. Looking up at the pale man, Richard felt the slow chill of realization crawl through his gut.

"*You* did this?"

His captor snickered and set the glass down on the coffee table. Kale leaned against the bar, and folded his arms folded across his chest. He didn't share his master's amusement.

"You could say I provided the necessary motivation to keep the board off your back. You may have birthed the idea, Dick, but I pulled the strings to make it happen. That's what I do, Dick. I pull the strings. You're all lifeless puppets to me. The show is, for all intents and purposes, *mine*. And now I'm here to take it to the next step."

He motioned to Kale. The bearded man nodded and left Richard's view.

"See, I can't have you thinking you have any sort of influence. That would only gum up the works." He turned and pushed the coffee table closer to Richard's chair. "And it seems only fitting that I demonstrate the significance of my creation."

Kale returned, carrying a square object with a long, black cord. Richard wasn't sure what it was until the small television was placed on the table before him. Kale picked up the cord and plugged it into a nearby socket.

The screen came to life, revealing a simple black and white outline of a door. Richard knew it well: it was his own design.

He looked up at his captors and laughed, "You broke into my house and tied me up to make me watch my own show? Really?"

The thirteenth man grinned what could have been a charming smile in the right circumstances, but Richard saw no charm. That lifeless smile chilled his bones.

"Yes, Dick, that's precisely right. You'll see just how special this show really is."

The Talking Heads came to a halt. Richard looked over and saw Kale standing at his stereo. He ejected the disc and snapped it in half, dropping the pieces on his way to the bar. There he stuck his hand into a fishbowl full of promotional buttons for the TV show. Grinning, he pulled one out and affixed it to his shirt pocket.

"Much obliged," Kale said.

The thirteenth man stepped out of view. Richard felt icy fingertips on his head, redirecting his attention to the small screen.

"You sit tight and watch this. When it's over, I think you'll understand the gravity of your mistake."

"Yeah?" Richard smirked, staring incredulously at the screen as the show's title sequence began. "What makes you think so?"

"Because," said the thirteenth man, now whispering directly into Richard's ear, "you're going to see just why you should've walked away when I gave you the chance, Mr. Henza."

His voice distorted as he said Richard's name, dimming in a flurry of white noise. The air in the room swelled once again, and he realized the thirteenth man's hands were no longer on his head. He glanced toward the bar and saw Kale was gone as well.

Richard struggled against his restraints until he could no longer bear the discomfort it caused, and when that didn't work, he tried calling for help. He had no family, and his housekeeper wouldn't arrive until the morning. Exhausted, he slumped against the back of the chair, and tried to rethink his situation.

Concentration proved difficult as the television flashed images of his TV show. Episode after episode of *Fading Out* played before him in succession. His thoughts of escape dwindled, and after the first episode's conclusion he found himself willingly glued to the screen. Richard was okay with this, despite the numbness creeping up his arms and legs.

Things began to change for Richard Henza at some point in the early hours of the following morning. The sudden onset of nausea snapped him from his fatigued trance. What began as a discomforting sensation quickly transformed into an invisible hand threatening to disembowel him.

And the noise, oh God, the noise was horrible. The low, thrumming drone of bells and static hissed together in his ears.

When he blinked, he found the darkness of the room was gone, replaced by a stark gray palette. Gone were his bar, sofa, and fireplace. The coffee table and TV were nowhere to be found. The room was empty but for the shapes of four tall figures. They stood before him, impossibly elongated like the drawings of children.

Droning bells faded from his ears, replaced with a series of dissonant mournful sobs. The shapes before him fell into focus, and Richard's bladder gave way.

The figures stood impossibly tall, with pale rubbery flesh stretched taut over bony frames. They towered over him, swaying lazily as though a breeze might blow them over. Their eyes were set back into their rounded heads like polished orbs of obsidian, and their mouths quivered hesitantly.

Richard Henza understood then what the thirteenth man meant by his warning. He understood it when the giant creatures opened their mouths, revealing rows of worn white teeth. He understood it when their jaws unhinged, stretching open to reveal four equally bottomless pits.

The closest figure quickly leaned forward, closed its jaws around the top of his face, and plucked his head from his torso. Richard Henza had no time to scream.

PART ONE

THE HESITANT MAN

Hesitation is his natural impulse in the face of exciting, terrifying new territory. He will stand on the line forever if allowed, a prisoner of his own inaction.

—Dr. Albert Sparrow
A Life Ordinary: A Comprehensive Study in Human Mediocrity

1

LESS DEFINED

Donovan Candle's cell phone rang as he exited the gas station. He carried a latte in each hand, with a glazed donut balanced atop one of the lids, and a copy of the morning newspaper tucked underneath his arm. The phone chirped again. Answering it involved a juggling act that ended with the loss of the donut, and he cursed when it hit the pavement. He stared longingly for a moment before answering the phone.

"Donna, you owe me a donut."

"I do?"

"Yes, you do."

Donna Candle laughed. The sound made him smile, and the donut, once a seemingly monumental loss, was now forgotten. He set the lattes on the roof of his car and fumbled for the keys.

"It's not like you need that donut anyway." Her playful jab was punctuated with more laughter.

Donovan unlocked and opened the door. "What's that supposed to mean?"

"I'm just teasing. I forgot to ask you to stop for me on your way home later today." He tossed the newspaper into the car, retrieved the lattes, and took his place behind the wheel.

"Let me guess," he said, starting the engine. "More pickles?"

"Yes, please."

"Sure. Any other strange preggo requests?"

"Umm, nope, that'll do for now."

She wished him a good day at work and hung up. He couldn't help but chuckle. After talking and planning for a couple of years, he and Donna had finally conceived a child. Now she was six months along and had been craving pickles for weeks.

Life for Donovan Candle was blissfully chaotic, thanks in part to that growing bump in Donna's belly, and he wanted it no other way. He'd spent the first part of his adult life meandering about in an effort to define himself as a husband, as a writer, as more than a blank face in the crowd—and now, at thirty-three years old, Donovan found himself comfortable with the idea of adding "Dad" to that list of definitions. It had a nice ring to it.

Smiling, Donovan put the car in gear and pulled out into traffic. When the morning commuters merged left toward the freeway, he went right.

He rolled down his window and let the morning air fill the car. With one hand on the wheel, the wind in his hair, and a latte in his other hand, Donovan Candle steered himself from the lifeless freeway into the bright summer green of the countryside surrounding the city.

He glimpsed the rearview reflection, watching the congested freeway ramp vanish behind a row of trees. *A year ago, I would've been sitting in that gridlock right along with them.*

His days at Identinel seemed like a lifetime ago, the company like another country across the sea. Distant, nearly forgotten, a bad dream from a long restless night of sleep. He'd spent nine years suffering through the same commute, toiling away at a thankless job, and compromising his hopes for what he thought was happiness. In the end, that bitter routine almost cost him his marriage, and his life.

But never again. I'm not going to live like that anymore.

The old farming road circumvented the city limits, flirting with the thoroughfares and avenues but never quite crossing those boundaries. He came to a stop sign, switching on the radio as he made his turn. A newscaster gave the latest local report:

"—case you're just tuning in, the city's still buzzing about the latest bombshell to drop. Richard Henza, creator of the acclaimed, locally produced reality show *Fading Out*, has been missing for a week now. He was last seen Thursday evening leaving the WBS building. Rumors of pending litigation between Henza and the network surfaced earlier this week; however, his attorney Joseph Rochester has not returned calls for comment. Authorities are asking for anyone with information on Henza's whereabouts to step forward. In other news—"

Too early for that. Not yet.

He changed the station. Pink Floyd filled the car, and he sighed. The countryside slipped away, its fresh air displaced by the stale fumes of smog. He sat in a line of traffic four cars deep and watched droves of people in suits and ties march to their jobs. Their blank faces reminded him of who he used to be. They looked like inmates walking the final mile to death row.

That's what I used to be. All blank and gray, headed toward my daily execution.

Traffic inched forward.

He was less than a block from the new office when someone knocked on his window, startling him from his thoughts. The snap back to reality made his heart race. A large man tapped on the glass, smearing some kind of black gunk across the surface.

Donovan looked down and made sure the door was locked. The traffic light up ahead was still red. He cursed under his breath and slowly cracked the window an inch.

"Can I help you?" An acrid stench permeated the car, catching him by surprise. He tried not to retch.

"Sure can." The homeless man's hair was black and knotted, and a huge shrub of a beard clung to his chin. He wore a tattered dress shirt with a small white button stuck to the breast pocket. In the center of the button was a black outline of a doorway.

The man stuck out his hand. A glint of light from a metal watchband caught Donovan's eye. He looked at it, saw it was a very nice watch for an otherwise homeless man, and pretended not to notice.

"Very hungry," he said. "Spare change?"

I'm sure that watch could fetch you a few meals.

"Yeah," he said, scolding himself for having such crass thoughts. He dug out a handful of nickels and dimes from the console, opened the window a little more, and gave them to the man.

"Much obliged."

The car behind him honked. Donovan looked up at the green light. He sped away without telling the man he was welcome.

"Good morning, Mr. Candle."

Donovan cringed. Rosie smiled up at him from behind her desk.

"Rosie, you can call me Don. Calling me Mr. Candle makes me feel weird. Like a teacher or something."

"Sorry, Mr. Ca—er, Don. Sorry Don."

"No worries. Any calls?"

She checked her computer. "Just one. Your brother said he's going to be out for most of the morning. Mrs. Beckman called him at home and said her husband left rather early. She thinks he went to meet with his mistress."

Donovan rolled his eyes. Mrs. Gloria Beckman was one of Michael's first clients. She lived in a mansion in Soaring Hills, and was forever convinced her husband, a network executive prone to working late hours, was cheating on her. Michael had yet to find a shred of evidence to prove this, but she was certain—as was her checkbook. Who were they to turn down steady work?

He opened the door to their office. Although the new place was ample enough for their needs, it wasn't excessive. They still shared workspace but were now afforded enough room for their own desks and computers. Donovan set his things down on his desk, booted up his computer, and took a sip of his latte. He went to put the second latte on Mike's desk, then thought better of it and offered it to Rosie.

"No thanks. I don't drink coffee."

"Give yourself a few years."

Donovan shrugged and set the latte on the corner of his desk, took a seat, and unfolded the newspaper. The headline read: SEARCH CONTINUES FOR FAMED TV PRODUCER. He skimmed the first line, recalling the radio announcer's broadcast. Richard Henza, creator and producer of the acclaimed reality show *Fading Out*, seemingly fell off the face of the planet a week ago.

Fading Out. He'd heard of that show. Never watched it—he rarely had time for TV these days—but he'd seen and heard its many advertisements. He set down the paper and called out to Rosie.

"Hey, what's that reality show you watch?"

"Fading Out?"

"Yeah, that's the one. Have you been following the news about the show's creator?"

"I have. I hope they don't end the show. It's one of my favorites."

He went back to the paper and looked for anything else that might be noteworthy. Not a week went by that he didn't read of someone else going missing. These notices were often accompanied by a smiling photo of the person, their faces home to eyes rendered blank by gritty newsprint. Given enough time, those faces would end up in files on his desk.

Michael assigned him to Missing Persons duty soon after making him a partner. "It's steady," his brother explained, "and should keep you busy. Been the bread 'n butter of the company for a few years now."

Bread 'n butter was only the half of it. Two months after he became licensed, Donovan found the volume of contracts growing. When he and Donna returned from their vacation at the shore, he found his brother taping paperwork to the wall of his home office. A conversation about file storage grew into a search for actual office space, and within a month they'd negotiated a lease.

The reports did not stop coming. His brother dismissed them as cut-and-dried cases—usually runaways, people who wanted to disappear and start new lives. Donovan wanted very much to believe him, but deep down he knew he could not.

After what he'd seen, the prospect of someone *wanting* to disappear seemed far-fetched to him. At first, he'd believed Michael was right. The first four cases involved runaway teenagers—all of whom he managed to track down over the course of a month. The fifth case, however, was the beginning of an unsettling trend: the first of many to go into his "unsolved" pile.

He lifted a file from the stack and flipped through its pages. Here was a straight-A student, cheerleader, and vice president of the National Honor Society. The young woman's senior photo smiled back at him. The local police had closed the case after only a month-long investigation, determining she was a runaway. Her parents weren't convinced and had turned to Candle & Candle for assistance. That was eight months ago.

Donovan stared at the frozen smile in the photo. *Where did you go?*

A familiar voice spoke in his head, one he'd listened to during many late-night writing sessions. And although this character existed solely due to Donovan's imagination, he considered him a real person. *You know it's not that simple*, spoke Joe Hopper. *Ain't nothin' ever is with you, hoss.*

Hopper spoke the truth. Donovan had a theory for all these investigations, but it didn't fit their circumstances, and the disparity didn't stop him from asking a pivotal question: *What if?*

Some of the cases on his desk fit his theory dead-on. Brian Owens, a subway operator, vanished from the locker room preparing for a day's work. Jaquelyn Ridgeway, mother of three and social security caseworker, left the office on her way to a client's place of residence but never arrived. Donovan's old boss, Timothy Butler, was in the stack, too. He'd disappeared from the offices of Identinel between the hours of noon and four. That was fourteen months ago.

These people all had the same thing in common: mediocrity. If there was one thing Donovan had learned in the last year and a half, it was that mediocrity is a disease. Enough of it would bring about a strange symptom called "the flickering." If nothing was done to end the saturation of mediocrity, the victim would flicker out of existence altogether. What lay in wait for them on the other side, however, was far worse than any death he could imagine.

Donovan knew this all too well. He'd seen it with his own eyes. It almost consumed him; worse, it almost cost Donna her life.

But this was different. In the last two months, he'd received similar cases from distraught parents whose daughters and sons seemingly vanished into thin air. All were in their late teens or early twenties. All had bright futures. Some of them held part-time jobs here and there, but nothing as strenuous and soul-sucking as the older subjects. He'd watched the pile grow one folder at a time, documenting the disappearances of these young adults. They were children by most respects, all of whom had no business vanishing into thin air, and that fact disturbed him.

He'd resisted the urge to bring his suspicions up to his brother, if for no other reason than the hole in his theory. Though Michael had followed Donovan into the abandoned subway line to rescue Donna, he didn't have the opportunity to see what Donovan saw. All he knew was the colorful world before his own eyes. Several months after the incident, and shortly before he and Donna left for their vacation, Donovan tried to talk to his brother about what happened. Michael, however, would hear none of it.

"I don't want to know, Don. We saved the day. That's all that matters. Let the past stay where it belongs."

Frustrating though it was, Donovan understood his brother's reasoning. Michael was always the one grounded in reality. He approached problems with logic rather than speculation, never looking beyond the realm of flesh and blood. Peering beyond that veil into the fantastic and impossible was Donovan's specialty.

He flipped back through the file and stopped on the girl's photo once again. *You're too young to flicker out. So where in this big scary world did you wander off to, kiddo?*

Donovan put the file back on the stack and looked at his watch. Forty-five minutes had passed. He pushed away the mystery of the missing kids, logged on to his computer, and went to work.

H e heard the door open and slam shut. It was the end of the day, and he had just shut down his computer. Michael Candle entered the office and stripped off his tie, followed by his dress shirt. Donovan leaned back in his chair and smirked.

"Rough day?"

Michael glared at him. "Don't even start with me."

"That great, huh?"

"Did Rosie fill you in?'

"Only that Mrs. Beckman called you again this morning."

Michael plopped down in his chair. Sweat dripped off his forehead. Rings of it stained his undershirt. Summer was in full effect and seeing his brother like this made Donovan glad he'd spent the day in the air conditioning.

"Yeah, she called," Michael said. "Because, as you know, her husband is screwing every bimbo in town."

"So she says," Donovan added.

"So she says. Damned if I can find any proof of it. Want to know where I've been all day?"

Donovan didn't say anything. Michael was on a roll.

"She calls me first thing this morning, tells me she thinks John's meeting with one of his *many* mistresses today, and proceeds to demand—not ask, but *demand*—I stake out the Spruce Lodge to make sure he's not 'bumping uglies' there."

"Why the Spruce Lodge?"

Michael threw up his hands. "I asked her the same thing. Her response? 'A hunch.'"

"And being the good detective you are—"

"That's right, Don. I drove all the way out there and sat in the friggin' hundred-degree heat all goddamn day. Don't look at me like that. It's not funny."

But Donovan was already laughing. Michael growled to himself. He rose from his seat, reached into a bottom drawer, and pulled out a fresh change of clothes.

"Good thing she pays well," he mumbled, turning back to Donovan. "What about you? Anything exciting happen today?"

Donovan shook his head. "Nothing new today. Finished some paperwork, made some calls, that's about it. I'm sorry to say it wasn't nearly as exciting as sitting in a car all day."

Michael gave him the finger, waited a beat, then asked, "Everything still on for tomorrow night?"

"Oh yes. She doesn't suspect a thing."

His brother chuckled, and Donovan bit his cheeks to keep from saying anything. Michael had proposed the surprise baby shower for Donna. He made the arrangements and sent out the emails, requesting that everyone keep it a secret.

Donovan didn't have the heart to tell him Donna already knew. She caught him one Saturday morning before he had his coffee and asked what she already suspected. He told her to act surprised, and he hoped like hell she would put on a performance worthy of an Academy Award. The hardest part was keeping her knowledge secret from his brother.

"She still thinks we're meeting you for dinner tomorrow night."

"Good. I can't wait to see the look on her face."

"Speaking of tomorrow night, is there any chance Jennifer will be joining us?"

Michael shook his head. "No, I think that's dead in the water."

"She pushed the marriage issue, didn't she?"

"What can I say? Just not my style."

They walked to the front desk. Rosie was already gone for the day. Donovan opened his mouth to wish his brother a good evening when Michael cut him off.

"Y'know, I meant to ask you something last week. Have you heard from any of those agents yet?"

Donovan swallowed and shook his head. "Nope. Still no word."

"Bummer. Well, I'm sure one of them will bite."

"Sure hope so," Donovan said. "Have a good night."

A gust of hot afternoon air smacked him in the face when he left the office, but it failed to sweep away the cloud hanging over his head. Truth was, in years past Donovan would have been thrilled by his brother's interest in his artistic endeavors. Talking about the story helped keep the plot fresh in his mind. He was amused by how quickly things changed. Now he did everything he could to avoid discussing his novel.

Thoughts of the book, its completion, and its future were set aside as he approached his car. A slip of paper was tucked under the windshield wiper. The flyer was small and rectangular, with the outline of a doorway printed in black and white. The words "Attend The Great Fade-Out!" were printed across the front. The details followed: "Join us in celebrating the show's second season by tuning in to a marathon of the first!"

The thought of watching reality television curdled his stomach. Watching an entire season's worth would be enough to turn any person into a drooling zombie. He crumpled the flyer and put it in his pocket.

Donovan took a different route home, suffering through traffic for all of five minutes before taking an old highway directly through the city's desolate South District. The area was familiar territory. Two blocks away lay the entrance to the subway's Yellow Line. It was not that large in comparison to the rest of the subway system, but to someone on foot it still amounted to several miles of track. The Blue, Green, and Red Lines received the most traffic, were considered the safest, and could take citizens just about anywhere within city limits.

Worn-out track, outdated cars, terminals in the slums of the city, and a rising deficit: it hadn't been hard for the council to rule in favor of closing this blight on the subterranean network. The tunnels, marked by a yellow stripe on the city subway map, were notorious for muggings and junkies. Growing up here, he'd often heard it was called the Yellow Line because it smelled like piss, and in his brief experience this wasn't far from the truth.

Passing in its vicinity always gave him chills, thinking back to that day he and his brother went into the dark in search of Donna. When he turned toward the highway entrance ramp, Donovan turned off the air conditioner and rolled down his window. He put on a pair of sunglasses and cranked the radio's volume. *Don't sweat it. It's beyond you. You're past it. Enjoy the reward.*

He was almost home when he remembered Donna's pickles, so he stopped at a local gas station and purchased a jar. The sun hung midway above the horizon, a lazy orange eye that might close at any moment.

Back in the car, Donovan took a deep, satisfying breath. This was life. This was *the* life he wanted. He felt complete. Catching a glimpse of his reflection in the rearview, he saw a smile looking back. It felt good.

Donovan pushed away his plate, letting out a low belch. Donna smiled at him while she chewed her food.

"That was good." He went to the sink and rinsed his plate. "How was your day?"

Donna swallowed her food and said, "Laid back. The baby was still for the most part. I did some work in the nursery, had a nap, then tidied the office."

"Sounds like a relaxing day. How's your hip?"

"Achy, but not as bad as yesterday. You know it is, the fibro pain comes and goes."

He smiled softly, trying to hide the worry on his face. Donna's fibromyalgia pain could only be managed, not conquered, and adding pregnancy to the equation only complicated matters.

"Don't look at me like that. I'll be fine, Don. I'm not made of glass." She turned from the table and faced him. "Why didn't you mail those query letters like you said you would?"

He paused. Water poured over the plate and his hands. He turned his head and caught Donna's stare. It was ice cold, and he stood frozen in its spotlight. A dozen responses flooded his mind, and out of them all he picked, "What, honey?"

She cocked her left eyebrow, upgrading her stare to an official glare, and Donovan knew he'd been caught.

"You heard me, Donovan Candle."

He shut off the faucet and put the dish in the drainer. When he looked back at her, he felt the full weight of her gaze bearing down on him.

"You're right. I did say I would."

"And?"

"And I didn't. I'm sorry."

She laughed and threw her hands in the air. "Don't apologize to me, honey. You're the one who worked so hard over that book. If you should say you're sorry to anyone, take a look in the mirror."

He wanted to spout off some witty retort, but nothing came to mind. Instead he sought a real answer to her question. Why hadn't he? The simple answer was that he'd forgotten, but it ran deeper than that. He'd spent six months working on that book, and another four revising it. He honed it down, chiseling Joe Hopper's visage out of white stone and black text, until he knew every single dimple, flaw, and pore.

When he was done, he spent another month researching the market, finding the right agents to query, and when he'd done that he found he still could not bring himself to mail the letters. It had been years since he'd let strangers read his writing, and he feared what their opinions might be.

"I guess I'm just not ready to send them," he mumbled.

Donna wiped her mouth and nodded. "I understand that, but you know what makes me a good wife is knowing when to act in your best interest."

"What do you mean?"

"I mean I found those letters while tidying up your desk, and I mailed them this morning."

His legs went limp. "You did *what?*"

Donna approached him with a snarky smile. She kissed the tip of his nose. "I mailed your query letters. After spending years watching you agonize over that book—which, by the way, I happen to think is brilliant—I'll be damned if I'm going to sit here and watch you chicken out now. So, I thought I'd do my spousal duty and give you a little nudge."

Donovan tried to find the words. She shushed him with another kiss. "You can thank me later."

He watched her leave the kitchen, and after a moment of gawking at the floor he finished the dishes. Donna's actions were the last thing he'd expected, and for a period of hours following dinner he found his small world turned upside down. Sure, he had written those letters and prepared them for mailing, but he'd not intended to send them. Not really. He retreated to the creative space of his office and stared at his computer, not quite sure what to do with himself. Donna had pushed him to that first step, and he found himself wondering if this was really what he wanted to do.

It's either this or the alternative.

Finishing that book had been part of his life pitch to Aleister Dullington, part of what saved his life from the horror of the Monochrome. Giving up on it now, after coming so far, seemed foolish. And yet timidity lingered over his head like a rusty halo.

Joe Hopper, the man to whom he gave life and through whose veins ran the blood of ink, was the one to reassure him—as he'd always been in some form or fashion: *Ain't nothing you can do about it now. What's done is done. Question is, what're you going to do about it when the tidal wave of consequence comes, hoss? You know it will, one way or another. It always does.*

Donovan sat back in his chair. He sighed. *Ride it out*, he thought. *Just like everything else.*

He carried that thought with him to bed. So what if the letters went out? So what if the agents didn't care for his book? He would query other agents if need be. He would ride the wave wherever it took him, whenever it decided to crash down.

His last waking thought was that of the wave itself and wondering if it would come. He had no idea how soon it would.

The wave of consequence came in the form of a cell phone chime. Donovan rose from a dream he could not remember, blinking away confusion.

The phone rang a second time. He rolled over quickly in fear that it would wake Donna. She'd not slept well these last few weeks, and the last thing he wanted was to rouse her from a meager slumber. He lifted the phone from the nightstand and answered the call. Donna stirred beside him.

"Hello?" His voice came out a low, dry rasp, and he looked toward the bedroom window. It was still dark outside. He lifted the phone away from his ear for a moment and looked at the screen. 3:31 in the morning.

"Don?"

The voice did not register with him at first. It was late, he'd only been asleep for a few hours, and he wanted very much to return to that unconscious state. Impressionist phantoms of color danced about the darkness when he closed his eyes. He found it difficult to resist the weight of his eyelids.

"You there?" The voice again. It was alert. Concerned. Donovan wondered who would be awake at this hour. "Don, for Christ's sake."

He forced open his eyes. Alarm in the caller's tone culled the image of a face from his sleepy mind: Detective Nathan Brock. Even in the haze of sleep Donovan could see the man's graying mustache. The ghostly smell of cigarettes hung about the image.

"Jesus, Brock, do you have any idea what time it is?"

"I do, and I'm sorry. I hope I didn't wake the wife."

Donovan glanced over his shoulder at Donna. He fell silent while he watched the bulge of her belly rise and fall beneath the sheet. "No, she's still sleeping."

"Good. Very good."

Donovan fought back a yawn. "Did you call just to make sure she's sleeping okay? You could've waited until morning for that."

"No, Don, that isn't why I called. I'm not sure I know how to put this."

He pulled back the blanket and put his legs on the floor. By some miracle, he found himself returning to full consciousness, but the cloudiness of sleep still hung about his head. The significance of Brock's trepidation was lost on him.

"We found some of those kids."

Donovan's breath caught in his throat. It stayed there for a few seconds, threatening to a burn a hole right through him. He let it out slowly and asked his friend to repeat himself.

"We found them, Don."

He rose to his feet with such force that it rocked the bed. Donna stirred once more but did not wake. Donovan put one hand out and pressed it against the wall. He'd braced himself for this phone call for the better part of a year, and he wasn't about to take it sitting down. *Please, please, please, please say what I hope you'll say.*

"Alive?"

Detective Brock hesitated. The catch in his breath over the phone was enough of an answer. Donovan felt his insides plummet. His legs were suddenly weak and limp, and he had to sit down on the edge of the bed.

"I'm sorry, Don."

"Me too." His eyes stung, and when blinking did not relieve their discomfort, he closed them altogether.

"Anyway," Brock went on, "I thought you should know. Give me a call in the morning and I'll fill you in on the details."

"Thanks, Nate."

Donovan ended the call. He placed the phone on the nightstand, but he didn't lie down. Instead he remained on the edge of the bed with his bare feet brushing the carpet. He looked back over his shoulder at his sleeping wife.

Thoughts came easily to Donovan Candle in the small hours. It was, he supposed, an inherent quality of his creative nature. Now it was his curse. He thought about the child growing inside her. He thought about all the dangers from which he would have to protect that child.

For the first time in a very long time, Donovan Candle felt something he did not recognize at first. It crept up the length of his spine and stopped at his shoulder. There it whispered things he didn't want to hear. It was an old friend, come to say hello, reintroducing itself as Doubt.

The wave had come, crashing down upon him and washing away the lines of his own self in a matter of minutes. He was now a man less defined, irrationally fearing for the life of his unborn child.

Donovan sighed. *Stop it. Get some rest. Long day tomorrow.*

He stretched out and pulled the sheet over him. Tomorrow would be a long day, but for now there was only the night, and he feared it would go on forever.

2

BAD OMENS

Donna woke as the first hints of sunlight pierced the curtains, splitting the room with bright, golden bars. She was used to these early mornings. Ever since she'd become pregnant, she found sleeping until seven or eight o'clock to be a chore.

What she was not used to, however, was waking to an empty bed. She ran her hand across Donovan's pillow and discovered it was cool. She sat up and called out to him, but he did not answer.

"Donnie?" She held her breath and listened. All she heard was the erratic thump of her heart. *Don't panic. You're just scaring yourself. Of course he's still home. He wouldn't have left without waking you. Stop being such a chicken shit. You didn't used to be like this.*

She didn't, but that seemed like a long time ago. A home invasion and abduction were enough to change anyone's perspective on home safety. That she woke to find her husband out of bed did not alarm her; that he did not answer was another matter altogether.

Donna fought her hesitations, braced herself against the aches in her muscles, and slowly climbed out of bed. The baby kicked in her belly, startling her, and when she steadied herself, she progressed down the hall. The bathroom was empty, as was the office.

"Donovan?" She waited. Nothing.

She was about to make her way downstairs when she noticed the light on in the nursery.

Donovan sat on the rocking chair, staring idly out the window. Their cat, Mrs. Precious Paws, was curled up in his lap, and he scratched between her ears. Donna stood in the doorway watching him. He seemed a hundred miles away.

"Honey?" She tapped on the door. Donovan blinked and looked up, startled from his thoughts.

"Morning." He watched her put her hand on her chest. "You okay?"

Donna nodded. "Just panicked when I couldn't find you. I called out, but you didn't answer."

"Sorry."

"It's all right." She walked over, stood beside him, and ran her fingers through his hair. "Are you okay, Donnie?"

He took a deep breath and shook his head. "No, I'm not. Nate called this morning. Some of those kids turned up."

She put her hand on his shoulder. "But that's good news!"

Donovan put his hand on hers and looked up at her. "They're all dead. Murdered."

Donna exhaled. Tears welled up in her eyes. "Oh Donnie, I'm sorry."

"Me too."

My God, she thought. *All those parents.* She imagined the police were now making their rounds delivering the bad news. A chill worked its way down the back of her neck.

Donovan squeezed her hand. He offered up a weak smile. "No tears. It's not your burden to bear."

"Are you—"

"I'm fine."

Liar.

She held his hand as they stared out the window together. Birds chirped, the neighbor's dog barked, and the street filled with cars. The world woke up and went about its way. Her heart ached for all those parents. She didn't know what she would do in their situation. The idea of losing a child was something she'd considered before, but she didn't want to think about it anymore than she had to.

Donovan was more deeply invested in those cases than he wanted her to know, but she saw and heard things he thought she wouldn't notice. There had been too many nights she'd awoken to hear him on the phone, discussing matters with the cops or tracking down leads that always came to dead ends.

Donna wasn't blind; she knew her husband and she knew how easy it was for someone to disappear. Her abduction had reshaped her views, and their effect on her still lingered. Some nights she woke from nightmares in which Donovan failed to find her. Some nights she found herself still locked in that utility closet, cold and hungry, terrified to the brink of insanity.

Of course, they were only nightmares, and she was thankful that the incident had reached a different conclusion. In the end Donovan *had* found her, and though she did not fully understand the circumstances behind her abduction, she understood his fear and determination.

"I should get dressed."

His words snapped Donna out of her trance. She was staring at two birds tottering along the electrical wire.

"Where are you going? It's still early."

"I need to start closing those files and make a few calls."

She followed him out of the room and asked if he wanted breakfast.

"No. Not today." He kissed her cheek.

"Call me if you need me, okay?"

"I will."

"Are you going to be all right?"

Donovan stared off into space for an instant, then squeezed her hand. "I'll be fine. Promise."

He kissed her again, and she smiled. She watched him walk down the hall to the bedroom. Donna turned back to the window and watched the birds out on the power line. Her husband's words tumbled back into her thoughts: *It's not your burden to bear.*

"But it is," she whispered to the empty room. "I just hope I can help you carry it as far as you need me to."

Her stomach grumbled, and the baby stirred. She drummed her fingers across her belly.

"Guess it's time to feed us, huh?"

She went downstairs to make breakfast, hoping the day would distract her from the uneasiness settling in the back of her mind.

"D on?"

He looked up from his paperwork. Michael stood beside the desk with a cup of coffee in his hand. Donovan nodded, took the cup from his brother, and sipped. The coffee was pitch black and he didn't care. He grimaced only once, savoring the burn and bitterness on his tongue.

Michael smirked. "Thought you could use that."

"Thanks," Donovan mumbled, wiping his mouth. He looked at the clock on his desktop: a quarter to noon.

"Why don't you take a break?"

"No." Donovan scribbled his signature on one of the work contracts, closed the file, and opened another.

"Don—"

He sighed and looked up at Michael. "What?"

"It's not your fault. None of this is. You did the best you could."

"Maybe, and yet I can't help but feel like that's not true."

"You can't do this." Michael pulled his chair over to Donovan's desk. He sat and gave his brother a hard stare. "If you take everything personally, it's going to eat you alive. This is just the job, man."

Donovan took a breath, feeling his blood pressure rise. Sometimes he wondered why his brother even bothered with this line of work.

"It's more than just a job, Mike. They were sons and daughters. Their parents trusted us to find them and to succeed where the police failed."

"I understand that, but you aren't accountable for what happened to them. No one expected this."

Donovan took another sip of coffee. "No, I suppose you're right about that."

He'd spent most of the morning trying to keep his mind off the discovery, but it wasn't easy. Detective Brock was kind not to reveal the specifics during his pre-dawn phone call, but he was less affable in the later morning hours. He'd called just before nine to discuss the gory scene in explicit detail.

Donovan barely got a word in before Brock had to go. All he was left with were a grim mental image of the scene as described by the detective, and a mounting fear building up in the pit of his stomach. There were fourteen victims clustered together in a back alley on the city's south side, dead of blunt trauma and multiple stab wounds. Some of them showed signs of post-mortem sexual assault. The coroner estimated their deaths had all occurred within the last twenty-four hours.

But where were they all this time?

This was a question that had eaten away at him all morning. The victims didn't fit the profile, but the way of the Monochrome was Donovan's only explanation for their sudden reappearance. They had all flickered out somehow, and for whatever reason Dullington had murdered them and—

The bodies. Why would they return? He keeps what's his.

The bodies. A trickle of nausea seeped into his belly, forcing Donovan to second-guess another drink of the coffee.

"I think…" He trailed off. Michael looked at him, waiting. *I know where they were,* he wanted to say. *I knew where they were all this time and I was too afraid to act. I knew, and I didn't do a goddamn thing about it. Because I was afraid.* The words were there, waiting for him to give them voice, but the chime of his cell phone spared him from the decision.

Michael moved the chair back to his desk. Donovan picked up his phone and answered. It was Donna's nephew, Quinn.

"Hey, Don. Are you free for lunch?"

"Uh, sure." He met Michael's gaze. His brother frowned. "I was just heading out anyway."

City traffic made the drive slow-going, and Donovan was fifteen minutes late when he parked along the curb behind a dusty brown Cadillac. He fed some coins into the meter and made his way into the small diner on the corner. The restaurant bustled with lunchtime activity, filled with the murmur of its patrons and punctuated by a mindless pop song on the radio.

Donovan didn't recognize Quinn at first. He scanned the scene, looking for a college student among the haystack of skirts and three-piece suits. He'd not seen Donna's nephew since Christmas, and when the stout kid in the dress shirt and tie beckoned to him, Donovan did a double take. He'd expected a college student in a T-shirt and shorts. No wonder he hadn't seen him.

"Uncle Don, over here." Quinn Upton stood from his corner booth.

Donovan met him with a smile and a handshake. "My God, look at you. When the hell did you grow up?"

"I guess working here in the city does that to a guy."

They took their seats. Donovan nodded. "Working in the city, huh?"

"Yeah, didn't Mom tell you?"

Donovan shrugged. In truth, he and Donna's sister Amanda hadn't always gotten along. They agreed to be civil for Donna's sake, but the terms of that truce did not include regular chats. Quinn got the hint and moved on.

"I got the internship."

"The one at the law firm?"

Quinn nodded, beaming. A waitress came and took their orders; afterward, Donovan sank back into his seat allowing himself a moment to relax. He watched Quinn speak, remembering what it was like to be twenty and carefree. Those days were long gone, but he liked to indulge himself with nostalgia from time to time.

"—the best part is that it's a paid internship. The whole thing has been eye-opening, for sure."

"I'm glad you're enjoying it. So, you think that's what you want to do after undergrad?"

Quinn nodded. "Definitely."

Good for you, Donovan thought. Quinn had wanted to be a lawyer for as long as Donovan had known him, and that went back to the days when the kid was in grade school. His penchant for arguing reinforced that drive. Seeing him today in the shirt and tie, looking so damn grown up, gave Donovan a sense of pleasant satisfaction.

"Oh, before I forget—" Quinn dug into his pocket. "This whole reason I wanted to meet with you today." He placed a small black box on the table.

"What's this?"

"I got it for Aunt Donna. It's a gift for her baby shower tonight."

Donovan opened the box. Inside was a necklace with a small red pendant.

"Do you think she'll like it?"

"I do." Donovan traced his finger across the jewel. Red was Donna's favorite color. "Where did you get this?"

"I didn't, actually. My girlfriend made it."

"No kidding? Is she the one who came with you to Christmas dinner?"

Quinn nodded. "Wendy. She makes jewelry in her spare time and sells it online. I told her about Aunt Donna's favorite color, and she made this."

"Well," Donovan said, closing the lid. "I think she'll love it." He slid the box back across the table and was about to speak when something outside the window caught his eye.

At first, he wasn't sure what that "something" was, and all he could determine was that something was there which wasn't before. When he turned to observe, he saw a slice of the city framed in glass, bustling with life and lunchtime rhythm. Crowds moved along the sidewalk while cars inched forward on the street.

And yet—

Yes, there *was* something off. Something that wasn't there before, and

Donovan now realized just what it was that abruptly stole his attention from the conversation.

A man stood at the corner, leaning against the side of a lamppost, his huge meaty arms folded across his chest. A matted beard swallowed most of his face. His clothes were tattered, covered in an oily grime Donovan could not identify. There was something else, too. He wore several small white buttons on his chest, affixed like medals on a soldier.

On any other day, Donovan wouldn't have given this man any thought. In fact, he would have looked right past the hefty figure, counting him as another blank face in the city's moving crowds when it struck him—he *knew* this man.

Much obliged. The transient from yesterday. Only the man hadn't been there before, he was sure of it. *Like he just popped into focus. Flickered, even.*

Quinn was talking, but Donovan couldn't hear him. He was too concentrated on the guy outside. Slowly, the man turned his head, and for an instant their eyes met. The big man nodded to his spectator with a grin framed by the tangles of his beard—and then promptly vanished.

Donovan refused to blink, keeping his eyes trained on the place where the bearded man should have been. The big guy's considerable outline remained within Donovan's vision, a specter of retinal trickery. He had trouble reconciling the fact that the man was no longer there.

The effect lasted only for a moment, and the bearded man blinked back into existence, still leaning against the pole, grinning. Now he held a rusty screwdriver in his hand, using it to pick his teeth. This sudden reappearance was enough to confirm Donovan's suspicions. His stomach plunged as a dozen questions raced through his mind, all clouded with the onset of utter confusion.

"—Uncle Don?"

Startled, Donovan turned away from the window. "I'm sorry, Quinn. What were you saying?"

"Our food," Quinn said, smiling. "It's here."

Donovan glanced up at the waitress and thanked her before turning back to the window. The bearded man was gone.

"What are you looking at?" Quinn craned his neck to look out the window.

"Huh? Oh, no, nothing. Just spacing out. Got a lot on my mind."

"Mom always said you were a brooding writer." Quinn smirked. "Guess this means you're a brooding detective now, too?"

Donovan paused, lightheaded as the adrenaline left his bloodstream. He looked back at the lamppost and nodded. "You could say that."

———————◆———————

After lunch, Donovan waited at the corner, watching Quinn jog across the street. When the kid reached the other side, he spun on his heels and waved.

"See you tonight!"

"Sure thing," Donovan said, forcing a smile. He waited until Quinn was out of sight before walking back to his car.

The early afternoon sun beat down on the city, causing heat to ripple from the sidewalk, but he couldn't shake the icy feeling in his gut. His sense of uneasiness went beyond the bearded man's vanishing act, drilling down into a core of memory.

If he was flickering, how could I see him?

Donovan had no idea how the odd state worked. He only knew the flickering occurred when a person became too saturated with mediocrity, boredom, or malaise. Dullington's minions, the Cretins, prevented others from noticing those who were flickering out. He remembered their tiny white bodies, their hollow eyes, and the way they whispered their jarring, backwards language into their victims' ears.

These creatures were the stuff of nightmares, but Donovan had witnessed them with frightening clarity. When he went to unlock his car, he realized his hands were shaking. He sat inside and tried to calm himself.

Who was that man? Why was he watching us?

People who flickered out—the Missing—were slaves to Aleister Dullington in the Monochrome. When Donovan made the exchange to save Donna's life, he was instructed to go to the Yellow Line subway, in the South District. The same area where the bodies were discovered.

His head swam with possibilities. *Might be something to your theory, hoss.*

Donovan put the key in the ignition, took a breath, and listened to his pounding heart. The Yellow Line was a place he swore he'd never go again, but his desire to know—to prove his theory was true—circumvented any promises he'd made to himself in that regard.

Terrified, he looked at his reflection in the rearview mirror. *You sure you want to do this?*

He turned the key. The car purred to life.

"Guess that's a yes," he whispered, shifting the car into gear.

Crowded streets gave way to empty parking lots and blind alleys. Sidewalks once filled with people were now abandoned and falling into disrepair. The city's South District contained the symbols of its heritage: empty storefronts, fenced-off lots, coin-op Laundromats—signs of a civilization that had moved on to better things. The living, breathing part of the city had grown up around its humble beginnings, leaving them to wither and rot.

He drove past the tattered shell of what used to be Winthorpe Station, a hub for the city's old subway system. New lines had replaced the old, and when operating costs became too high, the station closed. The building remained a mute testament to more elegant times, boarded up and forgotten.

Donovan's chest tightened. He circled the block once before overcoming his hesitation, parking along the curb in front of the aged structure. The building towered over him like the corpse of a giant. He got out of the car and took a breath.

"What am I doing?" he said to himself, waiting for an answer he did not have. What did he hope to accomplish by coming here? His suspicions were just that—suspicions. He had no way of confirming them without venturing down into the rotting labyrinth of the Yellow Line, and he wasn't prepared to do that. No one knew he was here, and he had no way to defend himself.

These facts didn't set his mind at ease. His thoughts ran rampant with possibilities circling around a central fear: that there was more to the murders than he once suspected. How he could see one of the Missing was something he couldn't answer, but that question didn't concern him as much as why the man was watching them in the first place.

He tried to calm himself. *Stop it, Don. Just have a look around and get the hell out of here.*

The building's windows had been shattered long ago, leaving behind fragments jutting from their frames, with sheets of plywood covering the openings like coins over dead eyes. Various symbols, possibly gang related, adorned most of the lower level.

One cryptogram caught his eye. It was small, just off to the right of the main entrance. Had it not been painted in neon pink he would have missed the design entirely, but its conspicuous color screamed for attention. To most it would have been an eyesore, but the image jumped out at him: crudely drawn—nothing more than three straight lines arranged to form double-Ts, and off to the side of the right line was an imperfect circle.

Here's what you missed on last week's Fading Out!

He recalled the narrator's voice, one he'd heard many times before in an amalgamation of background noise. Donovan walked up the short flight of steps and traced his fingers along the pink lines. Up close, he saw it was even more crudely drawn, with the grain of the brick showing through the paint. Squiggles of paint-drip accented the edges.

He glimpsed movement from the corner of his eye, but when he turned, he saw only a scrap piece of paper caught in the wind. It scraped across the pavement, down the steps, and under his car.

The door to the building shot open, startling him. A woman in a thick winter coat emerged from the opening. She stepped out onto the top step, lifted a handkerchief, and hacked into it for a good minute. Her coat was tattered and dirty, covered in some sort of gray sludge. The woman surveyed the empty street, squinting against the early afternoon light, then turned and coughed again. She wiped her nose and spat.

Donovan watched, unsure of what to do or say. The transient slowly turned her head. The wild look in her eyes gave him a chill. "The fuck do you want?"

When he spoke, his throat felt stuffed full of cotton. He fought to keep his composure, and after a few agonizing seconds he said the first thing that came to mind: "Do you know what happened to the children?"

She curled back her lip into a toothless snarl. "S'pose I do," hissed the crone. "Seen what he did, too, and good riddance to 'em all. Spies 'n traitors 'n everyone who don't serve the king burn in Hell. Did ya know that?"

"What king? Who is this 'king'?"

"The Monochrome King."

A pit opened in his stomach, threatening to swallow him from the inside. "You mean Dullington? He's here?"

The woman waved her hand to the sky. "Somewhere." She grinned that horrid grin like a rotting jack-o-lantern. "Somewhere over the rainbow."

Donovan's frown prompted her to let loose a wild cackle. He realized he wasn't going to get any answers and was about to walk back to his car when her laughter ceased.

She took two long strides toward him and stopped so close he could smell the stench rising from her body. "I know you," she said. "*He* knows you."

Donovan paused. "Who?"

"The king. He knows you. Knows us all. Over the rainbow, under it, other side of the darn thing where the colors don't show. He knows, and he knows *you*, and we'll all be seein' you soon."

Donovan stepped away from her. He suddenly felt very vulnerable, remembering he had nothing but his hands with which to defend himself. A scenario flashed before him: this filthy hag leading him into the depths of Winthorpe Station, where he would be cornered, robbed, and brutalized at the hands of an army of homeless people.

But they're more than just homeless. They're lifeless and empty, hoss. They're the Missing.

The hag cackled once more, and he recoiled from her acrid breath. He watched as she did an odd dance back across the pavement toward the open door. She sang, *"He sees you sees me sees you sees us all!"* as she went and stopped in the opening. Beyond it he saw what appeared to be stacks of televisions, what might have been an entire wall of them, all blank and gray and busy with static.

"The king sees us all," she finished, "and we'll all be seein' you *soon*."

She closed the door. Its hinges groaned. Then she was gone, and he was alone on the steps of the station once again. The exchange left him reeling, drained of his last ounce of determination.

He retreated to his car, realizing that he was not ready to make that descent after all.

———————— • ————————

K ale Abrams watched colors bleed from the world as the car sped away. When he turned back from the window, he found the upper floor of the station devoid of texture and detail. He took a deep breath of the stale air and smiled.

He was home.

Kale, spoke his master, *come to me.*

The bearded man obeyed, trudging down the hallway toward his king's chamber. The room used to be a manager's office, but the shades of the Monochrome had stripped its characteristics, reducing it to a husk of gray, flat geometry. Within the center of the room was a white fleshy mass of tendrils that stretched to the corners, suspending it inches above the floor like a perverse hammock.

His master slumbered within, resting for the tough days ahead. In their quiet hours together, the Monochrome King told Kale of his plans, revealing to him the fate of the Spectrum dwellers. Oh yes, there would be a great upheaval, a tip of the scales in their favor, and so far, everything was going according to plan.

There was just one last detail to be rectified, one more indulgence to be had.

Kale knelt before the rubbery mass. The white tendrils pulsed with a sickening gray light. His master stirred.

Did you follow the man I sent you to find?

"Since yesterday."

What did you learn?

"He's happy."

Of course he is. But not for long.

Kale smiled. "No, sir."

Why did he come here? Were you followed?

"Not sure." Kale closed his eyes, trembling. The fleshy mass pulsed, indifferent to his fear.

But he did not enter.

"No."

Too bad. You could have had so much fun, Kale. No matter. Everything in its time.

The bearded man exhaled in relief. "No matter."

He met someone today?

"Yes. Family."

Family. The mass stirred, pulsing brighter. *Yes, why didn't I think of that? This could work in our favor, Kale. Yes, it just might.*

The ropy tendrils slackened, allowing the white cocoon to touch the floor. Layers of the pale flesh slid back, revealing Kale's master. A pale man with gray eyes took a breath, savoring the taste of the air on his tongue like a serpent. He looked down at his subject.

"My son." The Monochrome King reached out his hand. Kale lowered his head and kissed his master's knuckles. "Tonight, you play."

Kale found he could hardly contain himself. He shook like an excited dog. "Blood?"

"Oh yes, Kale." A sharp grin spread across the pale man's face. "Lots of blood."

3

FADING OUT

"Do we really have to do this?"

Donna looked at her husband with big doe eyes. He smiled and shut off the engine. The car fell silent.

"It won't be that bad."

"You know I hate these social things."

"Come on, Donna. It's for the kiddo."

She sighed. "I know, but still. My parents are in there. My sister's in there. They're all going to be after the same thing."

Donovan laughed. "They've waited this long. I think they can wait another three months."

"That's easy for you to say. You can go hang out and drink with the other men. You don't know what it's like to be alone with these women. They're *ruthless*."

He leaned over, kissed her cheek, and patted her belly.

"Come on, Momma. You can handle them."

They entered the house to balloons, fanfare, and a singular shout of "Surprise!" She did her best, feigning shock and making a note to thank the Academy later on. Family and friends alike greeted her with hugs, kisses, and good tidings.

Michael pushed his way through the crowd, gave her a big kiss on the cheek, and led her to the den. He arranged his armchair in the center of the room so she would remain the focal point. *Oh you bastard*, she thought with a smile. He meant well but being the center of attention was the last thing she wanted.

The evening went on in a whirlwind of light banter, shouts of exclamation, and more pretend surprise. Over time, conversation migrated away from her pregnancy, and Donna was relieved to have lost the spotlight. She sank back in her chair, listening to the idle chatter, and observing the crowd.

Her sister, Amanda Upton, took a seat on the floor beside the armchair.

"How are you holding up?"

"How do you think?"

"Terribly." Amanda winked. "You're a bad actress."

"Oh well," Donna said. "You know I've never been one for these sorts of things."

Her sister took a drink. "I know. I'm not gonna lie, little sister—it made me giggle, watching you squirm."

"Thank you, big sister. You're too kind."

"I do try. So how are you, really? I haven't talked to you in a few days, and you've got that look on your face. What's going on?"

Donna sighed. She'd hoped to hide her concern, but Donovan's brooding didn't make it easy. "Today wasn't a good day. I'm sure you heard the news this morning. About those kids that were found in the city?"

Amanda nodded. "I heard about it on the radio. It's heartbreaking."

"Yeah, I've thought about it all day. I'm worried about Don, too. He had cases on most of those kids."

"My God." Amanda shook her head. "I don't know what I'd do if Quinn—" Her cell phone vibrated in her pocket, startling her. She checked the number, smiling at first, but her expression quickly transformed into a frown.

"What's wrong?"

Amanda shook her head. "Quinn just texted me. He isn't going to make it tonight."

"Why not?" Donna tried not to sound disappointed, but her sister was right when she called her a bad actress.

"He says some of the interns didn't show, and there's some big case tomorrow. I think it's got something to do with that missing TV producer. Quinn hinted at it a couple of days ago. They've had their whole staff working odd hours lately."

Donna leaned back in her seat, watching friends and family mingle. Quinn's was one of the faces she'd hoped to see tonight. She had a soft spot for the kid, having helped her sister take care of him when he was a baby. She was twelve when he was born, and she'd known from the first moment she held him that she wanted a child of her own.

"At least the internship is paid," Donna said, even though she knew the bright side would not ease her sister's mind. Amanda never liked the idea of Quinn pursuing a law degree; a medical degree was a nobler effort in her eyes, and one more worthwhile of her son's time.

Donna, however, was happy Quinn had managed to get his foot in the door of Rochester, Isley, & Moss. The firm was the oldest in the city, with a solid reputation. He would do well there. She was sure of it.

"Yeah, I guess that's something."

A few moments passed before Amanda took her phone and rose to her feet. "I'm going to call him anyway. Maybe I can talk to his boss or something."

"Amanda, don't be ridiculous. He's 20 years old, for heaven's sake. If he can't make it, he can't make it."

But Amanda wasn't listening. She stormed out of the room with the phone held to her ear. *So stubborn*, Donna thought. Her sister meant well, but Quinn was an adult now, and she'd have to let him go sooner or later. Such a terrifying thought, raising a child to adulthood and then letting them venture out into the world on their own. Donna wondered how she and Donovan might react once their child was old enough to "leave the nest." Surely Donovan would—

Donna blinked. Where *was* her husband? He wasn't among the living room crowd. She twisted in her seat, craning her neck to look back toward the kitchen, but he wasn't there, either. When she faced front, looking toward the patio doors, she remembered he'd gone out for some air.

She stood and went to the glass door. Patio lights illuminated a gravel pathway through the backyard toward a large gazebo. Donovan stood with his back to the house, looking up at the sky with his hands in his pockets. The lights cast a sad glow upon him. She knew the morning's news bothered him greatly, but beyond this, she feared some other storm was brewing in his mind.

He would tell her sooner or later, but for now she could only speculate, wondering just when that storm would break.

———————•———————

The night was warm and clear, but Donovan still had a chill. Arms folded, he searched the sky for shooting stars, but the city's polluted haze obscured any sign of them. He took a breath, savoring the stillness, listening to the low throng of laughter from within his brother's home.

The party would probably last into the late hours of the night. That was fine. He could stand out here until morning. It was a beautiful evening, with a canopy of stars twinkling overhead while a symphony of crickets played on. He was in good company, for the most part, save the uninvited thoughts dwelling in his head.

His doubts had lingered ever since last night's phone call, and the odd encounter earlier that afternoon had brought his fears into play. These fears were a cancer of the mind—a debilitating series of thought processes that could erode the soul—and sometimes they took on the voice of Aleister Dullington, speaking in low mechanical tones that gave him goose bumps.

Suppose, Mr. Candle, your child blinked out of existence. Suppose it was they who vanished for most of a year, only to turn up in a forgotten back alleyway, their clothes dirty and tattered, dead from head trauma and stab wounds. What would you do then?

"I don't know what I'd do."

What would you do? What could you do?

He took a seat on the gazebo swing. Sitting here reminded him of being a kid, when their mother had forced Michael to let him tag along to the playground down the street. Those were simpler times, but not much else had changed; being allowed to accompany his brother still made him feel invincible, important.

The sound of the party heightened as the glass door slid open. Michael stepped out onto the patio holding two bottles of beer.

"Thought I might find you out here."

Donovan leaned forward, watching his brother walk down the path toward him. "I needed some air. Her friends get on my nerves when they get together like this."

Michael plopped down on the swing and handed him a beer.

"Thanks."

"No prob. I had to get out of that noise, too."

Donovan sipped his beer, trying to forget his thoughts. The brothers were quiet for a few minutes, letting the crickets carry the conversation for them, but their silence quickly grew stale. Michael leaned forward and looked at his brother.

"What's on your mind, Don?"

He shrugged, took a drink. "Not a thing."

Michael chuckled. "You wouldn't be sitting out here if there wasn't. You look, uh, what's the word I'm looking for? Thoughtful? Deep in thought?"

"Pensive?"

"That's the one. Something's on your mind, or I figure you wouldn't leave the old lady in there to fend for herself."

Donovan looked to his brother, then across the lawn to the patio door. He saw a silhouette standing beyond the glass.

"She sent you out here, didn't she?"

Michael grinned. "I'll never tell."

"She's sneaky like that."

"She's just worried about you. So come on, level with me. I know you've had the day from hell. She knows it, too, even if you're trying to hide it."

"Donna's good at that."

"So talk, if you want to talk."

A moment passed. Donovan wanted to blurt out his troubles to his brother, spilling his guts on the gazebo floor to be examined one piece at a time. *Here's* the root of anxiety; *there's* the cause of his fear; and over here, well, *that's* an interesting specimen, isn't it?

But he couldn't give voice to the things bothering him. There were all those kids, and there was the implication of their deaths. There was the possibility he didn't want to face. He knew it was there, lurking in the shadows of his brain, the monster he'd spent the last year and a half trying to avoid. Naming the beast might wake it from slumber, inviting it to run rampant in the halls of his mind.

No, he wasn't about to ruin the evening by talking about it. When Donovan didn't say anything, his brother spoke: "Donna told me you didn't mail your letters to those agents like you said you would."

He sank further into his seat. His beer suddenly tasted warm, sour.

"As long as I can remember, Don, you wanted to be a writer. You worked your ass off to finish that book. Why stop now?"

"Mike, with all due respect, I don't need a lecture." Donovan shook his head. "The book has nothing to do with this, anyway. That's the *last* thing on my mind."

Michael shrugged. "Then tell me, man. What the hell is going on with you? Is it the murders? Didn't I tell you to stop taking it personally?"

"It's…" Donovan paused. *It's that I was too afraid to act on my suspicions,* he wanted to say, but he couldn't bring himself to speak the words. He sighed. "It's nothing. I'm just wondering if I'm cut out to be a father."

He washed the lie down with a gulp of beer but couldn't get rid of the bitter taste it left on his tongue. He didn't like lying to his brother but deflecting Michael's scrutiny was the only thing he could think to do. This wasn't the time or place to rehash a conversation which could only end poorly, and frankly, Donovan wasn't ready to talk about it in the first place.

Michael waited a beat, and then chuckled to himself. "Do you remember that one summer we spent at Gran's house?"

Thoughts of their grandmother's home in the country made him smile. "Of course I remember."

"There was that old tire swing at the lake. Remember when I tried to get you to jump?"

Donovan nodded. He saw that moment clearly, dusty though it was with age. There were dozens of times they'd ventured out there over the course of that summer, and every time he refused to go up in the swing. Finally, after two months of teasing, Michael finally persuaded him to give it a try.

His brother pushed the swing as high as he could, and shouted for him to jump, but Donovan couldn't. There was something about being at the zenith with the wind soaring through his hair and the creak of the rope against the old oak branch that made him seize up. He knew he only had a fraction of time to act, but in that moment—suspended above the water and the world—he froze and could do nothing but watch as everything moved in, out, and into focus once more.

"What're you afraid of, Don? Don't look down—just leap!"

He remembered feeling shame and self-loathing, unable to meet his brother's disappointed gaze. Over twenty years later, Donovan still didn't have an answer to that question.

Michael shook his head. "You wouldn't take that jump to save your life."

Donovan finished his beer. "Is there a point to this reverie?"

"There is, smart ass. *This* is your time. Don't let anything hold you back. Too many people get to where you are and stop. Don't be like them. Don't be afraid to jump."

"Thanks."

"No problem. Anyway, enough of that crap. Tonight belongs to you and Donna, and if we don't return to the party, we'll both be in trouble."

"Yeah, you're right. I don't want to spend the night on the sofa."

"What, like you were getting laid anyway?"

"Very funny."

Chuckling, they collected their empty bottles and walked toward the house. Michael put a hand on his brother's shoulder.

Donovan forced a smile, and he wore it like a mask.

———————————

"What do you want me to do, Mom? I'm not happy about it either, but I don't have a choice. I can't—No, you didn't let me finish. Can I finish? Please? Okay, thank you." Quinn rolled his eyes, collected his thoughts. "There is no one else here to do this, Mom. I don't know where the hell they are, okay? The other interns didn't show, and they didn't call in—for the second time, no, I have no fucking idea." He sighed. "I'm sorry for swearing, but you're frustrating the crap out of me. Tell Aunt Donna I love her, and I'll see her this weekend, okay? Thanks. Love you too, bye."

Quinn closed his eyes and leaned against the wall of the employee break room. The white clock on the wall ticked off the seconds, its hands inching closer to nine o'clock. He'd been there for a little over twelve hours.

He shoved the phone into his pocket. *Should've known better than to send a text. Like that would've done any good, stupid.*

At the time, staying late seemed like a great way to show initiative and put himself ahead of the other interns, especially when they didn't show up for the day. John and Erin always tried to one-up each other, currying favor with the firm's partners. Quinn kept to himself—he was just here for the experience, after all, and didn't care for office politics—but when the day began and their absence was apparent, their responsibilities fell to him, and he wanted to take advantage of the opportunity. He thought he could manage everything within eight, possibly nine hours, but now, twelve hours later, there was still work to do.

The offices of Rochester, Isley, & Moss emptied hours ago, just in time for Happy Hour, and only a handful of employees remained. Most of them were part of the nightly cleaning crew, but Quinn had spotted Mr. Rochester himself on the way back to his office. He wasn't surprised by this. Joseph Rochester was Richard Henza's attorney, and he'd been putting in long hours all week.

Quinn was glad he wasn't alone in the building. The hallways were dim in the late hours, and the pale fluorescent lights sucked the life out of everything, making the walls and carpets appear washed out, faded. Odd noises were more than apparent in the absence of the firm's workers—they were overpowering. These characteristics melded together in a perfect mixture of ambience, lending the halls and empty offices an eerie quality that often made Quinn jump at the slightest sound or shadow.

He listened to the hum of ventilated air and tick of the clock. *Get going. The sooner you finish, the sooner you can go.*

Quinn was about to leave when a man entered the break room. He was an older man, possibly mid-sixties by the look of him, wearing a gray suit and tie. Patches of silvery stubble dotted the top of his mostly bald head, glistening under the lifeless fluorescent lights.

"Hello there." He stuck out his hand. Quinn reluctantly shook it. The man's skin was cold, clammy. "I'm sorry if I startled you."

Quinn stared at the stranger for a moment, wondering what a client would be doing here so late. Then he remembered Mr. Rochester, and it all made sense.

"You must be here about the Henza case," Quinn said, smiling. The man seemed genuinely surprised.

"In a matter of speaking. I just paid a visit to old Joe to settle some business of mine."

A moment of silence moved between them, and Quinn took the opportunity to excuse himself. "Well, have a good night." Quinn began to step around the gentleman. "I still have some work to do."

He felt a hand on his shoulder. "Oh, don't go yet, son. Would you mind showing an old man to the door? I get awfully lost in a big place like this."

Quinn hesitated. "Uh, sure. If you hang a right outside the door and walk down the hall, you'll end up in the lobby."

The old man's grip tightened on his shoulder, and a spike of fear shot through Quinn's gut. A cold stare met his eyes.

"I didn't ask you to *tell* me, kid." His smile fell. "I asked you to *show* me."

Quinn's mouth went dry. For an instant he wanted to tell the man to remove his hand, but then remembered his place. One wrong word and he could say goodbye to his internship. He took a breath and forced a smile.

"I can do that. Follow me, sir."

The gentleman's eyes lightened, their hard edge replaced by the kind, elderly charm with which he'd entered the room.

"Why, thank you, son. Lead the way."

Quinn did as he was asked. The old man walked by his side. He did not remove his hand from the young man's shoulder.

An uninvited weight invaded Quinn's feet, making each step heavier than the last. He felt silly for being so apprehensive, but the way the man's demeanor had changed so quickly left him feeling uneasy.

The old man's grip tightened on his shoulder. "What's your name, kid?"

"Quinn."

"I like that name. It wouldn't be my first choice for a name if I had a son, but no, not a bad name at all. Say, do you like television?"

"I guess," Quinn said, wincing. "You're kinda hurting me."

The gentleman ignored him and went on talking. "I never cared much for TV, but it's a great way to spread a message. You might say it's a new hobby of mine." He reached into his breast pocket and pulled out a small white pin adorned with the black outline of a door. Quinn recognized it immediately.

"Do you work on *Fading Out?*"

The gentleman smiled. "You could say that. In fact, you might say I'm responsible for it." He pulled open the door and ushered Quinn into the lobby.

"But I thought Richard Henza was the creator?"

The old man released his grip. They stood in the empty lobby, staring at one another.

"We're all puppets, Quinn, but some of us have more strings than others."

"I don't—" he began but was interrupted by the appearance of a large man with a bushy beard. He entered the lobby from the opposite hallway, rubbing his hands with a dark rag. Quinn intended only to glance, but his eyes would not listen; they remained locked on the bearded man's dark hands and the blood that dripped from them.

"Did you take care of Rochester?"

"I did."

"Good. Let's prep our boy here for the transition."

"Yes, sir."

Quinn didn't have time to react. The bearded guy, big and lumbering though he was, moved with intense speed. He cracked Quinn's nose with a right hook. Stars exploded before the boy's eyes, and the last thing he saw before losing consciousness was a blurry image of two figures standing over him.

The bearded man smiled. "Sweet dreams."

Donovan packed an assortment of baby-related gifts into the trunk while Donna made one last round of goodbyes, gave her sister another hug, and worked her way to the car. Once inside, Donovan put the key in the ignition and turned to his wife.

"That wasn't so bad, was it?"

Donna closed her eyes and leaned against the window. "Just get us home, please."

He put his hand on hers and drove. She slept the whole way, and when they arrived Donovan had to give her a nudge to wake her. He helped her inside and up the stairs, kissed her, and put her to bed.

"Love you," he whispered.

"Love you D…" she mumbled and was fast asleep. He smiled, brushing strands of hair from her cheek. In the early days of their marriage, he'd lie awake some mornings, watching her slumber. They were short, peaceful moments, affording him a chance to focus his thoughts and reflect on things, something he hadn't the opportunity to do any other time.

Donovan stepped back and closed the door behind him. He found himself alone in a quiet house with nothing to keep him company but the turbulent thoughts in his head, and he wasn't ready to face those yet. Instead, he went about emptying the car.

When the last load was inside, Donovan locked the door and went back upstairs to the nursery. He sat on Donna's rocking chair, observing the assortment of packages spread out before him, a smirk on his face. *I think we're prepared.*

Except he knew he wasn't. He thought he was, but after the last 24 hours, Donovan Candle wasn't so sure of himself anymore. He replayed the morning's conversation with Detective Brock, imagining the gruesome scene in his mind with stark clarity, and wondering how the parents were coping with such grievous news.

Donovan felt a bottomless pit open in his gut. Fearing he might fall into himself, he rose from his seat, paced the room, and took a teddy bear from the crib. A baby was what he and Donna wanted. This was what they'd talked about for so long, and what he'd inadvertently stalled from happening for even longer. Now the baby was on its way, and he found the excitement he'd longed for was nowhere to be found—replaced instead by a colder, simpler emotion: fear.

Images of the missing kids flashed before him. He saw their photos, their smiles frozen in print. The details of the disappearances, the savage way they were murdered—all of these things looked simple in black and white to the untrained eye, but in the negative spaces between the facts was something else altogether. He knew what it was, had known the cause all along, and his willful ignorance sickened him. *I'm a coward. If I'd acted then, maybe they'd still be alive.*

He thought back to his brother's lecture. How many times in his life had he approached the apex of flight only to freeze up at the last moment? He knew what happened to those kids, but he was too afraid to make a move, and why shouldn't he be? He'd seen the horrors waiting on the other side of reality—they were pale, cold, with black eyes and maws that could swallow a man whole. One trip to the Monochrome was enough to suit him.

What if I can't protect my own child? he wondered, to which his brother's voice asked, *Why are you afraid to jump, Don?*

Donovan returned to his seat, where he slowly rocked himself into a daze. Mrs. Precious Paws crawled out from underneath the crib and hopped onto his lap. She curled into a ball, dug her head between his arm and thigh, and purred. He scratched behind her ears, staring off into space for a time, alone with the feline and his troubled thoughts.

He was so lost in his own head that he didn't hear Donna walking down the hallway. She stopped in the doorway and gave him a peculiar look.

"You're up late."

"Am I? How late is it?" He looked at his watch. It was a quarter past one in the morning. "I guess I am. Go back to bed. I'll be in soon."

Donna nodded, placing one hand behind her back and the other on her belly. She started to turn but paused and looked back at him.

"You okay, honey?"

"I—" he began, took notice of her face, and stopped. He thought for a moment, then said, "No, Donna. I'm not okay. No sense in lying to you. You'd know the truth anyway."

"It's those kids, isn't it?" She walked over and stood beside him. She ran her hand through his hair. "Tell me."

"It is," he said, "but it's more than that. I'm scared, Donna."

"Of what?"

He put his hand on her belly. She looked down at him, his words slowly sinking in, and put her hand on his.

"You're scared of the baby?"

"No," he sighed. "Not *of* the baby."

"Of what, then?"

Donovan leaned forward, staring at the floor. "I'm guess I'm scared that I'll fail."

"Fail? At what?"

"At protecting our child."

His lower lip quivered. He bit it back. *Don't*, he told himself. *Not now.*

"Donovan Candle, you can take this on my authority as your wife: you are not a failure. I wish you could see what I see, Donnie. I see a man who poured his heart into finding children that weren't his own. I see him torn apart inside because he couldn't stop bad things from happening to them."

"I couldn't—"

"You did what you could. You did what you had to. And I have complete faith that you will do whatever you can for our own child. The only person putting pressure on you is *you*, Don." She took hold of his chin and made him look at her. "I love you with all of my heart and soul, and I'll support you until the very end, but I can't help you through this. You have to find your own way."

He closed his eyes for a moment. "I know."

"Promise me something?"

"Anything."

"Don't give up. Not like you almost did before. Not again. I need you, Don. *We* need you."

He looked away from her and down at his feet, smiling when she ran her hand through his hair again.

"I promise." He stood and embraced her. When they let go, Donna took his hand and led him out of the room. He stopped her at the bedroom. "I'm going to watch some TV until I get sleepy."

"Suit yourself. You'll pay for it in the morning."

Donovan smiled. She was right. There wasn't enough coffee in the world to combat four hours of sleep. It was a battle he'd fought and lost many times.

"Don't be up too late."

"Yes, Mom," he mocked. She disappeared into their bedroom. He was sure he heard her say, "Damn right."

Downstairs, he stretched out on the couch and turned on the TV. The changing channels painted their living room a deep flickering shade of blue. He searched for something to occupy his mind and prevent everything he was struggling against from seeping in. Those thoughts still ran rampant through his mental attic, scurrying about like rodents nesting in the shadows.

He flipped through product infomercials, late-night movies, and re-runs of old sitcoms. His eyes drooped. Just before he decided to give in and turn it off, a familiar logo faded in on the screen, beginning with the simple black and white image of a door. At first, he thought it was an episode of *The Twilight Zone*, but the picture quality was too clear, and it lacked Rod Serling's iconic voice.

The door swung open, and the camera move forward into the light.

"Here's what you missed on last week's *Fading Out!*"

What followed was a series of scenes depicting various millenials lamenting about the lousy job market, unstable economy, their lack of prospects, and the struggle to make sense of it all. The show was, in a sense, a depiction of everyday life, only dramatized in the same fashion as every other reality TV show.

"Critics call *Fading Out* 'the most refreshing, realistic reality show on television!'"

You've got to be kidding me.

The commercial concluded with the doorway. It closed. An infomercial followed. Donovan frowned, rolling his tired eyes. "The shit they show on TV these days," he whispered, realizing that he sounded like his parents. He chuckled all the way back up the stairs. Sleep came quickly, and he soon forgot about the commercial, the party, and the thoughts plaguing his weary mind.

"Here's what you missed on last week's *Fading Out!*" The screens were already playing when he came to, casting him in a permanent glow, encompassing him in their shifting, bright light.

Quinn Upton opened his mouth to scream, but no sound came. His throat was raw, and his nose ached. The back of the folding chair dug into his shoulder blades.

The TV screens shifted in unison, transitioning from the *Fading Out* intro music to the show itself. *I've seen this episode before*, he thought. In fact, he'd seen them all, having watched the first season over the course of three months earlier that year.

Focus. I need to get out of here.

He craned his neck to the side and looked over his shoulder. He was bound to the chair with handcuffs. They dug into his ankles and wrists.

Where was the old man? And what about the huge dude with the beard?

He remembered the sucker punch, and his face throbbed with the memory. His mind was still lost in a haze, circling around the despair of his situation but never quite taking the plunge.

And the TVs were so damn loud. The shows repeated, caught in an infinite loop, and he soon gave up trying to think of ways out.

Quinn slumped back in the chair and watched TV, curious to know what he'd missed on *Fading Out*. He forgot about his restraints, losing himself in the haze, and the show played on.

-4-

BYSTANDERS

D onna came out of sleep in a startled daze, taking a few moments to piece together the reality of their bedroom. She plucked a word from the fog in her brain. *Phone.* She eased herself up in bed. Donovan stirred beside her for a moment, his form buried in the folds of the sheet.

The phone stopped. She listened to the silence of the house. A floorboard popped somewhere downstairs, and her heart began to race. It was the settling foundation, and she knew this, but in the haze of sleepiness, a single lingering doubt crept out of the shadows: *What if someone's downstairs?*

The abduction last year did more to shake her nerves than she would ever openly admit to anyone. There were times she woke in the night with memories of the man who broke in and knocked her unconscious. A year ago, she was agile enough to have avoided the whole situation if she'd not let her guard down. Now she was fifteen pounds heavier and carrying a child. How could she possibly fend off an attacker?

Stop it. It's the foundation. Go back to sleep.

Donna was starting to nod off when the phone rang again. Her eyes snapped open and she quietly cursed. The clock on the nightstand read twelve minutes shy of six. It was a Monday morning. Birds chirped outside. *No one calls this early.*

"Don." She nudged him. He grunted, scrunched up his face, and promptly rolled away from her. "Fine, I'll carry my pregnant ass over to the phone. You rest your weary head." The phone kept ringing. Sooner or later their voicemail would pick up. "Okay, okay, I'm coming."

She drummed her fingers across her belly. Then she braced herself against the inevitable muscle pain, got out of bed and hobbled down the hallway. The phone chimed at her from Donovan's computer desk. She answered on the sixth ring.

"Donna? It's Amanda."

"Mandy?" Donna heard herself say. She'd not called her sister that in years. "Sweetie, what's wrong?"

Her sister began to sob. It was only when Donna picked out the name "Quinn" that she knew the answer to her question. A confirming rush of fear coursed through her veins. Then, for the first time in a long time, she broke down and cried with her sister.

———————•———————

Two hours later Donovan found himself sitting at the kitchen table nursing a lukewarm cup of coffee. Donna sat across from him, her eyes puffy and face swollen from crying. The rise and fall of her sobs had finally woken him, and the sound of the phone clattering on the floor yanked him out of bed.

Mrs. Precious Paws rubbed against his ankles, restless for attention and seemingly aware that something was wrong. He offered an idle hand to scratch behind her ears.

Quinn was gone. He tried to wrap his brain around that concept. Three days had passed since their lunch at the diner. Donovan thought it was odd that Quinn missed the baby shower Friday night, but when he learned of the boy's work at the law firm he understood. Amanda's call to Quinn during the shower had been the last time she'd heard from him.

He sat there, going over the story in his mind as Donna recounted it.

When Quinn didn't come home, Amanda and Jeff suspected he'd spent the night with his girlfriend but calls to his cell phone went unanswered. The weekend came and went, and when the phone finally rang at dawn on Monday morning, Amanda was still awake. Panicked, she answered the call, expecting her son to be on the other end of the line. Instead the caller was a man who identified himself as Officer Douglas.

What followed was a mother's nightmare come to life: Quinn was missing. The police, answering an unrelated call at the law firm, had reviewed security footage in which an unknown assailant had attacked their son, hoisted him over his shoulder, and carried him out of view.

Donovan's curiosity circled around the missing facts: why were the police already there? And why would someone want to kidnap Quinn in the first place? Did he witness something? Was he in the wrong place at the wrong time?

He sat with Donna in the silence of the kitchen, mulling over the lack of information and the confusion it caused. Quinn's disappearance brought back memories of Donna's abduction. He thought about how lost he felt and wanted to say something to make Donna feel better, but comforting words would not come to him.

Some husband you are.

The phone rang, startling Donna. They stared at one another for a moment as it rang a second time. She reached out to answer, but Donovan stopped her. "Let me."

He took a breath and answered the phone.

"Candle."

Detective Nathan Brock. Donovan hadn't spoken to Brock since the morning after the bodies were found. The old man sounded haggard, like he hadn't slept in two days.

"Morning, Nate."

"I just met with your brother-in-law…" Brock hesitated for a moment. "Could you come down to the precinct? I need you to take a look at something."

Donovan glanced at his wife. She traced a pale finger along the edge of her milk glass.

"Would this have anything to do with that security footage?"

Brock grunted. "Can you be here in an hour?"

"I can."

"Good. See you then."

Donovan ended the call, his mind at work trying to piece together a puzzle he couldn't solve. He thought hard about his meeting with Quinn, and about the flickering bearded man watching them from the corner. *Why was he there? Why would Dullington let me see him?*

Possibilities flooded his mind, and he was overtaken with a wave of nausea. He took several deep breaths and waited for it to pass, but the sickening feeling lingered in the depths of his gut.

"How's Nathan?"

"He wants me to meet him at the precinct," Donovan said, feeling that familiar heat return to his face. *Just tell her. Tell her why you're scared. Tell her what you've suspected all along, and that you're too much of a chicken shit to do anything about it.*

They sat in silence, contemplating the endless vacuum between them. Donovan knew what this was doing to her. She'd helped take care of Quinn when he was a baby, and whatever horrors she felt could be surpassed only by Amanda's own fears.

He stood and dumped his coffee into the sink. Donna continued staring into space. Seeing her like this tore away at him from the inside. *Do something*, he thought. *Be useful.*

Joe Hopper whispered, *Jump.*

Donovan kissed his wife on the forehead before leaving the room to get dressed.

————————◆————————

H e met Detective Brock outside the precinct. The old man leaned against the brick building, puffing on a cigarette while heavy bags hung from his eyes. Brock offered him a short nod while dropping his cigarette.

"Candle."

"Nate, what couldn't you tell me over the phone?"

The detective gathered his thoughts, chewing his lower lip in the process. He scraped his shoe over the cigarette butt, mashing out the cherry. A tendril of smoke snaked lazily into the air. "I'll get to the point. I'm breaching protocol by doing this, but considering the news this morning, I think you need to know."

"Know what?"

"It's…better if I show you."

Donovan had last been inside the precinct almost a year ago when Michael had introduced him to the detective. He hadn't had a good reason to return since, but the building was as he remembered it: old, worn, its classiness wiped away years ago by the sins of the city's residents. Several men and women waited in the foyer to file a report or post bail. They sat along the wall; above them hung a large bulletin board covered in public notices and flyers. Donovan didn't need to look twice to recognize some of the faces on the tattered pages.

A uniformed officer behind the front desk nodded to them as they walked in. Brock returned the gesture, leading Donovan through a door to the side that opened up into the department's main offices. The room itched with activity. Desks were piled with case files, phones rang in tandem, and someone bitched about there being no coffee. Tension hung in the air like smoke.

"Mondays," Brock grunted, bypassing the rows of desks on his way to the stairs. He led Donovan to his office at the far end of the second floor and closed the door behind them.

"Okay, Brock. What's going on?"

The detective sat down at his desk. "Before I go any further, we need to have an understanding. What I'm about to tell you doesn't leave this office. Time isn't on our side right now. I expect someone will leak this to the press before the end of the day, but for now it's under lock and key. Okay?"

Donovan sat back in his chair and shrugged. "Of course."

Brock looked grim. He turned his computer monitor at an angle so Donovan could see it. On screen was a small, grainy window. "This is the law firm's security footage from Friday night."

The camera was positioned over a credenza and facing a pair of glass doors. Quinn entered the frame just as the screen began to flicker and jerk. A stuttering haze of static occupied the space next to the boy, obscuring a section of the frame. Quinn seemed to be staring at it. A few frames later, a large man entered from the left with his back to the camera lens. Quinn had no time to react. The assailant hit him with a right hook to the face.

Brock paused the footage, minimizing a window while maximizing another. "This is security footage taken just a few minutes before Quinn was attacked. It's…not pleasant."

He clicked on the play button. What followed was a series of frames shot in black-and-white, depicting a set of double doors, one angled halfway open. Beyond the doorway, Donovan saw a large executive-style desk with a set of windows behind it. Other details farther from the camera lens were too grainy to decode.

This scene remained unchanged for several frames before the opening widened, revealing a man crawling forward with one arm, while the other—twisted at an impossible angle—dragged along at his side. Donovan strained to decipher the details; the monochrome shades of the closed-circuit camera didn't make it easy. What happened next claimed his full attention.

A large man with a bushy beard entered the frame from beyond the door and stood over his victim. He planted his boot in the center of the victim's back, shifting all his weight to it. The poor man beneath him thrashed violently, struggling to get away despite the evident futility.

The bearded man smiled. A chill crawled its way down Donovan's spine.

The attacker pulled something from his pocket—a letter opener—and in one swift motion jammed the sharp end into the back of his victim's neck. A dark fountain gushed from the man's throat as he convulsed in agony, choking on his own blood. The bearded man lifted his boot and forced his weight against the back of the opener, shoving it farther into the man's flesh and holding it there until his victim stopped moving. A thick black puddle slowly spread around the body.

Donovan closed his eyes for a moment as he tried to process what he'd seen. *The bearded man. The man from last week, outside my car. Outside the diner, watching me—watching Quinn.* His blood went cold at the connection. The bearded man—no, the *flickering* man—was following him. But why? And why did he take Quinn?

"Could you pull up the first video?"

Brock did so. Donovan leaned forward, staring hard at the column of static standing beside Quinn and his attacker. Was there an outline in that static? He traced the lines of a head, shoulders, arms. *Dullington, what angle are you playing?*

"We've got some of the techies working on the interference, but it may just be an issue with the camera feed." Brock pulled up the second video. "This poor bastard was Joseph Rochester, one of the firm's founders. A friend of the mayor's." He sighed, rubbing his eyes. "And Richard Henza's attorney."

Donovan looked the detective in the eye. "Did you tell Amanda and Jeff about this?"

"Yes, to a degree. They know as much as we've told the press: that Rochester has been murdered, we're devoting all our manpower to tracking down the killer, et cetera."

"And?"

Brock reclined in his seat. "And that's all they know. *We* know a bit more than that, but we're not disclosing the information at this time."

"You didn't ask me down here just to tell me you have secrets, Brock." Donovan realized he'd raised his voice and calmed himself. "What do you know?"

"We lifted some prints from the scene. We're cross-referencing them with prints found at Henza's home and at the crime scene last week." He pointed at the screen. "Obviously that big bastard is our prime suspect."

"Who is he?"

Brock shrugged. "We don't know. We're working on that."

"Motive?"

"Working on that, too."

"Listen, Nate. I'm still not clear on why you asked me here. You've already got my cooperation. Was there something else?"

The old detective sighed. He closed the windows on his monitor. "Yes, and it isn't easy, Don. You need to understand something here. We're dealing with a cruel son of a bitch, and whatever his motive may be, your nephew's odds are not good."

Obviously.

Donovan waited, watching Brock work out his words.

"Considering your line of work, and your relation to one of the victims—"

"That implies Quinn is dead, Nathan."

The detective held up his hand in apology. "You're right. That's not what I meant. What I'm trying to say is that with your career and relation to Quinn, you might get it in your head to go try and track him down yourself."

Donovan nodded. "You're damn right—"

"I know I'm right. And that's why I need to ask that you refrain from involving yourself in this investigation."

He held his breath for a moment, eyes locked on the black background of the computer's desktop while Brock's words soured the air. Several replies came to him in rapid succession, each one a bullet meant to punch a hole in his friend's ultimatum, but he held back. His cheeks flushed with heat. *Watch yourself*, Hopper whispered.

Nathan Brock was sympathetic to Donovan's investigations, offering help when other officers wouldn't have bothered, and he'd taken a liking to Candle & Candle over the past year. The last thing Donovan wanted to do was piss him off, but the words that came to mind defied his intentions.

"Then why have me come down here and show this to me?" He tapped the edge of the monitor. "He's family. *My* family."

Brock leaned forward, shrugging. "Look, I don't like it any more than you do. Lord knows you're more equipped to aid us in this than most, but I didn't make this call. We've got people from the mayor's office screaming for blood, and the press is already riding the commissioner's ass. The last thing this department needs is more public criticism, and how do you think it'll look if it comes out that we've got a private dick helping us on the case?"

Donovan crossed his arms and clenched his jaw. He said nothing.

"Okay, you did your part with those missing kids. You took that personally—don't you look at me like that, son. I know you did. I understand it, too. When Evelyn disappeared, I wanted to do nothing else but find every person who'd vanished without a trace."

The detective stared off into space as he spoke, ignoring Donovan's gaze. *He's not talking to me. Poor guy's talking to himself. Rationalizing his actions, his defeat.*

Brock had accepted his wife's disappearance, resigned to the idea that there was nothing he could do, and this epiphany made Donovan sick to his stomach. The old man's resignation mirrored his own. He'd spent the last several months deluding himself, believing there wasn't more to the disappearances when he knew, instinctively, that something more devious was at work. Now those kids were dead, and Quinn was missing.

Donovan pushed back his chair and stood. "I think I've heard enough."

"Don, wait. This didn't turn out the way I'd hoped. I need you to understand me on this, okay? I don't need you running off and getting yourself killed in the process. This city's had enough innocent bystanders. Just go on home. Let us do our jobs."

His friend suddenly looked much older under the fluorescent lights, the shadows under his eyes more pronounced, the wrinkles dug out like trenches across his face. Brock was a frail old man, hollowed out by a cancerous apathy dwelling within his soul. Donovan wondered if this man was a reflection of who he might become in another thirty years: jaded, tired, and defeated.

"Just go on home? Let you do your job? Is that what they told you when Evelyn disappeared?" He paused, shaking his head. Something Aleister Dullington told him a long time ago bubbled up to the surface of his memory, and he slowly repeated it. "Actions birth definition, Nate."

Detective Brock sat back in his chair, stunned. Donovan didn't wait for his friend to respond. He turned and made his exit, taking the stairs two steps at a time.

———————

*T*hat *son of a bitch.*

A dull throb settled into the base of Donovan's skull, pulsing to the tune of his heart and plucking the chords of an angry riff. His conversation with Brock still resonated in his mind, and the early afternoon freeway gridlock didn't ease his irritation.

A waste of time. They aren't going to search for Quinn. Shit, they've already written him off as collateral damage. If it were up to me, Michael and I would—

His heart tumbled. The morning's urgency had swallowed him, and in his haste he'd forgotten to call his brother. While traffic inched forward, Donovan checked his phone. He had three missed calls from Michael and no messages. First, he tried his brother's phone, but there was no answer. When he tried the office, Rosie informed him that Michael wasn't there and had been trying to reach him all morning.

Donovan stared out the window at the row of cars beside him, his mind still ten miles back sitting in Brock's office. He knew what he was about to do could get him into serious trouble; worse, it could damage Candle & Candle's reputation.

He looked down at the cell phone, frowning. His brother wouldn't understand. The fear of Michael's disapproval had haunted him for most of his life, but there was something beneath the trepidation, something much greater: the promise he'd made to his wife. He wouldn't give up. Not again. He would follow the advice he'd given Brock, even if it meant risking his credibility.

Half an hour later he left the freeway and took a couple of back roads to his sister-in-law's neighborhood. He parked in front of their house beneath the shade of a willow tree. Amanda met him at the front step, her face flushed and eyes swollen. She was still in her bathrobe.

"Hey, Don."

"Hi, Amanda."

They were silent. Early in his relationship with Donna, Amanda had been one of his more vocal critics, and they'd had their share of shouting matches. But they were older now, and he was willing to extend the olive branch for Quinn's sake.

"Do you want to come in? For coffee? I can put the kettle on if you'd rather have tea."

He tried to smile. "Thanks, Amanda, but no thanks. I'm here on business. Is Jeff around? I need to talk to both of you."

She didn't respond. Instead she opened the door, retreating to the dining room. Donovan followed her, feeling the weight of the situation as he crossed the room. He'd not been in their house for at least a couple of years. They'd repainted their living room. New furniture. A new family portrait hung above the fireplace. When Donovan passed the kitchen, he saw more photos stuck to the refrigerator with magnets.

Jeff Upton stood at the kitchen sink, staring blankly out the window. He offered Donovan a quick glance and a short nod before returning his attention to the backyard. Amanda sat at the table and reached for an open pack of Marlboros. Her hands shook so bad she had a hard time lighting the cigarette.

Donovan cleared his throat. "Jeff, it might be better if you had a seat, too."

His brother-in-law nodded and took a seat beside Amanda. Donovan sat at the head of the table and collected his thoughts.

"Hanging in there?"

Amanda nodded, took a drag, and exhaled. The calming effect was immediate. Jeff fidgeted in his seat, his eyes bloodshot from lack of sleep. Donovan knew no amount of coffee would cure the man's lethargy.

"I filed the report with that detective this morning." Jeff paused, staring at the table. "He said they'd send a couple of officers over right away, but that was hours ago. Said the man who took Quinn may have killed someone at the firm. Some attorney, I think?"

Amanda took another drag from the cigarette and shrugged. "Rochester. He's been all over the news this morning."

Donovan nodded, weighing his words. "I met with Detective Brock about an hour ago—"

Amanda put her hand on his. "Are you going to help them, Don?"

"Yes."

She squeezed his hand, offering a glimpse of an empty smile. His response wasn't quite a lie, but it tasted like one. A ghost of the word soured on his tongue, a rapid-fire response that was out with the speed of a bullet before he could even think to stop it. *Not a lie. I am going to help the investigation—whether Brock likes it or not.*

Jeff leaned forward, putting his elbows on the table. "Is that official? Do they normally operate like this, involving third parties?"

"Honey, I'm sure Donovan's cleared this—"

"Technically," Donovan began, "no, it isn't official. In fact, I've been ordered not to get in the way." He studied their expressions. When they said nothing, he continued: "What I've been told was under strict confidence, but you're family. You deserve better, and honestly, if it were me in your shoes, I'd want to know." He dry-swallowed, ignoring the lump of cotton in his throat. "What they didn't tell the reporters this morning is that they believe Quinn's abductor is also the one behind last week's murders and that TV producer's disappearance."

Amanda offered her husband a quick glance. Jeff put his arm around her. She finished her cigarette. A tendril of smoke hung suspended before her face as she stamped out the smoldering filter in the ashtray.

Jeff drummed his fingers on the table. "So what happens now?"

"Officially, you wait. I imagine a couple of officers will come by to ask a few more questions and go through Quinn's belongings. They'll continue their investigation, searching for clues that might lead to Rochester's killer."

"And unofficially?"

Donovan stared at his brother-in-law, his mind drowning with possible replies he would never voice. *You'll wait for news that won't come. In six months when they still can't find him, they'll pull some nameless hobo off the street and pin it on him because the city needs a scapegoat, someone to be a blood sacrifice at the political altar. Quinn will be just another casualty, a bystander of a deranged killer. He'll be another cold case because I didn't trust my intuition. Because I was too afraid to act when I had the chance.*

"Unofficially, this whole mess is tied up in city politics. They're looking for Rochester's killer, not your son's abductor. Quinn is secondary to them. As far as the mayor's office is concerned, he's just another victim."

Amanda rested her head on Jeff's shoulder and closed her eyes. Tears fell down her cheeks. "Where's that leave you?"

"Without much time." Donovan sucked in his breath. *Put on your game face, Don.* Hopper's voice—gruff, cold, and hardened by experience, but not without a slight touch of humanity. "I need to see Quinn's room." He cut her off before she could question him. "Clues, Amanda. Please."

"They told you not to interfere," Jeff said quietly. "Couldn't you get into a lot of trouble for this?"

Donovan stood up from the table and looked at his brother-in-law, smirking. "Absolutely."

———————————•———————————

A manda stood with him for a moment while he scanned the room, looking for something, anything that might jump out. Nothing did. There were posters hung on the walls for various bands and movies; framed photographs of friends and family, including one of a young Donna holding baby Quinn; and various academic awards he'd won in high school. A couple of empty cardboard boxes were stacked up beside the closet.

Donovan pointed to the stack. "Was he planning to move?"

"At the end of the summer. He and some friends from school were going to rent a house for the semester."

He walked around the bed, nodding. Sometimes he played puzzles to pass the time on slow days at the office. Crossword puzzles, anagrams, anything involving vocabulary. When he struggled with a particular problem, he questioned himself: *What are you missing?*

To know what he was missing, he must first know what he had. He found he could apply this axiom to most situations. Sometimes it worked.

"What exactly are you looking for?"

He sat down on the bed, staring up at a large corkboard adorned with pushpins, notes, and flyers. Amanda remained in the doorway, absently chewing on her thumbnail.

"Amanda," he said quietly. "Would you give me five minutes here? I need to concentrate, and frankly you're making me nervous."

She stopped chewing on her nail. Her expression was a mixture of hurt and resentment. She was proud to a fault and taking orders from her asshole brother-in-law wasn't something she easily swallowed. He expected her to resist his wishes, but she didn't. Amanda closed the door without saying anything but made sure to shoot him a sharp glare just before bringing the door to its frame. *Duly noted*, he thought.

He went to work going through the boy's closet, bookshelves, and notebooks, looking for anything that might tip him off. *Think, Don. What aren't you seeing? Why would Dullington want Quinn, or any of those other kids for that matter? And what's the connection with the producer?* All the facts—the murders, Henza's disappearance, Quinn's abduction—suggested a bigger picture that defied everything he knew about Dullington and the Monochrome.

"None of this makes sense," he whispered, looking around the room again. The answers weren't here. He checked his watch. Michael would be furious by now, and before too long Donovan's phone would ring. He suddenly felt foolish for coming here, but—

Something caught his eye. The corkboard contained mostly phone numbers and reminders, but there was one thing that now stood out. It was a small square postcard, with black letters on a white background.

"Join us in celebrating the season premiere of *Fading Out!* You are invited to attend The Great Fade-Out!" Beneath that were the date, time, and channel: "Sponsored by WBS Media."

He freed the postcard from the pushpin and examined it. A small outline of a door was printed on the opposite side.

Donovan thought of the commercial he'd seen several nights ago, and the pamphlet left on his windshield. There was the graffiti outside of the old station, and the matter of the show's missing creator. He stared at the symbol, ruminating on the possible connections and the stake Dullington might have in a TV show.

I've got a handful of pieces to a jigsaw puzzle with no borders for context. Shit.

He tucked the card into his pocket and left the room. Amanda was back at the kitchen table puffing on another cigarette. Jeff leaned against the kitchen counter, sipping a cup of coffee. Donovan stood in the entryway.

"Does *Fading Out* mean anything to you?"

She answered without deliberation. "It's one of Quinn's favorite shows."

"Did you ever watch it?"

Jeff set down his mug and shook his head. "I tried to watch an episode once. Too boring for my taste. The other shows on TV, they have something going on, you know? There's a point. This show is just a camera crew following around a bunch of young millenials. I don't know how Quinn could stand to watch it."

Amanda put down her cigarette. "Why? Did you find something?"

"I'm not sure." He shook his head. "It could be nothing, but I'll follow up on it anyway. Listen, if you guys hear anything, you call us, okay? Day or night, it doesn't matter."

Jeff nodded. "We will."

He started for the front door. His sister-in-law didn't say anything, and he felt the weight of the place remove itself from his shoulders as he walked to the car. His phone vibrated in his pocket.

Michael's name flashed on the screen as the phone punctuated each ring with a short vibration. Donovan waited a moment, holding the air in his lungs until it began to burn. *Maybe I was foolish for thinking I could figure this out*, he thought, feeling his heart sink into the pit of his stomach. *Maybe I'm not cut out for this.*

The phone kept ringing. He slowly exhaled, waited a moment longer, and answered.

———————————•———————————

"Hey, Mike."

"Please tell me you aren't where I think you are."

His brother spoke in even tones, but the irritation in his voice was obvious. Donovan leaned against his car and wiped sweat from his brow. The afternoon sun was relentless.

"I'm just leaving Amanda's house. Why?"

"Goddammit. Brock called me after you stormed out of his office. Real nice, Don. Very professional. And when the hell were you planning on calling me, anyway?"

"I did. I tried your cell, and then I tried the office." He paused, searching for the right words. "Nathan called me right after I heard the news this morning, and I went straight over. I was caught up in the urgency. Sorry I didn't call sooner."

Donovan opened the door and sat down in the driver's seat. He started the engine, turned on the air conditioning, and leaned back against the headrest. The phone's dull hum filled his ear as his brother went silent. *Calm before the storm.* He felt a headache coming on.

"How're Quinn's folks?"

He glanced back at the house. "Surviving."

"And Donna? She's okay?"

"About as good as you can expect."

"What about you?"

Donovan blinked. "Concerned and confused."

"Confused," Michael repeated. He chuckled. "Sounds accurate enough. You *must* be confused—I mean, Brock *did* tell you to stay the hell away from this case, and where did you say you are? Oh right, Quinn's house."

"Mike, hear me out—"

"You *do* understand you could be arrested for this, right? Do you understand what that would do to business? Or to our fucking names?"

Donovan said nothing. The hum of the phone line punctuated their silence. Michael cursed under his breath and cleared his throat.

"Are you done now? Can I explain myself."

"I'm all ears."

"Quinn's part of our family, Mike. I'm not going to twiddle my thumbs while the cops chase their tails on this—and neither should you. Not when the department's already written the kid off as another casualty."

"There's not a whole lot we can do about it, Don. This is their investigation, and as Brock explained to you, they're under a lot of pressure to find this guy."

"They won't find him."

"You don't know that, Donovan. Look, you're good at what you do, but this is way more than either of us are equipped to deal with—"

"I *do* know," he said quietly.

"Wait. You think there's more to this, don't you? Just like all those other cases." Michael's exasperated laughter filled his ear. "Why do you insist on doing this?"

"On doing what?"

"This. Making it into something it's not."

His brother's jabs struck a nerve, igniting a deeply rooted anger that consumed the last of his patience. The words left Donovan's mouth with startling fury. "Because if I'm right, the same thing that happened to those kids last week is going to happen to Quinn. The same thing that could've happened to Donna last year, if we'd not done something about it. Believe me, I want to be wrong about this, Mike, but I have to be sure."

A cloud of heat surrounded his face, suffocating him. He leaned forward in his seat, taking deep breaths. After a full minute Michael broke the heavy silence, saying exactly what Donovan expected him to say, the same thing he always said. "We've been over this before, man. What happened, happened. I can't explain it, and neither can you. All that matters is that you're here, Donna's here—"

"Mike, look—"

"No, Donovan, *you* look. If you want to rationalize every disappearance, be my guest, but you have to accept the fact that every person who disappears isn't zipping off to some gray world you say exists. This bullshit is your imagination getting too carried away. If you want to write it all down, be my guest, but don't you fucking drag me into your delusions."

"Even after everything that happened? Even after the circumstances?"

"All I saw was a bunch of bums holding Donna for ransom. They wanted that hack doctor; we delivered. End of story."

You saw more than that, Donovan thought, recalling the nasty conversation Dullington had with Michael. *But you don't remember. Why would you? Dullington's Cretins took care of all that. They left me alone to bear the memories so I wouldn't slip again.*

Donovan measured his words, speaking slowly. "Don't you think it's odd we've been so busy lately? Doesn't it bother you that, more and more, people are vanishing without a trace?"

"People disappear every day, Don."

"No, I don't think they do, Mike."

"Of course you don't. That would be too easy, wouldn't it, Don? You seriously need to take a step back and examine this. Those kids were kidnapped and murdered. Don't misunderstand me Don, I'm scared to death for Quinn. But right now, there isn't anything we can do about it. Let the police do their jobs."

His blood pressure rose. This was all going nowhere. How could his brother be so obtuse about this? He thought of telling him about seeing Quinn's abductor outside the diner but decided against it. There was no point. Michael had already made up his mind on the matter.

"That's fine, Mike. We'll agree to disagree."

"You do that. When can I expect you in the office?"

"When I find my nephew," he said, and hung up.

———————————◆———————————

Dinner simmered on the stove when he arrived home. He stood in the entryway, shoulder against the doorframe while he watched his wife go about her business. She had her hair pulled back in a ponytail that swished and swayed whenever she turned, moving between the island and the stove while the radio broadcast a forgettable tune.

Watching her carry on with her day made him forget about his stress. He remained silent as she stirred the sauce, wrinkled her nose, and reached for spices. When she turned, she saw him standing there, and her smile was heaven.

"Hi."

"Hey there."

Blushing, she tucked a strand of loose hair behind her. "I didn't hear you come in."

He took her into his arms. "You okay?"

"Yeah." Her voice cracked a little, and she followed it with a chuckle. "No. Maybe. I just needed to take my mind off things."

He traced his thumb across her cheek, its ghostly trails of dried tears now hours old. Many times, he'd lost himself in those big brown eyes of hers, an act he'd never tire of.

"I love you," she said. He closed his eyes and kissed her.

"I love you too."

Donna went about her cooking while Donovan retreated upstairs to change and shower. Afterward he returned to take his place at the table, and they ate in silence. It wasn't until he'd pushed his plate away that she asked about the day's progress.

He surveyed her expression of hope, knowing he was about to disappoint her.

"It's complicated," he said finally, tearing his gaze from her and finding renewed interest in the mess of leftover noodles and sauce on his plate. When she said nothing, he forced himself to go on. "I stopped by Amanda and Jeff's house. I went through Quinn's room."

"She told me."

Her voice was hushed, dry. *Please don't cry*, he thought.

"I didn't find much there." His voice cracked. Invisible hands of heat smothered his face. He swallowed air, took a breath, and went on. He did not look at her. "I made a mistake this morning."

"What mistake?"

He paused, deliberating on what to say. He didn't want to repeat the conversation he'd had with Michael that morning. "Nate told me to stay away from the investigation. I didn't listen."

Donna stared at him, reaching across the table. She put her hand on his.

He offered her a weak smile. "Something about Brock just looked so defeated, like even he didn't believe the bullshit he was saying. He seemed more concerned about pleasing his superiors than finding Quinn. Still pisses me off."

Donna squeezed his hand. "So what happens now?"

"Now I'm in a world of shit with Nate, my brother's pissed off at me, and Quinn's still missing. I thought I could find some clue in Quinn's room, something to point me in the right direction, but—" he paused, frowning. "But I think maybe Michael's right. Maybe I ought to step back and let the police handle this."

Donna shook her head. She rose from the table, took their plates, and stormed off to the kitchen.

"Donna—"

She dumped the plates in the sink and turned on the faucet. "This is bullshit, Donovan. Who would do this? What did Quinn ever do? It's—it's j-just—"

"Honey."

Donna shuffled toward him, chest heaving and tears pouring down her face. He held her.

"It's just not fair."

"I know. Shhh."

Her sobs eased into heavy breaths. Donovan let go to turn off the faucet, then returned to her. She buried her face in his shoulder.

He put his arm around her, searching for the right words, something a good husband would say, but all that came to mind were hollow clichés. He wanted to tell her about the man at the diner and the odd connections to that damn TV show that he hadn't figured out yet. That their odds of finding Quinn were dwindling by the minute and finding him might mean going to a place that scared the hell out of him.

But he didn't. Instead he chose one of those dumb clichés, spoken a billion times before by a billion other men. He opened his mouth to reply when the pain of her nails digging into his arm silenced him. So did her shriek.

Donovan turned and froze. He felt a mixture of elation and shock as a block of ice wedged in his chest, feeding water to his veins. Donna squeezed his arm so hard he winced.

Quinn trembled in the doorway, his clothes tattered and face swollen, bruised. He raised the gun and leveled it at Donovan's head.

"Aunt Donna," he said. "Please step away from Uncle Don."

-5-
THE TRIAL

"Quinn," Donna gasped. All she could muster was a series of single-worded questions. "What? Why?"

The scene didn't register with Donovan at first. He was too shocked at finding his missing nephew standing in his home. Too shocked at seeing the boy's disheveled appearance: the layer of dirt on his clothes, the bruises on his face, a cut on his forehead. Utter terror filled his eyes, his filthy face streaked with tears.

"Sweetie," Donna said, letting go of Donovan's arm. She took a step toward their nephew. "What is this?"

Quinn pointed the gun at her, and Donovan's vision went red with an unsettling rage.

"Put it down," Donovan growled, balling his hands into fists so tight his knuckles popped. Quinn blinked, shifted his weight, and aimed his weapon at Donovan once more.

"For God's sake!" Donna cried. "What are you doing? *Stop it!*"

Shaking and sobbing, Quinn slowly lowered his weapon. He trembled in the foyer. The haze of red slowly cleared from Donovan's vision.

"Quinn." The boy did not look up; instead he continued to cry, staring off into space. Donovan spoke again. "Quinn?"

"Uncle Don, I'm sorry. I'm so sorry."

"Why don't you give me the gun? We can sit down and talk about this. Just give me the gun."

He glanced at Donna, caught her eye, then shot his gaze toward the phone on the wall. She nodded, frowning, her chin puckered as she fought a losing battle against the urge to cry.

Donovan stepped toward the boy. Standing in the doorway, caked in dirt and grime, he looked more infantile than Donovan could ever remember him being. Words came to mind. One was "Lost."

The other was "Missing."

He took another step. Quinn recoiled, raising the gun an inch.

"Don't, Don. Please. I have to do this. He told me to. It's the only way."

Donovan stopped in mid-step, his arms suddenly heavy. "Who?"

"He called himself the king," the boy muttered. "He said to tell you thanks. 'Thanks, Mr. Candle.' Oh God, I can't do this, I can't—"

Quinn began to sob, his body convulsing so hard the gun slipped from his hands. It clattered to the floor without incident. Several questions raced across Donovan's mind in that moment, circling around a memory of the hag at Winthorpe Station.

The king. He knows you. Knows us all.

He wanted to ask about this "king," but before Donovan could voice his questions Quinn snorted back his tears and snatched the gun from the floor. "I'm sorry."

Quinn flung open the door with such violence it slammed the adjacent wall, shaking the windows. Donovan turned toward Donna, still too shocked to react, and pointed at the phone. "Call the police!"

She reached for the phone and dialed. He was on his way out the door when she turned back.

"Don!"

He didn't stop. Not this time. He'd made a promise to her, and he wasn't about to break it. Heart racing, he forced his legs to move to its rhythm. He was a slave to the din pushing him, urging him forward into the evening. Clouds rolled over the horizon, darkening the day into a false night, and he saw a faint flash of lightning in the distance. Donovan stood on the sidewalk for a moment, head spinning, searching for a hint to where Quinn might have gone.

The yelping of a dog caught his attention. Mr. Cafferty's Labrador cried a second time, sparking Donovan's legs into action. He raced to the chain link fence separating their property and heaved himself over. His muscles screamed from the sudden exertion, reminding him of his years spent behind a desk, and he wondered why he'd not gone around the side.

Too long, Hopper said. His ankle twisted when he landed on the far side, but he grit his teeth and took the pain. *Go. Just go. Run. Catch him. Don't let him go. Run, you old bastard. RUN!*

A jolt of pain stabbed through him with every step, and his gasps for breath turned into quick heated yelps. He heard an outcry of *GO, GO, GO* chanting to the beat of his heart as he cut through Cafferty's backyard. A pair of overturned trashcans, the neighbor's Labrador cowering between them, indicated Quinn's likely path. Donovan heard leaves rustling in the patch of forest beyond his neighbor's house. Bobbing limbs in the foliage confirmed his suspicions, and he gave chase.

Donovan wasn't sure how long or how far he ran. The shock of icy water didn't faze him as he raced through a creek and over the hill beyond. Invisible teeth chewed his side, while his ankle throbbed, and his lungs filled with fire.

He paused long enough to catch his breath. When pain threatened to creep up, he started moving again, choosing to feel the numbness of adrenaline rather than the damage wrought on his aging body. The chant of *GO* continued in his head, and he hummed along to it between breaths.

He emerged beyond the trees on a rural road, the same one he often used to circumvent the city. Parked along the side was a brown Cadillac. It idled hard, sputtering black fumes from its tail pipe. Quinn stood beside it, arms behind his back, head bowed, and tears running down his cheeks.

Donovan stopped to catch his breath, wincing. The pain in his ankle finally caught up to him as the surge of adrenaline faded. Splotches of color burst before his eyes. He felt lightheaded.

"Quinn," he said between gasps. "Quinn, stop."

"I'm sorry, Uncle Don. I'm so sorry."

"We can talk about this."

Quinn shook his head. He sank back against the car, his arms crossed, staring at the grass. "No we can't."

The driver's door swung open, and the car's frame croaked in relief as a tall figure climbed out. The bearded man grinned at them. He clutched a dark bag in his meaty paws.

Donovan looked into the murderer's eyes, then glanced back at his nephew. Some of the pieces fell into place he felt like a fool for not putting them together sooner. *Puppets*, he thought, remembering the words of a desperate man just a short year ago.

The bearded man didn't waste time. He closed the gap between them in two long strides. Donovan tried to defend himself, but the loss of adrenaline turned his arms to jelly. His punch swung wide, missing its target entirely.

The bearded man sidestepped the attack, planting a boot against Donovan's foot. The momentum of Donovan's swing put him off balance, sending him sprawling forward. He hit the ground hard, knocking the wind from his lungs, and while he gasped for breath, the man known as Kale knelt beside him and slipped the dark bag over his head.

"Don't hurt him," Quinn pleaded, his voice now very small, a thousand miles away.

The bearded man grunted. "Shut up."

Donovan felt the murderer taking his arms behind his back, wrenching them together and pulling. There was a loud pop, and he suddenly found his breath, exhaling in an agonized scream. Everything swam together, colors of alternating shapes, senses of touch and sound, an amalgamation of all he felt entwined with the bitterness of bile in his throat and a churning sense of betrayal.

Quinn's words echoed from somewhere far off in his head: *"Thank you, Mr. Candle."* There was only blackness, and then nothing at all.

———————•———————

Donna waited. The rain came first, and then the police with their impersonal questions: Was Quinn alone? What was Donovan wearing? Did she see where he went? Everything had happened so fast she couldn't remember, and when she'd answered all she could the police reassured her they would do their best to find her husband and nephew.

After they left, Donna called Amanda, but there was no answer. She left a message, waited a couple of minutes, then called Michael and told him what happened. He said he'd be over as soon as he could.

Donna hung up the phone and took a seat by the window, watching the rain squiggle designs on the glass. She stared outside, absently biting her nails as the storm raged on, and when the phone rang, she didn't answer it. Donna knew it was her sister, but the thought of telling Amanda what had happened made her stomach turn. Quinn was right there, he was upset, he had a gun—and Donovan ran after him into the rain.

The kitchen clock ticked. Almost forty-five minutes had passed since she watched him run out the door. An unsteady calm settled over her as she watched the downpour. *He'll be back. He's coming back.*

A loud thunderclap boomed overhead. She rested her head against the glass, waiting.

Donovan didn't come back.

His head swam, afloat in a sea of agony and confusion, but he couldn't remember why. Clarity came when he tried to move: a lightning bolt seared across his shoulder and down his arm.

Donovan remembered the man binding his hands. He remembered the sickening pop of his shoulder separating from its socket. Thinking about it, feeling it again, made him want to vomit.

He was lying on his right side, pressed against something cold and vibrating. Confused, he tried to sit up, but the pain was too severe. He whimpered through clenched teeth, straining to keep from screaming.

His voice was muffled through the thick black fabric covering his head. When he swallowed, he felt the bag pulled tight around his throat. The realization made breathing more difficult, and for the span of a few seconds, Donovan thought he might succumb to claustrophobia.

Got yourself in a pickle, huh?

Donovan heard the gritty voice of his own creation inside his head. If he strained hard enough, he could even smell the phantom stench of Hopper's Camels.

I sure do. What would you do in this situation, Joe?

The answer was immediate: *I'd think my way out.*

It was a simple sobering idea, yet one he seemed to forget time and again. First, he should calm himself, deal with the pain. Then he could rely on his senses to determine where he was, and how he might manage to escape. These things, he realized, were far easier to imagine than perform.

Muscle spasms sent a sharp pain buzzing up and down the length of his arm, accompanied by the endless prick of ghostly needles. Colors sparkled and danced across the darkness. He felt himself starting to slip.

"No," he croaked. "Stay with it. Stay—"

There came a loud jolt, and he cried out as he was shoved forward. He didn't go far, less than an inch by his estimation, but the sudden movement escalated his pain to new heights. This new surge of agony made him aware of the loud hum filling his ears. A pattern of thuds overlay the hum, and the answer sprang out of the dark with the same exuberance as the spots of color before him.

I'm in a car.

He remembered Quinn standing beside the rusted-out skeleton of a Cadillac. He moved his leg, rubbing against something coarse and rounded on one end. *Spare tire.* He imagined himself bundled in the trunk while his captors drove him to some isolated location where he might meet his fate. He'd written a similar scene in his novel, and the whole scenario made him want to laugh.

Fighting his cynicism, he thought about how Joe Hopper escaped his captors.

Hopper didn't escape. He waited until his captors let him out. Seems like as good a plan as any.

He lay there, doing his best to keep his legs from falling asleep while moving his arm as little as possible. The car's acceleration and sputtering stops jostled him around, interrupting his concentration. He clenched his teeth as the car slowed, pushing him against the tire. The pressure on his arm shot fire down his bicep.

He thought about Quinn, struggling with a desire to strangle the kid, but he couldn't help remembering how his nephew had cried as he delivered the message demanded of him. Donovan knew his anger wasn't directed at the boy, but at the one who stole him away and used him as a pawn. That anger numbed the pain shooting out from his shoulder.

The pale humanoid face of Aleister Dullington crept into his mind like a spider, idly spinning a web entangling all his other thoughts. Dullington: the reaper of boredom, Keeper of the Monochrome. A demonic monk of some sort, perhaps, or maybe something else altogether—not that it mattered. What did matter was that people disappeared, seemingly plucked from the planet, and Dullington was the culprit. What mattered was that Donovan was powerless to stop him.

Why, then, was Dullington using his nephew to bait him into capture? And how was it connected to the other missing kids? He found himself facing the same shattered image and still missing a few vital pieces.

The car slowed, sputtering to a stop. The whole undercarriage shook as the engine shut off. He heard an irregular tapping against the car. He also heard muffled voices and footsteps. There came another click, and he gasped as fresh air and cold rain washed over his body.

"Is this the guy?"

This was a different voice, one he didn't recognize—shriller in pitch, high-strung. So far, he'd only seen the bearded man, another clear indication of the setup. He expected Quinn's voice, but if the boy was there Donovan couldn't hear him.

A man grunted. *That's Beardy*, he thought. He felt hands on his arm, and the shock of pain took his breath away. Stars burst before his eyes, and for a moment he felt as though he might faint. Their voices were a thousand miles away, lost in a painful fog shrouding his senses, and when the dim haze began to clear he heard the shrill tone of the first voice speaking to him.

"—suppose you got anything to say to that, huh?"

Donovan swallowed air. His throat was dry. When he tried to speak, no words came.

"Yeah, I thought so. Put him in the room, that's where the king wants him."

He felt a hand on his back pushing him forward. His foot caught against something hard, and he lost his balance. He came down on his shoulder, and the fire coursing through his arm surged into his lungs and out his throat in a scream that seemed to go on forever, masked only by the hiss of rain and the cackles of his captors.

"Guess you have a voice after all, don't you?"

Donovan sank below consciousness, reveling in the numbing dark, catching only pieces of the conversation between the two men.

"—easier next time—"

"—dislocated—"

"—fix it right up—"

Somewhere in that womb-like subconscious state, Donovan pieced together what was about to happen, but he was helpless to stop them. This was going to hurt. Rather than resurface, he dove deeper into those black numbing waters, leaving the realm of consciousness altogether.

The low throb of his arm yanked him out of those murky depths. He came to but discovered he still couldn't move his limbs. Dazed, Donovan felt sheer terror at his sudden paralysis. *They've cut my arms and legs off. Lopped them right off my body.*

Only that wasn't true. He *could* feel his arms and legs. He could wiggle his fingers and toes. Donovan tried to move and felt the hard back of a chair dig into his shoulders. His arms were bound behind the seat, and his ankles were affixed to the chair legs. Something coarse dug into his wrists.

The dark bag was gone. Donovan blinked away the blurriness and examined his surroundings. A closed door stood before him, and a single bare bulb offered the room dim clarity. A couple of empty shelving units stood against the wall, and a small brown bucket sat in the corner next to a pair of large push brooms coated in clumps of dust.

He craned his neck to get a better look but doing so made his arm hurt. The pain shooting through his shoulder was still present but lacked intensity. Bits of words bubbled up to the surface of his memory, painting a nauseating picture. *They popped my arm back into its socket.* Michael dislocated his shoulder once when he was in high school, requiring a sling and eventual surgery. Donovan feared he might need the same—his skin still felt tight, numb, and the sting was far from absent.

"Oh shit…"

His voice resonated in the small space. The sound seemed foreign, and for a moment he entertained the irrational notion that he had somehow awoken as a different person.

Voices mumbled beyond the door. He sucked in his breath, straining to listen to what they were saying. He didn't have to wonder long. The door snapped open, revealing the bearded man. Light glinted off an assembly of the familiar white doorway buttons on his shirt. A vicious acrid stench permeated the room, and Donovan wondered how long it had been since this man bathed.

Beyond the figure he saw a row of boxes with circular windows. *No, not windows. They're dryers.*

The large man entered the room, spilling light onto the machines beyond. What Donovan saw confirmed it: they were in a Laundromat, and this was a storage closet of some kind. A pushcart with a small television entered his view, followed by a short scrawny man in dirty jeans and flannel. He grinned at the sight of Donovan as he pushed the cart into the room. Large ashy boils spotted the man's face. They were round and puffy, and one seemed to pulse. The first word that came to mind was *leper*, and Donovan made himself look away from the man's rotting visage.

"Good to see you're awake. I'd offer to shake your hand, but I guess your hands are tied, huh?"

He squealed with laughter and slapped Donovan's shoulder. The pain was instant, but Donovan didn't cry out, resisting the blaze shooting down the left side of his body. He clenched his teeth, grunting.

Donovan had read stories of torture and interrogation in the news and in books, and he wasn't going to give them what they wanted. For all he knew, these were two sadistic men determined to inflict as much harm on him as possible. So far, their methods were working, but he wouldn't let them know.

The leper frowned. "Cat got your tongue?"

He slapped Donovan's shoulder once more. This time Donovan spoke, but it wasn't the cry they'd hoped for. He looked up at the man and the gray pox covering his face.

"I think they make a cream for that."

The bearded man let out a hearty laugh. The leper's face reddened. Donovan went on: "Don't pop it, though. It'll leave a scar, and then the girls won't have anything to do with you."

The leper grinned, revealing gums riddled with the weird gray pox. He put a hand on Donovan's sore shoulder.

"My friend Kale, he popped your arm out of its socket, and then he popped it back in for you as a courtesy. Keep runnin' your mouth, buddy-boy, and I'll see to it he pops it right the fuck off—along with some other things."

Donovan was about to say something but was silenced by the back of the man's hand. It wasn't a hard slap by any measure, and the words "You hit like a girl" were on the tip of his tongue, but he held them back. *Ease up*, Hopper spoke, *no sense in making things worse*. He swallowed his words and ignored the sting.

"See, me 'n Kale here, we figure you must be pretty important for the king to send for you. I mean, looking at you, you're not half the tall shit he made you out to be. Beats the hell out of me, but who am I to say, am I right, Kale?" The bearded man said nothing. He stood in the corner with his beefy arms crossed at his chest. "Still, if we got any hope of getting out of this prison, we got to listen to him and do what he says."

"What does Dullington want with me?"

The leper shot a glance at Kale, then back at Donovan. He fell into a laughing fit lasting a solid minute. "Dullington? Buddy-boy, what makes you think we serve Dullington?"

His answer left Donovan speechless. He stared at the leper, perplexed by the possibility that there was someone other than Dullington. The word "king" came to mind, and he wondered who—or what—could possibly be higher up the Monochromatic chain than Aleister Dullington?

"Dullington didn't give two shits about us Missing folks—but the king does. He promised us a way out of here. So, we gotta do what he says, and what he says is to leave you here watching the show."

The leper drummed his fingers across the top of the television. Donovan hadn't paid attention to it before, but now he set his eyes upon it. It was a relic by today's standards, small and wide, with rabbit ears jutting from the top and a pair of dials to the right of the screen. The leper reached over, turned the top dial, and stepped back. They watched as the old cathode ray tubes warmed and the screen slowly flickered to life. A fizz of static accompanied the screen's pale glow.

Donovan looked up at the leper, then at the bearded man, and back to the TV. The static hiss ceased as the screen settled on a single image, revealing the outline of a doorway. An announcer's voice came through the set's tinny speakers: "Tonight, on *Fading Out—*"

"Well, buddy-boy, I s'pose we'll leave you to your picture show. Come on, Kale."

Kale unfolded his arms, reached into his pocket and pulled out a handful of coins. He held them before Donovan's face and said, "Much obliged." He turned his hand and let the coins fall over Donovan's lap. Some of them hit the floor and rolled away. The two men shared a laugh and left the room, closing the door behind them. Donovan listened to their chuckles for a few minutes longer before they faded into silence.

The television announcer continued his monologue. Donovan ignored it, trying to figure out a means of escape, but a dull ache hammering into the back of his head made focusing difficult. He remembered the shock of seeing Quinn standing beside that car. *They tricked me. And I walked right into it. How could I have been so stupid?*

So you let your guard down, Joe Hopper spoke. *It happens, kid. Happens to the damned best of us.*

In fiction, he retorted, and then remembered he was having a conversation with a character in his head. Hopper's voice was *his* voice, *his* words. This wasn't fiction, and it certainly wasn't anything Donovan anticipated. The last thing he needed to do was argue with an imaginary friend. He was thirty-five years old and still well away from the depths of senility—or so he hoped.

"Okay," he said to himself. "Think, Don."

He thought about his restraints first, and he tried them. The rope was so tight it cut into his skin and struggling against it chewed up his wrists. His legs were bound just as tight, though his khakis kept the rope from biting his shins. *Beardy probably did the tying. Looks like a guy who'd be good at that sort of thing.*

The leper had called Beardy by name: Kale. Donovan couldn't recall that name, but he knew the man's face. After watching him flicker outside the diner and reviewing the gruesome security footage, he wouldn't forget Kale's face any time soon.

Fading Out began its intro scene on the TV. He paused to watch it for a moment. Focusing on the screen brought minor relief to his headache. A young woman by the name of Jeanna was introduced as a graduate of the state university, class of 2004. She walked down the front steps of her apartment and left the frame. The camera cut to a side shot of her walking down the sidewalk. She spoke to someone off-screen.

"Y'know, it's tough being in the job market right now. Everyone wants years of experience, but no one wants to pay for it." She stuffed her hands in her pockets, staring at the ground while the camera followed. "My parents told me college was my best option, but they couldn't afford it so I had to take on all these loans. I've been out of school for over a decade, and the best I can do is minimum wage. I feel like I wasted my time—and I'll spend the rest of my life paying for it."

The screen faded to black, revealing subtitles: "Jeanna graduated with a degree in Marketing. She has been unable to find a job in her field, instead taking a position at a local retail store."

He frowned. *Story of my life, sister.*

Another segment followed, focusing on the trivialities of her day, her goals and dreams, and the obstacles standing before her. More characters were introduced, along with their own segments detailing how their lives intertwined during the hour-long program. The show played out like a documentary on Millennial dilemmas but had just enough scripted elegance to keep it interesting.

"Interesting" was a loose term. Donovan found the show to be horrid. The concept of reality television was something he'd always considered an oxymoron. This show was no different, and but he saw its appeal. Everyone his age was struggling in some way or another, usually financially. Knowing there were others treading the same waters always soothed the pain.

He yawned, shifting in his seat, awakening the discomfort in his shoulder and the prickling sensation in his fingertips. He wiggled his fingers to keep them from going numb.

"Come on, Don. Think. *Think.*"

He settled his gaze on the shelving units on each side of the door. If he could somehow hop the chair across the room, he might be able to rub the ropes against the edge of the lowest shelf and slowly cut himself free.

It was a good idea until he tried putting it into practice. The chair wouldn't budge.

Probably bolted to the floor.

"Son of a bitch." He struggled against his restraints, allowing his frustration to get the better of him. "Who bolts a chair to the floor? In a Laundromat?"

The hopelessness of his situation began to sink in. No one knew he was there. Donna would be worried sick.

His mind raced with possible outcomes. He saw her pacing the floor of their kitchen, waiting like the wife of a sailor lost at sea, sinking into a mire of depression so deep that the health of their baby suffered.

Oh God, the baby.

The thought of their child growing up without his support terrified him. He saw his child progressing through life without a father. He saw an empty casket being lowered into the ground, his name carved into a marble marker. "Donovan Candle," it read. "Missing, presumed dead." He saw himself years from now, decomposed and still tied to the chair, his dusty rotted skull grinning in the empty luminescence.

Donovan screamed.

He screamed loud and long until his throat burned. His chest filled with fire, and the sounds escaping him singed the air. His screams turned to shrieks, then croaks. By the time he'd expelled his last ounce of energy, he lacked the voice necessary to call for help.

Spent, Donovan slumped in his seat. He saw the reality of his situation, and he knew he must face it: *You are stuck here.*

In his screaming fit, he missed the conclusion of *Fading Out*. The credits rolled. When they finished, the announcer's monologue started again, and a new episode began. The format was the same, starring a different face in a different situation.

Beyond the tired intonations of the episode's subject, Donovan heard little else. He tried focusing on his own thoughts and found it difficult. Buried deep in the dark folds of his brain, he heard the quiet chuckle of his creation offering its own suggestions to his question.

Who bolts a chair to the floor? Puppets do, hoss. They do what their master tells 'em, and if he says, "Seek out Donnie Candle, tie the bastard to a chair, and leave him to die," they ask when and where and how.

He thought about Aleister Dullington, about the fear and terror he'd experienced during that whole ordeal. He never imagined his own dull life would have such an adverse effect on those around him. Nearly two years ago he slaved away in a thankless job, selling identity theft protection, thinking he was making progress in life. So much had changed since then. He used to stick to a routine, and now he did as much as he could to avoid a routine altogether.

You used to be the guy running in place, but Dullington changed that for you, didn't he? Now look where you are. Your wife is probably worried sick. What's she going to do without you around, anyway? She'll be a widow raising a child on her own while you rot.

"No."

No? All right, then. You think it would make a difference if you were still around, safe and snug in your own comfortable life. What makes you think you can protect them? You couldn't protect Donna from being taken last year. You can't stop all those people from disappearing around the city, and you couldn't keep those kids from getting killed. What happens in twenty years when your own kid vanishes off the face of the earth and you're too old to jump to the rescue?

Donovan had no answer. A fading image of his wife hung in the frame of his mind: a photo of her taken during their trip to the shore. He remembered waking before sunrise. Donna was gone, and the strange surroundings threw him off for a few hazy seconds. When he realized he was alone in bed, he sat up and called out for her. She didn't answer.

Panicked, he scrambled out of bed, threw on some clothes, and went looking for her. At first, he thought maybe she'd ventured downstairs for the hotel's free breakfast, but it was much too early for that. When he didn't find her in the hotel, he went outside, and it was there he saw her.

She walked along the shore, absent to the world and lost in her thoughts. Donovan stood at the edge of the parking lot, looking down the slope at her tiny figure. She'd left her shoes in the sand, walking barefoot along the tide.

The sun slowly rose as he stood there, watching Donna make her way along the curve of the beach, and when golden morning light spilled over the world, she turned and saw him watching. Seeing her there was one of the most serene, surreal moments of his life. His panic subsided, and the warm comforting waters of safety took its place.

He clung to that image now. Donna's smiling face rose above the riotous anarchy of those crowded thoughts threatening to consume him. His doubts reached for him, asking their questions and presenting their damning possibilities.

What if he couldn't break free? What would happen to his beautiful wife? He would never know his child. The name "Donovan Candle" would appear in a short newspaper obituary, his legacy outlined by a 100-word character sketch. "Who was he?" they might ask on their way to the Sports section.

I'll tell you who he was. He was a shadow of a man too afraid to make a decision. He was a man who was given every opportunity to achieve happiness, but when it came down to the wire, he was too afraid to act. So afraid, in fact, that he couldn't do what he knew to be necessary.

Wasn't he a writer? Yeah, he thought he was, but he was too afraid to give himself a chance. He put his story in a drawer and forgot about it. His wife had to mail it out for him, because he was too chicken-shit to do it himself. Not that it matters. The book's obscurity mirrors his own. No one remembers either of them.

Donovan wanted to respond to this imaginary jury, again stopping short when he remembered it was all in his head. He took a deep breath, held the air in his lungs for a moment, then exhaled. The jury's words wrapped his brain like barbed wire, sticking in all the right places. All his demons had crawled up from the recesses to put him on trial for the one crime of which he was guilty: Inaction.

He thought back to Dullington's warning and the weight of its message. The life pitch. He'd had to prove he was above the mediocre life he'd established for himself. He had to catch up to the dreams he'd been chasing most of his life. He did catch up, and he held pace for a while, but he never surpassed them.

You have stagnated in your attempt, Mr. Candle.

Dullington's voice was clear over the litany of angry thoughts in his head.

Despite his efforts to break the cycle of monotony, Donovan had allowed himself to be bested by his own fear. He was afraid of the commitment of raising a child; afraid of facing rejection; afraid of doing what was necessary to find the missing people whose files accumulated on his office desk; afraid of admitting the truth to himself.

He was *afraid.*

The jury in his mind spoke up in a single roar: *Donovan Candle, we charge you with the crime of inaction. All you now endure, you have brought upon yourself, and this jury of your peers asks: what do you intend to do about it?*

Breathless, his heart racing and mind a blistering haze, Donovan closed his eyes and felt tears drain down his cheeks.

"I don't know."

The thoughts, the angry voices, even the ingrained intonation of Aleister Dullington fell silent at his response. He was alone except for the television and its interminable broadcast. Court was in recess, destined to return and judge him based on his response, and in the wake of the cacophony he slumped back in his chair. He thought of Donna and all the things he would never be able to tell her.

Tired, overwhelmed, and feeling like a pinnacle of human failure, Donovan Candle blinked away more tears and dove into the black emptiness of his mind. Minutes later, he slept.

———————•———————

The television and its showcase of *Fading Out* went on without interruption, bathing Donovan in the pale, white glow of one episode after another. He wasn't awake to witness the change when it happened but lost in the mire of his own dreams Donovan experienced it all the same.

———————•———————

He was alone on the shore. A soft breeze rolled in with the waves, kissing his face. Donovan wiggled his toes in the sand, squishing the grainy mush between them, and the cold water washing over his feet made him giggle.

The sun rolled past in its arc from East to West, followed by the moon and stars, then sun again. Donovan stood rooted in the sand as the cycle of days and nights moved around him.

At first, the passing of time didn't bother him, but when he reached up to his face and discovered a beard, he realized he was not exempt from time's influence. His hands were wrinkled and covered in brown spots. His fingernails grew into claws, brittle and yellow.

When he tried to move, he discovered the sand was concrete. The tide pulled away, exposing a damp gray landscape beyond. The gray muck around his ankles hardened with the passage of time, cementing him there like a statue.

"No." He shook his gnarled fists. "This isn't supposed to happen. Not like this. Not this soon."

The sun and the moon spun so fast on their celestial axis that their glowing orbs formed a singular path across the sky. Together with the stars they formed an infinite series of solid lines splitting the air above him. He felt himself grow old, his body shutting down with age. Unable to move, Donovan was forced to watch in horror as his own body decayed before him.

Who was that man? asked a voice. It echoed down from the sky and across the barren land. *Who was he?*

Donovan wanted to respond but couldn't. His body had decayed beyond the ability to function. He felt himself collapse against the hardened slab, heard his bones clattering upon impact. He was dead—yet his consciousness remained. His corpse lay there for eons until time slowed, and the waters returned, softening his tomb. His bones sank further into the muck beneath the waves.

Sometime later a bright light filled his skull, and he found his eyes had returned. He opened them.

He was in the backseat of a car. Donna sat in the driver's seat, her hair pulled back into a ponytail. The front passenger seat was empty.

"Where are we going, honey?" he heard himself ask, but his lips didn't move. His mouth wouldn't work. *That's odd.* He put his fingers to his lips, only to meet a blank slate of flesh. He hadn't spoken, because he didn't have a mouth.

"Donna?"

His voice seemed to be coming from a speaker somewhere in the car. A recording, perhaps? He wasn't sure. He couldn't identify the sound's source.

A tuft of Donna's hair lifted away from her neck, and a tiny white body crawled out from underneath it. The Cretin stood upon her shoulder, pointing at him, snickering. Donovan's heart froze.

"She cannot hear you, Mr. Candle."

He turned. Sitting beside him was someone he hoped he'd never see again.

"You," his recorded voice said. Aleister Dullington turned and offered him a grin. He wore a gray three-piece suit with a black tie.

"Indeed. And you cannot speak—or *can* you?"

Donovan's heart thudded in his chest. He wanted out of the car. He wanted to take Donna and run away from this place. Now, before something terrible happened.

"A riddle for you, Mr. Candle." Dullington reclined in his seat. He picked at his fingernails with a letter opener. "If Donovan Candle screams in the woods and no one is around to hear him, does he make a sound?"

"I don't know what you mean." Donovan stared into Dullington's black eyes. Sweat rolled down his forehead, and he realized he could no longer move his arms.

"You will need to figure it out, Mr. Candle. I am not making the rules this time. And neither are you, it seems."

Dullington leaned over so close Donovan could smell his breath, which reeked of rotten fruit. He closed his eyes and tried not to look into the lidless orbs sunken into Aleister's skull.

"I see a malignant light in there now, Mr. Candle. I see it like a dying ember in your head. A cancer that will eat you up one bloody bite at a time if you let it. And believe me, you *are* letting it."

"I don't know…I don't know what you mean."

"You do, Mr. Candle," Dullington hissed. "You know too well. You do, and did you know that in the end, the suicidal man pulls his own trigger?"

Dullington's words were a vibration in Donovan's ear. The back of Donna's head melted, swirling with the car's interior.

"You're insane." His voice hung in the air, stuck in the acrid miasma now filling the car, and he heard Dullington laugh.

"You are the insane one, Mr. Candle. You are the cause of your own failure. The question is, what will do you about it when the time comes? Well, I will give you a hint—you need to act." His black eyes glistened in the dim light. "You have been charged with the sin of inaction."

He reached across the seat and opened the car door. Donovan turned and looked out. The car sat on the edge of a cliff, and far below, black waters beat upon a concrete shore. Out on the horizon, far beyond the black sea, something glowed faintly. At this distance he couldn't be certain, but the object appeared to be a column pulsing with a faint glow. He felt the urge to reach out and grasp the light.

Aleister Dullington sat back in his seat, fingering the tip of the letter opener but saying nothing. Donovan looked at his wife and grimaced at the dripping void of her skull. She was still oblivious to everything happening around her. The white Cretin on her shoulder saw to that, whispering its menacing commands in her ear.

He turned back to the horizon. The glowing column was so far away, and yet he knew if he could just take a leap from that cliff, he might be able to reach it. Donovan climbed out of the car and stood upon the edge.

Behind him, Dullington leaned over the seat and said, "Actions birth definition, Mr. Candle. It is your decision." Then he slammed the door—

———•———

And a light knocking woke him. The ghosts of his dream still haunted his vision when he opened his eyes, but they were quick to scare away as reality set in. Donovan sat up in his seat, gasping at the pain in his neck, shoulders, and back. How long had he been asleep? He couldn't see his watch. The television was off. An odd staleness filled the air that left him with a strange taste on his tongue: familiar but carrying with it bad memories he couldn't quite reach.

Tap. Tap.

The noise startled him. He swallowed air, grimacing. His thirst was overwhelming.

"Hello?" His voice cracked on the second syllable.

A moment passed before he realized something was wrong. The lack of heat in the room gave it away. Before he'd fallen asleep, the room could have easily passed for a sauna. Now, when he craned his neck to look up, what he saw made his heart sink. The bare bulb was there, still on, but its light was no longer yellow. Instead it glowed a soft dull gray. He blinked to make sure he wasn't seeing things. It was still gray.

"Oh God. No."

The tapping at the door carried on in erratic bursts, as though dozens of tiny hands rapped upon the surface. The door itself had lost texture, as had the rest of the room. The television was nothing more than a gray box with dials and antennae.

There was a name for this colorless prison. Most called it the Monochrome.

He didn't have time to ponder his return. The tapping stopped, and a moment later the door opened. A dozen tiny figures marched into the room. Seeing them marching across the floor, standing at attention before him, brought home the reality of his predicament. They snickered and pointed at him, this guy who earned his second chance and blew it. If his captors were to be believed, it would not be Dullington who would come to claim him this time. No, it would be someone else. Someone in charge. This "king" of theirs. But if not Aleister Dullington, who?

"Mr. Donovan Candle. I told you I'd haunt you."

A figure entered from the gray shadows of the room beyond. At first, Donovan couldn't make out him out, but as the figure came further into the dim light, his features became more pronounced.

The face he saw not only angered but frightened him. The last time he'd seen this man in the flesh was on that subway platform, and their meeting was not a pleasant one. Time hadn't been kind to the man, and upon closer inspection, Donovan wasn't sure "man" was an apt description anymore.

"*You*," Donovan whispered.

Dr. Albert Sparrow looked down, grinning.

"Me."

-PART TWO-

-PART TWO-
THE CONTRITE MAN

When our weary traveler confronts his fears and realizes his wrongs, he has but two choices: repent and change, or wallow and die. He is left to stand on the edge teetering between the two, and neither choice will be made until he concludes the choice is his to make.

—Dr. Albert Sparrow
A Life Ordinary: A Comprehensive Study in Human Mediocrity

-6-
ABSENCE

Donna watched the sunrise from the nursery. Sleep tugged at her eyes but worry kept them from closing. Four days had passed since Donovan disappeared. Barring her abduction, it was the longest span of time they had ever been apart.

That span kept growing.

Her days and nights bled into one another, and she slept when her body made her, forcing herself to eat despite lack of appetite. Life without Donovan came to a stop.

"Morning."

Amanda stood in the doorway, wearing Donna's robe and holding a steaming mug of coffee. Her hair was tangled, her eyes puffy.

"Sleep okay?" Donna felt dumb for even asking. Her sister's appearance was answer enough. Amanda walked barefoot across the carpet to stand at the window.

"Never noticed the view from here."

"That's because you hardly visit."

Her sister fell silent. Donna hated small talk. Even more, she hated that all they had to talk about were their missing loved ones.

It had been Amanda's idea to spend the night. After consoling one another over the phone for most of the week, Donna was surprised to hear her sister ask to stay.

"Jeff's burying himself in his work, and I don't have the heart to keep telling Quinn's girlfriend there's no news," she'd said. "So I need a break, sis. Come on. It'll be like old times."

And it was. They'd planned a distracting evening of movies and popcorn, just like when they were growing up. The movie turned out to be drivel, the popcorn slightly burned, and when they realized all they had were each other and the common bond of missing people, things became uncomfortable. Amanda retired to bed early, but Donna stayed awake pacing the house with sullen steps. Just before dawn, she finally came to rest in the nursery.

Amanda sipped her coffee and looked down at her sister. "How are you feeling?"

Donna thought about it for a moment and said, "Very pregnant. Very, very scared."

She spoke in a morose tone that sounded foreign to her ears. Amanda said nothing and turned back to the window. Donna stared at the wall, her mind lost in a labyrinth of speculation.

Donnie, where did you go?

The last four days had gone by in a dim haze, the edges bleeding together to form a seamless, endless portrait of worry. None of those days were as defined as the first, however, and it was back to that first day that her mind constantly wandered.

Michael had joined the police in their search, combing the patch of forest behind Mr. Cafferty's house, and continuing onward even after nightfall. She insisted he wait until morning, but Michael wouldn't hear it.

"If Don's out there," he began, then paused and corrected himself. "He's out there, and I'm going to find him."

Michael returned less than an hour later. His face was pale, and he looked exhausted. Donna didn't ask about his luck, because she already knew. After sending Michael on his way, her imagination turned to more frightening possibilities.

She remembered the time Donovan tried to explain this "Monochrome" to her, several weeks after the incident. They'd gone for a walk after dinner, first through their neighborhood, then through the forest trail which ran behind their row of houses. He squeezed her hand as he spoke. She had a hard time fathoming the things he described to her.

These things, from the person he called Dullington to the creatures that lived in an opposite reality, were impossible. That it explained why a man named George Guffin forced his way into their home and knocked her unconscious was even more unlikely. And then there was his "Cretin" theory for why she couldn't remember certain details—such as his "flickering"—that seemed too convenient. She figured the blow to her head accounted for the gaps in her memory.

What if?

A simple question, but one her writer husband always sought to ask. She now found herself compelled to ask it as well. What if the things her husband tried to explain were real?

But really, white creatures that climb up on your shoulder to distract you? Giants called the "Yawning" that can eat men whole? Aleister Dullington, with big black eyes and jagged teeth? It's fiction, Donna. Things like that don't exist. They can't.

What if?

"Hey."

She looked up to the window, except her sister was no longer there. Amanda now stood in the doorway, and Donna didn't recall seeing her move across the room.

"Yeah?"

"How do you feel about breakfast?"

The thought of it made her stomach grumble, and the baby stirred in her belly. She climbed out of the rocking chair and braced her back. She smiled at her sister, and they went downstairs to eat. It was, as Amanda said, just like old times—if only for a little while.

"**D**o you mind if I smoke?"

Donna shook her head, gesturing to the window. Amanda opened the pane and lit her cigarette. She took two long drags before tipping the ashes into the sink. A gray tendril of smoke squirmed up from the cigarette's ember like a writhing snake in the morning sunlight.

"So...where do you think he is?"

Donna ran her finger across the rim of her glass. Her impulse was to change the subject and find something else to talk about, but the nagging voice in her head wanted otherwise. It wanted to bring everything out into the open, to tell her sister not just where she suspected they were, but what would happen to them if they remained.

Go on, that voice said, *tell her. What would it hurt?*

It'll just make things worse, and she'll think I've gone bonkers.

A year ago, Donovan, Michael, and she decided not to tell anyone what happened. They sat there at the same table and tried to sort things out. Donovan's story was beyond what she expected. There were concrete aspects—she was kidnapped, and they were coerced into doing the same to get her back—but the fantastic elements he described made no sense to her. How could they? An alternate reality? People who flicker and vanish from one to the other?

Now, in the absence of a more logical explanation, she found herself wondering "What if?" once again.

"Donna? You all right?"

She woke from her thoughts. "Yeah, I'm here, but not here."

Those were Donovan's words. Hearing them escape her lips made her heart ache. She looked up at her sister and offered a smile.

"Just lost in thought, huh?"

"Yeah," Donna said. She paused, measuring her words. "Amanda, honey, come sit down. I need to tell you something."

The pace of her heart shot up, and a thousand doubts raced through her mind in that moment. *What's the point of telling her? It will just confuse her. She won't understand. It makes no sense, not even to you.*

And then, behind them all, she heard Donovan whisper, "Tell her everything." It didn't make any sense, and it was almost stupid to think it would do any good, but something about it felt liberating, as if she'd been living with a lie all this time. She was alleviating a burden in doing this, and if it just made her sister even more afraid, then they would be more afraid together.

Amanda finished her cigarette. She gave Donna an odd look as she sat down at the table.

"This," she began, then stopped to think about what she was going to say. The words seemed so dumb, but so right. "Well, this is a story I need to tell you."

She reached out and took Amanda's hand.

"It's not going to make a whole lot of sense to you. Shit, it doesn't even make sense to me, but right now I don't have any answers, and this is the one thing I keep thinking maybe happened to Donnie and Quinn and hundreds of other people."

"Donna, what are you talking about?"

She took a breath, squeezing her sister's hand. "About a year ago, something happened to me. Happened to all of us, really, and it's something we decided not to talk about with anyone."

Amanda frowned. "Go on."

Donna told her story—the parts she could remember, anyway. As the months slipped by, the incident seemed more like a dream than reality. There were holes in her memory, places where the faded portrait of that weekend was wiped clean, and she did her best to stitch together the remaining images into a mosaic of coherent thought. Recounting the details became a chore as she struggled to remember. When she was finished, her sister stared at the table, drumming her fingers across its surface.

"We didn't tell anyone because, well, it would've just complicated things."

"No one would believe you anyway."

She looked at Amanda. "Do you?"

"If I didn't know any better, I'd say your husband made it all up. That's what he does, isn't it? Spends his time in the clouds, making shit up and writing it down?"

Amanda pushed herself away from the table and walked back to the sink. She pulled a cigarette from the pack and lit up. Donna wasn't sure what to say. What *could* she say? She felt dumb for even telling her sister the story, but that insistent voice kept nagging at the back of her brain, telling her she did the right thing, but damned if she could see what good it did.

"It's the honest truth." She rose from the table and went to stand beside her sister. "All I know is my husband's missing, and he believed in this 'Monochrome' world enough to turn his life around."

Amanda blew smoke out the open window. "You know how crazy this all sounds?"

"I do. Believe me." She put her hand on Amanda's shoulder. "Sis, it's the craziest damn thing I've ever heard, but I trust my husband and I believe he saw something you and I would never be able to comprehend."

"It doesn't explain why he's missing again. It doesn't explain where my boy is. It explains jack shit." Amanda crushed her cigarette in the sink. When she turned back to her sister, she was crying. Donna pulled her close and held her.

"Where did they go?"

"I don't know," Donna whispered. She tried to hold back the tears. *Donnie, where are you?*

The phone rang a moment later. She pulled away from her sister, wiped the tears from her cheeks, and kissed her forehead. "Stay strong, okay?"

Amanda nodded. The phone kept ringing. Donna let her hand hover

over it a moment, and she closed her eyes to make a wish. The voice of her conscience spoke up again, only this time it scolded her for getting her hopes up.

Donna answered, and she felt her heart plunge just the same. It wasn't Donovan.

———————•———————

Michael Candle waited for someone to answer the phone. He rubbed the sleep from his eyes, and when he moved his head, a sharp pain ran the length of his neck. He'd fallen asleep at his office desk for the second night in a row.

Clicks of Rosie's fingers on a keyboard came from the next room. They echoed in his head like a giant's booming steps. *Should've gone easy on the drinks last night*, he thought, glaring at the empty bottle of whiskey in the wastebasket. It would be another long day. The pounding in his head seemed to agree.

He was mid-yawn when his sister-in-law answered the phone.

"Donnie?"

Michael closed his eyes. "No, Donna, it's Mike. Sorry."

"It's okay," she lied. He couldn't hold it against her. "Any news?"

"No news yet. There's still no trace of either of them." He waited. Donna didn't say anything, so he went on. "That doesn't mean there *isn't* a trace somewhere. It's a big city, and I'm just one guy. I promised you—"

"It's okay, Mike. Really. I know you're doing everything you can. It means the world to me and Amanda."

"Did she stay with you last night?"

"Yeah, she's here. Do you need to speak with her?"

"No, no, that's okay. I don't exactly have good news for her, either."

"What happened?"

"Brock called me last night. They've matched the killer's prints, and they're working on the last known address. It's not much, but it's better than nothing."

Donna sighed. "I guess you're right."

"It's the best I've got right now. Been too dark these last few days, y'know?"

The line fell silent for a moment. He was about to say goodbye when she finally spoke up.

"Mike," she said, "I told Amanda. About, you know, last year. That weekend."

He pinched the flesh between his eyes. A thousand hammers struck his skull all at once. He looked at the empty bottle in the trash. *Never again.*

"I'm not sure now's the best time to start telling the truth about that weekend."

"I disagree."

Obviously. The headache surged.

"I think we should reconsider what Donovan told us, Mike."

"I thought we agreed not to talk about this ever again?"

"Things are a little different now, don't you think?"

"They *are* different now, Donna, but that doesn't mean we need to resort to ghost stories to explain them."

He could hear her thinking over the phone. They'd gotten along well enough over the years, but whenever they happened to clash Donovan was always there to break them apart. They didn't have that luxury now, and he feared his call was about to turn sour.

"Mike, listen to me. What if Don's right?"

"You have to be kidding. What Donovan told us was bullshit, and I've spent the last year trying to forget it. If you want to chalk it up to a momentary lapse in sanity or, hell, even post-traumatic stress, you go right ahead. But don't you dare tell me for one second that you think he's right."

The phone went quiet for a moment, and then Donna cleared her throat. She spoke slowly, evenly, making sure he heard every word.

"Tell me something, Michael Candle. What do you remember?"

"I remember enough."

"No, you tell me right *now*, goddammit. What do you remember?"

He sighed. "I remember Don showing up at my house that night. I remember talking to someone on the phone, but—" A flash of static buzzed through his head. What fragments of memory remaining were hazy, out of focus—just like they always were. His headache intensified.

"But you can't remember who." He heard the smirk in her voice. "I remember there were other people there with me down in that subway, but I can't remember a single name or face."

"What's your point, Donna?"

"I already made my point, Mike. I think Donnie's right."

"That's impossible."

"No, what's impossible is you, Michael Candle." He couldn't tell if she was crying or yelling now. Maybe both. "Your brother idolizes you. He'd walk through hell to help you. The least you could do is consider his point of view, no matter how crazy it sounds. And you know what I think? I think you're too afraid to admit he could be right."

"Donna, this is crazy. Listen to yourself. You need to calm down—"

But the phone was dead. He waited until the connection clicked over to a dial tone before hanging up.

Michael rubbed his temples. That was the second Candle he'd managed to piss off in the span of a week. *I'm on a roll.* He went to take a piss.

When he was finished, he popped a couple of aspirin and returned to his office. On the way, he stopped by Rosie's desk. She stared at the computer monitor, her eyes framed by dark circles. She wore a pair of ear buds. He walked around to see what she was watching.

It was a video stream of that TV show he'd seen advertised, and the one she was always talking about. *Fading Out.* He hovered over her shoulder and pointed to the screen.

"This what I'm paying you to do?" He tried to make it sound harmless, even forcing a smile as he said it, but it must not have come out right. She looked up at him and frowned.

"Sorry, Mr. Candle."

"No big deal. Been kinda quiet around here, anyway. Go ahead and watch it if you want. Just be sure to turn it off if someone drops in."

She smiled. "Thanks." She said something else, but a sharp hiss of static burst through his head, and he found he couldn't focus on what she was saying. The phantom hammer continued pounding a bed of nails into his brain. When Rosie stopped speaking, he smiled and told her he was going out for a drive.

"I'll be back sometime this afternoon to lock up."

Rosie didn't say anything. She was back to watching her video stream.

He drove with the windows down. The morning was crisp enough that some wore jackets, but he welcomed the cool air. It was a nice break from the week's humidity. Michael had no destination in mind, he just wanted to drive and clear his head.

Music from the radio gave way to the morning news report. There was a story about the city's proposed budget, followed by one about a shooting uptown. The reporter ended with commentary on the ongoing search for Richard Henza before cutting to commercial.

He thought of Donovan. He always told his little brother that people just disappeared sometimes, and their last conversation replayed in his head.

Stubborn to the end, old boy. Donovan's insistence that something ethereal was behind the disappearances irked Michael. The events surrounding Donna's kidnapping made little sense to him, but in the absence of reason he had to make do with what he could.

But there are too many gaps.

Donna's prying had uncovered this unsettling truth, and he had a hard time admitting it to himself. The suggestion that Donovan was right went against his entire code of logic. Up was up, down was down, and two plus two equaled four. There was little room for the "other side of reality" argument which Donovan so vehemently promoted.

Growing up, he'd always been a straight-A student. Language and vocabulary came easy to Donovan; Michael, on the other hand, was a math and science kind of guy. He excelled where his brother did not, and vice-versa. When Michael had trouble "verbing his nouns," as their father put it, it was Donovan who helped.

He'd developed a hell of a memory while growing up. He could still remember the quadratic equation, the first two rows of the periodic table, and if pressed he could recite all the presidents backwards to front in less than sixty seconds. Their grandfather once described Michael's memory as a "steel trap." When he chose private investigation and the cases began to accumulate, having that memory was a godsend.

He could remember endless minutiae, but he could not recall the details of what happened that weekend.

The truth was, not remembering scared the hell out of him. Donovan wanted to dig up those frightening facts and examine them, but Michael would have none of it. He'd lashed out at his brother like a frightened animal, and now he'd sparred over it with Donna, too.

"She's right," he mumbled, ashamed of his actions. Donovan admired him so much that he even based a character on him: the gruff detective Joe Hopper. He'd read an earlier draft of Donovan's book and enjoyed it.

But that was fiction, and Donovan had other stories. Neither he nor Donna believed Donovan, but they could see the fear in his eyes when he recounted his version of the events. Donna accepted it out of love for her husband, despite the possibility that the stress of the situation may have tipped him overboard. Michael, who was right there for most of it, chose ignorance. Now that choice haunted him.

Donna's voice resounded in his head. *You're too afraid to admit he could be right.*

He *was* too afraid to admit it. Everything Michael Candle knew of the world was based on a system of logic and reason, but now he found himself backed into a corner against impossible ideas. He'd spent most of the year building up excuses for what happened that weekend, but there were things he could no longer reconcile with logic.

Why was my brother so afraid? And why was he so convinced? What if he is right?

Michael steered the car onto the bypass and accelerated up the ramp. He entered mid-morning traffic and headed for a destination that, until a few moments before, hadn't even been on his mind.

For one of the first times in his life Michael Candle asked himself, "What if?" Then he asked himself if he could live up to the image his brother had painted of him.

Fearful, he spoke to the empty car: "Only one way to find out."

The entrance to the Yellow Line was as he remembered it. Trash littered its steps, and an acrid stench rose from the black depths. Michael stood beside his car for ten minutes, sizing up the place and waiting for someone to emerge. Last time he was here in the company of two others, but they hadn't been alone. There were homeless people living down there, and though he and his brother met no opposition, he was sure they could be dangerous if they wanted to be.

When no one came running out to greet or attack him, Michael opened the door, reached in, and pulled his Glock from its holster on the console. He'd purchased it after Donna's abduction, and only started carrying it with him since Donovan disappeared, figuring he could finally put that conceal-and-carry license to use.

He pulled back on the slide, chambering a round. Then he took a flashlight from the glove compartment, locked the doors, and walked to the top of the steps. He thought about calling out, but that voice in the back of his head suggested making his presence known to anyone down there might be a bad idea. Instead, he clicked on the flashlight as he descended into the derelict subway line.

The flashlight's short reach made the going slow, and he measured his breaths to ease the pounding in his chest. He took his time, feeling his way before taking a step. He wanted to believe he was alone, but there were things that told him otherwise.

Hushed voices lingered in the air. They ceased whenever he would turn to listen in their direction. Sometimes he caught movement at the edge of the beam, but when he redirected the light it was met by nothing but remnants of years past.

He crept down the stairs to each landing with increasing caution. The further he went down, the longer it would take to return to the top, and for a moment he pictured himself a lone explorer traveling deep into an uncharted cave system. Then he realized no one knew he was there, and that if something happened to him, he would be no better off than his brother. Or worse.

Stop it, he told himself, and kept on until he reached the token booths. He climbed over the turnstiles, nearly losing his balance on the other side. When he steadied himself, he moved his light over the causeway, and nearly fainted from shock at the sight of a human body.

Michael approached slowly, then kicked the mannequin, punting its wooden head across the room until it clattered against a far wall. He laughed, chiding himself for being so stupid, but when he paused to catch his breath the laughter continued. It went on for a solid minute, and he strained to identify the source. His heart pounded with tribal fury, and he had trouble keeping the light steady enough to discern shapes in the distance.

The laughter stopped. He wanted to believe it was a mere echo, but echoes didn't carry on for so long. He was not alone.

Michael followed a path of garbage toward the steps and descended to the next concourse. There was the platform. Beyond it was a good six-foot drop, a tunnel snaking its way underneath the city like a parasite. He couldn't remember how long it had been since the transit authority stopped using these rails, and he wondered when the first of the homeless laid stake to this unused territory.

A revelation struck him while he stood at the edge of the boarding platform. This was their place, and he nothing more than an intruder. If they attacked him it would be with good reason, and he wondered just what the hell he was doing down there in the first place. There was no sign of Donovan, Quinn, or his mysterious heckler for that matter. He was alone, and the longer he stood there, the more uneasy he became.

Michael made his way back to the street. He encountered no one, and the only sounds were that of his steps, his breathing, and his beating heart. The late morning sun pierced his eyes, and he squinted all the way to the car. There was still plenty of time, plenty of other places he could check, but one stood out in his mind: the alley where the murdered kids were found.

The alley ran between the Suds-O-Plenty Laundromat and the hollow remains of a storefront. The two buildings shared a parking lot, and the entire area was cordoned off with yellow police tape.

He circled the block once to make sure he was alone, then parked along the curb. A stiff breeze caught him off guard and sent a chill down his back. He was halfway across the empty lot when he realized he'd left the gun in the car.

Probably won't need it anyway. This whole place looks deserted—

Three men walked around the corner of the building. Two wore dirty sweatshirts and sweatpants; another—the largest of the three—wore the tattered remains of a button-down and slacks. All three men wore small white pins on their shirts, each adorned with the same black outline of a doorway, and the biggest man wore the most.

The trio cackled about something. Their voices carried across the lot: coarse, heavy, and drunk.

"Hey."

He raised his hand. The three men froze in their tracks, startled by his sudden attention. They glanced at one another nervously.

"Help you with somethin', mister?"

Michael didn't say anything. He was cataloging their appearances, noting their details, and effectively sizing them up. These three stooges all had their individual quirks. There was Larry on the right, with a large, gray mass sprouting from his forehead. It was the largest boil Michael had ever seen, and it seemed to pulse like an artery. He stared at Michael with a sly grin.

Curly, in the middle, had a nose that bent slightly to the right and a weird twitch in his eye. He was the first to speak, and now wore a smile spotted with missing teeth. The ones that remained were the color of malt liquor and nicotine.

The man on the right, Moe, was by Michael's estimation the most dangerous. He was the largest, with a beard sprouting from his face like a wild bush and a neck the size of a tree stump. He watched Michael with an intense stare that threatened to a burn a hole through him.

"Hi there, guys. Fine day, isn't it?"

"S'pose it is," Curly said. Moe crossed his arms and grunted. Larry said nothing.

"You see a man come around here by the name of Donovan? Dress shirt, khakis, maybe a tie?"

"No," Curly grunted, "can't say we have."

Michael smiled. "I see. So, *you* haven't. How about your friends here?"

Curly shot a glance at his comrades. After a moment of silence, Larry shrugged his shoulders. Moe, however, remained tacit, and kept staring. Michael felt a hint of sweat on his brow. He met Moe's gaze.

"How about you, friend? Cat got your tongue?"

"No," Moe grunted, "thinking."

Michael reached into his pocket and fished for some change. He pulled out a penny, held it up, and grinned. "For your thoughts?" He let it fall to the man's feet.

Larry put his hand on Moe's shoulder and cleared his throat. "Our friend doesn't talk much, so I'll speak for him. This man you're looking for, he could've had nice clothes and a good bit of money on him. He could've looked soft, and weak, and maybe some ugly fucks like my friends here could've done horrible things to him. Maybe they beat the shit out of him, took his money, and then beat him some more. Maybe they killed the son of a bitch."

Michael stopped smiling and locked eyes with Moe. "Maybe," he said. "And maybe it would be damned unfortunate if that happened. See, Donovan's my brother, and I'd kill just about anyone who hurt him."

Moe smiled, a thin line cutting across his face like a sharp blade.

"Can't say we've seen him," Larry said. "Now, if you don't mind, we'll be on our way."

He let loose a sharp squeal of a laugh that caught Michael off guard. Moe and Curly joined the laughter as the trio walked around him and across the parking lot. Michael chewed his lower lip. His shoulders were tense, and he discovered his hands were balled into fists.

What just happened?

There was something wrong about those men—that much was certain— but between the weird pox on Larry's face, the intense conversation, and their white pins, he couldn't decide which was more alarming. It was something he was not sure he would ever understand.

Walking back to his car, Michael felt confused and scared. He wondered if exploring the city's underbelly was a waste of time, or if there was any credence in the homeless man's affronting attitude.

He wondered if his brother was okay, or if he was lying dead in a gutter somewhere.

Michael climbed into the car. He sat with one hand on the steering wheel. The other traced the contours of the gun.

What if?

That question was what led him to this point. He was so intent on exploring one side of it that he failed to recognize the darker possibilities beyond its silver lining. Now, in the absence of an answer, Michael Candle discovered the other side of that question was a frightening place to be.

AMONG THE SHADES

The drab unlight of the Monochrome stung Donovan's eyes. He stared at the blank walls for a moment, frightened and confused, unsure of where he was. When the small white body of a Cretin scampered across the floor and crawled under the door, he remembered. Days of emotion rose from his stomach and into his throat, burning.

Muscles in his wounded shoulder awoke in agony, sending fire shooting down the length of his torso. He clenched his teeth, flexing his fingers and toes as best he could. His joints throbbed, and his neck was a knotted mess of strained tissue. Familiar pins and needles jabbed into his extremities. He wondered how long he'd slept, or how long it had been since they brought him here. He wondered if this discomfort was like what Donna felt during one of her fibro flares.

He wondered about her and his brother, and if they would come looking for him.

'Course they will, hoss.

He pictured Joe Hopper leaning against the wall, his battered trench coat stretched tight across his broad shoulders, fedora tipped down to cast a shadow over his eyes, and a cigarette hanging from his mouth. Donovan could almost smell the stench of nicotine. *They'll come lookin'. Can't say they'll find you, but they'll look.*

"Little consolation," Donovan grunted. His voice echoed in the vacant room. He blinked and stared at the place where he'd imagined Hopper once stood. *Losing my mind.* His stomach rumbled in agreement.

He hadn't had a proper meal in days. Sparrow's followers had fed him a total of six times since his capture. His visitors were all young men and women, in their late teens or early twenties. Some of their faces looked familiar. Each time they brought him a dirty bowl of gruel and a mug of lukewarm water. None of them acknowledged his pleas, sometimes refusing to look at him at all.

His stomach growled again, and he forgot about their lost faces. How long had it been since he'd had a visitor? He couldn't remember—it was hard to tell how many days had passed in this place. The Missing took his watch, and there was no sunlight with which to mark temporal passage. His head joined the aching chorus of the rest of his body.

They're starving me. This is what Sparrow wants. Though their reunion was short-lived, Sparrow's grating, nasally voice still filled Donovan's head:

"It is funny how sides have reversed. Just like flipping a coin, Donovan Candle, you never know which side will land face-up."

Donovan's memory of their conversation was fuzzy at best. He clung to details, searching for something to keep his mind off the growing discomfort in his belly.

"You look as though you've seen a ghost. You're white as a sheet."

Not a ghost. Something else. He'd stared into the sunken eyes of something wearing the face of a man, but he knew better. This was not the same Dr. Albert Sparrow he'd encountered before. No, this man was something else altogether.

"Have no illusions, Don Candle. This is going to hurt."

Sparrow was right about that. Donovan sank into a mire of fatigue and hunger, slowly weakening as one moment bled into the next.

Stay focused, hoss.

Donovan attempted to make mental lists of his observations. He restated the facts aloud to four bare walls, screaming for hours until his voice was gone, and his throat ached. He labored at his restraints again until he couldn't stand the pain any longer. After working himself into complete exhaustion, Donovan Candle began to cry.

Once he thought he heard Donna crying from somewhere beyond the door, and he was struck with the mortifying realization that whatever had made him flicker had also been done to her. As the crying grew closer, he realized that it wasn't Donna at all. That low, mourning sob was not of human origin. Memories of those gaunt figures known as the Yawning came rushing back, and he developed an acute series of shivers that would not go away.

The hours passed as they always did. Donovan found himself sinking deeper into a weakened stupor, and he reached for anything that might keep his mind sharp.

Think about the wife, Hopper said. *Think about the baby. Think about the book, about your brother, about the nephew. Stay with me, hoss.*

He looked up and saw his creation standing over him. Joe Hopper shared similar physical traits with Michael, right down to the stubble and rigid jaw. When Donovan thought about the bar fight in chapter two, a purple knot appeared just below Hopper's chin.

"That's some shiner you got there, Hopper."

You bet, old friend. Hopper knelt before him. *Hell of situation you're in, hoss. Any ideas how to get out of it?*

"Still trying to think my way out." His voice slurred, its echo slithering about the gray room like a drunken serpent. "No dice, though. Not since the last time you asked."

Too bad. Bein' lost here among the shades ain't no way to be, but I need you to stay focused, hoss. If you can't think your way out of this, we're both fucked.

Donovan reached deeper into the murk and grasped something. What came of it was a single white button adorned with the outline of a door.

Joe Hopper climbed to his feet and reached into his pocket. He produced the same button and held it before Donovan's eyes.

Doors open and close all the time. Ever thought about what happens when you stand between?

"I don't understand."

Hell, me neither. Just thinking out loud, hoss. I do reckon, though, this TV show's got something to do with it. Remember Quinn's room?

He did. He thought about the postcard affixed to Quinn's corkboard: *"You are invited to attend The Great Fade-Out!"* It had the same door logo.

Been seein' a lot of these lately, hoss. Maybe you ain't been paying attention, but I have. Somethin' else I noticed? All these kids sure look sorta familiar, don't you think?

Donovan sat up in his seat. The fog lifted from his mind, if only for a moment, and it was enough to offer some clarity on the situation. There were questions to which he still needed answers, but damn it all, he'd finally found the connection that had eluded him for months, and it had been in front of his face the entire time.

Hopper stuffed the pin back into his pocket. He leaned against the wall, folded his arms across his chest, and nodded. *'Atta boy.*

A loud knock came from the door, startling him out of his trance. He glanced back to the corner. Joe Hopper was gone.

The knocking continued. Before, the Missing came to feed him without notice or fanfare. Sparrow was the only one who bothered to knock. He braced himself for who might lie in wait beyond the door.

Quinn stepped into the room. His crooked nose was swollen, the surrounding flesh painted a sickly mixture of purple and yellow.

Donovan recalled the grainy footage of Quinn's abduction and smirked. "You look like hell. I'd hate to see the other guy."

Quinn looked away. His jaw trembled. "I'm so sorry."

Donovan shook his head. He understood now that Quinn didn't have much of a choice in recent events.

"Don't be." His stomach growled. The room took on the smell of warm fast food when Quinn entered. He looked down at the brown bag in Quinn's hands. "Please say that's for me. They're killing me with this gray crap."

Quinn snorted, recoiling from the stench.

"Haven't they let you up to, you know…" He motioned to the stains on his uncle's clothes.

"No," Donovan grunted, suddenly embarrassed. "I've had to sit here in my own shit." He watched Quinn retrieve a cheeseburger from the paper bag. His stomach growled.

"I hope the burger's still hot," Quinn said, holding it up so Donovan could take a bite. "I had to go all the way over to the restaurant on Front Street and bring it back here."

Donovan paced himself, mindful of what gorging might do to his insides, and when he finished the burger, Quinn offered him a cool bottle of water. After days of slurping gray slop and drinking warm water, this meager offering was a banquet.

"How did you get this food?"

Quinn's cheeks flushed. "I had to steal it. The others, they took my wallet, took Donna's pendant—"

"No, I mean, how did you get this food, Quinn? How did you bring it over when you flickered?"

"I don't know," Quinn whispered. "Flickered? What are you talking about?"

Donovan fell silent and thought for a moment.

"When I was here before—"

"You were here before?"

Donovan nodded. "Not in this room, but here in the Monochrome. It's a long story. Let's just say Sparrow and I have a history." He paused, collecting his thoughts. "Things were different. There was someone else in charge, and he only let the other missing people out once a day to feed. He wouldn't let them bring anything back over, either. Not unless he wanted them to."

He remembered using George Guffin's handgun against the Yawning. *Lot of good that did.*

Quinn took a sip of water, thinking. "Someone else in charge. Was his name Dullington?"

"It was. How do you know that?"

"I've heard the others whisper his name, but not much else. Sparrow forbids speaking about Dullington." A shiver crawled down Quinn's spine. He shook it off. "The others, they're afraid of Sparrow. The one they call their king."

"I'm not surprised." Memories of that day behind the bookstore came back to him. He remembered the cold metal of Sparrow's gun pressed against his forehead, the old man's snide tone. "Do you know what happened to Dullington?"

Quinn shook his head. "All I've heard is that things were different. One day they both vanished, and Sparrow returned sometime later. More water?"

He offered up the bottle. Donovan drank slowly, cherishing the cold, and thanked his nephew when he was done.

"Point is," Donovan said, "last time I was here, it felt different. It's hard to describe, but the air was tighter. There was tension everywhere. Being here felt like pulling on both sides of a piece of string, except you're the string. Now it doesn't." He stopped to think, then looked down at Quinn. "What happened after the big guy hit you?"

Quinn seemed surprised. Donovan chuckled. "We were looking for you. Well, I was. The last thing I expected was for you to come to me."

"Everything's still kinda fuzzy. I woke up in a large room. It was dark, but there was a wall of old TV sets in front of me, playing episodes of *Fading Out* over and over. I think I passed out sometime after that, and when I woke up everything was gray, and I wasn't tied up anymore. There were other people, too. They were dirty and scared, but mostly they just looked sad. Funny thing, though, they were all wearing these white pins—

" Quinn pulled back his shirt collar, revealing the same, circular ornament. "They put it on me while I was out. The ones in the room told me not to take it off."

"Or else what?"

The boy shrugged. "I guess I was too scared to find out."

A low guttural sob echoed from beyond the open door. Donovan sucked in his breath. The hairs on his arms stood up.

"It's the Yawning."

Quinn shot to his feet, scrambling to gather the food wrappers. He crumpled the paper bag in his hands.

"I've gotta go."

"Quinn, wait." Donovan fanned out his fingers as if to reach for the boy.

"I can't, Don. If they catch me here, we're both dead." He closed the door a few inches, then stuck his head into the room and said, "I'll try to make it back here, okay? Promise."

The door closed, and Donovan was alone again. He listened to Quinn's rapid steps as he ran through the building. Another moan echoed from somewhere beyond those walls, making Donovan's blood run cold. He held his breath to quiet his pacing heart.

The low cries died into silence after a few minutes, but his heart kept on racing. He'd seen what the Yawning could do to a person. Knowing that Quinn was alone out there with that thing terrified him.

He'll be okay, hoss. Donovan looked up, expecting to see Hopper leaning against the wall again, but he was nowhere to be found. *You didn't ask him about the TV show. Or why Sparrow has you here.*

"I've got my suspicions. Quinn's just a bystander in all this, anyway."

Just like the rest of those dead kids?

"Maybe. Can't say for sure. Need more facts."

A whole lotta good it's doing you tied up in this room while the pieces to the puzzle are runnin' 'round outside, huh?

Donovan closed his eyes and ground his teeth together. "A whole lot of good it's doing me sitting here, having hunger hallucinations and talking to a figment of my imagination parading as my conscience. You're not helping, Hopper. If you want to help, you figure a way out of this room for me while I take a nap. How's that sound?"

His words echoed off the walls. Donovan opened his eyes and waited. Joe Hopper did not respond.

"Yeah," Donovan mumbled, "that's what I thought."

———————•———————

Quinn saw the Yawning before it saw him. He froze in the Laundromat entrance. The white rubbery creature stood mere feet away alongside the building, staring across the blank street.

He sucked in his breath. The giant thing slowly rocked on its spindly legs, its knuckles scraping the ground in long slow arcs.

Shit, he thought, and doubled back to find another way out. He tiptoed between rows of cubes. Here in the Monochrome, the washing machines were just pieces of empty geometry that reminded him of gray cardboard. He wandered between the rows before turning a corner. There he found an exit, but the door was barred from the other side.

He spun around, his heart pounding a hypnotic beat that intensified when the Yawning uttered another sorrowful moan. Panic was a threat, creeping on the outer reaches of his mind, waiting for the right moment to take hold. He resisted it as best he could, fighting to stay calm. Sweat beaded on his forehead, and he wiped it away with his sleeve.

Another moan floated across the room. The Yawning lumbered past the entrance one giant step at a time. *It's looking for me*, he realized.

He waited, taking deep breaths to calm the bass drum in his chest. He thought of his girlfriend and the way her smile made him feel weightless sometimes. He wanted nothing more than to hold her again, and if he escaped this place it would be the first thing he'd do.

But you're not getting out of here if you cower in a hole. Quinn sucked in his breath and left his hiding place, tiptoeing toward the entrance. The Yawning was silent for a few minutes, but he could hear its slow shuffle. He waited, listening as its footsteps moved farther away with each stride. *It went around the corner. Down the street. It must think I snuck out the back.*

He learned early on that the Yawning were not the brightest creatures, and he likened them to simple-minded prehistoric beasts. The Yawning's unassuming demeanor, with the way it stared and wandered, hid its predatory qualities. Quinn learned this within hours of flickering into the Monochrome, witnessing a Yawning chase and devour a man in a single bite. Thinking back to that first day made his skin crawl.

He thought of his girlfriend again, desperate to maintain a fraction of sanity in this impossible place. The Monochrome was the stuff of fantasy. His presence here defied a reality he'd once accepted as fact, but that side of things—with its color and warmth—was long gone.

This side of town was foreign to him—after all, his parents had always warned him away from it, and what good was the dead side of town anyway?—but he knew enough to get his bearings. Just outside was a cracked sidewalk, and beyond that was a street full of potholes and fading traffic guides. Across the way was an empty slate of a building that, in another reality, was a hollowed-out department store.

In this place, everything was a copy of everything else, with no texture, no color, no life. This was limbo, and Quinn wondered if everyone here was dead.

I'll never look at things the same again, he realized, slowly peering around the corner of the doorway. The Yawning was gone. Quinn expelled the air from his chest and stepped out of the dilapidated building.

"Stupid thing," he whispered, and immediately wished he'd said nothing. He saw movement from the corner of his eye. His heart inched its way up his throat as he looked down at the curb.

Sitting on the corner was one of the tiny white bastards, with its arm supporting its head in a Thinker pose. It watched him with beady black eyes. When he stepped back, the Cretin tilted its head, grinning.

It leaned forward and rapped its fists against the ground.

What's it doing? He stood with his knees bent, ready to sprint if necessary.

The Cretin continued its rapid knocking. Its whole body fell into the rhythm, performing an odd savage dance to accompany the tiny pecks against the ground.

Another Cretin emerged from the storm drain, joining its counterpart in the strange ritual. Then another, and another. He counted fifteen before he broke free of his trance and finally turned to flee. More of them crawled out of the drain at the opposite corner, and he stepped on one as he ran. It squealed like a mouse.

This isn't happening. This is not *happening. I've lost my fucking mind. When I wake up, I'm going to be locked away in a padded room somewhere. This. Is. Not. Happening.*

The Yawning's low sob stated the contrary. It bounded along on its spindly legs from around the corner of a building. There it paused and raised its rubbery arm, beckoning to him as he ran past. Quinn's heart thundered as he pumped his legs to keep going. His chest burned.

Come on, it hasn't been that long since you were on the track team. Move your lazy ass.

He'd gone three blocks before complete panic set in. The Monochrome's lack of detail or texture was confusing. His landmarks were gone. All the gray buildings looked the same, and he couldn't remember which street he was on or where the steps to the Yellow Line station happened to be.

Quinn ran another block and turned a corner before stopping to catch his breath. He looked up at what should have been a street sign, but its panels were empty. *Corner of Nothing and Nowhere*, he mused, doubling over to vent the pressure from his lungs.

More moans filled the empty air, accompanied by a constant underlying drone. The incessant hum sounded like a hive of bees, but he knew better. Down in the subway tunnels, he'd seen the tracks covered with the writhing bodies of those little bastards, and the sound of them scuttling together made him shiver.

"Hey."

He didn't pay attention to the voice at first. He was still rooted in place, listening to the scratching drone of static headed down the adjacent street. The creatures of the Monochrome were looking for him, and if he didn't move soon, they would find him for sure.

"Kid. Hey. Over here."

Quinn searched the empty street for another sign of life in color, but nothing caught his eye.

"Up here."

Two floors up, in the building across the street, a scrawny hand beckoned to him. A head popped into view. He saw a red beanie covering strands of long black hair. The woman waved.

"Are you blind?"

He was about to reply when a rumbling in the earth ripped through the area. For a moment, Quinn had no idea what was happening. There was a pain in his back and bottom, and he realized he'd been thrown off his feet by the tremor.

When things settled and his clarity returned, he heard the woman shrieking for him to get up right now and move his ass. Amidst the droning and the trembling, he made out three distinct words: "Don't look back."

His instincts betrayed her warning, acting impulsively to do the very thing she wished him not to. Quinn climbed to his feet, looked back, and stood in awe. The creatures—thousands of them—rose in a singular mass, forming a chaotic rippling body like water.

The pale wave didn't move quickly or without purpose. Its white writhing surface rose to a crest along the street, crashing down in a methodic free-fall at the corner only to rear back just before impact. The wave hovered there, watching him with thousands of tiny black eyes that blinked in unison.

The fleshy mass writhed upon itself, building up one layer atop the next. Quinn's mind filled in the rest. He saw it crashing down upon him, an army of Cretins and Yawning chomping and scratching, consuming him one bite at a time until there was nothing left.

"*What are you doing? Are you fucking crazy?*"

His feet found the will, and they tore the rest of him free from the street just as the wave crashed at his heels. The woman in the building shrieked again, but he didn't make out her words.

That tiny nagging voice chanted in his head: *You can't run forever.*

I'll damn well try, he thought, shifting direction to the other side of the street. The wave crashed again at his heels. The whole world rattled and hummed beneath its weight, but Quinn didn't stop. He thought of his family, and he thought of Wendy. He saw their faces in the distance, through the burning red haze of his mind while he fled for his life.

Don't stop, they told him.

The wave of creatures roared behind him, and Quinn kept on running.

-8-
THE STRINGS

Albert Sparrow watched the boy through a thousand tiny eyes, feeling the rush of malignant energy sizzle through his fingertips. His pets were ravenous—he felt their aches, their urges resonating within him. They craved flesh and its many treasures. *Feed us*, they begged.

He was several blocks away when the Cretin saw the boy emerge from the Laundromat. Sparrow felt the creature's urgency, and within a moment its eyes became his. *Yes, the nephew. Another insect. I don't need you anymore.*

The children of the Monochrome pleaded with him, crying out for sustenance. *We do. So much flesh. Give him to us. Let us savor him.*

He peered through the emptiness, feeling the call of a thousand pale servants eager to please their king. Their eyes were like windows, and he saw them crawling beneath the streets, white rats ready to serve, to *feed*.

"Go then. Take him. He's yours."

The ground trembled beneath his feet as their bodies collectively shuddered in ecstasy. Their voices combined in a low hypnotic drone as they became one entity. *Music*, he thought.

His pets emerged from their subterranean home, congealing into a monstrous sea of eyes and teeth. Sparrow watched with glee as they pursued their prey. When they crashed down at Quinn's feet, Sparrow let out a shrill laugh that echoed off the surrounding buildings.

He watched through their eyes until the link weakened. Sparrow resisted, willing himself the focus to see beyond them, but his influence was already failing him. A few moments later they were gone, and he was alone once more.

A sudden fatigue washed over him accompanied by a gaping emptiness in the pit of his stomach. He'd once known that feeling as nausea, but that was long ago. Now the sensation was just a black hole pulling at his insides. He took a few steps toward the adjacent building and touched the wall to steady himself.

"You said the sight would come, but nothing was ever straightforward with you, was it?"

He closed his eyes, remembering the voice in the light.

You were once bound to humanity, a prisoner of its many tethers, but now I have freed you from that banal coil. You are no longer his *puppet. Now the strings are* yours. *Yours to pull. Yours to cut if you wish.*

Aleister Dullington promised him so much, but those promises were just more lies, gentle tugs on his puppet strings to guide him where Dullington wanted him to be. Lies to make him believe he was different; lies to lead him away from the city, across the demarcations, and into the true desert beyond.

Something happened when they reached their destination. A great light filled his eyes, and in that light spoke a voice he recognized. A voice he'd heard in his darkest moments, urging him to take the steps necessary to break free of his chains. The voice told him to sever his ties by taking a life. A blood sacrifice to prove his commitment and break the bonds of mediocrity holding him.

Something happened. The light filled his eyes, his mind, and then...

Nothing.

His memory was gone from him. He couldn't recall returning to the city. All he remembered was the voice, its truths, and the gifts it gave him.

The gifts. The sight, the power of will over the creatures of this existence, mastery over the chains binding Monochrome and Spectrum, and keeper of their keys. *But in time,* the voice told him. *I deliver you into this world like a young babe in the wilderness. You must grow strong.*

The cost of his weakness was already high. He'd lost a third of his army to the influence of a few rebellious minds. Those wretched few would suffer the consequences once he reached his potential. For now, they hid in the cracks and shadows, gathering the means to resist him. He'd not yet gathered the strength to exert control over the bonds between realities as his predecessor had done. Those wretched few brought whatever they wished over from the Spectrum.

Let them enjoy it. It won't last for long.

Oh, but to reach his potential! He struggled to remain patient. The gifts of his master were there, some just beyond his reach, others present but lessened so.

He saw through the infinite murk of the Monochrome's lifeless abyss for moments at a time. If he concentrated hard enough, he could pierce the veil and see through to the Spectrum, see things as they truly were and should be. He could see people, see through them if he wanted, gazing upon the riddle of flesh and tissue that made up their bodies. They were all there, just across the gray line separating the Spectrum from the Monochrome, oblivious to his desires and the mediocrity festering beneath their skin.

They were unaware, but not for much longer. Not after he had his way. Their strings were his to pull now.

A smirk cut across Sparrow's face. To think he had once resisted! *So naïve. I was a puppet of the flesh through and through.*

An ache crept through his frail body, vibrating in his joints like ghosts rattling chains. The threat of mortality still haunted him, but he felt it lessening with time, fading with the memories of who he once was. He crouched on the sidewalk and took a breath, tasting the stale air. His pets droned onward in the distance, searching for their prey. He tried to use their eyes, but nothing came of it. Their strings were beyond his grasp.

"Go, children. Take him and the rest of the Wretched. Devour them all."

The tremors in his body slowed. He leaned back against the wall to collect himself. *Should've known better than to push it*, he thought. He needed to be in prime form for his visit with the prisoner. They had much to discuss.

The Monochrome King closed his eyes, sank back into the gray mire of his mind, and searched for fragments of the man he once was.

Quinn ran along the sidewalk toward the intersection; there he took another left, rounding the corner with enough time to glance back. The wave of creatures built upon itself again, rising like a snake ready to strike. A cacophony of clicks, hisses, and moans followed. They saw him, they saw his course, and they would follow.

He was still looking over his shoulder when a hand shot out in front and nearly clotheslined him. The woman from the window yanked him into the alcove and put her palm over his mouth. She shook her head, flattening herself against the wall. Quinn followed her lead and kept quiet, waiting for the behemoth to pass them by.

The pale wave slowed as it turned the corner. Its bellowing drone rippled through the earth, sending tremors up the walls and into their bones.

The woman took this as her cue, gripping his shirt collar and yanking him up a flight of stairs. A hallway waited at the top along with a series of doorways and empty rooms. She shoved him into the first one and closed the door.

Quinn stumbled, caught his balance and turned to face her, hesitant to consider her a savior. Another violent tremor ripped through the building, and the wave's sullen murmurs echoed from beyond.

"What are you—"

She put her finger to her lips. The look in her eyes told him everything he needed to know.

The white beast's incessant whines intensified, swaying the building with its force. After a few minutes the deafening moan and unsettling vibrations diminished, leaving Quinn and the woman standing in the room, trembling.

Outside, the amalgamation of the Monochrome's bestiary continued its search, tearing through the gray streets.

When she was sure it had passed, the woman crept to the door and opened it. Quinn followed her. A large window stood at the end of the hall. Beyond it he saw the gray skyline of a lifeless city. The woman peered below, searching for the pale wave.

"Thank you," Quinn said. She ignored him, shifting from side to side, straining to get the best possible view. After another minute she stepped away, pushed herself against the wall, and took a cigarette from her pocket. She lit it and took a drag.

"What's your name, kid?"

He hesitated. There were others like himself in this place. A lot of them were young and frightened just like he was. Some were older, with weird gray zits on their faces. He stayed away from those people. There was something wrong with them, and it wasn't just their acne. They followed Sparrow—their *king*—like mindless drones, following his words like gospel. The stink of their devotion clung to them like an infection.

He couldn't see any trace of the gray pox on this woman's face, but that didn't mean it wasn't somewhere else. *Her whole body could be covered with them.*

She noticed, exhaled a plume of smoke, and laughed softly. "I'm not like the others, Q-ball." She stuck out her hand. "My name's Alice Walenta. Nice to meet you."

He was reluctant, but her demeanor was consistent with her claim. Quinn reached out and shook her hand. "Quinn Upton."

"That so?" A solemn look fell over her as she examined his face, noted his features. "I knew someone named Quinn once. Before all this. He'd be…" She trailed off, saw him staring, and changed the subject. "Cigarette?"

"No thanks. I don't smoke."

"Good for you." She took another drag. "Mind telling me what the hell you were doing out there by yourself?"

He opened his mouth to speak, but a single thought gave him pause. *What if she's like them?* He hadn't made any friends in the Monochrome, didn't think there were any to be made, for that matter. He wanted to believe her friendly disposition but living with the others had put him on his guard.

"I got lost. On my way back from getting food."

It wasn't a complete lie, but the words left a bitter taste on his tongue. His cheeks flushed. Wendy always told him he'd make a bad poker player.

Alice nodded. "Haven't been here long, have you?"

"A week, I think. Maybe longer? I don't really remember, to be honest."

"The 'chrome is disorienting at first, but you get used to it."

She finished her cigarette and let it fall to the floor. A lazy tendril of smoke rose from the smoldering nub. Quinn wrinkled his nose when he recognized the smell. His mom smoked the same brand.

Alice looked out the window once again. Angry cries from the pale wave echoed through the empty streets. Ghostly tremors rumbled beneath their feet.

"I've only seen those things do that a couple of times before. They must've really wanted you."

Quinn walked to the top of the stairs and looked down at the landing. He scratched his head, ran his hand across his neck, and realized his shirt collar was flipped up. He folded it down.

"I hoped to get back before Sparrow noticed I was gone. Guess I took too long."

There was a pause, then a dull metallic click. Quinn thought it was her cigarette lighter, but he discarded the idea when he felt something round and heavy press against the back of his head. He'd let his guard down a second time and now it was going to get him killed.

Slowly, Quinn raised his hands and turned to face her. The barrel of the revolver hovered less than an inch from his left eye.

"What—" he began, but Alice took a step closer and pressed the barrel of the gun against his forehead.

"Not another word. We knew he'd send others to find us. Didn't know it'd be a kid like you. That's a new low. What's the plan, then? Play the helpless victim, infiltrate our hiding place?"

"I—I don't understand what you're talking about."

"Bullshit." She grabbed him by the collar and yanked the white pin from his shirt. "He's marked you just like the rest of his slaves. All the king's men wear these."

Several words crossed Quinn's mind, but his lips wouldn't give voice to them. He was confused, scared, exhausted. What good would it do? Whether he died now or lived to do it later made no difference. His life was over, and there was no going back.

"Just do it. You've already made up your mind. I'm not going to argue."

She gave him a hard stare, pocketing the white pin. Finally, after a full minute, Alice lowered her weapon.

"No, you're not going to argue," she said. "But you *are* going to talk, Q-ball." She pushed him toward the stairs. "Now get walking."

———————•———————

*W*ho are you?

Sparrow reached back into the depths of the gray abyss, a vast expanse of mind and memory that he could not quantify. Here the strings were so apparent, each one ready to be guided, pulled, plucked, manipulating its host to his whim. Here he felt his followers, knew their desires and fears. Here he was a king—

No. Here he was a *god*.

But who are *you? Who is Albert Sparrow?*

"This is not the question," he said. "*What* am I? Yes, that's it. What."

He searched the strings, pulling himself toward fragments of memory, reaching for a sign he could read and understand. In the distance he saw a great column towering over the world. The vague obelisk was surrounded by the dense murk of the Monochrome's farthest reaches, and when he laid his eyes upon it, he remembered.

Albert Sparrow used to be a man. Yes, that's who he was—a pitiful man, a spiteful man. A *scheming* man. But that humanity was a phantom now, lost in that fathomless beast dwelling within the great column. He'd been remade—no, *reborn* in the beast's terrible unlight.

The Ungod will unmake you in its unlight, and then you will be perfect.

Perfect. His master's words stirred within him, dredging up memories of the change, the agony of his mortal body being absorbed in the light. He felt the violence of the transformation reach out of the murk, clutching at him like a desperate ghoul. He reeled at the memory of his mortal body dissolving, writhing in false pain as his existence was erased and rewritten.

Few things survived that pale fire. Most of who Albert Sparrow had been became one with the column and the nonentity slumbering within its chamber. The remnants of his existence tumbled through the Monochrome, lost in a dim haze while his vessel was reconstructed in his master's divine image. All that remained of Albert Sparrow were memories and knowledge, bits of electrical impulse and synaptic flares caught in a loop, screaming for context, purpose.

Were these pre-existing memories, or just constructs of the nonentity's collective unconscious? They were indistinguishable, now part of a greater whole, and he clung to them like a raft as he rode the violent waves toward a higher purpose.

Fragments of memory floated to the chaotic surface of his bodiless consciousness, reflecting an image: a young Albert Sparrow burning insects with a magnifying glass. He was their god, towering over them, deciding their fate on his childish whims. Such power and influence had once shaped a young man's mind, filling it with ambition to mold the world in his own image and rule it as he saw fit.

He saw an older Albert Sparrow, struggling to make ends meet as an adjunct professor. He saw a man forcing himself to get out of bed every morning, lying to himself about happiness just to make it through the day, only to repeat it all over again the next.

He saw a failure sleeping through life one day to the next, wondering what happened to the grand ambition of the child burning ants. What happened to the man who wanted to be powerful, influential? What happened to the boy who reveled in being a god?

Lost among the tumult, Sparrow saw his prize shining on the horizon of that rolling black sea, and he finally understood. Two words emerged like beacons from the chaotic depths. The first—his purpose—was a single edict given by the unlight, reaffirming what he already felt instinctively. That word was "Consume."

The second, a greater context culled from a memory of the man he once was—one of the few remnants of that lost soul—was "Candle."

His gray eyes flung open, awake with authority, focus. Revitalized, Sparrow rose to his feet, steadying himself against the slate wall. Few memories of his humanity remained, and these he clung to like talismans, aware of their power and influence. His meditation had revealed these artifacts, and they granted him the authority to act of his own accord, asserting his will over the strings.

People were insects, marching along the tethers that bound them to the banal coil of the Spectrum. He now held the strings, but there was something missing. A deeper desire buried within his shell.

Sparrow wanted to be more than simply the one who pulls the strings. He wanted to sever the ties and let the curtains fall. He wanted to consume them all and watch the coils burn.

He remembered his captive, his prize—and smiled.

So much had happened since that day back on the subway platform. In some ways he owed Donovan Candle gratitude for that day.

Something stirred within him as he continued his journey. Certain peculiarities of the flesh still resonated, empty impulses firing at the ends of dying nerves. Memory of the agonizing pain he'd suffered by Dullington's hand bubbled up to the surface of his darkened mind. He felt something like hatred for that man locked away in the room.

Sparrow gathered himself as he approached the Laundromat. He smiled.

Donovan Candle had put the magnifying glass back in his hand, and that good deed would not go unpunished.

He came out of sleep with a start. Fragments of the dream lingered at the edges of his blurred vision, but he couldn't reach out to grasp them. He stared at the ceiling for a time, trying to remember where he was.

"Sweet dreams, Candle?"

Donovan sat up, wincing as fire shot through his shoulder and down his arm. Albert Sparrow sat cross-legged on the floor in front of him. He blinked and focused on the man—*no, he's not a man anymore*—who had trapped him in this place.

His captor's eyes were colder than he remembered, colored dark gray. A sly grin spread across Sparrow's face.

"I slept," Donovan grunted. "There were no dreams."

His tongue was swollen, dry. He ran it across the roof of his mouth in search of moisture, wishing Quinn had left the bottle of water.

"Don't lie, Donnie. I've been here for quite some time, and I saw your feeble body twitch. I suspected nightmares, but when I tried to look inside your head, all I saw was darkness. I'm afraid the vision hasn't come to me just yet…" Sparrow trailed off, examining his cuticles. "But it will. In good time."

The vision?

"Something on your mind?"

"Nothing of interest to you." Donovan paused to search for a thought, then quietly chuckled to himself. His captor dropped the nonchalant facade and glared at him.

"Amused?"

"I was—I was just thinking," Donovan laughed, "I read that book of yours."

Sparrow smiled. "Did you like it?"

"No. It was horrible."

Donovan's dry laughter pierced the air. When Sparrow's expression fell, Donovan laughed even harder. Sparrow's eyes darkened, pulsing with a gray energy.

"*Enough.*"

His voice ripped through the building. The whole structure trembled. Donovan choked back his laughter, silencing himself as the tremors settled. He stared hard at his captor. *This is not the man I knew.* A chill crawled down the back of his neck.

"Do I have the laughing man's attention now?"

Donovan cleared his throat. "Yes, Sparrow, you most certainly do."

"Good. I want to tell you a little story, Donovan. You like stories, don't you? I would expect as much. We are both writers—or *were*, I should say. My career has slowed." He caught Donovan's stare. "Yours, it seems, never got off the ground."

Fair enough, old man, Donovan thought, although the jab stuck him more than he cared to admit.

Sparrow grinned. "Gather 'round, children. Your king has a tale to tell."

The walls shimmered, wavering in the gray gloom. To Donovan it looked as though the surfaces of the room were water, rippling with disturbances he could not see. Three Cretins pushed their way under the door. More followed, forming a Lilliputian crowd around their master.

They're worshiping him.

Cretin arms reached for Sparrow, desperate to touch him, and a moment later he levitated off the ground. Donovan blinked, realizing it was a trick of perspective. Sparrow was not floating off the ground; the Cretins were holding him. Sparrow remained seated in a meditative position, his pale wrists hanging limp at the edge of his knees. The Monochrome King's eyes glowed as he stared into his prisoner.

Donovan felt the man reaching into his mind, probing his secrets, airing out the skeletons. A thin smile spread across Sparrow's face.

"Once upon a time there was a man. A simple man, by trade, but one with high aspirations. He wanted to make something of himself. He wanted to reach out and touch others with his words. You might even say he was destined to do so. This man spent the better part of his life chasing that goal. He grew up, went to school, fell in love, and kept writing his little stories.

"But life is a cruel whore, and just as he reached the pinnacle of his talent, he fell into a rut. He was a newlywed by then, with bills to pay. His wife was ill, hobbled by chronic pain, and he needed the means to care for her He knew he would have to get a job—a steady job, a *committed* job—to take care of himself and his wife.

"He held on to that dream of his, though, and he kept at it in his free moments. Yes, those fleeting, precious moments. He allowed his mind to be poisoned with the promises of money and advancement. He became a *company man*, a slave to promises that would not be fulfilled, and still he clung to his goal—stop me if you've heard this one, okay?"

Donovan said nothing. Sparrow continued:

"Years passed. He grew older, but wisdom didn't come with age and one day he found himself fading. One day he found his whole world was turned inside-out, and he was forced to confront the last several years of his life. This man was given a simple ultimatum: rise to meet his ambitions or perish in obscurity.

"It was by the promise and demonstration of his willingness to change that the man saved his own existence. He avoided a fate befallen by so many before him, and he did it by trading the life of another." Sparrow's demeanor changed, his face contorting into a portrait of anger. He ground his teeth together. A loud hiss filled the room, and the walls around them rippled violently like a puddle in a storm.

"He chose another man to take his place, condemning that innocent soul to *rot* in a stagnant prison and *suffer* for past transgressions."

Sparrow paused. The rippling walls slowed, steadied. The Cretins shivered.

"But life went on anew for this man. He changed his direction, just as he'd promised, and accomplished a pivotal part of his goal. He helped conceive a child, establishing a lineage of blood to follow him, generations on. He forgot about the life he traded for his own."

"I didn't forget," Donovan whispered. Sparrow ignored him.

"Yet somehow, despite all he accomplished, despite the possibility of a bright future, the man jeopardized everything. Faced with the task of crossing over into uncharted territory where his dream might be realized, where he would begin a new phase of his life as a husband, a father, a writer, this man—this pitiful, scared man—lingered on the line between greatness and obscurity. He was afraid, a victim of his own fear, and rather than move into this vast unknown, he chose to remain on the edge." Sparrow snarled, pointing a pale finger at Donovan. "You *chose* to do *nothing*."

Donovan wanted to snarl back with a fitting rebuttal. Instead, all that came to him was an immensely rooted guilt that permeated every inch of his being. He remembered Dullington's words from his dream. *You need to move. Jump, Mr. Candle.*

He thought about everything he'd done to prevent the flickering from happening again. He left the shitty job at Identinel, he buckled down and wrote his book, he even went to great pains to break every routine he'd created for himself.

But that wasn't enough, hoss.

He realized he heard not the imagined voice of Hopper, but the sound of his own conscience. His actions weren't enough. He saw the path before him, saw what he was meant to do, what he should've done, and how he'd only met his life pitch halfway.

He wrote the book, but he was too afraid to take the next step. His wife had to do it for him.

He was too afraid to speak up to his brother about what happened that weekend, too afraid to pitch his theory about what was happening to the people who disappeared from the city. His obsession and concern over the fate of missing kids wasn't enough to urge him forward. No, he didn't find the will to act until Quinn's abduction, and by then he was too late.

The job, the book, the life he'd made for himself—Donovan realized, in that moment, that what he'd done was truly not enough. Sparrow, with all his conniving, seething postures and threats, was right about him. For whatever vision he lacked, Sparrow saw through Donovan with perfect clarity.

Never before in his life had he felt more defeated than at that moment. He was a man broken by hesitation and fear. He thought of his wife, the child she carried inside her, and how he may never see them again.

Tears slipped down his cheeks as he thought about the life Donna deserved, and how what he'd given her fell so far short. He conjured a picture of her, years after his disappearance, when she finally gave up and moved on with her life. He saw her with another man, faceless but handsome, successful, and able to give her all she deserved. He saw this faceless man being a proper father to their child, the sort of father who wouldn't be too afraid to act, who wouldn't hesitate to do what was necessary in *all* things.

Donovan saw the man he was supposed to be, the man he had failed to be.

"I'm sorry," he whispered, ignoring his putrid audience. "I'm so sorry."

"Those tears are wasteful, Donnie."

The Cretins set down their master. Sparrow rose to his feet and nodded to his white minions. They moved as one toward the chair; there, they climbed atop one another until they reached Donovan's restraints.

He felt his hands go free. His ankles followed. The urgency of freedom was not enough to move him from the chair. Sparrow extended a gnarled, pale hand.

"Come."

"Just end it," Donovan muttered. "Do whatever you plan to do to me."

"Oh I will. But there must be reason before action, Donovan. I want to show you *why*, and *what*, before I *do*." Sparrow's face contorted with rage, his eyes pulsing with a sickening glow. "Now get your ass out of that chair."

9

THE WRETCHED

Alice led Quinn at gunpoint across three blocks of empty streets, mindful of the pale wave's rumbling in the distance. Quinn thought about making a run for it but realized he had nowhere to go. Sparrow's minions were looking for him, which probably meant he'd served his purpose. The king's prize was back in the Laundromat, locked away and tied to a chair. What other use would Sparrow have for a college kid?

They carried on for another block until coming to a subway entrance. Alice perched herself on the railing to have another smoke. She kept the gun trained on her prisoner the whole time.

"You're going to make this a hell of a lot easier on yourself if you just tell me the truth, Q-ball."

He waved the smoke from his face. "You won't believe me no matter what I tell you, so what's the damn point?"

"Suit yourself." She grabbed his arm and shoved him down the steps. He cried out as he lost his footing and rolled to the first landing.

"Go ahead and do it, you crazy bitch. Just end it already." Quinn pointed at his forehead. "Do it. My life's over anyway. If you're so goddamn trigger happy, do us both a favor and put my lights out."

Alice dropped her cigarette, lowered her gun, and slapped him across the face. He looked at her, stunned and confused. Was she bluffing? Looking into her eyes, he wondered if she had it in her to kill another living thing. She was hardened and callous, but he'd seen his share of cold-heartedness in the last few days. Alice didn't possess the same look in her eye as the bearded man called Kale.

"You're no good to us dead. Suck it up, Q-ball, and get walking."

"Who's this 'us' you keep talking about?"

"Sparrow calls us the Wretched." She chuckled as she said it. "I guess you could say we fit that description."

"You mean there are more of you?"

"Lots, but you knew that already, didn't you? You wouldn't have come if you didn't know."

Quinn's face flushed with anger. He clenched his teeth. "For the last time, I don't know what you're talking about."

But Alice was already moving, and he had no choice but to follow. They moved past the ticketing booths, past empty gray cubes that had once been token machines, and over the turnstiles. There were signs of life down here: sleeping bags, empty food wrappers and containers, clothing, charred barrels. It looked like his new home, and the thought of it turned his stomach.

When they neared the steps that would take them to the boarding platform, Alice put her hand on his shoulder. Her gentle touch surprised him.

"Keep your voice down," she whispered. "If you speak up, we're both dead." She tapped the barrel of the gun against his temple. "And if it comes to that, I'll cap myself and leave you to fend off the Yawning on your own. Got it?"

He nodded.

"Good," she said. "Let's go."

They walked side-by-side, silent except for their footsteps. When they approached the edge of the platform, Alice motioned with the gun. He was hesitant, but the urgent look in her eyes forced him to move. He knelt first, then cautiously lowered himself onto the tracks.

He'd seen the tunnels fill with Cretins, and he'd seen what happened when someone was careless enough to fall into their torrent. It wasn't pretty, and he couldn't get the image out of his head. Memories of the poor soul's agonizing screams still haunted him.

Alice followed, dropping off the platform in a single motion. Quinn watched in amazement, envious of how comfortable she appeared to be, and he wondered just how long she'd been trapped here in the gloom. The question was on the tip of his tongue when he remembered her warning. She caught his eye, tipped her head toward the mouth of the tunnel, and started walking.

On his own, Quinn hadn't ventured far into the old network of railways, choosing instead to follow the other Missing whenever they went topside. Now he understood why. The tunnels stretched on forever, curving into straight pieces of track and back again. He knew that if they followed the tracks long enough, they would end up back at Winthorpe Station—ground zero for Sparrow's operations. Logically, this meant that if they could stroll into Sparrow's subterranean kingdom, the Missing could just as easily chase them down, and this thought bothered him. Where could they possibly go to hide?

When they came to the next platform, Alice hoisted herself up and offered him a hand.

"This way."

Quinn followed her to a door at the far side of the platform; beyond it was a short hallway that emptied out to another large tunnel much like the last, except it lacked railway tracks.

"What is this place?"

"Access tunnel. I saw the Spectrum side of it once. It's all pipes and cabling along the ceiling and walls. I think it runs parallel with some of the tracks."

"Do the others know about this?"

Alice didn't respond, kept on walking. Time down in the tunnels was hard to gauge, and after a while Quinn wasn't sure if they'd walked for twenty minutes or twenty hours. His face throbbed with every step. The groaning pit of his stomach didn't help matters.

"Almost there, Q-ball. We have food."

"You'd feed a so-called spy?"

"Just 'cause I said there's food doesn't mean we have to feed you."

Fair enough, he thought, and kept walking. Shadows colored gradient tones of gray danced along the tunnel walls. Quinn heard the crackling fire as they approached the bend—and voices murmuring beyond the flames.

The path curved into another station of sorts, except there was no boarding platform. Instead, he saw a sprawling shantytown constructed from cardboard, plywood, and other detritus. A single barrel sat in the middle of the clearing. The white fire cracked and popped within it, licking the air like a pale serpent. A group of figures huddled around the barrel, speaking in hushed tones. Their faces shifted and danced with the shadows.

One of them heard their approach and turned. "Who's there?"

"It's Alice."

"Who's that with you?"

Alice pushed him forward. The others left their post at the barrel and came to observe the newcomer, surrounding him with their inquisitive stares. Quinn's heart raced. *What are they going to do to me?*

They were men and women of varied ages. Dirty, haggard, dressed in tattered clothes—just like the others back at the old station. A few of them bore the markings of gray pox on their hands and faces. An elderly-looking woman appeared to be the worst of the lot, with large boils covering most of her face. Her skin pulsed in the dim light, and Quinn had to stop himself from staring.

"Found him topside being chased by a pale wave."

The ragtag group exchanged glances, murmuring to themselves.

"Is he a spy?" asked a man in a tattered three-piece. A larger fellow with matted hair and a droopy eye grabbed a fistful of Quinn's shirt and yanked him forward.

"Did Sparrow send you, ya little shit?"

"Easy, Frank." Alice put her hand on the boy's shoulder. She turned to the old woman and gave her the white pin.

"Only one way to skin a spy," said the other man. He reached into his trouser pocket and produced a slender blade that shimmered in the firelight.

"Frankie. Matthew. That's enough." The old woman shot Frankie a cold look, and he let go of Quinn's shirt. "He's got nowhere to go. Even if he is a spy, killing him won't do us any good."

"Evelyn, are you sure about this? After what they did to those kids—"

The old woman, Evelyn, shook her head. "There was nothing we could do, Matthew. You know that."

Quinn couldn't take his eyes off the sickly blemishes on her face. Some of Sparrow's followers had the same markings. *What's happening to these people? Is this what'll happen to me?*

Evelyn put her hand on his shoulder. "Young man, I'm going to ask you something, and I want the honest truth. If you can't give us that, we will have no choice but to return you to the surface and call out your position to every Cretin and Yawning in the area. We're not murderers, but we're not saviors, either."

Quinn swallowed back the lump in his throat and nodded.

"Do you serve Sparrow, the one they call the Monochrome King?"

"No, ma'am. I don't, and I never will. Not after what he's done to me. Not after what he's doing to my uncle Donovan right now."

Murmurs crawled along the crowd, and he heard Alice suck in her breath. He met her stare, but she was quick to look away, sinking back into the shadows.

Evelyn took his hand, looked him in the eye. He found no fear or anger in her stare, only a glimmer of hope and kindness and trust. She smiled.

"Your uncle Donovan. Would his last name be Candle?"

He nodded. Evelyn squeezed his hand.

"Well then," she said, "do you want a fighting chance of getting out of this hell?"

"Get up."

Donovan looked at Sparrow like a beaten dog. His pride was gone, his dignity erased, and all he wanted to do was cry himself to sleep. He no longer felt like an adult, but a child forced to face the evils of the world. Sparrow moved his hand over Donovan's shoulder.

"I see you as you were six months ago, Donnie. I can see you as clear as a photograph in my mind." Sparrow stared at the blank walls, lost in a daydream. "I see you getting the call. Your wife is pregnant. She's just come from the doctor. She's sitting in a car, her hands trembling with excitement, and I see you standing with the phone to your ear while she delivers the wonderful news. Now *your* hands are shaking with a fear you've never known. But you know that fear now, don't you?"

Donovan looked away.

"It must be a horrible thing, pulling yourself up only to realize you can't go any higher. Tell me, did you ever face the fact that you are a coward?"

"I'm not—"

Sparrow moved quickly, leaning in so close his crooked nose teased Donovan's cheek.

"If there is nothing else you believe, know that what I tell you is true. You *are* a coward. You doubted yourself into a corner, choosing to stagnate rather than embrace the changes in your life. You replaced mediocrity with a new addiction: complacency. In my opinion, that makes you a coward." Sparrow pulled back, sniffed the air, then let out a gruff cackle. "I find it rather fitting that you chose to search for those poor kids as a half-hearted way of facing your own fears."

Donovan's breath caught in his throat. *Those poor kids.* The words crept down his back one icy syllable after another. Sparrow met his gaze with a grin so wide it nearly split his face in two.

"Oh yes, Mr. Candle. You know who I mean."

His whole body trembled. Their faces flashed in his mind—smiling faces in photos taken during better times. They were students, sons and daughters, innocent bystanders in this sick game and oblivious to its rules. He remembered the night he learned of their fate. Dullington's voice whispered in his head: *This is where the wave crashes down, Mr. Candle.*

"You amaze me, Donovan Candle. For such a selfish person, you project a tiring amount of selflessness. What is it you're trying to prove, and to whom?"

Sparrow's words deflated Donovan's ego in a single burst. He felt his last bit of strength leave him.

"You spent so much time clinging to the hope that you might find them. What's worse, you even knew where they might be, but you were too afraid to do anything about it. So, you built yourself up as a concerned private eye, playing the valiant hero like a rubbish character from one of your stories, struggling to find the object of your obsession but conveniently hitting a wall at every turn."

"Stop," Donovan whispered, ashamed of the weakness in his voice.

"Those kids, those insignificant little shits to whom you devoted all those long hours, they were here the entire time. You knew it, and yet you did nothing. Too afraid of what your brother might say. Too afraid of what it might mean."

He tried to stand and face his tormentor, but the feeling in his legs faded, and Donovan sank to his knees. He sat there, the tears streaming down his cheeks, a broken man alone with his sins. *I am going to die here and I deserve it. I let those kids down. I let Quinn down. I let Donna and the baby down.*

Sparrow grabbed a fistful of Donovan's hair. "You let *yourself* down. My book was about men like you. Do you remember what I told you that day outside the subway? The day you returned me to this empty hell?"

"Happiness…"

Sparrow grinned. "'Happiness is the greatest con of all.' You will never have it because you are too afraid to do what is necessary to attain it."

He let go of Donovan's head with a sudden jerk. Donovan fell backward to the floor. *I'm so sorry, Donna. God, I'm so sorry.*

"You're a failure, Mr. Candle. Now get on your feet."

But Donovan didn't want to. The will was gone from him. He'd known depression, not long after he took the job at Identinel, and nearly every year after. The emptiness, the lack of will or desire, the placid acceptance of failure all defined him in those moments. And now, Donovan found himself amid such feelings once more. He remained on the floor, accused and convicted of inaction, and somewhere far off in the back of his head he could hear Dullington whispering, *Atone.*

That voice became Joe Hopper's voice. *Time to jump.* Donovan rubbed his eyes, wiped away the tears, and climbed to his feet. He stared hard into Sparrow's cold, gray eyes. "Why did you bring me here?"

Sparrow smiled. "To thank you."

"*Thank* me?"

"I had a good thing going in my previous life. I was happy, but you took that away. You ruined everything. In a way, *you* are the reason I am this way. And yet...*I like it.*"

The Cretins bristled at the sound of his voice, and their scuttling rose in volume as Sparrow held out his arms. The white army climbed their way up his body, forming a single squirming mass that coiled about his form like a snake.

"I lived and died here. I was reborn a god here. And with *Fading Out,* I will rule as king."

"What do you mean? What does this have to do with that goddamn TV show?"

Grinning, Sparrow turned and led the way out of the room. The small gang of Cretins followed, carrying their master along their tiny backs. Sparrow moved gracefully and without effort, willing them to move wherever he wished.

Donovan winced as he climbed to his feet. His shoulder throbbed. The dislocation seemed so long ago now. He was lost in quiet reverie, trying to recall how many days it had been, when Sparrow called for him. Part of him didn't want to go, but the other part—the more sensible, fearless part—knew he would never get out if he didn't leave that infernal room.

More stagnant air greeted him as he left the hollow shell of the Laundromat. Sparrow stood in a circle of Cretins with his head tilted to the side. The white creatures turned in place, searching the area for something they couldn't see.

"There is someone here."

Donovan smirked. "Can't you see them? Aren't you supposed to be Sparrow the Great and Terrible?"

Sparrow glared, his pale eyes sizzling in their sockets. "My vision is not where it should be. But that will change with time."

Again with the 'vision.' Dullington knew when and where someone was at all times. Maybe Sparrow's not quite up to it yet.

He didn't know how everything worked. Sparrow's state wasn't something he'd expected. All the rules he thought he knew were changing yet again.

A Cretin climbed its way up Sparrow's body and sat on his shoulder. He turned and whispered something in a language Donovan couldn't understand. The sound reminded him of skipping records turned in reverse. The Cretin nodded, leapt off its master, and scuttled across the street. It turned a corner and was gone.

"Now," Sparrow muttered, "let's be on our way."

The Cretin scampered across the street, following a peculiar scent. The creature turned a corner and paused. The master was right—there was someone here. But where? The Cretin stood in the building's shadow, scanning the empty street and rows of buildings.

Nothing moved. The only sounds were the fading voices of the master and his slave.

Focus, whispered the master. *Find the spy.*

Sparrow watched through its eyes. The Cretin walked, turning its head like a security camera, scanning every visible inch of the street. The smell intensified—a stark odor that filled the creature with a sense of revulsion. *Wretched*, thought the creature.

The master pulled away, turning his gaze elsewhere. The Cretin no longer felt Sparrow's burden behind its dark eyes. The creature continued its search, following the human stench to the end of the block.

No sign of the human. The Cretin looked both ways, pondering which direction to take. The stench was everywhere, as though—

The footsteps came from behind, and fast. Too fast. The Cretin spun around just as the smelly slave's boot squashed its head to the ground.

Joel lifted his foot and grimaced at the mash of white and gray innards. "Disgusting."

He dragged his foot across the edge of the sidewalk and scraped the Cretin's remains from his boot. He adjusted his glasses, stealing a glance over his shoulder. The street was still empty, but it wouldn't be for long.

The white things knew when one of their own was killed, and sooner or later a Yawning would lumber over to search for the killer.

Joel shivered and waited for his heart to stop pounding. It was getting worse, those shakes. He looked at his hands, at the pulsing boils spotting his skin, and frowned when he saw they were spreading down his forearm.

Pretty soon I'll be just like Evelyn.

He nearly jumped out of his skin when the first cries of the Yawning echoed through the air.

"Shit, shit, shit." He had to get back to the others. He had to get back and tell them Sparrow was moving the prisoner. When he looked over his shoulder again, he saw the figure of a Yawning looming in the distance.

Joel grit his teeth and began to run.

———————————◆———————————

Quinn watched gradient shadows dance across the gray ceiling. A fire popped and crackled from across the room. The others were gathered around the barrel, still murmuring about his arrival. One of them raised their voice a few times, but he couldn't understand it—nor did he want to.

Hunger and head trauma are my only friends in this place. That thought would've given him a laugh any other time, but all it did now was paint this grim reality a darker hue. *Shouldn't have told them about Don. The way they reacted when I told them who the prisoner was…God knows what they're going to do to him.*

He watched the group across the room. Sparrow called them the Wretched, and he could see why. They were dressed in rags, their skin spotted with rashes of gray pox. Unlike those in Sparrow's domain, most of the Wretched were older folks, and he wondered just how long some of them had been here.

Quinn thought about his parents and about Wendy, speculating if he'd ever get to see them again, and then he remembered what his uncle told him. If Donovan was here before and had escaped, surely that meant there was a way out. There had to be.

His mind ran wild with possibilities, but he had a hard time making sense of anything in this place. This Monochrome was a realm of abstraction, filled with impossible creatures, warring factions, opposing realities, and demigods. How *could* he make sense of it when it was all the stuff of fantasy?

But Don said things were different then. So what changed?

He remembered what his uncle said about Dullington, and about how the Missing couldn't bring things back with them when they flickered over. Now Sparrow was in charge and the rules were different.

Quinn looked up, peering further off in the haze at two figures standing watch at the mouth of the tunnel. He could just make out the silhouettes of their weapons. Where Sparrow had kept him, only a few of the Missing had weapons: mostly knives and blunt objects. These people had guns.

His chest tightened as panic took hold. *What are they going to do to me? And what are they going to do to Don? God, I just want to go home. I miss my parents. I miss Wendy—*

"Mind if I sit down?"

The old woman, Evelyn, walked toward him. She smiled.

"Go ahead." Quinn's gaze fell upon the sickly gray blemishes on the old woman's face. The small gray pustules throbbed, and Quinn found he couldn't stop staring.

"If it's my face you're afraid of, boy, you really ain't been here all that long."

Heat filled Quinn's cheeks, and he felt like a jerk. Evelyn patted his hand.

"Don't worry about it. You seem like a good kid. How old are you, Q-ball?"

"Twenty."

"Still a baby, yet." She looked back at the burning barrel. The crowd had dispersed. "Why don't we go over by the fire? The light helps me think, and there's something I need to talk to you about."

Evelyn stood and made her way over to the barrel. Quinn followed, taking a spot beside her. He held out his hands to warm them, only to realize the fire barely gave off any heat. Disappointed, he stuffed his hands in his pockets and watched the cold flames lick the air.

"You know, your uncle is something of a legend here."

"He is?"

She nodded. "A while back, he made a deal with Aleister Dullington."

"I've heard that name, but I haven't seen him."

"None of us have. Not since Sparrow came back." Evelyn thought for a moment, frowning. She stared into the flames. "Dullington's the one who brought most of us here—me, Alice, Frankie, Joel, Matthew. Those of us who've been here a while." She paused, smirking. "He'd say we brought ourselves, and I s'pose he's right in some ways. All of us lived dull lives. *This* is supposed to be our punishment."

She held out her arm and rolled back the sleeve. The skin of her arm was pulled tight across the bone, accentuating every curve and divot. Colonies of bumps and blisters spotted her flesh, pulsing in the firelight. Quinn's stomach clenched up at the sight of them.

"This is what happens when you've been here as long as I have." Tears covered her eyes for a moment, but she blinked them away.

"But what *is* it? What's happening to you?"

Evelyn pushed down her sleeve and folded her arms against her chest. "This place is happening. I figure I've been here for a long time. Longer than most. Some of the men and women who were here when I arrived…" She caught her breath. Her whole body trembled. "…they're not here anymore."

"Where did they go?"

"They disappeared. Wasted away to nothing, best I can figure. These pimples are just the start of it. It got worse when Dullington left."

She reached down, grabbed a small metal pipe, and used it to stoke the fire. The white flames surged, drawing long shadows across the walls and floor.

"Your uncle made his deal, and Dullington let him go. We'd never seen that happen before. Dullington wasn't a deal maker, so we knew there had to be something special about that guy your uncle brought here."

"Who?"

"You know him." She spat into the barrel. "We all do. Calls himself the king of the Monochrome. Sparrow."

"Uncle Don brought Sparrow here?"

Evelyn nodded. "They say he forced him here. That was part of their deal. Dullington had one of his own—he called us his 'puppets'—kidnap your aunt and bring her back here. He held her for ransom, and that ransom was Sparrow."

No wonder he's got Don locked up in that room.

"So, what happened? Where did Dullington go?"

"One day," she went on, "he left the old station with Sparrow in tow. They never returned. Something else did, though. Something that looked like Sparrow, or maybe what *used* to be him…"

Quinn watched her, watched the slight tremble at the edge of her lips, and noticed the sickening lurch of white bubbling up beneath her skin. *It's like it's alive. Something underneath, waiting to get out.* He recalled stories of flies laying eggs in living tissue. When the babies hatched, they fed on the host from the inside until they were ready to emerge.

"It's hard to explain, kid. We all saw him leave with Dullington, but the next time we saw him was in the old station. Upstairs, in one of the old offices, was this huge white *thing*." She demonstrated with her hands, miming a large, asymmetrical shape. "Like a big cocoon or egg of some sort. Sparrow was there, paler than a sheet, arms spread out like he was crucified to it."

"He just appeared out of nowhere?"

Evelyn shrugged. "Who knows how long he was there. He certainly didn't. It's like he sprouted out of the cocoon, grew right out of it like a flower bud. Must've been weeks before he finally woke up, too, and when he did, it was like Dullington all over again, but worse. Like he turned into the same thing Dullington is, or something like it. He can do some of Dullington's tricks, but not all of them. And he still has his eyelids."

Quinn cringed. "Dullington doesn't have eyelids?"

"No, but he's got the biggest, blackest eyes I've ever seen. So big they stick out of his head, like two lumps of coal. When Sparrow opened his eyes, looked at us the first time and flashed us that shit-eatin' grin, I knew things were about to get worse. Things were different after he woke up, and we learned soon enough just what those differences were."

"Don said something about this place didn't feel the same. The air's different, and people were only allowed to leave once a day?"

"Yes," Evelyn grunted, then began to cough. She doubled over as she hacked and spat. "Sorry. That damn cough gets worse 'n worse every day. Where was I? Oh right, the 'chrome. Your uncle's right, Q-ball. The air *is* different, and when Dullington was in charge, we only got to feed once a day. Some folks—newcomers like yourself—are still on a scheduled 'rotation' of sorts, but for us old timers, the flickerin' comes and goes at random. We do as well as we can to scramble out for food and back. Alice over there—" She pointed over to a small cardboard shack across the room. "—first discovered we could bring stuff back with us. Before Dullington disappeared, whatever we were holding just didn't cross over, but one day she was holding a can of soup and it came right over with her. Color 'n all."

"Is that when you started bringing guns?"

She nodded. "We brought over any sort of weapon we managed to steal. And we kept our secret as quiet as we could. The rest of the Missing folk, they were divided. Sparrow had his followers, and there were others like us who didn't trust him. He claimed he'd let everyone go if they helped him. He marked them with those white pins so he'd know who's who. The rest of us, when we didn't bow to him as our 'king,' he called us 'Wretched' and cast us out 'to the wilds of the Monochrome.'" She mocked his snide voice as she spoke. Quinn laughed, but when she put her hand on his arm, he saw she didn't find it very funny.

"He sent those white things to kill us. What you see here is everyone who survived. And we ain't going to keep doing that much longer if he has his way."

Quinn fell silent. He looked deep into the old woman's eyes. The gravity of their situation pulled on him with staggering force. "Do you really think killing Sparrow will reverse everything?"

"Best I can figure," she sighed, "both sides of this place are connected like parts of the same machine. Everything goes together, all tick-tock like, and when one moves, the other does too. When Dullington left us, that machine started to slow down." She paused, thinking. "Sparrow's not quite like Dullington, but he's getting stronger every day. One day he'll be just like Dullington was, and when that happens, I think the machine will start moving again like it's supposed to. Killing him might stop things altogether and weaken whatever's keeping us here. We need to act on it before he's reached Dullington's strength."

"What about my uncle? I can't leave him in that room."

Evelyn smiled. "Wouldn't dream of it. I was hoping maybe he could help us." She put her hand on his shoulder. "But I've done talked your ear off. You need to get some rest while you can, Q-ball. When things happen, they'll happen fast, and we'll all need to be ready."

She pointed out a row of empty sleeping bags. The need for sleep hadn't occurred to him before, but now the very thought of it prompted a yawn. Maybe a nap wasn't such a bad idea. He was halfway across the room when something occurred to him. He turned back to the barrel.

"Evelyn?" The old woman looked up at him from beyond the flames. "What happens when no one's there to mind the machine?"

She stared at him for a moment, her lips pursed into the beginnings of a frown that shifted in the dancing firelight. The old woman said nothing. When she stepped away from the barrel and back into the gray haze, Quinn had a frightening epiphany: *She has no idea.*

Sparrow led him down the empty street. His personal entourage of Cretins carried him along, giving him the appearance of a gray apparition. The white creatures moved quickly despite their master's burden. More Cretins climbed out of the sewer drains, joining their brethren and lengthening the white trail left in their master's wake.

"Where are you taking me, Sparrow?"

Sparrow lifted a wrinkled finger and pointed straight ahead. Donovan peered farther down the path. Vacant buildings stretched onward, featureless geometric designs standing tall like lifeless golems guarding the empty streets. Sparrow held his finger out for a moment longer before moving on his way, and it was then Donovan realized his captor was not pointing down the street, but beyond it. Above it.

The skyscraper was miles away in the business district of the city, standing higher than most. What caught his eye was not its size, but the abnormal white light emanating from its surface.

Déjà vu.

He stopped walking and stared. The intensity of the light rose and fell without pause, breathing like a giant white lung. There was something at the top of the structure he couldn't make out, its details obscured by the Monochrome's gray haze. Even at this distance saw the building's peak with the light's focal point.

Donovan remembered the strange gray column in his dream. *Can't be. That wasn't a skyscraper. That was something else...*

"The WBS building really is something to behold. Do you like television, Donnie?"

Donovan broke his trance and looked at Sparrow. "Not really. I used to, but I don't watch it all that much anymore. I have better things to do."

"Indeed." Sparrow began to move again, and Donovan followed. "The knowledge he passed on to me is limited, but that will grow in time. Not long after Dullington left this place, I was gifted knowledge of the strings. The tethers binding man to his many hopes and dreams, his many failures. And among those strings were the dreams of twelve men. Twelve powerful, wealthy men, with their mansions and their suits, all who were going to flicker out for one reason or another."

"So you made a deal? More puppets?"

"Of course. I've allowed them to live their lives as normal, but with the knowledge that I'll call upon them whenever I wish—or else."

The Cretins surged at the end of his sentence, chattering with laughter as they grouped into a writhing mass around Sparrow's feet.

"Who are they? Who are these twelve men?"

"Executives," Sparrow said. "Twelve bickering, egocentric executives who all think they're first in line on the chain."

Donovan looked up once more as they walked. The building was a little clearer now, and the light throbbed like a strobe in slow motion. He pointed to it.

"What is that thing? What does this have to do with the television network?"

Sparrow stopped, turning to stare at him. *Through* him. Donovan's cheeks flushed with heat.

"As Dullington's successor, I must feed on the boredom you humans exude. I could wait for you insects to flicker out one by one and live on your scraps. Or, I could force you over *en masse*." He lifted his gaze back to the pulsing structure in the distance. "Reality television is a perfect conduit, recycling your mediocrity back to you. It's like breathing the same air over and over again. Humanity deserves to suffocate."

Sparrow's words came together in Donovan's mind, connecting with a sudden jolt that left him reeling.

A perfect conduit.

He looked up at the WBS building again, squinting at its sickening light. There was only one thing that could be on the top of a building housing a television network's corporate headquarters. He remembered all the white pins bearing the same logo, the design painted outside Winthorpe Station, the promo card on Quinn's corkboard—all the pieces raced back to him, and he was astounded by how blind he'd been.

Every case file involving a missing kid rushed back to the forefront of his memory. Every seemingly unsolvable disappearance, with every disconnected piece of evidence, now fit so tightly together he wondered how he managed to miss it.

You got it, hoss. You can't find it if you don't know what you're lookin' for, and I'd bet the farm you just up and found it.

"You're using the TV show. That's why they're all flickering out, isn't it? You're forcing them over instead of giving them a choice. You couldn't bring me over because I wasn't flickering, so you forced me over with that reality show. This is how Quinn, all the others—"

Sparrow gave a slow applause. "Bravo, *Donnie*. Bravo."

Donovan pulled the promo card from his pocket. "What is this, Sparrow? What is this 'Great Fade-Out?'"

"It's a day-long marathon of everyone's favorite reality TV show. The broadcasts will force a mass flickering event. Anyone watching for the duration will transition into the Monochrome, and from them I will feed. I will *grow*."

An icy feeling seeped into Donovan's gut. The sheer number of viewers—not just in the city, but across the country—was staggering. His head swam with the possibility of such a large-scale disappearance.

"You can't—"

Sparrow's hand shot out and took hold of Donovan's throat. His eyes darkened in their sockets, sizzling with energy, and his voice echoed throughout the gray world, a booming baritone reverberating through the fabric of the Monochrome's reality. Donovan felt every syllable humming in his chest.

"I can. Henza thought he could stop me, and I fed him to the Yawning. I had his insect of an attorney murdered for the fun of it. The Great Fade-Out *will* happen, Mr. Candle, and there is not a goddamn thing you can do about it."

The Monochrome King released his grip. Donovan stumbled backward, gasping for air.

"Why Quinn?" he croaked. "Why not send someone else after me? Why involve the kid?"

"That's an easy one, Mr. Candle. I did it to fuck with you. No telling where he's run off to now, though. I sent my creatures in pursuit, and when they find him, they will consume him. He'll become one with us. With *me*."

Donovan glared at his enemy, feeling a boiling anger well up within him. "I swear to God if you've done anything to him—"

Sparrow waved him off. "Please, *Donnie*, enough posturing. You'll do nothing, just like you stood idle while those kids got theirs. Honestly, it's a wonder you aren't afraid of your own fucking shadow."

The words were a punch to his gut, knocking the wind and anger out of him. Donovan's face grew hot, his throat suddenly dry. "Why did you kill them? What could they have possibly done to you?"

"They were spies. Puppets of the Wretched."

"Spies?"

Sparrow tilted his head. "There are those who oppose me, Mr. Candle. They are wretched, vile things that think they can kill me, but they are mistaken. I may be weak, but I'm not mortal. And when I achieve my goal, I will feast upon them all." He looked back at Donovan, grinning. "They sent those brats to spy on me, to take advantage of my lack of...*vision.* Their death was a message. And I must tell you, Don, we enjoyed every minute of it—especially my associate, Kale. He did all the dirty work."

The old man spoke in steady rhythm, without remorse or emotion, and the blank look on his face infuriated Donovan. He found that anger rising again, but it was diffused by a simple, fragile thought: *I'm in over my head and sinking fast.*

"But enough of that. Now that you've had your twenty questions and your empty epiphany, I'm afraid I must confess something else. There *is* another reason I brought you here."

"I'm listening."

Sparrow's lips twitched, forming a malevolent grin that sent a chill scratching its way down Donovan's back.

"Punishment."

10

IN THE COURT OF THE MONOCHROME KING

E velyn stoked the fire, scattering white embers into the air. She questioned if she was ready to go through with her plans. *Our plans*, she thought. She hadn't come to this decision alone. The others were busy preparing for the assault on Winthorpe Station, gathering supplies and taking inventory. Their grim expressions told her what she already knew: none of them were ready for this.

"Hey, Evie."

She looked up and smiled. "Hey, Al."

"Where's the kid?"

"I told him to get some rest." Evelyn motioned to the far corner. "Matter of fact, we should wake him. We'll be ready soon."

Alice looked over at the young man. He lay on his side, knees drawn to his chest, asleep. She had a hard time remembering what it was like when she first came to this place. The Monochrome had a funny way of bleeding the memories from a person. This, she figured, was part of its punishing repertoire.

"Did you sleep, Al?"

"Not really. Couldn't close my eyes for more than a couple of minutes."

Evelyn patted her hand. "We all need the rest, honey."

"It's just nerves. Got a lot on my mind."

"Oh, please," Evelyn laughed, "you're too young to have nerves."

"Maybe, maybe not. My thirty-ninth birthday was just a couple of months ago. At least I think it was." That she could not remember the exact date was troubling, but she tried not to let it get to her. "We'll just say I'm thirty-nine forever."

Alice stared into the fire again. She *did* have a lot on her mind—more than just her age—and most of it revolved around what Quinn had revealed to them. They knew Sparrow had an agenda, but they didn't understand just how nefarious it was, or how deep it went. More curious, though, were Sparrow's intentions regarding the man in the room. After witnessing Donovan Candle's exchange with Aleister Dullington that day on the subway platform, she suspected Sparrow's plans for him were anything but pure.

Their rebellion against Sparrow's dominion was born out of a single revelation: the laws of the Monochrome were bending, maybe even breaking. This discovery was the first glimmer of hope she'd seen since Donovan's escape. Together, Alice and Evelyn had done all they could to keep that hope alive, recruiting other trustworthy souls in secret.

She thought about what they intended to do. They would break Donovan free from his prison, and with any luck find some way to kill Sparrow before he matured. The truth was, none of them knew if killing him would free them from the Monochrome, or if Sparrow could even be killed.

Now it seemed like a dangerous fantasy. They were on the verge of bringing their plans to fruition, and it scared the living hell out of her. There was more at stake now, more than she'd anticipated. Quinn's appearance into the equation wasn't what she'd expected. The last time she'd seen him, he was barely a teenager. Had she really been trapped here that long?

"Honey, if you stare any harder into that fire, you're gonna go blind."

Alice looked away. Evelyn put a hand on her shoulder.

"Talk to me."

Alice shook her head. "I keep thinking about Donovan locked up in that room."

"And to think, our newfound friend could've avoided a lot of trouble if he'd just told you who he was trying to help."

Things changed after that day on the subway platform. Those of the Missing who were there kindled the story of how Donovan saved his wife, spreading the fires of hope to the others. "Who is Donovan Candle?" became a quiet mantra among their group; a phrase whispered in the shadows to keep that vital hope alive.

Some of the Missing didn't share the same views. They scorned Donovan's name, blaming him for the upheaval caused by Dullington's departure. When Sparrow took his place as king of the Monochrome, they flocked to him, eating up the lies he fed them. They shared their new master's contempt for the man who was now their prisoner.

"Don Candle," Evelyn said. "Can't imagine Sparrow invited him back for cake and coffee."

"We'll need to act soon." Alice watched the others gather supplies. "They won't keep him in that room forever. Knowing Sparrow, he'll want to make an example out of Don."

"You mean a public execution?"

Alice nodded, frowning. "Great minds, old lady. I wish we were wrong."

"Me too, kiddo." Evelyn stretched her arms, tilting her head in Quinn's direction. "Speaking of kiddos, we should probably wake our new friend."

Alice was about to step away from the barrel when she heard heavy footsteps echoing down the corridor. Someone called out from the mouth of the tunnel.

A cold spike drove its way into her gut. She met Evelyn's gaze and frowned. "Stay here, old lady."

She jogged across the room to the tunnel opening, expecting to see Sparrow's followers marching toward their camp. Instead she saw Andrew and Eric, two of the men standing watch, and a third figure doubled over, gasping for breath. He took off his glasses and wiped sweat from his face.

"Joel?"

He looked up, eyes wide with urgency and fright. "Alice...we gotta go. We gotta go now." He broke into a coughing fit. "I ran...as fast as I could."

She knelt beside him. "Why, Joel? What's happened?"

"They're moving," he croaked. "Sparrow's moving the prisoner. If we're going to act, we gotta do it now."

Sparrow led him beneath the city. They walked in silence, the prisoner and his warden, and the Monochrome's denizens came out to watch the procession. Donovan had never seen so many before. Thousands of Cretins filled the tunnels, their rubbery bodies shimmering in the hazy unlight. The tunnel breathed with their movement, writhing frantically, chattering and scuttling with possessed urgency. Their master was walking with his prize, and they'd come to bear witness to his success.

A few Yawning lumbered their way through the masses, their giant spindly arms dragging the ground behind them. They peered at him, their mouths quivering with the erratic motion of a silent film. The Cretins didn't bother Donovan, but when he looked at the towering beasts it brought back horrible memories of what they could do. He knew what would happen to him if he got too close.

"They remember you, Candle. And when they see you, I see you. It's like watching a hundred-thousand TV screens."

The collective scratching and screeching reminded him of birds roosting before a storm. Donovan kept his head down, trying to block out the thunderous noise echoing within the tunnel.

They walked for what might have been miles, but Donovan had no concept of distance down here. His feet screamed with every step, his shoulder ached, and the hunger pangs would not be ignored. Worse was the fear he felt—not for himself, but for Donna and the baby. He felt afraid for them, and for Quinn, too. How could he have been so stupid? The answers were there all along, between the lines, and wasn't that where he was supposed to look first? Wasn't that his job? His responsibility?

Pityin' yourself ain't going to help things, hoss. It's best you think about gettin' yourself out of this mess first.

Hopper was right. He was always right.

Sparrow held out his hand and the Cretins carrying him slowed to a stop. Donovan lifted his head. They were out of the tunnels and between two boarding platforms that stretched back into the gloom.

"Where are we?"

Sparrow raised his arms. The Cretins piled upon one another, lifting him up to the platform. He stepped off and offered a hand to Donovan.

"The Nothing Place, Donnie. What you might remember as Winthorpe Station."

The old crone came to mind. *The king sees us all, and we'll all be seein' you soon.*

Donovan hesitated before taking Sparrow's hand. The old man was stronger than he should have been, pulling Donovan up to the platform with little effort.

The walls rippled and shook. Behind and below, past the edge of the platform, a river of Cretins screeched together in their backwards dialect.

Their chaotic drone was like the shriek of nails on a chalkboard played in reverse, and the dissonance made Donovan nauseous.

Sparrow's fingers dug into Donovan's maimed shoulder. White-hot fire shot through his arm, tearing through his tendons like a knife. Dark colors burst before his eyes as the pain washed over him in waves. He clenched his teeth, grunting, fighting to remain lucid.

"That's it," Sparrow growled. The old man's words were far away, lost in a droning haze of Cretin laughter and chimes. "You feel that? That's a fraction, Donnie. A *taste* of what's in store for you. When I'm through, you'll wish—"

"Dr. Sparrow?"

The weak voice carried across the platform. Sparrow loosened his grip, and Donovan swallowed back the pain.

A short fellow stepped into view. He was young, possibly Quinn's age. His matted fiery hair stood out like a beacon in contrast to their drab surroundings. Donovan's eyes were drawn to him. *Another one, just like the others. Another innocent kid. He had no chance to live his life.*

"What is it?" Sparrow barked.

"We—I mean, that is, me 'n Kale 'n Howard, we got those chains you wanted. It's ready for you, whatever it is you're gonna use 'em for, and—"

Sparrow clapped his hands together. "This is excellent. Perfect. Better than perfect. I love when things go right." The kid waited, unsure how to behave or respond. "Well go on, join the others. We'll be up soon." The boy stood in place, petrified with a kind of fear Donovan knew all too well. "*I said move, you worthless little shit.*"

The kid found his feet and ran like hell toward the stairs. The clip-clap of his feet echoed throughout the empty terminal. Donovan watched with helpless pity, his fists balled up, nails digging into his palms.

"Mr. Candle, if you please?"

Beaming, his eyes wide with delight, Sparrow gestured toward the stairs. The legion of Cretins collectively shivered down on the tracks. Donovan blinked, woke from his trance of thought, and looked to his captor.

They ascended together. At the top were turnstiles and ticketing booths, and beyond them the station: a hollow shell of its former self, long silent due to crime, apathy, and budget constraints. The walls, once teeming with bright artwork and character, were now devoid of color and life, sucked dry by the Monochrome's featureless hue.

And waiting for them there were the Missing: hundreds of them standing at attention, an army preparing for war.

Donovan saw faces both young and old, some clear and some covered in the sickening gray pox, clothes tattered and filthy. It was an army of the homeless, the forgotten.

Sparrow held out his hands. "Your king has arrived."

The room erupted in crazed cheers, laughter and applause not of the gleeful, but of the desperate and insane. They worshipped their king, a paragon of the mediocre, and the terrifying reality of their devotion gripped Donovan's mind like a cold hand. His heart plunged deep into a hole within his gut as the panic set in.

Oh shit.

Sparrow basked in their attention and spread his hands out like the king he claimed to be. His followers bowed their heads and parted, forming a path as he walked toward the center of the room. More of the Missing looked down from the mezzanine. He felt their eyes burning into his skin. He felt their hate.

"You see, Donovan," Sparrow bellowed, "here in my court I *am* king. And though you are my guest, I expect the same honor from you displayed so loyally by my subjects."

Donovan looked at his audience, noting their mixed expressions of loathing and unease, feeling their collective gaze pressing into his skull. "You want me to bow my head to honor you?"

Sparrow slowly nodded, smiling. He raised his hand again, and the whole room fell silent.

"No, I won't. Not to you."

"I expected as much." Sparrow walked further into the center of the crowd, and Donovan caught sight of the chains. He saw the bearded man known as Kale standing on the other side of the clearing, arms folded across his chest.

He took another look around the room. There was one face missing from the crowd. *No, not Quinn,* he thought, spinning in place, searching frantically for his nephew's bruised face. *He has to be here. He has to—*

But then Donovan remembered the calls of the Yawning outside the Laundromat, and he went numb. *I let another one die.* The emptiness inside got the better of him. His old friend Doubt crept out of that emptiness and slithered into his head. *You let another one die, and what makes you think you could bring a child into this world? What makes you think you could protect a child from monsters like these when you can't even protect yourself?*

He wiped his eyes. They stung.

"He's crying." Kale's voice broke the uneasy silence with a gruff roar. Those two words were enough. The king's court erupted into laughter, pointing and slapping each other's backs, cackling and hacking madly, mocking their pitiful prisoner.

"You see?" Sparrow boomed above them. "He is not the legend the Wretched make him out to be. He is a bitter, broken man. He deserves this hell more than *you* do."

Donovan blinked back more tears. Dullington's words echoed from within his mind: *You stand accused before a jury of your peers, Mr. Candle. How do you plead?*

"Guilty," he whispered.

Sparrow nodded to Kale, who knelt and prepared the chains. Hands came from behind, gripping Donovan's arms, pushing him down a path of scabrous lepers and innocents, souls who both belonged and did not belong in this gray hell. They hissed at him with teeth bared like feral animals. He recognized some of their faces—the soccer mom who never picked up her kids from practice, the financial analyst who never made it to his meeting, the bus driver who vanished at the depot.

Here, too, were the young men and women over whom he'd spent so many agonizing days, pooling his resources, trying to piece together a puzzle he couldn't see. The cheerleader, the musician, the math genius, the artist—they were all here, faces covered in grime and barely resembling the photos in their case files, unaware of their place in Sparrow's scheme. They were innocent bystanders caught up in his sinister plot, and Donovan wanted to feel hate for the bastard who had trapped him here—but such loathing paled in comparison to what he felt for himself in that moment. If only he'd acted sooner.

If only.

"Hey, Candle."

The voice was familiar. Donovan turned to his side and immediately spotted Timothy Butler. Time in the Monochrome wasn't kind to his old boss. A jagged scar ran the length of the man's face, but he still had that nauseating smile.

"Remember me? The king says he'll let me go if we help him. Nothin' personal—even if I thought you were a fuckin' loser."

Donovan turned away, letting his feet carry him toward the clearing. When they reached the end, Donovan discovered his fate would not be a kind one. Kale held up the shackles.

"Yes, Donovan, that's right." Sparrow approached the center, taking the shackles and chains from the bearded man. "No one escapes. Not I, and certainly not you. *No one.*"

He nodded to Butler. A sharp pain jabbed into the back of Donovan's legs, and he fell to his knees. Sparrow turned around, his hands raised in an eccentric pose, pleading with his audience.

"Everyone bows before the king," he beamed, and the crowd cheered. He looked down at his prisoner. "Strip him."

Donovan felt hands pulling at his shirt, tugging at his shoes, and then his slacks. He tried to kick them off, but there were too many holding him down. He gasped as they pulled his clothes from his body.

The air was cold against his naked skin, and his teeth began to chatter. He felt his balls shrivel up from the cool air and shame of exposure.

The first shackle clamped down on his ankle, slamming home like a gavel. *Clank.*

There were more voices over him now. He tried not to hear them, but when he saw their faces, his horror and defeat only intensified. There was the old crone from the station steps, with her pox-ridden face curled back into a jack-o-lantern grin. Beside her were two women he used to know well: Tammy Perpa and Tammy Quilago, Identinel's dual Human Resource coordinators. The last time he saw them was the day he quit his job, the day he made his life pitch to Dullington. They pointed and laughed at him, at the flab of his gut, and at his exposed manhood.

A scrawny leper with an enormous boil on his forehead snapped another shackle over Donovan's other ankle. He stood up and tossed a chain across to Butler, who held down Donovan's arms.

An urgent throbbing pain shot through Donovan's shoulder and down the length of his torso. He could no longer hold back the agony, whimpering through clenched teeth.

"It's like I said, Candle, nothing personal." Timothy Butler clamped the shackle around Donovan's wrist. *Clank.* "Never really liked you, though. You didn't fit with the program. You were too afraid to just go for it. You just went along with whatever we told you. We wanted leaders, not sheep. You always wanted to play it safe."

The final shackle closed over his other wrist. They were too small, the cold metal digging into his skin, cutting off circulation.

Kale stood over him, twirling an idle finger through his beard. He grunted. "Small balls."

The court burst into more laughter. When he looked up, he saw their faces peering down at him, down at this poor excuse of a man broken by his hesitation and fear. Defeated by his sin of inaction. He had failed to move, to leap, and now he would suffer.

Sparrow knelt over him. Donovan saw himself reflected in the old man's cold eyes, and he didn't like what he saw staring back.

"Now you'll know," Sparrow whispered, his pale lips hovering inches from Donovan's ear. "This is what oblivion feels like."

The Monochrome King rose to his feet, surveying his court before making his way through their ranks. He paused at the mezzanine's steps, turning to beckon to his flock.

"*Make him suffer.*"

Faced with his own mortality, Donovan found clarity in that moment. The crowd disappeared, his ears became deaf to their cries of hate, and he thought of Quinn. He thought also of the other young men and women whose lives were stolen from them; of his brother, and their parents; of his unborn baby. He remembered the promise he made.

Donovan closed his eyes and thought a silent prayer. Not to any deity, but to his wife: *I'm sorry for everything, Donna. I'm sorry I can't be there for you to help bring our child into this world. I'm sorry I can't be there to help you raise the baby. I'm sorry I can't be that man you thought you married. I'm sorry, and if I could do it all over, I swear on my love for you I would do it differently. I wouldn't lie to myself. I wouldn't be held down by my fear. I wouldn't be afraid to jump.*

He opened his eyes, saw their angry faces peering down at him, and braced himself for the onslaught of blows to come.

———————•———————

Quinn hadn't fired a gun before. He'd played his share of video games, and he'd played paintball once with friends from high school, but until a few days ago he'd never even held a real gun. Alice handed him the weapon as soon as they arrived at the station. He looked at her, helplessly lost with the firearm's simple mechanics.

"You're ready to go," she whispered. "Just aim and squeeze the trigger."

This can't be happening, he thought. *I can't do this. I can't just kill someone.* But he might have to. That possibility hadn't occurred to him until now.

No one noticed their arrival. The Missing were too busy paying tribute to their so-called king. The Wretched hung back in the mouth of the stairwell, lingering just at the edge of the crowd, heads bowed and eyes wide. From here they could see the center of the room. Sparrow pranced along the perimeter, speaking with animated gestures, fueling his court's rage.

Quinn couldn't see the cause of Sparrow's jubilance from the back of the group. He worked his way to the front, taking a place beside Evelyn. Until that moment, he never thought he'd have a reason to fire a gun, but the sight of his uncle shackled to the floor changed all that. His gut churned and he tasted bile on the back of his tongue. *Can I do this? If I don't—*

"*Make him suffer.*" The ground trembled with Sparrow's words, prompting the enraged crowd to move inward. Some of the Wretched shuffled nervously, looking to their leader for a sign of action, but Evelyn only watched, her mouth agape in shock and fear. Heart pounding, his mind a frantic race of possibilities, Quinn did the only thing he could think to do. He shut his eyes, pointed the gun to the ceiling, and squeezed the trigger.

The report filled the room with a deafening thunderclap. Sparrow's mob recoiled, reacting instinctively to the sound of the shot, and many of them dropped to the floor. Others refused to cower, standing defiantly over their prisoner.

Kale raised a meaty paw and bellowed for his master. "*The Wretched.*"

"*Now!*" Evelyn shrieked. The Wretched raised their weapons and opened fire.

Sparrow had reached the mezzanine when he heard the first shot. He turned just in time to watch his followers fall to the floor. A small group of people stood at the far end of the room near the stairs, and he knew who they were before Kale spoke. He saw Candle's nephew standing with a gun in his hand. Even from this distance, Sparrow saw the white pin affixed to the boy's chest. The old bitch, Evelyn, screamed what might have been a war cry, urging the others to attack.

How?

And then he remembered sensing someone outside the Laundromat. He remembered sending the Cretin, remembered watching through its eyes—

But then he'd looked away, tending to Candle's incessant questions and self-pity. Goddamn them all, they would not ruin this for him. He'd worked too hard to move these pieces together and he would not be denied his revenge.

"*SILENCE THEM!*" His voice boomed throughout the room, sending a violent tremor ripping through the building's foundation.

And the court did not listen. They scrambled and clamored over one another like insects, interested only in saving themselves. He felt hate burbling up within, not just for Candle or the Wretched, but for all of them. He did not need them. Not now. Everything was in place, everything was going to happen whether they were here or not, and when all was said and done the Monochrome would be teeming with more mediocre souls to feed upon.

Insects, he thought. *They're all insects.*

The crowd surrounding his prize was all but gone, scurrying away to the corners like rats, screaming and crying for help.

"*Help us, Sparrow,*" they pleaded. "*Save us, our King!*"

He watched the spectacle unfold before him, his anger and disgust growing with each passing moment. The bodies of his congregation sprawled across the floor as more gunshots filled the air, staining the Monochrome's empty palette a stark shade of crimson.

Candle resisted his chains, writhing in place like a fly without wings, shouting something Sparrow could not hear over the commotion. If only he possessed his master's influence, he could stop this massacre in an instant—

Quinn scrambled across the room, falling to his knees beside his uncle. They spoke to one another as the boy tried to pry the shackles apart. When they did not give, he began to search the bodies surrounding his uncle, turning out their pockets until he found the key

Sparrow ground his teeth together, watching helplessly while the little shit freed his prisoner. That was too much. He focused himself, focused his eyes on the millions of views that made up the Cretins and the Yawning. *Come, my pets. Come and play.*

But something else bubbled up within him. What he dismissed as his own anger was something else entirely. A dim energy rose in waves, pulsing, throbbing up his body, arcing across his bones in white searing jolts. His mind was suddenly alive with a new kind of awareness, a euphoric gift from the great column connecting him to something he could not see, something—

Yes.

The strings of the coil. The strings that bound them all, tied together in a single knot for him—and him alone—to pull apart at his leisure. They were there, beyond the gray veil, and he reached out with his mind to give them a pluck.

"**Q**uinn? What the hell?"

They both ducked as another round of gunfire burst through the air. Donovan scrambled to find his clothes, but Quinn yanked his arm.

"There's no time, Don!"

Another bullet whizzed by his head. Donovan did not argue. His nephew pulled him toward the turnstiles and the stairway beyond. He opened his mouth to speak but paused. The air went out of the room just as an unseen force pulled at his insides. The sensation left him reeling, and he put a hand on Quinn's shoulder to steady himself.

The flickering? No, can't be—

The screams froze him in place.

Long, horrific shrieks filled the room to its rafters, a collective wail of agony that sent chills scratching all the way up his spine. Donovan turned back to look at what was happening, and what he saw turned his stomach.

The congregation of men and women were doubled over in agony. Only the younger ones near Quinn's age were unaffected, and they stood frozen in place, terrified beyond comprehension.

"Alice? Evelyn?"

Quinn let go of Donovan's arm and took a few steps toward the two women. One held her wrist, biting her lip in pain while the other—a far older woman with a face full of the gray pox—was doubled over, clutching at her stomach.

Donovan looked away and caught sight of the suspected cause. Sparrow stood at the opposite side of the room, midway up the steps, his arms hanging rigid at his sides and his eyes closed. *Is he doing this? He has to be. But why?*

The next wave of shrieks answered his question.

A man's body lay just a few feet from where Donovan stood. Blood pooled around the corpse, his back riddled with oozing entrance wounds. The back of his arm was exposed, revealing a large cluster of the pulsing gray pustules. They throbbed with each series of pained shrieks, and

Donovan recoiled in horror as one of the malignant pods burst open. A white substance oozed out of it and collected on the ground.

Oh God, it's moving.

The sickening goo writhed and flopped on the ground like a maggot. Another pod burst, followed by another, and soon the whole cluster on the dead man's arm had freed itself of the white things growing within. The maggots squirmed together, entangling themselves upon one another, fusing into a single figure.

Donovan gaped in terror as he watched a Cretin form from the white maggots. The creature stood, stretched its limbs, and grimaced. When it saw him, it hissed and gave him the finger.

"Quinn!" he shouted. "Quinn, we need to get the hell out of here!"

But Quinn could not hear him over the screams erupting around the room. All the people afflicted with the gray pox fell to the ground, convulsing and crying through clenched teeth as the Cretin larvae worked their way out of their hosts. The army of Cretins grew, migrating to the foot of the mezzanine steps, faithful servants to the king who would soon set them free to wreak havoc upon those who were left.

Donovan grabbed Quinn by the arm. *"We need to go, NOW!"*

The younger woman held her wrist as she knelt over her elderly companion. The old woman convulsed with painful tremors. Another man with glasses lurched toward the two women.

"Joel," Alice cried, "we have to get Evelyn out of here."

Donovan pulled on his nephew's arm once again. Quinn turned to him with tears in his eyes.

"I can't, Don. I can't, I have to help them—"

"Oh Donnie. Where the fuck do you think you're going?"

The station shook. Back at the stairway the Cretins were climbing atop one another, molding into a lumbering form Donovan immediately recognized. He turned back to the man in the glasses—another familiar face from a long time ago.

"Joel, right? You can carry her. Come on, Quinn, help us."

Donovan helped them lift the old woman. She was frail, hollow. He tried not to look at the open sores on her arms and face.

"Here." He slung Evelyn's arm over Quinn's shoulder. "Get her to safety."

"But—Don, where are you going?"

Donovan looked back at the freshly formed Yawning. The behemoth raised its enormous white paw and beckoned to him. A low wail bellowed from its empty maw as it took its first steps toward them.

"He wants me. Now get the fuck out of here, Quinn!"

"Don—"

But Donovan was already running.

———————————◆———————————

His bare feet screamed as he raced down the cold gray tunnels. He had no idea where he was going and no map to guide him. The sounds of the Yawning echoed from behind and he pumped his legs faster, wishing he'd run track in his younger days, wishing he'd tried to stay fit instead of sitting at a desk for most of his adult life.

A burning ache occupied his swollen shoulder, throbbing its way down the length of his arm. He clenched his teeth and balled his hands into fists, wincing with every jostling step, feeling every pound of flab on his body smothering the meager muscles beneath. His lungs combusted long ago, fueling the inferno raging onward in his chest.

Go, his brain commanded. *Just go. Don't look back. Keep going. Don't stop. Never mind your feet. Never mind the stitch in your gut. Never mind the cramp in your calf. Just go. GO.*

He put one foot before the other, the bare pads of his feet slapping against the hard floor of the tunnel, while the pounding steps of the Yawning closed in behind him.

This is it. Out of the frying pan. I can't keep up. I can't. I can't—

He rounded the bend, and his heart sank into the pit of his belly. A large pile of debris blocked his way. He spun in a full circle, searching for an access door or platform, desperate for some means of escape.

No, not like this.

The Yawning emerged from the dim haze. Donovan backed his way against the rubble and cowered in the corner. The white lummox took one heavy step after another, its bulbous knuckles scraping the ground. When the creature saw its prey, it let out a call of triumph—a low, drawn out yawn filling the air with a stench of decay.

The beast closed the gap between them in three long strides. His heart raced a thousand beats, filling with adrenaline that would go to waste. The Yawning stood over him, its jaw quivering with anticipation.

Donovan shut his eyes. He knew what came next, and he didn't want to see it coming. He only wanted to think of Donna, and when he imagined her smiling face on the beach all those months ago, a strange sort of calm came over him. His heart slowed.

I'm sorry. If there were any way to make it right, I would. I swear it. God, I'm so sorry. I'm—

There was another tug at his gut, but it was different than before. A strange tickling sensation moved across his skin, tracing the contours of his body like ghostly fingertips, defining his shape in the gloom.

In that moment of unexpected serenity, Donovan smiled. He let go.

————•————

The Yawning's mouth opened, stretching until its jaw unhinged. The bottomless maw lowered to the ground, opening wide enough to accommodate a grown man. It leaned forward to fit its prey inside its mouth and met with disappointment.

The creature recoiled, snapping its mouth shut in confusion. It looked down at the corner where its prey cowered, but something was wrong. There was just the pile of rubble blocking the tunnel.

The space was empty but for the outline of a man, and in time, even that faded from view.

11

GHOSTS

'm sorry—

    A gust of air swept across his face. He opened his eyes, expecting to stare down the Yawning's obsidian maw, but what he saw didn't make sense. For a fleeting moment Donovan saw the outline of the staggering white creature. Its mouth contracted, settling into place while the beast stepped back in confusion. The outline lasted only a moment before fading out of sight.

    A chill crept down his naked body. He slowly picked himself up from the floor and looked down the tunnel. He blinked again—not because he couldn't see, but because he didn't trust his eyes.

    What the hell?

    The tunnel shimmered, pulsing with color, revealing fragments of the dingy, coarse walls. Every surface fluttered with ranges of the Spectrum he'd not seen in days. Watching the colors shift reminded him of the aurora borealis.

    He reached out, tracing his fingers along the wall. The surface—no, the *texture* rippled like water, shifting from flat geometry to bumps and ridges. The colors transmuted from gray tones to stark hues like peeling layers of paint. The effect had an odd physical quality to it, like slipping his hand into silt. The wall itself was still firm, and it resisted the pressure of his touch.

    Donovan followed the lights. They carried on like a coating of luminescent plankton on the surface of the sea. He walked for a time, lost in thought, transfixed by the bright colors flashing in waves around him.

Is this a dream? Am I dead?

No, that couldn't be right. Something had changed. Somehow, he'd flickered out just as the Yawning was upon him. One moment he'd cowered in a corner, watching as the creature unhinged its jaws to gobble him up in a single bite; the next he was here, still nude, still alone, and very confused.

You're not dead, hoss. Lost, but not dead.

A boarding platform fell into view as he came around the bend, and when the colors swam over it, he saw signs of life that would not exist in the Monochrome. There were old signs covered in cobwebs. The walls were adorned with graffiti—JIMMY B WUZ HERE—and he saw a dented, rusting soda machine long dormant and vacated of its cans.

He saw these details in a flash of color, and then the wave passed, returning the world to its shimmering gray self. Then came another wave, and he saw more than the first time. The cycle repeated and for a moment, standing there in perplexed awe, Donovan thought himself trapped inside a kaleidoscope.

He watched for a moment longer before pulling himself up the side of the platform. The movement came naturally and without effort—but he paused, suddenly aware of his shoulder.

Bracing himself, Donovan slowly lifted his arm, first stretching it to his side before lifting it into the air. Gone was the fire surging through his tendons, and the skin around his shoulder was no longer enflamed.

What the hell is going on here?

A cool uneasiness slithered into his gut and coiled around his insides, spreading a chill of panic all the way up his spine. He had to get out of this place. He had to find some clothes, get back to Donna, and stop Sparrow. He had to—

Calm yourself, hoss. Ain't no sense in panicking just yet. One step at a time.

Donovan took a deep breath and collected his thoughts. Hopper was right. Panicking wouldn't do him any good.

I need to get topside, he thought. *Figure it out as I go.*

Monochrome and Spectrum overlapped, coloring the room with vibrant tones. He caught a glimpse of a dented sign hanging above the stairwell: EXIT: 46TH STREET & HADEN AVE. Donovan sighed. 46th Street was at the far end of the South District. He was miles from the city limits.

One step at time. He crossed the platform toward the stairs, cursing Joe Hopper every inch of the way.

"**S**top here for a minute. I need to catch my breath."

Quinn leaned against the tunnel wall and doubled over, his chest heaving, trying to expel the cinders from his lungs. Joel slowed, turning with the old woman in his arms.

"But we're almost there."

"No, he's right." Alice struggled to catch her breath. "Rest will do us good."

Joel set Evelyn down and knelt beside her. They'd gone as fast as they could with their leader in tow, and when that slowed their progress Joel picked up her limp body, determined to carry her the rest of the way. He was stronger than Quinn, and after the stunt Sparrow had pulled back in the Nothing Place there wasn't much to the old woman anymore. Carrying her was no more difficult than carrying a cornstalk.

The Yawning's moans echoed from somewhere farther down the tunnels. They had a hard time telling just how far they'd gone in the gray haze. Alice put her hand on her weapon, but Joel shook his head.

"It's okay. They didn't see us."

"How can you be sure?"

"Because we'd be dead already."

Joel looked over Evelyn's unconscious face and frowned. The sores on her forehead, nose, and cheeks were open wounds. Blood had collected inside them like tide pools and was starting to clot. A sickly smell rose from her body. After living in the Monochrome for so long, he was used to the body's strange smells, but this was something different. The scent was almost sweet, like an overly ripe fruit, and his next thought made his stomach churn: *She's rotting from the inside.*

The old woman had helped them through so much and seeing her in pain like this ignited his temper. Hadn't she told them all to wait for her signal? He shifted his gaze to the new guy.

"What the fuck were you trying to pull back there?"

Joel pushed himself off the ground and was on Quinn in an instant, pinning him against the wall. He tightened his grip around the kid's throat.

"You dumb little *shit!*"

Alice rose to her feet. "Joel, don't."

Quinn glared into the eyes of his attacker with a mix of fear and anger. The man's fingers dug into his throat, and he began to panic as the ability to breathe was taken from him.

"*Don't!*"

The dirty man's hands loosened, and Quinn took that first precious breath as Alice pulled Joel off him. He fell back and stared. Tears carved paths through the dirt on his face.

"What's your problem?"

"You are," Joel spat. "We agreed to wait for Evelyn's signal. Why the fuck did you shoot?"

Alice stepped between them. She was crying. "It doesn't matter."

"I was…I was trying to protect my uncle."

"*Fuck* your uncle."

Quinn closed the gap between them, furious. "They were going to kill him, and she froze. If I hadn't acted, he'd be dead—and if Donovan hadn't lured the Yawning away, so would we." He paused, swallowing back the fire in his belly. Joel met his wild stare with equal fury. "I didn't mean for this to happen. No one did. But it happened, so let's just fucking deal with it, okay? Now get off my back."

Quinn stepped back, shaking. Joel stared for a moment, chewing his lower lip, but whatever venomous reply he had in mind was quickly forgotten. Evelyn raised a bloody hand to the air.

"That's…enough…kiddos."

Alice took her friend's hand and knelt beside her. The old woman's arms were bone-thin, and her face was deathly pale. Whatever Sparrow had done almost sucked her dry.

Quinn looked back at the two of them.

"Is she going to be all right?"

Joel scoffed. "The hell do you care?"

"I may not know her as well as you do," Quinn growled, "but she still tried to help me. Hell, she tried to help all of us—including my uncle."

Alice shot to her feet. "Enough! Stop your bickering. *Christ.*" She pointed down at Evelyn's shriveled body. "We have to get her back. She needs medicine."

Quinn looked over the old woman. They'd taken him in, shown him hospitality, and in return he'd led them all to their deaths. He cursed himself for not keeping his mouth shut. If he'd not told them about Donovan, they'd still be safe in their hiding place.

And Donovan would be dead. He could already *be dead.*

The thought made him shiver. He should not have let Donovan run off by himself. These tunnels were dangerous even when they travelled in groups. Going alone was suicide.

Evelyn came in and out of consciousness, mumbling nonsense words pulled from her feverish delirium.

"*Shit, shit, shit.*" Joel ran his hands through his hair. "Alice, what the hell are we going to do?"

"We need to get something for these wounds. My rotation is all messed up, but if I head to the surface, I can—"

"Alice."

She looked up at Quinn. "What?"

The fear in her eyes made him feel even worse. He spoke with a lump in his throat.

"My rotation is coming up. I haven't flickered since before you found me, and Evelyn told me it's still accurate for new people."

Joel rolled his eyes. "And what if your mental clock's off, huh, Q-ball? What if you're wrong? Then she dies, and if that happens, I swear I'm gonna come looking for you."

Heat rose in Quinn's cheeks, but he forced himself to ignore the man. "I can do this." He nodded to the dying woman. "If this is my fault, let me fix it."

Alice closed her eyes and took a breath. Then she looked at the mottled, bleeding wounds spread across Evelyn's skin. Seeing them made her body ache.

"Alice, you can't be serious about this." Joel knelt beside her. "You know what happened the last time we sent kids on our behalf. It was a bad idea then, and it's a bad idea now—"

She took a long look at Joel before returning her attention to Quinn. "There's a station up ahead. From there, you should be able to get to the edge of the city. Just a few blocks, tops. We'll need bandages, antiseptic—"

"Alice—" Joel began, but she held up her hand to silence him.

"Joel, we don't have a choice here. If we don't tend to her, she's going to die." She looked back at Quinn. "You're sure about this, Q-ball?"

A deep hollow widened in Quinn's stomach. He felt empty and scared, but there was a spring in his step. He wanted to do this. He *had* to do this.

"I can," he said. "I'll run."

"You'd better," Alice said. "Otherwise it'll be me who comes looking for you, kid."

Joel opened his mouth to add to the threats, but Quinn was already moving. He jogged around the bend of the tunnel. When he could no longer hear Alice and Joel behind him, he began to run.

Donovan had just crossed over the turnstiles when he saw an apparition limping toward him. The specter resembled a person, defined by a black outline that moved with the jerky qualities of a scratched movie reel. A sudden flash of color filled in the details, revealing an empty hallway covered in trash and graffiti; another flash returned the world to gray. The dark figure remained.

Startled, Donovan pressed himself against the wall and tried to ignore his pounding heart. The apparition stopped a few feet away and cocked its head.

"Who's there? Who is that?"

The dark figure reached out, intending to touch him. Donovan closed his eyes. *Please go away.* He'd never believed in spirits, but this was the closest thing to a ghost he'd ever seen, and it was scaring the shit out of him.

The black outline of a finger sank into his chest. He felt a weird tickle that made him open his eyes, and when he saw the thing sticking into his sternum, he let out a frightened cry. The dark outline fell backward, uttering a shout that echoed down the hall.

Frightened, Donovan leapt over the thing and ran. The apparition shouted a single word, which he heard loud and clear: *"Ghost!"*

Donovan looked back just as another flash of color left the world. He saw the outline fill in with the details of a raggedy old man, dirty and frightened, clutching a cloudy bottle of malt liquor. He backed himself against the wall, pointing in Donovan's direction—but another flash came, erasing the old man's outline altogether and silencing his terrified whimpering.

He slowed to a stop, waiting for his heart to cease its tribal thump. The place where the apparition touched him was ice cold.

"What the hell was that?" His hollow voice echoed down the corridor. The walls flushed with color before bleeding out into the Monochrome's gray tones, keeping to its odd kaleidoscopic cycle.

More faint voices rose from the silence, accompanied by the echoes of soft footsteps. He flattened himself against the wall once again as three specters ran past him, outlines flickering in time with the world's flashing colors, offering a fleeting glimpse of their qualities—light golden strands of hair, glasses, a crooked nose, dirty faces, scars. And then, just like with the old man, they promptly vanished into thin air, the whispers of their movement silenced by the shift between Monochrome and Spectrum.

I am dead. The Yawning killed me. Ate me whole. Cracked my bones and devoured every trace of me.

Donovan wasn't a religious man. He had no tethers to any one theology, but he'd read enough accounts of near-death experience to have some concept of the supposed afterlife. At any moment, he expected to see a bright light.

But what if that light doesn't come?

He was frightened by that thought. What if there would be no escape from this plane of reality? Was this what the afterlife was supposed to look like? Would he be trapped in this swirling purgatory, teased with the life he'd squandered?

He thought of Donna's smiling face, recalling his prayer back in the tunnel. He'd prayed to her for forgiveness. Was this the result of that prayer? Was he trapped here, caught between two worlds like an insect in a web?

Colors of the room swirled around him for an instant, taunting him with the Spectrum's vibrancy before bleeding out into a palette of grays. The Monochrome silently mocked him.

What sort of sick god would do this?

"No," he sighed, looking wearily to the exit up ahead. "Not a god. Just me."

Sparrow saw everything happen through the Yawning's eyes. Mystified, he watched as the naked man's outline lingered in the air like a free-floating drawing. The effect lasted only a moment, and then Donovan Candle was gone.

What's this, then?

There was no reason Candle should have flickered out. No one escaped unless escape was granted, and he only gave that to a select few. Something else had intervened. *Someone* else.

He retracted his mind from the Yawning and blinked away the disorientation. The walls of the Nothing Place dripped with the blood of his followers. Bodies littered the station's concourse, piled atop one another like kindling for a bonfire, and those who survived the summoning hid in the haze of shadows. They feared him, and rightfully so. Summoning his minions had renewed his vigor, filling him with a sudden surge of energy that resonated all the way down into his core. When the massacre was over, Sparrow found his hands were shaking—and he could not stop laughing.

His revelry was tainted by the loss of Donovan Candle, and when he thought of the man's unassuming face, rage bubbled up within him once more. Everything was coming together so well. Candle's suffering was but an ingredient in this dangerous recipe he'd concocted over the months. Not a vital ingredient, but one that would give things a better flavor.

That the Wretched were able to arm themselves was no one's fault but his own. He'd underestimated their resolve, turning his attention away from them to focus on other matters. They took advantage of his preoccupation—a weakness he would no longer allow them to exploit. Sooner or later his minions would find them; their demise was only a matter of time.

Albert Sparrow clenched his fist and slammed it into the wall, rippling the fabric of the Monochrome. If only he could mature faster, he would lock the coils in place and bring their daily feedings to an abrupt end. He would revel in their cries of agony while they slowly starved to death.

Oh, if only.

Sparrow turned away from the scene of the massacre, ascending the steps to his resting place. On another side of reality, the room used to be a manager's office; here the room was a barren square, unremarkable in every way except for a writhing tumor of white flesh affixed at the center.

The cocoon stretched from floor to ceiling, rooting itself into those surfaces like a weed with long, worm-like tendrils. They flared and stretched out to welcome him. These pale cilia ran up and down his body, feeling his presence. A sickly dim light emanated from the fleshy mass.

Sparrow stepped forward, surrendering himself to its tendrils. The rubbery arms folded over him, absorbing his body into its own and leaving only his head exposed. The effect was immediate. Newfound energy surged through his being, a subtle electricity that healed rather than harmed.

His mind drifted, but he fought the gray sleep for a moment longer. *Not yet*, he thought, reaching out with his mind. There was still the matter of Mr. Candle—and he had just the solution in mind.

"*Kale. Come to me.*"

At first his lap dog did not come, and he wondered if his faithful servant had been caught in his moment of rage. He felt something like sadness at the thought. A drifter and murderer, Kale had spent the last several years in an institution, whiling away the hours in a drug-induced haze until the flickering set him free into the Monochrome. Sparrow saw potential in the tacit man, and appointed Kale as his prime subject. The quiet man had proven useful so far and would do so once more—if he still lived.

Sparrow called again, and this time he sensed movement outside the room. The bearded man entered, knelt before the cocoon.

"You called?"

"Yes, Kale. I've a task for you. Candle escaped. Things will progress as intended, but I want you to do something for me."

"Of course."

"Since Candle has evaded me, I want you to hurt him in another way. He values someone else more than his own life."

A thin smile cut its way across Kale's face. "His wife?"

"Yes, my son. Hurting her would ruin Donovan Candle. In fact, I should've had you kill her sooner—but no matter. I want you to end her life, and I don't care how. Do what you wish with her. You've earned that prize. When you're finished, return to the WBS building. I'll be waiting for you there."

Kale climbed to his feet, offering his master a short nod of agreement before the flickering pulled him out of the Monochrome. Smiling, Albert Sparrow closed his eyes and relaxed. The cocoon closed around him, and he slept in its white womb, a cancer waiting to metastasize.

Detective Nathan Brock hated the city. He hated the traffic, the people, he hated the fucking smell, and he hated how old the place made him feel. He was fifty-seven, nearly fifty-eight, and felt every bit of seventy each time he reported for duty at the precinct. He decided long ago that the city was a blight on the countryside he remembered from his youth.

Back then, he gave a shit. Back then, he and Evelyn could rope the moon if they wanted, and for a while he almost believed they would.

The day was a scorcher, and the setting sun did little to break the heat. Brock put up the window and cranked the A/C. His cell phone vibrated just as he came to a red light. He pulled the cell from his pocket and frowned. MICHAEL CANDLE scrolled across the fancy screen.

"Son of a bitch."

By his count, Michael had called him three times that day. He had enough shit to worry about without adding to the pile, and Michael's incessant checking in was starting to grate on his nerves. He cancelled the call and looked up. The light was green. He grunted and stepped on the gas.

People were disappearing left and right, most of them just high school kids, and then that damned TV producer followed suit. Joseph Rochester's murder was the last straw, sending the whole city into a frenzy. Local media gave voice to the masses, pressuring City Hall to find the murderer, or else there would be hell to pay come election time. At some point, someone higher up the chain decided to put Nathan Brock on the case—after all, he knows all about those disappearing folks.

The thought made his stomach churn. Bile burned in the back of his throat. When traffic slowed, he reached over and plucked a roll of antacids from the console. He thumbed two into his mouth, chomping them to dust. He welcomed the chalky taste.

Fingerprints left on the murder weapon matched the prints lifted from Henza's home; those prints matched the ones found on several of the bodies from last week's crime scene. A search of their records returned one match: a man named Kale Abrams.

Brock shivered. He turned down the thermostat.

Mr. Abram's files revealed a history of mental illness and violence, both of which he'd adequately demonstrated on the law firm's security footage. The scene he'd left behind in the alleyway also corroborated what Brock already knew: Kale Abrams was a sadistic son of a bitch.

Even with details on the perpetrator's background, he couldn't begin to establish a concrete motive. Sure, he had his prime suspect in Kale Abrams, but *finding* the man was another matter altogether. Kale's last known residence was the county hospital where he was supposed to spend the rest of his days doped up on Thorazine, a permanent guest of the state due to an insanity plea.

But nothing's ever that simple.

No, nothing ever was. The hospital was a dead end. None of the hospital staff could recall what happened to poor Mr. Abrams. Some of them even struggled to remember, as if pulling those memories from their minds was an agonizing chore. They remembered the name, but wait—what *did* happen to Kale Abrams?

No one knew. It was almost like he'd vanished into thin air. A killer of missing people was a missing person himself.

He smirked at the irony and shook his head. *Shut it off, Nate. Call it a day, for God's sake.*

Evelyn used to be the one to help him sort out this shit. She was his anchor, his balance, and nothing was the same since she disappeared. Years ago, and long before his promotion, there were nights he'd come home from patrol, physically drained and emotionally shaken. She'd give him a glass of warm milk and sit up with him into the late hours, holding his hand and listening while he recounted the evening's happenings.

He'd ask her to go to bed, tell her it wasn't something she'd want to hear, but Evie always insisted.

"*You're my husband*," she'd say, a smile on her face and sparkle in her eye, "*and what troubles you troubles me. I ain't gonna sleep any better knowin' you're down here shakin' like a wet dog. So talk to me, darlin'.*"

She worked the loading dock at the textile mill. They woke up together, ate breakfast together, and left for work together. They couldn't have children, a fact that tested their mettle during the early years, but they'd endured. Their lives were simple, modest, and they were happy.

Even after he was promoted to Detective, earning more than enough money to sustain them, Evelyn kept working at the mill. He became engrossed in his new duties, and one day he came home to find things different. Evelyn wasn't herself. She was very quiet, very distant, and sometimes he couldn't remember a thing she said to him.

Remembrance of this fact stirred the acids in his gut. He took the next exit and guided the car down the ramp. There he waited at another red light, watching the cars come and go. Across the street, a stray dog waited for a break before limping across the pavement and into the tall grass of a vacant lot. The sun dipped between the skyscrapers of the inner city. He turned on the headlights.

God, he missed her. There wasn't a day he didn't think about her, and his resolve to find her was what kept him coming back. He could've moved out of this hellhole numerous times, but he didn't. Part of him wondered if she was still around somewhere, hidden in captivity or suffering from some sort of amnesia. Surely he was good to her? She wouldn't have walked out on him without at least leaving him a Dear John letter, right? He thought about the days leading up to her vanishing, how she seemed to stop talking to him altogether, and he always wondered if he'd unwittingly done something to hurt her.

These questions still haunted him. He could deal with answers, even if she turned out to be dead, but not knowing kept him teetering on a brink he did not want to face.

"Could use you right about now, Evie."

His words fell silent in the empty car. The light turned green, and he sped across the intersection into a gas station parking lot. He couldn't bring himself to cook in Evelyn's kitchen, and he'd not done so in years. The station's deli would have to do.

The air was cool inside the store. A line stretched from the register, and he nodded to the clerk as he walked down the aisles.

"How goes it, Nate?"

"Same shit, Bobby."

The register chimed as the till opened. "Different day?"

"You got it."

He wondered how sad it was that the employees knew him on a first-name basis. He'd sampled just about everything on the menu, and lately the turkey melt sub struck his fancy. He'd eaten it over a dozen times, and today when he pulled the frequent diner card from his wallet, he saw his next meal was entitled to a fifty-percent discount.

The woman behind the counter recognized him. She was a few years his junior, but not by much, and she flirted with him every time he came in. Her name was Janine.

"What'll it be tonight, hon?"

He handed her the card, offered up a smile, and gave his order.

"You got it, sugar."

Brock turned away from her while she took care of the order, wading back into the week's troubling waters. He thought of the last time he spoke to Donovan Candle.

Brock didn't see the harm in letting his friend assist with the investigation, but orders were orders. Donovan's tenacity was foolish, but also admirable. He was certainly a man of principle. What was it he'd said? Actions birth definition? *Whole lot of good that did you, bud. I tried to tell you not to get involved, and now look what's happened. S'pose that's why you fell off the face of the earth? Are you another one of the Mr. Abrams's victims?*

He sighed, and let the thought go. Off duty meant off duty. He had to stop doing this to himself. With his diet and non-existent exercise routine, he was on a short trip to a heart attack.

"Order's up, hon."

He turned and thanked Janine. He gave her a ten and told her to keep the change.

"Thanks, sweetie. You come back 'n see me now, 'kay?"

"Sure will," he said. He took the bag with his sandwich and made his way to the front of the store. He was so lost in his own thoughts that he didn't see the kid. They knocked shoulders, and Brock lost a handle of the bag. It fell to the floor with a light slap.

"Excuse me," he grunted, and knelt to pick up his dinner.

"Sorry," said the kid, though when Brock looked up at him, he saw he was hardly a kid at all. He was dirty and wore khakis that frayed at the bottom. His shirt was wrinkled and torn on one side. The young man was at least twenty, and it took Brock a moment to place the face.

He cradled two boxes of bandages, a bottle of rubbing alcohol, and several bottles of pain killers. A bag of cotton balls stuck out of his pants pocket. He looked down at the badge affixed to Brock's chest. Then their eyes met, and in that frozen moment Brock realized he *knew* him.

Well I'll be a son of a bitch.

The name was on the tip of his lips when a sharp pain ripped through his head. A buzzing, humming drone echoed in his ears, taking him by surprise. He strained to stay focused on the young man, thought he saw him crackle and flash like a movie missing a few frames. That wasn't right. He shook his head and stuck a finger in his ear. The droning dulled but did not stop.

"Quinn," he whispered, "don't move."

But the boy wasn't listening. He backed away from Brock slowly, his eyes wide and chest heaving to the point of hyperventilation. A bottle of pills clattered to the floor, rolled down the aisle, and stopped at Brock's shoe.

"I—I can't," Quinn said, taking another step back. Brock watched his gaze dart off toward the door marked Employees Only.

The old detective grimaced as the drone ripped through his skull. He held out his hand. "Son, you need to put that stuff down, okay? Come with me. I'm not going to hurt you. We can get this all sorted out."

"I can't," Quinn repeated. He gripped the items in his hands so tightly his knuckles were pale.

Bobby called out to him. "Everything all right over there, Nate?"

"Yeah, Bobby, we just got a misunderstanding is all. This young man and I are going to take our troubles out of your store. Isn't that right, Quinn?"

"What young man?" Bobby asked. The question took Brock by surprise. He turned to the side, thinking maybe the clerk couldn't see the kid standing between him and the deli counter. Bobby shook his head.

"Nobody there, bud. You sure you're not workin' too hard? Maybe you need to take yourself a little vac—"

Brock grimaced as the drone surged through his head again, swelling in his brain for a moment; when it subsided, he looked up and saw Quinn was gone. The door to the back room swung shut.

He cursed under his breath, drew his gun, and scrambled for the double-doors. The weapon's weight felt odd in his hands. He'd not used it in years. Holding it now was both exciting and terrifying, like reacquainting with an old flame.

The doors gave way to a small hallway filled with empty crates. An open door to the left led to a bathroom, but Quinn wasn't there. Farther down the hall was the entrance to the coolers, and at the far end was the manager's office. A closed-circuit camera perched above had a clear shot of anyone who might go in or out.

An emergency exit sat in the middle of the wall between him and the office, standing wide open. Moths fluttered inside, drawn to the lights above.

Brock's heart thumped out of rhythm, doubling its beats. He caught his breath, swallowing back bile. *Looks like I'm due for that heart attack after all.*

He stepped through the emergency exit just as Quinn made his escape. The kid's foot caught the edge of a Dumpster, and he landed on the concrete with a sickening crack. He cried out as the stolen items flew through the air.

Brock took a breath and raised his gun. He'd never pointed his weapon at a kid before. He had to keep telling himself Quinn wasn't a kid at all.

"Son," he huffed, "don't make this old man chase you down. That'll just piss me off even more."

Quinn slowly rolled on his side. Looking at him filled Brock's head with more of that ungodly static. He had to keep the kid in his peripheral vision; focusing directly on him made the drone surge so bad it hurt.

"Please, officer."

The young man locked eyes Detective Brock while reaching for the rubbing alcohol and bandages.

"Son, you need to pay for that stuff. I don't care what shit you've been through—stealing is stealing."

"It's an emergency. You have to let me go. Someone's going to die if I don't."

"Let you go?" Brock lowered the gun. "Do you have any idea how many people are worried sick about you? You've been missing for a week."

"I know, but…" Quinn's jaw quivered. "I have to do this. They're depending on me, and I need to make this right. She could die."

"Who could die?"

Quinn looked up. Tears streamed down his cheeks. "Evelyn."

The world sank back and ceased to exist. Brock's arms went limp and he let go of the gun. There were tears at the edge of his eyes, waiting to see if it was worth making the trip.

"W-Who did you say?"

"My friend Evelyn. She's hurt." Quinn winced, gathering up the items in his arms. "I have to go."

The static gushed in Brock's head. He tried forcing the drone from his mind, but the sound kept coming, a constant rushing hiss that drilled into his thoughts and inhibited his concentration. The world blinked in and out of focus, and the kid faded from view.

Detective Brock blinked. The surge stopped. He was alone behind the building. All that was left of Quinn was a single bottle of aspirin. He walked over, picked it up, then went back to retrieve his gun.

Bobby met him inside. He gave Brock his sandwich.

"What the hell was that all about?"

"Just a headache, Bobby. Nothing more." He gave the pills to the clerk and made his way out the front door.

Brock sat in his car for a long time. His hands were on the wheel and the engine was running, but he could not bring himself to put the car in gear.

My friend, Evelyn. Quinn's words ran laps around his head. What were the odds he was talking about the same person? Slim, seemingly impossible, but something nagged and pulled at him that he could not ignore. Why here? Why, out of all these places in the city, or even the state, did Quinn show up here, at this precise moment? The odds of that were just as great.

What if, he wondered. *What if she's still out there?* He rubbed his eyes, wrinkled his nose, and looked up at his reflection in the rearview. *You're too old to cry, but you're not too old to hope.*

The phone vibrated in his pocket. He took it out and looked at the screen. His old friend was calling for a fourth time that day. He thought about what had just happened, thought about how crazy it was all going to sound, but something told him that Mike just might believe him. He wasn't nearly as naïve as his younger brother, but those Candles, there was just something about them. They had a knack for things of this sort.

Detective Nathan Brock took a breath. He answered the call.

D onovan worked his way to the surface.

Glimpses of worlds cast in color and monochrome revealed bits of his surroundings. Once he saw the outlines of Cretins and Yawning lingering at the token booths as if standing guard. They felt his presence but seemed confused, unsure of how to react. He moved over and through them like air, his limbs tingling upon contact.

He emerged at the corner of 46th and Haden. The sky overhead swelled from gray to blue and back again, and with the colors came a hint of fresh warm air. There were sounds of the city, too. Cars idled and honked somewhere in the distance. He saw the sun hanging low within those short swells of color.

Donovan walked until he came to the edge of a shallow river. This landmark split the city from the suburbs and nearby countryside; he knew that if he followed it, sooner or later he would come to the bridge, and from there he would find his way back home. The sun lazed across the sky in a slow arc, advancing just a few inches each time the world shifted, and its gradual progression made him even more determined.

At times his feet sank into the muddy banks of the river. The sensations took him by surprise, and for as quick as they came, they were gone again. He lost his footing in the murk just as the world swelled with color, splashing down upon the riverbank. The water was cold, invigorating. After spending so long in that dingy room, feeling the water run across his naked skin was like heaven.

Then the world swelled again, and the color bled out. Gone was the water on his body. He was sitting on the empty shore of a gray riverbed.

Donovan smacked his hand against the ground and cursed. *"Fuck! I'm not supposed to be like this, goddammit!"*

Realities quietly shifted between Spectrum and Monochrome; the sounds of the living world on the other side bled through the moments in between. All were oblivious to his existence, and this only angered him more. He stumbled to his feet, arched his back, and screamed.

"I WAS MEANT FOR MORE THAN THIS!"

The rage spewed out his lungs like thick tendrils of smoke, taking flight in the form of words and echoing across a gray expanse before being drowned out by the colored sounds of life beyond.

"*It—*" he choked out, clamoring forward on rubber legs, "it's not supposed to be like this."

Donna flashed before his eyes, an angel in his private hell sent to tease him with the life he was supposed to lead. There she was, a floating face amidst the chaos of his mind. Unreachable. Untouchable.

He thought of everything he could've done. He thought of the missing kids, of Quinn, his baby yet to be born, and the plot Sparrow had set into motion. This was enough to get him fuming again. The arrogance of that man—no, the *thing* he'd become. He'd reached into Donovan's life and pulled the proverbial rug out from under him. First, he'd held up a mirror to make him see himself for what he was; then, just as he understood what was needed to redeem it, he'd taken his life from him.

It wasn't right, and goddammit, he would find a way to fix it.

Donovan climbed his way up the embankment. He was so lost in his own anger that he almost didn't notice the man standing on the bridge. At first Donovan thought he was just another specter from the living world—except things were gray, and this person appeared in full color just as he did.

He remembered he was naked, covered in dried mud up to his shins. He moved his hands over his manhood and tried not to look too embarrassed.

"Uh, hello?"

The figure stood on the other end of the bridge, leaning over the railing and looking down at the flashes of river below. Bald and tall, he wore a long, ashen robe that blended in with the world's gray median.

"Mister?" Donovan walked across the street with heavy footfalls. There was no way this guy couldn't hear him. His bare feet slapped against the ground. "Are—are you dead, too?"

The bald man cocked his head. Donovan froze in place and his heart stopped for that instant of time. The world and its flashing duality also stopped, and a thousand nightmares clawed their way out from the recesses of his mind.

Aleister Dullington turned and smiled back at Donovan with a grin full of jagged teeth. His black eyes jutted from their sockets and glistened with delight.

"No, Mr. Candle, I am most assuredly not dead, and neither are you." Dullington swept his hand through the air. The sleeve of his robe billowed with his movement, and the world flashed again with color. "Welcome to the spaces in between."

PART THREE
THE LIMINAL MAN

Søren Kierkegaard wrote of a leap every man must take in order to prove his faith. Our traveler is faced with a similar decision, but rather than take a leap of faith in the servitude of a nameless god, he must leap in declaration of faith in himself. It is the only way he can leave the precipice, but first he must choose to do so. He will remain trapped in both worlds until he makes this choice. Here he is bound; here he is empowered; and here, in his chains, he is free.

—Dr. Albert Sparrow
A Life Ordinary: A Comprehensive Study in Human Mediocrity

-12-
BALANCE

The world breathed around them, inhaling gray and exhaling color. In the moments of silence following his shock, Donovan thought he heard a telltale sigh with each swollen breath.

"Dullington?"

"You do not seem very happy to see me, Mr. Candle. Not that I blame you."

His appearance hadn't changed. He was still humanoid, his skin porcelain white, eyes bulging from their sockets like two large marbles.

Donovan felt faint. The adrenaline sustaining him through the horrors of the underground began to subside. He leaned against the railing, collecting himself.

There was much he wanted to say and ask, but he conserved his words. What he remembered of Dullington was not pleasant. Even though he influenced the changes Donovan made to his old life, he also perpetrated his own share of atrocities. Donna's abduction came to mind, as did the untold number of people trapped in the Monochrome. They may have committed their own crimes to end up in the gray prison, but Dullington was their warden and held keys to their cells.

The Monochrome's old master strolled to the opposite side of the bridge. Donovan followed.

"What are you doing here?" he asked, squinting as the world flashed. "And where is 'here?'"

"I told you, Mr. Candle, these are the spaces in between." When Donovan did not respond, Dullington turned and smiled. "We are in liminal space. For me it is a banal, tantalizing hell. For you, it is limbo."

"Am I flickering? Is that what this is?"

Aleister Dullington peered over the rail. "Flickering, Mr. Candle? You may call it that if you wish. I suppose, in some ways, you are in a constant flickering state between the Spectrum and Monochrome."

"How?" Donovan's voice cracked. He'd worked too hard to avoid the affliction a second time. This wasn't supposed to happen. "I did all you asked. I made my life pitch."

Dullington pulled back from the rail. "Indeed, you did. I cannot fault you for that. However, make no mistake about it, Mr. Candle. You are here because of your own doing."

His frustration rose to its pinnacle. He reached forward, gripping the edges of Dullington's robe. "I didn't *ask* for this," he growled. "I don't *want* this. Tell me how to get back to my own reality."

Dullington stared at him, through him, reading him as he was apt to do, and Donovan felt the adrenaline leave him once more. His muscles weakened, and he let go of the robe. Dullington spoke in calm, even tones.

"In another time, Mr. Candle, I would have had you skinned alive for that. But I am not what I once was. In some ways, I suppose I cannot blame you for your anger."

Donovan's knees buckled. He sank to the ground and sat along the edge of the walkway. The Spectrum surged in and out, ebbing like a tide pulled toward the Monochrome's empty shores. He saw the black, pencil-drawn outlines of people walking among them, past them, *through* them. He heard the phantoms of cars and smelled their exhaust. He thought he heard the mourning call of the Yawning from somewhere down below.

He ran his hands through his hair. All he could think about was getting back to Donna.

"She does miss you, Mr. Candle. Worried sick about you."

"Get out of my head, Aleister."

"I can take you to her if you like."

He looked up. Dullington extended a pallid hand, his white flesh shiny, stretched tight over bone. Looking at it reminded Donovan of a mannequin.

"You can take me to Donna?"

Dullington nodded, and Donovan reluctantly took his hand. "I can take you to her, but I cannot send you over. Where you are now requires a choice to be made, and you are the one who must make it."

"I don't understand."

Dullington pulled him off the ground. They stared at one another; then, without a word, Dullington let go of his hand and made his way toward the end of the bridge. With little choice, and a million questions running rampant in his mind, Donovan forced himself to action. He followed.

———————•———————

K ale Abrams shook away his disorientation and looked around the room. On the gray side, the station was a giant slate box, its concourse a connection of flat geometric planes without texture.

In the real world, however, the building was dingy, dirty, full of cobwebs, and dark. When he flickered over, the musty smell tickled his bulbous nose, and he fought back a sneeze. Sparrow's cocoon was gone, replaced by an empty desk and several overturned chairs. Light spilled into the room through a shattered window, an unwelcome invader in this dreary home.

He squinted at the bright orange streaks cutting across the floor. The gray world was easier on the eyes, and things were simpler there. He liked it that way.

In the Spectrum he was frowned upon for his unique tastes. They'd locked him away once, put him through all sorts of treatment, and he was forced to play along with their little games. Memories of the institution were a dim haze of faces swimming through his mind, eluding his grasp. If he focused, he could make out the faces of the nurses who kept him drugged, ensuring he would never be allowed to play again.

But that all changed when his master set him free. When the flickering first overcame him, he thought the sensations were side effects of the medication, and he resisted his stark, new reality—but the master helped him see through the haze. Master Sparrow opened his eyes, helped him to see.

They cast you aside, Mr. Abrams, but I accept you. You belong in the new world I'm going to create. You have a place.

For the first time in his life, Kale felt like he belonged. Finally, someone who *understood* his urges, his desires—someone who knew what it was like to taste taboos and yearn for more. Yes, things were so different now, and he owed it all to the Monochrome King.

Kale left the room, descended a flight of stairs, and stood in the grand foyer. He looked out over the concourse, remembering the deluge of bodies and blood. The ghostly howls of agony brought a smile to his face, and though he enjoyed the gray shades, the sight of blood made him feel giddy. He could still make out the dark pools stained black on the floor.

The ground level windows were boarded up, preventing the fading sunlight from entering. Two barrels of burning trash illuminated the large room, casting dancing shadows upon its discolored walls. He turned away from the decay. Along the inner foyer, a wall of televisions stacked up to his height. Some were turned on, revealing snowy static. Millions of white insects crawled behind the screens, feasting on some unseen carcass.

Others showed episodes of *Fading Out*. Kale did not understand how these screens were powered. The building, from what he understood, sat empty for years with no electricity. Seeing the screens served as a reminder of his master's growing power. Once the Great Fade-Out came to pass, Sparrow would be even stronger, and his promises to Kale would be fulfilled.

He flung open the door and looked at the remains of the day. The sun neared its vanishing point, casting long shadows across the empty city street. An old beat-up car sat along the curb, scratched to shit and pockmarked with patches of rust.

The old crone sat on its hood, standing guard over the station entrance. She chewed on the last bite of a chocolate bar. Her baggy winter coat was covered in dark splotches of blood from the open sores on her face. When Kale descended the steps, she turned around and grinned at him. Blood streaked down her forehead and dripped off her nose.

"Kale, Kale, Kale," she repeated, tossing the empty candy wrapper to the ground. "Jus' the lost soul I's been waitin' fer."

She reached inside her coat and retrieved two items. One was a set of keys, which he took from her without a word. The second item was a large Phillips-head screwdriver, and he said, "Thank you."

"Always had me a sweet spot fer ya," she said. Her airy rasp became a chuckle, which soon turned into a hacking cough that lingered for an uncomfortable minute. She spat blood on the pavement. "Me 'n the others got a bet runnin' between us. They says I can't git'ya to say more'n two words. Fancy I might prove 'em wrong tonight?"

Kale offered a smile through his tangled, black beard. He opened the door and climbed into the car, its suspension groaning beneath his weight. The old crone, whose name he did not know, ventured around to the side. The window was gone, shattered long ago by unknown trauma, and she put her arm through the opening. Her hand fell upon his shoulder, and the stench that rose from her ashy flesh made his stomach curl.

"Whatya say, biggie man? Ain't you got more'n two words fer me?"

He turned the key in the ignition. The rusty old thing sputtered to life, hacking exhaust into the air. The old crone stepped back, and he put the car into gear. Then he looked up at her, licked his lips, and smiled.

"No," he said. "Sorry."

The car sped away from the curb, its explosive exhaust accenting the raucous laughter bellowing from within.

———— • ————

They were out of the city. He could discern that much from the quick flashes between realities. There were more trees, more grass underfoot which tickled his bare skin in the moments he could feel it, and he noticed less and less sunlight.

Donovan stopped to rest, propping himself up against a guardrail alongside the road. Dullington continued for a few steps before turning back.

"Time does not wait for men."

"Just a few minutes," Donovan said, lifting one leg up over the other. He massaged his foot. "Don't you ever get tired?"

"I did, once. That was a long time ago."

"You were a man?"

Dullington doubled back and took a seat beside his companion. "Does this surprise you?"

"Yeah, a little." Donovan didn't feel comfortable sitting beside him. There was an aura resonating off Dullington's body that pulsed like the glowing light atop the WBS building. Looking at it made him feel nauseous, and he tried to busy himself with his sore feet.

"I have long forgotten the frailties of the flesh. Seeing you here, nursing your superficial wounds, makes me feel...*nostalgic*."

"Tell me something, Aleister." Donovan switched feet. He massaged the other. "What are you doing here? Why did you leave the Monochrome with Sparrow in charge?"

Dullington turned his head and stared. Donovan tried not to look at him, but the man's unblinking gaze was forceful. He looked into the empty, black eyes protruding from Dullington's skull.

"Something happened which I did not anticipate. I believed Albert Sparrow was the key to ending a feud between my predecessor and myself. I was wrong."

"Your predecessor?"

"The Monochrome has always been, Mr. Candle, and it will always be. It functions in tandem with the Spectrum. Together they work like a pocket watch, always ticking, always moving, the seconds, minutes, and hours equally measured. And like the watch, there must be someone to keep it wound. My predecessor did so, I did so, and now..." He turned away toward the horizon. "Sparrow believes he is destined to do the same. And so, the gears continue to turn for a time. It is the way of all things."

Donovan scoffed. "And where do we fit into that purpose? Why punish the ones who don't live up to their potential?"

"Men are trivial creatures with the aptitude for great things. Fulfilling their potential often advances their species. My reciprocal question to you, Mr. Candle, is simply this: *Why not?* If most of humanity actively chooses to stagnate, why should they be spared?"

He tried to find an answer but could not.

"Sometimes, it seems you fear your own achievements. Your fear, Mr. Candle, is a great adversary. We may even consider it the Great Detractor of the so-called 'human condition.'"

Donovan let out a frustrated laugh. He rose to his feet and walked into the middle of the road. The world flashed around them, revealing outlines of cars and Yawning milling about in search of prey. He turned and held out his arms.

"What are you to judge, Aleister? God? A demon? What?"

Aleister Dullington stood. "I am balance."

"Balance?" Donovan balled his hands into fists so tight they shook. "Is Sparrow your idea of balance? Tell me this, Al—if you're so goddamned benevolent, why are you letting Sparrow go forward with his plan?"

"What Sparrow does now is not my concern."

"Not your concern?" Donovan held up his hands, incredulous. "Not your fucking *concern?* What happened to two seconds ago, Mr. Balance? How is what he's planning to do any semblance of balance? What happened to choice? Those kids he murdered didn't have any fucking choice. My nephew sure as hell didn't have any choice."

Donovan was so angry he shook. After that speech about balance and the human condition, Dullington's attitude regarding Sparrow's intentions was ridiculous. The pale monk watched him without comment. His empty eyes and sullen features only infuriated Donovan even more.

"No, I get it. You thought you'd put someone else in charge and take a little vacation." Donovan waved his hand, gesturing to the fluctuating landscape. "How's this working out for you, Al? It's not exactly a beachside resort, but it's doing *wonders* for your complexion."

Dullington surveyed the swell of color and gray. He frowned. "I admit this is not what I believed would happen. It is not ideal."

"No, it's not. And for someone who can see everyone's secrets, you're too fucking blind to see the truth in front of you."

"And what truth might that be?"

"You're trapped here just like I am, only you don't want to admit it." Donovan shook his head and spat. "You're absolutely right, though. This is not ideal."

He turned and left Dullington standing in the middle of the road. His heavy footfalls slapped against the ground.

"Mr. Candle."

Dullington's voice echoed behind him. He kept walking, arms at his sides, determined to make it back to his home. He just wanted to see Donna, even if it was for the last time. Maybe he would be able to figure something out.

"*Donovan.*"

He looked over his shoulder, half expecting to be struck down for his defiance, but all he saw was a tired figure standing in the middle of the road. Seeing Dullington like that—with his face drawn, wrinkles carved across his forehead and shoulders hunched forward—gave Donovan pause. He turned. This supposed demigod looked like nothing more than a tired, old man.

The anger he held for Dullington left him. In its place was the last emotion he ever expected to feel for this vile creature. After all he'd been put through by this figure, Donovan discovered he felt nothing more than pity for him.

He is stuck here. *Just like I am.*

Dullington approached slowly. "'Stuck' has such infinite connotation. We are here by choice, Mr. Candle. That is all."

Donovan thought about this. He didn't know what choices Dullington spoke of, nor did he understand, but there was something he kept returning to in his own mind. Throughout everything, regardless of the means, Dullington only ever did good by Donovan. He was allowed a second chance, a shot at redemption when others were denied.

"Why me?" Donovan closed the gap between them. He stood before Dullington with his chin held high. "Why did you help me? Why are you helping me now?"

"I was a man once. The trivialities of the flesh may no longer be known to me, but fractions of the spirit remain." Dullington offered a short, timid smile. "You are kindred to me, Mr. Candle. An archetype human with the talent and fortitude to achieve whatever you please. Do you remember that day I reached out to you over the phone?"

Donovan nodded. "I said I was afraid I might disappear for good."

"I wanted to gauge your character, Mr. Candle. You pined for something interesting to happen to you. You sought change. Most of the people who find their way to the Monochrome are blind, unwilling to change until it is far too late. However, you wanted that change for yourself all along, and I knew you were capable. You just needed the proper push."

He sighed. "A lot of good that did, huh?"

"Defeatism does not suit you. You wear it like a bad hat. That you heeded my warning is a credit to you, but you did not move with it."

The conversation he'd had with Sparrow came back to him. Thinking about it made his cheeks burn with regret. "Is this why I'm here?"

"You were at your lowest down in those tunnels, Mr. Candle. Sparrow was going to watch you bludgeoned to death by his followers, and you accepted it. You felt you deserved it. And yet—"

"I wanted to fix things."

"Precisely. Your penitence, your desire to do better trumped the mediocrity forced upon you by Sparrow's shoddy experiment. It was, however, not enough to take you into the Spectrum." Dullington clapped his hands. The world around them continued to swell and pulse with color. "And now we must be on our way."

He moved past Donovan, who stood with a mixture of confusion and awe painted upon his face. There was far more to Aleister Dullington than he would ever fully understand, and that notion at once comforted and frightened him. He watched Dullington make his way down the old country road, painted gray with flecks of other-worldly colors. Dullington's words echoed in his skull: *We are here by choice.*

He was afraid of what that might mean and sought to follow up with his morose guide, but Dullington tore him away from his thought.

"You would do well to hurry, Mr. Candle. We have not much time."

Donovan jogged to catch up. "Why? Do you have a hot date?"

The joke was lost on his companion. Dullington did not crack even the slightest smile. "No, Mr. Candle, but you do."

There was a grim urgency in his voice. Donovan did not like the sound of it. It put him on edge.

"Do I?"

Dullington nodded. He turned and looked into Donovan with his empty eyes. "At this very moment, a man is on his way to your home. You are already familiar with his work."

The words burrowed into Donovan's ears, and he did not wait for his companion to follow it with more talk. They settled into the pit of his stomach like jagged nails, and Donovan Candle began to run.

The whiskey coated Michael's throat with a slick film of fire, burning its way down to his belly. He savored it for a moment before uncapping the bottle and pouring another shot. It went down quick, smooth. *Easy there*, he told himself, and held out his hand to watch its tremors slow as the booze worked its magic.

The phone calls to Brock had become something of a routine. They shared professional respect for one another but did not approve of the other's methods. Michael always took Brock for a disenchanted old man who'd experienced too much heartache in the business to feel much of anything anymore.

A while back, not long after he'd started the business, Michael and the detective had gone out for drinks. Brock retold his war stories with grim clarity, and just the memory of the way he looked at Michael gave him chills. That was back before Evelyn vanished, but even then, he was growing disillusioned with the job.

Evelyn's disappearance was the final straw. Detective Nathan Brock walked with his brow in a permanent furrow ever since, and he grew distant to all who knew him. Michael knew his insistence on staying in touch infuriated the man (and that was partially the point), but he meant well. He looked up to Brock as a mentor of sorts, an image of a man he aspired to be—and feared he might become, given enough time.

Michael sat back in his chair, sipping his whiskey and replaying their conversation in his head. He was in his car when he'd made the call, heading home after locking up the office. He'd tried reaching Brock all day without any luck. He didn't expect his friend to answer, was just about to cancel the call when there came a click, and Brock was on the line. He was panting, gasping for breath like he'd just finished a marathon.

"Hey, old man. Sounds like all those years of chain smoking are finally paying off."

"Mike, cut the shit. I saw Quinn."

Michael's smile left his face.

"Say that again?" He turned down the radio and turned off the A/C just to be sure. He wanted to hear this in full clarity. Brock caught his breath and spoke in slow, measured tones.

"I saw Quinn. Clear as day."

"Where?"

"In the Shop 'n Go."

"The gas station? Are you sure, Nate?"

"Sure as I'm sitting here. There was something wrong, something…" He trailed off. For a moment Michael thought the call dropped, but he could still hear the old man breathing on the other end. He sounded confused. "I—I don't know what happened. One minute he was there, the next he was gone."

"Nate, maybe you've just been working too hard, huh? Have you been sleeping all right?"

"Goddammit, Mike, I'm not going senile. I'm sleeping just fine."

"Okay, okay, just asking. Relax."

"I'm tellin' you, it was Quinn. I bumped into him. He was shoplifting."

Michael slowed the car and turned into his driveway. He sat there for a moment, listening to his friend's agitated breathing. He said, "How soon can you get here?"

"I'm already on my way."

That call was nearly an hour ago. He had leftover take-out from the previous evening, losing himself in his thoughts, trying to make sense of everything. The whiskey was the perfect end to a shitty day.

Quinn shoplifting from the Shop 'n Go? That didn't make sense. Brock wasn't the type to be easily shaken, either, so there had to be some credence to his story. Who he'd seen—who he *thought* he'd seen—was somehow pertinent enough to trouble him. That was enough to warrant investigation.

Over the last couple of days Michael attempted to resign himself to facts: the likelihood of either his nephew or brother being found was slim to none. It was a large city, with its own set of rules that most folks did not seem to understand. He was one of them. He thought of the men outside the empty Laundromat and the way they glared at him with malicious comprehension. People like that understood those unwritten rules. Somehow, some way, his own brother did as well—and now he was gone.

The doorbell rang. Michael set down the tumbler and left his office. Nathan Brock stood on his doorstep, looking exhausted, disheveled. They greeted one another with a handshake, and Michael noted the beads of sweat dotting the old man's brow. He led his friend into the kitchen.

"Coffee?"

Brock took a seat at the table. "Please."

Michael set the coffee to brew, then leaned against the counter with his arms crossed. He gave the detective a long look. "Are you okay, Nate?"

"Look, I—" Brock began, drumming his fingers across the table. "I'm not a literary man. I don't speak in metaphors, and I don't know my ass from page eight when it comes to Shakespeare, so bear with me a minute."

Michael nodded. "No rush."

When the coffee finished brewing, Michael poured his friend a cup. He set the mug down before the detective.

"Thank you."

"Don't mention it. Now, you were saying?"

Brock lifted the cup with a shaky hand and tasted the bitter brew. When he was finished, he recounted what happened at the gas station. The coffee mug was empty by the time he'd told his story. Michael absently chewed his bottom lip. He'd barely touched his own coffee and kept stirring it with his spoon.

"I swear it was like he was a ghost. Just thinking about it is givin' me the damndest headache."

Michael was quiet. He'd heard what his friend told him, but found that the more he listened, the more his mind drifted back to a fragment of conversation he'd had with his brother earlier that year.

These Missing people, they flicker over once a day to scrounge for food. Can you imagine how many homeless people we've glanced over might actually be the ones we're trying to find?

The question of belief was secondary to a simpler, weightier one: What if? That question again, rising from the depths to mock him. Was it so hard to accept that his brother might be right?

He thought of the night of the baby shower and what he told Donovan. *Don't be afraid to jump.* He supposed it worked both ways.

"I know this sounds crazy," Brock began, but Michael stopped him.

"You're right, old man. It does sound crazy, but you want to know something that's even more batshit crazy? I believe you."

Brock looked up at him, seemingly stunned by his admission. "You do?"

But Michael was already up and moving. He picked up his phone, dialed, then hung up and cursed.

"What are you doing?"

"Trying to reach Don's wife. Phone's busy. Quinn's mother's been staying with her these last few nights."

"Are you sure this is proper? I can't go over there and tell them I saw Quinn disappear before my eyes."

Michael set down the phone. He took his keys from a basket on the counter.

"See, that's where you're wrong, old man." He smiled. "Let's go."

Kale pulled over and parked the car. The sun was down, and fireflies sparkled to signal his arrival. The old road was empty. A field stretched on a hundred yards before ending at a tree line. To his right was a small embankment that dipped down to a thick line of trees. This would be his escape route should things go bad.

He got out of the car and breathed in the night air. This was one thing he missed about the world. Here the air was fresh, alive, and if he concentrated hard enough, he thought he could detect every living thing within his radius. Breathing the air here filled him with a lively energy. It sparked in his fingertips like electricity. He was ready to do this. The night was alive, and he would let it fuel his journey.

Somewhere along this road was where he'd brought the boy a week prior. At the direction of his king, he'd forced the boy through the woods and toward Donovan's home. Kale wanted to barge into the man's house and take him by force, but his master was too careful about leaving a mess. After seeing the one called Candle, Kale wasn't sure what the big deal was about him, but Sparrow held a cautious sort of respect for the man, the same kind of respect one gave a rattlesnake or wasp.

He had no idea where the Candle man was, nor did he care. He had his orders, and he would take great pleasure in carrying them out.

The screwdriver was heavy in his pocket. It reminded him of the traitors, and the honor it was to defile them at his king's command. They were a message to the others, those Wretched few who chose not to follow the king's wishes. Memories of that night brought a smile to his face.

He remembered their exquisite fear when they were found out, trapped by the rest of the Missing, and restrained to await their fate. They were marched topside like cattle to the slaughter, and he was happy to play his part as their executioner. He reveled in the shock of their own mortality as he took their lives, working his way down the line one puncture at a time. Even now he could feel the arterial spray coating his hands, its warmth like a blanket in the cool night air.

As he made his way through the dark forest toward the neighborhood beyond, Kale thought about Candle's wife. A lovely little thing. Pregnant, too. He considered himself a master of his craft, a painter about to create his life's masterwork. He would cut her open, remove the child and paint a tapestry with her entrails. He would pleasure himself over her corpse. Thinking about it gave him an erection.

He paused at a small stream and adjusted himself. The mere touch gave him pleasure, but he restrained his urges. He wanted to save it for the kill. It would be glorious.

The bearded man made his way across the stream. There he found a small, worn trail leading him the rest of the way through the brush. The woods were alive with the chirp of crickets and other nightly insects, masking his arrival. He found his way to the edge of the forest, which became someone's backyard. It wasn't the right house. He remembered the boy's sobbing description when they'd first interrogated him. No, this was the neighbor's—

A low growl caught his attention. He scanned the patio. A tall streetlight cast a bright, pale beam stretching along the house and into the backyard. It illuminated half of a smaller, pointed house, and he caught sight of a name hung above its tiny entrance: FRIEDRICH.

When he strained his eyes, he could make out the faint shape of the creature. A dog.

Friedrich the Labrador cowered within his home. He could smell the stranger, but he was a big stranger, and the last thing he wanted to do was get mixed up with a big stranger. So, he stayed in his house and growled, hoping his master would come to run this bad man off the property.

Kale slowly reached into his pocket for the screwdriver. It would not be much to stave off a dog protecting its home, but he was bigger than it was, and a simple twist of the neck would put an end to its attack. The ramifications of such a scuffle, however, could be detrimental to his plan. He needed the anonymity of the night, and any noises might draw the attention of interlopers.

"Good dog," he whispered. "Nice puppy."

Friedrich watched, but did not move from his house. His whole body shivered. The growls were half-hearted, weak attempts to warn away the big stranger. The sooner the better, too, for this bad man smelled of nasty things, like man-pee, man-sweat, and man-blood. The last scent troubled Friedrich the most.

The big stranger worked his way along the perimeter, careful to remain in the shadows of the tree line. The dog growled but did not leave his home. Kale prowled alongside the house until he reached the end of the trees. There he stepped over a shallow ditch and onto the sidewalk. Beyond the house was a chain-link fence, and then—

Kale smiled. He gripped the screwdriver. The lights of the Candle residence burned bright. Most of the first- and second-floor windows were, from what he could see, illuminated. The home looked warm, inviting. It was the sort of house he imagined living in once upon a time, before his urges put him on a better path.

He could always dream, though. Fantasize.

The bearded man stepped onto the concrete driveway. He was ready to play house.

———————————

Donovan stopped to catch his breath, unsure of his whereabouts, but when the colors shifted, he saw the street sign on the corner. He was close. Before the world changed again, he caught a glimpse of his home. It was dark out, the air filled with the lazy blinks of fireflies, and the lights were on. Donna was home.

Seeing this made his heart swell, made him forget about the fire in his lungs.

He couldn't stop now. Not with Donna so close. He jogged the rest of the way, up the sidewalk and across his own yard. There was no sign of an intruder, no faint pencil-drawn outline hovering in the air. It seemed strange, being back home but seeing it from this alternating reality. His house looked both familiar and foreign in a matter of flickering shades, and when he reached the front porch, he had a heart-sinking realization.

How the hell was he going to stop this man? His time in the Spectrum was limited as it was. What good would it do to lay his hands on the attacker only to fade out of existence and back into liminal space?

Hopper, long silent in his own head, finally had something to say. *Just roll with it, hoss. You'll think of something.*

"I wish it were that easy," he said, but Hopper made no reply. Donovan peered through the dining room window. The lights were on, but he couldn't see anyone inside. The day's mail was on the table, along with a plate of cookies. Donna baked when she was nervous. His absence surely would have driven her crazy.

The world flickered. Colors shifted.

Donovan stood on the threshold of his own home, unable to interact. He reached out to grasp the doorknob, but things went back to gray within an instant. The knob disappeared, replaced with a solid, monochrome wall. He beat his fist against it and cried out. Why had Dullington told him about this? Why tease him so, when there was nothing he could do to prevent it from happening? What did he have to gain from this misery?

"You are just in time, Mr. Candle."

He spun around. Dullington sat on a bench affixed at the far end of the porch, his arm stretched across the railing. Donovan opened his mouth to ask, but no words came.

"Being here is a matter of choice, Mr. Candle. You chose to blindly run off to save your wife. I chose to take my time and be here when you arrived. Liminal space is empowering like that. Had you waited, I would have told you that, and you would have been here much sooner."

Dullington smiled. Donovan had the stark urge to strangle him, but no good would come of it. He bit his tongue and looked back at the door. It shifted from featureless barricade to inviting obstacle as if to taunt him. He reached out for the knob once again and failed to turn it.

"All things in good time, Mr. Candle."

"You and your fucking riddles," Donovan growled. "How am I supposed to get inside?"

"It was no riddle." Dullington rose from the bench, straightened his robe, and proceeded to walk through the door in question. Donovan stepped back, shocked. His mind tried to compute what he saw, but so far it failed one process at a time. Despite his current situation, trapped in a reality that defied all manner of logic, he could not reconcile Dullington's passing.

"You see, Mr. Candle, that old saying of 'where there is a will, there is a way' is pertinent to these trying times." Dullington extended his hand through the wall. His fingers twiddled in the air, seeking Donovan's hand.

"You're kidding me."

"Absolutely not. Go on. Do you want to be inside?"

He looked at the window and thought of Donna, toiling somewhere within, and said, "Yes, I do."

"Then *will* yourself to be."

Donovan reached out and reluctantly took Dullington's hand. He closed his eyes. Slowly, steadily, he let himself be pulled toward the door. In a moment he was passing through it, its surface sizzling against his bare skin, prickling and fizzing as his molecules pushed the door aside. They occupied the same space for a single moment before separating again.

When he opened his eyes, he was standing outside the kitchen. Dullington stood beside him, grinning.

"You see, Mr. Candle, while you are between things, you are also empowered. The rules here are bent for a reason. Most people do not realize this, to a fault."

He ignored Dullington's banter and pushed on past him. He called out to Donna and felt foolish for doing so. The odds that she would hear him—and recognize it as him—were not in his favor. The kitchen, or what he saw of it, appeared to be in order. There were some dishes in the sink, and the dishwasher hummed underneath. He went from there to the dining room, past the table, and into the living room. The house filled with color, accompanied by the laugh track of an old sitcom on the TV.

He doubled back and went upstairs. He heard her before he saw her. Even when the world went gray, he heard the faint echo of her voice. She was singing to herself overtop running water in the bathroom.

She came out of the bedroom just as he reached the second floor. Her robe bulged from her pregnant belly, and her hair was pulled back. He could not make out the tune she hummed, but it sounded like a lullaby.

He pressed himself against the wall and watched as she opened the bathroom door. She reached down and fumbled with the knobs above the tub. The water stopped. She sat on the edge, lapping the water about with her hand while still humming her nameless song.

Donovan felt at once awkward and happy. He was a voyeur in his own home, a ghost haunting its halls and witnessing the life of his spouse when she thought no one else was watching. After all the time spent locked away in that damned Laundromat, wondering if he'd ever see her again, loathing himself for not following through on the promises he'd made to her—and to himself—Donovan felt weakened. His legs gave out, and he sank to the floor in front of the open bathroom.

He fought the tears welling up in his eyes and quietly said, "I'm sorry, honey."

After the journey to get there, all he wanted was to hold her in his arms. None of what came before mattered. Just this moment, just the two of them—

Quinn's still out there, Hopper reminded him. That stopped any emotional reverie in its tracks. He remembered the promise he made to her. He promised he'd bring Quinn back. He promised he wouldn't give up, not like last time.

Donovan climbed to his feet as the world swirled and changed around him. Dullington ascended behind him and looked down at his feet. Mrs. Precious Paws sat at the top step, glaring up at him.

"I see you replaced Guffin's collateral damage."

Donovan ignored his jab. "Tell me how I can bring Quinn back. There has to be a way."

Dullington looked beyond him and into the bathroom. Donna stood from the edge of the bathtub and closed the door. Her humming was instantly muffled.

"You can bring him back, Mr. Candle. In your liminal state, anything is possible. You can transition any time you wish."

"And?" Donovan shrugged. "That's it? I just will it and it happens?"

"You must remember what I said of balance."

Dullington turned and descended the stairs. Donovan followed after him.

"What the hell does that even mean?"

"It means, Mr. Candle, that you have a choice to make. That choice bears consequences. You may save your nephew, you may even save those Sparrow has wrongly taken, but know that something must be there to balance the weight. The Monochrome requires it."

Donovan paused on the final step. He watched Dullington move to the end of the hall and stand in the light of the dining room.

"You mean that if I bring the others out, I must stay in their place?"

The world shifted into color, and a crash filled his ears, startling him from his gawking state. Above and behind him, the bathroom door flew open. He heard Donna call downstairs.

"Mandy? Did you forget something?"

Silence permeated the house except for the ticking of a hallway clock—and the heavy footfalls of an intruder. Dullington turned back and looked at him.

"He is here."

Donovan scrambled down the hallway, shoving past Dullington into the dining room. The bearded man stood in the doorway, nursing a cut on his hand. Blood dripped on the floor. When the shift came, it left only a smattering of an outline that moved slowly into the room.

He forgot about the questions at hand. Something had to be done to stop the intruder from reaching Donna. He had to act.

Solemn and impartial, Dullington watched the violence without emotion.

"I have to stop this," Donovan pleaded, his voice cracking under the stress. "Help me stop this. *Please.*"

"The will to move is your own. Just be mindful of the reaction." Dullington began to fade as the world shifted once again. "Leap, Mr. Candle, or do not leap. It is your decision."

The intruder wrapped his hand with a napkin from the table. Blood soaked through the fabric, drizzling across the floor. When the colors shifted, Donovan found he was alone in the liminal space. Aleister Dullington was gone.

Donovan watched in heart-rending panic as the bearded man named Kale made his way to the stairs. His screwdriver glistened in the light.

13

THE LEAP

Donna stood atop the stairs, her bathrobe clinging to her wet skin as she shivered in the frigid blast of central air. She looked down in confused horror. She'd heard the crash from downstairs, and without thinking, called out to who she assumed was her sister—but Amanda left an hour ago, and didn't she say she wasn't coming back tonight?

Go, she thought. *Get to the phone!*

Below, the man's shadow stretched along the wall of the stairwell. She saw his weapon before he turned the corner: a screwdriver.

Then the man was standing at the bottom of her stairs. He was dirty, with a bushy black beard shrouding half his face, and the way he smiled up at her drove a chill down the back of her neck.

For a moment her mind shut down. This wasn't happening. Not really. Not again, not like before—except it wasn't like before. Last time the intruder caught her at the doorway when she was home alone, she wasn't prepared for it, and she and Donovan had since taken extra precautions to make sure something like this wouldn't happen again. But here was an intruder, plain as day, leering up at her and oh God, where was Donnie, why wasn't he here to protect her and the baby?

The bearded man pointed the screwdriver at her and laughed. "Play house."

From somewhere in the back of her head she heard Donovan screaming at her, begging her to run, and the child inside her womb gave a little kick, as if sensing her fear. Donna backed away from the stairs, and when she could no longer see the man, panic began to set in. She escaped to the nursery, slammed the door, and turned the lock—only to realize she'd forgotten the phone.

Shit.

The phone was still sitting on its cradle in Donovan's office. The intruder would be upon her before she could get there and back again.

Her mind racing, Donna braced herself against the door. The bearded man was big—very big—and it would not take much for him to break down the door. She looked around the room for something heavy: the bassinet, the rocking chair, the dresser. The last one would work best. Donna went to it as fast as she could, which could not possibly be fast enough. The day had been hard on her joints, and the hot bath was meant to alleviate those pains. Now she winced as she tried to push the piece of furniture a few feet toward the door.

"Come on," she gasped, putting all her weight against it. The dresser was an antique, passed down through her family for generations, made when things were built to last. Now it stood in her way, a big stubborn bastard of a thing that simply would not cooperate.

Pain shot up through her back, and the baby kicked again. She took quick, heated breaths through clenched teeth as the strength in her arms gave out. The dresser would not move.

Outside the room were footsteps, and a strange scratching sound like a pencil dragged across paper. Donna looked back at the window. She opened it, shivering at the twenty-foot drop before her. If she jumped, she would hurt herself and the baby.

Her heart raced. The man would be upon her any second now. She began to look for something—anything—to use as a weapon.

The hammer sat upon the nightstand next to the bassinet. She'd used it days before to hang a few picture frames, another meaningless project for the sake of distraction, and now it would serve a far better purpose. She crossed the room and clutched it like a religious artifact, whispering a silent prayer that it would protect her from this madman.

She pushed herself into the far corner. *Keep it together*, she told herself. *Keep it together.* But how could she? This man was coming to murder her and her child.

Donnie, where are you? This can't be happening. This can't—

There came a knock at the door. Donna began to scream.

The room shifted colors, but Kale's outline remained throughout. Donovan watched the intruder, his heart pounding, palms slick with sweat. He had to think of something, but what? What could he do to stop this? Dullington's own words echoed in his head. His insistence on speaking in vague riddles gave Donovan a headache.

"Mandy? Did you forget something?"

Donna's voice carried down the stairwell. When the bearded man turned the corner and looked up at her, she began to scream. He laughed—a deep, hearty guffaw curling Donovan's stomach—and raised the screwdriver in her direction.

"Play house."

Donovan swung his arm at the man's figure. It went through him as though he were nothing more than a projection in the air.

"Donna, run!"

She backed away from the stairs. He wasn't sure if she heard him, or if it was a coincidence—at this point he didn't care. *This is a nightmare*, he realized. Somehow, he had truly died. This was his punishment. He would remain here in limbo, forced to watch the demise of his love at the hands of a psychopath, and when all was said and done the reel would begin anew.

Best you stop thinkin' that, hoss. You get one turn at this, and if you don't get movin' he's gonna skewer your wife.

"But there's nothing I can do!"

Dullington's a bastard, but he's never done you wrong. Think about it.

Joe Hopper had a point. Dullington was fair, if vague.

The bearded man ascended the steps. A door slammed from somewhere upstairs. *That's it*, he thought, *buy yourself some time, honey. I'm coming. Somehow.*

Everything went gray. The man's outline became less pronounced. Donovan reached out, tried to grasp his form, but his hand passed through the same as before.

"Goddammit!"

The bearded man paused and cocked his head as if he'd heard something. Donovan ascended the steps, turned on his heels, and faced the man. Colors flooded the stairwell just as Kale reached the top, outlining his face with dark features. He took a couple of steps into the hallway, shifting the screwdriver from one hand to the other.

A specter of Dullington's warning hung in the back of Donovan's head as he mustered the strength to bar the intruder. *The will to move is your own.*

He reached out, straining in expectation of bulky resistance, but found his hands, arms, whole body fell through Kale's stocky frame. Donovan collided with the bedroom door and cried out in shock. He fell to the floor, stunned from the impact, and looked back down the hallway. The door at the far end was closed. The nursery.

Kale's outline paused at the opening to the office, peered in, then continued his way down the hall. He held out the screwdriver, tracing its end against the wall as he walked. Donovan heard the faint scraping sound of the metal tip as it peeled away a layer of paint. Chills scratched their way down his spine.

"Come on, Candle," he told himself. "Get up."

He was frustrated, at a loss for how he was supposed to stop this man from destroying everything he loved, and still Dullington's words ran rampant through his head like a vacant mantra: *The will to move is your own. The will to move is your own.*

How was this supposed to work? He thought of the way Dullington pulled him through the door moments earlier. Donovan needed a similar miracle; he needed to find his will.

Then Donna screamed, and he found it.

What happened next came in a sudden rush, a blur which later he could only reconcile as a series of impulses firing through his brain. The sound of his wife's shriek flipped his panic switch, releasing the floodgates and sending adrenaline shooting into his bloodstream with each aching heartbeat. Thought became action without fear of consequence.

He clenched his fists and ran toward the intruder's outline. A deep, rabid growl bellowed up from his lungs, forming a scream like an oncoming locomotive as he sprinted down the hallway. The world shifted, and there was that familiar, prickling tug at his gut.

"GET AWAY FROM HER, YOU UGLY FUCK!"

The grays bled away, and the flashing, turning colors of the house became sharper, vivid. They settled in place, and when Donovan's hands fell upon the man known as Kale, they did not pass through. The momentum of Donovan's weight carried him into the intruder, sending the burly man crashing against the door. The whole house shook from their collision.

His vision a hazy maroon, Donovan pulled the man to the ground, planted one hand on his thick neck, and slammed the other down in a balled fist. There was pain in his knuckles with that first punch, but Donovan didn't feel it. He shoved one knee into the big man's chest, pinning him in place.

Blood came away on his raw knuckles, but he paid it no mind. One punch became two, then three, and then he stopped counting. He pulverized Kale's face, shattering his jaw and his nose, blacking his eyes. Blood oozed from indeterminate wounds, covering the bearded man's face with a dark crimson matching the rage clouding Donovan's vision.

Kale took a single, gurgling breath, expelling a glob of bloody phlegm from his mouth. It landed on Donovan's face, and he recoiled in disgust, creating the opening Kale needed.

He pulled back and slugged Donovan once across the jaw. Stars sparkled before his eyes as he fell backward. Kale's ham-sized fist dropped like a sledgehammer.

A dense, black fog covered Donovan's vision, accompanied by the chime of far-off bells. He fought to stay conscious, forcing the swirling darkness away from his head, and when it cleared, he saw the bearded man climbing to his feet. Blood dripped from his mouth and nose in thick, black ropes. The hallway light caught on something small, something wet and shiny and off-white stuck in his beard. Donovan had a sickening, satisfying revelation as he pulled himself off the floor: he'd knocked out the bastard's tooth.

Kale ran one meaty paw over his face and smeared blood across his forehead. He glared at Donovan for a moment before remembering the screwdriver. It had fallen between the two of them during the struggle. Donovan followed the man's line of sight, saw the weapon, and moved to take it.

"Small balls," Kale snarled, charging into Donovan with full force. Both men fell to the floor. With Kale's full weight upon him, Donovan struggled to breathe. The man's sickly stench filled his nostrils, curling his stomach.

"Get off me," Donovan strained. He wedged his arms between them, trying to push Kale away.

Kale grinned, his remaining teeth stained dark red. The thick, dark fluid continued to ooze from the gaping hole in his gum line. Some of it spilled over his lips onto Donovan's face.

"Pretty wife," he grunted. "Play house. Play dead."

Kale raised his fist and slammed it against Donovan's head. More stars burst across his vision, and he felt himself go limp for a moment. Kale scrambled off him in a play for the screwdriver.

Colors swam before Donovan's eyes like a kaleidoscope, spiraling around in a circle that seemed to gain momentum with each turn. His stomach twisted with it. He thought he heard Donna scream again, but everything took on an odd hazy effect. Things moved about in blurred states, and he felt himself slipping back into liminal space. The world faded, bleeding out of its spectrum, and he heard Hopper's voice shouting from somewhere far away:

Focus, hoss. Goddammit, focus!

A thick hand of gravity pulled at his middle. He resisted it, racing back through the dark forest of his head and out of unconsciousness. *Stay with it*, he told himself. *Focus. Focus.*

The gray began to fill up with color again. The hallway ceiling regained texture, and the overhead light burned bright with yellow luminescence. Donovan felt himself back on the Spectrum side and saw in color once again—just in time to see the big man fall on him with the screwdriver.

The crash startled her so bad she dropped the hammer. Donna bent down to retrieve it, then paused as she heard the grunts and growls coming from beyond the door. There was someone else out there, too. And that scream just before the crash—was that a man's voice?

Yes, a man. His voice was deeper, determined, nearly animal in its conviction. Whoever it was, he was angry.

She remained huddled in the corner, clutching the hammer to her chest as though it might shield her from the violence outside. She heard the intruder, the dirty bearded man, say something about small balls, followed by more sounds of struggle. She was so caught up in the noise she almost failed to hear a car turn into the driveway.

Donna climbed to her feet, shaky from the adrenaline running through her body, and looked out just in time to see Michael's car come to a stop. She pushed back the curtain, put her head through the opening, and screamed for help.

Donovan raised his arm to stop the attack. The screwdriver's metal tip hung less than an inch from his eye. Heart pounding, his breath fuming from his lungs like a blast furnace, Donovan pushed against the bearded man's thick arm with everything he had. It was not enough. The screwdriver shook with the resistance, but Kale was the bigger man. The metal tip began to move. Donovan felt his eyelashes flutter against it.

"Small balls," Kale said again. Saliva and blood oozed from his open mouth. Donovan struggled to move his legs, found he couldn't—Kale had planted his knees firmly on Donovan's thighs—then discovered his other hand was free. He wedged it between them, then moved it down. The tip of the screwdriver was almost upon his eyeball.

"No balls," he said, and grabbed a handful between Kale's legs. The man's arm immediately went limp. Donovan tilted his head to the side as the screwdriver fell free from Kale's grip. He clenched his own fingers together, squeezing the intruder's testicles.

Kale howled, struggling to free himself. Donovan squeezed harder, uttering a primal growl fueled with his hatred for this vile man.

"Get out of my house," Donovan growled, and squeezed so hard his knuckles popped. The fabric of Kale's groin became wet. Whether from piss or blood, Donovan did not care. He wanted this man to bleed, to lose the last bit of dignity he had. He wanted to make him sorry to have ever set foot in his home. Sorry he ever set eyes on Donna.

Tears streamed down Kale's cheeks as he wrestled against Donovan's grip, both hands straining to pry his fingers free. When that didn't work, he brought his fists down against Donovan's chest. The impact was hard enough to knock the wind from Donovan's lungs. He released the pulpy remains of Kale's testicles.

Both men fell away in an agonized huff. Donovan sat up, struggling to regain his breath. Kale was sprawled out, both hands cupping his groin. A large, dark stain spread out along the inside of his pants, forming a dark halo around the edges of his fingers; from there it dissolved into tiny, dark threads trickling down the insides of both pant legs.

From somewhere in the back of Donovan's head, a hysterical voice quipped, *Our first castration!* He resisted a smile. He saw the screwdriver, and remembered what Sparrow told him back in the Monochrome.

Kale murdered those young men and women. He remembered the gruesome details of their ending. When he looked back at the burly man curled up in agony, he felt a sense of retribution.

For the kids. For their parents.

He climbed to his feet, ignoring the cries of his bruised flesh and aching muscles. Blood seeped from open wounds on his knuckles. His head swam, and he put out a hand to steady himself against the wall. The pull at his gut started again, and he forced himself to focus all his will against it. *Not yet. Not now.*

The hallway flashed gray for only a moment, but it was enough to disorient him, allowing his enemy time to pull himself off the ground. When things flushed with color once again, Donovan had enough time to register the looming shape coming at him from the side. He turned just as Kale's fist slammed into his jaw. There came another sound, a feeling of impact, and the whole world began to swim once more.

This is it. Let my guard down. The guy's a tank, and he's taken me down for the count. First, he'll kill me, then he'll kill Donna, then Sparrow will have his way and the whole world will vanish.

Joe Hopper rose from the depths of that black void. If Donovan concentrated, he could almost see the squared, grizzly jaw, accented by a cigarette hanging from his lips, a fedora tipped to one side on his head. *Ain't your time, hoss. Now you open your fuckin' eyes and get to it, or I'll pop you one myself.*

Donovan did as he was told, willing himself to open one eye, followed by another. The big man hovered over him with the screwdriver, his lips forming a bloody ring in the center of his bushy beard.

"Much obliged," Kale gasped. "Much—"

"Hold it, big boy."

Kale froze. He looked down at Donovan, then up at the interloper. Donovan turned his head and strained to see the owner of the voice. It sounded familiar, but older, tired.

Detective Brock moved his way up the stairs, gun drawn. Kale wheezed, eyeing the old fogey with the gun, then looked back down at his prey.

"Put the weapon down," Brock commanded. Donovan had never heard him sound so threatening. "Drop it, or I drop you. What'll it be, beardy?"

Kale weighed his options. His eyes darted between them.

"Put the goddamn screwdriver down."

Then Kale made his last decision. He gripped the handle and lunged for the old man. Donovan saw the flash of the report as the gunshot boomed in the hallway. The intruder collapsed beside him in a bloody heap.

From below: "You all right up there, old man?"

"Yeah," Brock said. He struggled for breath. "Not the first fuckhead I've had to—"

Kale's foot twitched, and his whole body began to shimmer with gray light. Detective Brock watched in transfixed horror as the bearded man's corpse twitched, sizzled, and faded from view. In a moment the body was gone, leaving only a large puddle of blood and brain matter on the carpet—and a nude, breathing body behind it.

Donovan clenched his teeth, then slowly climbed to his feet. He leaned against the wall. Detective Brock remained on the stairs, not quite sure who he was seeing. When he did not finish his sentence, the other voice called up to him. Donovan recognized it now.

"What's that?" Michael asked, but Detective Nathan Brock was no longer paying attention. He had his eyes focused on Donovan. He squinted hard. Donovan could not say anything. The words would not come. Instead he remained pressed against the wall, chest heaving, waiting for his heart to slow.

"Mary, mother o' Christ." He climbed to the top of the steps. "Don? Don, that you?"

Donovan smiled with half-closed eyes. He nodded. "Yeah, it's me."

"Where the hell're your clothes?"

After being lost in the liminal space for so long, Donovan forgot he was completely naked. He looked down at himself, opened his mouth to respond, but then the door to the nursery opened and he forgot what he meant to say. There was Donna, her arms wrapped around her robe, eyes wide with terror, tears glistening on her cheeks.

"Donnie?"

He forgot his nudity, forgot about the old man and his brother. After days of fearing he would never see her again, Donovan stumbled down the hall toward his wife. He fell to his knees before her, eyes filled with tears, his chest rising and falling in slow, deep sobs.

She looked down, ran her fingers through his hair, then sank to floor beside him.

"I'm so sorry," he rasped. "I'm sorry, God I'm so sorry."

Donna put her hands on his cheeks, wiped the tears from his eyes with her thumbs, and kissed him. They clung to one another, ignorant of their audience and the world around them.

Donovan held her face in his hands and cracked a tired smile. "At least it wasn't in a subway this time," he said, and pulled her close once more.

After their reunion, Donna retreated downstairs to put on a pot of coffee. Michael and Brock joined her, waiting impatiently while Donovan took some time to clean up. When he stepped out of the shower and wiped moisture from the mirror, he saw that he seemed somewhat older, yet strangely revitalized.

Is that my face?

Donovan's reflection smiled back. After all those hours spent tied to a chair, his body looked chewed up, digested, and shat out. Seeing himself in the mirror for the first time in a week was an odd experience.

Early makings of a beard covered most of his cheeks, lips, and chin. The whiskers made him look older, haggard. Experienced. He thought about shaving but thought better of it. There would be time for it later.

Being home, he felt normal again, as though nothing had happened— but he couldn't let himself fall into that false sense of security. That sort of thinking is what led him to this place, and he couldn't make that mistake again. Quinn was still lost somewhere in the Monochrome and Sparrow's plan was still in motion. And there was something else, something prickling at the back of his brain.

The will to move is your own. Just be mindful of the reaction.

He thought he knew what that might mean, and it didn't settle well in the empty pit of his gut, which grumbled in response. He realized he'd not eaten since Quinn fed him back in the Laundromat, but during his stay in the liminal space he'd not felt any hunger pangs. His time in between had healed his wounded shoulder as well.

Dullington echoed in his head: *While you are between things, you are also empowered.*

Had he willed the pain away? Donovan wasn't sure, nor did he care— all that mattered was that the pain had ceased.

Donna called up to him just as he finished dressing himself. Frowning, he stepped over Kale's bloodstain on his way to the stairs. *We'll have to deal with that later.*

At nearly midnight, he joined Donna, Michael, and Nathan Brock at the kitchen table. They sat in uncomfortable silence for a full minute before Michael got up for a drink.

"Don," he said, "you're the storyteller here, and I think story time is long overdue." He took a mug from the cabinet and filled it with coffee. "So, let's get on with it."

Michael and Donna were silent throughout Donovan's retelling of the last four days. Detective Brock took notes. When Donovan was finished, Brock set down his pen. He cleared his throat and flipped through his notepad.

"If this were any other day, under any other circumstances, I'd have called for backup an hour ago—but I'll be damned if I can even begin to explain what I've seen today. The paperwork alone would be a fucking nightmare. And your story…" Brock rubbed his eyes, slumped back in his chair, and shrugged. "Well, Don, if I hadn't seen the strange shit I saw earlier today, I would load you into the backseat of my car and drive you to the funny farm myself."

"What strange shit?"

Brock told them about seeing Quinn at the gas station. He hesitated as he finished the last bit about the boy's mention of Evelyn. Donovan remembered the bloody, old woman lying on the ground. He wondered if it could be Brock's missing wife but decided not to say anything.

Donovan sighed. "When Quinn disappeared, he was flickering back over. The static and the headache you felt were the effects of a Cretin whispering in your ear."

Donna shifted uncomfortably in her seat, gripping Donovan's hand. He looked at her and winked. She smiled, but it was short and worried.

Brock flipped back through his notes. "The Cretins are the ones that make you forget. Is that right?"

"How come we're not experiencing that right now?"

They all looked at Michael. He'd been silent up until that moment, mulling over Donovan's words and watching his brother's expressions. He knew when Donovan lied. He was terrible at it. This, however, troubled him. Donovan wasn't lying. He could see that plain as day, and though he'd resolved to entertain the prospect that what Donovan told them was true, it was not any easier to swallow.

Michael shrugged. "Why are we even able to see you right now?"

"I don't know," Donovan said. "I don't have a rule book, Mike. I'm only speaking from experience. Why can't you and Donna remember certain things about what happened last year? Why can I? I simply don't know." He thought a moment, knitting his brow. "Look, we have rules that govern our reality. Things like gravity and inertia. The Monochrome just has a different set of rules, with different consequences."

And those rules are about to change, he wanted to say, but held back the words.

"You understand how batshit crazy this all sounds?"

"Yeah, Mike, I do. It's not easy for me, either. I have theories, but they're not solid."

Michael put his arms on the table and leaned forward. "Try me."

It was not the response he'd expected from his brother. The last time they'd spoken was over the phone, when Donovan tried to pitch his theories about Quinn's whereabouts, his brother shot him down. Now his tone was intense and concerned. *He believes me*, Donovan thought. It thrilled him, but also frightened him.

"All right. When I was in liminal space, Dullington compared the balance between Monochrome and Spectrum to a pocket watch. He said someone must be there to wind that watch. You follow?"

"I think so."

Donovan nodded, and went on. "So Dullington left, and somehow Sparrow took his place. Which means Sparrow's become...whatever the hell he is now." Thinking of Sparrow's dark gray eyes sent a chill all the way down to his toes. "But whatever he's supposed to become hasn't happened yet. The lines between spaces are blurred, weakened. Sparrow kept telling me he lacked vision, and I think that has something to do with it. Things that are supposed to work aren't working right now. It's how the others were able to break away from his control and oppose him, gathering food, stockpiling weapons. It's probably why you can understand what I'm telling you, why the Cretins aren't blocking your thoughts."

Detective Brock shook his head and sighed. "This is horseshit. I can't believe I'm having this conversation."

Donovan ignored him. He held his brother's stark gaze. "What Sparrow has planned is going to speed up this process. What might take years is going to happen in the course of a day. It's—"

He paused. The sound of the television carried into the room. He heard an announcer mention *Fading Out*. Then he heard something about the Great Fade-Out, and he pushed himself away from the table. He ran into the living room just in time to see the date of the event.

"What day is it?"

"It's Friday," Michael called out, then paused for a moment. "Strike that. Saturday, now."

On the screen, against a backdrop of the eerie, familiar doorway logo, were the words: ALL DAY MARATHON THIS SATURDAY!

"Shit." He turned off the TV and unplugged it. He went back to the kitchen. There he unplugged the small TV on the counter.

"Honey?" Donna asked. "What's the matter? What are you doing?"

"It's the show." He nodded to Brock. "When they locked me away in that damn room, they made me watch *Fading Out* over and over again. The episodes never stopped. Somehow, Sparrow has figured out how to force mediocrity on people. He's *forcing* them to flicker out."

They said nothing, shooting looks at one another before directing their eyes back to him. It was frustrating, but he couldn't blame them. He took a breath, thought for a moment, and chose his words.

"This—" He pointed to the blank television. "This is the reason for everything. All the kids disappearing over the last several months, the murders, Quinn, *me*—all of it points to this show. What Sparrow is now, what he's becoming, he feeds off boredom and mediocrity. People will always flicker out, but they do so because of choices they've made. What Sparrow's doing isn't giving them a choice. He's *taking* them, he's going to feed on them, and when he's through, we'll be looking at possibly hundreds of thousands of people simply gone. Maybe millions."

Brock crossed his arms. "Millions? In a blink?"

"Yes, sir."

"Horseshit."

Donovan bit his tongue. After what he'd confessed to seeing, how could Brock ignore what he was telling him? *I'll tell you*, spoke that snide voice, *he can ignore it because it's insane. Crazy. Batshit psychotic stuff, Donnie.*

He watched as the old detective stood from his chair to stretch his legs. He clapped one big paw on Michael's back, mumbling something about calling it a night. He started to bid goodnight to Donna, too, when Donovan's anger bubbled over. He let it slip, what he wanted to say earlier: the only thing he knew that would make the old man listen.

"Brock," he said, "when I was in the station, just after the others rescued me, I saw a woman there. Older lady. About your age, maybe a little younger. She was wounded pretty bad. They called her Evelyn."

The air took on a harsh feel when those words left his lips. Detective Brock slowly turned away from Donna, his eyes squinted, the edge of his top lip twitching, curling back into a grimace. For a moment Donovan thought the man might snap, might rush the gap between them and clock him in the jaw, but he didn't. Instead he put out a hand to steady himself. He suddenly looked older, feebler, and Donovan had the irrational suspicion that his words had made the man ill.

"Don't tell me things like that, Don."

"I'm not making it up, Nate. I wouldn't make something like this up. I can't say for sure if it was her, but it makes sense. Evelyn *did* vanish without a trace."

His old friend took a long heavy breath, held it for a moment, and let it out in a slow gush. He rubbed at his eyes. When his hand came away, Brock's eyes were puffy, red. The sight of it shocked Donovan. *He believes me.*

"Ev—Even if you're right about this *Fading Out* thing, we can't waltz into the WBS building and stop the broadcast. We don't even have grounds for a warrant."

Michael stood and said, "I think we're well beyond the reach of the law." His words hung between the four of them for a few minutes. When it was apparent no one had a clear plan, least of all Donovan, it was agreed they should reconvene in the morning.

"The marathon isn't supposed to start until noon," Donovan offered. "We're all tired. We need sleep."

They came to unanimous agreement. Donna and Donovan saw them to the door. Detective Brock gave Donovan a firm handshake and a piercing look, but he did not say anything more. He didn't have to. Donovan knew that look, knew what it was meant to say, and he understood it all too well.

Michael gave Donna a hug, wished her goodnight, then pulled his brother aside for a moment. They stepped out onto the porch. He waited for Brock to walk on to the car before lowering his voice.

"You sure about all this?"

Donovan shrugged. "About Evelyn? Fifty-fifty. I may have just lied to the poor guy, but I had to think of something. We may need his help."

"No, no, not that," Mike said. "I mean about *this*. What you're talking about doing. It's not like you to run off and play hero."

"Sparrow's going to become what Dullington is. That's not an *if*, Mike. It's a *when*. He's got a grudge against me, and when he finds out we took care of his errand boy, he's going to send someone else after me. After Donna. After the baby. What the hell would *you* do?"

His brother did not hesitate. "I'd go after *him*."

"Exactly."

Michael wrapped an arm around him, gave him a quick squeeze, and said, "Call me in the morning. We figured it out last time, we'll figure it out again. I'm glad you're okay."

"Love you, too."

They exchanged smiles, and he waited on the porch until his brother was in the car. When they were gone, Donovan went back inside to his wife. They had only a few short hours until morning. He needed to make the most of them.

———————•———————

They lay in bed, Donna with her head on his chest, her pregnant belly pressed up against his side. The baby was still. He twirled a loose strand of her hair around his finger.

For a while they said nothing, merely enjoying the company of one another. A hallway clock ticked, filling out the empty spaces, and just when he was sure she'd fallen asleep, she would move as though startled, look up at him and smile.

"I love you, Donnie."

He kissed her forehead. "I love you."

She moved her arm over his chest and pulled him closer to her, tighter. She held him in that position for a few minutes as the tears came. He felt their moisture soaking into his shirt. He let her cry, knowing well enough from past years that trying to stop her would only make things worse.

I'm so sorry, he wanted to say. The words sounded perfectly fine in his head, but he couldn't muster the courage to speak them. All the thoughts plaguing him came rushing back. Donna's image kept him going, just as she had the year before. Even with the tables turned, he clung to her to give him purpose.

While she cried, he wondered if he truly was a failure of a man. Dullington was right—he *did* believe what Sparrow told him. He'd failed to act when it mattered most. He faltered on the edge, afraid to take that next step, the next leap.

Yet you leapt when you had to, hoss. Hopper's voice carried with it a memory of earlier that night, in the hallway just outside their bedroom. Donna's screams spurred him to action, sprinting down the hallway to stop her attacker, and somehow, he'd forced himself out of liminal space into the Spectrum. He didn't fear the act of protecting his wife—it was an action he understood.

Why, then, was he so afraid of taking other actions?

Donovan searched for the reasons while Donna's sobs calmed to whimpers. She clung to him like a baby, and he held her close. A memory came to him while he slowly curled her hair around his finger. It was of his brother that night in the gazebo.

This is your time. Don't be afraid to jump.

And then the answer came to him. It was so simple, like forgetting a pair of glasses atop one's head, and when he found it, a sense of calm resolve came over him.

I'm afraid to jump, he thought, *because I'm afraid of where I might land.*

He looked down at Donna and remembered a time when the thought of being a father excited him. It still did, in some ways, but after hearing what had happened to those young men and women—after failing to act on his suspicions because of his own fears—he questioned what sort of father he might be.

And yet it went deeper. He'd allowed himself to be sidetracked, distracted by another career that, while enjoyable, wasn't meant for him. He'd quietly let the memory of his novel slip away, its own character just a ghostly voice inside his head.

But he still wanted those things. He wanted to be a father. He wanted to make his career as a writer happen.

Donna stirred. She'd fallen asleep during the last few minutes, but he'd been too lost in his own thoughts to notice. She came awake, startled, looking around as though she did not recognize the room. Then she saw him watching her, and that smile returned, filling him with warmth.

"There you are," she said. Her voice was groggy. "Thought I'd lost you."

"Never."

"You shouldn't say that, love."

He went quiet. She had a point. He knew what waited for him in the coming hours. Quinn was still in the Monochrome, along with others who did not belong there, and he had to find some way to save them.

An echo of Dullington's riddle came to him: *Just be mindful of the reaction.* It called to mind the notion of balance. Taking one out meant rooting himself there for a period of time. And taking more?

Thinking about it made him nauseous. *It's a pickle, hoss, but what else is there to be done?*

"Donna," he whispered. "Still awake?"

"Barely."

He held her tight, kissed her temple, and said, "Do you remember what you told me the night of your baby shower?"

She nuzzled her head into his chest. "Sort of. Why?"

"I want you to know I mean to keep my promise."

"Your promise?"

"Yes," he said, softly. "I won't give up. Not like last time."

She patted his arm. "I know that, honey. You have too much to look forward to."

Yes, I do.

He waited for her to fall asleep again. When her breathing slowed, he put aside her arm and crept out of bed. He tip-toed down the hallway into his office, closed the door, and turned on the light.

Understanding always came to him in the late hours, making his creative nights hard to balance against the early morning schedule of his Identinel days. It was still tough, even while working for Michael, but he'd managed. Now, as he sat at the desk, words came to him without effort. He knew what he had to do; more importantly, he knew what he had to say.

He thought of the promises to Donna. They were his responsibility to keep, but to do so he had to come to terms with himself. He had to find the right place to land after taking his leap. He thought of those kids and their parents; he thought of Quinn and the others still trapped in the Monochrome. He had to do something to save them. In doing so, he would have to mind the reaction.

He left the note on the nightstand, kissed his sleeping wife goodbye, and then made his way out into the night. He breathed in the cool air and savored it before getting in the car.

Time to take that jump, hoss. Just mind that reaction. It's a doozy. He smiled. It was no longer Joe Hopper's voice. That voice was his own.

Donovan Candle started the car. He closed his eyes for a moment and resolved to take that leap. Where he might land, he did not know, and he didn't dare look down.

14

THE FOCUS

"It's time."

John Beckman awoke with a jolt, flailing his arms in disoriented terror at the nightmarish phantoms haunting his mind. He sat up, his heart thundering with panicked fury. *Just a bad dream,* he thought, closing his eyes. His mind swam in a haze of adrenaline and alcohol. The nightcap of scotch had worked, but not well enough.

"*John.*"

His eyes snapped open. He sat up, looking around the living room. "Gloria?"

His wife didn't respond. Of course not. She was in bed, probably comatose from her nightly regimen of sleeping pills.

John blinked away his sleepiness, yawning. The widescreen television hanging on the wall was muted, flashing with scenes from a late-night infomercial about hair loss prevention.

The tumbler on the end table still held a swallow of scotch. He reached for it and was about to knock it back when the voice spoke up again:

"*It's time, John Beckman.*"

The words startled him so badly he dropped the glass, spilling its contents across the white carpet. Gloria would be livid.

Heart racing, John leaned forward in his chair, eyes darting about the room. The WBS executive didn't scare easily—at least he didn't think so, but things had been different ever since the pale man came along. The transparent man. The board's mysterious thirteenth member.

"Who—who's there?"

He waited, listening to the shaky remnants of his voice echo off the high ceiling. The hallway clock ticked in tandem with the leaky kitchen faucet.

Tick-drip.

Tick-drip.

It's all in your head, he told himself. *You're half-asleep and drunk. Go to bed.* Yes, that was a logical explanation. He reached for the TV remote and pressed the power button. The screen filled with white static, blanketing the living room with dark, trembling phantoms.

John pressed the power button again. The television did not react, its screen a squirming hive of white insects, swirling and swelling, forming patterns in the noise.

"Mr. Beckman."

The static shifted in time with the words, rippling, vibrating as the disembodied voice spoke each syllable. John blinked, unsure if what he was seeing was real, or just a side effect of the booze. The buzzing white insects on the screen shifted once more, forming lips, a nose, and a pair of cold, blank eyes.

Oh God. No, not you. Not again. Please, God, let this be a dream. Just a dream.

He sank into his chair, drawing his legs to his chest. Sweat dotted his forehead. The face smiled, speaking in broken, electronic tones like a bad modem connection.

"You've work to do, Mr. Beckman."

"No…we did what we were supposed to do. What more do you want from us?"

"This is the final step," spoke the pale man. *"Your part is almost over."*

John Beckman, a multi-millionaire and one of the most powerful men in television, curled up into a fetal position, weeping like a terrified child. The static rippled, darkening, its face becoming more defined. The pale man growled from beyond the TV screen.

"You will go to the WBS building, Mr. Beckman. Together, we will light the world ablaze in white fire."

Beckman cried out, "Haven't I done enough?"

"I will decide when it is enough. Be there, Mr. Beckman." The static face surged, the tiny white and gray pill bugs crawling, scattering across one another in violent fervor. *"Our will demands it."*

A tremor shot through the mansion's foundation, knocking photo frames off the walls and overturning a lamp from the end table. John Beckman shuddered in agonizing terror, and when he finally mustered the courage to peek at the television, he saw the screen was black.

Shaking, he reached for the scotch. *Maybe it's time I change careers*, he thought, and turned up the bottle.

———————•———————

Fireflies winked along the country roads as he drove toward the city, the windows rolled down and music cranked so loud he could feel it in his bones. At this hour the radio DJ was one of few words, choosing instead to let the mellow tension of Faith No More's "Stripsearch" do all the talking. Donovan leaned toward the open window, the cool night air kissing his face as the ethereal tune washed over him.

At first, he was afraid he might lose his nerve as he'd done so many times before, but the calm stayed with him, and he felt strengthened by his choice to act.

The world came and went as he sped along the empty road. Whenever he focused his gaze ahead beyond the reach of the headlights, he saw the demarcation line separating Spectrum from Monochrome. Vibrant colors and gray hues intertwined for an instant, forming a jarring landscape of stark contrasts. He existed at a threshold now, a liminal creature walking between both realities, and when he relaxed, he felt the car slipping away from him, *through* him.

Focusing his thoughts, he came back into the Spectrum as a flesh and blood being, his hands still gripping the wheel, his foot still poised on the accelerator.

One farm road became another, and soon he found himself back on a familiar path, heading toward the hazy glow of the city. The traffic lights were in his favor as grassy pastures gave way to concrete sidewalks and steaming sewer drains. The fresh night air was replaced with a stagnant odor that refused to dissipate, even after he put up the window.

He turned away from the bright lights of the sleeping city and entered its derelict South District. Donovan was one of the few who truly understood the dangers lurking underground, down along the miles of unused subway track. Somewhere down there a group of people wanted him dead.

This thought made his heart skip a beat but did not deter him. He drove along the empty streets, noting the scattering shadows of watchers from beyond broken windows and boarded doors. Cretins and Yawning weren't the only ones watching his advances, and he would not have the luxury of anonymity for much longer.

Donovan parked in front of Winthorpe Station and looked up at the building's hollow carcass. The station appeared larger than it really was, a hulking monstrosity waiting to swallow up anyone foolish enough to trespass its dilapidated halls.

He waited a moment, listening to the silence around him. Something fell over across the street, hidden from view by an old wooden fence. A dog barked nearby, followed by the clattering of garbage cans. Beneath the stillness were faint murmurs, footsteps.

Let's see if I can do this again.

He closed his eyes and let himself slip back. He relaxed his focus and felt that familiar tingle across his skin. His stomach lurched as the world began to swirl and flash with a mixture of colors, illuminating the night with a subtle, gray hue.

Structures lost their texture and features, replaced by black outlines of perfect geometry. The car became nothing more than a series of scribbled lines, a sum of parts drawn with impossibly intricate detail down to the last nut and bolt.

Donovan took a breath. The world breathed with him, swaying like a twig caught in the wind. He waited a beat, listening to the nothingness around him. There *was* something, though. It was close, a murmuring that—when he focused on it—became louder, like someone had twisted a radio dial. There were voices, and when he turned around, he saw their outlines: three of them, two men and one woman by the sound of it.

"—the hell did he go?"

"Beats me. He was here a second ago."

"Think he flickered out?"

"Nah. Ain't no one who does that on command. Not that I ever seen, anyways."

They circled the car. When one of them came close, he put out his hand and let it slide through their outline. They recoiled from his touch.

"What's wrong?"

"Had a chill. Someone must've walked over my grave."

Donovan bit his lip to keep from laughing. He didn't understand how this worked, nor did it matter. All it took was a matter of concentration on his part, and if he could force himself into the Monochrome at will, there was an equal possibility of forcing someone else out.

Something must be there to balance the weight.

He could free someone from the shackles of the Monochrome, but at a heavy price—one he was prepared to pay if necessary.

"I'll cross that bridge when I get to it," he whispered. One of the outlined figures spun on their heels.

"D'you hear that?"

"Hear what?"

"That voice? Sounded like a man." The figure tromped out into the street. "Come on out, man. We don't want to hurt ya."

"You're crazy. First she's getting cold chills, and now you're talking to people who ain't there. Crazy, the both of you."

Donovan couldn't hold back the laughter this time. He let out a loud chuckle that carried into the Spectrum. A hush fell over the three guards for a moment as they exchanged glances. One proclaimed "Fuck this!" and began to run. The others followed suit. Donovan's laughter went with them.

They disappeared down the street. He thought about following to see where they might lead him, but a simple realization struck. He remembered the way he'd passed beyond the front door of his own home, the fabric of its existence swept aside like a curtain to allow him through, and now he wondered just how limitless his new ability truly was.

He trained his eyes on the ground, squinting in concentration as he scanned the flat surface. Color and texture changed before him from a gritty patch of road to a slate layer devoid of character. He strained his mind, felt himself moving outward without moving at all, cutting through some unseen barrier. Sweat formed on his forehead.

The street began to rend apart, its formless gray shape pulling away like a sheet of paper torn in two. A network of sewer drains and unused electrical lines lay before him, etched in black outline, shaded with graphite. For a moment Donovan wondered if he'd fallen into a pencil drawing, the folds of paper curling back upon themselves.

He renewed his focus.

The city's infrastructure beneath the street faded, revealing the subterranean tunnels below. And within them—

Donovan gasped. He saw them, all of them, the Missing and the bestiary of the Monochrome working their way through the tunnels, scattering like insects. Some ran for their lives from the gaunt, lumbering Yawning while others huddled together in small groups, struggling to survive in this vast, gray prison.

This is what Sparrow's lacking. This is the vision.

His stomach churned when he saw the Cretins. There were millions of them, writhing in the cracks of the walls, biting and clamoring over one another like maggots. He entertained a sickening notion that they truly were ill-formed larvae, feasting on the city from the inside out, and the grim imagery reminded him of what he'd witnessed just a day before.

Donovan refocused his attention, forcing the memory from his mind. A low throb emerged in the back of his skull, but he ignored it.

Sparrow said he cast out the others. They wouldn't be hiding with the rest of his court.

He slowly moved his eyes, scanning the area like a human x-ray machine. The ability was fantastic, but not without its price. A deep, searing pain bloomed between his eyes. He relaxed for a moment, letting himself bleed through into the Spectrum. The night air took him by surprise, and he gasped at its sensation.

The sky overhead had lightened. It was nearly dawn.

Get to it. Headache be damned.

He focused his gaze, moving along the sidewalk as he did so. The world transitioned beneath his feet, the sidewalk peeling away to reveal the city's squirming underbelly. He looked through the station's walls, saw the concourse where the massacred bodies still lay strewn about, and spotted the army of Yawning loitering over them. They knelt, picking apart the limbs and devouring those they liked most.

Donovan looked away in disgust. The spot between his eyes throbbed. He pushed on.

After walking five city blocks in the liminal space, he happened upon a tiny cul-de-sac within the network of tunnels. There was a large group of people down there huddled together in makeshift shacks. A tunnel dead-ended there, and above it was a small gated building. *Maintenance access,* he thought. The access tunnel intersected with a nearby line of track; this carried on to its various stops within the South District before circling back around to Winthorpe Station.

He looked back down at the group of huddled figures. *It's them. Has to be.* Why else would they sequester themselves so far away from Sparrow's center of operations?

The migraine pulsed within his frontal lobe. He tried his best to ignore it, focusing harder, projecting his will down into the street beneath him. Donovan gasped from the blinding pain slicing through his forehead.

When he opened his eyes, he found his efforts were working. The slow falling sensation made his stomach tumble. Donovan shut his eyes once more.

He sank.

Across the city, as Donovan found the will to submerge himself through the earth, a solitary figure watched the dawn from a window high up within the WBS building. Sparrow stood with his hand against the glass. He looked down at the street below, its lights marking the sidewalk and traffic stops along the way, then upward and outward to the horizon. A cool glow hung in the sky, and stars twinkled farther above.

Kale isn't coming.

He couldn't perceive what had happened to his faithful disciple, but he'd felt something like pain in his chest, and the sensation was not pleasant. Someone had cut the thread tying him to his master. Sparrow had felt a panicked vibration—then nothing at all. The stillness disturbed him.

If Candle was out there, he could not sense him. Nor could he sense if Kale had completed his task. The Spectrum's pull inundated him with nausea, stifling his reach.

He hated this place. Watching the world come to life like a blooming flower was sickening. The weight of the Spectrum tugged at him like a falling anchor, wrenching against his very essence. *I do not belong here. That much is clear to me now.*

After all the years he'd spent running from this destiny, that he resisted fate for so long seemed like a fool's errand. This was where he belonged, the king of a blank kingdom. Once everything was in place—which was so very soon now—he would reap the rewards of his plan, feasting upon the world like a parasite.

By tonight he would be impenetrable, inescapable.

Inevitable.

Sparrow turned from the window, grimacing at the strange nausea plaguing him, and took a seat at the head of the large table. He kicked back and put up his feet. *Just a matter of time,* he thought. Yes, it would be just a matter of hours. Hundreds of thousands would tune in to recap the exploits of their favorite lost souls, and by day's end they would belong to him.

The threads connecting recent events all led back to him. Sparrow closed his eyes, clinging to a memory of his former life that had survived the column's white fire. He remembered the day he looked down upon some ants charred by the focused beam of sunlight. Now he had that lens turned toward the entire world, and he would watch the insects burn.

He would harvest them all, absorbing their mediocrity as his own. He would grow, molting this carcass of flesh and emerging as something more, something greater than even Dullington could conceive. He would fulfill his natural purpose and consume the world one worthless soul at a time. He would set this banal coil alight and dance across its ashes.

And what about Candle?

Albert Sparrow opened his darkened eyes and looked beyond the Spectrum, staring deep into the recesses of the Monochrome's gray halls. An entourage of white creatures filled the room, eyes poised upon him, loyal to their master and his whims.

"*Soon. Very soon, my children. Not even Candle can hide from what is to come.*"

Sparrow rose from his chair and held out his arms. The Cretins let out a collective yelp before rushing toward him, climbing up his body, covering him like pale flies on a corpse.

"**D**rink this."

Evelyn opened her eyes and strained to sit up. Alice knelt beside her with a chipped coffee mug. She took it to her lips and tasted. The water was bitter, but after a timid sip she downed the whole mug. Alice smiled.

"We'll have you up and dancing in no time."

"I'm a terrible dancer," Evelyn rasped. She leaned against the wall and grimaced. "Feel like I was hit by a goddamn truck."

Alice frowned. "I think we could all say that."

Hours had passed since the boy returned with the bandages and medicine. What he brought wasn't much—nothing of prescription strength—but it was enough to dress her wounds and prevent infection from setting in. Evelyn regained consciousness shortly after Quinn returned. She tried to prevent them from covering her in bandages, and Joel had to hold her down while the others patched up the bloody, oozing holes peppered across her arms, hands, and face.

Quinn watched, whispering a short prayer for the old lady to pull through. He liked Evelyn and didn't want her death on his conscience.

Alice got up and joined him at the burning barrel. She was the first to approach him since his return. Those who survived the massacre kept their distance from him, and he wondered if he might fare better in the network of tunnels with the Yawning.

He tried to ignore her, focusing on the dancing flames, but when she didn't leave, he realized his efforts were pointless.

"How is she?"

"Sore, but it could be worse."

He nodded, watching the fire lick the air.

"You did good, Q-ball."

"Don't say that."

Alice put her hand on his shoulder. It was warm, lively, and made his gut twist into itself.

"I mean it," she said.

"No, don't." He looked at her now, trembling, blinking away tears. "She wouldn't be like this if it weren't for me. Saying I 'did good' doesn't change anything. She wouldn't need the meds if I hadn't fucked up."

Alice said nothing. She let her hand slide from his shoulder. They watched the white fire for a moment, silent, listening to the debris in the barrel sizzle and pop.

"We all fucked up," she said finally, a slight hesitation in her voice. "Me, you, Evelyn back there, Joel, the rest. We all fucked up some way. It's why we're here."

Quinn rubbed his eyes. "So?"

"So, we're no better than you. And that means you're no better than us. Most of these people—" She motioned out toward the grouping of shacks and the figures whose shadows danced across the walls. "—*they* don't even realize why they're here. They just know they woke up one day and were stuck in this gray hell. And because they don't know, they don't do anything to atone for it. They don't know to make it right. You understand?"

He nodded.

"What you did, Q-ball, was your way of making it right. You fucked up, and you know you fucked up. What matters is you tried to fix it. And I'm telling you that old woman over there, my friend, she could kiss you for what you did. She would be a hell of a lot worse off if you hadn't made your run to the top and back."

Quinn sniffled, wiped his nose on his sleeve. "What's your point?"

"My point," she said, "is that you did something about the bed you made. That's more than most of us can say for ourselves. So, stop your moping. It doesn't suit you."

He looked away, fighting the impulse to smile. It was the sort of thing Wendy might tell him but thinking of her made his heart ache.

Alice gasped. Her fingers dug into his shoulder, causing him to wince.

"Ow, what—"

"Heads up!"

Some of the men in the group came running, weapons in hand, the echo of their intermittent footsteps and panicked murmurs filling the vast room. Quinn turned away from Alice and the burning barrel, focusing his eyes on the access tunnel and the gray haze that obscured its depths. What he saw made his heart stop.

The figure was a sketch of a man, transparent but for a dark outline drawn into reality, with no face, eyes, or mouth. The shape slowly descended from the ceiling, a weightless phantom right out of a horror story. The transparent figure stopped at the floor, looking around for a moment as if lost.

The men of the group knelt and drew their weapons. Quinn watched, holding his breath until it began to burn in his lungs. He exhaled slowly, afraid that any sound might arouse the spirit's interest. After all he'd seen, his mind still had trouble accepting this. A ghost? Here? Ghosts were the stuff of fiction.

But his eyes said otherwise.

Quinn.

The outlined figure turned toward him, reached out with a crudely drawn hand, and beckoned. Its voice was distant, a whisper carried across the Monochrome's haze, but they all heard it. The men looked at him, frightened, unsure of what this meant. None of them had seen such a thing before.

Alice put her hand on his shoulder and began to pull on him.

"No," he said to the side, not willing to look away from this spectacle. The figure continued its advance, shimmering with a pale light that left spots in his eyes, illuminating the gloom with the intensity of a strobe. The closer the outline came the more of its features he could see.

It wore a shirt, jeans. A mop of dark hair sat atop the figure's head. The empty frame of a head became a face with a nose and eyes aged with the burden of experience. When the man moved closer Quinn's heart jumped, pulsing to a heavy rhythm. He *knew* this man.

Donovan walked out of the gray haze. "Hey, Quinn."

His nephew smiled, ran forward, and threw his arms around him. "I thought you were dead."

"Me too." Donovan pulled away from his nephew and looked at the tired group of men and women, their weapons trained on him, fear in their wide eyes. "I guess you're not all happy to see me."

"That's enough, boys."

The old woman's voice startled them all. They turned toward Evelyn, who stood with one hand braced against the wall. Alice went to her side and tried to coax her back to her sleeping bag.

"I'm all right, Alice. Really." She looked up at their visitor and beckoned to him. "Donovan Candle, huh? I've heard a lot about you."

He turned from his nephew. "Are you Evelyn Brock?"

The old woman's face went paler than their prison walls. "Y-yes I am."

"I've heard a lot about you, too."

They gathered around Evelyn's sleeping bag, despite her protests, and Donovan told them what he knew. He told them about his escape into liminal space, his visit with Aleister Dullington, how he managed to force his way between realities, and the grim truth of Albert Sparrow's plan.

"This event," Donovan said, "this 'Great Fade-Out' begins in just a few hours. If Sparrow gets his way, there are going to be far more people flickering out, just like you. I can't let that happen."

Someone in the group scoffed. When he looked up, he saw it was the one they called Joel. Donovan recognized him, the one who led him down into the station where they kept Donna captive all that time ago.

"We're already stuck here," Joel said. "Why should we care if a few more—"

"With all due respect, I don't think you have any concept of just how many people are at risk. I'm not talking about a 'few' here. This reality show is extremely popular around the world."

"So?"

"So that's a few million more people flickering out who aren't supposed to be flickering out. Most of you made your choices, but the ones Sparrow is claiming as his own haven't had a chance to stake their claim. It's a matter of balance."

Someone else said, "Balance, my ass."

Donovan sighed. "Look, I don't know what will happen, but I do know things are breaking down. Those weapons you've got aren't supposed to be here. The lines are blurring. What happens if all those people flicker out and the lines break down altogether?"

The group murmured. Now he had their full attention.

"What if Sparrow reaches his full potential, and the Monochrome will no longer bind him? Do you want the rest of the world to be overrun with Cretins and Yawning? What if your loved ones leave for work and find a Yawning at their front door?"

The thought of a pale, lifeless planet shrouded in gray chilled him—and strengthened his resolve. He would not let it come to that.

Evelyn was quiet throughout his tale but chose this moment to break the uneasy silence. She shuffled restlessly in her makeshift bed.

"Why did you come back here, Donovan?"

He looked down at his feet, remembering the peaceful look on Donna's face while she slept. *I could be back in bed. Sleeping beside her, comfortable, at ease—but then I couldn't keep my promise.*

"A long time ago," he said, "Aleister Dullington told me actions birth definition. I didn't understand it at the time, but in the past few hours I think I figured it out. Everyone—you, me, Quinn, *everyone*—we've all got a purpose, something we're meant to do. We're supposed to figure out what that purpose is, and act on it. We're supposed to define ourselves by those actions. A lot of people do, but then some of us lose our way. We forget what our purposes are, giving up on our dreams or deluding ourselves into thinking we've climbed as high as we can go—when in truth we're just afraid to take that next step, that next leap. Why did I come back here? I guess it's to define who I am. I made a promise to my wife that I wouldn't give up again, and I don't intend to break that promise. I only hope she'll understand what it is I have to do. I doubt it, but that's something I'll have to live with."

He paused, meeting the old woman's gaze. "Y'know, it's funny, I quoted Dullington to your husband about a week ago. You should've seen the look on his face."

Evelyn's face fell, and a full minute passed before she spoke again.

"Has the old man moved on?"

Donovan looked away, unsure of how to answer.

"It's okay, hon. You can tell me. I'm a big girl."

"Nate never stopped looking for you. He has never moved on, never remarried. He believes you're in this city somewhere, and he's still an old stubborn bastard." He met her gaze once more. "And he still loves you."

She put a shaky, wrinkled hand on his, and squeezed his fingers. "Thank you."

Looking into her eyes, Donovan took her hand, smiling. He reached out with his other hand, smoothing the hair back from her bandaged forehead. Dullington whispered inside his mind: *Mind the reaction, Mr. Candle.*

Evelyn opened her mouth to speak, but a bright light silenced her. Donovan pressed hard against her skin, focusing all his effort upon their contact, willing the old woman across the boundary. Something gave way as she slipped over, vanishing from the Monochrome and appearing in the Spectrum. Donovan felt an odd tension leave her body and enter through his hand. The sensation had weight, gravity, and made him feel sick.

For just a moment, a sickening aura slipped over him, clinging to his skin like a slimy film. Nausea swept through his gut, tightening in his chest as distant bells chimed in his ears. Colors—if they could be called colors—swam in amorphous clumps before his eyes. He feared he might vomit but the pain dulled quickly, settling into the bottom of his stomach and hardening like cement.

He blinked away the phantoms swirling before him. Alice and the others stared in awestruck horror. Joel's gun clattered to the ground. Uncomfortable murmurs filled the group as some recoiled in fear.

"Uncle Don?" Quinn whispered. "Are you okay?"

When Donovan looked back at the Wretched, he saw the mediocrity festering in their bellies, an off-white infection glowing just beneath their flesh like cancerous tumors. Some of them glowed far less than others—including Quinn.

Trembling, Alice Walenta stepped toward him. "My God, what did you do?"

"I gave her a second chance," he said, wiping blood from his nose. "Now it's your turn."

———————◆———————

Donna stirred in her sleep. She rolled on her side, legs twisting in the sheets, one arm cradling a pillow. The other fell upon the space once occupied by her husband. It was cold.

"Donnie?"

When he didn't answer, she opened her eyes. The room was dim, filled with a faint morning light giving the room a soft blue hue. She sat up and called out for her husband.

Again, he did not answer.

She reached for the nightstand to turn on the lamp, and that's when she saw the note. It was folded twice, with her name written on the outside in a scrawl that was unmistakably his. Only Donovan wrote that poorly, and she prided herself as one of the few who could decipher his horrid script.

"No," she whispered, her eyes scanning the note a second time. "No, no, don't do this to me. Don't."

Her pleas went unanswered. Donna did her best to scramble out of bed. She went into the office and found the phone. She dialed.

Michael answered after four long rings. "Hello?"

"He's gone." The words left a trail across her tongue. Her throat was thick with it, and she was crying before Michael could respond. "He's gone."

15

REACTIONS

Televisions flickered to life across the country as dawn became day, the morning hours willfully surrendered to a barrage of commercials, punditry, and sensationalist media by the overeager masses. The WBS Network expected high ratings. The *Fading Out* marathon—dubbed by some genius in the marketing department as the "Great Fade-Out"—would recap one episode per hour from noon until midnight with limited commercial interruption. It was a long enough stretch that even those who had prior commitments would, statistically, be able to watch at least one episode. Maybe two.

A two-hour special was aired that morning, serving as a "pre-game" of sorts, complete with a biopic on the show's missing creator, Richard Henza. This included interviews with the cast, crew, and pre-recorded segments with Henza in which he discussed the initial ideas spurring the show's creation.

The show was broadcast directly from WBS headquarters. In the daylight, the building towered over the city, a testament to modern architecture and a proud symbol of the city's culture. At its peak stood an array of satellites, triangulated and focused to the stars, beaming up its scheduled broadcasts twenty-four hours a day, seven days a week. To the naked eye the building shimmered in the light, its dark glass surface reflective of its surroundings.

In the Monochrome, the structure was a lifeless monolith jutting out above a dead city of empty geometric shapes. A white glow pulsed around the structure, beginning at its base and rising the length of the building in measured bursts. At its zenith, the light focused itself around the grid of dishes pointed skyward.

However, one would not recognize this satellite array. No, these structures were wrapped with thick, white masses of rubbery flesh, collectively writhing in time with each pulse of light. These tumors were a living extension of the Monochrome itself, connected by a single shivering vine that coiled its way down to the plaza below like a giant umbilical cord.

Albert Sparrow felt each pulse, every subtle vibration coaxing his deadened nerves back to life, reminding him they were there. Memories and instincts crawled out of his darkened mind, fantasies concocted out of his displeasure for the world and its many insects, and how he wanted to reshape reality in his own image. Beginning with the sky.

He hated the sky. Once everything was in place, and he had fed from the world's mediocrity, he would remove the sky's blue hue.

I will paint it the color of dead television while the world dies. It will be glorious.

Sparrow flickered back into the Spectrum. He turned, walking the boardroom's perimeter as the sun's sharp golden rays filtered through the blinds. All twelve members of the WBS Network's executive board were in attendance, summoned in the early morning hours by their pale master. They cowered in their seats, trembling with mortal fear of this creature parading as a man. Several of them prayed openly, calling out to their gods to save them, pleading for forgiveness.

"Gentlemen," Sparrow chided, "spare me your religion. I'm all there is now. If you want to pray for salvation, you pray to *me*."

John Beckman cowered with them, his face buried in his hands, quelling a hidden desire to cry out in defiance. The liquid courage of scotch had worn off a while ago; this was just brazen stupidity. He knew what the repercussions would be.

Not that it matters anymore, he thought, cradling his head. They were damned anyway, living on borrowed time by the good graces of the board's thirteenth member. The terrors of the Monochrome were more than enough to keep them in submission. Now, on the morning of Sparrow's final solution, John Beckman realized the gut-wrenching truth: there was no escaping their fate.

We were always meant to be used. We let this happen.

Sparrow paused once more at the window, tracing his slender fingers across the edge of the blinds. A low, guttural laugh bellowed forth from the old man, sending the others further into terrified despair.

A chill worked its way across John's arms, met at the back of his neck, and danced all the way down his spine. Sweat dotted his forehead.

My God, what have we done?

--------------◆--------------

Donovan braced himself against a wall, waiting for the sudden turmoil in his guts to pass. The drone of bells clanged in his ears, accompanying a display of colorful stars before his watering eyes, overloading his senses. His body's reaction to the sick energy told him all he needed to know: no human was meant to do what he'd done.

"Don?"

Quinn's voice echoed from somewhere beyond the roiling darkness. Donovan felt a hand on his shoulder.

"I'm fine," he muttered. "Just give me a moment."

Another minute passed before the sharp pain in his belly ceased, as did the chimes and the colors. He righted himself, leaned his head against the wall, and rubbed his eyes. *Well that was unexpected. Maybe too much at one time.*

He looked at his companions, now just Alice and Quinn. Some of the Wretched had fled his touch—fearful of what he had done to Evelyn, of what he had become. The others had embraced his offer to return and were now safely on the Spectrum side. He could almost hear their muffled voices from across the invisible line.

Steady now, Donovan took a couple of steps toward Alice. She pulled a dirty rag from her pocket and handed it to him. Donovan looked at it, puzzled.

"You're bleeding," she said, gesturing to his nose. He wiped his face with the cloth, staining it a shade of maroon so dark it was almost black. *The migraine,* he thought. It still lingered there between his eyes, a hammer threatening to pound away what was left of his brain.

"Thanks." He stuffed the bloody cloth into his pocket and gave her a long look, searching the corners of his mind for memories once stolen from him. "Y'know, we really ought to stop meeting like this."

Quinn turned away from the mouth of the tunnel. "You two know each other?"

"We used to," Alice said. "The Cretins took care of the rest. Do you remember anything, Don?" She hesitated, and then blurted out, "Does your brother?"

He shook his head. "All I remember is meeting you on the subway platform. Same with Mike. Anyway, I never did thank you for helping us."

Alice frowned. "Never mind that. I don't know how you're able to do whatever it is you just did, but if you want to see your wife again, I don't think you should do it anymore."

"It's not that simple."

"Yes, it is. You need to stop. If you don't, it's going to kill you. You're bleeding again, for fuck's sake."

Donovan felt the blood trickle down to his lip. He took out the dirty rag and held it to his nose. *She's right,* he thought, *but I've already made my choice.*

When the bleeding stopped, Donovan crumbled the rag in his hand and stepped toward her. She recoiled from him, not in fear but in protest.

"I'll stop when I'm done, Alice. And like it or not, you're going back to the Spectrum. Evelyn needs to get to a hospital, and I also have a favor to ask of you."

Alice considered his words, observing the agony illustrated so clearly by his body language. The sweat on his forehead betrayed him, exposing the pain he was so desperately trying to conceal. *You stubborn man,* she thought. *You stubborn, determined man. Just like your damn brother.*

"What's going to happen to you? Or your wife?"

"That's where you come in," he said, pulling her aside. He told her what he needed done, and when he was finished, she paused for only a moment before nodding in agreement.

Quinn watched their exchange, unable to hear them. When they were done Donovan put his hand on Alice's forehead, closed his eyes, and tensed up as a piercing light illuminated her body. For a period of seconds Quinn thought he saw the light emitting from beneath her skin somehow, like a flashlight underneath a blanket.

And then Alice was gone, leaving Donovan standing with his hand in the air, a contorted expression of pain on his face. He uttered a single groan before collapsing on the floor.

"Oh shit." Quinn rushed to his uncle's side. "Don? Are you okay? *Don?*"

Donovan's eyes rolled back in his skull as a strange, pale aura slowly spread across his body. Quinn watched in terror as his uncle began to flicker and fade, slipping from this reality into the next. Panicking, Quinn slapped his uncle across the face.

"Goddammit, Don, don't you fucking leave me here." Tears streamed down his dirty cheeks. *"I can't do this alone."*

Donovan's eyes rolled front, pupils dilating, struggling to focus in the Monochrome's low light. He reached up, took hold of Quinn's collar, and smiled.

"Don't count me out just yet," he whispered. "I'm not done here. Help me up."

Quinn took his uncle's hand and helped pull him to his feet. Donovan steadied himself against the wall once more, rubbing absently at his temples. Blood dripped from his nose, forming tiny dark puddles on the gray flooring. *Maybe Alice was right. This could very well kill me, but I can't let it stop me now. On your feet, hoss. Keep moving.*

"Look, you can't—"

Donovan held up his hand to silence him. "I have to, Quinn. Maybe not right this second, but soon. I need to get back to the street. Can you lead us out of here?"

"I—yes, I know the way. I just…you don't have to do this. Not for me. I'm not worth it."

"You may not think so," Donovan said, "but I do. And so does Donna. So do your parents."

"But what if this—whatever *this* is—what if it kills you, Don?"

"Then I'll die knowing I did what I could. Now let's get out of here."

Quinn did as he was asked, leading his uncle out from the depths of the access tunnels where the Wretched had set up camp. Donovan had to stop several times along the way, pausing to catch his breath while the migraine worked its way deeper into his skull like an icy drill bit. He'd had headaches before, but this was different. There was a force behind each agonizing throb threatening to punch his brain right through its cranial wall, and he discovered he had a hard time focusing on anything for longer than a couple of minutes. Blood loss from his persistent nosebleeds wasn't helping matters.

Mind the reaction.

Now he understood Dullington's warning. In freeing the prisoners of this reality, Donovan had taken on the burden of their mediocrity, becoming a prisoner himself. At the same time, he realized his new "gift" could also be used as a weapon, and with it he would end Sparrow's assault on the Spectrum.

They traveled in silence for a while longer, working their way through the network of tunnels beneath the city before finally emerging at the maintenance access hut Donovan had glimpsed earlier that morning. The dull haze of the Monochrome's empty skies met them with lifeless clarity. A low, pulsing drone filled the air, accompanied by a subtle flash of light. When he turned in the direction of midtown, he understood the source of the illumination.

Not long now. I need to hurry.

Quinn stepped off the curb, squinting into the distance. "That's new," he said. "I don't remember the light being like this."

Donovan joined him. "It's from the WBS Network building. I'm running out of time."

"You mean 'we.'" Quinn glared at his uncle, expecting agreement, but Donovan shook his head.

"No, Quinn, I've got a different job for you." He fished his car keys from his pocket and put them in his nephew's hand. "My car's just a couple of blocks from here, near the old station. I need you to get it and drive to the WBS building. Michael will be there."

He watched the epiphany work its way through Quinn's head, observing the disappointment and anger forming on his face.

"You're going in alone?"

Donovan nodded.

"But Don, you can't."

"I have to, Quinn, and I don't have time to argue about it. Now do what I've asked. Please. Go find Mike and tell him about the others." Quinn opened his mouth, but Donovan stopped him. "Just listen to me, okay? I choose to do this, and I don't expect you to understand. Look at it another way—a lot of those people I just sent over to the Spectrum are going to need medical attention. They won't all fit in my car. Mike can help you. Trust me."

Frustrated, Quinn dropped his gaze, his hands balled into fists. He couldn't leave his uncle here.

"They aren't the only ones needing medical attention," Quinn said. "Look at you, Don. You're bleeding, you're pale, and you fucking fainted less than an hour ago. I can't leave you like this."

Donovan sighed. He stepped forward, wrapping his arms around Quinn in a heavy embrace. "This is my decision, Quinn. When you see Mike, tell him I'm not afraid to jump anymore."

"Don, I'm not—"

Leaving you, he wanted to say, but his words were cut off as Donovan squeezed his arms tighter. Quinn struggled to free himself, punching Donovan's arms and shoulders, but to no avail. A bright, pale light filled his vision, washing out the world in a flickering glimmer of emptiness.

Donovan's arms folded inward as his nephew was finally freed of the Monochrome's shackles. He teetered on his feet for a moment, gasping at the sudden weight in his belly, tugging him to and fro like a ship lost on the waves. The world spun, swelling and pulsing with dim flashes of light in the distance. Chimes returned, filling his ears as splotches of color trailed across his vision.

A low tremor vibrated beneath his feet, but Donovan didn't notice. His eyes rolled back into his head as his arms and legs went limp. He collapsed in the street, sinking into a turbulent sea of nothingness while the walls of the Monochrome shivered under the stress of its malignant king.

Sparrow felt the shockwave. It ran through him like a chill, an exciting jolt of energy that made him cry out in surprise. He spun on his feet, reeling as a wave of nausea came over him, but he fought to keep it at bay. The pull of the Monochrome was greater than ever. He could feel his ties to the Spectrum severing with each passing moment. It felt like going home.

The board members of WBS gave each other concerned looks as the vibration tore through the room. The air suddenly became stale, thick with the tension of twelve men cowering in fear of powers that defied their comprehension. These men, kings of broadcast television, were reduced to the stature of beaten dogs, fearful of their master.

John Beckman sat at the far end, gripping the edges of the table until the quake finally ceased. He stared at his comrades, once respectable businessmen of honest pedigrees, now behaving like lowly "yes" men. A sickening thought occurred to him as he glared at their resigned faces: *I'm no different.*

Sparrow returned to the window, peering down at the plaza, clapping his hands as another tremor ripped through the building. His body faded in the morning light, taking on a transparency which Beckman knew all too well. The old pallid man who'd once introduced himself as Dr. Albert Sparrow had changed over the last year, his demeanor fading, becoming more erratic, violent, and impulsive.

A large painting at the far of end of the room collapsed to the floor, its hook shaken free from the wall. The flat-panel TV affixed to the adjacent wall toppled forward, hitting the floor with a solid *whump* as sparks burst from the back of the unit.

He looked up at Dr. Sparrow. Still clapping, the old man flickered in the morning light, vanishing from one end of the glass wall and reappearing at the other.

A loud crash erupted within the room, startling them all. The company's CFO fell out of his chair, crying out in shock as he hit the floor. John looked around, confused. The sound was like thunder, a sudden explosion that did not stop. The noise filling their ears quickly turned into a scratchy tearing sound, like Velcro slowly pulled apart—and that's when he saw them.

He didn't believe it at first. There were other figures in the room. He'd seen them before, seen them lurking in the dark corners of his vision. They were the silent sentinels, always watching, waiting. Sparrow never made their presence fully known but used them as a warning should any of them decide to defect.

The white creature emerged out of thin air, its arms and legs slightly transparent for a moment before solidifying into reality. It marched along the edge of the table, its tiny eyes surveying the world as if for the first time. A thin black slit of a mouth widened in awe of the room. John Beckman looked at his cohorts, curious if he was the only one seeing this impossibility, but their reactions told him he was not.

Sparrow paused his erratic jubilation. He stopped when he saw the Cretin on the table.

"Welcome, little one."

The creature saw its master and scampered across the table's surface. He put out his hand and allowed the white thing to climb up his shoulder like a domesticated rodent. It stood beside his head and leaned toward his ear. He chuckled.

"Yes, I know this place looks horrible. It won't for long. Just until the day is over, and then we'll remake it into something more suitable." He looked up at the board members. "Them? Oh, they're nothing to worry about—what's that?" His face darkened. He turned away from them and approached the window once more. "Is that so?"

Sparrow put his hands upon the glass as he peered down at the street.

"Yes, I can feel him. There *is* something different, isn't there? Hmm?

Oh no, I would not be concerned. I can feel it happening much faster than expected. It's like holding electricity. Like being born."

He turned away from the window, head tilted to one side, listening to the whispers of the demon on his shoulder.

"Them? I suppose I don't *need* most of them. Just one—and only until the broadcast is finished."

Sparrow monitored the members of the board, taking in their expressions of anguish and terror. They were fat, greedy men with more money than they would ever need, prime examples of human excess. These were the men responsible for filling the airwaves with mindless drivel, brainwashing the masses into believing their brand of entertainment was best.

These were the men in charge of polluting the world—and people loved them for it. Sparrow smiled, pleased with his convictions. Humanity certainly deserved to suffocate and burn.

"Mr. Beckman," he said, "take me to the roof. As for the rest of you, well, I no longer need your company."

The men of the WBS Network's Executive Leadership Team looked up at their master, at once stunned and relieved, their faces a mixture of elation and disbelief. John Beckman shared their disbelief, but for different reasons.

"The roof? Why aren't I free to go? What the hell did I do?"

Sparrow flickered as he crossed the room quickly and was on Mr. Beckman before the executive could react. His gnarled old fingers dug into the flesh of Beckman's throat, who kicked his legs as he was lifted from his chair. Sparrow held the man over the table.

"You pull the strings here," Sparrow growled, *"and I pull yours. You aren't free to go because I fucking said so."*

His booming voice made the windows crack. Beckman struggled for air, resisting the dark spots of color arcing across his vision as Sparrow tightened his grip. Then, with a flick of his wrist, Sparrow threw the man like a ragdoll across the room. He collapsed in a heap, coughing for air.

Sparrow turned toward the others. He smiled, speaking in calm, even tones. "All of you are wastes of skin. You are better served elsewhere."

John Beckman struggled to pull himself together. He looked up just in time to watch Sparrow wave his hand through the air. He blinked as it left a rippling trail like the wavering effect of heat rising off asphalt. For a moment the entire room shifted, its textures and colors bleeding out of existence before returning to normal.

Heart racing, John watched in stupefied horror as more of the white creatures materialized. They were much larger, taller, their heads nearly scraping the ceiling, with arms that hung down to their feet. They looked around in lazy wonder just as the smaller one had moments before.

More of them came, one for each board member, stepping into reality as one might step beyond a curtain. Their master clapped his hands together, rippling the air like water.

"Children," he said, "please acquaint them."

John Beckman wanted to look away, wanted to run screaming from the boardroom, but his limbs wouldn't respond. He watched as the white monstrosities knelt over the men seated at the table. Why they didn't try to run he would never know, and the urge to cry out stalled on the tip of his tongue. *Go*, his mind screamed, *get away from them!* The other executives were either too scared or too stunned to move. They cowered in their seats as each of the Yawning's jaws unhinged and stretched to the floor, revealing blackened, bottomless maws lined with rows of worn, white teeth.

Together they pounced, consuming the men whole—chairs and all—lifting back their heads to scarf down these rich delicacies. One closed its jaws early, tearing the company's senior vice president in half. His dismembered legs splattered on the table, drenching the polished surface with a thick coat of blood.

Finally, John Beckman found the will to look away, but the sounds remained. He heard the crunching of bone as the creatures chewed their prey. He realized he had pissed himself, and for the first time in decades he wished for nothing more than his mother's safe embrace.

But she was dead, and so were the members of the board. He feared he was about to join them.

Sparrow stood over him and extended a hand.

"Mr. Beckman," he said. His voice was calm, collected. Jovial. "Please take me to the roof."

———◆———

Donovan opened his eyes, staring up at a gray, muddied sky. His throat was parched, and when he sat up, a jolt of pain shot through the back of his skull. He thought the crippling nausea was gone, but when he climbed to his feet that familiar wrenching sensation returned, working its way up from the pit of his stomach and into his throat.

Clutching his belly, he doubled over and vomited. A viscous, gray liquid splattered on the street in a gelatinous puddle flecked with dots of blood. The strange substance burned his throat and tongue, coating his mouth with a slick film. The taste was vile, and the smell was even worse, like rotten garbage left out in the rain. He almost hurled a second time from the sight of it but turned away before his guts could churn again.

Hunched over, bracing his hands on his knees, Donovan Candle groaned in agony. When the nausea finally passed, he opened his eyes and stared at the dark specks of blood on the ground. More droplets fell from his nose.

Not good.

Standing tall, Donovan shrugged off the uneasiness that had come over him. He wiped his nose on his sleeve and turned in the direction of the WBS Network Plaza. Finding the building wouldn't be difficult here in the Monochrome maze: he need only follow the nauseating light pulsing into the sky.

A tremor shook through the earth, rattling his teeth. The quake startled him so badly he almost lost his balance. When the vibrations settled Donovan collected himself, struggling to bury the turmoil in his gut.

He put one foot in front of the other, trudging down an empty street in the direction of the WBS headquarters.

16

THREADS IN THE TAPESTRY

Aleister Dullington saw everything with unblinking clarity. Mr. Sparrow and Mr. Candle, two souls whose strings had become intricately entwined. A pluck here, a pull there—the strings were resilient, easily stretched and wound. So much effort had gone into arranging this moment.

More than effort. Sacrifice. Diligence. His adversary's recent moves in this long game of theirs had taken Aleister by surprise, the latest in this centuries-old tête-à-tête. Feigning wounds and retreating into liminal space was his only move at the time. From there, however, he'd regrouped and waited, watched.

And then his adversary tipped his hand, perverting the Ungod's light and transforming the former Mr. Sparrow into a true puppet of impulse. Blind to his own strings, fueled with the fire of human ego, ambition, and lies, Mr. Sparrow had acted much as Aleister suspected he would.

There, in his former prisoner's actions, was his enemy's true intentions made known.

If Aleister were to triumph and set things right, he would need a puppet of his own.

No, he corrected himself. *Not a puppet. An avatar.*

Someone he could guide. Someone who had proven their dependability. Someone with something to lose.

Mr. Candle had done everything he was supposed to. Now there was only the matter of confrontation, and Dullington already knew how that would go. Mr. Sparrow's retention of hatred for Mr. Candle was more than fortuitous; Aleister saw it as a mandate from the Ungod itself. A quiet plea from the nonentity's dream state to stop the disruption of the strings.

His adversary had spent centuries manipulating the threads from afar, corrupting them, pulling and twisting and knotting wherever possible. Centuries of defilement had led to countless nightmares across the Spectrum, horrific atrocities for which there were no precedents, an ocean of blood spilled to satiate one man's desire.

Now his adversary had enacted a new strategy, focusing on the Monochrome instead of the Spectrum to tip the balance for good.

His old master's words floated through his mind like ashes in the wind. *Man must be made to face his nightmares. I will hold open his eyes so that he may see and despair.*

Aleister Dullington gazed upward at the expanse of threads demarcating the sky. He thought of his fallen brothers, of his former life. All sacrificed for the greater good, to protect the sanctity of the Ungod, Great Weaver of the tapestry threading both realities together.

A tremor rumbled through the cityscape. Aleister felt the vibration and witnessed the repercussions of Sparrow's scheming. The strings above shifted, frayed. His adversary's laughter carried on the wind in triumphant mockery.

Your move, old friend.

Down below, Donovan Candle marched toward the epicenter and his fate.

Aleister Dullington watched. He waited. Not long now. Not long at all.

-17-

HE WHO
WINDS THE WATCH

The WBS plaza sat in the middle of the city's business district, just a few short blocks from the edge of the south side. The plaza itself was ornate by design: several free-standing bronze sculptures adorned the area, and two large triangular fountains stood on either side of the walkway, directing foot traffic toward the plaza's main centerpiece, the WBS building. The structure jutted out of the ground like a giant needle, tethering earth to sky.

Donovan recalled these vivid details from memory, but what he saw in the Monochrome was something else altogether, something that defiled those memories and left him speechless.

Flat textures replaced the skyscraper's decorative symmetry. A thick, organic rope coiled its way down from the structure's zenith, wrapping around like a giant, albino umbilical cord while bright, piercing light surged upward from the foundation. The sickening energy swallowed the top of the skyscraper in its luminescence, hovering like a malign halo. Rather than disperse into the gray sky, the aura slowly worked its way back down, forcing a violent tremor throughout the surrounding area.

Standing guard at the foot of the building were the Missing, their gazes fixed upward, drawn toward the arcane energy resonating up the building like a lightning rod. There were many of them—easily a hundred—but the white creatures far outnumbered their ranks. The entire scene squirmed with life. The Cretins covered every possible surface, clamoring over one another like rats. Their backward chatter coalesced in a muffled roar, filling the air with their nonsense and awakening the migraine sleeping within Donovan's head.

A sharp, searing jolt sliced through his mind. He recoiled, slipping back into liminal space and its ever-shifting palette of colors. The building's visage remained constant—a gargantuan monolith with darkened windows, constricted by the snake-like tumor and glowing with a pale, nauseating aura.

Closing his eyes, Donovan focused himself back into the Monochrome. He braced for the migraine, clenching his teeth as he lowered his gaze to follow the growth down to the bottom level. There it fused with the ground, indiscernible from the flat shades of the plaza.

The umbilical cord shuddered as another pulse of light surged upward, climbing the length of the building while the earth trembled below. An uneven drone filled the air, rising and falling in tandem with each flare. While he observed the bizarre structure, Donovan was struck with an unsettling thought: *It's breathing.*

A chill scraped its way down his spine. That the Monochrome might be alive—or even *sentient*—disturbed him. He suddenly felt very small, a traveler marching to his death, ready to be digested in the belly of a giant.

He listened to the horrific breathing for a few minutes longer before finding the will to move.

Don't stop now. Keep moving. Almost there.

He took a breath, clenched his teeth to hold back another wave of nausea, and traveled the final block toward the WBS plaza.

No one noticed his advance at first. They were too busy, too focused on the waves of energy shooting up and down the building. He'd reached the first set of steps that led up to the main thoroughfare between fountains before the young woman saw him.

She was easily Quinn's age, possibly even older, another victim of Sparrow's nefarious plot. Donovan wasn't sure if she was the subject of one of his investigations. Blonde hair hung in thick dirty clumps obscuring most of her face, and like the younger members of the Wretched, that same dim light filled her belly, glowing from underneath her clothes.

She sat on the edge of the fountain, looking frantically around to see if anyone else was paying attention.

Donovan raised his hand to calm her. "It's okay," he whispered. "I'm not going to hurt you."

Wide-eyed, trembling, the young woman rose from her seat and took a step backward. Donovan kept his hands out in a gesture of goodwill. All he needed to do was get close—

"He's here!"

She looked away, pointing in his direction while heads turned to face him. Donovan sucked in his breath as his heart lodged into his throat. Silence descended over the plaza as every pair of eyes fell upon him. Even the Cretins ceased their incessant chatter, watching him, waiting for someone to make their move.

One of the Missing—a gaunt fellow with a bandage over his right eye—beckoned to him with a crowbar. Another stepped forward brandishing a sledgehammer. He recognized some of their faces; the same mindless drones had hovered over him back at Winthorpe Station, ready to bludgeon their prisoner to death.

Nothing had changed. He slowly exhaled and closed his eyes, loosening his grip on this reality.

Donovan heard their collective gasps for just a moment, a sensation like muffled noise under water—and then he was in liminal space, the colors shifting between Spectrum and Monochrome. Specters of the crowd littered the area, and if he focused hard enough, he could still hear their confused muttering just one reality away.

The young woman was still the closest. Even in the fluctuating space, Donovan could see the mediocrity glowing dimly beneath her spectral flesh.

Will this work here? Curious, he walked toward her darkened figure, put his hand to her forehead, and concentrated his thoughts. *Only one way to find out.*

The gaunt man dropped his weapon in shock. The crowbar clattered on the ground, but no one in the crowd noticed. Their attention was focused on Shelly, the young girl who'd alerted them to Donovan Candle's intrusion.

Except Shelly wasn't there anymore. She was gone, erased from existence in a bright flash of light. They'd all seen their friends flicker back into the Spectrum for their daily feedings, but this was different. No one flashed when they crossed over.

They were so stunned by her sudden disappearance that none of them noticed the dark shadow wandering among them. Had they noticed, they would've seen a specter in the shape of a man, sorting them out, selecting the youngest of their group.

Someone closer to the building entrance cried out, pointing to the space where a young man once stood. Throughout their ranks, more of the Missing cried out in alarm, swearing that so-and-so was just there a minute ago.

All around them, the Cretins and Yawning grew increasingly erratic, fidgeting in the presence of the interloper. They could not see him, but they *sensed* his presence, could almost smell his sweat and hear the blood coursing through his veins. Something was not right about this intruder. Like the Missing, the creatures of the Monochrome felt uneasy. Desperate, they tried to communicate with their master, but he would not answer their call. They were resigned to watch the dark specter take those he wished, sending them across the veil into the wretched Spectrum world.

The taking stopped after several minutes, and although the cattle known as the Missing couldn't sense it, the Cretins felt the sickening relief and joy from those who'd crossed over. Now they understood their master's reverence for this man called Candle.

For the first time in their existence, the white monsters discovered a new sensation that sent a collective shiver through each of their frail bodies. The feeling was at once simple, unwieldy, and entirely, uncomfortably human: Dread.

———————•———————

Michael Candle loitered outside, waiting for some sign of his brother. The call from Donna that morning had left him more than shaken; he was terrified. It wasn't like Donovan to do something like this.

At least not without talking to me first. The act of little brother seeking big brother's advice was a staple of their childhood that had followed them into their adult years. Michael didn't mind but had often wished Donovan would act on his own at times. Now he wondered if that wish had come true.

The plaza in front of the WBS building was mostly empty except for a few pedestrians admiring the display of sculptures. A young couple, probably on their way to the park nearby, stopped to admire the fountains. Traffic circled the roundabout, cars and trucks braking and speeding along to their destinations. For a Saturday, the business district was incredibly dull.

He'd been there for an hour already, waiting for some sign of Donovan.

Once or twice he felt an odd tremor beneath his feet, but they were slight, and he passed them off as the rumblings of nearby trucks braking to a halt.

He pulled out his cell phone and paged through the numbers. He thought about calling Detective Brock but figured the old man had had enough adventure for one weekend. He decided he would call only if Donovan did not show.

And when would that be?

The hands of his watch approached noon. *Soon*, he thought, but as the minutes wore on a cold, unsettling feeling moved into the pit of his stomach. Something wasn't right here, beyond Donovan's absence. Wherever Donovan was, he wasn't safe. Michael was certain of that, even if he couldn't explain why. Their mother used to call it brotherly intuition, swearing he and Donovan shared some sort of link. The feeling in his gut made him entertain the possibility.

What if?

Such a powerful question. He laughed to himself, surprised at how easily he'd taken to considering the prospect.

He was still chuckling when his brother's car screeched to a halt on the roundabout. A young man emerged, leaving the car parked in the middle of traffic. Several drivers screamed at him, blaring their car horns, but the young man didn't pay them any attention. He raced up the steps between the fountains, eyes wide, spinning on his feet to take in his surroundings. He almost lost his balance, stumbling against one of the bronze statues before steadying himself.

Michael felt a chill creep down his back. The boy looked like hell, clothes tattered, torn, covered in dirt, his face bruised—and awfully familiar, too.

"I'll be damned." He cleared his throat and called out across the plaza. "Quinn? That you?"

The young man turned away with a start, searching for the one who called out his name. Michael's heart slowly crept up into his throat. *It is him.*

"Mike?"

Trembling, Quinn closed the gap between them. He met Michael halfway across the plaza, collapsing to his knees.

"Hey," Mike said. "Easy, man. You're okay."

"We have to go. We need—I need—"

Michael took Quinn's hand and helped him to his feet, surveying the large bruise across the bridge of his nose. The young man had clearly been through hell.

"Calm down," Michael said. He looked back to the roundabout. Traffic backed up behind the parked car, honking in disapproval as other drivers waited their turn to merge out of the lane. "Is that Don's car?"

Quinn nodded. "He told me to take it. Said I'd meet you here. He said—"

"You saw Don? Where? What did he say?"

"He said that he's not afraid to jump anymore."

His words dug into Michael's mind like hot needles, tearing him out of this reality and dragging him back to the night of the baby shower. The familiar, unsettling feeling that something was very *wrong* seeped into the pit of his stomach, and now he feared more for Donovan's safety than ever before.

Michael squeezed Quinn's shoulder. "Listen, Quinn, I need you to take me to Donovan right now, okay? Go get his car and meet me at the parking garage. We'll go together."

"It's not that simple." Quinn looked up at the WBS building. "He's gone on alone. I wanted to stay and help, but he wouldn't let me."

"Gone on alone? I don't understand."

Quinn shook his head, frustrated. "You don't have to, Mike. He sent me here to get you. There are others that need our help. Alice, Joel, Evelyn—" He paused, looking down at his feet. "Do you feel that?"

"You need to slow down," Michael said. "Let's take this one step at a time—"

The shockwave ripped through the earth with a loud groan as the building's steel girders swayed to the vibrations. Michael pushed Quinn away from the building just as a large crack splintered across the pavement, working its way toward one of the bronze statues. The effigy of a nameless businessman toppled forward as the ground collapsed in on itself. A loud clang filled the air as the sculpture collided with concrete. More cracks formed across the bottom row of glass windows as another tremor tore through the foundation.

And then, as the vibrations settled, Michael Candle experienced something that made his blood run cold. The plaza had been empty just a moment before, but now—

He blinked. Now there were other people—dirty, disheveled, their clothes nothing more than rags—standing in front of the building, terrified and confused. He saw one of them—someone he could've sworn was one of their Missing Persons cases—materialize in front of him like a ghost.

His mind froze in that moment, unsure of how to process what he was experiencing. The city was nowhere near a fault line, and for as far back as he could recall there had never been an earthquake in the area. He could deal with that. Tectonic plates shifted all the time in unlikely places. The quake was tangible.

But these people, these bodies of flesh and blood who weren't there just a moment ago but now stood mere feet away, defied any modicum of logic he could muster. This was like something out of his brother's stories—something so bizarre, so strange, it defied explanation. Now he was living in such a moment, and he couldn't begin to explain what he saw.

Michael stared, refusing to blink, afraid he would miss the chaos before his eyes. As he watched, a thick cloud began to lift from the back of his mind, freeing the memories hidden from him and filling in the gaps he'd struggled to uncover just a day before. He remembered, with unsettling clarity, watching as his brother flickered in and out of existence, speaking on the phone with a strange man named Aleister.

More men and women flickered into being, staggering backward in shock with tears in their eyes. Some fell to their knees, sobbing, praying, thanking a higher power, praising the one who set them free. Another shockwave rocked the plaza, but it didn't last quite as long as the previous two.

Quinn said something, urging them to leave and meet the others, but Michael was too enraptured by what was happening. With a hand on his phone and a faint smile on his face, he watched as the last of the crowd flickered into existence. For the first time, Donovan had done something Michael never thought possible: He made Michael believe.

Donovan fell to his knees as the building shuddered and groaned around him. The pain in his stomach was agonizing and his head would not stop pounding. He'd taken as many of the Missing as he could before the pain became too great, and in a final rush of strength he forced himself through the doors and into the lobby.

He rolled on the floor as the world shifted and swelled with color, clutching his belly and growling through clenched teeth.

Indigestion from hell, he thought. The prospect was so absurd that he choked out a short laugh, followed by a burst of vomit. His stomach convulsed, the muscles in his abdomen burning with each wet heave.

Donovan waited for the nausea to pass. He saw colors, heard the chime of bells in his ears, but he kept going, crawling across the swirling lobby floor. The whole world trembled around him, quaking with every inch of his advancement, and by the time he reached the stairwell the tremors were so bad he thought the building might topple over.

He climbed to his feet, wincing at the sharp pain wedged into his ribs like a hot needle boiling his insides. The room pulsed in conjunction with the tremors, welling up with color before bleeding out into a haze of grays. Looking up, he peered through the building's skeletal framework of steel and plaster, and felt his body leave the ground.

Donovan ascended as far as the third floor before the pain became too much. He slipped out of focus, out of liminal space, and collapsed beside a water fountain. He touched his fingers to his nose. They came away covered in his blood.

This won't do, he thought, wincing at the sharp pain drilling itself between his eyes and into his stomach. He looked at his surroundings: an empty hallway adorned with framed artwork and promotional posters for many of the network's properties. Three elevator doors stood side by side across from him.

"Guess I'll go the old-fashioned way."

He climbed to his feet and pressed the call button. Another tremor vibrated the building, knocking some of the framed artwork off the wall.

Donovan flattened himself against the opposing wall. He wiped sweat from his forehead and rubbed his temples. A deeper discomfort lay buried beneath the violent nausea, migraine, and nosebleeds. This heavy sensation pulling at his insides felt like every day he'd worked at Identinel compacted into a lead ball, sitting in his gut, unmoving. That feeling was synonymous with a lot of things: Malaise. Ennui. Boredom. All of them were perfect descriptions of what he felt, and he was so caught up in his reverie that he didn't notice the Cretin wander across the hallway in front of him.

When the creature's erratic movement finally caught his eye, Donovan did a double-take. He thought maybe he'd transitioned again without realizing it, but the color of the Spectrum and the reality of what was happening did not mesh. The white bastard leaned against the opposite wall and looked up at him. When it noticed him looking, it spoke something in its broken, backwards language, then gave him the finger and scampered off.

Donovan blinked. He remembered what he told the Wretched just a few short hours before making his journey. The lines truly were blurring.

Another tremor filtered down through the building's girders. The elevator dinged as it slowed. The doors opened, and Donovan reluctantly stepped inside.

———————•———————

S parrow stood among the array of satellite dishes with his arms stretched outward as he received the white signals filtering through the air. He felt himself pulled from one reality to the other, his stomach performing somersaults within its space. The sky above morphed from sickening azure to hazy gray. Simultaneously, he saw both clouds overhead and pale energy encircling the building, felt both warm concrete and cold, writhing flesh beneath his feet.

"*Mr. Beckman,*" Sparrow crowed. He turned away from the horizon and back toward the sorry shit now cowering like a beaten dog. His body flickered in and out of the Spectrum as he walked, arcs of light moving between him and the dishes channeling their energy. He stopped at the end of the row and beckoned to the defeated man.

"*This is no nightmare.*"

The vision was upon him. He felt it just as easily as he could hear Beckman's thoughts. Sparrow stepped back within the array's white aura. It filled him from head to toe, a searing, nearly painful jolt of energy that he could not articulate within his own mind. The energy simply *was*, simply *his*, and he claimed it as a birthright.

With this, he would pull the collective strings of the world. He would entwine the strings, binding them together into a single fuse he would set alight. The world would burn, and he would rule over the remains, dancing among the ashes.

Dr. Albert Sparrow raised his hands to the sky and laughed. As he did so, black cracks splintered out from the corners of his eyes. They made seams in the flesh of his face. *Yes, let it happen.*

He felt the vision pushing between his eyes. Sparrow refocused his efforts, channeling energy into his body, feeling the spot between his eyes grow heated. Black viscous liquid oozed from his nostrils.

He lowered his hands from the sky and took them to his face, fingers digging into the flesh around his eyes. The nerves of his old body were still there, and they sang as he took hold of his eyelids, tugging, *tearing*. His flesh gave way with little effort, separating from the rest of his skull with a sickening rip.

Sparrow wrenched his eyelids free from his face and screamed. His voice was not that of a man, but an electronic interference imbued with human traits, a horrendous screech amplified in reverse, the sound of a thousand dying rats. The shriek filled the air, echoing out over the city, causing a tremor so violent that the top story windows exploded in a storm of glass.

Beckman curled himself up into a ball, slowly rocking, babbling once more that this was not happening. The stairwell door burst open. A man emerged. Dried blood caked his nostrils and upper lip.

"Sparrow," Donovan said. His jaw dropped when he saw what the old man had done to himself. "Oh no."

The Monochrome King lowered his hands, revealing a pair of black, bulbous eyes, two large obsidian marbles bulging from his skull. Black goo trickled from his exposed sockets. Patches of white flesh slipped from his fingers, falling to the ground with a sickening *plop*.

"Hello, Mr. Candle. Nice of you to join us."

———————————•———————————

D onovan braced himself. If he was too late, so be it. He could not simply walk away now. Whether or not Sparrow had attained his full power he did not know, but the man's resemblance to Dullington was striking. When Donovan focused and peered through the layers, he perceived the nauseating light emanating around the satellite array. The sight of the fleshy growth covering the rooftop made his stomach twist into itself, and he forced himself back over to the Spectrum to avoid the effects.

Sparrow hovered above the ground, cackling madly to the sky while basking in the sudden influx of energy. His body flickered, fading between Monochrome and Spectrum.

John Beckman rocked back and forth like a frightened child. "Wh–Who are you?"

Donovan pointed to the array. "Do you know how to shut off the broadcast?"

"I–I don't—"

"Go pull the plug. Pull all the plugs. Do whatever you have to do. *Just go.*"

"But I—I mean, we can't just—"

Donovan reeled back and struck Beckman across the cheek. *"If you don't fucking do it, everyone you love is going to suffer. Do you understand? Just go, goddammit."*

Clarity flashed across Beckman's face as he came out of his stupor. He waited a beat, met Donovan's eyes, and nodded. "Okay," he said. "I'll see what I can do."

He shot Sparrow a fearful glance before scrambling for the door. Anything to get away from that madman.

Donovan turned back toward his enemy, fading into liminal space. Sparrow hovered like a spirit between worlds, soaking up the uncanny energy arcing between the satellites. Colors blossomed and decayed around them in frantic bursts, swelling in time with the pale aura surrounding the building.

"So, this is how you escaped from the tunnel," Sparrow said. He glanced down, sizing up Donovan with those unblinking black eyes. "You slipped between the cracks. If only I'd known. Before I remove every trace of you from this earth, tell me, Donnie: how ever did you find your way into these spaces between?"

Donovan moved toward Sparrow, stopping only when he was within arm's reach. He thought for a moment, considering the old man's words. "I chose to make things right."

He reached out and touched Sparrow's pale, gnarled hand. The effect was instant, a searing jolt that coursed across Donovan's fingertips and into the pale man's skin. He howled in pain, clawing at the scorched surface. His body shimmered, flickering back over to the Monochrome, and Donovan followed.

When Sparrow saw Donovan's outline materialize in the gray world, he gnashed his teeth and spat a gob of gray phlegm on the ground. From it sprouted an amorphous lump that slowly constricted into four large, clumsy hands; these hands braced the ground as arms took shape. Two Yawning slowly pulled themselves out of the puddle one limb at a time, standing between master and prey.

Sparrow retreated to the edge of the building, commanding his children to take care of the interloper.

Donovan's heart raced. Standing atop the building and peering into the lifeless eyes of the white creatures reminded him of the first time he encountered the beasts. He looked up at them, the way they swaggered in place, and surprised himself by walking toward them. Their jaws quivered, began to unhinge, ready to accept this prized meal.

Only that did not happen. Donovan reached out and channeled his bizarre energy into them. Both Yawning bellowed in agony as their rubbery bodies began to dematerialize, melting back into a puddle of grayish-white goo.

Blood gushed from Donovan's nose. The place between his eyes hardened, threatening to burst out of his head while he fought against the crippling nausea, his stomach twisting into itself.

Keep going. You can do this. For Donna. For the baby.

While the Yawning dissolved into a burbling puddle of phlegm, Donovan turned his attention to the first writhing tumor surrounding the nearest satellite. The hulking, gelatinous mass sensed his presence, quivering frantically as he approached. The others joined in the trepidation.

He put his hand on the shivering thing, closed his eyes, and focused his mind. The roiling nausea seated so deeply in his gut paused for a moment as he imparted his will upon the tumor. The weight of the malign energy he'd absorbed in the last few hours lifted in that brief instance, alleviating him from the burden as it surged through his fingertips.

When he opened his eyes, he saw the white cocoon shrinking, eaten away by a strange light emanating from his touch. The tumor shriveled up into a wrinkled, gray husk and fell from the satellite like a dead tick. A short, violent tremor shot up through the building, causing the steel framework to groan from the stress.

A calm fell over the other cocoons, slowing their rapid gyrations, their pulses of light dimming. Donovan had no idea what he'd done, but the effect was immediate. The other tumors were slowly shriveling into empty husks. The broadcast, however, was still going strong. Light pulsed up and down the building, beaming its malicious signal into the atmosphere.

Sparrow watched, helpless, while this arrogant insect destroyed his creations. He backed against the edge, nursing the wound on his hand where Donovan had touched him. An outline of fingerprints glowed on his pale flesh like a beacon.

Donovan turned away from the first satellite, walking slowly down the row between arrays. He met Sparrow's empty stare.

"When I left you here," he said, "I thought I'd done something horrible. And you know what? I was right. You've caused so much pain, and for what? Power? Tell me, Sparrow—did you ever consider why you ended up here in the first place?"

The world shifted as Donovan approached. The two men transitioned between both realities, the sky flashing from blue to gray, the sensations of heat and wind starting and stopping with each change. A violent tremor tore through the building. The roof shuddered, and a low metallic whine erupted from somewhere below. The light surrounding the mass of tumors intensified.

"Stay away from me, Candle."

"You flickered out because you didn't want to try. You expected the world to just hand everything to you, like you deserved it. You didn't want to try, and because of that, you stagnated. Just like I did. Just like everyone."

"*I did fucking deserve it,*" Sparrow growled. "And now I'll have my retribution. I'm going to burn this fucking world, set my children free to devour everything. I will consume this place—starting with *you*."

Sparrow climbed up on the edge of the building, flailing his scrawny arms. At first Donovan thought he was losing his balance, but that would have been much too easy, too simple.

The backwards chatter of the Cretins filled the air, rising to a dull roar, filling the world with their jarring ambience. The building trembled once more. Sparrow shot his adversary a quick grin, then stepped off the edge.

Donovan rushed to the side and looked over. He expected to see Sparrow's smiling face as he plummeted to the ground below. Part of him *wanted* to see it, but that isn't what met his eyes. The city, painted the color of Monochrome, spread out before him toward the horizon, its streets dissecting city blocks into neat, uniform squares. Filling those streets was something white and viscous, a thick burbling river of bodies that ebbed and flowed as a single entity.

It rose and fell, crashing over and against anything in its path as it headed toward the WBS building. Sparrow splashed down into the wave just as it reached its crest and broke against the structure's side.

The building's framework swayed from the impact, straining with resistance as more windows shattered below. The wave crashed around the building's foundation, effectively drowning the plaza in a sea of Cretins.

Something bubbled up within, and the drone of reversed chatter grew to deafening volume. The white, malleable mass collapsed upon itself for a moment before shooting outward in a long, gray column. A guttural cry echoed from within the mound of flesh.

"*Candle,*" it said.

"Oh shit."

The column, he realized, was an arm. The stump on its end broke apart in a series of digits that reached toward the side, digging into the windows for traction. Realities shifted, and Donovan saw the damage through Spectrum eyes. Glass shattered inward from the pressure of the unseen force. He focused back to the Monochrome in time to watch another arm emerge from the writhing white pool.

The creature pulled itself out of the sea, made up of millions of the little white monsters. A head crowned from the swirling mess below as the monstrous abomination birthed itself into being.

Donovan's blood ran cold as the giant thing emerged from the pool and began to climb up the side of the building toward him. Tentacles squirmed over a pair of empty black sockets. The monstrosity crashed into the side of the structure, one hand after another, pulling itself up out of the pool and toward its prey.

"*You are* nothing, *Candle. A pitiful waste of a man. Fearful. A coward. A slave to your own devices.*"

The behemoth continued its ascent. Donovan stumbled away from the edge as it reared up its terrible head. The cilia over its eye sockets beckoned for him, reaching out and tasting the air. The mammoth beast let out a roar when it saw him, clamping one hand on the edge and wrenching itself upward. It raised its other hand into a balled fist. Donovan gasped, turned, and began to run.

"*I should have killed you when you were tied to that chair. Now I will rectify my mistake.*"

Donovan ran as fast as he could. The nausea he felt in his stomach was like a lead weight pulling him down. His mind screamed, *RUN, YOU OLD BASTARD*, and run he did. He ran until his insides were on fire, until he reached the stairwell. There was nowhere else to go.

The creature brought down its fist, crashing into the row of satellites pointed toward the gray heavens. There was an inhuman scream as a surge of white energy illuminated the rooftop. Donovan dove to the side, crying out in pain as he landed on the ground. Sounds of metal wreckage came to his ears. He turned just as the first satellite wrenched forward and fell to its side.

"*NO!*"

Arcs of energy burst between the dishes, shooting up into the sky and connecting with the behemoth's limbs. Pieces of its skin flaked off, falling to the ground below, and Donovan watched as the gross aura ate away at the giant creature.

The reversal, he thought, remembering the energy leaving his body.

Had he corrupted the force dwelling within the array? He had no time to contemplate the possibilities. Another roar bellowed out of the creature's bottomless maw.

The beast looked up in surprise, stunned at what was happening, as though it could not fathom its own demise. Its arm detached from its body, severed by the glowing aura, and degenerated into a puddle of half-formed Cretins crying out in agony.

"You're coming with me, Candle. We'll rot together."

Donovan looked up. The other arm hovered over him with fingers fanned out like claws. Pieces of it chipped and fell in a pale rain.

He tensed, closed his eyes, and held up his hands to shield himself. A swift, crackling energy swept through his body as the behemoth's flesh met his, pulling at his insides. Donovan uttered a cry of agony as his stomach hardened and the migraine resurfaced, punching through the walls of his skull one aching throb at a time. A din of chimes filled his ears, but somewhere beyond them he thought he heard a man screaming.

Low light surrounded the rooftop, illuminating the Monochrome's hazy atmosphere with a gray aura. Whatever abysmal energy had collected within the creature was now absorbed through Donovan's touch, his body serving as a conduit, siphoning the power from its host. White arcs of electricity sizzled across his skin, raising the hairs on his arms and neck and filling his eyes with the blinding light.

The energy surged, building up into a final, climactic burst with such force that Donovan was thrown backward against the stairwell door. The impact knocked the air from his lungs, and for a few frightening seconds he feared he might suffocate.

All he heard was his pounding heart and the erratic wheeze of his lungs. Gone were the droning roar of the creature and Sparrow's crowing banter. The Monochrome was still.

A voice pierced the silence.

"Ever the puppet, Albert Sparrow. I am certain your master is quite pleased."

———•———

John Beckman threw open the door to the control room. A group of engineers and interns looked back at him, startled.

"Shut it off. All of you, shut it off *now*."

They looked at one another, unsure of what they just heard. Surely, he wasn't asking them to turn off the marathon. Not after all the marketing dollars that went into promoting its airtime—

Beckman grabbed the intern and screamed. *"SHUT IT OFF!"*

They scrambled to the controls. Within moments, the broadcast was off the air. The Great Fade-Out was over.

D onovan found his breath. Head swimming, his belly in knots, he slowly rose to his knees. Aleister Dullington materialized from the gray haze, his robe billowing behind him in the stagnant air. The white creature recognized its former master. Donovan was certain he saw a smile on its face as it broke apart, pieces of its body collecting in a gooey pile of rubbery flesh.

The white aura surrounding the rooftop dimmed, flickered, faded from view.

Albert Sparrow spilled out of the aborted mess onto the rooftop just as the creature's head caved in upon itself. He rolled away from the edge as the behemoth finally disassembled, its giant husk of a body slipping over the edge.

"Goddamn you," he growled. "This is *my* place now."

"No, Sparrow. May the Ungod damn *you* as you have damned yourself."

The feeble man climbed to his feet, staggering toward his old master. He was drenched in a thick gray sludge, leaving a trail in his wake.

"I did…everything…I was meant to. The strings were mine…to burn."

Dullington stopped before his beaten subject. "Yes," he said, "you did do everything you were supposed to."

Sparrow's pale wrinkled face lit up, his black eyes bulging from his skull. "I served—"

Dullington reached out, gripping the old man by the throat. He held him effortlessly in the air and stared into his eyes.

"You served your master well, Mr. Sparrow." He turned toward the horizon, lifting Sparrow like a prized trophy. "Now it is time I did something I should have done long ago."

Donovan leaned back against the door, blood leaking from his nose. He was lightheaded, and colors swam before his eyes as he struggled to remain conscious, watching as Dullington held the old man in the air. Sparrow began to scream, but Dullington's albino hand muffled his cries.

He heard Joe Hopper's voice from somewhere in the back of his head. *You did it, hoss. You stopped the son of a bitch.* But he could not share his creation's excitement.

Chimes filled his ears, dulling the tightening pain in his abdomen, and despite his effort he could not hold back the blackened waves of unconsciousness coming to claim him.

Donovan Candle closed his eyes, relinquishing himself to the dark tides, drowning in their violent undertow.

EPILOGUE
THE DEFINED MAN

Colby flung herself across the door, barring his exit. She could not let him go. Not now. Not after all of this.

Joe Hopper crossed the room and took her in his arms. He gave her a deep, heartfelt kiss that left her weak in the knees. A kiss that rekindled the fire between them, even after all they'd been through. He looked her in the eye and smiled.

"It's just somethin' I gotta do. Won't be for long, darlin'. I'll be 'round and back before you know it. Just you wait and see."

Colby held back her tears as she dropped her arms. Joe Hopper left the room, left her life—if only for a time—but he did not leave her heart.

—Donovan Candle
Monochrome Dream

Nathan Brock fell into his armchair, cell phone in hand. He'd been trying to reach Donovan all morning, but when the hours slipped into early afternoon, he refocused his efforts on reaching Michael. Neither answered their phones. *Real funny*, he thought. *Those goddamn Candle brothers will be the death of me.*

Resigned, the old detective uttered a long, frustrated sigh. He picked up the remote and turned on the TV. A reporter for the local news station stood outside the WBS building; several police officers and firefighters lingered in the background, craning their necks, staring upward at the building. Brock turned up the volume.

"—absolute pandemonium downtown. As you can see behind me, there are rows of windows completely shattered, and—Jake, can you zoom in?" The camera shakily panned upward, surveying the broken glass jutting from the window frames like shattered teeth. Entire sections of the building's face were caved inward. Brock leaned forward in his chair, slack-jawed with shock. "This is just a fraction of the damage, Susie. These holes occur all the way up the side of the building."

The screen split in two, revealing the news anchor, Susie Winters, back in the studio.

"Tom," she began, "have the authorities been able to ascertain what caused this structural damage? Are we dealing with a potential terrorist attack?"

"Well, Susie, the police have made no official statements, but several eyewitnesses reported feeling severe aftershocks following—"

Brock's cell phone rang, startling him so bad he nearly fell out of his chair. The screen lit up, flashing the name MICHAEL CANDLE in bold letters. Blood pressure spiking, he muted the TV and answered the call.

"What the hell did you *do?* We were supposed to meet this morning, talk things over. Now I've got the TV on and there's fucking chaos—*what?*"

Detective Brock paused, his heart beating so fast he had to catch his breath. There was static on the line.

"You still there, old man?"

"I—I'm here, Mike, but you're breaking up a little bit." Brock sucked in his breath, waited for his heart rhythm to slow. "Would you mind repeating what you said just a second ago?"

"I said I'm at the hospital with Evelyn. How soon can you get here?"

The wind rushed out of him. He felt as though someone had delivered a sucker punch to his gut. Shaking, he told Michael he'd be there as soon as he could and ended the call.

On TV, the reporter Tom Ashland interviewed a young woman, presumably homeless by her appearance. She was crying. Brock waited a moment, forgetting he'd muted the television, staring off into space. He felt lost, numb. Was this a joke? Couldn't be. Michael wouldn't be so cruel.

He found he was too weak, too afraid to move at first, but that nagging curiosity sparked in the back of his mind. The need to know flared in the folds of his brain, catching fire, burning his fear to cinders. The old man climbed out of his armchair, grabbed his keys, and went out the door to his car.

I'm comin', Evie.

He barged into the lobby, shouting for Evelyn, and only after hospital staff calmed him down did he manage to dictate who he was looking for.

"Evelyn Brock. My wife. She's been missing for—oh God, is she here?"

The clerk typed away at her keyboard, worried her answer might provoke another outburst from this crazy old man. When the search came up with a name, his knees nearly buckled.

"Room 703," she said. "Seventh floor. Take a right off the elevator. Can't miss it."

He wiped tears from his eyes, nodded in gratitude, and walked swiftly toward the trio of elevators at the far end of the lobby.

This could all be a misunderstanding. Maybe they picked up someone with the same name. Maybe this person looks like my Evelyn. Maybe—

The elevator chimed, pulling its doors apart. A lump rose in Nathan's throat, filling his mouth with cotton. *Go on,* he told himself. *Get this over with.* He stepped inside, pressed the third-floor button, and ascended.

Michael waited for him in the hallway, leaning against the wall beside a water fountain. He was tired and worried about his brother but lingering at the forefront of his mind were concerns about the old detective. They had so much to discuss, but those matters could wait just a little while.

The elevator announced its arrival. Detective Brock stepped into the hallway, trying his best to maintain some semblance of composure even though he knew he wasn't doing a very good job. Michael could tell immediately. The old man's eyes were red, and his hands shook.

"Where is she?"

Michael put a hand on Brock's shoulder. "This way."

They walked just a few short steps past the nurse's station. A woman and young man stood outside the door for Room 703. Brock didn't know the girl, but he knew the boy.

"Quinn," he said, confused. He shot a quick glance at Michael. "How—?"

"We'll hash out the details later, Nate. Someone wants to see you."

"Are you sure it's her? Please don't fuck with me like this, Mike."

"I'm not," Michael said, smiling. "Go on."

Nathan Brock offered his friend a simple nod, took a breath, and swallowed back the butterflies fluttering about in his stomach. He peeked inside, looking at the old woman lying on the bed. She had heavy bandages around her forehead and arms, but he could recognize that face in the dark if he had to. Hers was a face he'd only seen in distant memory and dreams, a face he'd vowed to find again. A face that he struggled not to forget every agonizing day of her absence.

She turned to him. "Hi, old man."

Evelyn smiled up at him. Brock felt his legs go weak. He closed the gap between them, collapsing beside her bed. She moved her hand, ran her fingers through his silver hair.

"Is it really you, Evie?" he said, choking back the tears.

"Yes," she said, softly. "It's really me."

Nathan Brock took his wife's hand and squeezed. He would never let her go again.

Smiling, Alice Walenta slowly closed the door. They had watched the Brock reunion for long enough; now the old couple needed their privacy.

She turned to Michael Candle, studied his face. "Do you remember me?"

He glanced at her, "No. Am I supposed to?"

"No," she said, "I guess not." Alice closed her eyes, held her breath. *Keep yourself together. Focus on the now. Focus on the debt you owe to his brother.*

Alice exhaled. "We can't wait here. I need to see Donna."

"Look," Michael began, "before we do anything, I think we all need to sit down and talk about what the hell just happened downtown. There are questions that need to be answered—"

"That's the idea, Mike."

Quinn stepped between them. He'd had enough tension for one lifetime. "Let's just go, okay? The doctors will take care of everyone else. We need to go."

They stepped away, walked down the hall toward the elevator. Michael called out to them.

"But...why Donna?"

"Because," Alice said, calling the elevator, "this concerns her, too. She needs to understand what's happened to her husband—and so do you. Now are you coming or not?"

Donna Candle spent most of the day cooped up inside, busying herself with household chores and the task of clearing the bloodstains from the upstairs carpet. Several times the radio was interrupted with breaking news updates about the latest details to emerge from WBS plaza. The network's board members were missing, and for reasons unknown, the company's CEO had interrupted the highly anticipated broadcast known across the country as The Great Fade-Out.

She waited for a phone call that never came, and by the afternoon she'd had her fill of the news. She shut off the radio, listening to the stillness of her house, the tick of the kitchen clock making her anxious one minute at a time. When she could no longer stand the silence, she decided she would go for a walk. The fresh air would be good for her and the baby. Besides, she needed time to clear her head and focus her thoughts.

Donna walked along the trail, kicking aside small pebbles half-buried in the dirt. She breathed deep the scent of the forest, relished its cleanliness, its purity. It was alive around her. Birds cawed overhead while limbs rustled in the breeze. The afternoon sunlight filtered down through the boughs, casting a broken orange pattern upon the underbrush.

What if he doesn't come back?

Of course he'll come back. He's got a baby on the way, and he loves me too much not to. Right? Oh goddammit, Donnie. How could you do this to me again?

She was crying when she reached the stream. It was paradise here, the way the water babbled over the rocks and cut through the gully. She reached into her pocket and pulled out the piece of paper. Her teary eyes scanned its words even though she already knew them by heart:

Donna,

Well I've gone and got myself into a mess here. I think I can find a way out, but you can't come along. I don't expect you to understand. I don't think I even understand. I just know I have promises I made that need to be kept, and I can't do that if things aren't right with myself.

I love you, darlin', and I won't be gone forever. Not if I can help it. I'll find you when I've done this thing I have to do. I'll find you. I always do.

Your love,

D.

Trembling, fighting to contain the aching sob welling up inside her, Donna Candle crumpled her husband's letter into a ball. She stood on the edge of the narrow stream, her tears falling into the babbling waters, the paper ball clutched tightly in her shaking fist.

Her husband's words rose from the shadows of her memory: *It's not your burden to bear.* But it *was* her burden to bear, and she'd resolved to help him carry it, but not like this. Not on her own. She couldn't do this on her own.

He left me. He left us when we needed him most.

She raised the paper ball, preparing to toss it into the brook, but could not make her fingers relax. They refused her wishes, holding on to the crumpled letter, that one final remnant of her husband's presence.

Donna stuffed the letter into her pocket. The heavy sob she'd tried so hard to hold back finally worked its way up her throat, announcing her frustration to the surrounding forest. All the fear, sorrow, and anxiety built up over the last week were finally given voice, echoing through the woods in a single, aching cry.

She stood there for a few minutes, waiting for the sobs to pass, heaving in quick convulsions. When she had calmed herself, the baby stirred in her womb. The subtle sensation of movement plucked at her heart, giving her the strength she needed in that desperate moment.

I can do this. Donnie would want me to. For the baby.

Donna wiped her eyes and nose, composing herself as she followed the trail back home. A soft breeze picked up, cooling her feverish mind as she emerged in the clearing between houses. She was so lost in her thoughts that she didn't notice the pair of cars sitting in the driveway.

"We were wondering if you were home."

She looked up, snapped out of her silent reverie by Michael's voice. Three figures stood on her front porch—two men and one woman. Her heart gave pause when she realized one of the cars in the driveway belonged to her husband.

"Is Donnie with you?"

Quinn stepped off the porch and met her on the sidewalk. The bruise around his nose had yellowed since she'd last seen him, but his face seemed lighter, happier. He threw his arms around her in a frantic embrace, stuttering and sobbing.

"He wouldn't let me stay," he cried. "I'm so sorry."

Donna fought back her tears, patting her nephew on the back. "Shh, it's okay." She pulled away, looking up at her brother-in-law and the woman standing beside him. A spark of recognition flared in the back of her mind, illuminating a dusty fragment of memory filed away long ago and forgotten.

The woman with long black hair stepped forward. The mid-afternoon sunlight reflected off a few silver strands in her otherwise darkened mane, and that spark in the back of Donna's mind grew brighter.

"Mrs. Candle, I doubt you remember me…"

Donna stepped away from Quinn and moved closer to the porch, squinting at this woman, a stranger and yet so familiar. A gray haze lifted from her mind like a low-flying cloud. She *did* know this woman. Knew her well, in fact.

"Alice," she said. "Your name is Alice. You helped me some time ago. You helped me and Donnie both."

A thin smile spread across her face, perking up at the edges. "Yes, I did, Mrs. Candle. We should all go inside. I need to tell you something."

Still reeling from the emotional overload and shock, Donna Candle led them inside. Michael helped himself to some coffee while Quinn and Alice took seats at the kitchen table. Donna took her place at the head of the table, noting the malaise written across their faces. Quinn must have lost at least ten pounds, and Alice was equally scrawny.

"What happened to you?" she asked. Alice and Quinn exchanged glances, unsure of how to begin. Michael joined them with a mug of coffee in hand. He sat back in his chair, sipping the brew, waiting for one of them to speak.

Alice Walenta cleared her throat and told her story as best she could. Quinn interjected, providing his own account to fill in the gaps, painting a bleak picture of the same world Donovan had tried to explain so many times before. Donna listened with an open mind, desperate to understand what had happened, but no matter what they said to allay her fears, she could not keep her anxiety at bay.

Donna wept quietly as they told their tale of Donovan's actions. When she was finished, Alice reached across the table, put her hand on Donna's arm, and gave her a light squeeze.

Alice smiled softly. "Donna, I don't know what's happened to your husband, but I can tell you what I believe. I believe he's still alive. You don't understand what happened last year, the significance—"

"Then *help* me understand."

"None of us had hope before Donovan came along. But then he changed everything last year when Dullington let him go. He...*proved* there was still a chance at redemption. People who go to the Monochrome, they're there for a reason. We—I—deserved to be there. I gave up on my dreams, squandering it for a job I hated, and in the end all I did was hate my own life. But your husband, he gave us all a second chance."

"But why did he stay, Alice? I'm six months pregnant. I don't have a job, and my fibro issues...I can't do this all on my own. I can't—"

Donna burst into tears. Michael and Quinn stared at the table, unsure of what to do or say to make her feel any better. Alice measured the uneasy silence, collecting her thoughts, searching for the right words.

"Before he sent me back, Donovan asked me to tell you something. He knew you wouldn't understand, and he didn't expect you to." Alice waited while Donna wiped her eyes with a tissue. "He said to tell you this is the only way he could keep from giving up. That he made a promise to you some nights ago, and the only way he could keep that promise is by making things right again. He said that not doing what's right was just another way of giving up."

Donna shook her head. "Not doing what was right?"

Alice sighed, brushing hair from her face. "My grandfather used to tell me something from time to time when I was a kid. He used to say, 'What you do in this life defines you, Allie. Never forget that.' I think that's what Donovan is doing, Mrs. Candle. Defining himself. Because he has to."

"But what if he doesn't come back, Alice? What if..."

Michael shuffled uncomfortably in his seat, ruminating on the dangerous implications of the day while Quinn stared into the table, unsure of what to do. After all that had happened, they hadn't thought that far ahead yet. What *if* Donovan didn't return? Were they just supposed to go about their lives, knowing he was still stuck in the Monochrome? *Could* they?

Donna looked away, and slowly rose from the table. She walked out of the kitchen and stood at the back door, staring out the window. Her reflection hovered off to the side, staring back longingly in the glass. She saw a woman of contradiction, of frailty and strength etched out in the patterns of her eyes.

She leaned forward, bracing her forehead against the cool glass. "I can't do this on my own," she whispered. "Donnie, please come back. Please. I'm drowning here without you."

Donna Candle closed her eyes and waited.

———————•———————

Colors swam in the darkness, a gray mist rising and falling over his mind with each weakened breath. Bits of memory and feeling returned to his nerves, sparking to life an orchestra of aches spread out across his muscles and joints.

Donovan opened his eyes, watching the haze of the Monochrome's dead sky roll past in a lazy parade of emptiness. He sat up, wincing at the sharp pain in his neck. Grimacing, he managed to right himself, leaning back against the flat surface of a door.

The rooftop. I'm still here. Not dead.

"No, Mr. Candle. This is the second time I have had to confirm your mortality."

Aleister Dullington sat on the edge of the roof, resting his chin on his fist in a thinker's pose, watching the world below with calm curiosity. Donovan groaned as he climbed to his feet. The unsettling pain in his abdomen had lessened but was sure to make its presence known every time he took a breath. Clutching his stomach, Donovan shuffled across the rooftop, stepping over the faded wreckage of the satellite array.

As he neared Dullington's perch, he saw a mangled body spread out on the other side of a shattered dish.

Albert Sparrow—or what used to be Albert Sparrow—lay on the ground, his body twitching erratically while a dim, pale smoke snaked upward from the bubbling remains of his face. Donovan merely glimpsed the oozing visage of his enemy before turning away in disgust.

"What did you do to him?"

"Nothing he had not done to himself, Mr. Candle."

Sparrow's fingers twitched.

"Is he dead?"

"Yes. He will trouble us no more, although we will witness his legacy in time. The damage has been done, and I fear we have only bought ourselves a matter of days." Dullington lifted his chin and peered up at Donovan. "I sense you are quite different now, Mr. Candle. You made a choice and discovered the reaction."

Donovan met Aleister's blackened stare. His stomach lurched, cramping inward in a fury of hot, invisible needles. "I guess so. Balance and all that crap."

Dullington nodded briefly before turning his attention to the horizon. Donovan followed his gaze, peering out over a dead city of empty shapes patterned in a grid. Beyond the reach of the Monochrome's endless haze, a large column stood in the distance, surrounded by an enormous, swirling maelstrom.

The column from my dream, he thought.

"The very same, Mr. Candle."

"What is it?"

"A place where you must go."

Donovan stepped back from the edge, his hands balled into fists. The only place he had any intention of going was home. He closed his eyes, focusing his mind to the Spectrum, but the veil did not lift.

When he opened his eyes, he found Dullington staring at him.

"I am afraid your choice to act has shifted you out of liminal space, Mr. Candle. In freeing the others, you have anchored yourself to the depths of this world."

His thoughts turned to Donna and the baby. He knew this was the price to be paid, but that knowledge didn't make it any easier to swallow. After everything he'd done, after finally taking that jump, to remain here was heart-wrenching. This was not the landing he'd expected to make.

"I can't... Is there any way?"

Dullington stood, pointing to the horizon. The great column glowed like a beacon.

"Only the Ungod can sever the ties that now bind you to this place, but I fear the great nonentity still slumbers."

Donovan approached the edge, staring out at the giant obelisk. "Is there a way to wake it up?"

He lifted one pale hand and put it on Donovan's shoulder. "My former master hid himself away in its chamber long ago. If we are to wake the slumbering beast, we must confront him. We will not be welcomed there, but in the wake of Sparrow's onslaught, I suspect we may prevail."

A chill crept its way down the back of Donovan's neck, splintering and spreading across his arms like the march of a dozen spiders. The weight of Dullington's touch pulled on him with a gravity all its own, and the pale man's unnatural stare left an unsettling feeling in Donovan's stomach.

He thought of Donna's beaming smile, and of their unborn child. He thought of Quinn and Michael, his family, and friends he might not see again. This epiphany struck him in the heart, sending an ache that resonated all the way to his toes. If he had any chance of getting home, this was it.

"If that's what must be done, Aleister. I'm trusting you here."

"This is not a matter of trust, Mr. Candle. It is a matter of duty and constitution." A thin smile spread across Aleister Dullington's pallid face. His empty black eyes pierced Donovan's heart. "A defined man always knows how to act."

"Well..." Donovan Candle turned away from his host in resignation. "Let's get to it, hoss."

Out on the horizon, the great column stood, its slumbering nonentity waiting within while a tempest of its dreams raged forever onward.

"Yes," Dullington said, his smile fading. "Let us."

NEEDLE AND LOOM

Vibrations rippled through the cosmic strings, awakening him from his meditation, his precious dreaming. Hate, anger, betrayal, confusion—he recoiled from the emotions flooding his mind, torn away from his manikin of flesh with the violence of ultimate death, and opened his true eyes for the first time in centuries.

The cradle's chamber hadn't changed. Why would it? He'd sealed the entrance ages ago, shutting off the maelstrom of dreams from stirring the sands of sleep within. The severed hand of a former brother lay half-buried in the sand at the foot of the chamber's entrance. White bone broke the surface, pointing in accusation at his betrayal; Brother Thomas was the last to glimpse his master's intention before the seal claimed his hand.

So long ago now.

Entwined in the Weaver's loom, he'd lost a sense of mortal time. From here in his cocoon, he was impartial to the plight of man, for the hopes, dreams, and nightmares of all who had ever been and would ever be were all within reach.

Time was a construct for the frail and forgotten. Here in the center of all things, time had no relevance.

His body, withered to a husk and mummified by the slow passage of time, remained entangled in the umbilicus of strings woven together from the opening far above. Long-dormant nerves twitched with life, singing a falsetto movement of operatic agony.

After all this time, a misstep, and his enemy was there to capitalize on it.

Just as I taught you. You were always an observant pupil, even if you hated me so.

Gods, his eyes hurt. The haze of the Monochrome permeated even this stagnant place. He forced his gaze downward upon the sleeping creature below. Nestled in its cradle, the Weaver slumbered for all time, suckling on the dreams of man like a child to its mother.

Even with the knowledge he'd stolen, he could not say which had come first: man, or the nonentity here in the great needle. For it *was* a great needle, designed to complement the loom and the sleeping beast, the nonentity, the Great Weaver. He'd overseen its construction a millennium ago when he followed the whims of so-called philosophers.

Shield the creature from the influence of outsiders.

Allow its slumber.

Never meddle in the tapestry of man, his dreams, his failures.

Fools. Arrogant, insufferable fools.

If he'd had the forethought, he would've slaughtered them all on the spot. A glimpse of the greater human tapestry gifted to him by the Weaver had confirmed everything he feared. War, disease, blasphemy against the gods, a perversion of the earth and sea and sky. Man would destroy himself in the end without understanding why.

I will force mankind to gaze upon his failures and despair.

He'd spoken those words long ago when the Order was disbanded. When he'd cast out Aleister to the Monochrome wastes.

So resourceful, his former pupil. Aleister's victory over his manikin may have taken him by surprise, but the damage he'd sought was already done. The tethers of Monochrome and Spectrum were frayed, swaying in the cosmic winds, and soon they would become one.

And then man will know his failures. He will see his sickness in the flesh.

He will despair. He will suffer. He will succumb to the ravenous hunger of his own nightmares.

Aleister's victory was for nothing. He and his avatar would learn this soon enough.

Satisfied with his resolve, the man once known as Pontius Vile wove his hands among the coiled umbilicus feeding the Great Weaver. He closed his ancient eyes and sank back into the space of gods, away from the time of mortals.

He waited.

Elsewhere, a groan of thunder tore through the Monochrome sky, and cracks formed upon the horizon like splintered glass.

He dreamed.

BOOK III
NONENTITY

-PROLOGUE-
CHILDREN OF THE UNGOD

Circa 1313 CE

Bitter winds brushed back Aleister Dullington's cowl as he trudged across the gray wasteland. The lone monk clutched the sleeves of his ashen robe as a fleeting chill sank into his bones.

Trembling, he peered up at the Needle, offering a reverent glance to the strings beyond. A thick glowing tendril of woven threads rose from the structure's center, stretching to the sky where it dispersed into a million fading lines. *Please,* he prayed silently, *do not let me be too late.*

Word of their master's absence had spread among the Order, and while the elders debated on his intentions, their lord Pontius had set his plan into motion. His proposal of leaving one of their own behind in the Monochrome went against the Order's core purpose, his suggestion of this lonely soul communing with the Ungod was heresy, and his goal of being the one to remain was pure insanity.

Without warning, the Order's master vanished into the wastes to pursue his prize, and the elders rallied the monks to stop him. No one was above the laws of the Order, not even its master.

Aleister was the last to transition and the last to arrive, and as he emerged from the storm of the Ungod's discarded dreams, he saw he was now the last of the Order. He watched as small ghostly cyclones tore dusty trails across the plane, whirling with fits and stops, scattering gray sands across dark pools of blood. He paused and uttered a soft cry as he made sense of the chaos before him.

The bleeding bodies of his former brethren lay scattered across the sands, their eyes milky white and staring forever upward in terror. A few still clutched to life, driven mad by the agony pushing them toward the precipice of oblivion.

Aleister sank to his knees and cursed his master. All this bloodshed, and for what? To punish his fellow man for transgressions yet to be committed?

"Pontius, you have succumbed to your own madness." His words fell flat in the soft breeze, and he fought back the emotions stirring within. He mustn't lose his focus, not now. He was the last; the Order's purpose now rested upon his shoulders. He would protect the Ungod from corruption, even if it meant taking the life of his master.

"My dear Aleister."

Gray light spilled from the cracks in the column's crumbling façade, pulsing in time to Pontius Vile's booming voice, and coating the bodies of his fallen servants in its corrupting haze. The strings above rippled at the sound, shivering across the heavens.

Aleister lifted his gaze and quietly wiped the tears from his eyes. "You have lost your mind, Pontius."

"I assure you, Brother Aleister, my sanity has never been stronger."

He stood, approached the remains of his former brothers in silence. Some of them were already half-buried in the gray sands, a severed leg exposed here, a twitching hand there. Each pallid face was another reminder of his inaction. How long had he suspected the master's defection? Months, now, and yet he'd been too afraid to speak out.

Now the repercussions lay strewn about in pieces. Former friends. Brothers.

Aleister paused when he found Christopher among the deceased. His head and torso were all that remained of Vile's onslaught. Aleister knelt, closed his dead mentor's eyes. *I'm sorry, old friend.*

He felt the vibration of the great strings above, rippling like the disturbed waters of a pond, and together they sang a song of warning: there was a usurper within. The whole world groaned in protest.

Christopher's milky eyes flicked open and stared up at him. *"Do not avert your eyes, Aleister. Drink of the pain you have wrought. Drink it deep, but do not fill your belly. There will be more to come."*

Aleister looked down at his fellow acolyte's remains. The eyes were open, rolled upward in a frozen rictus of shock, and the raspy voice passing lifeless ashen lips did not belong him. Vile's voice spoke through the other dead, a hollow army bellowing the commands of their master.

"We are more alike than you would admit, Aleister."

"I am nothing like you, Pontius. I know my place."

Low cries echoed from the horizon, punctuating Vile's words with a sound of grim melancholy. *"My children have returned to feed. Come, children. Finish what was begun."*

Aleister turned, his skin prickling at the sight of the horrid beasts. Gaunt figures marched together across the empty plane, congregating at the center of their reality, ravenous for the flesh of man. They lumbered across the sands as an army of tiny pale beasts poured between their limbs like water.

He'd crossed over knowing he might not return, and he'd made peace with the possibility. If he met his end here, then he would do so serving his purpose. He thought of his family, the wife and son taken from him so long ago, and struggled to fill the hollowness inside himself. Dying here would mean an eternity in obscurity. No name, no memory. Nothing but dust.

Another gust of stale wind swept down from the ancient pylon, stirring sands over the bodies of the fallen. Aleister stood his ground as the creatures approached, but to his surprise, they were not drawn to the allure of living flesh. No, they wanted the leftovers of their previous meal, and sauntered across the sands for seconds.

His dead friend's corpse uttered a choked wet laugh. Blood erupted from Christopher Dullington's graying lips, coating his cheeks in a coagulating mess. *"We are all children of the Ungod, Aleister. You know this. We are all bound to this banal coil, and somewhere in the tethers that feed the slumbering beast, you and I are entwined whether you like it or not. That is your place. So it has been and so it shall be."*

Aleister frowned, peering back up at the Needle. The broken structure loomed over all creation, built to keep the slumbering entity inside safe from the malign influence of man—and now his old master had sealed himself within, entombed with the beast and free to do as he pleased.

"I will not let you do this, Pontius Vile."

"And I will not let you stop me. I will find a way. Even if it means keeping you here."

What few bodies were spared from the creature's bottomless maws erupted into laughter. Aleister closed his eyes, trying to drown out the cacophony of the dead, struggling to remain sane when all means of sanity were stolen from him.

"Let me show you the failures of our kind."

Aleister opened his eyes, glaring upward at the Needle's pinnacle, the drab unlight seeping from the cracks. The light coalesced at the column's summit, forming a singular beam which cut slowly through the throng of beasts toward him.

Christopher Dullington's gray face contorted into a bloody grin of victory as Vile spoke through him. *"I have seen where the strings will lead, Aleister. These are the hopes and dreams of a dying planet. Man must be forced to confront his failures—"*

The corpse was silenced with a crunch beneath the weight of Aleister's boot. Another gust of wind erupted from the Needle's fractured summit, carrying with it the faint echo of an old man's rage. The concentrated beam of light continued its path toward him, searing a trench into the gray sands, but against all impulses he remained still.

Aleister Dullington bowed his head and waited. Alone, he said to the wind, "Not until I confront mine."

-1-
STRANGE DAYS
Present Day

Donovan Candle lost his footing as another shockwave tore through the earth. He fell to one knee, hissing in pain from the impact as the fabric of the Monochrome shuddered around him like a billowing curtain. He collected himself, gritting his teeth to hold back the sharp needles stabbing into his kneecap, and rose to his feet. An aftershock caught him off guard and almost sent him sprawling to the street again, but he found his balance in time, wincing at the pain in his stiff knee.

He looked back at the swaying skyscrapers and frowned. *Getting worse.*

More tremors underfoot. Donovan took a step, expecting to feel the needle of pain buried in his knee, but the sensation was muted. In another minute, the pain was gone altogether. His mental fatigue, however, remained front and center, culminating in a dull throb at the center of his skull.

Dullington had told him the effects of liminal space would linger. Walking toward a nearby bench—what might've been a bus stop in the Spectrum—Donovan shook his head and smiled to no one. *Dullington told me a lot of things. How much of them are lies?* He sat and caught his breath, felt the subtle shift of the earth beneath him. *And he never said anything about this, whatever it is.*

In truth, Dullington hadn't said much of anything after Donovan's confrontation with Sparrow. One minute they were there, staring out toward the mysterious column on the horizon, discussing the journey ahead; the next, Donovan was alone but for the simmering remains of Albert Sparrow's ruined body. He'd stood there long enough to watch the old man's corpse dissolve into a pool of bubbling white. Just long enough to make sure the old bastard was truly dead.

Yes, let us. Dullington's words echoed back in his head, accompanied by his own. *Let's get to it, hoss.*

Joe Hopper's words finally given voice, as good a war cry as Donovan could muster given the circumstances. If he'd known he'd be crossing into enemy territory alone, he would've asked more questions. Not that he'd experienced any resistance. Quite the contrary, in fact—most of Sparrow's followers had either been devoured by the Yawning or had dispersed into hiding among the empty buildings of the dead city.

Those who'd remained were more of the city's missing teens, and he'd sent them back to the Spectrum without a second thought, despite Aleister's foreboding warning.

In freeing the others, you have anchored yourself to the depths of this world.

A necessary sacrifice, or so it had felt at the time. Who he was the day before was a distant effigy of the man he'd become. He'd lost a piece of himself in the fight with Sparrow, he understood that now. It was apparent with each step, each breath, each heartbeat. There was a hollowness inside him, a piece of his soul missing from the greater portrait, and while staring into the great gray nothing before him, he wondered if he would recognize his reflection. Would he know his own face?

Donovan rubbed his eyes, tried to force those uneasy thoughts from his mind, but they always crept back in.

Would Donna recognize me? Would she forgive me for leaving her again?

God, he didn't want to think of the answers. Nothing terrified him more. He thought of her smiling face, aglow in the shadows of his memories, and held it there while keeping the anxiety at bay. Donovan doubted she'd ever understand the weight of responsibility he now carried upon his shoulders. She would be angry, she might even hate him for what he'd done—and he wouldn't blame her. She had every right.

Of course, he knew such anger could only manifest from her love of him, her fear that he wouldn't return. And yet if he could somehow get word to her, maybe he could at least let her know he was still alive. The last thing he wanted was for her to worry, for the sake of her health and their unborn child.

And what if he *didn't* return? What would she do then?

Awfully arrogant of you, hoss, thinkin' she can't do without you.

Hopper's southern charm had worn thin in the last several hours, but Donovan had to admit he was right. Donna was anything but weak; he'd watched her suffer through the worst nerve pain imaginable and still keep a smile on her face. She was the stronger of the two, no doubt about it, and he loved her more than anything else.

"I've done an awful thing," he said quietly, listening to the lonely drone of the Monochrome humming in his ears. "I should've stayed…"

But then Quinn would still be trapped here. Sparrow's plan to force everyone to flicker out would've come to pass. Would you be able to live with yourself knowing you'd traded millions of lives to save your own skin?

No, Donovan realized, he wouldn't. He looked to the sky and discovered he'd been crying. After wiping his eyes, he climbed to his feet and set off toward the edge of the city.

———•———

Another tremor, another aching groan from the structures around him, punctuated with more moaning cries from creatures out of sight. *Strange days,* Donovan thought. *It's like the whole goddamn world is falling down.*

Maybe he was right about that. Dullington told him there was no one left to keep the balance in place, which raised several questions, but Donovan hadn't had the chance to ask. Instead, he was left alone to speculate, and while he was uncertain of most reasons, of one thing he was sure: Dullington hadn't told him everything. Not at all.

He knew only to head toward the column on the horizon, beyond the confines of the city. Easier said than done; the blank city was a maze without its features, signs, and landmarks. His time in liminal space had at least afforded him the occasional glimpse of the Spectrum. Now, anchored here in the Monochrome for good, he hadn't much to go on.

After wandering in circles for a few hours, he'd finally set his sights in one direction and walked. The buildings grew smaller, farther apart. There were still remnants of the Missing in the city, even on its outskirts, and they fled whenever Donovan called to them. Twice he encountered Yawning, but they were occupied with their helpless prey, and he'd closed himself off to the human cries for help.

Ain't nothin' you can do for them, hoss.

But that wasn't true. He could send them back, take on their mediocrity himself. Free them by imprisoning himself.

Not that it matters. I'm already a prisoner here.

And deeper down, buried beneath all those good intentions of martyrdom, was an element of selfishness he didn't want to face. Whomever he saved from the grip of the Monochrome would become his messenger, for better or worse. Someone to find Donna and tell her he's still alive. Someone to tell her he's trying to get back to her, one way or another.

Someone to tell her he's sorry for what he's done.

Bein' a coward doesn't suit you much, hoss.

Hopper was right. Having someone else apologize to her on his behalf wouldn't mean shit. He'd suffer with the guilt, live with the agonizing reality he may never have a chance to say it to Donna's face—or that she'd never forgive him. Maybe that was his penance.

"HELP ME!"

The shriek startled him from his thoughts. He'd been so caught up in his own head that he'd tuned out his surroundings; now, he heard the pounding steps of the Yawning just ahead in the haze. There was movement in the distance—a smaller figure on the run. Another one of the Missing. A young man, by the look of him, not quite Quinn's age and draped in rags.

The lumbering beast uttered a triumphant groan as it followed its prey between two buildings.

Get to it, hoss.

Donovan didn't wait. He darted off in pursuit of the creature. *"Hang on! Don't let it get close!"*

He wasn't sure if the person heard him over the Yawning's droning cries, wasn't even sure this was a good idea at all, but he had to try.

The beast turned a corner at the alley's end. Another muffled shriek echoed down the narrow path. Donovan grit his teeth, forced himself to move faster until his muscles were screaming. Fire filled his lungs.

He reached the corner, ready to steal the creature's attention—and his gut dropped away. A body lay at the Yawning's feet in a puddle of blood. The beast reared back and swallowed what looked like the torn remains of an arm.

Too late. Goddammit, too late.

"Hey!"

The Yawning pivoted on its heel, revealing an elongated mouth ringed with blood and droopy black eyes. The lanky thing stared at him with a dumbfounded expression, as though it didn't recognize what it was seeing.

"That's right, big guy. Come here and try that with me."

Days ago, he considered these creatures a serious threat. Watchdogs of the Monochrome, preying on the Missing and consuming anyone who crossed their path, and used by Dullington as a means of enforcement.

Now, after facing far worse in the form of Albert Sparrow, Donovan felt no fear. They were walking shapes of sentient mediocrity and nothing more.

The Yawning swayed in place before taking its first step. Donovan smiled. "That's right. Over here."

One more lengthy stride brought the creature before him. It looked down at him without emotion or concern, its mouth already shivering as its jaw unhinged, ready to devour one more hapless human in its path.

Donovan reached out, placed his hand on the creature's abdomen, and focused his mind. A dim arc of light erupted between them, and within seconds, a pulse of energy shot through the creature. Its pale body blew apart, the remains splattering the back wall like white paint. Pieces of the creature slid down and collected on the ground in a wet clump.

He stumbled backward against the alley wall and steadied himself. His whole body hummed with energy, the tips of his fingers numb, his head filled with a rush of static.

Warmth on his upper lip. Bleeding again. He wiped the blood on his sleeve, took a deep breath, and waited for the static to clear. He stared at the young man's lifeless body and the pool of blood. Dirty sweatpants and a torn T-shirt covered in stains.

Too late, Candle. Good try, though.

Donovan collected himself and sighed. Next time he'd be faster. Next time—

The body stirred, sat up, shook its head in confusion.

"Oh my God." Donovan jogged over to the young man, knelt to help him. "Easy, man. Don't move, that thing took a bite—"

Out of your arm.

Only the young man's arms were intact. One of them was covered in the pale slime of the Yawning's remains. There were bite marks in the skin, deep gashes pooling with blood, but nothing had been severed. Donovan shook his head, questioning what it was he'd seen the Yawning eating.

Puzzled, the young man looked up at his savior. Deep scars mottled his face, but Donovan was too startled by the piercing gray eyes to notice the jagged lines crossing the kid's face. He'd never seen eyes so gray before—or had he? The color triggered a memory too far buried, itching at the back of his brain.

"Thank you," the young man said. A white sheen clung to his skin like cellophane, coating him in a strange, pallid glow. He pulled himself to his feet. Blood seeped from the wounds and pattered on the ground like soft rain. "I will be okay."

Donovan frowned. "Are you sure? I mean, that thing took a huge chunk out of you..." *More than a chunk. A whole bite and then some. I'm sure of it.* He stared at the kid's arm. "You need to put some pressure on that. Clean it if you can—"

"I will be okay," he said again. The blood slowed to a trickle. "You see? All is well now."

"Sure..." Donovan forced a smile. "My name's Don. You got a name?"

"I do have a name." He turned away from Donovan and examined his arm, flexing the muscles, stretching his fingers. The viscous remains of the Yawning slowly faded from his exposed skin. "You may call me...John. John Black."

"Okay, John. You nearly got yourself killed."

John turned back. His gray eyes glistened in the unlight. "Indeed."

———————•———————

Donovan knew something wasn't right about the kid he'd rescued. "Kid" was a loose term—John Black had the figure of a twenty-year-old, but the longer Donovan stared, the more the boy's face seemed to age. His face had sagged in the ensuing minutes, his skin a rocky planet of scars, wrinkles, and strange spots. Birthmarks, maybe, or remnants of the gray pox.

"It is a good thing you came along, Mr. Don." John kicked at the gelatinous remains of the Yawning. "He would have consumed me for sure."

"Yes," Donovan said, staring at the young man's mannerisms. He had a twitch, almost like a drug addict in need of his fix, and his body shuddered in odd intervals. And then there was his speech. Slow, deliberate—almost like a certain monk he knew, but not quite. No, something was different, something he couldn't place.

"Mr. Don—"

"Just Don."

John smiled. "As you wish, Don. I was going to ask if you are Donovan Candle?"

"Yeah, that's me. Do we know each other?'

"Oh no, not at all. Not exactly. I have only heard your name among the others. The great liberator. The one who walks between. They ask, 'Who is Donovan Candle?' like a mantra. A great existential question. Who *is* Donovan Candle? Well, I suppose I have my answer now. He is you."

Donovan looked away, his face flushed with embarrassment, trying to hide the stupid grin on his face. The great liberator? Please. He was no hero. When he thought of Donna, he certainly didn't feel like a hero—he felt like a traitor.

"I'm sure Sparrow had plenty of nice things to say about me."

"Oh yes," John said, grinning. The smile took Donovan by surprise. It was unnatural, the way the man's lips pulled back, revealing too much of his gums and teeth. It was the rictus of a porcelain doll, frozen forever in false joy. The thought sent a chill down Donovan's spine. "One would believe Sparrow was your number one fan by the way he ranted about you." John approached the corner, peered into the gray haze. "But no longer."

"You don't have to worry about him anymore."

"A shame."

"What do you mean?"

"He made life here interesting. Brought...color to the place, if you can believe it."

Donovan thought of the spiteful old man and all the pain he'd caused, remembered Sparrow's beady gray eyes—and froze.

Gray eyes.

"I must hand it to Aleister, he chose well. My manikin was resilient to a point, but you, Mr. Candle, have proven to be an insect who cannot be crushed." John reached out, placed his hand upon Donovan's arm. A soft white glow lit up between his fingers. "But I am not beaten so easily."

Donovan recoiled, tried to wrench himself free of the man's touch, but the light held them together. The surging nausea of mediocrity coursed through him as the light grew brighter, and within moments, John Black dissolved before his eyes.

The light ceased, and his gut was filled once more with a leaden weight. Donovan doubled over and retched, evacuating the pulpy gray contents of his stomach. Blood trickled from his nose, dotted the ground before him. A searing pain lit up his arm. A reddened outline of John's hand was etched into Donovan's skin.

"What the hell..."

Donovan shuffled forward a few steps, intent on resuming his journey out of the city, but the twisting pain in his gut would not relent. He staggered through a kaleidoscope of sparkling colors before losing his balance and falling into a deep, dark nothing. He was unconscious before the sidewalk broke his fall.

———————·———————

Donna Candle recoiled with a jolt and dropped her glass. The small tumbler fell to the floor and shattered, spilling a crystalline mixture of water and blue glass across the kitchen tile. Amanda stuck her head into the room and saw the mess on the floor.

"Donna? You okay, sis?"

"Yes." The response was involuntary, robotic. "I'm fine." She rubbed her forearm, tracing the pain resonating from her wrist down to her elbow. The sensation was as sudden as it was brief, but the effect lingered in her marrow, and following in its wake was a quiet, solemn thought: *But Donovan is not okay.*

She couldn't explain it any more than that—not to herself, and not out loud. *Just another fibro flare.* She knew the pain all too well, but after living with fibromyalgia for the better part of her life, she'd never experienced such a palpable anxiety along with it. The two were indelibly linked, one pain transforming into another, calling out the emptiness in her chest.

He'll be fine. He's got too much to come home to.

The reassurance from the voice in her head was unprompted and unnecessary, but not unwelcome. Any other time, she would've believed that tiny voice in her head, but not today. Today it didn't sound so convincing. *It lacks conviction,* Donovan might say, if he were here, and not—

The baby kicked, startling Donna from her anxious reverie. She placed a hand on her belly and gave her sister a timid smile. "Really. The baby's just restless. Nothing to be worried about."

Amanda frowned. "You're sure?"

"I am." She forced her smile wider, pulling down a happy mask to hide her worry. Amanda stared for a moment longer before averting his gaze to the broken glass.

"Let me clean that up."

"Do you mind?"

"Not at all. Do you still keep the broom hanging behind the basement door?"

Donna nodded, turning away from her just as a tear slipped down her cheek. "Thank you."

"No problem."

Donna smiled as her sister went about cleaning up the broken glass. She was grateful; the last thing she needed was to overexert herself and slip into the clutches of another panic attack.

How many attacks had she suffered since Michael and Alice left for the city that morning? Two? Three? She'd lost count—not that keeping count even mattered now. All that mattered now was her child and her health.

And the man you love, she thought. Of course, the man she loved mattered. But did he love her? That question had never entered her stream of consciousness before. Donovan had run off to fulfill some foolish mission, leaving his pregnant wife behind to fend for herself. Was that love? Would love drive someone to do that?

Donna wasn't sure anymore. The more she thought about Donovan, the more her heart raced. In prior years, she would've considered that a trait of her ongoing love and devotion, but after all that had happened in the last forty-eight hours, she wondered if there wasn't a hint of bitterness there, a smidge of resentment, a dash of anger.

She turned on the faucet and ran cold water over her wrists to cool herself. Her heart was racing again and sweat beaded on the back of her neck.

Think of the kiddo. He'll come back. He has to.

Either he would or he wouldn't. Deep down, she knew this, and she wanted to believe with every fiber of her being that she hadn't misjudged him in some way. That the man she'd married all those years ago was still in there somewhere, and that wherever he was, he was fighting to get back to her. To them.

She stared out the kitchen window and into the backyard. Thick gray clouds had rolled in, draping the sky with drab overcast hues and leeching life from the world. Had the weatherman called for rain? She couldn't remember. This day had slipped from her grasp as she sank deeper into a mire of despair with each passing moment.

What she could remember confused her. The dark-haired woman who'd returned with Michael and Quinn yesterday was only the start of that confusion.

Alice Walenta, the missing woman from years ago, the same woman who watched over her while held captive down in the subway tunnels—she was at once a stranger and a sudden friend, known and unknown, her face wiped from Donna's memory and redrawn with distinct clarity. Where there was once a series of blank spots was now a jumble of memories thrown into her mind like confetti: office parties, conversations over dinner, talks about her parents, her travels. They *knew* each other—only they didn't. They couldn't.

The temporal dissonance made her head throb, and she closed her eyes. Everything that had happened since yesterday had come and gone in a blur, from the moment she awoke to find Donovan's note on her nightstand to the moment Michael returned with Quinn in tow. She suddenly felt faint, and she reached out for the edge of the sink to steady herself.

There were blurry spots staining her memory. Great big gray splotches of conflicting information, in which she saw herself sitting alone at their dining room table, while at the same time sitting across from a man who might have been her husband. His face was obscured in the haze, his features barely visible as if pressed against a thick invisible drapery. When she concentrated, she could almost see him there, and it *was* her husband—a silhouette of him, transparent, fading, flickering in and out of reality, paradoxically present and absent at the same time. Seen and unseen.

The throbbing in her head intensified. She chewed her lip, struggling to maintain the memory of Donovan sitting across from her. He was speaking something, his words muffled, punctuated by bursts of static that ripped through her mind like nails. *He's calling my name. Or trying to. And I couldn't hear him. Why couldn't I remember this before?*

What had Donnie said about that place he called the Monochrome? It had its own set of rules, with a different set of consequences. People who flickered out were supposed to be forgotten by those who remained here. *Maybe*, she mused, *we're not meant to remember. Maybe we never were.*

The clatter of glass shards startled her, and she opened her eyes just as Amanda dumped the last of the tumbler pieces into the trash.

"All done," Amanda said, tapping the dustpan against the edge of the bin. "Now—oh, shit."

Amanda's face went pale. Donna frowned. "What's wrong?"

"Your nose," Amanda said. She scrambled to the kitchen counter and thrust a dish towel into her sister's hand. "You're bleeding, honey."

Puzzled, Donna raised the cloth to her nose and examined the deep crimson blossoming across the fabric. Something was droning in her ears, a distant hum of bells, and shapes were present in her kitchen. There were others besides she and her sister, drawn in flickering outlines like figures in a silent film.

"Donna?"

Amanda's voice, a mile away and submerged underwater. Heat flushed Donna's cheeks, the back of her neck, her forehead. The droning of bells surged, and the shapes in her periphery coalesced into a darkened blob slowly clouding her vision.

"I need…"

To sit down, she heard herself say, only the words didn't escape her lips.

"Oh shit, Donna—"

A phone was ringing. Her phone. Somewhere else. The kitchen counter, maybe. *Answer it,* Donna wanted to say, but the kitchen was sinking away from her, the darkness clouding her world in shadow. *It could be Donnie…*

The room faded, the drone of bells and a ringing phone the last things she heard before sinking beneath the waters of unconsciousness. There was no bottom, no undertow, only a soothing warm embrace—and then, nothing.

-2-
RECLAMATION

Michael Candle waited until the phone switched over to voicemail, and when Donna's chipper voice asked for a message, he canceled the call. They were parked in a garage across the street from the city's transit authority, "regrouping" as Alice put it, but he saw it as nothing more than wasting time.

Alice opened her eyes. "No answer?"

"No. I'll try again in a few."

Quinn stirred in the backseat, rolled onto his side, and snored softly into the upholstery. Michael looked back at the kid and smiled. *Guess he's not a kid anymore, not after what he's been through.*

The young man's insistence on joining them hadn't gone over well with Amanda, but Michael suspected she'd seen the same change of maturity in her son. Whatever he'd been through had aged his soul, and his mother had quickly realized her protests and commands weren't going to work this time.

That was several hours ago, and in the time since, they'd scoped out the subway terminals around the business district, hoping to catch a glimpse of Donovan, or more importantly, someone who might've seen him. The whole plan didn't sit well with Michael, felt too much like a dead end, but he'd acquiesced to Alice's demands anyway. He'd never admit it, but he didn't have any better ideas. There was something else, though. Something he couldn't quite put his finger on.

Alice sat with her door open, stretching her legs. The sour city air filled the car with a warm miasma of exhaust fumes, sweat, and piss. He looked at her, struggling to find the right words to voice the thoughts racing through his mind. He wanted to ask her to close the door, wanted to know if there was somewhere else he could take her because he worked best alone—but mostly, he wanted to ask her if they knew each other.

Michael struggled to make sense of what he was experiencing, had done so since that morning, like a whole piece of his mind had suddenly woken up. The feeling of recognition, a stark certainty that he knew this woman, would not relent. Not from Donna's abduction years ago, but from something else just out of focus, like the feeling of a word on the tip of his tongue, there and just out of reach. He'd wrestled with the sensation all day.

Alice turned in her seat. "Listen, I think we're—oh shit, Mike, you're bleeding."

He looked up in the rearview, saw dark red trickling from his nose, and pointed to the glovebox. "Napkins in there."

After he stopped the bleeding, Michael lowered his window and tossed out the bloody napkin. "That was weird. Haven't had a nosebleed in years. Anyway, you were saying?"

"I think we're going about this the wrong way."

"How so?"

She gestured to the transit authority across the street. "We aren't going to find Donovan by driving around to the different stations in the city. I know you want to find your brother, but he isn't going to stroll out of there like nothing's happened."

Mike looked away, shook his head. He'd promised Donna he wouldn't stop searching, promised himself that he'd find his brother one way or another. Returning to the city, staking out its many entrances to the subway network made the most sense to him at the time, but now he wasn't sure. He'd witnessed people blink into existence before his eyes, watched sections of a skyscraper implode, and felt the earth rumble beneath his feet. The world he knew was falling away in pieces.

Don, what the fuck have you done?

"Mike?"

Her voice pulled him back to the present. When he looked at her, met her bright gaze, he felt a flush of warm remembrance. A hint of familiarity. Déjà vu, but ten times stronger. He knew her but couldn't understand how.

Alice blushed, and he realized he was staring.

"Sorry," he said. "I was lost in my own head. I'm honestly at a loss here, Alice. My brother is gone, his wife's on the verge of a breakdown, and frankly, so am I." Tears stung his eyes. A foreign feeling, this emotion, but something he welcomed; it reminded him he was alive, still present of mind.

She reached out, wiped a stray tear from his cheek. He took her hand and held it there against his face, unsure of what he was doing, terrified of what he was doing, and yet the touch of her cool skin felt right somehow.

Alice sighed, traced her thumb along his cheek. "You don't remember me, do you?"

Mike shook his head. "No, but I know I should."

"Give it time." She withdrew her hand. "Besides, we need to look for your brother."

He collected himself, blinked away his tears. "I'm open to ideas."

"I don't think we're going to find Donovan down there...but I do think there's a way to get the word out. When in doubt, leave a message on the message board." She winked at him and climbed out of the car. She tapped the backdoor window. "Wake up Q-ball. We're going for a hike."

———— • ————

A menagerie of shadows fills her mind, driven to the beat of a synthesized drone pulsing overhead. She is lost in the chaotic darkness, unable to move as other bodies twist and squirm and press against her. Somewhere in the tangle of limbs is Donovan, not yet her husband, and barely her boyfriend.

There's familiarity in the urgent panic climbing through her chest. Donna's had this dream before many times, the setting and crowd and noise always the same, but now something isn't right. This is how it happened that night, and yet not. They're still two babes in the wilderness of the crowd, barely old enough to grasp the complexities of the love they've claimed for one another. All those feelings and fragile understanding will grow with them in time—but here, now, they've been separated in the chaos.

She feels her way through the darkness, reaching for a hand that isn't there. All she finds are other bodies writhing in time to the beat, and in the logic of this dream, she knows she needs to find him, or else—

And there's the difference. This isn't how it happened at all. That night at the concert, it was she who was caught in the crowd, nearly crushed to death by the swell of bodies scrambling toward the stage. Armed with this epiphany, Donna doubles her efforts, pushing with all her strength against the men and women around her. The crowd moves as one, inhaling and exhaling in panicked gusts, churning like violent waves crashing upon rocks.

They were separated, she remembers, pulled apart by the surging crowd as the band took to the stage.

Now she fights that rush, pushing her way deeper into the throng of men and women in search of her love. He's lost in here somewhere, struggling for air, struggling to keep his head above the tide. He has taken her place, and on the heels of this realization is a cold, stark reality: if she doesn't push forward, Donovan is going to be crushed in the undertow of this human tidal wave.

The drone pulses overhead and generates a rhythm. Strobe lights flash in time and fog drifts over their heads. The band reaches their song's first crescendo and the world slips away into chaos. She's lost in the gray slate pulled over the world like a thin curtain, barely there, just beyond her grasp. Fragments of memory float up from some dark abyss, hinting at what is to come: the two of them sitting alone in the park, bloodied and bruised from their escape, quietly embracing one another for comfort. There's a chill in the air, and as Donna closes her eyes, she hears Donovan tell her he loves her.

But those events are yet to come. Donna is back in the dark, clamoring among the bodies in search of a man she's only just begun to know. As she works her way through the menagerie of silhouettes, their faces change in the flashing strobes. Human features melt into impossible proportions with bulging black eyes and jagged teeth. Their bodies shrink and stretch into a pale amoeba of gelatinous flesh. They are all parts of a whole, one conglomeration of entwined limbs, a ball of white rubbery flesh and sharp teeth intricately woven together into a single blockade.

And beyond this pallid wall is Donovan. She can see him now, just his head poking above the surface. He's calling out her name, searching frantically for her.

Screaming. He's screaming.

Donna tries to respond, but her voice is a whisper compared to the synthesized chaos pulsing overhead. She pushes forward, shoving her arm into the rubbery mass and cries out in pain. A million pinpricks dig into her skin, tasting her, eager to leech the life from her veins. She grinds her molars as the flesh of her forearm is chewed and scratched, her fingers slowly gnawed down to bone.

Donovan turns to her now, locking eyes with her, and smiles as an errant wave of pale skin crashes over him, drags him down below the roiling surface.

She screams his name, screams "I would for you," and plunges headfirst into the ravenous tumult. She opens her mouth to scream his name—

———•———

—A nd gasped as Amanda rolled her onto her side. Her sister yelped in surprise and fumbled her phone.

"Oh, thank God. Donna? Donna, honey, can you hear me?"

Donna opened her eyes, puzzled by her view of the kitchen. The world was blurry, her throat was dry, and the back of her head throbbed. Amanda knelt beside her, pale-faced, with beads of panic sweat dotting her forehead. She picked up her phone and dialed.

"I'm calling an ambulance—"

Donna reached for her sister's phone. "Don't. I'm—I'll be fine."

"You just fainted, Donna. There could be something wrong with the baby."

The child in her womb kicked as if on command. Donna winced and held out her hand. "Help me up. I'll go to emergency, but not in an ambulance."

"Donna—"

"I can't afford it," she said. "Our insurance—I mean, with Donovan gone—oh, just fucking help me up, sis."

Amanda frowned, but said nothing more and did as Donna asked. She walked Donna into the dining room and sat her in a chair.

"Does anything hurt? Does anything feel wrong?"

Everything feels wrong, Donna thought, but didn't dare say anything to her sister. Amanda would assume she meant it in a physical sense, but in that respect, Donna felt somewhat fine except for the lightheadedness. Emotionally, however, she was anything but fine. And that dream—

"I'll pack some things. Stay put."

Donna smiled faintly. "Yes, Mom."

She watched Amanda jog upstairs, waited until her sister was out of sight, and buried her face in her hands. The tears came easily enough, but their release was less of a comfort than she'd hoped. She hadn't thought of that night at the concert in years, so why now?

I can't deal with this. I'm a fucking nervous wreck.

It wasn't just the concert. There were other memories surfacing now, bubbling from the depths of untold pockets of her mind: Donovan sitting across from her at the dinner table, haggard and depressed with dark circles below his eyes, pleading for her to acknowledge him. Donovan wandering through their home like a ghost, trying to get her attention the way a child might, waving his hands and shouting at the top of his lungs.

The memories were ridiculous, and maybe in another time she would've thought them fragments of forgotten dreams, but not these. This jumble of memories was real, these scenes had happened, and she'd tucked them away like unused plastic bags in a kitchen drawer. Holes in her memory, holes she wasn't even aware existed, were slowly filling in, fading into focus.

There were others, of course. Other people of whom she'd forgotten completely. Mr. Bolton, the mail carrier who'd delivered parcels to her parents; Mr. Vasquez, one of the sanitation workers who frequented their street weekly; Mrs. Daugherty, her former manager at her last retail job in the mall—faces she'd known and seen on a regular basis but were erased, now returned to their proper places in her mental tapestry.

A flood of memories overcame her, coursing through her mind like a film reel at double speed, neighbors and coworkers and family—

Chris, my cousin. Oh my God, I had a cousin.

Her head thudded, pulsing to the tune of her heartbeat, and a drop of blood plopped on the table. Donna touched her nose, frowned as her fingertips came away crimson.

"Amanda," she called. "We need to go. Now."

———— • ————

After years of living in the cracks of society, foraging for food while evading the Monochrome's dangerous bestiary, the last place Alice wanted to visit was another goddamn subway tunnel. But it was also a world she knew all too well, more real to her than the vibrant Spectrum side of reality, and in some ways, she supposed, it was one which made more sense to her.

The city's subway system had a life all its own, with a unique culture insulated from the greater populace above. Down here, the rules were unwritten, unspoken. No nepotism, no bosses, and no bullshit. Bartering was the only currency, and without the drive of greed, there was no concern of status. Anyone who chose to live down in the tunnels and between the cracks of the city's foundations wasn't concerned about race or social pedigree.

Down here, all were equal in the gloom, and all were driven by a basic desire to survive.

Alice kept this in mind as she led Michael and Quinn into the transit authority terminal and downstairs to the boarding platform. As the central transit hub for the city, the Blue Line was busy at all hours of any given day, but the crowd didn't worry her. She'd grown well adept at being invisible over the last decade, and she doubted anyone would trouble them when they left the platform.

"Over here." She pointed to the far edge where the platform gave way to an impenetrable darkness in the tunnel beyond. "When the next train departs, we're going to hop the gate and drop down. Stick to the wall and follow me. Don't cross the rails."

Quinn tilted his head, peered into the tunnel. "You're serious?"

"Yup."

Michael shook his head. "There's no other way to get where we're going?"

"Would I be doing this if there was?"

"Fair enough." He looked back at Quinn. "Stay close to me."

They waited near the edge, watching the crowd of well-dressed men and women squeeze themselves into the subway cars. A moment later, the doors slid closed, and the train was on its way into the opposite tunnel. Warm, stagnant air blasted their faces. Alice wrinkled her nose. She knew that odor but would never get used to it.

She looked back, nodded, and dropped down into the darkness. After some hesitation, Quinn followed, and Michael reluctantly did the same. Alice waited for them just beyond the terminal's end, hidden in the gloom except for the faint glow of a red light from somewhere farther down the track.

"Stay along the wall. If you step on the track…" She pointed to the infamous third rail. "Don't step on the track."

Quinn nodded, looked back at Michael. His uncle said nothing and didn't have to; his face betrayed any sort of stoicism, revealing a grim nervousness too palpable to conceal. Alice noticed Michael's expression, gave him a short nod, and slid along the wall into the dark.

She supposed Michael's reticence was warranted. After what they'd collectively witnessed in the last twenty-four hours, and especially after hearing hers and Quinn's retelling of recent events, she suspected his firm grasp on reality had been lost. Stories of the creatures living down here in the tunnels, of men and women choosing sides and battling one another, of the demigod who lorded over them—it was enough to scare anyone away from the subway lines for life.

But here they were, trekking into the darkness where they weren't supposed to go. A year ago, she would've shared his caution, but now they had the safety of the Spectrum on their side. There would be no danger from the Yawning, no fear of being spotted by the Cretins. Down here, all they had to worry about was the fear of electrocution and confrontation by their fellow man.

Alice kept this in mind as she led them further into the dark, slipping along the damp tunnel wall and around the curve ahead. Michael and Quinn followed her closely in silence, too afraid to step out anywhere but in her shadow, too afraid to breathe for fear of something—anything—noticing them.

She held her hand against the tunnel wall, feeling for the slightest vibration, a sign that another train was approaching. Ten minutes into the gloom, she received one such warning, and hissed for the others to flatten themselves against the cold brick. Seconds later, another train southbound from the business district sped by mere inches from their faces. Alice held her breath and closed her eyes, waiting for the roaring wind and shrieking rails to abate, and counting the nervous beats of her heart.

Four. Five. Six.

She counted to seven before the train was gone, zipping off into the shadows in a rush of stagnant air.

"Holy shit." Quinn sudden gasp gave her a start, but she welcomed the levity in his voice. Down here there wasn't much laughter to be heard, too fewer smiles to be seen.

Michael pushed the boy forward. "How much longer, Alice?"

"Not far. See that light up ahead?" They followed her finger toward a dim red glow beyond a bend in the tunnel. "There's a fork in the rails. Old track that isn't used anymore. What we're looking for is about a half a mile beyond."

"You going to tell us what we're looking for?"

Alice smiled. "It's better if you see it. You'll understand."

"All right. Let's get going then." Michael looked back in the terminal's direction. "I don't want to get stuck against the wall again."

Alice nodded, turned away, and inched her way forward into the dark.

O n the derelict southside of town, not far from the abandoned Laundromat, a homeless man by the name of Clancy Jones was halfway along the crosswalk when a memory emerged from a dark cobweb-laden recess in his mind: Patty Winslow washing her hair in a restroom sink at the 12th Street terminal. Lord, that was years ago, long before they closed down that old Yellow Line for good. He shook his head, scratching his ragged beard with a free hand while he pushed his shopping cart across the street. The memory was a domino, and when that first one fell, so did the others: Patty, lying naked in his arms; Patty, teasing him about the beard he'd grown; Patty, telling him everything would be all right, that he'd find work eventually, to keep trying the unemployment office.

Except none of that had ever happened. Had it?

Confused, Clancy Jones stopped in the middle of the street and stared up at an uncaring overcast sky. Earlier that morning he'd overheard a couple of businessmen in expensive suits discussing rain in the near future.

Maybe that would be for the best. A little rain would break up the tension in the air; maybe even dampen the anxiety that now weighed on his heart.

Patty Winslow. Where had she come from? His mind and his heart were at odds with one another: Patty didn't exist, he'd never even heard that name before—except he *had* heard the name before, he'd known her face and touch and smile and voice long ago, and there were even more memories lurking deeper in the folds of his brain, memories that became more pronounced with each passing moment.

The blaring horn of a taxicab yanked Clancy out of his daydream with a jolt.

The driver slapped his hand on the side of the door. "Whaddya doin', you crazy asshole? You gotta death wish or somethin'?"

Someone honked behind the cab. The cabbie turned back and gave them the finger. Clancy stared at him, frowning. The cab driver turned back and held out his hand. "You got a problem, pal? Move yer ass. I got fares to collect."

Clancy lowered his gaze, shook off the reverie, and offered the angry cabbie a light smile in return. "Sorry, mister. I'll be on my way."

The lie burned his tongue. In his youth he might have provoked the angry fellow, but his years of middle age were waning and lately all he wanted to do was find a place to bed down and sleep. Maybe even die.

One or the other, it didn't matter to him anymore, and with the sudden resurgence of Patty Winslow in his mind and heart, he found he was driven to the latter emotion even more.

He gripped the handle and pushed his cart of belongings across the street, his jars of paint rattling as the rickety rubber wheels clattered along the asphalt. He paused on the sidewalk and watched the crosswalk signal turn to red. The cabbie sped off, leading a charge of traffic down the boulevard.

Patty was gone. He knew that now but didn't understand why or how. The heartache of her disappearance gripped him with its inescapable gravity, and for a few minutes Clancy leaned against the lamppost and sobbed.

Where had she gone? He'd last seen her at the soup kitchen next to Our Lady of Sorrows, her dusty brown hair pulled back, eyes wide but burdened with a lack of sleep, and strung out beyond comprehension.

Do you see them? she'd asked, but Clancy hadn't responded. All he could recall was a deep inset buzzing noise like an old television signal gone wrong and a sharp pain between his eyes. He remembered wanting to reply, but some backwards voice told him no, ignore her, she isn't there anymore, and she doesn't love you.

Clancy wiped his nose on his sleeve. She was real and he'd loved her and now she was gone.

A drop of rain pelted the back of his hand. He looked up and blinked as a few more drops fell into his eyes. The businessmen in the fancy suits were right, and if he didn't get moving soon, he'd be spending his evening trying to stay afloat.

He pushed his cart to the end of the sidewalk and turned a corner into a blind alley. A row of Dumpsters lined one wall of dingy bricks; the other side was adorned by a series of scaffolding platforms set aside for what appeared to be an abandoned painting project. There was just enough clearance for him to take shelter.

A stiff breeze swirled through the passage, ushering a chill down his back, and he was struck with a flashback of Patty in his arms. They were in the city park. Snow was on the ground. They'd huddled together under a tree, and Patty couldn't keep warm. She wouldn't stop shivering.

Clancy bit his lip to hold back his sorrow. Where was this coming from? Was he losing his mind? Had living on the street finally got the best of him?

"Leave me be," he muttered, crossing his arms to hold back the irrational chill tearing across his body.

But Patty's ghost wouldn't leave him alone. Her face haunted him until he could no longer stand it; he reached for his pencil and notepad, and within a few hectic moments he had sketched the outline of her face across a torn, water-stained page.

How do I know you? From when? I don't understand—

The painting. For years he'd carried a painting, unable to recall where it had come from. He'd set it out on the sidewalk during the days when he busked for money, offering to paint portraits for a dollar a page. Hers was the most detailed, the most exemplary of his talents, and he'd turned down offers to sell it for reasons he never quite understood. God knows he could've used the money, but some part of him couldn't bring himself to part with that beautiful face. *No sale,* he'd tell people, *she's the lady of my dreams.*

And she was, but now he realized she was real, dammit, he had held her in his arms and loved her and—

"Now she's gone."

Clancy was so lost in his languishing confusion that he didn't notice the pulsing light emanating from the end of the alley. Not at first. Patty Winslow was still on his mind as he set aside the notepad and dug through his cart, sifting through a stack of painted, wrinkled pages wrapped up in a sleeping bag until he found her immortalized in bright acrylic colors. There she was, her sandy brown hair defined in swirling brushstrokes, her green eyes speckled with flecks of unmixed blue and yellow. He traced his finger across the smudges that formed dimples in her cheeks as his eyes were swallowed in tears.

Thunder cracked overhead, tearing through the alley with a deafening boom, shaking him to his core. The tremor worked its way down his legs, and a moment later he was struggling to keep his balance. He dropped the painting as a shockwave tore through the earth, rattling the paint jars in his cart and the skeletal framework of scaffolding overhead. Windows high above exploded outward, raining down jagged shards of safety glass like a downpour of razorblades.

He flattened himself against the wall, heartbroken and terrified as the world fell down around him, but no sooner had he closed his eyes did the violent quake cease. Elsewhere, cars honked and people shouted, punctuated by the piercing, redundant chirp of a car alarm.

Another earthquake. Just like what happened downtown at that TV station yesterday. He opened his eyes and winced. A grayish light strobed from the alley's dead end. *Broken bulb? Must be a short or somethin'.* He couldn't recall seeing a light there before, but what did that matter anyway? His memory wasn't what it used to be—

Where's Patty?

He searched for the painting, but it was no longer at his feet. The wind had swept it further down the passage; he spotted its bright colors tucked under the side of a tin garbage can. Clancy stepped out from the safety of the scaffolding with rubbery legs. Fragments of broken glass crunched underfoot as he walked deeper into the alley, each footstep punctuated by a growing pressure behind his eyes. He was two strides away from reclaiming his painting when the pale man materialized before him in a surge of static and light.

Panicked, Clancy stood transfixed in a collision of awe and growing horror, his mind torn between curiosity and the instinctual urge to run for his life. The painting was just a few feet away. If he was quick—and he used to be—he could snatch the paper and be on his way before trouble came calling his name.

The pressure behind his eyes was sharp and blinding, two big hands pushing to break free from the prison of his skull and unite with the sickly light surrounding the stranger.

The pale figure shuffled forward and braced himself against the nearby wall. A series of fractures splintered all the way up the building and across the alley floor. Clancy nearly soiled himself when he realized the man—was he a man?—had no face. Where a face should've been was a soft mound of white flesh, sodden like clay or even dough—but the longer Clancy stared, faint human features slowly formed in the swirling mess of tissue.

For the second time in his life, Clancy forgot all about Patty Winslow, and he discovered he wasn't as quick as he used to be. He was in mid-turn when the first pale hand fell upon him, and he was unable to cry out as the faceless thing pulled him forward. Clancy struggled, but the creature's grip was impenetrable, its fingers digging deep in his frail shoulders. His feet dragged the ground as the pale man pulled him close.

"Servus meus es tu."

It pressed a blank cheek to Clancy's face. A searing pain shot through his eyes as thin white tendrils felt their way across the gap between them, and for one agonizing, terrifying moment Clancy felt himself become one with the creature.

The tendrils wormed their way behind his eyes and into his mind, filling his head with that same jarring light and a babbling voice that was not his own. He uttered a cry of mortification, bellowing forth the horror seeping into his core, and the faceless thing finally released him from its hold.

Clancy Jones fell backward, grimacing as bits of glass sliced into his dirty palms, but he was too stunned by the drone echoing within his own head to notice the pain.

The thin, faceless figure stepped toward him, draped in the tattered remains of dirty jeans and a gray T-shirt. Clancy kicked away from the pale thing, dragging himself against the safety of the nearest Dumpster.

"What—what the fuck *are* you, man? *Who* are you?"

The creature's swirling mess of a face took shape, forming gray eyes, a hooked nose, and scars so deep they ran chin to forehead like railroad crossties. The pale man looked down and spoke. "John Black. But to you, insect, you may call me *master*."

-3-
LITTLE SPARROW

*H*ello, old friend. We almost made it, did we not?

The old rowboat was where he'd left it centuries ago, planted firmly in the gray sands, the oars half-buried in small dunes built over time. Aleister traced his fingers along the boat's rim. The gritty sand and harsh winds had smoothed the craft's wooden surface, rounding out the battered edges, polishing it to an unnatural sheen.

Here, near the last of the metachasm's demarcations, the boat's presence was an anomaly in an otherwise empty world; and yet, for Aleister Dullington, its presence was a monument to a young man's determination—and his arrogance.

So, too, was it a symbol of his adversary's cruelty. What served as a scathing lesson should have also served as a warning of Master Vile's growing madness. To break the tenets of their order for any reason was considered a grave crime—perhaps the greatest of crimes—but to do so with such contempt and for the sake of discipline went beyond the scope of right and wrong. Even his mentor, Christopher, recognized the disintegration of Vile's reverence for the laws. All his brothers had noticed the change in their master's demeanor, the severity of his rage, the growing disdain for all humanity, and yet none of them took measures to end his reign.

Aleister considered his complicity in Vile's eventual corruption and betrayal. Like his brothers, Aleister Dullington was not innocent, and in time he had paid penance for his inaction. He was still paying, and there were moments in his long life when he feared the debt would never be settled.

Damn me for not stopping him when I had the chance.

Such was the regret of a demigod. That, and the sadness he'd buried long ago—a sadness which punctured his dead heart with every breath, every step, every quiet moment of reflection.

Aleister lifted his robe and stepped over the side into the boat. He sat, stared at the pair of oars, and silently wished he could close his eyes just once more.

———·———

Howling winds blast his face with sea brine as he heaves the boat against the tide. The waves crash against his knees, soaking his robe, inhibiting his movement, and urging him backward. *Stay,* the sea whispers, *stay or be damned.*

Only it isn't the sea which beckons to him. It's his master, calling to him from across the gray wastes of the other place. What the master calls the *Monochrome.* Somewhere beyond the veil of human understanding, hidden to all but the initiated—and the damned.

Aleister of the Dullingtons—formerly of Gloucestershire—presses on until the rowboat is free of the sandbar and hoists himself over the edge. He rolls onto his side, gasping for air, staring upward into the darkening clouds of the coming storm. Exhaustion tugs at his eyelids, calling him to sleep, but he resists. The young man is far from free. Months of planning have led to this moment; to forego his constitution now would be foolish and potentially fatal.

And so the young man forces himself upright and takes hold of the oars. He begins to row against the current, away from the isle of the Order and his brothers. Away from his vows.

A voice calls to him from the shore, weakened by the incessant gale blowing down upon them. He turns back, knowing whose face he will see. Christopher of the Dullingtons stands in the surf, hands cupped around his mouth, calling out his brother's name.

"—beg of you, brother, do not do this!"

Aleister wants to respond, wants to cry out to his brother and plead for accompaniment, but the drive to escape is far too great. To return to shore now would mean risking punishment per the laws of the Order. No, he would rather face the currents and risk death in the channel depths than return and suffer at the hands of Master Vile.

Reluctant, Aleister closes his eyes and shields himself from Christopher's beckoning. *Stay true,* he tells himself. *Remain steady on your path. Vile cannot touch you here.*

Oh, if only he'd known of the dangers that awaited him on this accursed isle. He'd blamed Christopher for a time—after all, it was he who'd recruited Aleister in the village market so long ago—but his brother of the Order was doing as commanded. Pontius Vile would not suffer insubordination; Christopher was as much a puppet of the mad man as the rest of the Order.

Aleister fell for the Order's allure like so many others before him, rejoicing in promises of a new way beyond the religious doctrines of their time. A true meaning, a true purpose, a way to directly influence the nature of all things—the Order promised all this and more, if only he would make his vows and submit to the Master Dullington himself, Pontius Vile.

The last year slips across his memory like droplets of rain into the sea. Memories of the beatings, the mandated silence, the soul-cleansing rites spent in total isolation and meditation. The road to every salvation is paved with penance, but in the eyes of the Order, salvation is only the beginning. To truly see the world beyond the veil, one must shed all luxuries of life, all love, all hope, and slowly wither in the quiet spaces of solitude.

Only then will he become a true brother of the Order and an acolyte of the Ungod.

After nearly a year of seeking the means to calm the raging storm within his soul, Aleister of the Dullingtons has mustered the courage to forsake his vows and regain his identity. He has come to terms with his foolishness, realizing in those moments of silent meditation that there is no greater meaning to life than that of love.

He's clung to thoughts of his wife and son to keep him going all this time, suffering a different sort of torture in his soul for thinking his departure was a wise decision. Now he is set to rectify his mistake. He never should have left them. He was selfish to do so, but now he would cross the channel to the mainland, collapse at their feet, and beg their forgiveness.

Where are you going, little sparrow?

A voice booms overhead like a crash of thunder. Aleister turns skyward, bracing himself against the smack of harsh winds and sea spray, and a sharp chill cleaves through his core as he spies a face among the clouds. The visage lasts for only a moment, but it is long enough for him to glimpse the features of his master.

Panicking, Aleister clenches his teeth and rows faster against the waves.

This can't be, he tells himself. *Master Vile is across the metachasm somewhere in the Monochrome, communing with the Great Weaver—*

Lightning splits the sky overhead, painting the world in bright white, and the mainland along the horizon fades into a blur. Aleister rows as fast as his arms allow, forging ahead against the current until his muscles are on fire.

You are mine, little sparrow. Your old life is beyond you now. Those were your vows to me. To the Ungod.

"That name is not for you," he grunts, pulling the oars through the waves. An inferno burns in his chest, set alight by the fire in his soul and the ache in his heart. Sparrow. The pet name his wife Agnes gave him during their courtship. Hearing it spoken by his adversary fuels the rage inside him. He cries out as he pulls against the current.

Aleister hears her voice in his head, crying for her sparrow to return, to not abandon them for a foolish crusade. *You have all you will ever need here with us,* Agnes sobbed. *What is it that you are so lacking? What peace would you seek? Please, my sparrow, help me understand.*

"A peace not given," he says now between gasps. "A peace that must be found. A peace...that I'm lacking."

A peace that does not exist. You are a foolish man, Aleister Dullington, and you have learned nothing in your time with us. All must be forsaken if you are to honor the vows of the Order. If you would not cease your escape, then allow me to clip your wings.

Another flash of lightning cracks the sky overhead, and the winds begin to slow. The spray of brine upon his face ceases, and the sea's endless resistance falters against his efforts. The world shifts and blurs around him, and within moments his boat shudders to a halt. He looks back over his shoulder and feels his insides drop away.

Gone is the mainland, the churning waters, the clouds upon the horizon. In their place is a great swirling tempest of sand and light, a wall of dead dreams culled from the Ungod's eternal slumber. The boat is lodged firmly in gray sands, and there is no sign of the churning sea, the waves driven away by the whim of something greater. Something ancient, neither living nor dead, the power of something that should not be channeled into an unseen entity—and controlled by the man he once called master.

"Feeble sparrow. You have forgotten your lessons. I draw the boundaries and bend them to my whim."

A lone figure emerges from beyond the wall of swirling sands. He is draped in gray robes customary of the Order, his cowl pulled down to hide the scars over his face. Pontius Vile stands tall amid the emptiness, his presence like a once-noble statue now left to crumble and rot. He lowers his cowl and reveals a smiling rictus which forces a chill down Aleister's spine.

Old scars from the conquest of Britannia line the man's face. They are visible reminders that he has known the kiss of a blade and witnessed the horrors of man. His eyes are gray, focused, and when they fall upon Aleister, the young man withers beneath his master's gaze.

"You have forgotten your vows, brother Aleister. The laws of the Order demand punishment for your breach."

Aleister closes his eyes. He knows he is caught, and there is no escaping this monster. His hopes of seeing Agnes and Thomas once again crumble to dust.

"I…" he begins, but what is there to say? Master Vile knows what lies in his heart and mind, has been blessed with the gray sight by the Ungod. There is nothing which Aleister can hide. Instead, the young man blinks away errant tears and faces his captor. "I underestimated you, Master."

"Indeed you did, little sparrow, as did I. Most of your brothers lost their will to escape *in primo anno.* But not you. No, you cling to love more than your duty. It is the root of your stubbornness to submit. A lingering hope that your old life awaits you, that your wife and son still hold love for you in their hearts." Vile approaches, stands before his scolded subject, and smiles. He takes Aleister's chin in his hand. "Leave it to me to cure your malady, little sparrow. I am well adept at crushing hope."

Two figures emerge from beyond the wall of the storm. Tall, robed, they walk erratically on unsteady legs. Aleister does not recognize them, nor can he recall ever seeing fellow monks of such height. When they grow nearer, his stomach lurches at sight of them. No, why would he recognize them? They aren't human at all—nor are they the familiar monstrosities lurking here among the gray wastes.

Their skin is alabaster, their faces devoid of eyes or noses. Mouths are their only human quality, careless rips in the empty canvas of their faces, both peeled back to reveal darkened gums lined with jagged fangs.

Pontius Vile notes Aleister's horror and turns to greet the faceless figures as they approach. "The Great Weaver honors me with the will to create. Man and beast together as one. My perfect servants."

"They're abominations."

"Indeed, little sparrow, that they are—but they are also obedient. In that respect, they are your superiors."

"The Order—"

"I *am* the Order, insect. I am its laws made flesh, its judge and its executioner. And you have crossed me for the last time." He nods to his servants. "Take him to the Needle."

"No matter your punishment, Master Vile, I will not be defeated so easily."

"Too true, my little sparrow. Yours is a spirit not so easily crushed, but I have my ways of striking at the heart of matters." Vile flashes a grim smile before pulling the hood over his face. "If you want to see your wife and child again, far be it from me to stop you, Aleister Dullington. Come. Let us go see them together."

———————•———————

Aleister turned away from the grounded rowboat and faced the unending tempest along the horizon. Long ago, before his transformation, he would've felt the pangs of guilt and regret, the profound emptiness of loss. But no longer. His emotions were stolen from him like his wife and child, lost to time, cast across the vast Monochrome desert with so many other grains of dust.

That his adversary chose a puppet by the name of Sparrow was no surprise. In hindsight, Aleister supposed he should have expected such a slight. Vile could've chosen anyone to serve as his manikin and set off this catastrophic chain of events. Selecting a man like Albert Sparrow to bear his influence spoke volumes of Pontius Vile's putrid nature.

Little sparrow, come closer. Witness the misery of your loves once more. They are here with us, waiting to display your failures yet again.

Vile's snide mockery carried on the wind. Aleister clenched his jaw, readying himself for the trek through the tempest and the nightmares it would reveal to him. He'd made this journey several times since his attempted escape all those years ago. Each time he witnessed the fate of his wife and son in crystal clarity, culled from the only dreams he had left to bear, phantasmagoric reminders of the price he'd paid in search of greater purpose, peace.

"Your sparrow is coming, Agnes. I beg you do not hate me."

Aleister pulled the cowl over his head, turned away from the storm, and knelt beside the old boat. Somewhere beyond the demarcations, Donovan

Candle made his way toward this juncture. Aleister would wait for him here to serve as his guide. Unaccompanied, the poor man might lose his mind in the hurricane of nightmares ahead.

You have served me well, Mr. Candle. I will do what I can to return the favor, even if it is not the outcome you so desire.

Aleister of the Dullingtons crossed his legs into a lotus position and stared forward into the gray haze, waiting for his companion to cross the demarcations. *Alone,* he thought. *Some journeys we must always make alone.*

-4-
PILGRIMAGE

A lifeless haze swam before him when he opened his eyes. Donovan stared up at the grim expanse of emptiness for a few moments as the rest of his body woke up, and a faint lattice of lines slowly drifted into focus. They crisscrossed and stretched for as far as he could see, an orderly webbing covering the world.

As he watched, a tremor ripped through the earth beneath him, and thin hairline cracks splintered across the sky like black lightning. They intersected the skyward lattice, interrupting each line's path, creating chaos among the uniform pattern. The cracks widened in place, revealing a black void beyond. From somewhere above, a howling wind swept over the dead city, ushering a chill across his skin.

First the quakes, and now the cracks. What the hell did Sparrow do?

Donovan tried to move and gasped. A throbbing ache took up residence in his skull, and his gut churned when he tried to move, but the worst was the taste in his mouth. Pulpy, thick, bland—the taste of chewed paper, with a hint of sour bile lingering in the back of his throat.

He sat up, spat a wad of gray phlegm on the ground, and tried to collect himself. Something had happened. The man with gray eyes had forced himself across the boundary and into the Spectrum. But was he a man? No, he was something else. Something Donovan hadn't seen before.

Should've known something was off. The gray eyes, a dead giveaway. So stupid. Need to stay focused, stay sharp. Need to keep moving. Another quake ripped through the world, and the city's structures groaned in agony. *This whole city's going to fall down.* He shook his head and forced himself to his feet. As he did, two unsettling thoughts occurred to him: If these tremors and quakes were getting worse here, what was happening in the Spectrum? And who—or what—the hell had he just unwittingly sent back?

Troubled, Donovan tucked those questions away as he exited the alley and continued his journey out of the city. According to Dullington, he would find something called the demarcation lines beyond the city's boundaries. *You will know them when you see them, Mr. Candle.*

"Cryptic bastard," Donovan muttered, shoving his hands into his pockets as he trudged onward through the city streets. Overhead, thin cracks followed an erratic course toward the horizon.

————— · —————

"**I** thought you said this thing was half a mile up ahead? We've been walking for almost an hour."

Quinn smiled, fought the urge to laugh at his uncle's whining. Instead he looked back and saw Michael's haggard face cast in the pale glow of safety lights lining the tunnel corridor. Heavy stubble, circles beneath his eyes, a thin rim of crusted blood around his nostrils—Quinn couldn't remember the last time he'd seen Michael look so rough.

"It's been a while," Alice said. "Quit whining and keep walking."

Michael grunted in disagreement but said nothing more. Quinn shook his head, peered forward into the dark.

Time down here lost most of its meaning. There was only above and below, and all the shifting shadows in between. They had indeed crossed the barricade nearly an hour ago, following a breadcrumb trail of fluorescent tube lighting on one side of the decommissioned tunnel, pale fingers pointing the way toward some unseen goal. Only Alice knew where they were headed, and she kept her mouth shut, remained focused on the destination ahead.

Quinn hadn't spent as much time in the Monochrome as Alice had, but what he'd experienced was enough to know how time faded without the guidance of the sun or moon. After Donovan's capture, Quinn lost all hope of escape, and all sense of time slipped away from him.

And now I'm back down here again, listening to these two bicker like a married couple...

He stopped in his tracks, nearly tumbled forward when Michael bumped into him. A sudden ache shot through his forehead, filling his mind with a flash of blinding light, and he cried out in pain, pinched the bridge of his nose.

"Q? What's wrong?"

Alice was a thousand miles away, her words muffled and distorted as though held underwater. A cacophony of words occupied his mind, different voices merging and dissolving, forming whole sentences out of the ether. Two voices, Michael's and...Alice's? They were younger—*he* was younger—and they were talking, bickering over something stupid, something like dinner, maybe.

"Quinn?"

Michael this time, and closer by the sound of him. Quinn felt his uncle's hand on his shoulder. "Just...give me a minute. Headache out of nowhere."

But it was more than a headache. It was a wave of memories crashing upon the shores of his mind, occupying the nooks and crannies of where they used to be, places that had since grown over and filled in with the sediment of other times, places, people. So many memories that had once been lost were washing up in the tide, and in them he saw Michael and Alice, younger and smiling and happy, saw them embracing, kissing. He saw them at a birthday party—*his* birthday party—when he was younger, barely in high school. Donna and Donovan were there, too, younger, happier—

"Jesus, his nose is bleeding now." Alice pressed a napkin to Quinn's face. "Tilt your head back."

"That doesn't work," Michael said. "Pinch his nostrils—"

"I'm sorry, I didn't realize you were a fucking nurse."

"Who the hell do you think you are, talking to me like that? Who—"

Quinn pushed away from them, wiped the blood from his nose, and blinked away tears. The blinding light slowly abated, giving way to the gloom of the old subway tunnel. Michael and Alice stood before him like worried parents, their bickering forgotten in favor of his health. He looked at them both and shook his head, smiled.

"She's your fiancée."

Michael's face glowed red even in the poor lighting. He opened his mouth to speak, managed nothing more than a short laugh of uncertainty.

"That's...I mean..." He turned to Alice, but she'd moved on, heading further down the tunnel.

"Come on," she said. "We're almost there. We can..." She paused, looked back at Michael. Her eyes glistened in the light. "We can talk about this later."

Quinn watched Michael follow her, weighing the outcome of their exchange, wondering if he should've kept his damn mouth shut. *If that's a memory, what else have I forgotten?*

He waited a couple of minutes, lost inside his own thoughts, before lighting out toward them.

———•———

S omething had changed, and it wasn't just the sky. Donovan had been walking for what might've been an hour, maybe more, and the city outline stretching before him never changed. Buildings large and small jutted from the rudimentary streets like the bones of a long-dead giant, eroded over time, and destined to fade into dust. The buildings grew shorter but never ceased, the streets continuing their unbroken parallel pathways without convergence or curvature, and the faint column on the horizon remained constant.

There were few things of which Donovan prided himself more than his sense of direction. He couldn't remember street names to save his life, but after traveling to a destination once, he would likely find his way back with ease. When they were younger, and before smartphones and GPS functionality were commonplace, Donovan's sense of direction had often saved his and Donna's many road trips out of state. Those trips, whether to visit college friends or to get away for a long weekend after class, were always something he looked back on fondly. They were adventures, just his and Donna's alone, the two of them against the universe.

He thought of those drives, traveling into the unknown until nightfall, stopping at a shady motel for the night, drinking beer and eating pizza, making love until they inevitably passed out, only to rise and repeat it all the next day. Those were days in their twenties when getting lost seemed like the greatest thing in the world.

Because he never truly felt lost. Not with Donna at his side. Those were happier times, when the world still made sense. His sense of direction hadn't failed him before, not even here in the Monochrome, but now he was beginning to doubt himself.

Keep it together, hoss. You got out of the city once; ain't no reason you can't do it again.

Donovan thought of that walk through liminal space, naked and vulnerable, racing to get back to Donna before Sparrow's servant could murder her. He'd had no trouble finding his way then, and that had been no more than a couple of days ago.

Now something had changed. He thought about the strange man he'd encountered before, thought about Dullington's weird way of being wherever he wanted to be at any given time.

"Dullington, goddamn you." He spun in place, looking for a difference in his surroundings. Even the street behind looked the same. He might as well have been walking in place for the last hour. "Now I know how the mouse feels in the maze."

Frustrated, Donovan sat down in the middle of the street and tried to calm himself. *Something doesn't want me to get out of this city. Paranoid, maybe, but given everything else I've seen here, I wouldn't be surprised.* "Follow the demarcation lines," Dullington said, *whatever the hell that's supposed to mean. Another damn riddle.*

He thought back to that night he saved Donna from the bearded man. He'd willed himself through a closed barrier, much like he'd willed himself into liminal space without thinking about it. Like he'd forced himself back into the Spectrum to stop Donna's would-be murderer.

What sort of magic had he conjured then? Nothing literal, of course. This sort of magic was internal, not far removed from all the lies spun by New Age infomercials on late-night television. *Believe in yourself, Donovan Candle. Believe you can do it and you will!*

"Bullshit…"

Cynicism don't suit you, hoss. It all sounds like bullshit when you get right down to it, but right now it's all you got. Best keep that in mind.

He sighed. Joe Hopper's ageless southern wisdom crept out from the shadows once more to speak a truth Donovan already knew. Here the metaphysical crossed paths with the physical, and something as simple as a desire to better oneself was enough to transcend states of reality. Here the will to act was paramount, and Donovan was no stranger to the concept.

"You're thinking realistically again, Don." He climbed to his feet, staring at the column on the horizon. His voice rang hollow across the empty street. "So…there's a demarcation line somewhere ahead. I don't know what it looks like, and that doesn't matter much anyway. All that matters is that I need to cross it. I will cross it." He closed his eyes, walked forward. "I will cross it, because I choose to. Because I have to. Because…"

I will.

I am.

I do.

He pictured Donna in his head as he took another blind step forward.

I would for you, Donna. I will for you. I am for you. I do—

The air surged around him, the Monochrome world uttering a gasp as a massive weight was released by his crossing. Donovan opened his eyes, startled to find he was no longer standing on the city street, but on the edge of a vast gray desert. A large group of figures marched across the sands ahead of him.

He turned back, found the city's outskirts were half a mile away in the distance and far less defined. Buildings were rendered as fading skeletal lines, the smooth featureless walls now absent, a shivering silent film of childlike drawings. A wall of air shimmered before him like heat rising from the asphalt. He held out his hand, felt a slight tickle on his fingertips like a loss of circulation. *Demarcation lines,* he thought, watching as other Missing emerged beyond the boundary.

Men and women, young and old, some with faces covered in open sores and a scattering of gray pox, wandered forward into the desert with forlorn expressions. *Lost in mind and soul,* he thought, watching as they brushed past him. Some of them still wore the *Fading Out* logo pins on their tattered clothes, marking them as remnants of Sparrow's army.

An older woman with a hood pulled over her ashen face caught his eye. He called out to her, asked her to hang on a minute.

"I need to get moving, mister."

"Me too, but tell me, where are you going?"

She lifted an emaciated hand and pointed toward the column in the distance. Dark, roiling clouds obscured the structure's base. "Only place we got left to go. It's calling us home."

"What is?"

But she was already moving along, her footprints fading in the sand. Donovan shoved his hands into his pockets and followed the other pilgrims across the gray sands.

"Here it is."

Alice hoisted herself up the decommissioned platform, dusted off her hands, and offered one to Quinn. Michael followed them, grunting as he pulled himself onto the cracked tile, and paused in wonder at the décor of the old station.

The tunnel opened into a series of ornate archways, each decorated in a mosaic of colored tiles. Cobweb-covered chandeliers hung between each arch, their old bulbs still giving off dim light, painting the station in the gloom of nostalgia. Their shadows stretched along the far walls like giants.

Alice smiled as she took in their surroundings, relishing the old décor, silently yearning for a return to this artistic form far removed from today's soulless, bottom-dollar design. She used to come here in her early days of imprisonment, sometimes skipping her daily meal in favor of basking in the dim light and color. Topside, the city was a lifeless grid of concrete and advertisements and exhaust fumes; down here, she felt at home among the coloration, no matter how chipped or faded, with graffiti to brighten the cavernous room. Especially the graffiti.

She wasn't sure how long the other Missing had been coming here to leave their messages. Surely old Dullington had known about it, although she doubted he cared about such trivial things. *Let the prisoners have their little hopes,* she supposed. *Let them have their own Wailing Wall.*

But this was less a place of pilgrimage and more a rudimentary message board. Street addresses for places to find easy meals or clothing, the names of kind souls and the like, and more importantly, the names of others not trapped in the Monochrome. The names of loved ones left behind, writ in layers of paint along the far wall. A list of names decades old stretched from one end of the station to the other. There was power here, power in the names of those to be remembered and those to be found, they who might be contacted and asked to recall the ones they've lost. Most of the Missing came here at least once in their tenure, others much more often, and if there were any left who might be tethered to the 'chrome, she hoped she would find them here.

Quinn broke the silence. "What is this place?"

"Old station that was closed seventy or eighty years ago. See the curve in the track? Modern trains can't take those turns. Too narrow."

"So they just sealed this off?"

Alice nodded. "Shame, isn't it? It's beautiful."

"It is," Michael said, "but what are we doing here, Alice?"

She walked to the foot of the terminal stairway where a neon green milkcrate sat filled with cans of spray paint. "We're here to leave a message."

"A message?"

"Uh huh. On the Memory Wall." She plucked a can of white paint from the crate and shook it. The noise of the rattling ball bearing within echoed across the station like the marching of metal feet. "People used to come here when I was trapped in the 'chrome. To leave messages for loved ones, mostly. Hope goes a long way down here."

She went to work with the paint, crafting one letter after another with enough patience to ensure they were legible. Some spots were so thick they dribbled, but the message was still clear enough, with letters so large the entire message spanned the length of the terminal.

"What's Donna's phone number?"

Michael crossed his arms, half-smiling and half-confused by what she was painting. "For what? Why?"

"Just trust me, please."

Quinn nudged his uncle. "Come on, Mike."

"Ugh, fine." He fished his phone from his pocket and read off the number from his contacts. "Happy now?"

She winked at him and went back to work. When she was finished, Alice returned the can to its crate and wiped white paint on her jeans. She surveyed her work:

Quinn frowned. "Who's this message for, Alice?"

"Anyone," she said. "Donovan's name is well-known in the Monochrome. Anyone who comes here, well, maybe they've seen him. Maybe they know someone who has." She shrugged. "It's our best shot at reaching anyone with ties to this place. Besides, if the worst happens and he flickers out forever, maybe this will help someone remember. We have to hope there's a way to break that cycle."

Michael rolled his eyes and turned away. Alice followed. "Where are you going?"

"Back to the surface. Back to my car. Back to the real fucking world, Alice."

"Look, I know this sounds crazy, but—"

He spun on his heel, finger in the air, a drop of venom on his tongue. "But nothing. We've wasted half the goddamn day chasing dead ends.

Donovan isn't down here and leaving Donna's phone number on a wall so every crazy hobo can call her isn't a solution."

Alice scoffed, gestured to the emptiness beyond the boarding platform. "This is better than waiting for him to magically appear. Better than staking out a dozen stations."

"At least a stakeout is something productive. It's something that—"

Quinn cleared his throat. "Guys…"

"Makes sense? God, you haven't changed in all these years. If something doesn't make sense to you, it must be a lost cause or a waste of time." Alice saluted in mockery. "Just the facts, ma'am—unless those facts go against your accepted paradigm. No wonder you and Donovan never got along. Fuck, I'm starting to wonder…"

Why I was gonna marry you, she wanted to say, but found the words stuck in her throat. A sudden heat flushed her cheeks as she realized what she was about to say. She'd given up on ever seeing him again, made peace with that fact years ago, but when he'd appeared two years ago on the heels of his brother down here in the dark, a light of hope was rekindled in her heart.

Staring at him now, Alice realized she needn't wonder at all. She still loved him, even if he was a stubborn bastard. Even if he never again remembered what they'd meant to one another. Somewhere across the terminal, she'd once scratched their initials into one of the tiles. It was probably coated in layers of paint now, buried beneath the hopes and dreams of others just as desperate as she'd been. But it was still there, somewhere, etched into the old stones like his name in her heart.

"Well? Go on, Mystery Woman, tell me. I'm waiting."

God, she hated when he did that. His snark pushed every button she had, but now, after so long, she couldn't bring herself to stay angry.

She realized she was crying, wiped her eyes, and looked away. Quinn caught her eye. "What is it, Q?"

"Do you guys hear that?"

Alice didn't. Not at first. She was too caught up in her argument to notice anything but the aching rage in her heart. And when she finally did hear the sound, she tried to rationalize it away as something else. Something which made sense down here. The howling wind from a subway car, maybe, but that didn't make sense because they were too far from the working rails. Maybe it was someone crying out from down the tunnel.

Maybe—

Michael tilted his head to one side, listening. "Sounds like someone moaning."

"No, it's not that at all." Alice's words were thick in her throat, drunk from the anger and sadness. But her mind was still sober, still sharp, and the words she could not bring herself to voice raced a marathon in her head. *This can't be. Not here. Not now. Not possible. Not possible. Not possible—*

A thin pale figure walked clumsily into the dim light from around the tunnel bend. Spindly legs

(oh God there's too many legs)

carried an awkward torso that bubbled and churned erratically, sprouting appendages, sprouting more legs to support the creature.

Because it *was* a creature, something Alice hadn't seen before. Something caught in the divide between Monochrome and Spectrum, not quite small enough to be a Cretin or large enough to be the Yawning. This was something in between, its existence an infection upon this reality, and even the creature seemed to share such sentiment. It peered around the dim station, confused and angered by its presence here, offended by the bright coloration of the Memory Wall's various messages.

The impossible thing chittered in a clipped language that was no longer reversed, and the sound drove a spike of ice through Alice's gut. God, she *understood* parts of its speech, fragments of names and simple commands

(do not see, do not remember, do not believe, do not seek, do not speak, do not hear, do not know)

repeating in a constant hum of noise punctuated with a painful moan echoing throughout the room.

"What the hell is that?" Michael raised his flashlight, trained the beam on the fidgeting creature. Alice made to stop him, to tell him to leave it be, but she was too late. The pale thing focused on the beam, winced from the light, and let loose a shrill cry which echoed back through the abandoned tunnels.

A chorus of shrieks and whines answered its call.

They watched in horror as the thing changed before them, mutating into something worse, something beyond impossible, something that *should not be.* Nodules on the creature's belly sprouted into more legs, accompanied with the crackling noise of snapping bones, and its head inflated to the size of a basketball. The bulbous appendage grew into a massive tumor that was little more than a pale fleshy mound filled with eyes and jagged teeth.

Alice slowly reached out, put her hand on Quinn's shoulder, and pulled him close. She looked at Michael, who watched in perplexed fascination as the pale thing changed before their eyes, and said in a hushed voice, "We need to move. Now."

The creature skittered on its legs—Alice had lost count after ten—across the dead rails and walked right up the tunnel wall. It stopped halfway up the damp brickwork to contemplate its next move, turned in place, and let loose a grating hiss when it saw them.

Alice snatched the flashlight from Michael's hand, pushed him toward the platform's edge. *"RUN!"*

He almost didn't listen to her. The odd creature's mournful voice fascinated him in a way he didn't understand, and in the moments before Alice pushed him, Michael felt himself lured forward. *Do not listen,* its buzzing words echoed in his head, *do not remember, do not believe…*

A voice so familiar somehow, and he'd wanted to press forward, sit down on the tracks, listen to the strange thing sing its siren song—but now Alice was screaming in his face, urging him to run, run for his goddamn life, and his legs were pumping him forward.

Is this happening right now?

Michael's head swam, trapped in a fog he couldn't outrun, and as they raced down the narrow tunnel, he began to laugh. *Am I stoned?* Everything felt lighter, the pull of gravity loosened somehow, and the world around him had grown fuzzy, visually dissonant, like two overlapping images slightly askew.

A shrill hiss echoed down the tunnel from somewhere behind them. Quinn shouted something but Michael couldn't hear the boy over his own laughter. There were hands at his back, pushing him forward, and in his limp state he could do no more than follow the shaking beam of light dancing ahead.

"You keep your shit together, Michael Candle, you hear me?" Alice's voice growled in his ear. Sweet Alice, he loved her more when she was angry. "Do not fucking fall apart on me now. I need you."

I need you too, he wanted to tell her, even if the thought, the words, felt so foreign and familiar. They were words he'd spoken to her before even if he couldn't remember when, their sound and weight full of a power he wasn't yet prepared to voice.

The odd fuzziness surrounding his vision began to clear, the static hum in his head dissipating and giving way to the noise of scuttling legs not far behind.

Michael began to look back and Alice stopped him. "Don't," she hissed. "Try not to listen. Just keep going."

Silent, Michael did so, resisting the urge to turn and gaze upon the monstrosities in pursuit. Because there was more than one now, more than the multi-legged thing from just a few minutes ago—the singular hiss had blossomed into a growing chorus of dissonant chatter, a pattering of tiny legs swelling into a rampant drumline. He imagined a hive of those spider things, creamy white as the moon, blind from living down here in the dark, disturbed and hungry and so pissed off.

Quinn yelped as he stumbled forward, scattering dust and stones across the old rails, and Michael knelt to lift him up. He looked back in reflex, drawn to the fury of noise following them down the tunnel, and immediately wished he hadn't. Bone white, scrambling across every inch of the tunnel surface like giant maggots, the spidery things hissed and gargled and spat in violent anger, uttering guttural chirrs which might have once been words. Now they were mere ululations of rage broken into frothing syllables, choked with a hatred that had been building for eons and now loosed upon the world.

They moved erratically, gnashing teeth with a hundred mouths and flailing limbs as one being, swarming toward them in a raging river of pale white. Michael yanked Quinn to his feet, pushed the boy onward, and doubled his pace.

He lost track of how far they had to go before reaching the main subway line, laser-focused on every step and every breath and the flames licking the inside of his lungs. How long had it been since he'd subjected his body to such physical strain? Years, maybe. Two at least, not since he'd chased Donovan down into the dark—

Another memory bubbled up to the surface: A young woman standing among a crowd of transients, staring at him from across an abandoned platform with a sort of yearning which he didn't quite understand, which had made him uncomfortable in fact, and now he realized he knew that face, knew it intimately—

"Michael!"

Alice's cry ripped him from his reverie, forced the world into focus before him. The earth rumbled underfoot, a surge of wind blew back his hair, and he realized what was happening.

Train.

One word, enough to ignite a blaze in his aching muscles and quicken his pace. There was Alice on the other side of the track, at the mouth of an intersection near the active station. Quinn was just ahead. He darted over the tracks and toppled into her, shouting as they collided against the grimy tunnel wall.

The rumbling increased, accompanied now by a shrill whine of metal, a popping of sparks. And behind, the ravenous shrieks of something which shouldn't be.

Come on, old man. Pick up the pace.

Michael pushed himself, giving everything he had left to cross the gap between himself and the tunnel mouth. Each step became a labor of fire and will, as the rumbling underfoot grew more violent and the shrieking behind even louder.

Three strides now, maybe four.

Alice stared at him, wide-eyed, a stagnant breeze blowing back the hair from her shoulders and sweaty forehead. They shared something in the silent moments that followed, when time slowed and the world ceased its turn. It was just the two of them in that instant, he rushing toward her across some unseen boundary which wasn't meant to be crossed. But he'd cross it, one way or another, because she needed him to. *He* needed to.

Come on, Michael. Don't leave me again. Her voice in his head, carried across the expanse between them and communicated by a simple gaze, and yet he heard her clearly. His whole body felt the impact of that voice, but nowhere more so than in his heart.

The fire in his lungs faded, the agony of unused muscles forgotten, and with a final leap, Michael dove across the subway tracks just as the first car reared its head into the tunnel. He collided with the wall, the impact on his shoulder and back stealing his breath as a sharp pain shot through his body.

An instant later, the pale wave of ravenous things crashed into the side of the subway train. The shriek of metal filled his ears as the emergency brakes were engaged. The impact was too much, however, and the engineering car derailed at the interchange, sending sparks and clouds of dust washing over them.

Panicked, his veins filled with adrenaline, Michael pushed through the pain and threw himself over Alice and Quinn. He clenched his eyes shut and braced himself against the chaos erupting around them.

———— • ————

John Black felt a tremor beneath his feet as the infected Mr. Jones led him through a maze of back alleys into the heart of the city. He paused, surveying the narrow walls coated in old advertisements and chipped paint, watched as a line of metal trash cans rattled in the earthly vibration. Clancy Jones stopped long enough to lean over and vomit. Thick strings of gray phlegm erupted from his mouth and nose, splattered on the concrete. He heaved for some time, his body struggling to expel the viscous infection now filling his insides.

When he was finished, Clancy wiped his mouth and recoiled in horror at what he'd just coughed up from his lungs. A sickly gray puddle sat at his feet, and it was *moving.* Plump wormlike tendrils writhed in the viscous mess amid half-digested chunks of a previous meal. John Black watched with amusement as his new servant struggled to understand what was happening to him.

"Pieces of a whole, Mr. Jones. What you see is not a sickness but a part of you, and soon it will be all you are—a living failure, a reflection of your soul." John strolled on toward the street ahead. "Come, my servant. Let us spread the message."

They were nearing downtown now, where the streets teemed with life and traffic. At the edge of the alley, John closed his eyes and took in the sensations. The smell of exhaust, food, sweat, the salty stink of old sex from somewhere in the shadows—here the world had not changed in the centuries since he had walked its roads. Rome had fallen but been rebuilt a thousand times over, the great city evolved by technologies beyond comprehension, and yet its people were still base, repulsive things. *Maggots on the dying corpse of civilization.*

Here were sounds of anger, frustration, sickness, utter banality spoken for the sake of noise. Human cattle busying themselves with their daily business, ignorant of a greater purpose each neglected without realization, blind to the strings above, their path so obvious and yet unseen.

He saw the phantom threads lifting off each of their heads, stretching toward a yellowing sky of smog. Somewhere beyond, hidden from mortal eyes, was a loom of strings constantly woven and tied and severed, leading each hapless soul toward its inevitable end. To clutch one would be to see the path that soul might take; to clutch them all was to see the path of humanity.

And he had done so many times now. Their trail toward oblivion had not faltered in a millennium.

Here among their daily toils, the manikin calling himself John Black observed the ignorant and careless, the void of compassion and empathy, the sick and the callous. Humanity was a disgusting stain on the greater fabric of the universal tapestry. He would use their failures against them, force them to face the mediocrity inherent in their being, and wipe this necrotic reality from existence.

One step at a time, he mused, recalling the tremor a few moments before. The merging of Monochrome and Spectrum was at hand, his children already finding their way across the boundary, and soon he would unleash a hell of humanity's own making.

Smiling, John Black gestured for his servant to join him. Together, they vanished into the city's afternoon miasma.

-5-

DISSONANCE

The emergency room at St. Lucien's Hospital bustled with activity, every lobby seat filled with another suffering soul. Broken limbs, a few sniffling children, an old woman complaining of an unrelenting migraine—and at least ten people, by Donna's count, afflicted with sudden nosebleeds.

She sat near the entrance while Amanda returned the requisite paperwork, one hand on her bulging belly and the other rubbing at her temple. There, just below the thin patch of skin, was an invisible spike driving its way deeper into her skull.

An infant shrieked in displeasure from across the room, and the sudden noise drove the nail deeper into her head. The child in her womb delivered a swift kick in reply. Donna smiled despite the pain. *Can't win. Guess I'd better get used to this.*

Amanda returned, knelt next to her. All the other seats were occupied. "Lady at the front desk says it could be at least an hour, maybe more. Old bitch wouldn't let me get a word in edgewise."

"That's fine."

"No, Donna, it isn't. You need attention, like, right now. If you'd let me call for an ambulance like I wanted…"

Amanda shook her head, and Donna looked away, let her sister seethe in silence. She hadn't felt the need to explain her reasoning when they'd left her house an hour before, nor should she have to, but now she considered it just to keep Amanda quiet. *She's gonna judge anyway. Might as well give her a reason.*

But then Amanda's judgment would lead to other questions, other worries, more stress which Donna couldn't handle right now. That she was terrified of an unplanned medical expense should've gone without saying, especially given her husband's absence, but Donna still felt the pressure to spell it out, give it voice, make it real. *No, Amanda, I can't afford the ambulance, and I doubt the insurance will cover the ER visit, not over a silly nosebleed, but…*

Always a *but*. Always an extraneous reason which might—*might*—turn out to be serious, and with a child on the way, she couldn't afford to take her chances. *Damned if you do, damned if you don't, girl. Guess you need to suck it up, buttercup.*

At least her obstetrician, Dr. Warner, was based here. That knowledge comforted her, albeit briefly. Donna tried to place her mind elsewhere, focusing on the television mounted to opposite wall, but then she remembered how Donovan had unplugged their television the other night. *He was so worked up about that reality show, certain it was the cause of all the missing kids. Still can't wrap my mind around it. He was so certain, so determined, and then…*

Then he'd left her in the night, and that was the last she'd seen of him. He'd been missing for days, appeared out of thin air to rescue her from an intruder, only to vanish once more. She'd not given herself enough time to process all that had happened, not really, and had it not been for the resurgence of memories from her own abduction two years before, she might have discarded his actions as lunacy. But she couldn't do that now, because she remembered things she wasn't supposed to. Things that were blocked from her mind, painted over in blinding white light. She remembered both versions of events, times when Donovan was there and not there simultaneously, speaking about visions and creatures and then nothing, silence save a reverberating noise like a record spun backwards.

Her head throbbed. Amanda gasped, plucked a tissue from her purse, and thrust it into Donna's hand. "Your nose again."

Donna pinched her nostrils, pulled the tissue away, and frowned. Scarlet splotches blossomed across the tissue's surface.

"We interrupt this program for a special news report." A newscast interrupted a talk show on the television. Half the room looked up at the sound of the familiar sound of a news bulletin. Donna watched their reactions, thought them disturbingly Pavlovian, and closed her eyes to block out the piercing light streaming through the lobby windows.

"—regret to report that WBS president and CEO, John Beckman, was found dead in his home this morning—"

Donna looked up after all, struggling to process the newscaster's words. *Beckman. Husband and father. No foul play suspected. Suicide. Thoughts and prayers.*

"Jesus," Amanda whispered. "Poor bastard."

The talk show returned to the air, and Donna looked away, wondering once more about her husband. He'd left in the middle of the night to go to the WBS building. He was going to stop their planned broadcast. Had he met the late Mr. Beckman? Did Donovan have anything to do with the man's demise, or what happened at the plaza yesterday?

Stop it. You're going to drive yourself crazy thinking like this.

And she did stop. For a while, anyway. More people trickled into the emergency room, complaining of horrible headaches, and in a few cases, nosebleeds. Men, women, some children—there was no discrimination for the afflicted, and as the afternoon wore on, Donna began to wonder about yesterday's events.

Two hours had passed by the time she was called back to see a doctor. On her way to the exam room, she overheard an elderly woman explaining to her husband that they had a child, a son named Charlie, and he'd disappeared twenty years ago. The husband lifted his head of white hair and looked about the room seeking answers. Briefly, Donna met his gaze, and then she looked away, turned the corner, and followed the triage nurse.

Me too, she thought, picturing his confused eyes wrapped in tears. *Me too.*

———•———

In his centuries on this planet, in this reality and the next, the one calling himself John Black had grown to believe in a cosmic synchronicity of events. The strings above were constantly threading, entwining, knotting themselves together as souls became entangled, often at his whim for pure amusement or to serve another purpose; however, there were times when the strings wove themselves together so perfectly that he could not help but acknowledge the beauty of cosmic providence.

His selection of a manikin known as Sparrow, for example, was one such instance of entanglement. That he would find a suitable subject with which to manipulate and create dissonance between realities was a given; but to find one who would serve as a living mockery of his adversary's weakness, well, that was the universe aligning in his favor. Some strings tied themselves.

John Black contemplated this seldom-witnessed truth as he traveled along the sidewalks of mankind. Men and women parted a path for him, unsure why they felt the need to avoid this odd pale-faced man but cognizant of his wrongness just the same. He relished their aversion, their inherent fear of his nature.

To think he had once been one of them, the servant to an empire by another name, banished to a far-flung land for the sake of territory and expansion, the sake of one leader's pride above the needs of his people. And the atrocities he had witnessed in his time! Mankind disgusted him. Barbaric, parasitic things, battling one another over pieces of dirt, shitting and fucking themselves into oblivion like so much cattle—and this was before the Ungod had opened his eyes, showed him humanity's destination at the end of the strings.

He'd stolen a glance at forbidden knowledge, witnessing the destination of all those threads, a sight not meant for human eyes. Seeing what could not be unseen changed him, changed his nature. Mankind wasn't meant to see such truths, and so he became something more than man. Something else.

Something godlike.

And now, just as before, he found himself repulsed by the nature of mankind. They gathered and swarmed along the streets of iniquity, pledging their lives to named nonentities for the sake of riches, selling their time to the highest bidder, selling their souls, hopes, dreams.

Soon, they would drown in a sea of filth, beneath waves of their own making.

Clancy followed like a submissive dog, fearful of John's intentions, of the things festering inside him. John felt that fear prickling at the tips of his fingers, heard the mental anguish coursing through his subject's mind like weakened shouts on the wind, and he relished the sensation. *There will be so much more to come,* he thought, *once the failures of this cursed landscape are set free. One soul at—*

Screeching tires and squealing brakes ripped him from his reverie. He turned, stared at the silver hood and flashing lights of a police cruiser inches away. In his reverie he had crossed the street into traffic. Cars beyond the cruiser honked erratically, signaling their annoyance.

"Mr. Black," Clancy whispered, too afraid to raise his voice, "you're in the crosswalk and the light's green."

"Christ, I could've killed you!" A cleanshaven man in shades and a blue patrol uniform climbed out of the cruiser, leaned on the open door. His flushed face screwed up into a concerned frown. "You walked right into traffic!"

"Tell him you're sorry," Clancy whispered, "that you weren't paying attention."

"Be quiet, insect." John Black walked toward the officer. "I did, but I don't..." He searched the man's face, dove into his mind as one might dip their hand into a flowing river in search of pebbles. He found one easily enough, right on the surface without having to dig too deep. A tiny white pearl of irritation snuggled between tattered folds of esteem and pride. "...I don't stop for fascist pigs, Mr. Redford."

Officer Redford blinked, looked at Clancy incredulously as if to say *Did you hear this?* His face flushed a deep dark red like a bruised plum as he straightened and slammed the door. The car behind him honked again, but Redford shot a look at the driver with such disdain the poor man behind the wheel shriveled in his seat.

Redford approached the sickly man, sucked in his breath, and measured his words. "What did you just say to me, sir?"

"I called you a fascist pig." Mr. Black smiled, leaned forward, and spat a wad of writhing phlegm on the officer's shoe. "I spit on pigs. Pigs like you, Mr. Justin Redford."

Clancy shuffled forward, clutching his gut, his forehead spotted with sweat. "Mister, he don't know what he's sayin', he—" The poor man trembled, and he doubled over in pain, vomiting a softball-sized wad of wriggling white things. It splattered on the pavement, and a few of the pedestrians behind them gasped.

Officer Justin Redford frowned in disgust, took a step back. "Your friend..." He kicked one of the pale maggots away from his shoe. "He looks like he needs a doctor."

"He is allergic to swine."

"Okay, enough, there's no reason—"

"You are a pig. Your father was a pig. And his father before him. A family of fascist swine, all of you." Mr. Black took a step forward, and the officer's hand went to his holster in reflex.

"Gonna ask you to take a step back, sir. Or else—"

"Or else you will arrest me, pig?"

Before Officer Redford could respond, John Black smacked him across his face. There was a moment when time ceased, the air sucked out of every onlooker watching from a distance, a salient instant before an inevitable explosion when everyone knew what came next.

In the next moment, time sped up as the officer readied his reply. He took Mr. Black's arm, twisted it behind his back, and subdued the pale man over the front of the cruiser. He was halfway through reciting the Miranda warning when John twisted his head in Clancy's direction and smiled.

"Attack him, insect."

Clancy trembled, shook his head in protest, but his limbs would not obey. The older man watched helplessly as his body acted on its own, pulled by strings he could not see but certainly felt with every twinge of muscle, every flare of nerves. Each time Clancy resisted the pull he was met with a searing pain across his skin, his tendons, deep in the recesses of his skull.

"N-No, Mr. Black—"

John laughed as his puppet struck the officer on the back of the head with a loud slap. The audience of pedestrians and drivers erupted in a singular gasp of shock.

Minutes later, as they sat cuffed in the backseat of the cruiser, Clancy turned to him. "Why did you make me do that, Mr. Black? I ain't done nothin' to you."

"Because I have use of you, and this will get us there faster. Now be silent or else I will make you gouge out your own eyes."

Clancy trembled, opened his mouth to speak in reply, but thought better of it. He turned away, pressed his forehead against the window, and snorted back tears.

Officer Redford climbed back into the cruiser, called in the arrest, and shot Mr. Black a glare in the rearview. "Call me a pig all you want, sir, but I'm not gonna let you badmouth my daddy."

John Black smiled grimly. Their intersection of paths was not planned—least of all by he—and yet here they were, suddenly entwined and traveling toward the same destination. That the Great Weaver would see fit to thread their strings was yet another sign of good fortune. They needed quick travel toward the 12th Precinct, near the center of the city, and so the Weaver had delivered unto them a chariot of easy provocation: a man of short temper, low esteem, and heightened sense of pride, one so easily manipulated by a simple selection of words.

Mr. Black leaned toward the window, looked up to the sky at the cascading array of strings above, and the faint hairline cracks beginning to show behind the clouds. *Sweet synchronicity,* he thought.

———————•———————

"**G**rab my hand."

Wincing, Quinn took his uncle's hand and helped to pull himself over the side of the toppled subway car. A low vibration rippled through the metal surface, and when he joined Michael and Alice, he thought he heard muffled cries for help coming from inside the car.

Flickering lights from the windows gave the tunnel a pale strobing effect, and in the brief moments of illumination, he saw the damage wrought by the swarm. The subway train lay mostly on its side, filling out the tunnel like a dead snake, and faded into a cloud of dust and smoke. The erratic lights formed phantom columns in the dust, punctuated with the tumult of frightened voices echoing within each car. He heard the slapping and pawing of innocent hands clamoring for a way out of their tomb, and when Quinn realized the nature of what he heard, he wished he hadn't been so insistent on joining Michael and Alice in their search.

They're trapped inside. Oh God, we have to…

He looked away, and Alice read his face easily enough in the gloom. "We'll call for help as soon as—" She looked in the direction of the transit authority terminal. The last subway car lay on its side across the tracks, blocking their exit to the station. Fluorescent light seeped between the cracks, painting the tunnel mouth in a melancholy hue. Alice looked back, studied his face. "As soon as we get out of here. But we're not going that way."

"No shit," Michael grunted, wincing as he clamped a shaky hand over a bloody gash in his elbow. His shirt sleeve was ripped halfway down, exposing an atlas of fresh scratches and scrapes, and the injured limb hung loose at his side like a piece of taffy. Quinn watched his uncle, saw the look in his eyes, and wondered if the mutated Cretins, the crash, all this chaos had done something to the poor man's mind. There was a distance in Michael's eyes, two vacant mirrors obscuring his struggle to process all that he'd seen, all that had happened in the last half hour. Blood seeped between his fingers.

"Jesus, Mike, are you okay?" Quinn made to reach for his uncle's arm, but Michael shied away.

"I'll be fine."

Alice shook her head, rolled her eyes. "Such macho bullshit. You're bleeding. Here." She yanked a hanging piece of fabric from his torn sleeve and slapped his hand away. Michael scoffed, tried to turn away from her, but Alice would have none of it. "You always were stubborn, Michael Candle."

Quinn snorted in amusement. "Just like a married couple."

Michael ignored his remark, pulling away from Alice and rubbing at his makeshift bandage. "Anyway, how far's the next station? The next working station, I mean. And do you mind telling me what the fuck those things were?"

"Cretins," Quinn said. The word surprised him, its sound unnatural here on the right side of reality, like giving voice to a bad dream. He walked along the side of the train car, away from his companions, following a scuttling noise emanating from the dark. "At least they *were* Cretins. Don't know what they are now, but..." He stole glances at the windows and squinted at the interior lights flickering erratically, filling the cavernous dark with strobing beams. "I've seen them change before."

He tilted his head, listening to the urgent scrambling happening below them, ahead of them, the whole tunnel seemingly alive with movement.

"But not like that," Alice said. She joined him, put her hand on his shoulder, and whispered, "I hear it too."

"I'm the odd man out then. It—they—whatever the hell they were, their words did something to me. To my head."

"That's what they do," Quinn said, barely above a whisper. Shapes, nearly indiscernible from the shadows that birthed them, flickered in and out of the light as the subway car trembled violently beneath them. Shrill screams ripped through the darkness, and something slammed against the nearby window, fracturing the glass in a spiderweb of cracks.

Time slowed as panic took hold. Quinn's breath clung to his throat. He glimpsed the thing inside the subway car. A fraction of a second caught in the flickering pallor of failing lights revealed all he would ever care to see, a shape which might haunt him for the rest of his days if he could only escape this place—but his mind rooted him there, frozen, unable to correlate what he saw.

A man wrenched at something clinging to his face—a membranous white thing, slippery with blood from an open gash in his forehead, squirming and dripping like pale oil.

In that moment before the light died once again, Quinn thought of an old B-horror film he'd watched on late night TV as a teenager. *It's the Blob,* he thought, *or something close. Something*— He remembered the onslaught of mutated Cretins, remembered the way they'd merged and spread like a roaring tidal wave. *Oh God. They seeped into the train.*

The lights flickered and sprang to life once more, illuminating exactly what he feared: faceless men and women and children, crawling over and crushing one another as they struggled against the viscous things coating their skulls. They were human-sized maggots, faceless and blind, seeking escape from their prison as their screams gave way to gurgling phlegm, retching, muffled whimpers of agony.

The light died, and their voices died with it—only from the darkness erupted a chilling sound he'd hoped to never hear again. The low, sorrowful moan of the Yawning, or something close to it. Wet, not quite as guttural, but unmistakable.

Quinn turned back to Alice and Michael, was about to tell them to run when a bloody hand smashed through the glass. Droning murmurs filled his ears, words spoken in reverse by human tongues, and he found he could not take his eyes off the bloodied appendage seeking purchase, seeking *him* beyond the window's rim.

Alice pulled him away from the shattered window. "Get moving. We need to get back to the street."

"They're…" Quinn began, but Alice was shoving him toward the gap, toward the next car. He crossed the space with a long stride and panicked when he saw flickering shadows dancing within the next pair of windows. *They're people,* he'd wanted to say, but time had caught up to him. Time and panic created a dissonant rift in his mind, clashing the edicts of "real" and "unreal" against one another with his psyche trapped in the middle.

Only moments ago, he'd accepted their presence here in the Spectrum, could even accept their odd mutation—after all, they didn't belong here. Why wouldn't this reality alter their nature? But to see this, to see them infecting the innocent had broken something in his mind. The world—his reality—no longer made sense.

Not that it mattered now.

Now he needed to get the hell out of the subway.

When he looked back, Quinn wasn't surprised to see Michael gawping at the disembodied hands clutching for the air. Alice was the only one who seemed unfazed by this startling development, but as she pulled his uncle across the gap to join him, Quinn thought he saw a hint of fear in her eyes.

Get it together, Q. You don't have time to lose your sanity.

He took a breath, shook his head, and trotted across the subway car toward the opening in the tunnel. Alice and Michael followed.

Behind them, angry sobs and shattering glass echoed in the dark.

Something tightened in Clancy's chest, squeezing a low cry from his emaciated frame. A dozen hands all clenched at his guts, and the interior of the police cruiser went white for a few seconds, the whole world coated in pallid splotches like God had splattered paint when She made the clouds.

And there were voices now, a rolling thunder of voices chattering over one another, frontwards and backwards in languages he could not comprehend. Voices and bells and a mechanized drone in his ears. He wanted to vomit.

No, he wanted to die. Death was preferable to this hell. He was one more innocent life caught up in the turbulence of a world that didn't care.

But his new master, like his pain, was ever present in his mind. They sat inches apart, and while Mr. Black's mouth did not move, Clancy heard his voice loud and clear in his head: *You are not allowed to die, Mr. Jones. Not unless I wish it. You belong to me now, and when I am done with you,* then *you may die. But not a moment sooner.*

"Please..." Clancy moaned. Officer Redford looked in the rearview, and Clancy appealed to his fellow man. "...he put some kind of sickness in me, mister. You gotta take...gotta take..."

To the hospital, Mr. Jones? Do you truly want to waste your final hours on this infernal plane of existence wasting away in a waiting room? There is no doctor on this earth who can cure what I have given you. Only you possess the cure, but the time for remedies has past. All I have done is awaken the failures within you. Soon they will grow, mature, and become *you. You will be nothing but your failure. So shall your fellow man.*

"Quiet down back there," Officer Redford said. "Only place you're going is to jail. Now shut up."

Clancy sank back into his seat, grimacing as waves of wrenching pain washed over him. He cast a desperate gaze toward his master, made a silent plea for release. John Black cracked a smile. His eyes glowed even in the bright sunlight of the day, and a thick dollop of white seeped from the man's ear. It plopped on the seat between them, wriggled and squirmed away.

My children are waking up, Mr. Jones. Can you hear them? Down below, where you and Patty and so many others were exiled by your fellow man. Yes, I know about Patty. My children took her from you once, all your memories and dreams of her, washed away in the rains of time like all the tears you have shed for reasons you could not understand. I heard your cries, tasted the tears that drenched the earth beneath your feet, and feasted on your dreams. They were delicious.

The cacophonous chittering in his head quieted, and the pulling, tearing, churning sensation slowed in his gut. Clancy blinked back tears and spoke in a low whisper. "What are you, mister?"

Cracks formed in the center of John Black's forehead, splintering outward in thin lines which seeped the same gray light as his hollow eyes. His smile widened, more cracks formed at the corners of his mouth, and when he opened his mouth, Clancy glimpsed something inside. Something gray and malign beyond the coat of flesh. He saw another mouth in the man's throat. It was smiling and filled with the same dim light. Its lips moved, and he heard John's distorted voice in his head once more.

I am the end of all things, Mr. Jones. I am the mirror in which man will see his reflection.

"I don't understand," Clancy whispered.

You will, and soon. For now, enjoy your escort to the police station. And then, my servant, you may die.

Clancy turned away, watched the city pass by from the cruiser window. The voices and drones returned, and when he closed his eyes, he saw his master's gray light in his head. He felt the pull of hands in his chest, the gnashing of teeth at the back of his throat, like something alive biding its time before making an escape.

Silent, Clancy prayed for death and wept.

6

ROUGH BEASTS

Donovan followed the remnants of the Monochrome's Missing across gray sands. A flat expanse of earth stretched toward the horizon in all directions. Behind them, he saw the faint outline of the city, its towering structures barely visible now in the hazy curtain of nothingness.

Forever, maybe. Feels like forever. Hard to tell in this place anymore.

Indeed, his concept of time had faded. How long had he been gone now? Days? Hours? And how long had any of them been walking? Years, by the look of the others. The woman he'd met just after crossing the demarcation walked ahead, hunched over, her tattered hoodie hanging loose from her scrawny figure like excess skin.

We are the rough beasts, he thought grimly, *and our time has come 'round at last.*

The woman sensed his stare and looked back, nodded. A strange gesture, one he found oddly comforting given the circumstances, as though she was checking to make sure he was still with them. He was one of them now, one of the Missing. Ever since this awful nightmare began, he supposed his status as a member of their ranks had never really changed. He'd been pending for too long; now it was official. Bring on the merit badge and induction ceremony.

All he needed now were a few holes in his clothes, a stench of soiled trousers, the sour scent of weeks-old body odor. With enough time he'd have the proper uniform.

"How far do you think we have to go?"

His voice surprised him, the words an embarrassing jumble of small talk, but he pushed the shame away. The old woman turned back and slowed until he caught up to her. Stringy gray hair half obscured a face ridden with a bulbous pumpkin patch of gray pox and a mountain range of wrinkles. He hadn't truly seen her face before, only a silhouette against the haze, and now he wished he hadn't. He thought of the old hag in front of Winthorpe Station

(*he sees you sees me sees you sees us all*)

and a shiver crawled over him. One of Sparrow's white *Fading Out* buttons was pinned to her hoodie.

The woman shrugged. "Don't know. All's I know is I gotta walk there."

He kept pace with her for a few minutes, walking forward to the horizon, watching the other pilgrims slink across the gray wastes. "Why?"

A question so simple, so innocent, and yet he regretted asking the moment the word left his lips. She glared at him, snarled like a wounded animal. "The voice. Don't you hear it? Ever since Sparrow vanished, we've all been hearing a voice telling us to leave the city, to travel to that big building out there…" She pointed toward the glowing column and lowered her voice. "…It says *he's* going to be there."

"He?"

"Yeah. The man who murdered my husband." Tears wrapped her eyes now, and when she spoke again, her voice strained against a tide of sorrow. "My George. He was only doin' what Dullington told him to do, and what did he get for it? Eaten by one of those things."

Slow realization spread through Donovan like a cold wildfire. *George. Eaten by the Yawning.*

Flashes of that night atop the parking garage filled his head in rapid succession. The man he met at Rossetti's diner. The man who held him at gunpoint. The man Dullington sent to kidnap Donna.

"I'm…sorry to hear that," he said. His voice rasped like sandpaper, and he dropped his eyes to the sands, suddenly interested in the many grains underfoot.

"Me too. The voice says I'll meet the man who was there, who caused George's death." She pulled back her hoodie, revealing a handgun tucked into her waistband. "So that's why, mister. That's why I'm walking."

She turned to him, and Donovan resisted the urge to meet her stare, afraid he might admit everything to her right then. A dozen scenarios played out before him, all of which ended with him eating a bullet. *Best keep to yourself, hoss. Ain't no reason to stir the pot just yet.*

The woman snorted back her tears, cracked a smile. "Name's Margie, by the way. Margie Guffin." She held out her hand, and Donovan shook it out of reflex. "You got a name, mister?"

"Uh, yeah." The name came to him instantly, the only one which seemed right given the circumstances. A lie for the greater good. "Name's Joe Hopper."

"Well, Mr. Hopper. What do you suppose that big storm is up ahead?"

He glanced away, toward the roiling tempest along the horizon, now much larger as they approached. Dark clouds of dust and sand and something else, something *fluid* swirled within, and if he concentrated, he could hear something on the wind. Voices, maybe. Songs. Or were they cries?

Donovan shrugged. "I don't know, but I think we're soon going to find out."

He looked back at the expanse of gray and the clusters of hunched men and women trudging toward the same destination. He wondered how many of them held a grudge, how many were brainwashed into believing he was the enemy. How long it would take before one of them recognized him.

Somewhere ahead, he hoped he'd find the monk waiting for him. It was the first time he'd ever hoped to see Mr. Dullington, and the fact wasn't lost on him.

He was a pilgrim lost in the wilderness. Hope was all he had now, and it did little to mask the truth of his situation: he was alone here among the wolves.

Donovan took a breath and kept on walking.

———————•———————

The pale monk sat waiting at the edge of the storm, meditating on the promise of battles to come. Before him, the tempest of mankind's dead dreams, failures, and regrets swirled endlessly, swelling and collapsing in upon itself, a constant explosion of emotion made manifest. Voices of the dead and the forgotten living collided with one another in a cacophonous hum which droned throughout the Monochrome. After seven hundred years, he was used to the sound, but he had not grown used to the nightmarish tapestry the gusts of sand occasionally revealed.

He saw Agnes in there sometimes. He saw Thomas with her. Dark reminders of his failures as a man. If he possessed any remnant of mortal fear, however irrational, then he would find it lost among the chaos of dreams and sand.

And somewhere beyond, Aleister heard his old master laughing in mockery, taunting him for clinging to the fear and a shadow of his humanity. *Dreams come here to die,* Vile once told him, *and so does man's hope. The Ungod will devour and defecate them in a storm of rage and hate and fear. Hate me all you want, Aleister, but you know I'm right. This storm is as much a part of you as it is the rest of your ilk.*

Crossing through the tempest was a burden, a journey he had made many times over the centuries, each trip another attempt to coax his master from the Needle. Every time he crossed the demarcation, he met his wife and son, and every time he lost a piece of himself along the way.

Now he would do so again, and soon. Only this time it would be the last. Win or lose, Aleister Dullington would not abandon his charge.

Across the wastes, he sensed the presence of others. Lost souls he had helped inter here, and others stolen during Sparrow's reign, all called toward the Needle. He'd heard Vile's voice on the wind, vibrating among the strings, whispering his lies to lure them here. Aleister had his suspicions, but they were not his focus, and he would deal with them in time if he had to.

For now, he was pleased to sense Mr. Candle among them. A thin smile crept across his pallid face. The man's journey was far from over, but crossing the first demarcation was a critical first step. *The will to be,* he mused, *is always the will to overcome.*

Aleister Dullington climbed to his feet, put his back to the storm, and crossed the sands to meet his manikin.

————— • —————

Alice led them in silence along the stagnant tunnel, following the dim glow of red signal lights spaced along the ceiling like a devilish breadcrumb trail. Her silence was not for a lack of things to say, but for the indecision of which to voice first. So much had happened in the last two hours, more than she could process at once, and she chose to retreat into her thoughts as they walked along the subway line.

Her boys, as she'd come to think of them, walked behind her in silence, no doubt traumatized by the crash and the emergence of the Monochrome's beasts. At least Quinn was somewhat mentally prepared for the latter; Michael, she could see, was struggling with what he'd witnessed. The trauma and the blood loss were secondary when one's reality was visibly called into question.

She remembered that mental dissonance, trying to come to terms with an accepted view of reality. Trying to come to terms with what she'd done with her life to end up in a place like the Monochrome. How many days had she wept? Weeks, she was sure, more for the loss of her loved ones than for herself.

Maybe that's your problem, sister. Always thinking of others first, never taking the time to take care of you.

The guilt and shame resurfaced, and for once she was grateful for the gloom so that her tears and flushed face were hidden. She thought of the time she met Donovan, introduced at Identinel's annual office potluck, and later meeting he and Donna for drinks during Happy Hour after work.

Alice glanced back at Michael's sulking figure, looked at the way the red lights above outlined the contours of his body. He looked up at her, and she turned away.

Swore I'd never date another man. And then Don said he had a brother, that he was driving over to join them for a drink.

Walking, daydreaming, Alice smiled when she remembered the gruff demeanor, the grumpy expression on Michael's face. Something about it had seemed so endearing, like a child determined to take on the world. It was all a façade, of course; she knew it as soon as he sat down and ordered a bottle of cheap beer. A month later, she asked him what was on his mind that night he walked into the restaurant. They were lying in bed, legs entwined, the dew of sweat still fresh on their naked skin.

"You'll laugh."

"No, I won't. Promise."

He looked at her, grinned sheepishly. "I was trying to think of a reason to bail early."

"Why?"

"Didn't want to be there. Me and Donna don't really get along, but I try to keep the peace for Don's sake. Figured if I could pass off a bad mood, they wouldn't mind if I left early." He nuzzled his face into her neck. "And then I saw you."

Alice swallowed back a sob.

And then I saw you…

And then I saw you standing in our bedroom, looking right through me as I begged you to hear me. I saw you walk out of our house, out of my life, and then I saw you years later on that subway platform with your brother.

I saw you, you didn't see me, and I hated myself a little more for it. Because

I'm the one who put myself there in that prison. I stayed at Identinel too long, I didn't leave when I swore I would, but I was too caught up in trying to meet our sales goal, meet our number, meet our quota.

She blinked away tears, resisted the urge to spin on her heels and collapse into him. Her heart ached worse now than it had when she'd first flickered out.

How do I reconcile this? I never expected his memories would start to come back, and now those awful things are crossing over and—

"Alice?"

"What?"

Quinn recoiled, and she realized she'd snapped at him. She offered a timid smile. "Sorry. What is it?"

He pointed toward the faint light around the bend ahead. "I think that's our station."

"Should be." She looked back at Michael. "How're you holding up?"

"I'll live." He winced as he clasped the gash on his arm. "Might need stitches though."

"We can get a cab back to the transit authority and get your car. Hospital's not far from there."

Michael nodded, ushering in a silence which fell over them as they approached the station ahead. Alice squinted as the station's lights came into view, shielded her face from the stark glare of fluorescents overhead. The eastbound subway train sat idle between the platforms, its operator having a somewhat nervous and animated conversation on her phone. If she saw them approach, she gave no sign, not that it would've mattered. Alice led their tiny procession up the access ramp and onto the platform, ignoring the crowd of annoyed commuters, their stares of judgment and disgust.

How disgusting they must be, having ventured into the city's bowels and survived a derailment. She looked back, took in the kid and her former fiancé, and stifled a laugh. They were both coated in dust, their faces smudged with something black like soot. A shred of Quinn's jeans was missing, revealing a calf covered in dried blood.

Now we really do look like the Missing.

Topside, Quinn hailed a cab, and a minute later they were on their way back to the transit authority. Alice took a closer look at Michael's wound. He hissed when she grabbed his arm.

"Would you take it easy? This hurts like hell."

"I bet it does. Let me look at it anyway." She pried his fingers away and felt the blood drained from her face. The gash was deep, nearly cut down into the muscle of his bicep. Michael turned away, blinked back tears.

"How bad is it?"

She stared at the bleeding wound for a few seconds, stunned to silence by its severity, and remembered the time she had to extract a piece of glass from Michael's foot after he stepped on a bulb.

She'd pulled the glass from his foot easily enough and watched as a stream of crimson gushed from the cut. He'd nearly fainted from the sight of it and had cried out when she cleaned the wound with alcohol. When she was done bandaging his foot, he'd looked her in the eye, pale-faced, and asked with stern clarity, *"How bad is it?"*

"You don't handle blood so well, Mr. Detective. And you're in luck. No amputations in your future."

"You're squeezing too hard."

Alice blinked, released his arm. She shook her head. "You never did handle blood all that well. I don't think we'll have to amputate or anything, but..."

She met his gaze, and she saw that same clarity in his eyes, only there was something else. Something more. An epiphany. A memory.

He opened his mouth to speak but stopped short and clenched his jaw. Alice let the tears come this time. She'd had no choice in the matter; she couldn't hold them back anymore.

Say it. Tell me you remember. Please tell me you remember.

Michael took her hand and gave her a light squeeze. "This isn't the life we dreamed about, is it?" Then his eyes rolled back, and he fainted into the cab's backseat.

"Typical," she whispered, and faced front. She tapped the driver's shoulder. "Hey, change of plan. Take us to the nearest emergency room."

The cabbie nodded, flipped on his turn signal, and took the next right.

———•———

"Well, your blood pressure looks a little elevated, but it's nothing I'd call abnormal." Dr. Moreno flashed Donna a reassuring smile. "Trips to the ER tend to cause spikes."

"No kidding," Donna said sheepishly, feeling the heat of embarrassment rising in her cheeks. She looked at her sister sitting in the spare chair across the exam room and wondered how much worse her stress would be if she'd followed Amanda's advice. "I still thought it better to be safe than sorry."

Dr. Moreno pulled a penlight from her breast pocket. "I understand completely. Tilt your head back for me?"

Donna did so, and a moment later, the doctor told her to relax. "The nose bleeds came out of nowhere this morning."

"And the fainting," Amanda quipped. They both looked at her with some minor annoyance. "Don't forget you almost cracked your head open on the countertop. If I hadn't been there to catch you—"

"Yes," Dr. Moreno cut in. "Possibly due to the sudden blood loss. I saw no lesions or signs of sinusitis, but I'd still like to take some blood and a nonstress test. I'm sure Dr. Warner would like to see those results as well. And, like you said, better safe than sorry."

Donna nodded, forced a smile. She thought about the old woman in the waiting room, pleading for her husband to remember. She thought of the people who entered with tissues pressed to their noses, and she considered asking about them. *What if there's an epidemic? Is it viral? Am I infected?*

"A nurse will be with you shortly. Unless you have any questions for me, I'll be on my way—"

"Actually, doctor, I do." Donna cleared her throat and nodded her head toward the door. "I saw a lot of folks walking in with nose bleeds. Is there something going around?"

Dr. Moreno chuckled. "I assure you, Mrs. Candle, it's not a virus, if that's what you're worried about. I think I heard the pollen count is really high. Probably just a lot of overactive allergies."

They said their goodbyes, and when the doctor was gone, Amanda rose from her chair to stretch. "Pollen? Really?"

"Yeah, I don't know." Her mind was already drifting back to Donovan and the troubling resurgence of memories she'd forgotten long ago. The nosebleeds hadn't started until the memories returned. When Donovan disappeared. *You're going to drive yourself crazy, Donna. It'll be fine. You're fine. The baby's fine.*

But what about Donovan?

Something tickled the back of her brain, a soft fluttering of intuition. An image of her husband tackling her captor, falling over the edge of a derelict subway platform. A slow-motion silent film reel played back in her head, the frames scratched and skipping, and in a span of seconds she saw Donovan vanish, reappear, and vanish again as though he were a shadow caught in the light.

She'd witnessed all of this, and yet she suddenly felt like a voyeur in her own life, witnessing something she wasn't supposed to see. Or remembering something she wasn't supposed to remember.

Donnie, what have you done? How did you get mixed up in all this?

There were no answers. Only more questions.

A chime filled the silence of the room, and they both looked toward Amanda's purse. Her sister retrieved her phone and frowned.

"It's Quinn. They're on their way here."

"Here?"

"Michael's hurt. Something about a subway crash?"

"Oh my God." The world dropped out from beneath Donna's stomach, and for an instant she was in freefall. "Is he okay? I mean—"

"Quinn said they'll be here in a few minutes. I'm telling him we're here."

A moment later, there was a knock on the door and a perky nurse wheeled in a heart monitor. Donna reclined back in her seat, watching as the nurse went to work placing electrodes, but in her mind, she was a hundred miles away.

When Donovan looked back again, he saw even more pilgrims had joined them, their heads down in reverence, their faces solemn in acceptance of whatever grim fate awaited them. The only thing which had changed was the city skyline, now barely present in the haze, a thin drawing upon the world's canvas.

He'd lost track of time and distance. In the Spectrum, his limbs and feet would be aching, but here there was no pain. Here he was caught in a web of time and suffering in constant stasis. Maybe Dullington's Ungod could fix this. And maybe Dullington was full of shit.

Margie Guffin remained at his side for a time, long enough that he feared she'd seen through his lie and knew who he really was, but as the storm drew nearer, she picked up her pace. Donovan took the opportunity to fall back among the crowd of taciturn figures on their lonely march across the sands. She posed a danger he hadn't anticipated, and while he was safe for now, he was certain someone sooner or later would recognize him. *Best to blend in, hoss. Let her keep the lead.*

Donovan did for a while, until she'd blended in with the group of wayward souls ahead. George Guffin's screaming rictus flashed before him, forever frozen in a state of fear before the Yawning devoured him whole.

He'd not thought much of the man after what had happened that weekend. Admittedly, memories of him had slowly withered from Donovan's mind, one more casualty to the work of the Cretins, but now he recalled everything in crystal clarity.

She thinks I killed him. Hell, maybe I did. I didn't pull the trigger, but he was only there because of me, because of what Dullington...

A baritone voice spoke up inside his mind, slow and certain, the sound of God to an insect. *I used George Guffin, Mr. Candle. He was necessary and expendable.*

"Doesn't mean you had to kill him," Donovan whispered, darting his eyes to see if the others noticed he was speaking to himself, but they gave no sign. "And it doesn't reassure me you won't do the same to me when we're done with...whatever it is we're doing here. Where the hell are you, anyway?"

Keep walking, Mr. Candle. Toward the tempest before you. You will see me soon enough.

Donovan lifted his head, peering out above the river of lost souls, and saw the storm was closer now. Thick clouds of dust swirled across the horizon, blotting out the haze of dim light emitting from the column ahead, and now he saw there *was* something roiling inside its chaos. Dozens of thin, gelatinous tendrils colored mother-of-pearl moved lazily along the surface of the cloudy curtain, tasting the air, sliding over one another with hypnotic effect.

He thought of Sparrow and the way the mad man conjured a wave of the creatures, forming and shaping them like a child with clay

(we'll rot together)

and shoved the image away, back to a dark corner in his mind where it belonged. The things inside the storm revealed themselves beyond the clouds of dust as if to mock him, and he thought he saw the contours of Sparrow's face for an instant. His nose was the size of an airliner, his empty eyes like small moons, and his grin stretched across the horizon. The visage was there and gone again in a blink, but the memory remained burned into his brain, an echo of a monster once lost in the dark.

Donovan shook his head, shook off the tremor racing down his spine. The ceaseless tumult of wind and sand and pale flesh continued its shapeless journey, destroying itself and rising from the dead once more.

You're one thing I don't regret, Sparrow. You got off easy.

Hopper's words resonated in his head but spoke with Donovan's voice.

Amused, he wondered how long before he and Hopper became one, the creator and creation merging to become someone else altogether. *Maybe after the third book, if I live to write it.*

He smiled, but the levity drained away in passing moments, sucked dry by the arid Monochrome wasteland. There would be no joy here, and as he drew closer to the tempest, the terrain became rocky, jagged, the sands obscuring something just below their surface.

Curious, Donovan stopped and dug a trench with his shoe. A lump of cotton appeared in his throat, his mouth suddenly dry, the air in his lungs an inferno ignited by blinding white panic.

Bones. He'd unearthed bones. The remains of a rib cage, a rigid jaw full of brittle teeth, and what looked like fingers. They were petrified, polished smooth by the sands and bleached white.

Donovan stared at them for a moment, sobered by his discovery, and utterly terrified. The pilgrims parted and marched around him. If they saw the bones, they gave no sign, and he suspected they wouldn't care either way.

Get a grip on yourself, hoss. Keep movin'.

He swallowed back the lump in his throat, kicked sand over the remains, and continued on his way.

7

BLACK, JOHN

Officer Redford marched them through the front door of the precinct. As they crossed the threshold, the afternoon heat was replaced with a stagnant atmosphere of recycled air, old sweat, and panic. Dozens of men and women loitered in the foyer, waiting their turn to speak to the frazzled woman at the front desk. Phones rang from the offices beyond, punctuated with the occasional bark from an officer's radio. Someone murmured about a subway crash downtown.

John Black savored their collective anxiety, felt it crawl across his vessel's skin, and relished the bone-deep shiver it wrought. So primal that sensation, the unspeakable fear lingering on the tip of every tongue. Every glance at their fellow man was an unspoken communication, a silent knowing of their mutual end without truly grasping the reality of their inevitable oblivion.

Somnambulist cattle. Thousands of years of civilization reduced to these sleepwalking fools. Slaves to their new gods of commerce and frivolity. It is time for you all to wake up.

Officer Redford took in the chaos as he herded them forward and nodded to the young woman behind the desk. "Tracy, I've got two more for booking." He looked back, "You okay up here?"

She glanced his way. "Carl's on break. Should be back in a few. Go on, we got this." And then, to the old woman next in line, "I'm sorry, but let me make sure I understand this correctly. You *think* your husband's been missing for over ten years?"

The old woman clutched a tissue to her nose and nodded. "That's what I'm trying to tell you, officer—"

Redford mumbled to himself, something none of the people in line heard, but John Black heard every syllable loud and clear. "Whole damn city's going to shit."

As Redford pushed them into the main office for booking, John Black grinned and said, "You have no idea, officer. No idea at all."

———————•———————

Clancy followed Mr. Black down an aisle of desks decorated with stacks of files, loose paper, computer monitors, and paper cups full of steaming coffee. All around them were other officers of various rank, slumped in their seats while listening to men and women regale them of tales about people they thought had been missing for years, people they'd suddenly remembered.

Just like Patty. How could I have forgotten her? A rumbling drone sprinted through his head, the room sizzled around him with burning white light, and the pain squeezed his gut.

Something warm trickled down his upper lip, and when he looked at his feet, he saw dark splotches of blood dotting the scuffed tile floor.

Am I dying? Did that man put a cancer in me?

He'd watched his mother be eaten away by cancer when he was just a kid, swore he'd kill himself before succumbing to such indescribable suffering, and yet here he was, each step taking his breath away as a surging agony seized his center.

"You two. Sit." Officer Redford pointed him toward a nearby chair, and he sat on command.

Clancy knew the drill. Last time he'd been arrested was a little more than a decade ago, a few months after the market crashed and the packaging facility where he worked shut its doors. Public intoxication, they called it, but he liked to think of it as four bourbon shots too many. *Always know your limits,* his daddy once told him, and for the better part of his life, Clancy thought he had himself figured out, limitations and all.

Then the warehouse closed, and he missed a mortgage payment. Having a few shots of bourbon seemed like as good an idea as any other. Turns out, that was the only true lesson he'd needed about his limitations.

A solemn night in the drunk tank afforded him enough time to contemplate the turns his life had taken in a matter of months. No job, soon to be homeless, and now he had a record. All because some greedy assholes gambled big with his money and lost.

Or something like that. He could barely balance his checkbook, much less grasp the implications of a stock market crash, so he spent the late hours working on a different sort of arithmetic.

Twenty-two years. He'd given most of his adult life to the company, working sometimes twelve-hour days six days a week to meet goals which, to him, meant nothing more than a few extra cents on the dollar. *I make a dime and the boss makes a dollar,* his coworkers used to say, but Clancy was grateful for that dime. He rolled it into his pension, planning to retire early and live out the rest of his days in comfort.

And then the crash happened, and all those dimes he'd saved over the years nearly vanished overnight. What little he had in the bank was quickly devoured by bills and late fees. One foreclosure later, he was officially homeless.

He looked over his shoulder, surveyed the busy offices, listened to the dissonant trilling of phones. A board at the far end of the room was littered with Missing Persons photos. Their ends overlapped one another, partially obscuring the faces in both color and grayscale, until it was impossible to see where one ended and the other began. The board was a massive banner of lost souls.

She's there, somewhere in that mess. I bet if I peeled back some of the sheets, I'd find her. That's where I found her before, last time I was here.

Clancy remembered Patty, almost saw her ghostly outline waiting on a nearby bench parked in front of the bulletin board. She was there with her other friends, waiting while their pimp paid their bail, and they'd locked eyes as a cop led him toward the exit. Hungover, his mouth full of cotton and his head full of cement, Clancy couldn't remember much about that day, but he'd always remembered Patty's emerald green eyes.

He ran into her some months later outside of town, underneath the bridge where others had set up a makeshift camp. She was skinnier and sported a fresh bruise around her right eye, but he'd have recognized those green eyes anywhere.

They'd hit it off easily enough, became fast friends in the cracks of society. Life with her made their situation bearable, and there was a time when Clancy thought himself happy, all things considered. Patty saved him from despair, at least for a while until she vanished from his life. She'd showed him the ropes, showed him how to adapt and survive on the streets, which shelters to visit and which ones to avoid. They'd fallen in love, or at least he thought they had—that much was still blurry in his memory, but the *feeling* was there, deep down in his heart like a perennial seed hibernating against the cold.

A seed of love buried in a soil of sorrow, one taking root in the other where it would grow and live and die, perpetuating an endless cycle of life and loss. *Patty's words,* he thought, recalling she'd always had a penchant for poetry.

Yet there was nothing poetic about his life now. Not here, with the infection his horrible companion had imparted upon him. Clancy felt it now, stirring deep down in his gut, a thousand hands pushing from the inside out. And not just hands, but teeth too—he felt fangs of jagged glass cutting, tearing their way free of their prison, tasting his innards and gnawing on bone.

His belly squirmed and bloated, and he twisted in his seat as the cramping became unbearable. Clancy farted a thin squeak of air like a punctured balloon. A few laughs broke through the constant hiss of chatter, but Officer Redford wasn't amused.

"If you puke again, I'm gonna make you clean it up."

"No sir," Clancy grimaced, blinking tears from his eyes. "I might…I need a doctor, officer. Mr. Black did something to me. Put somethin' in me."

"I'll get to you in a minute. Just sit there and keep quiet."

Something thick inched its way up the back of Clancy's throat, and he swallowed it down with a muffled gag. *Feels like a worm. Oh God, it feels like a worm.* He looked to Mr. Black for answers, possibly relief, or perhaps an end to this discomforting nightmare, but his new master only stared at him, through him. *He can see what's happening,* Clancy realized. *He knows because he put it there. What did you do to me, you fucking monster?*

John Black studied his face before cracking a smile—and suddenly Clancy heard the awful man in his head. *Your time is almost nigh, Mr. Jones.*

Clancy frowned, shook his head. "Get out of my head, mister." Officer Redford grunted but did not look up from his computer.

How fortunate you are to be the bearer of an ending for all mankind. Feel privileged, insect. This is the greatest moment of your worthless life.

Finally, Officer Justin Redford looked away from the screen and back to them both. John Black met the officer's stare and smiled. "My friend will be quite all right, Officer Swine. No need to worry about him."

Redford's cheeks flushed red, but he held back his temper with a deep breath. "Fine, we'll start with you. What's your name?"

"This vessel's name is John Black." He licked his lips, and a pale aura circled his eyes. "And I am here to deliver your reckoning."

The light from Mr. Black's eyes grew brighter, and Clancy squirmed in his seat, tried to put some distance between them, but a wave of pain washed over him. His muscles locked together in a singular spasm as his body revolted against his will. He sat upright, arched his back so hard and far that his spine snapped with a series of sickening cracks.

The world fell away in a flash of brilliance, the voices of the room silenced to murmurs, and something broke free inside him. He felt the pull, the tension, the struggle of a thousand tiny claws working their way out of his guts.

In the silent moments before his world faded to black for all time, Clancy Jones had a fleeting thought: *Maybe I'll get to see Patty now.*

Then his body burst with a thick wet pop, and all hell broke loose.

———•———

Officer Redford tried to shield himself when he realized what was happening, but his mind wasn't fast enough for the things breaching his prisoner's gut. *Things.* The only word he could muster in the ensuing seconds—there were claws and teeth and black eyes and far too many limbs, things ripped straight out of a nightmare, and now they were pouring out of this homeless man's guts.

He fell backward in his seat as Clancy's body exploded in a red mist of bone and viscera and spiders. His mind seized on the image, finally able to make sense of the awful bestiary crawling from the gory remains—pale spiders with far too many limbs, tiny heads full of eyes and teeth.

One of them scuttled along the top of his desk, uttered a triumphant shriek, and flopped down on Redford's chest.

"Jesus Christ." He made to slap it from his chest, but the pale thing bit off a chunk of his finger. Blood gushed from the wound as white-hot pain settled into his nerves, forcing his muscles to react. He squeezed the tiny thing in his fist until its head popped like a ruptured boil. Thick, gray phlegm erupted from its open neck, and he nearly vomited when he saw it was squirming.

Redford scrambled to his feet and unbuttoned his holster, was about to draw and fire when he saw one of the spiderlings leap from the neighboring desk and into the mouth of Officer Reid.

The hefty man's eyes bulged as he clutched for his throat. Thick rivulets of white foam dribbled from the corners of his mouth as the creature worked its way down his gullet. Officer Redford reached out to his friend, a man he'd known for all of his five years on the force, and recoiled in horror when he saw the ropes of foam weren't liquid at all, but veiny tendrils sprouting out of the poor man's mouth.

More screams erupted around them as the spiderlings spread across the room. Redford turned, took in the chaos surrounding him. Men and women struggled against the spiderlings, trying to pull the foreign bodies from their mouths to no avail as a layer of membranous white veins coated their necks, faces, skulls. One by one, officers and civilians alike suffered the same fate, each invaded by an impossible creature.

"This isn't happening…" His words were faint, barely audible, the strength pulled from them like the air from his lungs. A sudden and painful throb rose up deep in his skull, embedded between his temples, and he heard the low buzzing drone of static. Blood dripped from his nose.

"It is happening, Officer Swine."

Redford turned, prepared to draw his weapon on the one called John Black, but the strength was gone from him. His limbs would not move. He felt drunk, and the world before him dissolved into a haze of searing white light. *His eyes,* he realized, staring into Mr. Black's pale face. *The light's coming from his eyes.*

"Indeed." John Black approached, took Redford's face in his hands, and turned the officer's head back to face the tumult. "Gaze upon the failures of your kind, mortal. I have simply awakened the despair in you all."

Bulbous mounds of sickly gray membrane slowly grew over the faces of the fallen, molding to the contours of their skulls. Redford watched with revulsion as facial features were slowly erased, their identities swallowed up by so many swollen tumors, and he thought of the strange man's words. *Awakened the despair in you all.*

He wanted to ask what John Black meant by that statement, but when he looked back, Mr. Black vomited a wad of writhing gray phlegm into his face. His world bled into scathing white, and he sank to the floor as something took hold of his consciousness. He tried to retch, tried to spit out the disgusting matter infecting his mouth, but his muscles would not cooperate.

Redford lay on his back, watching in terror as he felt something rubbery and wet inch its way down his throat. John Black knelt over him and smiled.

"For centuries I have watched you squander your talents, watched you torture your fellow man for pieces of earth, and watched you suffer in willful slavery in pursuit of unattainable wealth." Redford twitched as his nerves were attacked by something within, something rising from the pit of his gut to meet whatever it was sinking down his throat. He struggled to breathe, to cry out for help which, deep down, he knew would not come.

"Take a breath, Officer Swine. That sickening stench in your nose and bilious taste in your throat is nothing more than your own failure awakening inside you."

Light seeped through hairline cracks in Mr. Black's skin. A piece of flesh fell from his face, revealing a hazy gray void underneath. Officer Redford met the man's stare, and for an instant, he felt Mr. Black's presence inside his thoughts.

Who are you?

"I am your reckoning, human. Your judge and jury. Before your time on this earth is done, your peers will know the name Pontius Vile and weep."

More strips of Black's skin fell to the floor like chipped paint and revealed the glaring light within. His purpose complete, the manikin calling himself John Black slowly disintegrated into a cloud of dust, leaving behind a pile of stained clothing.

The time of Pontius Vile had finally come.

———•———

Elsewhere, beyond the demarcations and the immeasurable expanse of the metachasm, Aleister Dullington halted his walk and craned his neck upward. The strings were vibrating so violently he could hear them hum. And above them, somewhere, laughter echoed across the tempest winds.

He reached out with his mind, touched one of the trembling strings, and recoiled in disgust. In that instant he saw his adversary's recent conquest, and he finally understood Vile's method of attack. But how had he managed to sneak a manikin into the Spectrum?

A voice called out to him from across the sands.

Aleister retreated from the strings, steadied himself, and turned toward the crowd of lost pilgrims marching toward the storm. Donovan Candle approached, somewhat haggard since their last encounter, but the confidence on the man's face was apparent.

Vile's voice boomed overhead, a triumphant growl so deep and loud it shook the world. The earth trembled beneath them, and somewhere above, dark cracks splintered the sky.

I used the monster you made, little sparrow. Look upon ye mighty works and despair!

A warm wind swept through the wastes, stirring the sands, and blanketing the pilgrims in a thick gray curtain. Donovan shielded his face.

"What the hell is happening?"

Aleister Dullington frowned and faced the tempest raging behind them. "Our time is short, Mr. Candle. Follow me."

-8-
CRACKS IN THE SKY

Violent shockwaves ripped through the police station's foundation. Girders buckled, windows shattered, and with a creaking groan, the structure split in half. The upper floors collapsed inward, their stunned occupants and loose furniture tumbling into an abyss of torn wiring, glass, and broken pipes. Thick clouds of dust erupted from the destruction, blanketing the bruised and bloodied bodies of those trapped in the rubble. Many were already dead, and those who clung to life were quickly suffocated by the pale insectoid things climbing their way between the cracks.

Outside, those in the vicinity of the building witnessed its brick-and-mortar frame crack and split down the middle. Pale beams of light shot through the shattered openings, carried by screams of agony along the dusty wind, and those who were there thought they saw something in the luminescence.

Thin lines like spools of thread stretched across a loom, vibrating erratically. Above the noise of crumbling stone and spirit rose a violent hum, light at first but growing in power with each passing second until the sound bellowed across the city in even, droning chords.

Glass shattered, blanketing the streets as windows across the city were blown out by the sound.

Another shockwave tore through the earth, and the bisected remnants of the police station were swallowed in a single cataclysmic gulp—but the fragments of light remained, unnatural ribbons blanketed across the sky. The strings illuminated within were vibrating so heavily now they were starting to fray.

Pontius Vile felt the vibration of every fiber, heard the subtle *plink* as one string snapped in two, and then another. He ran his desiccated tongue across lips that had forgotten the taste of water, savoring the hint of chaos on the air. Sweet. Delightful.

At last, after centuries of stalemate, he had finally gained the upper hand. His manikin might be dead, but the damage Sparrow had wrought was more than adequate. The balance was crumbling, the veil between Spectrum and Monochrome tearing away, and now his children were waking up to deliver his message to the world.

He strummed a gnarled hand across the strings, and his mind lit up with the image of a city painted in impressionistic splotches of pain, dabs of confusion, and broad strokes of fear. And yet deep down he felt the contents of their hearts, inside every trembling soul a cold slab of regret covering a sober, primal understanding that this horror they were experiencing was deserved somehow. For the way they had squandered their lives, had neglected the greater human tapestry, foregoing the larger picture for the sake of I and Me. Their laziness had awakened their inner mediocrity, a gray malignance nurtured by the evolution of society's apathy and drunk on humanity's self-made comforts. Man had forgotten the fear of stasis, grown complacent with his many achievements, and suckled from the tit of convenience until he was ready to burst.

Across the withering divide between realities, eight billion souls cried out in terror, prayed to the gods of their making, and struggled to understand the cataclysm ripping through their world.

Alone in the Ungod's cradle, Pontius Vile cracked a smile and threaded his fingers through the strings.

He strummed.

———————————•———————————

Michael regained consciousness halfway through the suturing procedure amid trembling walls and a shaking floor. The nurse stitching up his arm sucked in her breath, waited for the aftershock to pass before slipping the needle back into his arm. He felt nothing but pressure and the tug of skin, and he tried to sit up when he realized what was happening.

"Easy, Mike. Stay still."

A warm hand braced his shoulder, slowly pushed him back down onto the table. He recognized that voice. Warm. Comforting. Its cadence stirred hazy memories in his head, some lodged so deep he'd forgotten they were even there.

Another tremor rocked the building. Lights overhead flickered twice before dying into darkness. A moment later, the backup lighting kicked on with a sharp hum.

"Generator," the nurse mumbled. "Lived in this city for thirty years, never felt an earthquake until yesterday. Now the whole damn place is falling apart. Are things that bad outside?"

"You have no idea."

A familiar voice. Alice. His fiancée. She'd disappeared one day, never returned home. Less than a year until their wedding day, and poof, she's just gone. And why hadn't he remembered until now? Her entire existence had been erased from his mind. Did she have belongings at his house? Mail? He thought he'd remember such things, but no, those memories were wiped clean from his mind.

Cretins, Mike. They make us forget.

His lost brother's voice spoke up in his head with a distant echo. Donovan was a phantom now, haunting them every step of the way, and everything he'd tried to warn Michael about in the last two years was coming to pass. He remembered the last time he saw Donovan the night before things went to hell, remembered the way his brother looked different somehow. Changed. Whatever he'd been through had done something to him. Tempered him, maybe, but at a cost. And whatever Donovan had set out to do hadn't worked out the way he'd hoped.

Lingering on the edge of consciousness, dipping his toes into the waters of oblivion, Michael was struck with the notion that something had gone wrong. Inexplicable, an itch so far down his back he couldn't reach it, the notion that he'd helped his brother set something in motion that day in the abandoned subway.

The nurse slipped the needle through once again, and Michael fell headfirst into the icy murk of nothingness. Down here in the dark there were impossible things all tethered together in a vast network of woven threads. There were gray lights—*unlight,* he thought, an impossible word for an impossible place in an impossible time. The entire world was droning now, a sound like the grating of old gears slowing to a halt, and he caught a glimpse of something on the horizon of his dreamspace. A massive column, chipped and weathered with time, surrounded by vast gray dunes, and below those ancient sands was something else lost to time. The column was just an exposed artifact of a much larger treasure, a massive network of architecture built to protect and house a monster.

No, not a monster. A god.

He finally understood. The column wasn't a column at all, but a needle driven into the earth, and all those threads were looped through a hollow space inside, tethered together in a cradle of stone, and feeding the Great Eater of Dreams.

All dreams, malignant or benign, were devoured here. Their triviality tasted and judged and knotted together to form a massive tapestry of human experience. But something was wrong. The sky was fractured, shattered by an unimaginable cataclysm, and the slumbering entity within was slowly choking, its umbilicus of dead dreams coiled around its throat and pulled tight by human hands—

"All done."

The nurse's voice yanked him free of the dreamspace and the gray wasteland hiding beneath its waves. Michael opened his eyes, looked around the room in a daze, expecting to find the remnants of his dream had followed him into reality.

Instead, he watched a silver-haired woman in green scrubs toss her latex gloves in a nearby receptacle and wash her hands. When she was finished, she saw he was awake and smiled.

"You're all set, hon. The anesthetic should wear off in a bit. You're welcome to relax here until you get your bearings."

Michael closed his eyes, waited for a wave of nausea to pass. Half his torso felt like tingling jelly. He grimaced when he tried to swallow. His throat was raw, felt like he'd been gargling sand.

Sand.

A wasteland flashed before him, but its significance was fleeting, and it slipped easily from his grip. *Need to get moving,* he told himself. *Need to find Donovan.*

He tried to sit up again and gasped as the room swam before him. The nurse frowned.

"You lost some blood, hon. I'll go get you some juice. Be right back."

"Alice," he rasped. "The woman who—"

"Oh, the pretty thing who brought you in? She said something about going to see a friend. You hang on to her, she's a keeper."

"A friend…" But the room kept spinning, and Michael allowed himself to relax. "I'll wait for that juice."

The nurse smirked. "I'd say you don't have much choice."

———————•———————

The stairway door closed behind her, and Alice paused long enough to catch her breath. The elevators were out of order due to the recent tremors, and while the task of taking seven flights of stairs was an annoyance, she preferred the fatigue to being trapped in a box suspended between floors.

Evelyn Brock's room was just beyond the nurse's station down the hall. A stocky fellow in purple scrubs sat behind the desk with a phone nestled against his ear. He gave Alice a passing glance before grumbling into the receiver, "Yeah, I get that, but is it an earthquake or not? My shift doesn't end for another six hours, babe, so I can't—hello? Hello? Josie?"

The nurse returned the phone to its cradle, shook his head, and looked up. "Yes, can I help you?"

"No," Alice said, lowering her gaze. She realized she'd been staring. "I'm just here to see Evelyn Brock."

"Yeah, 703. Just down the hall. Say, do you mind if I borrow your cell? I just got cut off from my wife."

She shook her head. "Sorry, man. Don't have one."

"Thanks anyway," he said, but shot her an odd look before turning back to his computer. Alice's cheeks warmed from a brief flash of embarrassment. The world had changed so much in the time she'd been away. TVs were thinner and phones were smarter now. *Now I know how my mom felt,* she thought, and realized she'd not thought of her mother in years. This sudden reemergence in her memories only bolstered the storm looming over her mind. *I should go visit her grave, maybe when this is all over. If this ever ends.*

She faced the door to room 703 and wished she'd brought flowers or something.

Evelyn's husband, Nathan, opened the door on her second knock and welcomed her inside. He looked older since she'd last seen him, his face drawn with heavy bags below his eyes, but she suspected the fluorescent lighting wasn't doing her any favors either.

On the wall, a muted TV was tuned to the news. A reporter stood across the street from the transit authority, and a red ticker along the bottom said something about an explosion downtown. "Authorities are not ruling out a terrorist attack," it read.

A small armchair sat in the corner covered with a mound of blankets and a pillow. Alice's heart lightened when she saw it. He hadn't left her side.

Evelyn looked the same as before, bundled comfortably in her bed and covered in a scattering of bandages. "Hey, Al. You clean up nice."

Alice smiled. "A shower works miracles. How're you feeling, old lady?"

"Not too bad, all things considered. Except this old man here snores way more than he used to."

Nathan returned to the hospital bed, took Evelyn's hand in his and gave it a squeeze. "I could say the same about you, my dear." To Alice: "How's the tenacious Private Eye?"

Alice opened her mouth to speak, but the words faltered on her tongue, and she second-guessed what to say, how much to tell him. So much had happened in the last twenty-four hours that she'd barely had enough time to unpack it herself. The last thing she wanted to do was drop a bomb on the happy couple, especially after being apart for so long. "He's doing okay. Downstairs in the ER if you can believe it. Needed some stitches for a bad cut on his arm." Concern lit up Detective Brock's face, but Alice raised her hand to calm him. "Relax, he'll be fine. He passed out before the nurse had a chance to give him an anesthetic. I don't think these quakes will wake him."

"Yeah," Evelyn said, "we felt the building shake." She waited, searching Alice's face. "How bad is it?"

Alice glanced at Nathan, and then back to Evie. He looked at them both and nodded. "Girl talk. I get it. I'll leave you two ladies to it then."

When he was gone, Alice took Nathan's place beside the bed. She knelt, and the tears were flowing before she could open her mouth. Evelyn squeezed her hand and softly shushed her.

"What happened?"

Alice told her about the day, from the resurfacing memories to the subway crash and the spiderlings underground. She shivered as she recounted the things glimpsed in the darkness of the wrecked subway cars. She cried harder when she spoke of her frustration with Michael. None of this was fair. She'd lost her future husband, then her identity, nearly lost her life while trying to survive in the Monochrome for years, and now that she was finally back, the world was ending.

Her sorrow reached a crescendo point when the words stopped coming and were replaced by heavy sobs, her chest rising and falling in hitches, the tears cooling her burning cheeks. Evelyn squeezed her hand through it all, did what any good mother would do, and let the poor girl cry it out.

"Al, honey..." Evelyn swallowed back tears of her own. "God, I don't know what to say to make you feel better. I don't know if I can."

Alice forced herself to smile, wiped her eyes. "Of course you can't, old lady. You're bedridden in a hospital."

"You know what I mean, smartass."

"I do…I just can't help thinking I'm being selfish for feeling this way. Michael's brother is still missing. The world is falling apart. And here I am being all 'woe is me' while something horrible is happening out there. Maybe everywhere." She cleared her throat, thought for a moment. "I've never felt so small in my whole goddamn life. It's like you said before…the machine is slowing down."

"I've never wanted to be more wrong." Evelyn sighed, looked toward the window and the fractured skyline beyond. "It's odd…not an hour ago, I was asleep and having the strangest dream."

"What about?"

"About a needle. A huge needle sticking out of the earth. There were all these threads connected to the eye, and Donovan was there, watching while some old man tried to cut them all."

"That is strange."

Evelyn shook her head. "No, that's not even the strangest part. There were cracks in the sky, like it was a big dirty window. And I could see pieces of blue in the opening—"

Another tremor shook the building, followed by the sonic crash of an explosion somewhere nearby. The windowpane splintered in a hundred tiny cracks, segmenting the city beyond like a drab kaleidoscope. Plumes of smoke drifted lazily into the sky. Overhead, the lights flickered, dimmed, and then brightened once more. Alice realized she'd been holding her breath.

"—and then I woke up, and I see shit like this happening outside and on the news."

Alice approached the window with trepidation, fearful another quake might shatter the glass entirely, but her curiosity held her tightly in its clutches.

Strange bands of light split the skyline in odd intervals as if someone had placed spotlights all over the city. Stranger still was their visibility in broad daylight—and yet even that seemed diminished, like a dull curtain had been pulled over the world. More troubling than the odd light, however, was the appearance of massive dark cracks spread across the sky above. From a distance, she'd mistaken them for splintering glass; up close, she saw they were real despite their impossible nature.

The sky was a smashed television screen, hazy with static and the Monochrome's unlight seeping through the cracks. The ribbons of light revealed faint lines, woven threads tethered to something unseen and stretched so tight they vibrated with each earthly tremor.

Alice's heart sank into a well of despair as she watched a thick fissure spread across the horizon. She looked back to her old friend and found words she hadn't been brave enough to voice in front of Michael and Quinn. "Evie, what if Donovan failed? We put all our hope in him because… because he could do what we couldn't, but what if that wasn't enough?"

Her words hung in the air between them as silence filled in the gaps. The implication of whatever was happening in the city, perhaps even across the world now, was that Sparrow had won. The balance was tipping, and the machine was slowing down. The Monochrome was colliding into the Spectrum. Those things below the city were proof of that, and soon they were going to reach the surface if they hadn't already.

"No," Evelyn said. A sly smile spread across her face. "I don't believe that. I can't. The man I met down in those tunnels had a fire inside him. He had something to prove, and not just to anyone. He had something to prove to himself."

Alice sank into the armchair and closed her eyes. "My gut tells me he's dead, Evie. Or worse, maybe Sparrow's done something to him." She sighed, shook her head. "But my heart…my heart says you might be right. He's still in the Monochrome trying to make things right. That's the Donovan I remember, the one I still know."

Evelyn smiled. "And there's the headstrong woman I've known all these years." She reached out her hand, and Alice took it. "But you promise me something, girl."

"Of course, Evie. Anything."

"Whatever's happening outside, don't you try to save me this time. I'm back where I want to be."

Alice opened her mouth to protest, but the old woman gave her a look that could crack stones.

"I mean it, Al. I'm back where I belong, and my husband is still here. We have each other. It's times like this we have to have faith, just like when we were down in those tunnels scraping by day to day. I'm not talking about gods or temples, but about faith in each other. I'm talking about faith in you, in Mike, in Donna and Donovan. *In each other.*" She punctuated her words by squeezing Alice's hand. Tears swallowed her eyes. "Well. Leave it to this old bitch to get sentimental. Hand me a tissue, would you?"

Alice did as she was asked, and then she planted a kiss on the old woman's forehead. "Thank you. You always know when to kick my ass."

The room shivered as another tremor tore through the earth. Evelyn smiled and patted Alice's hand. "Any time, Al."

"**D**id you feel that?"

Donna eased herself out of the exam chair and looked at her sister, but Amanda was too preoccupied with her phone. She'd been glued to the screen throughout the nonstress test, and even when the nurse had proclaimed all was normal, Amanda had offered little more than a hurried nod. That her sister hadn't felt the strange shuddering in the floor wasn't all that surprising.

She snapped her fingers. "Amanda. Hey. Come back to earth for a minute."

Amanda looked up from the screen, her face drawn with worry. "Sorry. What is it?"

"That vibration. It felt like an earthquake."

"I didn't feel anything. I was reading the news reports. About the subway accident, and something else happening downtown. One of the police stations…isn't there anymore."

Donna slipped on her shoes. In her concern over the baby's health, she'd pushed the train derailment from her mind. The exam room felt too warm, the walls too close, and she wondered how much more stress she could really take. "Not there anymore? Like, it was destroyed?"

"I'm not sure. It's still developing. They said there's a lot of smoke and dust and no one's sure what's really going on. And the emergency crew that went into the subway hasn't returned yet."

"That's weird."

"Right? You'd think there'd be something more by now." The phone buzzed again. Amanda was already out of her seat with purse in hand. "Quinn's headed back to the lobby. I'll meet you there."

"Sure," Donna whispered, not really hearing her sister. Her mind returned to the vibration she'd felt a moment earlier. The sensation had unearthed something in her memory, a half-buried artifact left for her to find, and when she projected herself into that daydream state, a sudden jolt snapped her back to reality.

Another tremor, this one strong enough to rattle the loose paraphernalia in their jars on the counterspace. *Getting closer,* she thought, and remembered a story Donovan read to her once, about villages of people tethering themselves together into massive giants. She'd always imagined the footsteps of gargantuan beasts might sound like the crash of thunder, but this was different. This was heavier somehow—

The intercom speaker crackled to life overhead. "All hospital personnel: Code Triage." Donna held her breath and waited. The alert repeated itself twice more and was accompanied by the pattering of feet outside in the hall.

What if it wasn't an earthquake? Those tremors were quick, short—oh shit, what if they were explosions? What if it's a terrorist attack? She clutched her belly absently. Mere thought of a such a disaster kicked her maternal instincts into overdrive.

And then she remembered why she was there in the first place. Panic and anxiety, a fainting spell likely sparked by immense stress, and she'd just completed a nonstress test for the baby less than ten minutes before.

Cool it. She tried, took a few breaths, and focused her mind. *The code is probably just for the subway crash.* Of course there would be a surge of wounded people in need of emergency services. But what of the tremors? What of the—

Another shock rumbled through the floor and walls, rattling anything not bolted down. The lights flickered overhead, and from somewhere outside the room, someone yelped in surprise.

Donna walked to the door, gave a silent prayer, and stepped into the hallway. A pair of nurses exchanged hushed concerns, but their expressions melted into smiles when they noticed her walking by. She hadn't heard much—something about downtown, a police station—and then she was moving on down the hall. The double doors ahead swung open, and several EMTs rushed in a man on a gurney. Donna flattened herself against the wall, told herself to look away, but her eyes wouldn't listen.

My god, his face. What is that on his face?

A thick white mass covered half his head, but as they neared, she realized she couldn't tell where the membranous tissue ended and the patient's face began. Multiple lumps along the ridges suggested what might have once been legs or arms, but they'd softened and fused themselves to the poor man's skin.

His clothes were blackened with blood and his arms jerked against their restraints. One of his legs kicked upward with such force his shoe dislodged, hit the ceiling, and fell with a dull thump on the tile floor. The

EMTs ignored it, kept wheeling him down the hall where they were joined by the other nurses. Donna remained in place and stared at the orphaned boot.

Something stirred inside it; a moment later, a white spider crawled out and over the loose shoestrings. The insect was larger than any she'd seen before, at least as big as her hand, and the longer she stared, the larger it seemed to grow.

A memory pushed its way to the surface, suddenly free from the obscuring mental detritus weighing it down, and forced itself into the front of her mind. She'd seen something like this before. Yes, she was certain of it—she recognized the round knobby head, the eyes, the way it wrinkled its face into a sneer. She'd seen one on her shoulder, days before she'd been kidnapped, while standing at the bathroom mirror brushing her hair. The creature's appearance was sudden, and yet it hadn't seemed out of place, and in the ensuing minutes she forgot it was even there. It had whispered something to her then, something that had seemed almost soothing—

Do not listen. Do not remember. Do not believe.

A searing white spike wedged itself in her brain and drove the memory away. She uttered a gasp at the sudden ache, turned away, and saw two drops of blood splatter on the tile. There was a familiar warmth on her upper lip, and when she ran her tongue across it, she tasted copper. The headache surged, building a stormfront of pressure at the base of her skull, and slowly working its way forward.

Do not speak. Do not scream. Do not run.

The words filled her mind in a droning cadence, lighting up places of her mind she'd not realized were there. A single word bubbled to the surface: *Cretins.*

Were these the things Donovan had told her about? No, these were different. Changed somehow.

The frantic tapping of spindly legs on tile pulled her from her trance. Donna winced as she forced herself to look toward the creature. An onslaught of stiff robotic commands filled her head, but she braced against them, focused her vision and mind on the pallid creature scuttling toward her. It was bigger now, easily the size of a kitten, and now she could see its jagged teeth. An eerie white light emanated from its dark eyes.

She thought of the bloodied man and the tumor on his face, and just as the spiderling readied itself to leap, Donna crushed the monstrosity beneath her shoe. There was no satisfying snap of bones or crunch of exoskeleton;

instead, a gurgling plop of viscous gray goo shot out from both sides like a lanced infection.

Donna lifted her foot in triumph, relieved the headache was gone, but when she saw the jellied remains and smelled the pulpy stench of old paper mâché, her stomach churned. A drone of clanging bells filled her ears as dark colors flashed across her vision in dazzling starbursts. She swallowed the taste of bile and told herself she would not get sick here. Not now.

When the nausea passed, she marched forward to the end of the hall and pushed her way into the ER lobby.

The room buzzed with panic, every face a canvas of anxiety and fear, and the nurses at the front desk struggled to keep up with the demand of in-patient processing.

Donna spotted her sister across the room, standing with Quinn. When she joined them, Amanda handed her a tissue and frowned.

"Another nosebleed. I knew we should've asked for another exam. Let me go find that nurse—"

"No." Donna put her hand on her sister's arm, shook her head. "We need to leave. We need to get away from this place."

"Tell me about it. It's a madhouse here, and we almost lost power from those quakes. Not to mention they're on alert for anyone caught in the subway crash…" The grave look on Donna's face was enough to give Amanda pause. "What is it? What's wrong?"

"You don't understand." She turned to Quinn, put her hand on his shoulder. Tears wrapped her eyes and her whole body trembled with fear. What she was about to say meant a forfeiture of reality and acceptance of what Donovan had been trying to warn them about. Even now, with the words on the tip of her tongue, she felt herself resist the implication, knowing this was a drastic leap from which there would be no return.

"What is it, Donna?"

"It's…the Cretins, Quinn. They're here. I—"

A scream sliced through the room and silenced the lobby to a jumble of stunned murmurs. Their eyes were collectively drawn to the windows and the parking garage beyond. A trio of bloodied figures—two EMTs and what might've been a victim from the subway—staggered their way around a derelict ambulance.

White tumors clung to their heads.

Out in the hallway, the intercom sprang to life with static, and a panicked voice announced Code Gray.

-9-

MAGGOTS

"Before we enter, I must give you a warning."

Donovan heard his companion but didn't look away from the gathering crowd of pilgrims. The city had all but vanished, was little more than a distant outline on the horizon, and yet no matter where he turned there were more of the Missing journeying across the desert. They approached, heads bent and eyes focused forward as if in a trance, drawn toward the edge of the massive storm ahead.

"Mr. Candle."

"Do they know where they're going? I mean…" He thought Guffin's widow. She'd seemed conscious enough, although not entirely sane. "They're walking right into that thing."

Aleister nodded solemnly. "It is where we must go if we are to reach the Needle."

"The Needle?"

"The column from your dream. It has possessed many names over time, but those in my order called it the Needle. It is where the strings of mankind are woven into the tapestry above." He gestured to the sky. Among the backdrop of darkening fractures was an infinite expanse of faint lines. "All strings lead to the Needle and the Great Weaver within."

"You mean the Ungod?"

"Indeed, Mr. Candle. The tempest beyond us is the final demarcation before we approach the center of the Monochrome. It will be our crucible."

Donovan looked up at the swirling mass of dust clouds. He'd seen photos of microburst storms, but this was far larger, a massive swirling wall of violent air and sand obscuring something hideous and strange beyond. He'd glimpsed the tangle of pallid vines roiling over one another like a swirling nest of snakes and thinking of them now spurred a chill from his head to toe.

"It isn't just a storm," he said, more to himself than the old monk.

"Indeed, Mr. Candle. It is the cause for my warning."

"You've been inside that thing?"

"Several times now. It is…" Dullington's face slackened as he lost himself in his thoughts. After a moment of silence, he sighed. "Most unpleasant."

"Why not do your disappearing act? You know, *will* yourself over there the way you left me on that fucking building." The words were harsher than he'd intended, but the meaning was the same. The inner voice of Joe Hopper said to trust Dullington, but Donovan found he was tired of being led along with only pieces of the picture. It was a seething kind of anger he'd tried to bury deep down after leaving the WBS building however long ago that was now. Hours? Days? Hell, it could've been years. Would Donna even remember him when he returned? *If* he returned?

"Even I have my limits, Mr. Candle. And I am not telling you everything for your own sake. Some burdens man is not meant to bear."

"See," Donovan snapped, "that's what I mean. 'Some burdens man isn't meant to bear.' And yet here we are, Al. I'm standing at the foot of an impossible storm in an impossible place on my way to wake up a god. I think we're past the point of 'what man is not meant to bear.'"

"Mr. Candle—"

"The *only* reason I'm following you, Dullington, is because I have no other choice." He turned and sat down in the sand with his back to the old monk. "So go on and patronize me some more. Why not. It's not like I have a life to get back to, or a wife, or a child…"

The anger fizzled out at his utterance of those words, leaving in their place a cold ache that resonated through his heart. Donna and the baby. That's all he wanted, his only reason for going on at this point.

Aleister Dullington sat next to him, and for a time they watched the pilgrims march around them.

Donovan searched their surroundings, desperate for anything to tear his mind away from the thoughts and fears nibbling at his resolve. He settled on a small mound of sand not far from them and realized something was protruding from the short dune. Recalling the errant bones he'd seen further back, Donovan allowed his curiosity to lift him to his feet, and he crossed the gap. As he neared, he realized what he was staring at, and its existence here disturbed him more than the storm's looming presence.

A boat? Here? How…

He turned back and watched Dullington approach.

A flurry of words swept through Donovan's mind, all of them barbed and venomous and aimed at the only friend he had in this place. "Friend" was such a dubious term, but what else could he call him? He was certainly not his enemy. Not entirely. A memory surfaced of his college days, one of the many English Lit courses he'd attended. The many lectures on Faust and the devil, Mephistopheles. The entire semester on Dante and Virgil as they journeyed down the circles of Hell.

There's always a guide, hoss. Always one to follow into the darkness, one to lead you through to the light.

Of course Hopper was right. Wasn't he always?

Donovan sighed, looked at his companion. "I'm not going to apologize, Aleister."

"I know, Mr. Candle. I deserved your words."

"You going to explain this?" Donovan kicked the edge of the old dinghy. A cloud of fine sand slipped from its bow. Dullington's lips spread thin in a faint grimace as if he'd tasted something sour. He gave the boat little more than a passing glance before turning away. Donovan took note of his companion's reticence and filed it away for later.

A rumbling tremor shook the earth beneath them while dark fractures split the sky along the horizon. Donovan thought of Donna again, wondered if she was safe.

"I cannot lie to you, Mr. Candle. She is not safe. None of them are. And the longer we wait here—"

"Yeah, I get it." Donovan dusted sand from his jeans. "What's your warning?"

Dullington pointed toward the tempest. "This is a storm of dead dreams, Mr. Candle. Inside you will be confronted with your fears, your failures, every nightmare you have ever experienced. Inside, they are real and they will attempt to consume you." He set off toward the rim of the storm. "If we become separated, and I suppose we will, ignore their calling and continue forward."

Donovan followed him to the edge. Violent winds blasted his face with coarse sand. He raised his hand to shield his face. Dullington said something else, but his voice was lost in the gale, and a moment later he was gone.

"Dead dreams," Donovan whispered, but his own voice was stolen in the tumult. He thought of Donna again. *I would for you, love.*

He sucked in his breath and marched into the storm.

———•———

Detective Brock heard the first code announcement as he trotted down the hall, but his mind was far away, lost in a blur of thoughts and elation. He was still high on the sudden reappearance of his long-lost wife, and still struggling to make sense of the strange curiosities he'd witnessed in the last forty-eight hours. The detective in him, bolstered with decades of training and experience, suggested he have his annual psych evaluation early this year; and yet there was another part, buried deep down and long forgotten, whose words now filled his mind like a chilled breeze: *Roll with it, old man.*

But he didn't hear the words in his own voice. This voice was younger. Stronger, maybe.

Nathan sighed and shook his head, wished he could smoke here. There weren't many people who could stir up a craving for nicotine faster than Donovan Candle. *You've disappeared off the face of the planet and you still won't leave me the hell alone.*

He walked past the nurse's station, which now stood empty—presumably because of the code he'd heard, although he couldn't recall what it was for exactly—and approached the window at the far end of the hallway. What he saw beyond the cracked glass stole the breath from his wheezing lungs, yanked him back from the euphoria of recent days.

Pillars of smoke obscured fractions of the city. Jagged sections of the sky were missing, colored over in a dark gray hue which made his head hurt whenever he tried to focus on it.

You stupid old man. You've locked yourself away in Evie's room all damn day and ignored your duty.

The guilt he felt was fleeting, however, when a sudden indignation reared its head from the depth of his soul. Goddamn right he ignored his duty. After years of thinking her dead, his Evie had returned to him; leaving her to do something as trivial as protect a city intent on eating itself was out of the question. The only reason he'd dodged retirement was with the hope that he might find her one day. *Mission accomplished, Captain. I'll take my leave now, thank you, sir.*

And yet he was afraid to take off his badge so soon. Buried beneath all that indignation was something he didn't want to admit. He'd locked himself away with her in the hospital room, an old man caring for an old woman, terrified that if he so much as closed his eyes, she'd vanish again. He was so paranoid that he'd haggled with hospital security over keeping his service weapon in his holster instead of handing it over at the entrance. Cost him a hundred bucks to make them look the other way— that and name-dropping his captain—but his peace of mind was worth every penny. He knew it was a foolish thing to do, and even Evie said as much when she spotted the shoulder holster underneath his suit coat. She was here, all right, and she wasn't going anywhere.

They'd sat up into the late hours, talking about nothing, talking about everything in the years between. She'd told him of all that had happened, all she'd done, the good and the bad, the thieving and hiding and, in a few cases, the killing—self-defense, she'd said, and he believed her—and he'd listened with rapt attention even if his dusty mind had trouble making sense of some parts.

Even if he'd heard some of it before while sitting across the table from Donovan just a couple of nights ago.

And still the fear lingered. A fear he couldn't put into words even when she suspected something was wrong. *I may have been gone for years, honey, but I'd know that look anywhere. What's on your mind?*

He'd almost told her, almost spilled his guts about the stupid dream he'd had that first night after her return, but the old detective in him forced it all back into the shadows. *Best not to give it voice,* he'd thought. *It's just a crazy dream, probably nothing more than indigestion and stress. More gravy than grave, isn't that what old Scrooge said?*

Now, staring out the window at the city shivering in the wake of an unnamed cataclysm, Nathan Brock swallowed his pride and admitted to himself that something else was going on. Something beyond his scope of understanding.

The dream played out before him in vivid clarity: the city was on fire, earthquakes were shaking the foundations, and somewhere down below, there was Chaos with a capital C. Thousands of people—but *were* they people anymore?—walked lazily across a shattered hellscape of cracked pavement and glass. Their heads were covered in strange white growths, some so thick and distorted that their faces were unrecognizable. They were coming here, coming to make everyone see something.

No, to *face* something. That's what a booming voice had said before the sky overhead shattered in a million jagged pieces and covered the world. *All will become their failures,* that voice had said, and he'd awakened in the comfy armchair with a frantic kick. He'd found Evelyn fast asleep in the hospital bed beside him, the gadgets monitoring her vitals beeping in a steady rhythm. The dream was so out of the ordinary, so outlandish, and yet in the following hours he'd watched the sunrise because he couldn't bear facing the horrific landscape again when he closed his eyes.

Now, he watched out the window as the scenery of his dream happened in high-def clarity, and Brock realized he'd been right to keep his service weapon on hand.

He pulled out his phone from his pocket and turned it on, cursing himself for cutting off his ties to the department. It was hasty, unprofessional, and—

The screen brightened to life. He had eight missed calls and twenty-three messages. When he checked the latter, he saw they were from his captain, his fellow detectives, even a few of the rookies with whom he'd had drinks on occasion.

> Nate where are you?

> Need you on duty ASAP
> -call me

> Subway derailed near
> transit authority

> ANSWER UR PHONE!

> 12 PRECINCT
> ATTACKED!

> WHERE ARE YOU?

Detective Brock pocketed the phone and closed his eyes, listened to his racing heart. The fear within seeped to the surface where it lingered, coating him in a sheen of panic sweat. He felt disgusting, wanted to tear off his clothes and skin and shower for a thousand years, wanted to pack up his wife and get the hell out of town before things got worse.

But you can't, he told himself, *because what's happening out there might be happening everywhere. You know it is, because that's how it happened in your dream.*

He opened his eyes, took a breath, waited for his ticker to slow. "Not a dream," he whispered to the hallway. "A living nightmare."

Overhead, a panicked voice sprang from the intercom and announced a Code Gray.

Nathan broke free of the fear holding him at the window, pushed himself forward toward his room, his wife, and the service weapon which might—God willing—protect them from the Chaos outside.

The door opened just as he reached its threshold. The young woman, Alice, stood before him with something in her hand. He lifted his gaze from her hand to her face and saw they shared the same urgency, perhaps even the same intentions.

"I need to borrow your gun." She cocked her head in Evie's direction. "Your wife said it's okay."

"My wife—wait, my gun? Just hang on—"

"Let her go," Evelyn said. "I need you here with me."

His cheeks flushed with heat. "Should I give her my fucking badge too, Evie? Christ."

The ladies shared a laugh, and Brock knew he wouldn't win this argument. And perhaps that was just as well. He felt his age in that moment, and the idea of passing the burden on to someone else, someone younger and stronger, filled him with such a rush of relief.

"Honey, come here." Evelyn held out her hand, and he brushed past the young woman into the room. He took her hand, felt comfort in its warmth. "I need you to trust me, old man. There are things happening downstairs that you aren't prepared for. Neither am I, for that matter—but she is."

"Evie, can she even use that thing?"

"Of course. Who do you think taught her?" Evelyn grinned. "Ain't that right, Al?"

Brock turned back, watched Alice pull back the slide and check the chamber. "Well, shit." He pointed to his overnight bag next to the armchair. "I've got two extra mags in there."

Alice began to cross the room once again, but he stopped her, put his hand on her shoulder. He tried to hold back the tears, but the stone-faced façade he'd spent decades carving finally began to crack. *Keep your shit together, old man.* Only he couldn't, he knew he couldn't, and that knowledge made it so much worse.

He collected himself, wiped his eyes, and stumbled through his words.

"You be careful, young lady. Evie says you saved her life more than once, and I suppose I owe you for that."

"No, detective, that's where you're wrong." Alice smiled, patted his hand, and retrieved the spare magazines from his bag. "You don't owe me anything." She bent and planted a kiss on Evelyn's forehead. "Just promise me you'll stay here and keep her safe."

Brock shook his head. "How am I supposed to do that when you're taking my weapon?"

Alice made her way to the door. "Because, dear detective, you've got a spare revolver in your bag just below your undies." She tilted her head to Evelyn and grinned. "Girl talk, remember?"

The color drained from Nathan Brock's face. He watched the young woman leave, and when he turned back to his wife, Evelyn burst into a fit of laughter. A moment later, he joined her, and for a while they forgot about the world falling down around them.

———————•———————

After Donna left them to find Michael, Quinn stayed behind with this mother in the lobby. He observed the disgusting things lumbering outside with the warm fascination of a child, his face nearly pressed against the glass despite his mother's nagging.

There were more of them now. Hideous things that used to be human, remnants of men and women unfortunate enough to be in the wrong place, wrong time, wrong reality. Aunt Donna said the Cretins were here, and while he believed she'd seen something, he knew better than to believe they were Cretins. The things he'd witnessed down in the tunnels were something else entirely. He recalled their ravenous hate and all those scuttling legs.

They came straight for us. Not to make us forget, but to consume us, and they would've if it hadn't been for the subway train. A shiver crawled down his neck and along the length of his spine. *The train didn't stop them. They seeped into the train. And what they did to the people inside—*

One of the tumor-headed things walked into the locked automatic doors with a dull *splat*. It teetered back, swayed in place like the Yawning, and then tried again. *Splat.* A film of white residue seeped from the bloated flesh coating its host's face. Spiderling limbs fanned out of the victim's mouth and buried themselves into the tender skin of a blood-caked throat. Human traits ended at the bridge of the nose; from there, a cluster of pulsing white growths had consumed the victim's head. Quinn thought it looked like a rotting gourd.

"*Please* get away from the window." His mother again. He nodded to signal his intent, but he wasn't alone in his fascination. There were other men and women pressed against the glass to get a better look, and all of them shared a common revulsion. Except him, of course. He was the only one in the room with a greater context, a young man who'd glimpsed the impossible, witnessed the greater horrors of what lie beyond the veil.

But despite their familiarity, Quinn found he was drawn in by their differences. Their lazy movement, the way they shivered and swayed, was just like the Yawning, but their blind wandering sparked a memory. Mr. Jewell's biology class, junior year. The lifecycle of a housefly.

They're just like maggots. Blind, squirming, looking for food. And they had to hatch from somewhere. Inside us, maybe, just like that weird mediocrity shit Sparrow drew from all those people at the station and used to make the Yawning.

Another heavy *thunk* as one more swollen half-human thing walked into the glass. Quinn finally turned away, was about to share his revelation with his mother, and saw a man in dusty jeans and a sweat-stained T-shirt reading "Foley Construction" eagerly walk toward the automatic doors. A mop of dirty blonde hair sat atop his head, he wore a fresh cast on his right forearm, and a pair of wild blue eyes complimented the cocky smirk smeared across his face. A brunette woman—his wife, maybe, though she wasn't wearing a ring—tugged at his arm, begged him to stop.

"—don't know what those things are," she said. "Please, Dustin—"

"Let go of me, Kelly. I don't have no time off left. If I don't get back to the site, the foreman will can my ass for good. Anyway, just look at 'em, will ya? They're harmless. *I said let go of me!*" He yanked his arm free of Kelly's grip and smacked her. Several people in the lobby grumbled uncomfortably. Quinn looked to his mother, but she averted her eyes, shook her head for him to do the same. She should've known better.

"Hey." Quinn stepped forward. "Didn't anyone teach you not to hit women?"

"Mind your own fuckin' business, dude. Kelly, you comin' or not?"

Kelly held a hand to her face, hiding the eye where she'd been struck, trying to hold back the tears but failing. She met Quinn's stare. He shook his head and mouthed *Don't,* but she had already taken Dustin's hand.

"Look, you don't know—"

Dustin pointed and spat at Quinn's feet. "You don't know shit, kid.

Anyone else want a piece of my mind?" He surveyed the room, waiting for someone else to step up, but they all withered under his nervous gaze.

"Let him go," an old man said. His elderly wife nodded silently, gripping her cane as if ready to defend herself. Others grumbled in agreement, and Quinn felt his mother's hand on his shoulder.

"Not your fight, hon."

"No," he whispered, "but that doesn't make it right."

Satisfied with their silence, Dustin pushed open the first pair of doors and pulled Kelly into the foyer with him. She closed the doors behind her, and before she turned away, she gave Quinn a quiet nod as if to say thanks.

He frowned, his face flushing with heat and shame. *She doesn't want to go. Hell, it's right there on her face, and no one around me did a goddamn thing about it.*

Over the last week, he'd been exposed to the darker side of humanity's innate drive for self-preservation. Sparrow's followers versus the misfit outcasts, each one choosing a side out of fear and hope. *How quickly we turn on ourselves when the chips are down. Another day and we'll be eating each other. Maybe the world deserves to crumble.*

Dustin unlocked the outer doors and pushed them open. Kelly lingered a moment longer, still questioning if she'd made the right decision, before he yanked her outside. He turned to her, said something that might've been "See, nothing to worry about" if he'd been able to finish the sentence.

Quinn already knew what awaited him when he turned back to the lobby windows. The eruption of gasps and screams all but confirmed it, and he'd already steeled himself against the bilious reflux of horror rising in his gut. A dozen instances of the Yawning's grisly meals flashed before him, but after he witnessed the end of the poor couple outside, he thought those lanky monstrosities merciful by comparison. With the Yawning, everything was over in a single chomp.

With these half-human things, consumption wasn't as simple or clean—and like their taller monstrous cousins, their sluggish, dimwitted gait was deceptive.

When Dustin and Kelly began their trek across the rotunda toward the parking garage, the few creatures near the entrance all seized in unison. Their fingers flared and curled, and the clusters of tumors obscuring their faces began to pulse erratically. They pivoted, watching—no, *tracking* the arguing couple across the pavement.

And then the one nearest the doors, the one in a bloody EMT uniform, broke into a crazed dash toward them. It tackled Dustin, diving headfirst into his back like a tumorous arrow. Both sprawled forward into a landscaped median, crushing flowers and shooting tufts of mulch into the air.

Kelly screamed for help, but no one in the lobby was prepared to go outside. How could they be? Even now their eyes struggled to make sense of what they witnessed. Only Quinn had the slightest idea, and even he remained frozen, unable to act out of sheer fear. The risks were real now. Maybe they always had been, but just a couple minutes ago, he was prepared to defend that poor woman against her abusive boyfriend. Now he stood by with the rest of the onlookers, ashamed and afraid and unwilling to help her as she begged for her life.

There were others now, closing in on their position with the same mad scrambling of legs and pale pulsing flesh. Dustin tried to regain his footing but to no avail; the first creature pinned him to the ground, driving its knees into his back as it lowered its head toward his. One of the giant tumors swelled and popped like a malignant bubble, and the same thin residue seeped from the wound over the back of Dustin's skull.

A pause slipped over the scene as the nerves in Dustin's body woke up, and in an instant, the cocky construction worker began to scream. It was shrill and wet and lasted for what felt like years, and then Kelly joined him. She'd tried to run for the garage, but not with those white heels she was wearing. Her ankle had twisted as soon as she'd left the pavement. Now she lay in a crumpled mess, kicking and crying against the faceless abominations as they crowded around her.

Her screams lasted only a few seconds longer before silence fell over the world once more. The first creature climbed to its feet, hefting the twitching remains of Dustin's body effortlessly into the air, and Quinn's gut curled into itself when he finally made sense of what he was seeing. Their two bodies were conjoined at the head, one cluster of tumors forming another, like a finger trap of blood and viscera and pale goo.

Hushed silence fell over the ER lobby, punctuated by the occasional quieted sob. When Quinn looked back to his mother, he saw she'd vomited into a small wastebasket. She wiped her mouth and shook her head. He read the terror on her face. There were no words to express the utter horror she was experiencing, and for all that Quinn had seen in the last week, he found even he struggled with what had just transpired.

The world slowly blurred and went glassy, and he realized he was crying. Amanda reached for him and he embraced her, unashamed of the emotions flooding his mind and heart, unashamed that he now felt like a young boy all over again. He'd once thought himself strong and ready for whatever the world might throw his way; now he felt ill, weakened by the knowledge of things beyond his understanding.

"I don't know what's happening," his mother whispered, and he squeezed her tighter. He shook his head, but inside he had a good sense of what was happening and realized there was a deeper root to his sadness, a cause for all the unease happening around them. *Now would be a good time to come back, Uncle Don.*

Quinn held his mother close until the tears passed and he could think straight again. He looked out the window one last time and saw the tumorous figures had turned their attention to the ER entrance. More had appeared from the parking garage and were shambling toward the windows.

He closed his eyes and turned away. *They're being consumed, eaten alive from the inside. God, if they're maggots, then what are they going to become?*

FEAR OF A BLANK PLANET

Donna's heart raced as one sterile corridor turned into another. Visions of the seizing patient flashed before her, fueling an ever-present dread which would not relent no matter how much she reassured herself things would be fine.

But how could they be after what she'd seen? The implications shattered her perception of the world. After the EMTs staggered into view outside the lobby, she'd retreated out of instinct, promising her sister and nephew that she would return once she found Michael. Now there was screaming and it sounded like it was coming from behind. *You could always cut and run,* a voice whispered, *get yourself and the baby as far away from here as possible. Take your chances. Steal a car, get away, start over. Donovan's not coming back. He's either dead or abandoned you, and did you really need him anyway? He's the worst kind of baggage, honey, a walking panic attack too afraid of his own dreams. All he's doing is weighing you down. You don't—*

"Fucking stop." She stamped her foot on the tile floor. The ensuing clap echoed down the hall, and a gray-haired woman stuck her head out from one of the exam rooms.

"You okay?"

"I'm fine," she said, the response an automatic reflex. Any other day she might've smiled, averted her eyes, and kept right on walking. "I'm—

(scared)

—I need to find my brother-in-law."

"Is he a patient here?"

"He was brought back here not too long ago. Had a deep cut on his arm."

The nurse stepped into the hallway and smiled. It was a forced expression, but one she'd probably spent years honing in the face of true emergency. "I know the one. Big baby, that one." She pointed onward. "Round the corner at the end of the hall. First door on your left. Just listen for the whimpering."

Donna smiled, looked at the woman's badge affixed to her scrub top. "Thank you, Carina."

"Not a problem, hon." Nurse Carina glanced at Donna's belly and grinned. The older woman's wrinkles furled, revealing a warm kindness that reminded Donna of her late grandmother. "How far along are you?"

"Second trimester," she said. Again, the words felt automatic, a recording playing on repeat. "Thank you." Donna wanted to go on about the nuances of pregnancy, something she supposed most women had in common, but the familiar ache in her skull slowly began its tribal beat once again. She clenched her jaw, forced a smile, and kept on walking while the world shifted around her like two overlapping images knocked out of sync. She reached out to steady herself against the wall.

Donna tried to focus ahead through the visual dissonance, but the world seemed to fall out of place, revealing a hazy facsimile of itself. She turned, was about to cry out to the nurse when she saw Carina had shut her eyes, was putting pressure on her temples.

Not just me, she thought. *It's everyone. What the hell is happening to us?*

And then Carina was gone. Donna blinked out of reflex, her mind unable to correlate the sudden absence, and she even saw the nurse's outline like a faint shadow. The woman's silhouette slowly faded into a backdrop of gray walls. An awful synthetic drone pierced Donna's ears, reverberating in time to the heartbeat throbbing away in her head. She blinked again, shook her head, frantically looked around the hallway for something familiar, but there were only gray shapes and dark outlines and that goddamn awful noise filling her head.

Movement from the corner of her eye. Something small, blurry. She tried to focus, but the throbbing in her head had stolen her energy, attention. *What is happening to me?*

And then she saw it. Small, bipedal, and pale. She thought of a famous doughboy mascot and almost laughed until the little thing moved closer to her. Where had it come from? Was it always there? It looked so familiar somehow, its general shape sparking a long-forgotten memory—

No, this *is a Cretin. Not the spider-like thing I saw before. That was something different.*

As if it sensed her epiphany, the pale creature leered up at her and gave her the finger. A flood of words churned through her head in reverse, forming a terrible sound that clouded her thoughts. She stepped back, wanting to run

Then it tapped against the wall, and something stirred from beyond the boundary, a scrambling, gnashing sound like too many feet and teeth.

"I've lost my mind," she whispered, and the Cretin slowly shook its head.

The world fell out of focus once more. Color flooded her vision, revealing the figure of Carina, who was now huddled in the doorway of the exam room. She covered her face with her hands and slowly shook her head. Donna thought she heard the poor woman sobbing, was about to retrace her steps and comfort the nurse when she realized the Cretin was still there.

The creature blinked, examined its surroundings in a puzzled stupor, and suddenly convulsed. It cried out in pain before doubling over; an instant later, a trio of limbs sprouted from its back.

Donna sucked in her breath, terrified of what was happening to the awful thing, terrified that she'd been right all along. *They* are *Cretins, but something's happening—*

Its small frame arched backward with a sharp crack, accompanied by a series of popping noises as its head slowly rotated in place. Jagged teeth extended from its mouth as more limbs sprouted across its torso. The mutation occurred in seconds, but to Donna the change lasted for years as adrenaline flooded her veins. She watched with a mixture of fascination and revulsion, at once hesitant and eager to comprehend this creature's transformation, much less its existence at all.

When it was finished, the spiderling lifted its twisted face to her and glared. *Do not believe, do not see, do not hear, do not remember, do not tell, do not love, do not hate, do not seek...*

She heard its words clearly now, a commanding drone which stoked the pain in her head, prompting it to rise with newfound fury. Warmth dribbled across her lip and fell to the floor with a soft plop. Donna ignored the bleeding and turned to run, but then she remembered the kind nurse who'd helped her only moments ago. She looked back and felt her stomach drop to the floor.

The creature hissed in triumph as it scuttled along the tile toward Carina. Donna tried to cry out and warn the old woman, but a sharp tearing noise from the adjacent wall stole her attention. The paint cracked and bulged in spots as something pushed against the drywall from within.

Oh God no.

Paint split and cracked as thin limbs pushed their way free.

Down the hall, Carina screamed, but her voice was quickly muffled and displaced with a deep gagging that churned Donna's gut. She pressed herself against the wall, frozen in terror by what she was seeing. More of those things were pushing through from the Monochrome, inching their way into this world, and when they broke free, they'd change just like the rest.

Get out of here. Find Michael and leave. You have two feet, so use them, woman.

Her own voice this time, the voice of who she could be if she'd remained composed, focused, sane. The voice of an expectant mother in the face of imminent danger. That was the woman she needed to be now; she couldn't allow this sudden breakdown of reality to get in the way of that.

The old nurse's body convulsed as the spiderling wedged itself into her mouth and drove its limbs into her cheeks. Donna gasped, turned away from the poor woman, and was about to move when a piece of drywall dropped to the floor, followed by the soft thump of a pale-bodied monstrosity.

You little bastard.

Donna reacted out of reflex, didn't give the spiderling time to get its bearings in this new colorful world. She took a step and punted the creature across the hall where it struck the wall with wet squelch. A muffled cry of pain escaped its ruined remains as a sickly mound of goo slowly dripped down the wall.

Another Cretin broke free, surveyed the hallway from the breach, twisted its head around to stare at her, and hissed in triumph. She looked up and watched its face mutate. The sight was enough to spur her to action, and in an instant, she was running down the adjacent hall, shouting her brother-in-law's name as loud as she could.

———•———

"**M**ike!"

He heard his name, but it was so far away, and he was so comfortable here. Donovan was with him, or some version of his brother, really nothing more than a silhouette painted against a dimly lit desert. The sands were gray and there was a storm raging off in the distance. They'd been having a conversation, but as he grew aware of his surroundings, he found he couldn't remember much of what they'd said.

Something about strings and weavers and a massive tapestry of human experience, whatever the hell that meant, and an ominous warning. *You're right to fear a blank planet.*

And then his brother's shadow left him there, buried up to his arms in sand, buried so deep he couldn't free himself, and all he could do was watch Donovan wander alone into the storm. There was more to it, but the shrill repetition of his name—

"Michael!"

—tugged at his presence in the dreamspace. It was the spiders that finally drove him back into consciousness, however. He couldn't see them, but he *felt* them, and with paradoxical dream logic he knew what they were: small mutant spiders, just like those things down in the subway. The desert was full of them, and he felt them nipping at his fingertips and toes. Little gray monsters full of teeth and sludge and all the negative things we bury within ourselves, vessels full of failure, living manifestations of all the horrid things humanity had ever done and would do—

"MICHAEL!"

He opened his eyes and stared at the pair of fluorescent lights humming overhead. Fragments of the dream hung there in the pale light, the sensation of burial still present, and the lack of grit between his fingers was confusing.

Michael sat up and reeled from a sudden wave of nausea. Pins and needles jabbed at his arm, and when he tried to lift it, he discovered it was little more than a tattered limb filled with jelly. He looked down and surveyed the row of sutures down the length of his bicep. Jagged pieces of memory floated to the surface. He remembered Alice was there and then not there, replaced by a nurse who was both kind and firm, and then nothing. He'd passed out again, rocked to sleep by the gentle sway of anesthesia and blood loss and sleep deprivation.

The room, its instruments, the floor and the exam table and all the cabinetry possessed a hazy quality, like the world was wrapped in cellophane. He shook his head, rubbed his eyes. The layer remained, robbing the walls of their texture, painting everything in a thin coat of gray.

I'm still dreaming. I'm back home, maybe, and Alice should be home from work any minute. Her absence opened a pit inside his soul, one that might have been there already except he'd filled it in years ago. He had no time to dwell on it—there was a figure standing in the doorway now, and she was shouting his name.

"Donna?"

"We've got to get the hell out of here, Mike, we—" she paused, glanced around the room. "Where's Alice?"

"I don't—wait, what's going on? Slow down, everything's still kinda—"

Fuzzy, he wanted to say, but he was stunned to silence when one of the spiderlings crawled across the opposite wall in the hallway. He stared at it, at once incredulous and fascinated by its appearance. These things were torn right out of his dream. Shit, he still felt their teeth nipping at his fingers and toes from somewhere below the surface of consciousness, and now they were here, they were *right here,* and this one in particular looked pissed off.

The spiderling hissed, bared its teeth, and readied itself to leap. Donna saw his wide-eyed expression, turned to see what captivated his attention—and cried out in shock as a gunshot exploded in the hallway. Michael flinched as the spiderling exploded into a thousand chunks of goo.

He climbed to his feet, pulled Donna inside. "You okay?" She stared at him in shock, eyes vacant, her ears no doubt ringing from the heavy report. Finally, she regained her composure and nodded slowly, focusing on something just beyond his shoulder.

"Sorry, Donna."

Michael turned and felt butterflies flutter upward from that bottomless pit inside himself. Alice approached, gun in hand and one finger in her ear. He stared at her, transfixed by her appearance, as if he was seeing her for the first time. Maybe he was.

She met his stare. The corner of her mouth curved up into a smirk. "Glad you're awake. Shit's hitting the fan."

"Quinn and Amanda," Donna rasped. She steadied herself and absently rubbed her belly as if to comfort the child within. "They're in the lobby. Those…things are outside. I think they used to be people."

Michael stuck his head outside the room and took in the hallway. A squirming nest of spiderlings congregated near the corner, chattering in that odd clipped language, a reversed recording played forward once more. He remembered their words from the abandoned tunnel and the way they made his head hurt. *Donovan was right. I'll be goddamned, he was right.*

"Mike? You okay?" Alice touched his shoulder. Her fingers were warm from gripping the weapon.

He smiled, put his hand over hers, and kissed her. Alice didn't recoil; instead, she leaned into him, and their touch ignited a wildfire of memories across his brain. Dates, birthdays, parties, all the quiet moments they'd spent in silence with one another. A whole other life, one that had been stolen from him and now returned in the strangest of ways, and despite the fear lurking at the back of his mind that everything he knew was turning upside down, he felt that he could face it with her.

Alice pulled away, closed her eyes, smiled. Michael grinned. "I am now," he said. And then, to Donna: "Let's get going."

———— • ————

Quinn recognized the jarring shift and didn't want to believe it. The way the room overlapped itself was all too familiar. He heard the faint mechanized drone in his ears, even tasted the stale air on his tongue, and while the remaining patrons in the ER struggled against a barrage of surging headaches, Quinn looked on. The billowing silver curtain separating Monochrome from Spectrum was beginning to pull away.

Crack.

The noise was subtle, barely audible beneath his mother's gasp of pain, the tumult of panicked voices and muffled cries, and all the goddamn droning. He hated that sound the most. It was a constant reminder that something wasn't right, wouldn't be right ever again, an ongoing alarm of synthetic tinnitus digging down his ears and drilling into the mantle of his skull.

Snap.

Quinn regained focus and saw a mob of those consumed men and women and—

He did a double take, his heart plummeting into the void of his gut. There were children among the mob, their tiny faces obscured by clusters of bulbous tumors, pulsing erratically with sickening fervor. They were drawn to the ER entrance like a scene from the hundred-plus zombie films Quinn had watched when he was a kid. Only this was worse. They didn't want to eat the living; no, eating would be so much better than what had happened to Dustin and Kelly. More than a dozen faceless creatures slapped and clawed at the panes of glass separating them from their prey.

A thin crack shot across the length of the window. Quinn registered what was happening and clutched his mother's hand. *We need to go,* he was about to say, *we need to find Donna and Mike and Alice and get the hell out of here.*

But Amanda pulled away from him, nearly stumbled and fell to the floor. She caught herself on one of the plush waiting room chairs and lowered herself into the seat.

"Oh my God," she said, rubbing her forehead. Quinn knelt before her and saw blood dribbling from her nose. "I think...Q, I think I'm having a migraine. Hand me my purse, I need some aspirin..."

And like the obedient loving son he was, Quinn reached to do just that. In the coming hours, he would reflect on that moment, wishing he'd acted differently. Wishing he'd been more attentive. Aspirin was the last thing she needed, and he knew it. Instead of reaching for her purse, he should've pulled her to her feet and fled the room. Just like his gut screamed for him to do.

But he did as she asked anyway, his obedience little more than a reflex, reaching for her purse just a few seats away. It was one of those expensive designer handbags, overpriced for its size but it's what she'd wanted for her birthday a couple years ago, and he and his dad had saved money to buy it for her. The kind with the logo embossed on a silver medallion. He curled his fingers around the straps—

—and the window shattered, raining fragments of glass upon them both.

What happened in the ensuing moments played forward in a slow-motion reel of images, his brain suddenly overwhelmed with a rush of adrenaline so fierce he was barely conscious of his actions. His survival instinct took over, and there was no time for anything except self-preservation.

Amanda cried out in surprise and covered her face. A shard of glass struck Quinn's cheek, shooting a bright stinging flash of white across his vision.

The room exploded in a cacophony of panicked screams and fractured glass as the mob stumbled blindly forward. The tumorous things expelled a thick phlegmy gurgling noise like a series of clogged drains, and the smell—God, the smell was pungent like rotting compost, so acrid it brought tears to Quinn's eyes.

Amanda shrieked, stumbled from her seat as one of the consumed monstrosities reached for her. She collapsed on the thin gray carpet and kicked herself forward like an infant, struggling to regain her footing in the ensuing panic.

Quinn watched in frozen terror, already seeing what was about to happen, already calculating what could be done, what should be done. He reached out for her, intending to yank her to her feet—

One of the creatures fell upon her, crushing the air from her lungs in a pained wheeze. She met his glassy stare. He saw the horror in her wide eyes, saw that she was hyper-aware of what was happening, what was going to happen, and the despair writ upon her face drained him of his resolve.

Amanda Upton mouthed one word to him—

(Go!)

—before the pallid creature's pustules exploded a sickly gray residue across the back of her skull. The gelatinous substance writhed and crawled across her scalp in search of her forehead, fusing itself to her skin, and coating her face like putty. Her airways were sealed off from in a single hissing rasp.

Quinn froze, unable to move as he watched the remains of his mother slowly stolen from him. The world around him faded away, the chaos of the lobby dulling to a muffled hum, and for the first time since Donovan had rescued him from the Monochrome, Quinn wished he'd never left. Maybe then his mother would still be alive.

Bits of glass snapped underfoot as more of the faceless mob of human maggots breached the opening, wandering blindly toward their prey.

-11-
TEMPEST

An oily light coated the world inside the storm, and Donovan felt it cling to his skin like a layer of sweat. Here the shadows had weight, imbuing the air with an oppressive gravity which tried to pull him down with every step. He'd crossed the churning wall of violent wind and sand, bracing himself for a stinging blast to his exposed skin, but now there was only an eerie calm amongst the slithering shadows.

Thick curtains of fog hung before him, obscuring the darkening silhouette of Dullington's figure as he trudged across the placid dunes. Donovan gave himself a moment to settle his nerves, found such a task was impossible in this place, and followed his companion's footprints into the haze. The old monk's words played an ominous refrain in his head as he focused on each step, desperately trying to ignore the shifting shadows within his periphery.

Inside you will be confronted with your fears, your failures, every nightmare you have ever experienced.

Every nightmare, fear, and failure? He crossed off a mental list, trying to estimate how many of each he'd accumulated in his short life, and found the count too overwhelming to truly quantify. Who would take the time to balance such a grim ledger?

His late parents were the religious sort, something which he and Michael had never followed in their youth, but after all he'd seen and experienced these last few years, Donovan found himself wondering if his many downfalls were being measured. Someone—or *something*—was keeping score. He thought of the ancient myths and cultures he'd learned about in school over the years, thought of the weighing of one's heart against a feather or the passage of souls through a needle's eye. Was this storm the method of his crucible?

Donovan was so lost in his thoughts that he'd failed to notice the crowd of figures congregating up ahead. They'd appeared as mere shadows, there and not there again, constantly shifting in the broken light like indecisive phantoms. Only when he was upon them did they take form, dim stone-like figures cast in various poses, their facial features weathered away over time. Pieces of broken limbs lay strewn about their feet, half-buried in the sand.

He stood beside one of them, examined its unsettling appearance. Man or woman, he couldn't tell. The figure was faceless, its arms raised in the air, one leg stretched and bent before the other as if bracing for something. The others held a similar gait, all facing in one direction toward something he couldn't see. He wasn't sure he wanted to.

And then he heard the sound. A heavy thudding beat pounding a rhythm he recognized. Moving further into the stony crowd, Donovan began humming a melody that confused him as much as it excited him.

A song. He *knew* this song. A tune from his youth filled with distorted guitars, machine gun percussion, and a synthesized bassline, one so violent his mother had threatened to take his stereo if he didn't turn it down. Only this wasn't a recording playing now—this was being performed live, and he was somewhere in the midst of a concert crowd. The hazy light had darkened, and he could no longer see the sand beneath his feet or the cracked veneer of the frozen concertgoers. It was just him in the dark, listening to a band from a million years ago, somehow driven from obscurity by recent events.

Shadows flashed and danced upon the walls—since when was he indoors? He couldn't remember—projecting the distorted images of elongated arms and heads and a violent performance happening onstage. Strobing lights erupted from somewhere overhead, giving life to the petrified crowd, their appearance shifting and turning as he worked his way between them to the stage. More of them now, packed in tighter, so tight he had to suck in his gut in places. As the song reached its violent chorus, a voice broke through the sonic assault. A voice he knew so well and yet tuned higher in pitch, a voice belonging to the woman he would someday marry. She was ahead somewhere in the chaotic darkness, screaming for his help. Screaming because she was about to be crushed underfoot by the suffocating crowd, a thousand faceless monsters trying to take another step, gain another inch closer toward that goddamn stage.

Donovan pushed against a wall of stone figures, struggling to squeeze his way between them but to no avail, and the young woman just beyond was screaming his name now, screaming that she was going to die. Screaming with a visceral fear he'd never heard before, accusing him of letting her go. Accusing him of leaving her in this awful place to suffer at the hands of a thousand faceless things.

No, he wanted to scream, *I didn't—this isn't how it happened. I pulled you out of that crowd, we left the show, I was the one who got hurt—*

A sharp crunch overpowered the music and the screaming stopped. The lights faded on, illuminating the gray veil pulled over the world. All the statues were gone save one: a figure sprawled out on the sand, twisted in a pose of eternal agony.

He staggered forward, sank to his knees beside the stone effigy, and quietly sobbed. The wind stirred around him, sending dust devils spiraling into the haze, and from somewhere far away, he thought he heard the jagged lilt of croaking laughter.

———————— • ————————

*F*or every trespass we must give a piece of ourselves.
Christopher Dullington's teachings replayed in Aleister's mind as he marched ahead into the dreary fog, and he wondered how much of himself he'd left here in the stillness. Too much, perhaps, but in a region where no creature was meant to tread, a toll must always be paid.

Such was the nature of the Monochrome: a balance to be maintained, nothing given without something taken. He had left a portion of himself here with every crossing just as Christopher warned him all those years ago. Now Christopher was dead, another victim of their former master, and Aleister was alone but for the sins of his past given flesh in this perpetual storm. Even he wasn't immune here. The ethereal tug at his own strings were at their most palpable here, amounting to the equivalent of a prickling of skin, the faint tickle of gooseflesh across his arms and neck.

Donovan's sobs carried on the wind, and Aleister reconsidered his approach. Should he have made more time for which to prepare his companion?

Time was not a resource to be spared, not since the balance had shifted and the metachasm began its withering. Pontius Vile would succeed in his apocalyptic desire to reconcile both realities. Even now the Ungod was choking in its cradle. He sensed its weakened breath in the stillness.

The manikin known as Candle would struggle to rationalize and question. Too much time would be wasted to explain the cruel nature of this place. Telling a mortal man he is the maker of this place, much less the nightmares dwelling within, would not be enough to sate his appetite for knowledge. Most men, perhaps, but not this one.

He will persevere, Aleister thought. *It is not in his nature to relent.*

Indeed, Mr. Candle had proven himself once more a most valuable asset. His determination to save others, save his loved ones, and perhaps even to save himself was an admirable quality to which Aleister felt kinship. He had been filled with such fire long ago, a raging inferno deep inside that would have consumed him if not for Christopher keeping the flames at bay. Now all that remained were ashes of the man he was long ago. Ashes, and buried somewhere below, cinders.

Candle's sorrow faded into a light breeze, his cracked voice elevating in pitch until it was no longer recognizable as male. This voice Aleister knew all too well. Hearing it now pulled at the hollow space where his gray heart once beat.

She was already calling his name, crying out for help he would never be able to grant. That time had long past; all that remained now were echoes of his failure, amplified by the cruel nature of this place.

"Free me, husband. Please…I suffer so."

Her voice gave him pause. Something so pure did not belong in this place, and though he knew what he would find waiting for him here, her presence never failed to make him hesitate. The centuries had not dulled her suffering, every passing moment as agonizing as the last.

Dark shapes slithered into formation just beyond the curtain of fog. For a moment, Aleister considered turning back, wishing to witness this horrendous display no more, but the duty of his charge weighed heavily upon him. There was too much at stake now to turn back.

Go, then, and gaze once more upon the moment of your surrender. May it be for the last time…

———————•———————

A pair of T-shaped crosses emerge on the horizon as he is escorted into the storm. Two figures—one tall, one short—are suspended in tandem, arms tethered apart and legs tied to the single supporting beam.

The shorter figure's head droops at an unnatural angle, the muscles in its neck limp where there should still be a sturdy resolve.

A nod to the Greeks, he thinks, and then in a flash of epiphany, realizes it is the pose of the Christian Saint Anthony. *Not in honor but a mockery.*

The faceless servants urge him forward, and as they crest a final mound of sand, Aleister's heart finally falters, plummets to his empty center, and silently shatters in a million fragments.

"No...not my boy..."

Thomas's lifeless face gazes down at the pile of his entrails in a kind of lazy shock, forever surprised that his insides could be so darkly red and so numerous. The child's lower half is missing, one coil of intestine piled at the foot of the cross in a mound of gore as dark as tar, and the tatters of his torn gray tunic flap carelessly in the tempest's deceptive breeze. Aleister struggles to compose himself and fails. He retches and empties his stomach upon the sand, his robe, his bare feet.

"My sparrow..."

Agnes's voice is weak, barely more than a whisper. He looks up to her, a pilgrim in supplication to the only true god he has ever known, and he finds his words are stolen from him. He cannot express the sorrow seeping from his broken heart. All that crosses his tongue are invectives aimed at his master, venomous barbs dulled by the weakness of his resolve. Pontius Vile has seen into his soul yet again and stoked the agony of an open wound that refuses to heal.

Tears cling to his eyes as he struggles to reconcile the scene before him. He is struck with a desire to crawl inside himself, hide his gaze from the misery displayed before him, and yet he fights against the urge as it would only fuel his regret. These are her last moments, he realizes with cold clarity, and this will be his final opportunity to take in her beautiful face before life is drained from it forever.

The servants lead him to the foot of the cross. They let go, allow him to fall to his knees in the sand, inches from where her blood has watered the wastes.

"My love..." He cannot bring himself to say more. He is unworthy to speak in her presence, a failure of a husband, a betrayer of the vows made in their union.

Agnes struggles against the ropes cutting into her wrists, tries to lift herself for another precious gasp of air, but her strength is fading. Her biceps bulge, quiver, and fail. She slumps in exhaustion and slides down an inch. Her chest heaves against the strain of her own weight.

"Enough," Aleister pleads. "I'll remain. Please, let her down. Free her from this place."

Pontius Vile approaches and kneels beside him, whispers in his ear. "In times of bleeding, it is necessary to cleanse a wound with flame. In times of poisoning, it is necessary to remove a limb to prevent its spread." He lifts Aleister's chin, meets his gaze with the cruelty of untold centuries framed behind two hateful eyes. "I will be your savior, Aleister Dullington, and someday you will learn this love is merely a weakness. She is an icon of your old self. The new self you must become has no place for her in the tomb of your heart."

Agnes struggles for another breath. She tries to pull herself up once more, but exhaustion and suffocation have taken their toll, and she slumps down yet again.

No, my love, I can fix this, I can—

Two hollow pops divide the silence, and her body goes limp, wilting like a dead vine upon the cross. Her arms have dislocated from their sockets, her muscles torn apart by her weight, and a faint line of spittle slowly drips from her slack lips. Her eyes are half-closed, the light in them dulled and unfocused, and when Aleister finally forces himself to look at her, he finds only an empty shell of the woman he loves.

Pontius Vile climbs to his feet and looks to the faceless beasts in waiting. "Take him," he says. "It is nigh time this little sparrow's wings are clipped once and for all."

———————•———————

"*O*nly *your damned spirit would not relent.*" Aleister Dullington looked up at the visage of his late wife strapped to the cross, dead for centuries yet now alert, her eyes glowing gray. Pale liquid oozed from between desiccated lips and pooled on the sand below. Small tendrils rose and twitched from the surface, tasting the stale air and sensing his presence.

Agnes's corpse had lain in wait for him each time he journeyed through the tempest, a signpost left to torment the remains of his soul and test his resolve. He had always paid her tribute, said the words he had always wanted to say but never could when they mattered. He'd prayed for her forgiveness in those silent moments, and for a time he believed his enemy had left her merely as a mute reminder of failures past.

"*Look at me, servant. Gaze into the eyes of your destroyer.*"

Aleister did so and felt the stirrings of the fire deep in his core. After centuries of sorrow and indulgence in his wretched state, driven by a desire to right the wrongs committed during his mortal years, he once again felt a warmth he had not known since the day Pontius Vile stole his humanity.

He knew that warmth all too well. It was the one piece of his soul the Ungod's corrupting light could not extinguish. A small flame nurtured and sustained over the interminable years. A reminder of his charge, the point of his continued resistance to this monstrous usurper he had once called master.

"You will not stop me, little sparrow. The Ungod will suffocate, and I will fill the metachasm with the corpses of man."

"As you have said," Aleister whispered, hearing once more the agonizing sobs of Donovan Candle lost along the wind. "For centuries now, Pontius Vile, you have spoken the same tiring rhetoric. Spare me now. We both know you will not stop me from trying."

More cries on the wind. He sensed Donovan's impending madness and turned his back on Agnes's possessed corpse. Her voice spoke Vile's words, another empty warning: *"He is lost in his failures, Aleister Dullington. He is beyond saving. Come, now, and face me alone."*

Alone.

Now Aleister understood Vile was merely biding his time. This was yet another calculated move, a twist of the knife stuck in his side all those years ago. A distraction meant to slow him down. He looked over his shoulder at the preserved remains of his beloved wife. Her face was slack once more, her taut skin coated in a thin layer of sand, and the light was gone from her eyes.

"In due time, my love."

Aleister tempered his resolve and moved toward the sound of Mr. Candle's voice.

M argie Guffin lowered her head and forged onward into the storm. She'd become separated from the others, lost in the confusion of swirling shadows, dust, and wind.

This way, the voice said. *Follow me toward the Needle.*

She'd half-expected to meet this stranger speaking inside her head. Here, the abstract storm of dreams seemed as likely a place as any. Years ago, she would've questioned her sanity in the face of such experience.

Then George vanished, and not long after, she began experiencing the flickering herself. Now the real world made less sense to her than the Monochrome did.

Here in the gray, Margie had witnessed her share of oddities. Impossible things culled from the gray pox which riddled her body, creatures big and small grown right out of the sickly pus. Even now she felt them stirring just beneath her skin. They'd been nibbling away at her insides ever since Sparrow disappeared, covering her body with an interminable itch that would not relent. Some of the other Missing experienced the same thing; they'd been here just as long as she had, if not longer, and none of them had felt this before.

And when she heard the voice, she didn't question its existence. Along with everything else in this insanity, why not a disembodied voice for good measure? It whispered directives, urging her to leave the city, to walk into the storm. And like the others, she'd done as she was told. What else was there? Dullington was gone. Sparrow was gone. Things had changed in the Monochrome, and not for the better.

Serpents of doubt crawled along the back of her mind and questioned her blind servitude. What if this was another one of Dullington's tricks? Her George had fallen for it, and all it earned him was a slow digestion in the belly of the Yawning. What guarantee was there the same wouldn't happen to her?

But the voice was insistent. Worse, it was convincing.

She tucked her hands into her hoody, fingered the gun barrel, and thought about the chaos of the plaza. Her husband's killer had been there, mere feet away from what she was told, and she'd missed him entirely. All she saw was the back of his head, and then poof, he was gone. Vanished like a ghost into thin air. Then others started disappearing, mostly the youngsters Sparrow had recruited for his army, and after that, the quakes began. She'd barely escaped, certain the whole world was falling down, and for a while she'd holed up in her quiet corner at the back of the old station.

And after, the voice crept in. Sweet, quiet, and charming, it reminded her of George when they were dating all those years ago. He always knew what to say, and so the voice did as well.

He will be there, it told her, *the man who took your George away. Dullington's puppet. The one called Candle.*

She'd asked, "What should I do?"

Trust me, child. Follow my instruction and I will deliver you unto your vengeance.

Now she was lost in a strange storm of sand and shadows. Several times she glimpsed the figures of other pilgrims in the distance, but she had no desire to approach them. The voice hadn't told her to do so, and she wouldn't unless it did.

Nor was she truly alone, either. A persistent feeling of presence had accompanied her ever since she'd crossed into the tempest, as though her shadow had substance in this place. A phantom companion of some manner, hovering just beyond her sight, and speaking in the voice of her dead husband.

You just listen to what the man tells you, George said. *He'll lead you where you wanna go, honey. Just promise me one thing. Can you do that for me, Marge? Can you grant me a teeny-tiny promise?*

"Of course, George." Her voice seemed lazy, tired in her own ears. Not quite drunk, but not sober either, and only half-conscious. She was in a trance, she realized, her feet carrying her on autopilot, one heel down into the sand after another.

When you put that bullet right between his eyes, you tell him it's for me. You tell him he never should've crossed George Guffin. Will you do that for me, babe?

Margie nodded in agreement as she walked forward into the thick curtain of fog. From behind, just over her shoulder, right inside her ear, her husband and the voice became one. They spoke together with a hint of jubilation, and the sound made her smile in reflection.

Good girl, it said.

———•———

His wife's stone effigy crumbled to dust as Donovan tried to cradle the figure in his arms. He sat in dumbfounded terror as he watched her remains crack and disintegrate. When a gust of wind covered him in a cloud of ash, Donovan found the strength to scream. Primal, a blistering fusion of anger and sadness, the sound carried across the hazy expanse with a fury to match the tempest itself. He screamed until his voice fried and his throat burned to a charred husk.

A dozen voices whispered on the wind, taunting him for his failures, accusing him of leaving her to wither and rot.

"Should've stayed, should've made a better choice, should've said something else, should've tried, should've tried, should've tried—"

To the wind, he said, "I did try."

"Not enough, never enough, should've done more, should've lived, should've lived more, should've stepped out of your shadow."

Should've lived. He couldn't argue there.

Oily shades slithered into existence, dimming the world before his eyes, and formed a collage of moments he recognized:

The last time he saw his parents alive before their fatal car crash. He heard the words he'd wanted to say played back like a bad recording, full of static and glitches and yet his voice was unmistakable, all the times he could have said "I love you" and didn't.

All the arguments he'd ever had with his brother, from the day of their parents' funeral to their last phone call about Quinn's disappearance. He felt every moment of disappointment like a sucker punch to the gut, the pain of futility and regret lingering in his mind and strangling every nerve. And then his own voice emerged from the darkened display with accusatory force, stabbing into his ego with each syllable: *All I've ever done is let you down.*

At least they can't see you now, eh hoss?

Joe Hopper's chummy cynicism filled his gut with lead. The southern detective's voice was so clear and familiar, and yet tinged with a hint of something else, a sense of the unknown like a reflection in a dirty mirror. Distorted somehow, filled with a sort of accusing rage.

Donovan shook his head. "That's not you."

Of course I am, hoss. I'm a part of you. The voice you gave your conscience, a part of your gut. I'm an idea of the man you wanna be. I'm the you you'll never be.

Hopper's shape materialized in the shadows. Donovan smelled the acrid blend of cigarettes and liquor, saw the lazy tendril of smoke rising from beyond the grizzled figure's fedora.

I'm the only one you can trust, hoss. And believe me when I say you won't ever be satisfied. You'll never be content. That's the rigged game Sparrow tried to warn you about years ago. It's a con. You can fill one void and another will just tear itself open. Show me a happy man and I'll show you a goddamn liar. By my measure, you've been lying for a long fucking time.

Hopper's visage dissipated into a stream of smoke, replaced with the outline of a familiar scene: Donovan's home office. Desk in the corner, lights out save the drab glow of the computer screen.

And there he was, sitting alone in his office, hunched over a keyboard while imagining life experiences filtered through a lens of characters who would come to represent everything he lacked, corner pieces of a puzzle framing the shape of a man, and only just. Everything in the middle was missing, those vital fragments stolen by time, regret, and fear. That man at the keyboard was a shadow of the man he could be, always chasing a better state of being, forever seconds late in a race that spanned his entire life.

Days of futility played on in a cosmic gag reel, every night of frustration and failure presented in stark clarity. He saw himself delete page after page, all while telling himself this would be the one, this would be the story, this one, this one *right here,* this is the one that takes me to the next level, the next phase of my career, this will be the one that fills this emptiness inside me, this staggering pit that's always been there threatening to swallow me whole, this impossible gauge against which I always measure myself, this one, this is the one that will *make me proud of me.*

Years became decades. He was still there, pecking away at a keyboard, beating his head against a wall of self-doubt. Donna was there in the background, watching him from the doorway of his office, her hair gone gray and her skin withered with time. She shook and winced with the constant nerve pain slowly destroying her body, her resolve, her will to keep going. *This is the one,* he told her, *and once I sell it, we can afford to get you proper treatment.*

A flash of light filled the scene, and Donovan's shadow was no longer sitting at a desk. Instead, he saw himself at Donna's bedside, weeping over her lifeless body. Bottles of pills lay strewn across the floor. *I'm so sorry, please don't go, don't leave me here, without you I have no purpose, I can't go on, I don't know how to be if you aren't here, I'm too afraid, I'm too afraid, I'm too afraid—*

Donovan shook his head, forced himself to turn away. He took a few steps in the opposite direction, determined to find his way out of this damn storm, certain that if he found its boundary, he would be free of these phantoms.

But would he? Weren't these the very ghosts locked away in his own mind?

"Aleister," he called out. The word weighed heavy on his tongue, as though mentioning the name was admitting defeat. "I can't—I can't do this. I'm sorry, this is too much, I can't..."

I can't. I'm afraid.

His gut lurched. Was he too afraid to stand on his own? After coming all this way, was he too afraid to go on alone? Too afraid to see this through no matter the outcome?

Donna's face flashed in his mind. Her sleeping face, so peaceful in the moonlight cast from the window. The last night they were together before he made a foolish decision to try and do the right thing. Another regret, another failure, another stupid decision made because he thought he could handle the task.

The air thickened around him. Tendrils of shadow slithered away, seeping down into the sands and between ripples of air. A pale glow emanated from the surrounding haze, and the tempest's winds calmed to a light breeze. Donovan wiped his face on his sleeve, took a deep breath, and exhaled. He cupped his hands and called for Aleister once more.

Now there was silence, the paradoxical storm overhead suddenly calm despite its violent swirling nature. He shouted again, and the lack of an echo across the dunes sent a chill crawling down his spine. The air thickened with a stale, cloying heat.

"Hello? Is someone there?"

A man's voice. Faint and frail. Higher in pitch, not the booming baritone of the pallid monk. Confused, Donovan turned and froze when he spotted the shape walking toward him through the grim fogbank. A cold hand took hold of his gut and squeezed.

A robed figure emerged from the gloom, its cowl obscuring a starkly pale face.

"Who're you? Where's Aleister?"

The monk offered a weak smile as he raised his chin and gave Donovan a tired once-over. It was a meager gesture, there and gone again, wiped clean from an expressionless slate.

"My name is Christopher of the Dullingtons. The Ungod sent me to find you, Master Candle, and save you from the usurper."

"Master Candle? Usurper? What are you talking about?"

"Yes," Christopher said, pointing forward into the fog. "The usurper called Aleister. I will show you the way."

THE LINES BEGIN TO BLUR

The sands quaked beneath Dullington's feet as he doubled back through the storm, a tremor so strong that he paused to consider its implication. He looked upward into the mess of wind and dreadful dreams, searching for any sign of the strings beyond, but all he saw was a roiling stew of shadows. A lack of sight was not enough to inhibit him, however; even now, he felt a stirring of energy on the wind, between it, an electric vibration so strong it conjured gooseflesh across his arms and neck.

There were eyes upon him. Foreign eyes that did not belong here—and yet were familiar to him. He saw a shimmering of color mingling with the dulled gray tones of the world, the air itself wavering and blending and blurring, a mirage of Spectrum bleeding into the Monochrome. And beyond that hole in the fabric of reality, he glimpsed a familiar figure.

Donna Candle, at long last you see.

She stood in the portal, transfixed by the impossible world beyond, while behind her erupted a different sort of chaos. Gunfire. Screams. The unmistakable screech and groan of the Monochrome's bestiary distorted and corrupted by a reality they were never meant to inhabit.

The demarcations are bending, he thought. *Breaking, merging. To reconcile these two realities is utter madness. Does the well of Vile's contempt for humanity have no bottom?* He turned away from the rift and forged ahead into the gloomy haze, troubled by the answer which came to him all too easily. *No, of course not. No man could see what he has seen and escape unscathed.*

Another tremor, this one powerful enough to shift the surrounding dunes. Loose sand was swept away in the chaos, revealing the long-forgotten bones of the souls who had come before, lost within the storm like sailors across the sea. Drawn to the Monochrome by their own failings, and then to this storm by a corrupted siren's call, these nameless men and women were robbed of their last chance at redemption. These bones beneath his feet were all that remained of them. Pale, polished to a dull sheen by the centuries of sand and wind, forever preserved here in a Golgotha of failure and misery.

This will be Mr. Candle's fate if I do not hurry.

Aleister lifted his hood and braced himself against the wind, pushing against the forces of a storm which tried to seize his mind with each step. Tendrils of shadow slithered and coiled in his periphery, and when he spotted the twin figures in the distance, he suspected the tempest was having its way with his fears again.

But as he neared, heard their voices, recognized their features even through the haze, Aleister realized this wasn't the storm's doing. Once again, his adversary had been one step ahead.

He sank to his knees and hid himself beyond the rim of a nearby dune, watching as the two figures conversed. Candle's voice and silhouette were unmistakable; the second figure was yet another phantom of Aleister's past, an old friend lost all those centuries ago.

He remembered Christopher's face that day on the shore, remembered how his mentor had pleaded for him to reconsider abandoning the Order. Aleister was so sure he could make it to the mainland and escape the repercussions of his choices. If only he had listened, perhaps Agnes and Thomas would not have met such a cruel fate.

In his quiet moments over the years, when his duty to the Monochrome became too heavy a burden, Aleister would retreat into himself and indulge in a fantasy of possibility. In those rare moments, he preferred to think of the lives his wife and son might have led had Vile not intervened. Would Agnes have moved on? What sort of man might Thomas become?

He wanted to believe she would have found love again. Perhaps someone who was stronger and less foolish, someone who could be content with her love and a simple life. Someone who wasn't driven by a desire to find their place, who wasn't kept awake at night by the existential nightmare of understanding their purpose. Someone who wasn't afraid of raising their only child.

All of those hopes and dreams withered in an instant, reduced to nothing more than grains of sand across this lifeless expanse of nothingness.

Afraid.

So much of his life had been dictated by fear. A human emotion burned away in the Ungod's light centuries ago; in the years since he had spent every moment of his nullified existence working to answer for that fear and right the wrongs he had allowed to happen.

Agnes. Thomas. Christopher. And now Donovan.

He allowed himself this moment of despair, a passage of warmth from the cooling cinder of humanity down in the void where his heart once beat. Once again Aleister Dullington wished he could close his eyes if only for a moment so that he, too, might shut off the horrors of his predicament.

The usurper wearing Christopher's face offered to lead Donovan out of the storm. And Donovan Candle, ever the desperately hopeful soul, took him on his word.

Aleister watched and waited, and when they were but ghosts on the horizon, he rose to his feet and set off after them.

Donna thought she heard her husband amid the screams and gunfire. His voice was a phantom in her ears, not truly there, and yet she detected it through the chaos. No, between it. Around and beneath it. And the world before her was slipping away like liquid, an ethereal tide pulled back by unseen gravity, revealing all the damp sand underneath.

One moment she was standing in the hospital hallway while Alice and Michael retreated to the ER lobby, the next she was staring at a vast expanse of desert. A sand dune lay just beyond the entrance of an open exam room across the hall, the sands covered in a thin layer of fog, while a darkening cloudbank rolled overhead. She stared in disturbed wonder, questioning everything she was seeing, questioning her sanity, and yet beneath her doubt she felt the tickling certainty that this was really happening.

Wind blew back her hair, and she winced as a blast of sand struck her face.

Aleister?

The sound raised a lump in her throat. Donovan's voice. She was certain of it.

Donna approached the portal, raised a hand to protect her face from the blowing sands, and peered through the opposing gloom. Twin shapes stood in the distance. One of them, she was certain, was her husband. Which was a foolish thing to do, teasing herself like this, believing Donovan was right there standing in an impossible desert. Standing there, taunting her from the safety of a hallucination.

And yet—

Who're you? Where's Aleister?

His voice was so clear, even from this distance, carried on the back of a grainy gust of wind. The other shape took form, and when it spoke, she heard two voices: one calm and reassuring, and the other, a nasally voice of greater pitch. One spoke before the other, not quite in synchronicity, and overhead she thought she saw a bundle of lines stretching down from the storm.

Marionette, she thought, thinking back to a children's TV shows from her youth. *He's not a real man, but a puppet.*

The second voice, she realized, belonged to the puppeteer. Unseen, beyond the roiling clouds above, guiding this figure's actions. Instructing him to speak to Donnie.

"Donna!"

She turned, watched her nephew Quinn nearly stumble and fall as he entered the hallway. Michael followed, slamming one of the doors against the wall for Alice as she fired a round into the room. The report gave Donna a start, dulling the noise in her ears. Michael shouted something, and Quinn tugged at her arm. *No,* she wanted to say, *Donnie's over there, he's right—*

Donna looked through the doorway and saw an unused exam room. No dunes, no storm, and no figures in the distance. A dull beat announced itself in her head, thudding away at the front of her skull, and her vision blurred. Low clanging bells filled her mind, a droning chime slicing through every thought, and every screaming joint in her body joined in a chorus of flaring pain. The world swam in and out of focus, and although she was vaguely aware of the chaos erupting around her, she retreated inward in a desperate attempt to center herself.

Keep it together, girl. Focus.

She fired questions at herself in a desperate attempt at reclaiming her lucidity. How long had it been since she'd taken her meds? How long since she'd eaten? How long since Donovan had disappeared?

Hours. Since this morning. He disappeared less than forty-eight hours ago. Maybe more. I can't remember. Wake up, Donna. Wake up and face this. Your nephew needs you—

"—Donna, are you with me?"

Michael's voice. Was that his hand on her arm? She shook her head, pushed the droning chimes away, pushed against the encroaching darkness clouding her vision.

"—don't have much time—"

"—can't hold the door—"

"Michael, look out!"

Another gunshot. Another eruption of ringing in her ears. The shadows cleared and she found herself leaning against the exam room's doorframe. Quinn pulled at her arm, pleading for her to move. His cheeks glistened with tears. Michael braced himself against the double doors while something pushed from the other side.

And then she saw Alice, saw the weapon in her hand, and the pale squishy thing flopping in pain on the floor. *Cretin,* she thought. *One of those things from the Monochrome.*

Monochrome. The desert. Donovan's place.

Things were spilling over, merging somehow. Whatever lines separated their realities were beginning to blur. All those nightmares he'd told her about were crossing over now.

Gotta move, girl. Swallow the pain and move.

Donnie's voice culled from a distant memory. The first time she'd experienced a series of flares so severe she'd been bedridden for two days. He'd never spoken to her that way before, his words tinged with a stern tone of exhaustion and worry.

You can be mad at me later, but right now you need to move, Donna. You're going to the doctor. One step. That's it. Now give me another. There you go. I know it hurts, honey, but this is the only way. It's for your own good.

Donna stood upright, winced, and did as she'd done all those years ago. She swallowed back the pain, clenched her teeth, and took one step after another. *This is for my own good,* she thought. *For me and for the baby. Anything for the baby.*

She took hold of Quinn's hand, and when he met her gaze, she asked, "Where's your mother?"

The young man opened his mouth to speak but his words faltered. He lifted his mother's purse in offering, and Donna accepted it without hesitation. She was still too stunned by his expression. The young man's face said all it needed to, and though Donna felt the understanding with the force of a sucker punch, she dared not let it get the better of her now.

The lobby doors shuddered against Michael's weight, and he called out to her in panic. *"Parking garage. Now!"*

Alice looked back, caught Donna's terrified gaze, and nodded. "We need to get moving. Are you okay?"

No, Donna wanted to say, *I'm absolutely not fucking okay.* Instead, she sucked in her breath and nodded. "I have to be. Let's get going."

They were halfway down the hall when Michael sprinted away from the lobby entrance. A moment later, both doors swung inward and struck the walls with such force Donna felt it in her bones.

Behind Michael was a sight dragged from her nightmares: a room full of those bulbous white things that used to be people. Arms flailing limp at their sides as they shuffled into the hallway. Some were still in the process of absorbing their victims, stumbling out of the lobby like toddlers learning to walk, their centers of gravity skewed by the dangling pairs of legs jutting upright from their torsos.

A cry of horror rose in her throat, but she swallowed it back. *No pain and no fear, girl. You stay focused. One foot in front of the other. Keep going. For me, okay? Do it for me. Do it for us.*

I will for us, she thought, and followed Alice around the corner to the emergency exit.

———————•———————

Alice doubled her speed as she took the corner, ready to barrel through whatever lurking horrors might be waiting for them. Instead, all she found was a short empty corridor and a single overhead sign lit in red letters: EXIT. Outside, a smoking area gave way to a set of steps and a sidewalk leading from the hospital grounds to the neighboring parking garage.

Her mind had shifted to panic mode long ago, and what few thoughts found their way through the hyperreal focus of Now were singular directives.

Move.

Slow.

Breathe.

She reached the door, raised Brock's weapon, and peered through the glass. The path to the garage was mostly clear, with only a few of those infected abominations wandering blindly along the walkway.

In the span of seconds before Donna, Quinn, and Michael finally caught up to her, she allowed herself the clarity to observe the cystic bodies of what once were people. A pair of them had merged, one supporting the other with an elongated torso of writhing white flesh, the other's legs dangling limp and wild. Bubbles of sickly goo inflated and pulsed across the tumorous mass. Some of the ichor dribbled to the ground. A moment later, a thin tendril of smoke rose from the pavement.

Thunder clapped overhead, accompanied by another shuddering quake beneath their feet. When she trained her eyes skyward, she saw holes where clouds should be. Fractured portals of gray crosscut with faint lines like looking through a mesh screen.

It's bleeding through. Everything's collapsing into itself.

She wasn't sure she could even call it a sky anymore. That term failed to hold meaning now. Instead, what she saw overhead was breaking glass, the sky merely a one-way mirror obscuring the Monochrome beyond. Fractured, shattering one piece at a time, and soon there would be nothing left to stop them all from crossing over.

Alice looked back, felt her stomach lurch as a scuttling nest of white spiderlings erupted from a bulging hole in the wall.

"We've gotta move, Alice!"

Michael. She heard him, met his panicked stare, and slipped back into focus. She pushed open the door—

—and gasped when she stepped into the Monochrome. The droning noise filling out the empty spaces of silence was unmistakable, as was the sudden rush of stagnant air. Panicked, she looked back to make sure she wasn't alone, and felt selfish relief when she saw her companions were with her. Among them, only Quinn recognized the crossover; Michael and Donna walked outside, squinting into the fragmented haze of gray light, visibly struggling to make sense of their surroundings.

No texture, no detail, no color—here were the planar streets of a dead city fading into a monochromatic haze, the negative spaces of a place they once thought familiar, where the lost so easily fell through the cracks, and were so easily forgotten. Here, where they might meet the same fate if they weren't careful.

Alice squeezed the grip of Brock's weapon as she surveyed the space before them. Apparitions of the faceless creatures faded in and out of view, crossing from one reality into the next without warning. Thin fluttering spaces of air shimmered around them, swelling with telltale signs of a colorful world beyond. One of the creatures crossed into the space and was illuminated in coloration and detail, every bubble of swollen skin suddenly focused in high definition.

"Alice…"

She turned, saw the fear in Quinn's eyes. Saw the tearstains on his cheeks.

"It'll be okay, Q. Just keep moving." And then, to Donna and Michael, "Follow my lead."

They nodded, still not sure what was happening, and their fear wasn't lost on Alice when she turned back. *Counting on you here,* she told herself. *Keep your shit together.*

Alice took a breath, listened to the rhythm of her racing heart, and slowly exhaled. She walked carefully, as quietly as possible in case those blind things couldn't hear them here in this plane of reality, and led them down the steps. Figments of the faceless things wavered in and out of existence, at once appearing in full detail and again dissipating like smoke, reduced to thinly drawn outlines. One of them shuddered and turned as she grew near, and she held out her hand to signal a stop.

Just wait. Wait. See, it's turning away. It can *hear us, but maybe it can't* find *us. Take your time, and if you just mind your steps, you'll be all right.*

And she wanted so desperately to believe it, but with the sky literally cracking and falling, with the very fabric of reality tearing itself threadbare, where could they really go? Was there truly any escape from this?

Get that shit out of your head right now, Al. You didn't come this far to bite it in the Monochrome. Stay focused and worry about the next move when you get there.

Alice clenched her teeth and slipped between the two phantoms, mindful of the dangling limbs convulsing violently in the air. Neither one of them seemed to notice her.

She looked back, was about to motion the others forward—

The air around them swelled, its gray features darkening and losing focus for a moment before color blossomed in great splotches like ink across a wet canvas. Suddenly the world was in full spectrum once again, the air lighter and warmer, the sounds of a fire alarm shrieking from within the hospital and sirens in the distance, the musty smell of smoke and something stagnant like sickness.

Alice recognized that smell, recognized the pungent stench of life clinging to its final moments. It was a smell she'd experienced as a little girl when her grandmother wasted away from cancer. The smell of something dying from within, a body slowly eating itself. Only this stench was everywhere now, a thick aroma of failing life clinging to every breath, coating her nose and throat and lungs. It was all she could to do to keep from vomiting.

One of the faceless abominations twitched, swiveled in mid-stride, and rotated toward her.

Time slowed as Alice's mind slipped back into acute focus, issuing single word directives, willing her to act.

Back.

Gun.

Fire.

Alice raised her weapon and fired. The bullet tore a hole through what used to be someone's head. Bits of gelatinous ooze erupted across the grassy median. A beat later, the bloated mass of tumorous flesh slumped to its knees and folded into itself. Pieces of the congealed skin slipped free of its host, unwrapping from the person beneath like a banana peel, and revealed a woman's face in twisted agony. Milky eyes locked in terror for all time. A mouth stretched far too wide, so wide the skin had ripped along the seams into a hideous false smile. A pool of bubbling goo slowly seeped from the cavity of her mouth and drained down her throat.

Donna gasped, and Michael reacted instinctively, held out his arms to hold her and Quinn back. Alice looked away from the corrupted body long enough to meet his eyes and read the fear writ upon them.

Shit, shit, shit.

She turned just as the second creature charged into her, knocking the wind from her lungs as they both collapsed on the sidewalk. The world spun before her, and in the ensuing chaos, she saw Spectrum and Monochrome interweave in a bizarre amalgamation of color and lifelessness. Through it all, the creature's outline and grotesque features remained constant, and in the time her neurons fired back a response, a single mantra chanted repeatedly in her head.

Don't let it touch me don't let it touch me don't let it touch me if it touches me I'll scream don't don't don't—

The faceless thing reached for her, raked its fingertips across her stomach. Something bubbled to the surface of its tumor and popped, dribbling a gray fluid that hissed when it reached the earth. The stench was at once sweet and stagnant, a ripe scent of death and cancer, and she thought of her dying grandmother once more. Deep inside the faceless maw of that thing was a person, a real person who had hopes and dreams, loves and losses, now choked and consumed with a lifetime of fear and failure made manifest.

Deep inside, a gurgling cry worked its way through the folds of flesh, the last gasp of the dying soul within.

Alice screamed. She screamed for herself and for her grandmother and for every other person caught in this chaos. The terror in her throat quickly dissolved into a fried croaking rage, and before she'd regained her sense of self, Alice had rolled away from the creature's grasp. She found Brock's weapon in the grass, shot to her feet, and fired a round.

A clump of earth erupted beside the scrambling abomination. Alice focused, caught her breath, and squeezed the trigger. A thick chunk of the creature's head vanished in an explosion of smoke and viscera.

She fired again.

Again.

Her scream returned, fueled by a fire of lost lives and lost years. All those days and nights spent living in fear and regret, wondering if she'd ever see Michael again, wondering if her parents would even remember her, all those countless hours in limbo ignited in fury. She screamed until there were no rounds left in the gun, the gelatinous tumor subsided, and the poor man's horrified face a scattered mess of bone and blood.

And still she squeezed the trigger. Tears streamed down her face. Michael put his hand on her shoulder, and she wheeled around with her fist raised, ready to pummel her next assailant. He caught her wrist.

"It's done, Alice. It's done."

She fell into him, buried her face against his neck, and allowed herself a moment to breathe. "I can't keep doing this."

Michael didn't say anything. She pressed her face against his cheek, felt the sandpaper scruff of his five o'clock shadow, and smiled faintly. *This isn't the love I ever dreamed of,* she thought, *but if this is how it's going to end, I'm okay with that.*

Somewhere nearby, the familiar moan of the Yawning rose up against a backdrop of sirens and gunfire. Alice's skin prickled at the sound, and when she pulled away from Michael, she saw Quinn standing beside his aunt, shuffling his feet, ready to run.

"Alice? You okay, hon?"

She looked at Donna, wiped her face, and nodded. "We need to get moving."

More of the faceless abominations were shuffling their way across the ER rotunda toward them. Alice took a breath, reached into her back pocket for one of Brock's spare magazines, and reloaded the weapon.

Michael shook his head and cracked a smile. "Where did you get that thing?"

"A girl's gotta keep some secrets."

She set off for the parking garage.

———◆———

"You said Aleister is a usurper. Of what?"

Donovan's voice echoed in the stillness as he followed Christopher across the sands. The storm overhead had fallen silent, if such a thing were possible; when he looked up, the clouds still rolled violently into one another, and he had the impression they were in some sort of bubble, insulated from the greater chaos unfolding around them.

Christopher of the Dullingtons looked over his shoulder and spoke. "Of the Ungod itself, Master Candle. Whatever Aleister told you is a lie. I assure you, he is using you as he used the rest of our Order to gain entrance to the Needle and the Ungod's cradle."

Donovan considered this, considered everything he knew about the pale monk, and all that had unfolded since their paths had crossed. He'd never felt at ease around Aleister, not really, but the monk had followed through with his promises—albeit in obscure and tricky ways. And of course there was the late George Guffin's warning just moments before the Yawning devoured him. *He's using us, feeding on us.*

Using? Definitely. Feeding? That remained to be seen.

Lying? By omission, maybe, but never directly. That much Donovan knew for sure. His presence here in the Monochrome was proof of omitted facts, yet he also couldn't say Aleister hadn't tried to warn him.

"Do not feel sullen, Master Candle. He betrayed us all to steal the power of the Ungod."

"Us?"

"The Order of Silence. We protected the secret of the Monochrome—of the Ungod's existence—from the world for centuries. Once Aleister was chosen to be the Monochrome's Keeper, everything began to unravel." Christopher looked back again, cracked a thin smile that drove chills down Donovan's spine. "I should know. I was there."

"So you knew him before."

"Indeed. I was his mentor. I showed him the ways of the Order. Ordained him as one of the Dullingtons. And for nothing. He left me for dead here in the wastes of the Monochrome. Abandoned me to be devoured by his creatures like the rest of his brothers. I have worked to oppose him ever since."

Faint words rose to the surface of Donovan's mind, a memory of something Dullington told him back on the rooftop of the WBS building. *My former master hid himself away in its chamber long ago.*

He opened his mouth to voice a question, but Christopher raised his hand and cut him off.

"Ah, here we are. Behold, Master Candle, the Needle."

The storm's foggy haze dissipated as they crossed the final demarcation. A flat expanse of desert spread out before them, littered with stony protrusions, piles of bones, and remnants of man-made structures like the hulls of ships, exposed wheels of buried chariots, and something that looked like—impossibly—the wing of an airplane.

In the center stood the Needle, a massive column of chipped marble driven deep into the earth and stretching as high as Donovan could see. Faint shimmering lines were tethered and bound in thick clumps, spooled together from every direction across the sky amidst a backdrop of black splintering cracks. A strange pale light surged within, shining through errant holes in the structure. Beams of light stretched out across the sands like thin pallid arms searching for something unseen. The light slowly climbed the structure to its zenith where it dissipated in a singular flash.

"Inside, our Great Weaver the Ungod slumbers and binds together the strings of fate. Only a willing human soul may enter, Master Candle. It is for this reason I have led you here. Aleister Dullington cannot follow, nor can he see inside. You will be safe from him within."

Donovan heard the man's words but was too perplexed by the surrounding detritus of the ages to pay them any attention. His mind ran rampant with questions as he walked atop bones, suits of armor, weapons of antiquity. Swords and shields, pikes and bows and discarded quivers, even a crank-driven machine gun. How many battles were fought here? How many men slain? And for what? He looked up once more at the Needle and thought of the Crusades, of millions clashing in battle to defend or conquer an expanse of earth deemed "holy" for its history.

Christopher observed this battleground with the same tired smile. His eyes were obscured by the drape of his cowl, and Donovan suspected they had seen their share of this place's bloody history.

All this bloodshed to gain access…or to defend it from breach. Was this sleeping thing inside really so important? Someone certainly thought so.

Even now, as he walked among the remnants of the dead, Donovan felt an odd energy in the air. An electric sense of gravity pulling at his limbs, tugging with the faint touch of needles. Urging him toward the center with a promise of knowledge and experience. Was this the origin of the strange pull of the flickering? The droning hum of the Monochrome itself? He suspected as much, and yet the possibility excited him despite all the horror he'd witnessed in this reality.

Help me.

Donovan looked back. Christopher had turned his attention back toward the storm's edge. There was only the wind, the hum of energy, and—

Help. Me.

The words tickled his ears, spoken in a whisper through the energy of this place. Enunciated slowly, a careful vibrating hum forming the sound of words meant only for him. The sensation prickled his skin with gooseflesh.

Bones crunched underfoot as he walked toward the base of the column. A small outcropping of stones was positioned along the base, framing an apparent entrance covered with a thick slab. When he neared, Donovan saw something had been chiseled above the entrance. Rigid glyphs carved with precision and utmost care. Latin, by the look of them.

ACTA NON VERBA

He stared up at the message and tried to puzzle out its meaning, but here the energy was at its strongest, and he found he had trouble focusing on anything. The intense hum in his head was paramount, churning the same words over and over in a vibrating cacophony of *help me help me help me help me*—

A low rumble tore through the earth beneath him. The stone slab shuddered, unseating clouds of dust into the air, and slowly slid aside to reveal a corridor coated in murky light.

"The Ungod awaits, Master Candle."

Christopher's words gave him a start. Donovan looked back, was about to chastise his companion for sneaking up on him, when he spotted a lone robed figure emerging from the storm. Christopher studied his face and followed his gaze.

"Donovan!"

Aleister's booming baritone voice echoed across the wasteland like a clap of thunder.

"Get inside, Master Candle. I will hold him off as long as I can."

Donovan looked at the open portal waiting for him, beckoning to him, pleading

(help me help me help me)

for his assistance. He took a step, then another. Joe Hopper spoke up inside his head. *Better get on with it, hoss. Ain't no tellin' what Dullington's gonna do if he catches up to ya.*

Donovan stopped. Confused, he turned back and watched the pale monk race across the boneyard toward them. A dozen instances of that inner voice disguised as Joe Hopper replayed in his mind, all of them urging him forward, telling him to trust Dullington, that he's never lied, and now—

Now I'm not supposed to trust him. Is this really me? Beneath all of it, is this really me?

Donovan cleared his head, listened to his gut. Joe Hopper was silent now. All that remained was an uneasiness and uncertainty. He thought of the young man back in the city. Thought of his eyes. His gray, glowing eyes.

"Christopher," he said. The hooded monk looked back.

"Inside, Master Candle. You are wasting time. What—"

Donovan crossed the gap between them and pulled the hood back from the man's face.

A pair of sunken eyes the color of dishwater stared at him. The obscured half of the man's face was more skull than flesh, a plate of bone mottled with cracks from which a thin viscous liquid wept. What little flesh remained was pale white, rubbery, and pulsed to the beat of a malignant heart.

"Step away from him, Donovan!"

Christopher of the Dullingtons flashed a bony smile of brittle teeth. "I told you to go inside, insect."

The monk raised his hand, and before Donovan could reply, a violent flash of light sent him sprawling backward through the air. He slammed onto the stone floor of the exposed corridor and struggled to breath. The impact drove the wind from his lungs, and as he gasped for precious air, a shadow fell upon him.

The stone slab slid back into place and cut him off from the Monochrome beyond.

-13-
VILE

"Is nothing sacred to you?"

Aleister approached Christopher Dullington's robed corpse, his pale skin prickling with energy as a stormfront of fury crashed over him. The times he'd felt such anger since being robbed of his humanity were few, and even then, they had been little more than plumes of flame in an otherwise cold hearth.

Now the fires raged, consuming everything that was not already dead inside.

"Did you expect me to stand idle while you made pilgrimage to my doorstep? Oh, little sparrow, you never learn—"

Aleister raised his hand and expelled a crackling ball of light. The remains of Christopher Dullington exploded backward, painting the cracked column with bits of rotted flesh and brittle bone. A thick white residue seeped down the pitted surface, collected along the rim of sand, and slowly seeped into the earth.

Aleister approached the stone entrance, and in a fit of rage, slammed his fists against the slab. "*VILE!*"

His voice echoed across the demarcations, the expanse of the Monochrome, and even the metachasm itself. The strings above quivered, and elsewhere in the Spectrum, many were struck with an unexplainable shiver that left them reeling. Windows shattered and foundations cracked, yet the phenomena went unnoticed amidst the greater turmoil as both realities merged.

All around him, worlds shivered in distress at his sudden anger, a violent rage powerful enough to silence the cosmos and ignite stars—and yet for all his fury, the entrance to the Ungod's cradle would not move.

Vile's cavernous laugh echoed from deep within.

———————•———————

The darkness swallowed him whole, and for a time, all Donovan heard was the sound of his racing heart thumping away in his chest. He was grateful for the dark. It hid his shame.

He'd let himself be deceived a second time. Seeing the reanimated corpse of Aleister's mentor put everything in perspective now. The young man back in the city, the so-called John Black, really had been killed by the Yawning.

He thought of the strange white sheen coating the man's arm. *It wasn't his arm. Not really. It was that white stuff, mediocrity or whatever, molded in the shape of an arm. God, I was so blind.* So Dullington's adversary could reanimate the dead, or perhaps even inhabit the mediocrity within. The implication of that possibility terrified him. John Black's words replayed in his head. *"My manikin was resilient to a point, but you, Mr. Candle, have proven to be an insect who cannot be crushed."* The context wasn't lost on him. Sparrow was being controlled after all. Donovan supposed that made sense; the real Albert Sparrow he'd met years ago at the bookstore never seemed like the sort to plan and orchestrate the Great Fade-Out.

No, the real Sparrow was a coward, one who'd rather save his own skin. He wouldn't have put himself in harm's way again. The Sparrow who weakened the balance was nothing more than a puppet in the truest sense. Just like John Black and the one called Christopher.

Dead puppets used for manipulation. Donovan looked around the dark corridor now that his eyes had adjusted. A gray glow lit up a stone passage deeper into the structure. *It's time to meet the one pulling all those strings.*

A dozen what-ifs raced through his mind as he climbed to his feet, and he forced them back into the shadows. Now wasn't the time for anxiety. He'd languished in the hell of his own fears for too long.

Help me.

That voice again. Faint, little more than a strained whisper, inhabiting every surface, every breath, the air itself. It was nowhere and everywhere at once, two syllables echoing forever in the expanse of Donovan's mind. Another ruse? Dullington's adversary had already proven himself to be a voice in Donovan's head. He would never again trust the voice of Joe

Hopper, a revelation which was at once freeing and terrifying. Had the character ever been his own? He tried not to think about all the times he'd trusted the Hopper-voiced instincts to guide him along this bizarre journey.

Please.

Donovan followed the dim light down a long corridor and traced his fingers along the stone wall to keep his orientation. At its end, the corridor opened into a massive circular chamber carved from great stone slabs. In the center was an elevated slab decorated with ornate etchings, symbols he didn't recognize, perhaps the letters of a dead language long forgotten. A fleshy white membrane protruded from within the slab, and as he struggled to make sense of it, a word leapt forward from his racing thoughts: *cradle.*

Yes, a cradle for whatever lay within. Was it the Ungod? He wanted to move forward and peek inside, but his fear held him there while his heart thundered.

The membrane inhaled slowly with a rattling gasp; a moment later, it exhaled a pulse of gray light from its center which filled the chamber, illuminating carvings along the walls. Armored figures stood in etched portraiture, each one gazing solemnly at the stone mass in the center. Sentinels who'd once guarded this sacred place—or perhaps they were jailers, posted here to ensure whatever rested within the cradle could not leave.

Movement stole Donovan's attention, and when he looked back toward the center, he saw the light surging upward along a pallid bundling of thick cords woven tightly together. He followed the light as it crawled upward along the gnarled path, growing in brilliance until a tangled mass suspended above blocked its progression.

Donovan strained to make out what was caught in the cords—the strings, he realized—and took a couple steps forward for a better look. Another breath of light swelled and collected, rose and lingered at the foot of the entangled figure long enough for him to see.

There was a man entwined in the strings above. Remnants of a tattered robe protruded from the knot, two bare feet, one arm woven tightly to the side and the other partially free and suspended in the air. Gnarled arthritic fingers twitched erratically in the gloom, painting a spindly shadow along the walls like a massive spider. A grizzled beard framed a wrinkled and scarred face, and from somewhere inside the man's chest arose a pleasured hum as the light washed over him.

His eyes opened. Two wild gray eyes, full of maddening knowledge and purpose. Donovan's entire body erupted in gooseflesh as the man lowered his gaze and smiled.

Pontius Vile licked his lips. "Come forward, Donovan Candle, and meet your liberator."

———— • ————

They were nearly to Amanda's SUV on the garage's second floor when Donna was struck with a gut-sinking realization: Amanda wasn't with them.

Their trek into the garage and up the stairwell had gone unnoticed so far, and for those fleeting moments she'd thought the worst behind them. Once they were mobile, they could drive off into the sunset and escape these monstrosities—only now she realized that was a pipedream, because she'd gotten too far ahead of herself. In all this chaos, she hadn't had time to come to terms with her sister's sudden absence or the pale, lost expression on her nephew's face.

Donna clutched her sister's purse to her chest, fearful she might lose it somehow, this last physical connection with the overbearing woman whom she'd resented at times and loved despite their differences.

She reached into the purse and fished out Amanda's keys. A flood of emotion crashed against her resolve, clouding her sight with tears, and drowning her heart in aching despair. Her sister was gone. How, she did not know, but she suspected one of those things in the hospital had something to do with it. One of those impossible things torn straight from someone's nightmares.

Quinn looked back, noticed she was lingering in the stairwell entrance. "Aunt Donna?" He turned, called out to Alice and Michael. "Something's wrong, guys. Hold up."

Donna shook her head, tried to wave them off, but her words faltered. The tears welling within her eyes spilled down her cheeks, and for a time, she struggled to keep her hitching breaths from evolving into sobs. *Keep yourself together. Now is not the time for these goddamn hormones to get the better of you, woman.*

Easier said than done, however. She glimpsed Michael, saw him shake his head and look away, and his annoyance lit a fire in her chest. The urge to scream rose in her throat, and if given the chance, she knew she would smack the shit out of him.

Michael looked back, frowned. "We really don't have time for this, Donna."

Alice plucked the keys from Donna's hand and threw them at him. "Go scout ahead. I'll take care of this." He tried to speak again, and she shushed him. "Quinn, go with him and keep him out of trouble. We'll wait here."

Once the boys were on their way, Alice exhaled and muttered, "He can be such an asshole sometimes." And then, to Donna: "What's wrong, hon?"

"It's Amanda," she whispered, and everything else she wanted to say—*She's gone, Quinn's mom is gone, she was my best friend*—crumbled into a fractured stream of consonants. Alice wrapped her arms around Donna, pulled her close, and whispered in her ear.

"I know. Shh, I know. And I know this hurts, Donna, but there is nothing you can do about it. Nothing I can do about it either. But there is something you *can* do, okay? Keep it together for Quinn. The poor kid has been through nothing but hell these last few days, and losing his mom is the cherry on top."

Donna closed her eyes, swallowed back another sob, and nodded. "You're right. I'm sorry, I—"

"Not another word." Alice stepped back, smiled. "You've always been stronger than you give yourself credit for, Donna. When I realized it was you down in the tunnels all that time ago, I knew you had a better chance than most."

She stared at Alice, took in the kind features of her face buried beneath a mask of stone. A familiar face, its remnants of memory just below a thin layer of fog, and yet—

I knew her, Donna realized. *She used to work with Donnie. Used to date Mike. They were going to get married. God, how many hours did I spend on the phone with her? Complaining about the guys, gossiping about our jobs—was it really that long ago? When I was still working, before all the fibro issues really started?*

Something warm dribbled across her upper lip. She wiped the blood away and smiled shyly. "You—I think I remember you."

Alice grinned. "It's about time, Mrs. Candle. We've shared too many glasses of wine together."

A silver SUV sped toward them and screeched to a halt. Quinn threw open the back door. *"GET IN!"*

Before Donna could question her nephew, Alice shoved her into the backseat and screamed for Michael to drive. The SUV lurched forward as something struck it from behind. Alice slammed the door behind her and cursed. *"Goddammit, go!"*

Michael stepped on the gas. Tires squealed as the SUV rocketed forward, away from the unseen danger behind them. They were around the corner and on the garage exit ramp before Donna looked back. All she saw was a lurching shadow one level above—and something that reminded her of wings.

———— • ————

*W*ings. *My God, they have wings.*

Michael's mind raced in time with his pounding heart as he slammed on the gas pedal. Even in the face of what must be insanity, he struggled to make sense of what he'd seen, to correlate the impossible beast and file it away in some fashion that made sense. Quinn, Alice, and Donna screamed words he couldn't understand, their voices forming an unintelligible shriek as he focused on exiting the parking garage as fast as possible.

Tires squealed as he took the corners and sped down the ramp. There were more of those things lumbering in the lower levels, turning toward the noise of the engine as Michael drove past them. At the first-floor entrance, nestled inside the ticketing booth, was a gelatinous mass of quivering flesh, seizing erratically as it adhered itself to the glass window.

Alice gasped. "What the fuck is that?"

Michael answered by gunning the engine and driving through the crossbar. The SUV shot forward onto the adjacent street, and the tires voiced their distress as he took a left toward the freeway.

What the fuck was that thing?

There was no time to react or process what he'd seen between the parked cars further down the garage lane. After all he'd witnessed in the last ten minutes—hell, the last forty-eight hours—he wasn't prepared for the transformation taking place when he turned the corner beside Amanda's SUV.

Michael had opened the door, spotted movement, froze. What happened next did so in a series of fragmented images, his mind switching into autopilot to save what was left of his sanity.

A pile of white flesh.

Human limbs sprouting from its center mass.

A series of mouths opening and closing, gasping for air, tasting his scent.

And wings. Membranous tissue sprouting from the cocoon—because that's what it was, he realized now. A cocoon. The spider-things nested inside people, did something to them, and then they grew into—what? He failed to conjure a name. A human insect held aloft by these new appendages sprouting from its back, the host's body barely recognizable from the pallid tissue engulfing its mass. Almost like a locust emerging from its shell.

A gourd-shaped head formed from the mass. Mouths—he counted three before slamming the SUV's door—grimaced and bared jagged teeth. Two bulbous eyes opened, squinted, sized him up.

"What is it?"

Quinn had climbed in beside him, couldn't see what Michael saw over the hood.

And then the pallid thing had climbed to its feet, flapped its translucent wings lazily, testing them for the first time. Feeling the lift of air, the weight of gravity in this new world, readying itself for flight. *For flight.*

Quinn had shouted something, and Michael had started the SUV. Everything after was a blur, a series of emotions more than a montage of images. Incredulity, denial, fear—he went through those motions as they sped toward the city, away from the winged beast that had hatched before his eyes.

"—plan?"

Michael blinked, looked into the rearview, and met Alice's wide-eyed stare. "What?"

"Where are we going? What's the plan?"

He turned the wheel, swerved to avoid a collision in the intersection. The avenue leading to the freeway entrance was a maze of derelict cars and loping pale figures.

"I don't know," he said. "Away from here. Out of the city…" His words faltered, faded on his lips.

But, he wanted to say. *But they could be everywhere.* How many people were going about their day when this began? A hundred thousand? Five hundred thousand? Every person was a vessel for one of those things, and he didn't have the heart to tell them they didn't have enough gas or bullets.

They sped up the freeway entrance ramp. A pair of winged monstrosities stirred beside an abandoned tractor trailer, no doubt disturbed by their approach, and tested their wings. Michael swerved away from them, afraid of catching their attention.

In the last moment before the SUV passed, he saw one creature spread its wings and leap into the air.

---·---

The old man's words echoed across the vast chamber, disturbing the shadows, the emerging light, rippling the air itself. "You have traveled a long way to see me, Master Candle. Ever the loyal manikin."

Donovan stood his ground, portrayed his best poker face, but inside he was trembling. After his trek across the Monochrome, he had yet to consider what he might say in the face of Dullington's adversary. The Great and Powerful Oz Himself. Only here there was no man hiding behind the curtain, no deceiver or charlatan. Here was the real thing, a man who had literally tied himself to the strings of fate, and for what? To upset the cosmic balance between both realities? The *Why* question circled his mind without an answer.

"Your mind betrays your silence, young Donovan. I hear your thoughts and I have seen your dreams. This, here…" Vile raised a hand and stroked a thin fiber from the series of thick knots entwining his body. "This was one of yours. I have saved it for some time, knowing we might come face to face one day."

He twirled the string around his finger and pulled. It gave way with a tiny *plink,* and a slight stab of pain in the center of Donovan's skull gave him a start. He rubbed absently at his head, ran his fingers through his hair.

"I would not expect you to remember, Master Candle. That was but one of your many dreams, one from your youth before your parents were stolen from you. Before you fell under your older brother's overbearing shadow. Oh yes, I know you, Donovan. I have always known you, even when you were but a cell in your mother's womb."

"I've heard that line before. You think you're a god?"

The strings slowly loosened, breaking apart the knots suspending Vile in the air. He drifted downward like a wingless angel with arms held out in a welcoming pose. The strings receded from him as his bare feet touched the stone floor; a moment later, they entwined themselves together and rejoined the massive umbilicus rising toward the vast ceiling.

"No god, Master Candle." He looked back, gestured to the stone cradle and the stirring mass of flesh within. The membranous form recoiled from his gaze. Donovan thought he heard a whisper from afar

(help me)

but Vile spoke once more and the weak voice was silenced yet again.

"The only god is the one you made. An Ungod in between existence and the void, forever slumbering, and sustained on the dreams of man. You think this place a prison, when in turn it was man who built it. The Monochrome only exists because man is incapable of facing his failures. I suppose you know something about that, do you not?"

A thin smile cut across Vile's haggard face. Donovan's cheeks flushed with heat, and he clenched his jaw in an effort to hold back his emotion. Vile's sudden laughter echoed throughout the chamber. The air quivered around them in response.

"Settle yourself, Master Candle. Aleister prepared you for a confrontation, but I am only offering you conversation. Unlike your droll guide, I will give you answers without riddles. You question my intent, and I give you my answer: I want to show man his true nature."

"True nature?"

A low moan of agony rose from the stone cradle, followed by a soft pulse of light which resonated up the umbilicus and into the great hollow above. Donovan watched the light trail its way along the strings until it faded from view.

"Each string connects to a soul, and a mere touch reveals where that soul has been, where it is, and where it will go. And the Great Weaver, what you know as the Ungod, binds these threads into the very fabric of reality while it slumbers. A perfect machine unknowingly created by man to consume that which man is incapable of facing himself." Vile returned to the cradle, took hold of the umbilicus, and plucked another fiber from the coil. "Here is a dream conjured by a soul full of fear. It is a dream unrealized, one that will never come to pass. This hapless soul will never know the crushing weight of their failure to act, will never know the repercussions of that failure—but I do. I have seen where all strings lead, Master Candle, and that is why Spectrum and Monochrome will become one."

Vile held out the thread, let it fall to the floor, and crushed it beneath his foot. Donovan watched in silence, wondering if the thread's owner sensed what had happened. Wondering if that dream was forever gone from them now.

"You think you know what's in store for mankind? That's what all of this has been about?"

"I do know, Master Candle. I can see mankind's future because he follows the same routine. Once I doubted myself, wanted so much to believe the contrary, and so great was my desire that I broke the covenants of my Order. I stole myself away to this chamber and communed with the Ungod. Here I learned my fears were true." The haggard man knelt beside the stone cradle and stared longingly at the pulsing mass of skin. "Fear and a failure to act on dreams that would better mankind. Pain. Famine. Disease. Endless conflict. Everlasting agony for the sake of gods and greed. I have seen how adept we are at brutalizing one another, and I have taken part in spilling oceans of blood."

Vile dragged his fingers across the scars on his face. This close to the light, Donovan could see the old wounds with more clarity. Ribbons of skin were missing, flayed away by blades from a bygone era. All that were left now were wrinkled trenches etched into a time-worn face. If not for the man's crooked smile, his features might have been worthy of portraiture in stone. Donovan thought about all the half-buried weapons he'd seen poking out of the sand.

"I once clung to the absurd notion that man was meant for more than his lot, but the Ungod swept aside such self-perpetuated lies. Concepts such as happiness and hope are but symptoms of man's greater disease, his consciousness."

"You think consciousness is a disease?"

Vile recoiled as if struck, his face contorting in a portrait of rage, and Donovan truly saw the insanity in the man's wild eyes. The crazed monk crossed the space between them and spat at Donovan's feet.

"Of course. How could you not? Would you pursue happiness or live in hope of another day if you were not aware of yourself? *Cogito ergo sum,* Master Candle. You *think,* therefore you *are.* You *are,* therefore you *do.* It is in your nature to find meaning in your actions. Without the meaning of hope or promise of happiness, what are you, Master Candle? An empty vessel. A shell. *A manikin."* Vile realized his anger, unclenched his fists, and stepped back. He took a seat against one of the carved stone pillars and wiped sweat from his brow.

There was a sick kind of desperation in his eyes, an eagerness to believe in his convictions. Donovan had seen it before, painted on the aged face of a self-help guru while standing outside a subway entrance. In the pale gloom of the chamber, he realized there was little difference between Vile and his former puppet, Albert Sparrow.

Donovan stood over the frail old man, looked down at him with a mixture of resentment and pity. He chuckled quietly to himself. "An old acquaintance once told me happiness is the greatest con of all. Was that him talking, or was it you speaking through him?"

Vile cracked a smile. "Would it matter? Happiness is the lie you tell yourself to give meaning to your existence. A story you tell your children so they may sleep at night and not fret over the truth: that their lives have no meaning."

"And what of our actions? What of mine? It's mighty bold of you to sit there and tell me all I've done to get here means nothing. That my existence is meaningless along with the rest of humanity. I was—"

"Meant for more than this, yes? Spare me, Master Candle." Vile sighed and rolled his eyes. "Your life has no meaning, ergo you construct a lie so convincing even you must believe it. You construct gods to give yourself direction, and you construct happiness to give yourself a reason." He waved his hand toward the stone cradle. "You construct a being to devour what you could not achieve."

The threaded umbilicus quivered, and a weak gasp for breath rose from the chamber center.

Help me, a voice rasped.

Donovan looked away from his adversary, toward the desperate sound wheezing across the room. *If I can wake it, I can end this. I don't know how, but I have to try.*

He started for the cradle, and Vile caught his wrist. "You cannot stop what has begun, Donovan. The metachasm has been bridged. Even now the Spectrum and Monochrome are becoming one. Even now, mankind is facing what's dwelt inside him all along. You believe a man as stubborn as you can reset the balance?"

"No, I don't, but I have to try."

He shook himself free and climbed the chiseled steps toward the glowing opening in the center. Heart pounding, his breathing suddenly labored as the air thickened around him, Donovan approached the glowing epicenter. Whatever lay within was his ticket home to Donna and their child.

A lithe figure took form in the light—

(help me)

—and a sudden force propelled him forward, over the cradle and into the swirling umbilicus of threads. He cried out as searing fire spread through his eyes, his forehead, his mind, blinding him to the chamber and his surroundings. Struggling, Donovan kicked and pulled against the tangle of threads, but his restraints had come alive in a span of seconds. They weren't threads at all, but eyeless snakes moving to the whim of their new master, squeezing the air from his lungs with each tightened inch.

"I have grown bored of this conversation. You cannot delay the inevitable, and while I do applaud your spirit, our time for parlay has grown thin. I must attend to my former pupil as I should have done so long ago."

Vile's voice echoed across the darkness and between the splotches of color exploding before Donovan's eyes. He saw color and shadow and thin lines stretching on forever, burning a pathway into his brain like a massive loom. Each individual thread murmured with a voice, joining a chorus of dissonance spreading across an endless expanse of stars.

Donovan tried to scream, thought he did, but could no longer tell. He felt removed from his body, his essence separated from the vessel entangled in the coiled umbilicus. Across the void, Pontius Vile's voice boomed with the fury of all the burning stars before him.

"You want so badly to see your loved ones. It is, after all, the reason you came all this way. You might say it is the meaning you have given yourself. So be it, Master Candle. Allow me to give you what you desire."

The lines converged, the stars morphing into a singular ball of searing light. Donovan felt a familiar tug at his gut, but the sensation appeared elsewhere—his eyes, his mind—pulling him forward into a great unknown. The chorus of voices slowly died away, and now he could hear the sound of his body crying out in agony.

Now he heard his own screams. They followed him forward into the light, and like the rest of his mind, slowly disintegrated into oblivion.

-14-
COSMA

The blinding pain dissipated within seconds, and Donovan opened what he thought were his eyes. The sensation of muscle memory was gone from his being, replaced by a feeling of intense dissolution from himself into a million tiny pieces. And yet his senses were still there somehow, suddenly far more acute than they'd ever been, sharpened to a knifepoint.

"Conscious. Disembodied. Not dead. I am still here. I am still alive. I am. *I am.*"

His thoughts vibrated across an infinite expanse of threads like the strings of a strummed guitar. He saw their sounds, felt them in his bones like an itch that would not relent, and tasted the sparkling coloration dancing before him as he traveled. To where, exactly? He did not know.

There were billions of strings for as far as he could see, stretching out to a singular point of shifting light. A massive kaleidoscope of color circulated at their focal point.

Curious, Donovan reached out with his mind and traced a phantom finger across one of the threads. Light surged in his head, filling him with the consciousness of someone else, someone he didn't know. He felt their fear and anxiety, saw them trembling in a hospital exam room while something pounded on the door. The chair used as a makeshift barricade shifted from the force. Donovan felt the hope slowly drain from them, saw the spark of epiphany light up the shadows of their mind for a brief instant.

The string ended abruptly and was soon replaced by another tether in the weave. Donovan retracted himself, freed his mind of those emotions, and wished he could wipe his eyes. He felt his fingertips twitch, but they were distant, somewhere far behind him.

"Attached to my body," he realized, and felt the full weight of his detachment. "I'm still there in the chamber, and I'm here too. Traveling somewhere. Across the strings. Across the metachasm."

The metachasm.

Knowledge of its existence lit up his mind, the understanding needed to grasp its nature all at once present, and he wondered if it had always been there. Locked behind a door in his brain, maybe. Here, unburdened of his corporeal self, he was free to view existence without filters and taste the knowledge hidden from most. The knowledge reserved for someone like Aleister Dullington or Pontius Vile.

Leaden fear seeped into the corners of his consciousness, questioning if he was meant to see and know these forbidden things, but were eventually silenced by his unbridled wonder. There was so much here to know. He felt drunk with the possibility, but a flash of Sparrow's grinning face sobered him in an instant.

Donovan instead turned his gaze from the strings and down into a stygian gulf of darkness below.

"A sea of dreams as thin as paper and as wide and deep as the darkest pit of every human heart."

The voice from before. Neither male nor female. Weak and whispering, yet he heard it clearly over the roar of his thoughts vibrating across the strings.

"You're the Ungod."

"I am the Great Weaver. I am the sleeping beast. I am the Ungod. I am Cosma, and I am a dying flame."

"Cosma." His essence mouthed the word, and the threads reacted violently, shuddering with the force of a power chord. "The Great Weaver."

"Weaver of all strings, all dreams, all fates. Every string a tether of fate. Every fate bound by a balance of fears overcome and fears unmoved." The shimmering cable of entwined cords vibrated, hummed in perfect harmony with the Ungod's words. *"The slumbering beast which guards you from yourself."*

Donovan felt each syllable deep in his essence, an unsettling bassline submerged in marrow and spirit, and he wished to avert his eyes from the swirling light illuminating the horizon. But he had no eyes, no ears, no physical shell with which to turn away. The Ungod was in his mind, however ethereal, and he supposed that were he able to turn away, the nonentity would still be wherever he looked. Facing him with a blank infantile face, peering with unblinking black marbles for eyes, the most hideous porcelain doll he'd ever seen.

"That was you calling out to me, wasn't it?"

An apt question given his circumstance, but the uncertainty and trepidation in his voice made him second-guess himself. Deep down, he supposed he already knew the answer.

"Yes. Pontius Vile has corrupted my purpose. Knotted the strings I must weave. Choking me in my slumber, using the power of the strings to manipulate and weaken the balance."

Donovan thought of the tangle of strings suspended above the Ungod's cradle. "He's damning us all for things that haven't even come to pass."

"Pontius Vile glimpsed a possibility and took it for fact. No fate is intact. Every thread may be knotted or split. Every thread may diverge and change. When he took hold of the umbilicus, he saw one of many outcomes and was driven mad by it. His madness has blinded him to my fallibility."

If he still had a body, Donovan would have scoffed. "I thought God was supposed to be perfect, immutable? Every action or inaction not without its reason?"

"I am a sum of many parts, all derived from the need of humanity. Your minds are powerful engines, Donovan Candle, capable of immense potential. Capable of solving the greatest of problems and birthing the most horrible machinations. I was made to sift through those dreams, the fears, the failures. I was made to guard you from yourselves."

"Made by whom?"

"By you and the rest of mankind. In the liminal spaces of the dreaming, when your minds wander into the dark, a subtle cry in the face of all you cannot process. I was made in those shadowed moments, from the stolen breaths of all your fears. You made me, a thing through which all your unwanted fears and failures would pass, so that your minds would not make them manifest in the flesh. As I am made from man, so too am I imperfect. You want to believe your gods are omniscient and perfect, desperate for something to give meaning to your existence and context for the decisions you make. You have told yourselves a great lie, that your fate is beyond your control. That is the lie which Vile believes.

Silence followed as Donovan contemplated the Ungod's words. A low ache settled into his mind, behind where his eyes might be. All this metaphysical discussion made his head hurt.

"You are not expected to understand, Donovan Candle. You are expected to act."

"How can I when I'm…like this? When I'm back in the Needle?" Donovan's mind filled with the Ungod's strained screams, with the image of an umbilical cord wrapped around an infant's throat. He struggled to withdraw from himself and found there was nothing from which to do so. His essence was all that remained in this vast space. There was no looking or turning away.

"Vile believes he has trapped you in the loom of fate. Even now your presence is drawn across the metachasm and into the Spectrum. Soon you will take the place of one of his minions. It is there he wishes to trap your mind. You will be helpless, and he will be free to achieve his goal."

He reached forward, felt his disembodied fingers glide across the expanse of threads, and marveled at the way they hummed. "I can help you, Cosma, but you need to help me out of this. I need to get back to my wife. I need to go home. Dullington said you can do that." A long silence. The band of shimmering strings splintered into a thousand separate lines and spread out across a dark horizon. "Was he lying?"

"All things serve a balance. One scale cannot outweigh the other. If Vile succeeds and I expire, the scales will tip for all time. The reality you know will wither and fade, and mankind will be consumed by the gnashing teeth of all he fears."

"You aren't answering my question."

"I can help you, Donovan Candle, but the balance must be restored. You must stop Vile. Life for life."

Donovan searched his heart, weighed his options, and realized how much he'd relied on the wisdom of a false creation. Joe Hopper always knew where to guide him, but even that was a façade. The thought of Vile being in his head all these years made his skin crawl—or gave him the sensation, anyway. He felt violated in the worst way.

Nothing I can do about that now. Cosma's words don't exactly inspire confidence, but what other choice do I have? I have to try. For Donna and the baby. For me.

A flashing light pierced the dark, projecting a shifting kaleidoscope of color across the narrow sliver of threads. Donovan became aware of the speed at which he was traveling, felt the surging wind and cool air against skin that wasn't his own.

"Even now you push forward into the unknown, unbound by the fate Vile has bestowed upon you. I can see why Aleister of the Dullingtons chose you to be his avatar. I will help you, Donovan Candle. Now listen carefully—"

Donovan did as he was told, bracing himself for the destroyed world rushing forward to greet him.

WIDOWS

Margie Guffin crossed the demarcation and out of the eternal storm. She walked with some trepidation, confused by the sudden absence of cloudy haze, and allowed herself to focus on the blasted landscape. Gray sands mottled with the occasional half-buried piece of junk spread out before her. A massive column stood in the center against a backdrop of violent cloudbanks, pulsing a weird light that hurt her eyes.

Other pilgrims wandered across the clearing, the ones who'd managed to find their way through the storm. She'd been so focused on her journey across the wastes that she had failed to grasp the size of their number. Now, watching them slink forward with hunched gaits toward this maddening epicenter of oblivion, Margie was puzzled by their presence. She knew why she was here, but what about them? Why had an entire city of the Missing been called here to this desolate place?

Across the expanse, along the opposite rim, she spied the movement of other tiny figures. *Not just the city. Others beyond the city. Maybe the entire world.*

More emerged from behind, brushed past her on their journey forward to the column. She studied their faces, took measure of the vacant stares, the lines of trauma carved into their faces. Even after all these years struggling to survive in the Monochrome, this goddamn place still had new horrors to share.

Indeed, even she had questioned her sanity in the storm, facing off with the phantom of her dead husband. He'd appeared to her in the oversized coat he'd worn the last time she saw him, when Dullington sent him on that fool's errand—only he was covered in blood. One of his arms was missing, and there was something wrong with his face, his skin waxen and reshaped as if by a child kneading clay. His eyes were too pale, and they wavered in their sockets like a candle flame caught in a draft. She'd found she couldn't bring herself to look too long, terrified that his eyes would go out, leaving only the stark blackness of empty orbits. Silent, expressionless, imposing. Accusing.

"George." Her words had hitched in her throat and stayed there, like she'd swallowed a wad of chewing gum. A bitter taste lingered in her mouth. Metallic.

Kill the one who did this to me, he had said, and she'd forced herself to keep moving forward. He'd turned to follow her as she went on, trailing behind her in eerie silence. When she'd finally worked up enough nerve to confront his bloody visage, she'd turned to find herself alone but for the swirling dust devils conjured by the silent storm above.

There were other horrors—phantoms of past decisions, a ghost of the child she'd given up for adoption before she'd met George, the money she'd stolen from her parents and the resulting hardship, the drugs indulged in her youth—but only her husband's bloody figure truly shook her. *That damn fool, volunteering to be Dullington's puppet thinking he could escape this place. Thinking he could bargain with a monster.*

"All life is a bargain with a monster, honey. Everything in between is just negotiation, and at the end, the monster always collects." George's bloody figure staggered out of the storm and stopped beside her. He gestured to her waist. "You're that monster today, babe. Candle's luck has run out."

Margie removed the weapon from her waistband, wrapped her fingers around the grip, and lightly traced her fingertip along the trigger. "I'm that monster," she repeated, grimacing at the rise of emotions like acid in her throat, the agony she felt the day she learned her George wouldn't be returning to her. When she finally lifted her gaze to look at her dead husband, Margie discovered she'd been crying, her vision cloudy like dirty glass in the rain.

"Will you be that monster for me today, Marge?"

"I'll be whatever you need me to be, hon." She wiped her eyes. "I'll be any monster you want."

George Guffin smiled. A mixture of blackened gore and gray ooze seeped from his mouth, dribbled down his chin. The lights in his eyes flared. "That's a good girl." He raised his remaining hand and pointed beyond the column. "I want you to think really hard about that for me. Concentrate all that hate you're feeling, keep that murderer in the center of your mind, and keep walking that way."

She followed his finger and squinted into the distance. The storm swirled and folded upon itself, a never-ending monsoon of dust and dead dreams. It towered over the clearing, over the group of figures emerging from its tumult, and was rivaled only by the column itself.

"Is he here?"

"He is close, and you will find him if you have the will. I know you do. It's brought you this far, my dear. It can take you a little further."

"And when he's dead?"

"Then," George Guffin said, walking backward into the churning wall of the storm, "you and I can be one together once again. All of us will…"

His words faded as the storm swallowed his body. Margie blinked, shielded herself from the errant sands stirring in the wind, and found her dead husband was gone. Only a spotted trail of gore marked his retreat across the sand. Margie stared at the nearest pool of bloody sludge, relieved that he'd been real.

Terrified that he'd been real.

Together once again, she thought, turning back toward the column and the storm beyond. *If I have the will.*

She squeezed the handgun's grip, measured its weight, and rested her finger against the trigger guard. Margie set off in the direction of her husband's killer.

———— • ————

Overhead, thin hairline fractures cracked and splintered across the hazy gray sky. They widened in places, revealing a shimmering band of color beyond. The heavens trembled, and the earth held its breath in waiting.

———— • ————

Donna screamed, "Here they come!"

One of the winged creatures clipped the SUV's backside, crushing the bumper and knocking the vehicle askew. Michael jerked the wheel too late, cried out in shock from the impact, and tried to correct their course along the highway. He glanced in the rearview out of reflex, but only saw the backs of Donna's and Quinn's heads.

"How're we looking back there?"

Quinn looked back, met Michael's eyes in the mirror, and shook his head. "Still just the two. Can this thing go any faster?"

Michael pressed the clutch and shifted to the next gear. The engine growled with displeasure.

A row of cars sped past them in the adjacent lane, their drivers no doubt trying to escape the chaos erupting in the city. Michael glanced to the side, noted the faces of terror and frigid tension on their drivers and passengers. *Good luck,* he thought, and immediately wished he hadn't.

One of the flying abominations swooped down, landed on the hood of the first car, and smashed the windshield. The driver—a balding man in a green T-shirt—lost control of the vehicle in his panic.

Michael let off the gas just in time. The car swerved across the lane and slammed headfirst into the center divider.

"Christ," he whispered. A heavy tremor hitched through the cabin's frame. He squeezed the wheel hard, draining the blood from his knuckles, digging his nails into his palms.

Come on, hold yourself together, old boy. Just long enough until—

A blast of cool air washed over him. Alice had lowered the window, was unbuckling her seat belt.

"What the hell are you doing?"

She raised Brock's weapon and cracked a smile. "Cover fire."

"The fuck you are." He reached over, took her free hand, and squeezed. "You're a good shot, but this ain't the movies."

"Just admit you're worried about me."

"Of course I'm worried."

Alice raised the window and buckled her seatbelt. "Feels good to hear that again—"

A trio of winged abominations landed in the center of the highway, their jagged teeth bared from a series of grimacing mouths, wings and limbs fidgeting in anticipation of their oncoming prey. For a brief instance, Michael's impulse was to slam on the brakes, but the creatures were too close and they were driving too fast. Slowing down, swerving to miss them wasn't an option.

Instead, he stepped on the gas, and the SUV lurched forward as the engine RPMs topped out.

"Shit! Everybody hold on!"

At least that's what he thought he said. The following moments blurred together in a jumble of automatic actions and firing neurons, disrupted by the ever-shifting world around them, and the violent trembling of the earth below. The SUV plowed through the trio, shooting one of them up and over the hood. Its gourd-sized head shattered the windshield and exploded in a mess of dark blood and gray ooze and broken teeth. The creature's body remained glued to the frontend like a demonic hood ornament. A second monstrosity slipped beneath the wheels, forcing the vehicle to buck slightly in the air.

The third creature, sensing its imminent mortality, forced itself upward with the lift of humming wings. Its feet pattered across the roof with the frantic pace of a sprinting toddler. A guttural shriek erupted from somewhere above them, but its immediate ferocity diminished as they sped on.

The SUV shuddered, hitched in protest. Thin trails of smoke rose from below the crumpled hood, coating the fractured windshield and broken creature's body. Michael was struck with the ridiculous notion to switch on the windshield wipers, perhaps in a comical gesture to clean the filth from view, but the moment was fleeting. He was about to exhale burning air from his lungs when he spotted something through the streams of smoke and broken glass.

Something huge, much bigger than those winged beasts. Tall, spindly, with what looked like an enormous mouth—and it was racing to greet them head on.

This time Michael had no choice but to slam on the brakes. Alice shrieked something that sounded like "yawning," but he didn't have a chance to ask for clarity. He yanked the wheel, intending to swerve away from the creature, but the SUV's speed and momentum pulled them forward.

Tires shrieked along the asphalt. A moment later, they left the road altogether, and Michael's world began to spin.

The tempest's roiling curtain slowly dissipated as Margie walked beyond its boundary, revealing not the wastes of the Monochrome, but the bright Spectrum world she'd once called home. Even here the depressing miasma persisted, spilling into the real world like paint down a canvas.

The world she'd once known was shifting somehow, its color and texture fading into muted shapes, little more than empty structural geometry.

What details remained suggested she was somewhere on the city's outskirts, near the highway bypass which ran overhead of the city's derelict slums. She had come full circle, traveling miles in what felt like seconds. Graffiti decorated the overpass's concrete supports. Years of faded lettering overlapped, one artist's message shouting over those who came before, but a pale doorway caught her eye amidst the screaming mural. Its drip-dried lines had been painted over the different colorations and distorted lettering.

Margie traced her hand across the surface and savored the feel of grit and grime on her fingertips. A cool breeze greeted her, stirring the hairs on arms while a chill crawled across her body, and she lifted her dirty face to the fractured sky above. Thunder rolled in the distance. A flash of lightning lit up the city skyline. Hairline cracks in the sky widened, deepened into fissures, and revealed the blank haze of the Monochrome sky beyond.

The world she knew and the world she'd known were crashing together, two massive tectonic plates of reality colliding to form a perfect union of imperfect souls. Now the world would know the truth and share her prison.

For an instant she forgot about her mission, forgot all about her late husband, and entertained the prospect of making her escape. Dullington was gone. Sparrow was gone. Who was left to tug on her chains and drag her screaming back to the gray wastes? Not that escaping meant much now anyway.

You can still be free, babe. As soon as you've done that little thing for me, you can do whatever you wish. All the gods, all the kings, all of man's previous societies will crumble. No one will be left to stop you from doing whatever—or being whomever—you wish. Remember that dream we shared?

Margie opened her eyes, watched new hairline cracks spread across the sky before they were obscured by a passing thunderhead. "I remember, George. We were gonna leave this shitty town, sell our shitty condo, and move out to the country."

You still can, Margie. All that's standing between you and that dream is a dead man walking.

"But I don't know where he is," she whispered, the sound of her voice like a faint dream in her own head, muted and miles away. "Is he close?"

George did not respond. Instead, the sound of shrieking tires filled the air, followed soon after by the rapid thudding crunch of metal.

Margie smiled. "Never mind, babe. I'll be right there."

She pulled the weapon from her waistband, pulled the slide, and chambered a round. Just like her George had taught her to do all those years ago at the shooting range. *You can never be too careful, babe.*

Lightning flashed, lit up the threadbare world around her, and thunder crashed above. Rain pelted her face and masked her tears. Smiling, Margie Guffin shuffled dreamily toward the highway entrance ramp.

———————•———————

Dull ringing filled Michael's head. Something soft cushioned his face. And there was a smell of exhaust and rubber and something else. Gas? He wasn't sure. His senses were overloaded, pushed beyond their limits, and somewhere in the back of his mind he heard himself laughing. *Day's not over yet, old man.*

Movement. Cracking glass. Shifting limbs and hushed breaths.

The world swirled around him, and when he finally opened his eyes, he struggled to make sense of what he was seeing. A white balloon of some kind. *Airbag,* he realized, and the last five minutes raced back to him in a storm of shattered images.

He tried to move and hissed from the pressure on his bad arm. The seatbelt was locked tight around his waist and chest, his arm wedged between his body and the strap. His head swam. He was upside down.

Voices and words blended together, muffled by the dull chime of bells from deep inside his head.

"—is everyone okay?"

"—Donna, my seatbelt is stuck, I can't—"

"It's okay, Quinn. We're gonna get out of this—"

"Mike, are you okay? Please answer me—"

He cleared his throat. "I'm okay," he croaked. "Need to get out of here."

Alice said something else, but her voice was muffled by the airbag. He wouldn't have heard her anyway. The chimes in his ears were growing louder as more blood rushed to his head.

Michael gulped air and clenched his teeth. He freed his bad arm, waited for the sparking colors to subside from his vision, and slowly fished his other hand beneath the airbag. A moment later he found the seatbelt latch. Another breath, and he disengaged the lock. Gravity took over. The top of his head struck the roof with a deep thud, and his neck popped as it took on the weight of his body. He grunted in pain.

"Jesus, Mike—"

Alice froze in silence. A low sob erupted from somewhere outside. Michael thought it sounded like a cat in heat.

"The fuck is that?"

He grimaced and slowly turned his head as far as he could. Alice met his stare from beyond the rim of her airbag. The fear in her eyes drove a chill all the way down his back.

"It's the Yawning. It shouldn't be here. None of these things should be here."

Michael wanted to reach out and hold her. The panic in her voice set his mind on edge. What he remembered of her—what he'd always *known* about her—was her tough-as-nails attitude. She never rattled. Not like this.

"Where's the gun?"

"I don't—I dropped it when we crashed."

"We'll worry about that in a minute. Need to get out of here first."

She said something else that might have been an apology, but Michael wasn't listening. He was too focused on ignoring the screaming pain in his arm. The anesthetic the nurse had given him in the hospital was wearing off, and the throbbing ache across his skin suggested he'd pulled some of the sutures in the crash.

Teeth clenched, Michael fished his hand behind the airbag and felt for the door handle. Seconds later, the driver door swung open, and he crawled his away across oil-slick asphalt riddled with shards of broken glass.

Droplets of rain pelted his back as thunderheads rolled overhead. When he climbed to his feet and looked up, he was stunned to see widening fissures crawl across the sky. Drab light emanated from within, illuminating a flock of flying monstrosities crisscrossing one another over the city skyline. *Flies buzzing over a corpse,* he thought. *The city's dying. Maybe everything is.*

Another sob echoed from across the highway. He lowered his gaze, following a thick plume of black smoke back to the exposed engine of a crashed car, its hood buckled in half like a folded playing card. A pale gangly figure reared back its deformed head and choked down a pair of bloody human legs. Michael stared in disbelief, frozen by a crawling fear which sneaked its way into every muscle and bone, holding him in place.

He'd never been one to give much time to his dreams or nightmares—that was always Donovan's preference—but staring across the median at this abominable monstrosity ignited a memory from childhood. One filled with gnashing teeth and seeking hands. He'd had the dream the night his parents died in the car crash.

The Yawning snapped its jaws, severing its meal at the ankles. Two bloody feet clad in stained sneakers clattered to the asphalt. The creature pivoted, twisted its massive head, and peered in his direction. It raised a spindly limb and beckoned to him. The flying abominations in the cracked sky above swerved in a curved pattern, redirected themselves, and set a course directly for the highway.

Oh fuck. He looked at the SUV, upended and derelict in the center of all this chaos, and felt a wave of panic crash over him. He needed a weapon, something to defend himself from these things, but even that would be an act of desperation. What he truly needed was to get his family out there and to safety, wherever that may be.

His family. Those words broke through the panic and spurred him to action. He stumbled to Alice's side of the SUV. She tilted her head and looked up at him, saw the mask of terror affixed to his face.

"How bad is it?"

"Never mind that," he said. "I need to get you out of there. Right now."

Michael tried the latch, which gave way without resistance, but the door itself wouldn't budge. *Come on, don't do this now.* He braced his foot against the fender and pulled as hard as he could. Metal whined in protest, but it would not relent. He staggered backward and nearly lost his balance.

"It's okay," Alice said, "I can crawl out the window. Help me pop this goddamn airbag."

He dropped to his knees, intent on handing her a piece of shattered glass, and cried out when something brushed past his head. The hum of beating wings filled the air as one of the monstrous flies swept over him. He reeled back and watched the pale thing slow to a hover twenty feet away.

"I need that gun. Right now." He met Alice's stare, saw the fear in her eyes, and scrambled toward her. "I'll pop the airbag, but you need to find that weapon, Alice. *Focus!*"

He didn't wait for her to react. Instead, Michael took a shard of glass and punctured the airbag. Free of her restraint, Alice pawed blindly along the roof of the vehicle, searching for Brock's weapon. *Come on,* Michael thought, watching the creature size them up. He wanted to turn and take stock of its fellow swarm but was too afraid to peel his eyes off the thing. The way its mouths opened and closed erratically unsettled him to his core.

"Found it!"

Quinn's jubilation took him by surprise. He heard something clatter inside the vehicle, and an instant later, Alice's trembling hand offered up Brock's weapon.

The flying creature belted a piercing shriek, thrust its arms back, and shot forward. Michael snatched the handgun, resisted the urge to check the chamber and mag, and aimed for the beast's center mass.

The first round struck the monstrosity's pulsing chest, knocking its mass off course. Michael watched as the creature crashed to the pavement a few feet away, its limbs writhing nervously, its mouths contracting in shock.

Relieved, Michael wiped panic sweat from his brow and walked toward the wounded thing. "Didn't see that coming, did you?" Two black eyes stared at him, emotionless. Thick gray fluid seeped from the wound in its chest. Michael stood over it, aimed the weapon for the creature's head. "This is for my brother, you piece of—"

Something barreled into him, knocked the wind from his lungs, and sent him sprawling backward. He lost his grip on the weapon, heard it clatter across the pavement.

Alice screamed.

Michael shook his head, stunned by the sudden impact, and peered up at a giant gangly figure looming over him. This close, he saw the Yawning in all its horrific glory. Enormous spindly arms hung low at its sides and dragged the ground as the behemoth swayed in place. Soulless black eyes stared down at him, and the creature's stoicism was betrayed only by a slight tremor in its bloody jawline.

He tried to crawl backward away from the towering beast. Flapping wings and stale air fluttered overhead. A moment later, four of the flying abominations landed several feet away, trapping him in place.

A memory crawled forth from the shadows of Michael's mind. His brother, drenched from a downpour, sitting in his living room explaining the Monochrome. Explaining the giant creatures that had chased him through the city. *They swallowed Donna's captor whole, Mike. Like he was there and then he was gone in one bite.*

Thunder crashed overhead. Rain fell in thick sheets, pattering the asphalt and the upended SUV, heavy drumbeats of a requiem Michael hoped he wouldn't hear for some years yet. Alice shrieked for him to get up, to run as fast as he can, but Michael knew he didn't have a chance of outrunning this thing. Its legs were cut from pure muscle. Even if he managed to get away, those flying bastards would catch him.

"Mike, please get up!" Alice again. She was halfway out of the SUV, crawling across glass and concrete toward them. He held out his hand to stop her.

"Get Donna and Quinn out of there." He couldn't bring himself to look at her, didn't want his last image of her face to be one of horror. "Don't worry about me."

He held his focus on the Yawning. Stared as hard as he could into its empty eyes. "Go ahead and do it, motherfucker. I'm right here."

The Yawning's quivering mouth slowly opened, revealing the pitch-black nothingness within.

Michael curled his hands into fists and readied himself for oblivion.

———————•———————

Donna turned away, couldn't bring herself to witness her brother-in-law's gruesome death, but then movement caught her eye. The creature Michael shot moments earlier slowly climbed to its feet. Its gait was all wrong, standing upright and balancing on two legs. Its features melted like warm putty, the gaping mouths sealing up into its torso, the wings collapsing into its back. The oversized skull shrank into something almost human.

A strange light pulsed around the pallid figure, and as it moved closer to them, she realized it was human. Sort of. A faceless figure coated in white skin, absent of any defining features, like a living statue dipped in wax. *Oh God,* she thought, *what is it now? I can't take this anymore.*

The strange figure surveyed its surroundings, spotted her watching from the shattered window, and paused. It swept its hand over its bald head, as if brushing back hair. As if trying to decide how to act. As if—

Alice screamed once more for Michael to get up and run. The faceless man turned away from her, jogged across the highway toward the Yawning, and placed his hand on the creature's back. A deep cry of pain bellowed from the gaping maw, and within seconds, the looming beast began to dissolve.

Donna watched in disgusted wonder as the once-towering figure was reduced to a pile of smoldering goo. Satisfied, the faceless man stepped over Michael toward the other winged creatures.

Alice scrambled across the pavement and knelt beside the window. "Gonna get you two out of there." She reached inside. "Take my hand, Donna. Careful now."

But Donna didn't hear her right away. She was lost in her thoughts, watching the strange figure assault the flying monstrosities in the downpour. Studying the way it carried itself. The way it moved.

Even as Alice pulled her free of the wreckage, Donna couldn't take her eyes off the faceless man. The similarities were too great. She'd know that silhouette anywhere.

Donnie?

———— • ————

The body—at least, the one Donovan had willed into being—wasn't quite a facsimile of his own. There were enough differences that his consciousness didn't feel at home inside it. He was painfully aware of his presence in this foreign body, like a splinter lodged in his skin. Except in this case, his mind was the splinter, and every movement a reminder that he did not belong.

But he wouldn't allow the discomfort to stop him from saving his brother. Even as his nerves flared to life in a symphony of screaming aches and pains, even has he took in the grim landscape of the highway and wreckage and the Monochrome's machinations, Donovan found his anger was overpowering.

All of this had come to pass because one man had lost his mind and decided to condemn mankind for its consistent failures and innate mediocrity. For atrocities born of both and not yet committed.

He was already in a raw mood before his banishment to the strings; seeing his wife trapped in an upended SUV and the Yawning looming over his brother ignited a powder keg of fury deep inside his soul. *Damn me if you must, Vile, but I won't let you hurt my family.*

The Yawning was a familiar adversary, a dimwitted beast too focused on its next meal, and its dissolution was over in seconds. Donovan wasn't sure if stealing the creature's mediocrity would work with this body, not until he placed a hand on the Yawning's back and felt that familiar sensation in his gut, saw the dismal light erupt between his fingertips. Heard the beast's bellowing pain.

He watched his brother scramble away, wanted to tell Michael to get everyone off the highway as fast as possible, but he lacked the means to make a sound or any expression for that matter. This body was pure mediocrity, the only substance over which he had any control. So be it, then. He would use it to shield them from the trap Vile had sprung.

The other machinations, the ones with wings and multiple mouths, were new to him. Human-Yawning hybrids, by the look of them, and equally nightmarish. They were made of the same matter and met with the same demise as their Yawning brother.

In the end, Donovan found himself standing in the center of their battleground, surrounded by smoking piles of grayish-white flesh. Some of the mediocrity stirred, twitching and squirming as pools slowly congealed and washed away in the downpour.

Donovan watched with satisfaction. The rage-red haze clouding his vision slowly dissipated. For the first time since his return, he saw the chaos of the world around him. Towers of smoke littered the city skyline. He saw massive fractures in the sky where the storm clouds broke. The highway asphalt trembled as aftershocks ripped through the landscape.

Vile's plans had worked. Stopping Sparrow hadn't changed anything. Or had it? He suspected only the Ungod could answer that question. Or perhaps Dullington could if he ever saw the old monk again.

In the distance beyond the wrecked SUV, a lone figure approached from the highway entrance ramp. Donovan was too lost in his own thoughts, contemplating the destroyed landscape and its implications. Even when the figure drew closer to his brother, even when he finally took notice and recognized her haggard face, his mind was too slow to react and force this new body to action.

Donovan ran.

He heard the old woman ask, "Candle?"

And Michael, invoking the earnest manner which had earned him a solid reputation across the city over the years, looked away from Alice. "Yes?"

Margie Guffin had already drawn the gun from her waistband. Donovan had no mouth to scream.

———————•———————

Alice didn't hear the gunshot at first. She didn't even see the strange woman approach. She'd been too focused on Michael, the man she'd lost for so long, the man she never stopped loving despite his stubbornness. The man she'd almost lost again to the Yawning.

One moment he was smiling, holding her with one hand around her waist. That moment would remain frozen in her mind for the rest of her life. All the details—the warmth of his body a respite from the cool rain, the smell of his cologne mixed with the odor of sweat, the subtle tremor in his voice when he asked if she was okay, that half-dazed look in his eye when he realized how close he'd come to mortality—would be etched into the darkness behind every blink, every sleep, every dream. She loved this man with every fiber of her being, and for as many times as she would replay this moment in her head, no amount of love could prevent the next few moments. Even in her dreams she couldn't stop the old woman, the gun, the bullet. Their fates were always interwoven and knotted in strange ways, together for as long as they were held apart, two occasionally parallel lines intersecting until one, inevitably, was severed.

"Candle?"

A dry voice, aged ahead of its time, starved of sustenance and sunlight. A determined voice, uncertain and yet driven to a purpose they would all soon know.

Michael looked away from Alice, confused. "Yes?"

When Alice finally turned to follow his gaze, she saw the old woman with mud caked into her wrinkled face, saw the stained clothes and straggly hair. Saw the familiar white button affixed to her stained hoodie and the handgun muzzle protruding from one dangling sleeve.

"This is for my George."

The gunshot struck Michael in the throat, forced his body into a clumsy pirouette before he collapsed. Donna and Quinn's screams were muted by a blast of thunder overhead. The only cry Alice heard amidst the tumult was her own.

She dropped to her knees at Michael's side, shakily placed her hands against his throat to stop the bleeding. He was trying to breathe, his mouth opening and closing like a beached fish, while gouts of thick crimson seeped between Alice's fingers. She held his hand, squeezed. "You're gonna be okay, it'll be okay, just keep your eyes open for me. We're gonna get through this. Mike, just look at me, okay? We—"

The strange faceless figure rushed past her, darting headfirst toward the old woman. Another gunshot ripped through the air. Alice turned from her dying husband just as the figure's waxen body crumpled to the asphalt and liquefied in a puddle of goo.

"Al—" Michael's voice drowned in all the blood. She looked back to him, saw the light in his eyes fading. He raised a trembling hand to his face, pointed to his eye, and then to his heart. His eyes rolled up and his body slackened.

I love you too, Alice thought, as her tears pelted his bloody face.

"Are you the bitch he was sent to find?"

The old woman's voice distorted in the rain. A demonic force sent to punish her for escaping the Monochrome, a remnant of Sparrow's followers. How dare Alice try to move on, reclaim the life that was stolen from her. She turned away from Michael's body, looked up at his killer, and clenched her teeth.

"I don't know who you are."

Michael's killer raised her weapon. "Margie Guffin. Your husband killed mine. I'm just settling the score."

"Michael never killed anyone," Alice said. "He didn't kill your husband. *And you fucking murdered him!*" She shot to her feet, intent on rushing the old woman, but Margie raised her gun.

"You just stay put, missy. You tellin' me that's not Donovan Candle?"

Alice's head swam as a slow numbness spread out from her core. Her limbs were loose, filled with jelly. This wasn't happening. Couldn't be happening. *If this is it for me, then I'll die by his side. I'm sorry Donna. Sorry, Quinn. I—*

"Hey. Bitch."

Margie spun around. Donna stood behind her, one hand clutching her pregnant belly, the other holding a large chunk of broken asphalt.

"You killed the wrong man."

She didn't give Margie a chance to respond. Donna bashed the side of the old woman's skull with the rock. Margie's weapon clattered to the ground, and Alice darted for it in a fit of rage.

Michael's killer lay sprawled on the asphalt, clutching the side of her face and gasping in pain. Donna stood over her with the rock in hand. Blood dripped from her fingertips as tears streaked her soaked face.

"He killed my husband," Margie groaned. "He was just doing what he was told to do." Her eyes found their focus and settled on Alice. "Go ahead, you bitch. I'll see you both in Hell."

"Alice? Donna?" Quinn approached from the side of the SUV. "We need to go. I—" He glanced at Michael's body. His jaw quivered. "—We need to keep moving. Those things are still out there." He pointed toward the sky, and Alice followed. More of those flying things were in the vicinity, black stars swirling about a dismal sky.

"Go on," Alice said. She gestured to Donna. "Take the ramp and get off the highway. We'll find another car."

Donna waited a moment, staring intently at the woman on the ground, before turning away. She placed a hand on Alice's shoulder. "I'm so sorry," Donna whispered, and kissed Alice's forehead.

Alice waited until Donna and Quinn were on their way before firing three shots into the air. In the distance, the swarm of flying beasts changed course. Margie Guffin began to laugh.

Minutes later, after Alice rejoined Donna and Quinn on the street below, the old woman's laughter turned to screams.

-16-
ACTA NON VERBA

The gunshot blasted Donovan's consciousness out of his makeshift form. He'd seen the bullet in his heightened state, knew its trajectory would rip through his skull, but he didn't care. The rage burning away in his mind was far too great, his desire for vengeance blinding rational thought. His brother had taken a bullet meant for him, dredging guilty memories of so many conversations from their twenties, after their parents had died. Michael swore Donovan would be the death of him.

It wasn't supposed to be like this. I did what I could...

One moment he was charging forward, the arrogance of his anger enough to make him believe he was impervious to a bullet. He forgot about seeing Donna, forgot about the terror writ upon her face as she witnessed the slaughter unfold. Everything slowed to a fraction of a second, the rain decompressed into individual droplets, the report of the gunshot a white muzzle flash of combusting gas and powder residue, the old woman's half-blinking eyes and toothy grin, and then the bullet itself, piercing the air, driving itself forward to his faceless cranium.

Momentum was not on his side, however, and he had only time to observe the startled, contorting face of Alice Walenta as drops of her fiancé's blood spattered her face.

Her fiancé. Oh my God.

The epiphany was a light shining through caverns of memory, revealing all the Cretins had hidden in shadow. She was more than just a former co-worker. This sudden discovery was more kindling on the inferno building inside him, forcing him forward, determined to rip Margie Guffin's head from her body.

Then came the bullet.

Reality dissolved, displaced by a fleeting glimpse of a string at the end of its run. Michael's string. Donovan tried to reach for it but realized he no longer had arms, hands. A body. His consciousness surged back across the metachasm along a never-ending tether of fates, and with no physical mind to filter the rage, he let loose a psychic scream so terrible the strings themselves shuddered in his wake.

Donovan was meant to take that bullet, the false death of a false body, so that his mind would be freed of Vile's trap. Only a megalomaniac would believe his creatures impenetrable, another flaw in his thinking, and the Ungod had prepared him for the onslaught waiting in the Spectrum—but he didn't know there would be Yawning and other beasts in ambush. That wasn't part of the plan.

"No fate is certain," Cosma said. The Ungod's voice whispered from all directions, devoid of emotion or urgency, and its flat quality further enraged Donovan.

"You knew this would happen." His voice echoed across the infinite. "I could've changed it. Goddamn you…" Donovan's voice broke, crumbled into a gut-wrenching sorrow. Somewhere on the other side of the great tethering, tears streamed down his cheeks. "I could've changed it."

To this, Cosma said nothing.

Donovan waited for a time, allowing the anger to subside, a fire that would never truly die. In a span of minutes, he'd been within arm's reach of his wife, seen her beautiful face once again after what felt like years. And when she saw him, he felt for an instant that she *knew*. *She saw me. She knew it was me.* He recalled the way her face lit up with recognition moments before Alice screamed for Michael to run. And after, there was only terror. How long had Donna been without some form of peace? And how much was his fault?

I did what I had to do. I can't—stop thinking that, Don. You did what you could. To save Quinn and the others. To save Michael and Alice and everyone else. Everyone.

A soft voice spoke from somewhere within, a voice he recognized all too well. The voice of smoke and liquor, dripping with cynical wisdom, a southern drawl he might have created but had since been stolen by a usurper in his mind.

At what cost, hoss? Your brother's dead. Guffin's old bitch probably smoked the rest of 'em while she was at it. And for what? All this pain and anguish is so much wasted effort, another failure in a long line of failures. In the end that's all you'll be, hoss. One more notch on humanity's belt. A lonely failure. Faceless. Forgotten. Another pile of ash in the wake of the smoldering fire spreading across the world one person at a time.

Donovan ignored Vile's taunts, focused all his energy on the strings ahead, and the journey across the metachasm. A chirring laughter rippled across the expanse, forcing a shudder down the tethering of fates, and stoking the flames of Donovan's anger yet again. He forced his mind elsewhere, thought of Donna's sweet

(pale and gaunt and terrified)

face the last time he'd seen her when she was sleeping soundly in their bed. The night he left to return to the city. The night he willingly trapped himself here.

The cost of my soul, Vile. If I have to lose myself to end this, I'll do it. I'll burn myself to cinders if it means stopping you. He thought of Donna again, stirring the hurt and flames in his heart. He thought of their unborn baby. *I would for you, love. I will.*

When all that remained of his rage and sadness were embers, he called upon the nonentity once more.

"Show me my thread. Show me where it leads."

More silence, and at first, he feared the Ungod would not grant his request. Finally, Cosma spoke: *"Heed my warning, Donovan Candle. No fate is certain, but all fates lie at your feet. Acta non verba."*

The inscription above the Needle's entrance. His grasp of Latin was rudimentary at best, but the meaning was clear enough, an extension of Aleister's simple sermon from what felt like so long ago. *Acta non verba,* he thought. *Actions without words. Actions birth definition.*

Ahead of him, a single string entangled in the coil glowed softly. Light pulsed along its length like the malign tumors atop the WBS building. He reached out with his mind and touched the bundle of string, and all secrets were known.

------·------

*D*o *you hear their cries, little sparrow? Can you feel their strings giving way?* Aleister had grown numb to Vile's ceaseless taunts over the centuries, but now he felt the bile of despair rising in his throat. His inability to glimpse his adversary's plans had proven to be his downfall once again. With both Donovan and Vile concealed beyond the Needle's walls, Aleister found himself once again at the beginning without direction. In an effort to curb the frustration welling up within, he walked away from the structure and assumed a lotus pose among the sands.

He drifted, projecting himself across the metachasm and parallel with the strings. They trembled with a violence he had not seen before, and when he touched them with his mind, all he felt was pain and fear.

In his past, before Vile stole his humanity, Aleister prayed twice to the slumbering god in the great column. First, for an intervention and a means of escape, a means of seeing his wife and son once more. He did not yet understand the nature of the strings, that his memories and fears and dreams could be intercepted, observed, experienced. Those prayers had cost him his wife and son for all time, a painful reminder of his selfish naivete.

And the Ungod remained silent, even as his wife and son were crucified before him. Even in the months of flagellation that followed. The Ungod offered nothing in return.

The second prayer he made on the eve of their brotherhood's journey into the Monochrome. A brief prayer for a successful confrontation. A prayer for the safety of his brothers.

Master Vile had abandoned them by then, fleeing across the demarcations into the wastes to corrupt the Ungod's purpose, and the Order had no choice but to keep their oath of protection. Their order was established to protect the Ungod from influence, to keep its existence a secret from the rest of humanity. So it had been since the days of antiquity, long before Pontius Vile assumed his role as the Order's leader, and so it would always be.

Or so they all thought.

Not all of his brothers took Vile's mad intentions seriously. The Ungod was safe in its cradle, they'd argued, enclosed in the Needle which Vile's ancestors had built, and sealed away by the power of human will. Not even Vile himself could open that barrier. Only a willing soul could breach the entrance, a wise check to Vile's power as the order's keeper—he had forsaken his humanity when he took up the mantle long ago, an act also thrust upon Aleister at the time of Vile's final betrayal.

His second prayer carried the same result as his first: silence, disappointment, and pain. Aleister hadn't prayed to the Ungod since, had felt no compulsion to do so.

Now, with the Monochrome and Spectrum on the brink of collision, he reconsidered his apathy toward the slumbering nonentity within the Needle.

I have served you tirelessly. Everything I have done has been to preserve the covenants of the Order. Now I am asking for your guidance, Great Weaver. Please give me a sign. Show me the path I am to follow.

Aleister retracted his mind from the metachasm. He bowed his head and listened to the roaring winds of the ongoing storm. Sands stirred among the graveyard of derelict structures scattered across the expanse. He listened, desperate for a word or signal, and all he heard was the vast emptiness of the Monochrome itself.

But there was something else now. Distant murmuring. Voices.

He lifted his gaze and sighted the pilgrims marching across the littered clearing. Their names were known to him, their crimes of mediocrity and fear etched into his dead heart, a thousand lost souls driven across the demarcations and through a storm of living nightmares. The Missing and Wretched alike, some of them bystanders in the war waged across a lifeless city, all pilgrims led astray for a more sinister cause.

They crossed the wastes toward him, congregating among the detritus of ancient battlefields where broken armies clashed, bled, and died. Armies that had come to breach the barrier, and others to defend it. Now another army had come, and Aleister was alone.

So be it.

He stood, watched in silence as they formed a skirmishing line across the clearing. They stared mindlessly, each one a lamb driven willfully to this killing floor, no doubt promised their freedom by his adversary in exchange for their keeper's end.

Was this the Ungod's answer to his prayer? One more obstacle stacked before him, the reward for centuries of fulfilling a purpose thrust upon him. Any lesser soul would crumble, run, or plead for amnesty. He had been cruel in his charge, using innocent souls as pawns in this cosmic game, and had lost himself somewhere along the way—until Donovan Candle helped him turn the tide, showed him there was still hope. If he would answer for his cruelty today, then he would do so without shame. *I did what was necessary. I will do what is necessary.*

Standing before an army of the Monochrome's prisoners, Aleister Dullington remained steadfast in his duty. He would not let them breach the Needle.

And you will not have to, little sparrow. The Ungod will not answer your hopeless prayers, but I will. Let this be the sign you so desperately seek.

From behind, the stone barrier slowly unseated itself and slid open. Aleister turned and glared at his former master.

Vile stepped outside the Needle, sinking his toes into the sands for the first time in centuries. He raised an arthritic hand and ran gnarled fingers through the scraggly patch of beard. His battle scars framed a crazed and broken smile.

"All this trouble to open a door." Vile clicked his teeth. "All you had to do was knock."

"Levity will not save you," Aleister said. He clenched his hands into fists and channeled the power of the Monochrome. A pale glow lit up his face as the buried anger of countless years rose from his core. "You will answer for your crimes, Pontius Vile. Crimes against humanity. Against the Order. My wife and son. *Me.*"

He leapt toward the old man with fists raised, ready to drain whatever power Vile possessed—and realized his action was yet another miscalculation. Vile extended a hand and Aleister froze in the air, two figures enshrouded in a pulse of the Monochrome's unlight. The former keeper's face darkened, his eyes aglow with gray energy, and stared deeply into the empty abyss of Aleister's glare.

"You are in no position to charge anyone with crimes, old friend." He cocked his head, glanced over Aleister's shoulder. "Yet *they* are."

A blast of light erupted between them. Aleister shot backward, digging a trench through the sands before slamming into an overturned chariot. The impact left him stunned, a long-forgotten sensation now shoved to the forefront of his memory, and he spent the ensuing seconds struggling against the hazy fog draped over his vision.

Pontius Vile strolled across the sands and beckoned to the congregation of lost souls. "What say you, then? He has kept you here, stolen your lives, treated you with every indignity. What of *his* crimes?"

The throng of pilgrims answered with a dissonant roar of fury. Aleister heard their cries, felt the beating of their footsteps in the trembling earth.

He climbed to his feet, ready to see this through once and for all.

The thread he touched wasn't his own. Donovan's mind lit up with fragments of light which coiled around his consciousness, filling his mind with a slideshow of memories recalled through other pairs of eyes. Instantly he felt himself pulled away from the strings, away from any semblance of reality, and jettisoned somewhere else.

Somewhen else.

Sumwhanne.

Pieces of an archaic tongue. Words he'd never heard before, in a language at once foreign and familiar. Someone else's thoughts melded with his own

(cannot abandon Agnes and yet I cannot be at peace with myself)

in a jarring transmission of secrets and desires, ambitions and fears. Soon other senses drifted into place, each one offering a puzzling context to the foreign consciousness entwined with his own.

A smell of dung and other bodily odors. The stench of livestock. Woodsmoke. A sensation of hunger gurgling in his disembodied belly when he detects a hint of meat cooking on a spit. The feel of coarse fabric, damp with the morning dew, hanging loosely from his limbs. Chill wind, and little warmth from a morning sun drenched in fog.

He wasn't himself. Only this wasn't like before, when he'd inhabited a body of his own creation; now he was in the mind of someone else, stalking their memories and trespassing on their senses.

A crowded marketplace. Vendors hawking their wares. Men and women in medieval dress. A couple of soldiers in full suits of armor. Murmurs in the crowd. Heads turning, bodies shuffling away, parting a path down a mud-caked lane.

Donovan saw them, recognized their garb, the way they carried themselves.

Gray robes. Six men with cowls pulled over their heads, their faces cloaked in shadow and mystery. Women pull their children away, tucking them behind their legs like mother hens. Men bristle as the cloaked figures pass. A word murmurs from somewhere in the crowd: Dullingtons.

"You there, friend. Do you seek a higher purpose?"

He recognized that voice, that face. The one leading the group. Christopher of the Dullingtons.

The images froze, distorted across a chasm of empty space. Donovan heard thoughts that were not his own. Felt emotions that were not his own. Heard words spoken centuries before which set events in motion—

Aleister of Gloucestershire hesitates. The hooded figure before him is an outcast, one of the strange worshipers from the monastery off the coast. Even now he feels the eyes of his neighbors upon him. He hears their whispers, their gossip. Their judgment makes his skin crawl.

"Pardon?"

The strange man offers a curious smile. He removes his cowl. Dim sunlight reflects from his bald pate. "You possess a kind of melancholy I have seen before, friend. You feel lost, without a sense of purpose. You feel unfulfilled. We can help you find what you are missing. A peace hidden from you." He sweeps his gaze over the staring crowd. Some of them recoil in terror. "A peace hidden from most."

Aleister considers the stranger's words, feels them in his bones. For too long he has felt lost, barred from a hidden path he believes he is destined to find. Languishing in a state of stagnation, brimming with unfulfilled purpose. Each day he labors on his family's failing farm. Each night he lays awake dreading the coming winter. He fears he is unable to provide for his wife and son. He fears the dark, and the world it conceals. He fears he is meant for more; fears he will never achieve a higher purpose. He is afraid he will live, he will die, and there will be no memory of him when he is gone.

The stranger nods at Aleister's silence, replaces his cowl. "Consider my words, brother. Our vessel departs at dawn. I hope to see you there."

The thoughts and scenes shifted before Donovan could process what he'd experienced. A vortex of whispers and shouts swirled across his consciousness as he felt himself pulled deeper into the shadows.

Memories stir and flit about like moths in lamplight. Aleister struggles with confessing to his wife about his melancholia, the discomfort he feels in his own skin, and the unsettling belief that he does not belong. It is a belief that keeps him awake at nights and distances him from his peers during the day. He believes he is meant for more than this, fears he will never fulfill his duties as a husband and father, fears that he will never know a greater peace of mind and soul.

On rare occasion when he has opened up to Agnes, she has tried in vain to ease his spirit by suggesting prayer and deepening his relationship with God—another cause of anxiety, as he has not felt a kinship with the Church or the Almighty in some time. He feels adrift, lost among the waves, and he cannot bring himself to admit the truth to her: that meeting the monk in the village was the first glimpse of hope he had seen in years.

Admitting this truth to her would mean admitting all of his shortcomings to himself: that he is alone in this cold, uncaring world, and no loving embrace will thaw the glacier in his soul. Only he can light such a fire, and to do so would mean a pilgrimage of body, mind, and spirit. It would mean losing all he has in order to find himself again. He is terrified of this notion for he is uncertain if he could find his way back.

In the dawn, he kisses Agnes on her forehead as she sleeps. She stirs, smiles faintly in slumber, and rolls on her side. He kisses his son and smiles when the young boy snores. Finally, he scrawls a hasty note by candlelight across a patch of linen, struggling to formulate words from his limited vocabulary, and agonizes over fears that his intentions will make no sense.

A fragment of sunlight breaks through the dawn haze. Aleister snuffs the candle, places the note on their table, and leaves his home for the last time.

A pebble struck Aleister in his temple. One of the approaching mob, a slack-jawed young man in tattered clothing, spat on the ground. "Five years you cost me, Dullington! I'm gonna beat those years out of your fuckin' skull!"

Aleister raised his hand and expelled a bolt of unlight. The young man exploded in a red mist of viscera and bone. Drenched yet undeterred, his accomplices moved forward over a darkened pool seeping into the sands.

"Uncouth even for a peasant like you, little sparrow." Vile clicked his tongue. "Are you going to kill them all?"

"Only if I have to." Aleister spun and fired another bolt of light. Vile anticipated the move, raised his own hand in deflection, and for a moment the two monks were encased in a struggle of light.

"I have spent years drinking from the well of the Ungod's sustenance. This is but a drop."

Light streamed from Vile's eyes as he gnashed his teeth and raised his other hand. The beam strengthened, doubled its force, and in an instant, blew Aleister backward into the mob. He collided with the front line, knocking them off their feet. The next wave of Missing collected around him, eager to inflict punishment upon their warden and exact a toll for all their collected years lost.

Aleister struggled as the world dimmed around him. Was this pain? After all this time he thought himself impervious to the frailties of body. No, this was something else. A weakening of his spirit. Vile's essence was corrupted, infected with the power of countless nightmares. Even now Aleister felt something eating away at his being like acid.

Hands fell upon his robe and cowl, pulling, gripping for purchase across his pallid flesh. A concerted effort of muscle and rage heaved him off the ground, and he was carried away by the mob of souls whom he'd condemned to languish in obscurity. He resisted, but no matter how much he struggled, he could not regain his center of gravity, could not pull himself free of them all.

They turned to Vile for direction. The scarred legionnaire nodded in approval and smiled.

"Crucify him."

———— • ————

*W*aves *lapping on a rocky shore. Morning mist obscuring a plain stone structure on an island hilltop. The smell of brine and vomit and fear. Mostly the fear.*

Always the fear.

Aleister watches the sea, hoping for a clear day so that he may glimpse his former life across the channel. Even now he hears the voice of his new master resonating in his mind, ever present and always taunting. What life you had is no more, little sparrow. I have seen to that. Why do you insist on making this more difficult than it needs to be?

He still remembers Agnes's cries. So much confusion and terror. So much sorrow. You brought this upon me, *her face said.* I gave you all the love you would ever need, and still you could not be fulfilled. You had to go find yourself, and look at me now, my sparrow. Look at the pain you have wrought.

Her voice, but not her words. Vile again, manipulating his thoughts, driving the blade deeper into his soul.

"Have I not suffered enough?" *He spoke to the sea, the lapping waves, the unforgiving current of time.*

No, little sparrow. No amount of suffering will ever be enough. No one forsakes their vows, and no one defies me.

"*Then why not punish me?*"

Oh, little sparrow, is this not punishment?

Laughter in the distance, carried along the breeze with the flapping of seagull wings. A siren's song of mockery.

Donovan was overcome with sadness, a sudden and agonizing emptiness in his essence that was at once cold and crushing—and yet buried underneath was a flickering signal of light in the void. A solitary burning cinder of rage fueled by an unyielding desire for justice. A flame that would over time spread to consume its host, even as the rest of his humanity was slowly stripped away in a ceaseless corrupting beam of light.

Years later.

A deepening fear of the madness overtaking their Order's master.

Pontius Vile has grown obsessive over the last several years, distancing himself from the rituals set in place by his predecessors, rites performed in honor of the balance they are all sworn to preserve. Rumors slip between the cracks of the old monastery as easily as the whisper of winter's chilling winds, but they are far colder in their implication.

Rumors of their master's insanity. The uneasiness and uncertainty. The anxiety of something growing on the horizon, an inexplicable thing they can all feel and yet cannot name. An unspeakable act none of the Dullingtons would ever consider a possibility.

A recollection of events in fractured sensory impulses and images: The muffled slap of footsteps. Hushed whispers in the night. Flashes of candlelight in the dormitory hallway, seeping beneath the crack of the door. A silent panic in the air.

"He took Brother Marcus," someone says.

"To the Monochrome?"

"For what purpose?"

"Against his will—"

"The Great Weaver's chamber—"

Members of the Order are summoned. Brother Christopher will lead them to the Needle in search of their master. If they have not returned by dawn, a second party will dispatch.

The anxiety of standing guard in the scrying chamber, waiting for their brothers to reappear. Watching the light of dawn slowly creep over the horizon and burn away the fog. The terror of knowing they must cross the tempest's demarcation to reach the Needle.

The uncertainty of what awaits them on the other side.

Aleister follows his brothers into the Monochrome, hesitant to warn them once more of the abominations their master has conjured. None of them were there the day his wife and child were murdered. They did not witness the creatures or their obedience—and they did not believe him when he confessed their master's brutal punishment years later. Impossible, they told him. Master Vile would never steal such power from the Ungod. To do so would violate his oath to the balance.

Yet here they are, traveling into the forbidden wastes of the Monochrome in search of a master whose defection once seemed beyond consideration.

Their screams guide him through the storm, one bloodcurdling shriek after another, pleading for help from their brotherhood. They have met the creatures at Vile's beck and call, and although Aleister is spared the gruesome details of their meeting, he is witness to the devastation as he crosses through the storm.

———————•———————

The corruption ate its way through Aleister's insides, igniting a sensation of pain he had not felt since his transformation. He felt little else but the festering heat inside him, inching into every pore, saturating the mediocrity from which he was made. Even in his final moments, he was denied any true agony, an agony of mortal flesh, something with which he might relate to his wife and son one last time. Long ago, he'd watched as their lives were stolen from them in the most barbaric way possible. To share their fate seemed almost poetic, if only he could feel what they felt.

Shades of the man he once was clung to the contours of his spirit, the defined etchings of a man weathered away over time. Aleister of Gloucestershire, once a meager peasant, husband, and father; another lost soul seeking a greater purpose in a dismal world of pain and uncertainty. He still felt the hollowing regret even after all this time, the sting of epiphany that comes with understanding, in hindsight, that all he ever needed was in front of him. There was no greater purpose, no higher meaning, than the duty he had vowed to his wife and son. What he had hoped to find on his journey was overlooked, had been there before he ever set foot outside his home that dismal dawn—and in the years since, in his desire to achieve the only purpose he had left, he had condemned another soul to the same fate.

Agnes. Thomas. Donovan.

He repeated their names as the mob fashioned the means of his torture. The petrified remains of a destroyed trebuchet were lifted from the sands, the beams splintered with the force of a hundred arms driven with justified rage. Theirs were names he could not bring himself to speak, nor could he recount the names of the millions whose lives he had stolen over the centuries.

They spread out his arms. Fastened him to the crude crossbeam with a spike driven through his flesh, one stone's strike after another, inching the sharp edge deeper.

Aleister felt nothing but the festering corruption eating away at him from the inside, and the hollowness of regret left in its wake. Even when there was no more left of him, the regret would always remain, and its presence the only pain he would ever feel.

The prisoners hammered their warden into place. He let them.

———————•———————

Donovan witnessed the aftermath of a bloody massacre through Aleister's eyes. Smelled the blood and felt the grit of sand blasting his face. Half-chewed limbs were strewn about the clearing, arms and legs tossed aside like driftwood on a crimson shore. Dark trails crisscrossed the sands along the graveyard, signs of one more battle in a long history of skirmishes—but as Donovan traveled forward through the monk's memories, he saw signs that this was less a battle and more of an ambush.

They didn't know about the Yawning or the Cretins. My God, they walked right into it.

Sadness curdled into a bilious rage, filling his phantom throat with a roiling inferno of venom, and Donovan felt himself on the brink of explosion. Even now he wondered how Aleister had held his emotions at bay, remaining calm even in the face of this apparent coup, burying the melancholy as he stepped over the remains of his friends. His brothers.

Donovan watched as Aleister approached the Needle, witnessed the macabre conversation between the monk and Christopher's remains. He saw the piercing light erupt from between the cracks of the Needle's marble façade.

"Not until I confront mine," Aleister said.

Aleister Dullington bows his head and waits for his death. The light from the Needle is swift, piercing, and burns with an immense heat. He sucks in his breath—and exhales in a blast of pain as his skin bubbles and blisters.

Time ceases to exist as the light fills his eyes and the searing pain consumes his mind. His robe burns away, each thread a fiery patchwork across a palette of charring skin, and soon his flesh follows suit. The agony ceases as his nerves die, his sight burned away as the light disintegrates his eyes, the lungs he used to breathe forever deflated in this boiling white inferno, and somehow his consciousness survives. Even after his mortal body is destroyed, his mind carries on in a state of shock, unable to process all that it is seeing: an endless array of threads, the strings of fate woven by the Great Weaver, crisscrossing for all eternity in an unbroken latticework of life and death.

"We will be bound together, little sparrow. You will keep the Monochrome in my absence. So it is my will, so it shall be yours."

The shimmering trail of threads fades from view, drifting into the back of his mind as new sensations spring to life. His vision returns, displaying the gruesome killing fields once more, and he feels the grit of sand between his naked toes.

He surveys his body, feels the prickling of energy in his fingertips, and gazes through an infinite sea of eyes waiting just beyond the wastes. Creatures conjured from the physical failures of man, their nightmares given shape and form, and eager to devour whatever lay in their path.

Aleister Dullington lifts his unblinking gaze to the Needle's summit. Light seeps through flaws in the façade, sweeping over him in quick flashes of heat, each one a reminder of this great price paid in full.

"You have won nothing," Aleister says.

"Perhaps." His master's voice booms across the wastes, shaking the slate heavens above. "And neither have you."

Donovan felt something pull at his essence, and in an instant, was dragged further along the thread. Images of the centuries flashed through his mind, a montage of cruelty in service to a misplaced duty. Aleister's rage and sadness distilled into lifetimes of hate and resentment, a growing sense of futility as each attempt to usurp Vile's place in the Needle was met with failure.

A history of painful anger and sorrow unfolded before him in seconds, the cruel years a violent undertow dragging dozens of innocent victims beneath its crashing waves. A cosmic chess game played between two warring entities, with innocent men, women, and children playing the pawns on a board balanced atop the Ungod's Needle. He saw Albert Sparrow's face, from his early days as a professor until the moment Donovan relinquished him to Aleister's control. He witnessed Aleister's trek across the Monochrome with the old professor in tow.

You tried to use him, he thought, while the memories played on. *To open the door. But Vile stopped you. Banished you somehow and used that light to change Sparrow. Not like you, no, but something close to it. Was that his plan all along? Cosma, is that what you wanted to show me?*

The memories shuffled forward, and Donovan was dragged further along the thread. He saw himself in liminal space and felt the sadness in Aleister's heart. It was a familiar feeling, something the monk had experienced centuries before. That same melancholy on the day he left his wife and son. The day he joined the Order in search of a greater purpose.

I do not want this for him, he heard Aleister say, a phantom voice carried across the thread by ethereal winds. *I cannot go through this again, and I cannot bear to confess the outcome. If we are successful in stopping Pontius Vile, there is only one way to send him back, and it is a price I do not believe he is willing to pay. For him to come this far only to be forgotten by those he holds most dear is not something he will accept.*

A slow numbness crawled across Donovan's mind, and somewhere far away, he felt that familiar sensation of his gut dropping. He found his voice and cried out to the void.

"No…is this true? Cosma? *Answer me!*"

Silence but for the hum of a distant wind, and as the seconds crawled on, Donovan resisted the inertia carrying him along the thread.

"Cosma? COSMA!"

Light filled the metachasm below and blinded his mind's eye. He struggled, cried out to the void as gravity found him and pulled with force. Everything dropped away—

———————•———————

—And he screamed as the coils released him to the marble foundation below. He gasped for breath and swallowed air, triggering a gag reflex that made him vomit a thick gray goo. His head swam as his senses fired to life once again, the dim chamber's features drifting in and out of focus, the gritty taste of mediocrity on his tongue, the needle-pricks of blood returning to his extremities.

You do not have much time. The metachasm is shrinking.

Donovan climbed to his feet and wiped his mouth. He first looked to the chamber entrance, then back to the Ungod's cradle. The light pulsing from its hollow had dimmed.

"No, *fuck* the metachasm, and *fuck* you. Why did you lie to me?"

I did not lie, Donovan Candle.

"I'll be forgotten. By everyone."

An effect with every cause. A reaction with every action. Humanity often boasts of action without commitment. Few possess the constitution necessary to proceed in the face of annihilation. Few are willing to acknowledge the truth.

"Yeah, what truth is that?" He spat on the floor, tried to rid himself of the awful taste in his mouth.

That you must lose everything to gain everything in return. Your whole life has been driven by fear of action, Donovan Candle. Fear of losing something for your action. Most men fear this precipice of reason. Are you one of them?

He considered the Ungod's words, weighed them against the sour taste in his mouth and the bile roiling in his gut. Memories of Donna's terrified face flooded his mind. He saw with vivid clarity the fear in her eyes, the superficial cuts on her forehead from shattered glass, a mortal terror overtaking her that not only was her life in danger, but so was the life of her child. *Their* child.

Regardless of his anger and fear, the world was collapsing under its own weight, inching toward a reconciliation of realities that would cancel out one another. Vile was winning. Would he sit back and wallow in his despair or do what was necessary to save his wife and child? Even if it meant losing himself in the process?

Donovan wiped tears from his eyes. He swallowed back the sorrow. *I haven't come this far to let them down now.*

He didn't wait for the Ungod to respond. Instead, he gathered his wits and made for the chamber entrance.

The passageway stood open. There was movement in the distance, a mob of figures clamoring across the gray dunes toward some sort of totem, but he couldn't make it out from here.

Pontius Vile bellowed a directive, and the pilgrim mob erupted in cheers.

Donovan looked back across the antechamber. Cosma's fading light barely lit up the room.

Are you one of them?

"No," he whispered, "I'm not."

-17-
THE MAN, THE MONK, AND THE MONSTER

Donna frowned as she swept bits of broken glass from the passenger seat. There was blood on the upholstery and across the dash, thick streaks that might have been chocolate syrup under any other circumstances, but she knew better. The car sat with the engine still running, its front fender caved in and coated in that bizarre grayish matter, and its driver was long gone. Most of them, anyway. A few severed fingers lay on the crumpled hood, the source of a bloody tributary washed away by the rain.

"This is our best bet," Quinn said quietly, opening the back door. Alice followed, climbing into the driver's seat. Donna clutched her belly as she took her seat, trying to forget the blood, the glass, the chaos. Trying to forget Michael's horrific death. She looked at Alice, opened her mouth to speak, but no words came to mind. Nothing that would bring comfort or soothe the pain of loss.

"Quinn," she said, turning in her seat. "Are you okay?"

The young man's weary tear-streaked face told her everything he couldn't bring himself to say. He was a college kid who'd aged twenty years in the course of a week. The dark circles under his eyes and the five o'clock shadow spread over his cheeks and chin were a glimpse of the man he would become: worn, tired, and haunted.

She reached out, took his hand. He blinked back tears and looked away. "I hope my dad is okay."

"Me too." Donna gave his hand a squeeze. "Once we get somewhere safe, we can figure out how to reach him. Right, Alice?"

Alice had reclined against the headrest, eyes closed, her chin a quivering levy about to break. Donna placed her free hand on Alice's shoulder.

"I'm…I've lost…everything."

And the levy broke, freeing a tumult of emotion in a series of heaving sobs. Alice buried her face in her hands and cried with deep shuddering breaths. Donna leaned over and held her. There was nothing else she could do except provide physical comfort. A moment later, Quinn leaned over the seat and put his arm around them both.

They sat like that for a time, holding one another while the tears came and the world fell apart around them. After all the horror she had witnessed, Donna found a brief moment of comfort in the embrace. *They may be the only family I have left,* she thought, and the realization forced her stomach to drop. Was Donovan still alive? If that were him back on the highway, inexplicable thought it may be, could he have survived the gunshot?

I don't know. God, I don't know.

The baby kicked as if in reply. Donna let go of Alice, leaned back in her seat, and half-smiled. *Maybe you're right, kiddo. I should know better.*

A minute later, Alice wiped her eyes and collected herself. She turned to Donna and nodded. "Where do we go from here?"

"Out of the city," Donna said. She looked out the window at the fractured sky. The cracks had widened, visible now even through the downpour. "As far away as we can." And then, to Quinn: "What do you think?"

He frowned, nodded solemnly. "I think it's best."

"Sounds good to me," Alice said, shifting the car into gear. The vehicle hitched and the engine sputtered, a sound that made them all hold their breath, but a moment later they were on their way.

Quinn leaned over the back of Donna's seat and whispered in her ear. "Dad will be okay. He has to be. Right?"

Donna nodded, patted his hand, but looked away. She couldn't bring herself to lie.

———————— • ————————

A brisk wind swept over him as he exited the Needle. Goosebumps prickled his skin, and a cold serpent tightened around his gut. The old battlefield surrounding the needle was full once more, with a massive mob of pilgrims from all corners of the Monochrome. Those he'd seen on his journey toward the tempest was but a fraction; what he saw across the expansive wastes was a mob that numbered in the thousands, if not more.

Vile's army, he realized. *Calling them all here to stop us. To stop me. I wonder if they even know they're being used.*

Halfway across the expanse, Vile stood before his people like a crazed puppeteer, arms outstretched and waving erratically with frantic gestures. A mad conductor directing an orchestra of rage.

Donovan saw the anger writ upon their faces as he drew nearer. Expressions contorted in a rage-induced madness, the faces of the hateful and the betrayed—their bodies clamored over one another, eager to glimpse the source of their disdain, to spit upon their enemy propped up in the center of the masses. Aleister Dullington's body hung limp from the spikes of an impromptu cross. Sickening ribbons of fluid oozed from his wounds. His head hung down, chin to chest. If he saw Donovan, he made no sign.

They killed him. My God.

The sight gave him pause, and all he knew of the dead figure once known as Aleister of Gloucestershire raced through his head, filling him with an unexpected sorrow comparable only to the loss of his brother. He thought of what he'd said hours before, back before entering the storm. *It's not like I have a life to get back to, or a wife, or a child.* After all he'd seen in the metachasm, the weight of his words struck him with the force of a runaway truck, and his face flushed with shame.

Like Michael, Aleister had been a tenuous companion, at times grating, smug in his patronizing righteousness—and yet he had steered Donovan in the right direction, even if the reasoning was often cryptic, the destination vague. Now Donovan was alone, and he wished both men could stand at his side once more.

They were gone forever, two more casualties of this cosmic game, and by the look of the broken sky above, there was soon to be many more. Colors swirled beyond the fractures in jarring contrast to a hazy gray expanse. Soon, he suspected those colors would stabilize, revealing a blue sky beyond.

And then what?

Singularity, maybe. He was beyond the scope of rational speculation. What man could offer conjecture for the collision of parallel realities?

Donovan pulled himself away from the sky, refocused on his task at hand. He walked toward the mob and their prisoner. Pontius Vile had vanished amidst their ranks and was lost in the turmoil.

No, not lost. He was in there somewhere. Donovan heard him speaking.

"—were always one of my puppets, little sparrow. Even when I shredded your humanity and formed you in the Ungod's image, even after you were gifted a greater sight, you still remained blind—"

Donovan hesitated at the mob's border, unsure if he was ready to do this. Worried they might recognize him. Afraid he might suffer the same fate as his late companion. A few of the ragged men and women turned as he approached, gave him a disinterested once-over, and returned to their mindless milling. Donovan wondered if they had any idea of what they were doing. Were these really people anymore, or just more of Vile's puppets? He suspected the latter. *Leave it to a megalomaniac to throw his own victory party.*

He took a step and nearly tripped on something in the sand. A rod of some kind lay half-exposed at his feet, one end fashioned into a polished wooden handle. The blunt end was wrapped in strips of woven leather. Donovan knelt, fished the object from the sand, and was stunned to find a blade at its other end. A sword, still sharp by the look of it despite the untold years and spotted with dark stains. Another object of antiquity cast aside here in a battle without name or record, unmentioned in the tomes of history. He raised the sword, tested its weight, and cast his gaze across the wastes. Its owner was here somewhere, a bleached skeleton buried just below the shifting sands. Perhaps he would meet the same fate this day.

He thought of Michael and the look of shock on his face when the bullet struck his throat. The utter surprise and confusion. The blood.

And then he thought of Donna and the terror painted on her face, upside down and framed by the shattered SUV window. She was defined in that moment by her panic, eyes wide and mouth agape, unable to speak or move. It was the same face he'd seen years ago, when she'd nearly been trampled at the concert—only now she was afraid for more than just her own life.

He squeezed the hilt in his fist and swallowed back the feeling of ridiculousness welling up in his throat. What did he know of swordplay? Not a goddamn thing. Nothing beyond what he'd seen in countless fantasy and historical films. But now wasn't the time for fear, or the doubt born from it. He could stand here until the world he knew collapsed into itself, or he could act in the face of his fear.

Now or never, he told himself. It was his voice he heard, and unlike the uncertainty pooling in his gut, it sounded strong. Confident and furious.

There it was. The fire of his youth. The flames that ignited and fueled his spirit that night at the concert, when he'd set aside panic and acted to save the woman who would become his wife. The same fire that propelled him through the city in search of Donna, and later, in search of Quinn.

The fire that would burn forever until he put an end to this for all time.

Donovan forged ahead into the mob, the gladius raised and ready to strike at any sign of resistance, but the tattered pilgrims barely paid him attention. They moved aside without care, offering only the slightest curiosity, calm as a herd of cattle.

He was halfway toward their center when a path parted ahead. Vile moved forward at the far end, arms held out in mockery to the crucified figure ahead, an insane priest wading into the churning waters of baptism to be born again. The pilgrims on either side allowed him to pass through their ranks, mindless manikins held by the strings at their master's whim. Donovan took advantage of their blind following and moved swiftly toward his enemy.

"—to think, after all this time you would lie down like the beaten mongrel you are. I expected more from you, little sparrow. I expected a confrontation worthy of the Goths—"

"You're going to get one."

Donovan clenched his teeth and shoved the blade beneath the old monk's shoulder blade. Vile's words withered away in a pained gasp of breath. He slowly sank to his knees, one hand reaching aimlessly for the sword, seeking an itch he couldn't quite scratch. Blood seeped from the wound, stained the length of the old monk's robe, and drizzled on the sands below.

"*You…*"

He stepped around Vile's crumpled body and met the man's stare. "Me."

———•———

Vile's mouth curled into a weak smile. A thin trickle of blood escaped his lips and dribbled across his pale cheek. He stared at Donovan with words on his tongue, but the only sound he made was a soft gurgle of air forced through the blood filling his lungs.

"That breath is more than you gave my brother." Donovan clenched his teeth, struggled to keep the rage at bay. He wanted to pummel this monster into the earth, beat him until nothing was left but a pulpy mess of blood and bones, but time was not on his side. If he hoped to save Donna and the baby, he could not linger for long. Instead, he swallowed back the fire and turned away.

The surrounding mob of lost souls stood in place, their faces full of confusion and fear, struggling to make sense of their whereabouts. Whatever spell Vile had cast upon them was fading. Murmurs spread amongst them as those closest to the bleeding monk and his murderer realized what had happened. Donovan heard his name spoken more than once as he forced his way through the crowd toward Aleister's body. *Candle,* they said through hushed whispers. *Dullington's puppet. The walker between worlds. The liminal man.*

He stopped at the clearing where Aleister Dullington was hung in punishment. The monk's pale face hung limp to one side, his lifeless black eyes staring endlessly into the crowd of his accusers, and thick dollops of gray sludge seeped from the wounds in his wrists. Donovan stared up at the figure in silence, still in disbelief that something like this was even possible. *What happened to you,* he wondered. *How did Vile ever get the better of you?*

"His…corruption…"

Donovan gasped. Aleister slowly lifted his head. Dark veins crawled across his exposed neck.

"We…not much…down…"

Strained breaths broke up his words, but Donovan gathered their meaning, and he leaned his shoulder into the base of the cross. The old wooden beam groaned against his force, but after planting his feet, his weight finally gained the upper hand. A moment later, the plank toppled to the earth, disturbing a cloud of dust upon impact.

He went to work pulling the spikes free from Aleister's wrists. Once free, a strange dark fluid seeped from the wounds and pooled in the sand. Donovan had seen many oddities here in the Monochrome, but this was a first. Was this what Aleister meant by corruption?

"Candle…" Aleister struggled to sit up and reached out his hand for help. Donovan pulled him upright. "What happened to you?"

"Me and the Ungod had a chat, but there's no time for that right now. Let's get you on your feet."

"Vile…his corruption is eating me from within. Not much longer. Is the Needle—"

"It's open."

A peaceful acceptance brightened the monk's face. For a fleeting moment, Donovan caught a glimpse of the young man Aleister had once been, and a piece of his heart shattered. A life wasted in service to a misplaced sense of duty, now atoning for all the wrongs to make things right again. He saw more than the man Aleister had been. He saw a reflection of himself.

"Please forgive me, Mr. Candle—"

Donovan pulled Aleister to his feet. "Put your arm over my shoulder. We have to get you inside that column."

"You do not understand, if I do this…"

"I understand there's no choice. If you don't wake up the Ungod, all of this will have been for nothing. I can't—I won't let my brother's death be in vain." His eyes burned with unshed tears. He blinked them away. "I won't let my choice to come back here be the end of my wife and child."

"I am sorry. For everything."

Donovan carried Aleister past Vile's bleeding body. The madman had slumped forward in an awkward pose, half the blade jutting from his back, his face buried in a hardening pool of blood and sand. Aside from a few morbid spectators, the massive crowd had begun to disperse, their thirst for revenge forgotten on the phantom wings of a bad dream. Now they wandered aimlessly across the vast clearing, lost and confused.

"What will happen to them?"

Aleister shook his head. "I do not know. Everything beyond the Needle is new even to me." He squeezed Donovan's shoulder. "You must know, when I wake the Great Weaver…"

"I know. The balance must be preserved. You can't get something for nothing."

"That is not what I mean. You may be forgotten, but it does not mean—"

Cries of shock erupted from the crowd of pilgrims, or at least that is what Donovan thought. When he turned back, he saw some were all doubled over in pain, clutching their bellies, some on their knees, others writhing on their backs. Above, a crash of thunder rocked the sky, and pieces of the heavens shattered like glass.

A piercing scream ripped through the world, so sharp it cut through every atom and was felt in every living being, Spectrum and Monochrome alike. Donovan felt it in his bones, a trembling sensation of fear and agony, the breaking of ribs encasing reality itself. The effect was so unsettling it took his breath away.

The shriek of agony dulled to a muted vibration and was soon overpowered by a powerful tremor in the earth. A shockwave rippled beneath them, sending both men sprawling to the sand, and the groan of earth moving below drowned out everything else.

Donovan cried out as a monolith of stone broke free of the earth mere feet from his head. He rolled away, shook off the panic, and scrambled toward Aleister.

Another stone pillar shot up from the earth. When he looked back across the sands, he saw similar monoliths rising from the ground. Among them were the writhing crowds, only they were significantly less human than they had once been. Their bodies appeared to be melting—no, not melting, but excreting a familiar substance in an act he'd witnessed not so long ago in the abandoned subway station. Their mediocrity was drawn from them so violently that their bodies could not withstand the force. A nearby pilgrim's head ripped free of his torso, and a geyser of the sickly white sludge shot from the gaping wound.

He wrapped his arm around Aleister's waist and pulled him to his feet. "Come on, we've gotta get you inside."

"Agreed."

They shuffled forward on unsteady earth. Chiseled blocks of white stone rose up around them, marking off corridors of a structure long hidden below the sands, and not seen by human eyes in a millennium. Undeterred, Donovan urged his companion forward to the opening ahead, a path narrowing with every step as more stone structures shot up before them.

They were a few yards from the entrance when a powerful tremor knocked Donovan from his feet. He fell backward, struck the side of a chiseled block of stone, and cried out as sparkles of pain clouded his vision.

"Donovan!"

He shook his head, waited for the daze to clear. "Keep going," he called out. "You have to wake it up!"

Aleister said something else, but his words were muffled by the appearance of another barrier. The granite monolith broke through the sands and cut off both men.

Donovan winced as he climbed to his feet, his whole right side still tingling and sore from the collision, and approached the barrier. The adjacent stones formed a dead end. He beat his fist against the smooth surface and called for Aleister. No answer but for the rumbling earth and screams of agony from those still alive.

Goddammit.

He turned and found the configuration of stone monoliths had formed a kind of hallway. A thick haze of dust and sand obscured the far end, and as he walked along one side, he found some corners opened up into opposing paths. They stretched onward for as far as he could see until they, too, either ended abruptly or connected with other passages.

I'm in a fucking maze, he realized. *What the hell is this?*

A guttural voice echoed from beyond the cloudy haze ahead. "A relic of the Greeks, built to prevent interlopers like yourself."

Donovan's blood ran cold. *Can't be.*

He glimpsed a silhouette ahead. A man standing in the center of the passage. Barely more than a shadow, and it was changing each moment he watched. Distorting. Twisting in upon itself like a disturbed reflection in a pool of water.

"You think a pinprick is enough to end me? Let this be your first lesson."

Something flew through the air, clattered against the nearby wall, and landed with a soft thump in the sand. Donovan approached slowly, kicked the grains away from the gladius. The blade was coated in blood.

———————•———————

Aleister stumbled to his knees. He grimaced from the discomfort in his chest, coughed, and expelled a black wad of phlegm from his throat. Vile's twisted energy was eating him alive with every second, a living emptiness slowly spreading until there was nothing left of him to consume. The sluggish disintegration of being was something that should have terrified him, but terror was a mortal emotion, a reflection of the spirit's resistance to parting the body. After centuries of existence without a human vessel, the promise of actual oblivion was almost a blessing. Finally, he would rest in the embrace of nothingness, his struggle completed and duty fulfilled.

But not yet. No, he could not die yet.

He looked back at the granite slab with some reluctance. Would Donovan be strong enough to confront Vile? Or to resist the madman's manipulation?

You know better, he told himself. *You did not choose him lightly.*

He peered up at the massive column. Light pulsed weakly through the cracks in the marble façade and cast long shadows across the sands, draping him in a faded gloom. The Ungod lay within, but its time was drawing near, each breath growing more labored. He felt its weakened pulse beneath, each rattling inhalation accompanied by a tremor in the earth, the wind, the fabric of this precarious reality shuddering more than the last.

The Needle's entrance stood open just a few yards away. Finally, Vile had played his hand, a move that hinged upon a single miscalculation: that Donovan Candle lacked the fortitude to resist and overcome.

A thick and guttural growl echoed from beyond the labyrinth of granite monoliths. He looked over his shoulder and whispered a silent prayer to the Great Weaver.

Be with Donovan now.

The words clung to his trembling lips, and he did not have the energy to give them voice. Instead, Aleister collected what little strength remained, and crawled across the sand.

———— • ————

Donovan slowly knelt and retrieved the sword, afraid to take his eyes off the mutating shape in the distance. Vile's silhouette grew in mass with each passing moment, his torso bubbling and throbbing erratically while his limbs stretched, thickened, and contorted. He watched, frozen with fear as the figure grew beyond the limits of a mortal human body and into something *else.* A monstrosity standing as tall as the granite monoliths surrounding them.

The haze slowly cleared as the dust settled, and he saw the true face of his enemy for the first time. What had once been Pontius Vile was now a gargantuan beast with a body of pulsating mediocrity. Thick tendrils of the sickly white pus-like substance wrapped around his limbs, forming an exoskeleton of writhing sinew and muscle, and as its blackened eyes fell upon Donovan, it reared back its head and let loose a bellowing growl.

A voice in the back of Donovan's head shrieked for him to turn and run, but within moments it was silenced by the crackling embers of fire in his soul. He hadn't come this far to lose his nerve. *Spent my whole life being a coward. That ends now. For Donna. For the baby. For Michael.* He raised the blade, tightened his grip on the hilt. *For me.*

"Aleister," he called out, uncertain the dying monk could hear him. "I'll buy you time as long as I can."

Vile uttered a distorted cackle so powerful the earth trembled. *"Foolish man. I have already won."*

And that might have been the case, but Donovan wasn't going to give the bastard the satisfaction of knowing, nor would he make it easy. Sword in hand, he steeled himself and darted forward into the fray.

———— • ————

Across the narrowing expanse of the metachasm, Donna Candle reclined her head against the passenger window and closed her eyes. She'd remained alert while they sped out of the city through the storm, on the lookout for more of those flying freaks, ready to warn Alice of impending doom—but their path along the city's side streets through its derelict south side was mostly devoid of encounter. The Monochrome's invasion had not yet spread this far.

But it would. She knew that, and with each passing mile, as the confines of the city gave way to the surrounding countryside, she wondered how long before they spread elsewhere. Or worse, was this already happening across the world? *Oh God,* she thought. *Is this the world my baby's going to grow up in? Always on the run from those things?*

That unsettling thought followed her down into the waters of sleep, a leaden weight dragging her deeper into inky depths without a bottom. Waiting for her there, just below her feet, was a massive pattern of twists and turns and dead ends. A maze of some kind, the sort she might see in a puzzle book, but not nearly as refined. This one was built from thousands of stone pillars, some closer than others, creating channels and byways between for navigation.

And down there, closest to its center, was a man sprinting inward to something she couldn't make out. A tumor of some kind, bloated and pulsing with thick appendages that filled the passage with its festering corruption. They were fighting, a tiny Theseus versus a gargantuan Minotaur, one attempting to crush the other.

She sank closer to the maze, watching with dreamy wonder as the festering beast tried to crush its opponent, as the man darted between the creature's legs, as he turned a corner and fled deeper into the maze. *Don't,* she wanted to tell him, *you were almost out and now you're going to get lost again.* But she was just an apparition in this place, drifting on a current of dreams and tethered by an unseen cord—

She awoke with a jolt as the car crossed over a pothole in the road. Alice glanced at her, asked if she was okay.

"Yeah, just startled. Sorry I drifted off to sleep."

"It's fine. Haven't seen another car for half an hour now. Eerie."

"Mmm." Donna leaned her head against the window and watched the countryside roll by. Suburban neighborhoods slowly transformed into miles of farmland, fields of corn and untilled earth, silos and barns. Familiar shapes blurred and distorted by the barrage of raindrops on the glass.

They drove on in silence for a time, moving further away from the city and deeper into the country, past the backroads which would lead them back to her home.

Sleep had almost claimed her once more when Alice brought the car to a shrieking halt. Quinn cried out in surprise as he was thrown forward against her seat. Donna sat upright, bleary-eyed and confused, her heart thudding away on overdrive.

"What is it? What's wrong?"

Alice gripped the steering wheel and cocked her head toward the windshield. "That's what's wrong."

Donna wiped her eyes and looked forward. Half a mile up the road and through the pouring rain, the air shimmered and rippled like water, the effect of heat rising from pavement on a scorching day, but this was something else entirely. Pale light seeped from this apparent tear in reality, a hole that was growing wider with each passing moment right before their eyes. The road stretched into the rift and vanished, fading into an expanse of desert and—impossibly—a giant structure on the horizon. A column, by the look of it, surrounded by a series of stone monoliths and sheathed in a pearly glow.

She looked at Alice, and then back at Quinn. "What is that?"

"I don't know," Quinn whispered. "Never saw anything like that when I was in the 'chrome."

Alice slowly rubbed her temples. "Me neither. Looking at it is giving me a headache."

Donna leaned forward, squinting, trying to unearth an artifact of memory irritating her brain. She had seen something like this before, back in the hospital. A doorway of sorts, revealing figures marching across a vast desert. And then there was her dream, fragments of which had returned with her to the surface of consciousness. A maze-like pattern. A man and a monster.

"Donovan…" She opened the door and climbed out of the car, ignoring the protests of Alice and Quinn alike. The ongoing storm washed over her, cooling her skin and drenching clothes that had only just begun to dry. She relished the pattering on her skin, a tabla percussion in tandem with her racing heart.

What are you doing, lady? Have you lost your mind?

Maybe she had. Maybe they were all hallucinating. Maybe this was all a dream, and she was on the floor of her kitchen, bleeding from a headwound while her sister called 911 in a panic. It was a nice thought—at least then her sister would still be alive. Michael would still be alive. The world would still be whole.

But Donnie would still be gone. You'd still be on your own, fretting over how to pay the bills and support this child while suffering from all the pain in your muscles and joints. Your heart would ache no less than it does now. You would still be stuck trying to figure out why he would leave in the middle of the night.

Donna looked up and let the rain wash the tears from her face. Quinn lowered his window and called out to her. "Aunt Donna, please get back in the car. We don't know what's out there. It isn't safe!"

She smiled at him, and then to Alice. "I need to see this for myself, guys. I need to understand why he left."

Alice stepped out of the car. "Donna, please. Quinn's right. We can double back, find another way around."

"I need to do this. I don't expect you to understand…" She trailed off, frowning. "…but I think you already do."

Alice's face softened, and even through the rain, Donna could see the tears welling in her friend's eyes. A bolt of lightning lit up the sky above, followed by a sudden clap of thunder. Donna nodded, turned back to the widening tear ahead, and walked on alone.

18

FATES UNTETHERED

Donovan raced between the monstrosity's legs, narrowly escaping the swing of Vile's deformed arm. The bloated fist obliterated a chunk of a nearby monolith, scattering the passage with a cloud of granite shrapnel, and was followed by another guttural roar.

"Run, Candle. It will make your death so much sweeter."

He ran as fast as he could, his heart pounding, fueling the inferno burning away in his lungs. His whole body was an engine of steam and pistons driven by the singular desire of survival. The earth trembled beneath him as the monstrosity that was once Pontius Vile lumbered in pursuit.

One passage became another as he moved deeper into the labyrinth. The detritus of all the wars waged here had been driven to the surface by the stone monoliths, and as he moved further inward, Donovan found the paths increasingly littered with human remains. Bones were strewn across the sand, skeletons half-buried in the dunes, ribs and femurs and skulls protruding in a grim suggestion of his fate.

"You were meant to remain in the mind of my minions. Did the Ungod show you a way out? No matter. I underestimated you, Master Candle, but I will not make that mistake again—"

A blast of stone exploded behind him, and the gargantuan beast emerged from the cloud of dust. Donovan dove headfirst into a nearby passage, praying Vile hadn't seen him. He regained his footing, pressed himself against the stone wall, and tried to catch his breath.

Keep yourself together, Don. You can beat this thing. Buy some time for Dullington.

Vile's booming steps drew closer. A nearby pile of bones rattled and collapsed into itself. The sands vibrated and shifted apart, revealing another layer of the dead. Donovan closed his eyes and waited for his heart to slow.

He thought back to when he was a teenager, and Michael was on the verge of graduating. It was the year of high school when Donovan was plagued by a pair of bullies. Always picking on him. Always ridiculing and threatening to kick his ass. Michael had been the one to stand up for his little brother, but now he would be going off to college. He wouldn't be there to save Donovan anymore.

You need to learn to stand up for yourself, Don. I can't be there all the time. These guys, they're bigger than you, yeah? Use that against them.

A lifetime ago, and yet his late brother's words were more prescient now than ever before. He'd managed to get the upper hand in high school, ducking a swing aimed for his face, and planting a fist in the bully's gut just like Michael had taught him. A sucker punch wouldn't take Vile down, but maybe he could get behind him—

Vile's fist broke through the adjacent monolith, scattering the corridor with chunks of fractured stone. A moment later, the behemoth stepped into the crossway, mere feet from where Donovan stood against the wall. This close, he saw with sickening clarity the snake-like vines of mediocrity woven together to form the beast's tendons. Somewhere inside the writhing mess was a mortal man possessed of an impossible power and forbidden knowledge. A man driven insane by glimpsing the unknowable and corrupted by the influence of a drowsing, fallible god.

"These walls were built to serve as a tomb. One last attempt to keep out those who might want to interfere with the Great Weaver." Vile turned away, lifted one of his massive trunk-like legs, and kicked a hole into a monolith across the passage. Half the giant stone block crumbled to dust. *"Every civilization played a hand in building this place, every society contributing to its barricades, every man and woman contributing to the need. All this time, none of them thought to question why."*

Vile marched on, crushing another monolith to bits. Donovan exhaled slowly, crossed to the other side of the passage, and peeked around the corner. Nothing but another sand-covered crypt of the dead and defeated. He walked lightly, sword in hand, following the sound of Vile's destruction along a parallel path.

"Why must we keep the Ungod safe? What secrets could it possibly possess that we were not meant to know? I had to understand this for myself, you see.

I had to comprehend the point. And all I found—" A sinuous fist crashed through the monolith ahead, crushing half the structure to powder. *"—was an endless cycle of hate and suffering, atrocity after atrocity, bloodshed and bigotry and genocide. Mankind was not meant to be safe or sane, happy or content. We are a stain on time itself. Insects on the corpse of the earth. Why continue this cycle when it can be broken? Why must we allow a nameless god to feast upon our fears and failures when it is we who should be choking on them?"*

Donovan hesitated, gripped the sword in his hands, and finally called out. "You're insane, Vile. And you're wrong. The Ungod has a name."

A pause in the tumult, followed by a shudder in the earth as the beast turned in Donovan's direction. He darted across the passage and into the shadow of the adjacent monolith. Vile crashed through the wall of stone, and the rubble fell where Donovan had stood only moments earlier. He watched from beyond the corner, adrenaline pumping, ready to run once again.

"What you know—what you think you know—is but another lie you have told yourself. Much like your precious happiness. Much like the life you think you are meant to have, and the meaning you so desperately seek to know."

He held his tongue this time. Instead, he reached down and lifted a fractured skull from the sand. He threw it across the path where it shattered against the stone. Seconds later, he moved to the opposite corner and waited for the beast to follow his lure.

"You are no different than the rest, Candle. What have you done to reach this present state? You led George Guffin to his fate. You abducted Sparrow in trade for your wife. How many condemned souls did you free in the plaza? And your brother, Michael. Even he suffered by your hand."

Donovan bit his lip, clenched his teeth to hold back a retort.

"You knew Margie Guffin was a threat. You were the one she wanted. But you chose to conceal your identity. If you had faced the consequences of your actions, your brother Michael would still be alive."

He slid along the wall to the next corner and peered around just as Vile moved to investigate. The beast crunched the pile of bones underfoot and beat its fists against the wall. Cracks ripped through the stone surface. Donovan watched them spread to the corner where several chunks fell to the sands below. He stared at the indentations and then the top of the monolith, calculating the height, wondering if he could be fast enough— or strong enough—to scramble up the side.

"Everything you have done has been an act of selfishness. The pitiful truth is you do not even realize it. Do you truly believe you are trying to save humanity? Are you so blind in your righteousness that you cannot see you are no different?"

The deformed beast turned away, squeezing itself down a narrow passage between two nearby stones, and Donovan saw his chance. He raised the sword, reared back, and heaved the blade over the top of the monolith. It clattered across the surface and out of sight.

"Is that you, Candle?" A heavy vibration tore through the granite slab as Vile doubled his efforts, squeezing himself faster between the stones. *"Ten thousand men could not find their way out of this labyrinth. Your hubris is astounding."*

With his heart pounding and a nauseating flutter in his gut, Donovan took a running leap at the wall, digging his foot into the first crumbling indentation and reaching for the next. Bits of stone slipped between his fingers, and for a terrifying instant he feared it would give way—but then he took hold with his other hand, and with a panicked heave, lifted himself along the cracked surface.

As soon as he hefted himself over the edge of the monolith, Vile freed himself of the narrow path and returned in search of prey. Donovan lay on his back for a moment, trying to catch his breath while ignoring the burning ache in his hands and feet. The sky above was riddled with holes, revealing the swirling kaleidoscope of liminal space and the threads of the metachasm beyond.

Any day now, Aleister.

Vile continued his patrol between the stone monoliths, one earth-shaking step at a time. Donovan waited until the monstrosity had passed once again before climbing to his feet. He moved to the center of the structure and retrieved the gladius.

"Even now you are trying to justify your reasons, lying to yourself that your actions are for the benefit of the many." Vile returned, slammed his fist into the stone wall across the way, and growled. *"Face the truth, Donovan Candle. You are acting for yourself and no one else. Just like the rest of our kind."*

Donovan approached the edge, shakily lifted the blade, and readied himself. For the first time in his life, there was no voice of doubt whispering in his ear, urging him to reconsider his intentions. No take-backs, what-ifs, or might've-beens. This was now or never.

"You're right about one thing. This time it's for me."

The beast slowly turned. One sinuous arm reared back, ready to strike. Donovan raised the blade and leapt from the slab—

A fist of rubbery tendrils caught him mid-air, squeezing the breath from his lungs. Vile raised Donovan into the air in triumph, a distorted cackle freeing itself from his throbbing, bloated head. *"As I told you before, Donovan*

Candle, I have known you your whole life. Every pivotal turn in your life was but a tweak of the strings, pulling you here or there, guiding you to this moment."

Donovan struggled to breathe, squirmed against his restraints as dim colors burst before his eyes and phantom pins prickled his fingertips. He squeezed the sword's hilt so tight his knuckles ached.

Vile raised his fist to his face. Two milky-gray eyes bulged from hollow sockets, completing a bloated visage of the madman's true face, a façade carved from man's failings. His face quivered as bloated lips peeled back into a rotten grin.

"I spent lifetimes wrapped in the strings, seeking the right pawn, a manikin with whom Aleister would find kinship. Someone with whom he would attempt to stop me. Someone who would ultimately fail. And after centuries of searching, I found you."

Fingers as thick as tree trunks compressed, squeezing Donovan's fragile body so hard he could not help but cry out in pain. Vile laughed, expelling a gust of rancid breath.

"Every fateful twist in your life was my doing, Donovan. I want you to know that." He brought Donovan closer, until all the man could see was one of Vile's glossy eyes, a swirling void of gray like sour milk left to curdle. The stench of his breath made Donovan's eyes water. *"Donna's chronic pain. The crash which stole your parents. The advertisement for the job you hated. Your brother's death. And let us not forget your laughable creation, Joe Hopper. I take immense pride in manufacturing that guiding voice in your head. These were but a few careful plucks of the string that binds you, Donovan Candle. I am the designer of your fate—"*

A searing light erupted from the far end of the passage, blinding them both. Vile recoiled in surprise, raising his free hand to shield himself. Donovan squinted to make out what was happening. Another burst of light filled the dead end, followed by the familiar colors of real life seeping inward. A hole ripped in the fabric of reality. Beyond the tear he saw a winding road and a car some distance away. Storm clouds overhead draped the world in sheets of rain.

A lone figure approached the rip. A woman holding her belly. Pregnant. Two figures followed after her, crying out her name.

Could it be her? He strained to see. Between the flashing lights of creeping color and the spreading downpour, he couldn't make out her face from this distance. But he *felt* her. In his heart. His soul. Any relief he might have felt was quickly displaced by the horror welling up inside him. She shouldn't be here. Not here. Not now. She had no idea how much danger she was in. If Vile saw her—

He found a burst of strength, pried himself free of Vile's relaxed fist, and worked the blade free of its restraint. Time slowed in the following moments, Vile's reflexes too sluggish to catch his prey a second time.

Donovan teetered on the edge of the beast's hand, raised the blade, and spoke through clenched teeth. "I make my own fate."

He gripped the hilt and plunged the blade deep into Vile's eye.

———————— • ————————

She peered through the rip with horrified wonder. This place, this Monochrome, was unlike anything she had ever seen. No color, no texture, nothing more than a series of corridors partitioned with massive stone structures like protruding teeth. This was beyond what she had witnessed back in the hospital, and to see what she had glimpsed in the depths of her dream now in stark clarity set her mind alight.

There was the man, held tightly in the grip of the bloated monster. The cancer which she knew with impossible rationale was the cause of all this turmoil. The source of so much pain and suffering and utter terror.

Rain beat down upon her, obscuring her vision, and although she could not see his face clearly, she knew that man was her husband. She *felt* him somehow. In her heart and in her soul.

"Donnie," she whispered, and her words drowned in the rain.

"Donna, get away from there!" Alice's voice, also muffled in the storm. Her warning went unheeded as Donna approached the rift.

She watched the man free himself, heard him shout something at the beast before raising a sword and stabbing its eye. The cancerous brute recoiled in pain, tried to shake the man loose like a bothersome flea, but Donovan held fast. He yanked the blade free and shoved it into the creature's other eye. A roar bellowed from the monstrosity, the sound of a million dissonant voices screeching in pain, and this time it shook its opponent loose.

Donovan flew back, collided against the opposite wall with a sharp thud, and fell to the sand below.

Oh God, no. Donnie!

"Aunt Donna, please!"

She ignored Quinn. Heart racing, Donna mustered her courage and stepped beyond the rift into the Monochrome.

19

THE DAY
THE WORLD WENT AWAY

Aleister heard the chaos of battle as he crawled across the Needle's threshold. Violent spasms rocked the foundation while a creature roared in the distance. He paused just inside the entrance and collected his wits. The corruption eating away at him had spread to his extremities, filling his fingers and toes with an odd prickling sensation, and when he raised his hand, he watched two of his digits disintegrate to dust. Bits of skin and bone drifted away, caught in an errant breeze.

The discomfort swelling in his chest had spread to his throat, and he had to stop and expel more of the dark infection from his mouth. When he was ready, Aleister tried to regain his footing and stand, but one of his legs would not work. He looked back, raised the hem of his robe, and saw half his foot was gone. A pale and bloodless stump rested against the floor, disintegrating before his eyes.

Must keep on, he told himself, and resumed his crawl despite the ache which had emerged in the wake of his missing parts. *This is my end,* he realized, but refused to give in to despair. He was beyond such emotions, had suffered a lifetime of them; to succumb to them now would be fatal, and not just for himself. Instead, Aleister fixed his gaze on the archway across the antechamber. He focused on the fading light pulsing beyond the room.

Help me…

He raised his head, listening. The voice was weak, barely there, strained of breath and choked of life.

Aleister pulled himself forward to the chamber entrance. He wrapped his hand around the corner and watched another finger slip away into nothingness.

"I am coming, oh Weaver. At long last…"

———————•———————

The hairs on Donna's arms and neck stood on end. Everything here vibrated on a different frequency. The air was heavy, stagnant. An insidious drone hummed in her ears like a synthetic tinnitus, and she was certain that if she remained for a lengthy period of time, it would drive her mad.

Straight ahead, the sinuous beast writhed and clawed on the earth, blindly seeking the means to gain its footing, and failing to do so. Pieces of its body unwound and fell to the sand like dead branches from a diseased tree. She wasn't sure what it was—or, impossibly, *who*—but kept her distance anyway. She followed the path along the sand, stepping over the broken remains of those who had gone before her, and hurried toward her husband.

Donovan lay on his back, groaning. His left arm was swollen around the elbow, likely broken. Blood stained the sand and oozed from a wound on the back of his head. Donna gasped when she saw the state he was in, wincing when he tried to move and recoiled from the pain in his arm.

"Donnie, oh God, honey…" She knelt beside him, tears already welling in her eyes, and placed a hand on his cheek. "I've gotta—you need to get to a hospital." That word lingered in her throat when she remembered the chaos of St. Lucien's. No, they couldn't go back there. But if not there, then where?

She looked back, saw Quinn and Amanda standing beyond the edge of the tear. Their hands were cupped over their mouths, but she could not hear their words.

Donovan's eyes slowly opened, looked up at her. His pupils were dilated, vacant, and his eyes drifted around her as though following something she couldn't see.

"Don, it's me." She took his good hand and squeezed. "We can get out of here. I can take you home. Everything's going to be okay—"

"Donna…" He rasped, tried to pull himself up and hissed from the pain in his bad arm. "Give me a minute. I need to catch my breath. I…" Clarity filled his eyes, and he stared at her with a sudden thirst, unsure if she was really here or just a mirage conjured to torture him. "Honey? Is it really you?"

Tears slipped from her cheeks and plopped on the sand. She took his hand and kissed him deeply. "It's really me, I'm really here, and…"

What could she say? Michael was gone. Amanda was gone. The whole world was on fire and being devoured by an army of abominations.

"Is he…" Donovan struggled to sit up and cried out when he tried to move his broken arm. Donna helped him to his feet, waited until she was sure he had his balance before letting go. He looked at her, absently rubbing the back of his head. Blood covered his fingers.

"You probably have a concussion," she said, frowning. "Come on, Don, we need to get the hell out of here. There's—"

Something wrong with the world, she wanted to say, but the hopelessness in those words stalled her voice. Instead, she watched him stumble toward the hulking remains of the strange beast and kick aside some of the fallen appendages.

The creature lay in a smoldering pile across the path, thick tendrils spread out like massive roots ripped free of the earth in a deadfall. A body lay half-buried in the sinuous vines, one hand limply held out in offering. Part of an old man's face was exposed. One of the eyes was missing, the socket an empty orbit of blackened gore. A sword protruded from the other socket, impaling the old man's brain.

A sharp clap of thunder erupted above them, followed by a piercing shriek as cracks splintered the sky. Soon after, a violent tremor rippled through the earth beneath their feet. Donovan looked up at the glowing column and frowned.

"Donna, honey, you can't be here. You shouldn't be here. I…" He turned to her, his face flush with shame, his eyes sunken with a sorrow she'd only ever seen in the mirror these last several days. "You weren't meant to see this place. None of this."

"I saw you," she said. "In my dreams. And then we were trying to leave the city, and I saw you again, but this time…" Donna looked back at the massive tear in reality. Quinn and Amanda waited in the storm, arms crossed, watching. "I came to get you, Don. We can go home. We can…"

Start over, she wanted to say, but voicing those words seemed so foolish now. She'd lived with him long enough to know he had already made up his mind. Seeing that look on his face made her want to scream.

On those nights during his absence, when she could not sleep for all the worry clouding her brain, Donna had rehearsed what she might say to him if she ever saw him again. She heard herself screaming, threatening to leave him, *promising* to leave him, throwing every justified barb she could to pierce through his selfish resolve—and now all those words withered and died on her tongue. All her love and resentment were driven by a singular fear of loss and born from a sacred place of love. She wanted so badly to hate him, but she loved him too goddamn much, and that in itself infuriated her.

All this time she had questioned his reasoning for leaving, questioned his need to take up this stupid cause—but after witnessing his actions in person, after stepping into this place which had seemed, at best, another one of his fictional creations, Donna found herself burdened with the heavy realization that his actions weren't selfish at all. She took measure of his state, studied the deep lines of worry on his face, the perpetual frown, even the faint traces of gray in his sideburns and stubble. He had been gone less than forty-eight hours but had aged ten years. This burden he had shouldered himself would kill him over time if he allowed it to.

And he would, too, because the man she married, the man with whom she had fallen in love all those years ago, did not leave matters unfinished. Not if he could help it. It was a quality she admired in him, even if he personified it to a fault. Sometimes he never knew when to quit—and this time, of all times, was one she recognized he needed to see through to the end.

This time she would not let him do it alone.

"Then take me with you. Whatever's left for you to do, let's do it together."

"Honey, if this could be any other way…"

"You haven't seen yourself, have you? Do you have any idea what this place has done to you? What it's *doing* to you now, even as I stand here?"

"This isn't about me. It's about you, and our little one." He rested his hand on her belly and frowned. "This place is dangerous, and I haven't come all this way for something to happen to you now."

She raised her hand, wanted to smack him, but instead placed her palm on his cheek. "This is what I get for falling in love with a stubborn bastard."

He closed his eyes, smiled, and leaned into her touch. "You deserve someone better, but I'll always be grateful you chose me."

"You stupid man. You *are* someone better." They embraced. Her lips found his, and they kissed for what felt like the first time. When they were done, she took his hand and squeezed. "But you forgot something about me, Don. I'm just as stubborn as you are, and you can't get rid of me that easily." She smiled. "So. Where are we going?"

Donovan sighed. He looked back at the glowing structure piercing the shattered sky. "There. We have to go wake up a god."

———•———

She helped him fashion a sling from the tattered remnants of his shirt. Once his arm was immobile and the surging pain had finally quieted to a dull ache, Donovan pointed the way. His memory of the twists and turns was hazy at best, but the late Pontius Vile had left behind a memento in the form of a bread crumb trail.

The path of destruction led them back through the labyrinth, chunks of fractured granite marking the way. They walked side by side in silence between the stones, hands interlocked like the young lovers they used to be, their steps almost sluggish in the journey. That was Donovan's doing, taking things slow, if only because he knew what came next. He had seen it in the metachasm, a glimpse of the path where his thread would lead, and although the circumstances had changed slightly, he suspected some events remained constant in the fate he made for himself.

For now he was content to remain by Donna's side. Her presence was a respite from this greater responsibility no matter how fleeting, and he intended to bask in her glow for as long as he could. Twice she caught him staring at her, each time blushing like the college girl with whom he'd fallen in love, and although he smiled in return, he secretly wanted to break down, plant his feet in the sand, and refuse to move. Because refusing to advance meant she wouldn't follow him into the Needle, meant the Spectrum and Monochrome would become one, and all reality as they knew it would collapse.

Nothingness. The concept eluded him. A philosophical conundrum not unlike dividing one by zero. It would never compute. Not in this state of being, anyway.

But for as much as he wanted to remain here with her as the world fell down around them, he knew doing so would be the ultimate act of selfishness. To remain would mean robbing their unborn child of a life to live. To remain would rob humanity of the opportunity to redeem itself, to prove Pontius Vile wrong.

And so, when the shrieking sky grew louder in pitch and the fractures overhead widened to reveal the purplish haze of their world at dusk, he resisted his instincts. He gripped her hand tighter and hurried her along, out of the labyrinth, toward the fate they had chosen for themselves.

"Wait a second."

They stood at the Needle's entrance, where a slimy trail of black ichor led the way inside. Donna hung back, arms crossed above her baby bump, staring at the Latin inscription.

"How old is this place?"

Donovan shook his head. "Hard to say. The Romans built this place—or maybe it was the Greeks? The only one who knew for sure is back there in the maze." He leaned down for a better look at the dark substance. "I think this is blood. Or something like it."

Standing now, he took Donna's hand and led the way into the antechamber. The Ungod's pulsing light was almost gone, barely detectable even in the musty darkness. Donna clung to him as they entered the shadows, and he felt a shiver ripple through her body. He turned and put his arm around her.

"Aleister?" His voice echoed across the antechamber. "Vile is dead."

No response. He called out again, startled by the trepidation in his voice. After all this time, he had taken Aleister's presence for granted. He and the Monochrome were one in the same in Donovan's mind, one an extension of the other. Of course he knew better now. After his time in the metachasm, he knew Aleister was as much a victim of this place as everyone else. He recalled the monk's memories, the heartache, the anger. The urge to make things right.

Donovan was about to call out again when a weak voice spoke. "Here...I am in here..."

He exchanged glances with Donna before following the sound into the Ungod's chamber. Weak light slowly lit up the room before failing into darkness, each swell of illumination a fraction of time shorter than the last, the Great Weaver's breaths a countdown to oblivion. In the brief glimpses offered by the fading light, they witnessed the end of the figure tied so closely to their fates.

Aleister Dullington had made it as far as the marble steps leading toward the cradle before his body gave out. His robe lay wrinkled on the floor, obscuring what Donovan suspected to be a gruesome absence of form. All that remained of Aleister was his head, an arm, and the upper half of his torso. When the light swelled once more, they witnessed the last of Aleister's pale hand dissolve into dust. A black puddle seeped from beneath the monk's remains.

Donovan left his wife's side and crossed the room to kneel beside his friend.

Friend. A word he'd never expected to relate to the once villainous Aleister Dullington. *No,* he thought, *that isn't his name. And he was never a villain. He was just trying to make things right again, no matter the cost.*

Donovan took what remained of the monk's arm and set him upright. Aleister slowly turned his head, peered at Donna's timid figure, and offered a smile. "Donna Candle...at last, you see."

She walked toward them, frightened and repulsed. Donovan reached out and took her hand. "It's okay," he whispered.

"What's happening to him?"

"I think he's dying."

Aleister's arm slowly vanished one piece at a time. He tilted his head up toward Donovan. "The Ungod...it is up to you now, Mr. Candle."

"How? I..."

Can't do this, but those words rang false in his head. He knew he could, understood he would have to no matter how much he resisted the idea. The true savior of the balance had met his end mere feet from his goal. If not Donovan, then who?

The monk turned his head and hacked up a mouthful of black bile. A thin stream of the dark gore trickled from his lips. His dark eyes widened as he strained for breath and more of his robe slowly sank inward.

"Do not...be afraid. A defined man..."

"Always knows how to act." Donovan forced a smile, but on the inside, he was screaming. *And I'm fucking terrified.*

The slow rot infecting Aleister's body finally reached its pinnacle, first dissolving his neck and crawling upward to his chin. Soon his face was gone, leaving a gray void in its wake before it, too, vanished from reality. Aleister of Gloucestershire, last of the Dullingtons, was gone.

Donovan lowered his head and waited for the wave of emotions to crash. A lone voice spoke up in his head, culled from a days-old memory he had almost forgotten.

Time for you to take that leap, Michael whispered. *This is your time.* That night in his brother's backyard. Donna's baby shower. A lifetime ago, and yet oddly prescient in his current circumstance.

"Acta non verba," he whispered.

Donna took his hand. "What?"

He pulled her to him, and then led her up the steps toward the Ungod's cradle. Together they stood over the opening, awash in a pallid dying light from the slumbering nonentity below. Donovan wanted to ask her if she saw the same thing he did, but the words would not come. He was too enraptured by its presence, frozen in awe and terror.

A humanoid infant the size of a man and pale as the moon, a creature utterly alien and familiar, at once alive and dead, forever awake in its dreams. A contradiction through which all humanity's failings passed, were measured, and were consumed. The filter saving us from ourselves.

The umbilicus of strings which had once cocooned Pontius Vile was wrapped around the creature's throat, and its breathing grew more labored with each passing moment.

Donna squeezed his hand, cleared her throat. "It's...this is a god?"

"The god we made."

"I think it's dying."

"It is, but not for long." He turned to her, trembling, his eyes glossy with tears. "But you need to understand...every action carries a price. Something taken for something given. A balance in all things."

She shook her head. "I don't follow...Don, what do you mean?"

He let go of her hand, brushed her hair away from her forehead, and kissed her. "I want you to know I will always love you. You and the baby."

"Honey, you're scaring me..."

"You're my whole world, Donna. I wasn't me until I met you, and I won't be me without you."

The Needle trembled around them. A massive crack splintered its way up the wall and into the gloom above. Soon after, an enormous piece of marble crashed to the floor, barring the only exit.

"Don't...don't do this to me again, Donovan Candle." She beat her fist against him, and when he didn't react, she smacked him so hard a red handprint blossomed on his cheek. When she tried to turn away, he wrapped his arm around her and pulled her close. Donna shivered against him, her chest hitching, holding back sobs he would not be there to comfort. "You don't get to do this to me again. Goddamn you..."

Tears slid down his face. He kissed her forehead and let her go. "I'll find you when this is done."

She wiped her eyes. "You always do."

He saw a hint of a smile. It was there and gone again, buried once more in her anger. God, he wanted to stay here with her, hold her forever until the sky fell and the stars burned out, but this was not to be. This was as far as he had glimpsed, as far as the Ungod itself could see, and what happened afterward was anyone's guess. For the first time in his life, Donovan Candle had no strings to bind him, and he was free to lose everything if only to find himself once again.

He turned back toward her. "I love you, Donna Candle."

And before she could respond, he hopped down into the cradle and took hold of the threaded umbilicus.

"*Cosma,*" he shouted, unraveling the cords from the nonentity's throat. "*Time to wake the fuck up!*"

———————— • ————————

The Ungod gasped for breath, opened its black eyes, and with a deafening roar, unleashed a bolt of light from its mouth. The pale beam encompassed all, filled the cracked chamber with its brilliance, and pierced the Needle's zenith. The light tore through the shattered heavens and into the Spectrum, seeding the earth with the fearful fury of billions, and birthing a stormfront that transcended dimensions to cleanse the living fears from their makers.

Rain fell in the Monochrome, washing away the dust and bones of countless lives lost in battle, a history of pointless bloodshed wiped clean. Dark lightning crackled across the slate sky and crashed upon the earth, breaking the stones of the monolithic labyrinth, and chipping away at the marble façade built to imprison the Ungod's presence.

Within minutes the great Needle was no more, reduced to fractured rubble surrounding the cradle. Cosma stared dreamily toward the light and the strings stretching across the metachasm. Soothed by the tears of countless souls, the Ungod closed its eyes once more, breathed deep, and slipped once more beneath the waves of slumber. There were no dreams, and there was no bottom.

There was only peace—and a fluttering thought sent vibrating along its savior's solitary thread.

———————— • ————————

Donna opened her eyes and looked to the sky. The storm had finally relented, but in the fading light of sunset, she saw a strange white light among the clouds. Shimmering, almost, like a child's idea of stardust. Fireflies blinked lazily as they rose from the field, and she laughed when one of them hovered just above her nose.

She traced her hand along the tops of the tall grass, relishing the tickle on her fingertips, while something tugged at the back of her mind. Something had happened. But what? A cool breeze swept over her, and she felt dampness on her cheeks. She wiped her eyes and discovered she'd been crying.

Was I dreaming? I feel like I was dreaming. But what about?

Whatever had happened eluded her, burrowed deep into the shadows of her mind, just out of reach. This mysterious thing felt like something important. Something close to her, and yet lost somehow.

"Donna…"

A man's voice tore her from her thoughts. She blinked, looked further off into the field, and saw a man approach. He was shirtless, with something wrapped around his arm like a sling, and looked like he hadn't eaten in months. Dark half-moons clung to his eyes, and she suspected he might fall over at any minute.

"Do I know you?"

The man slowed to a stop, looked away. Failing sunlight reflected off the moisture in his eyes. "No," he murmured, shifting his weight. "No, I guess you don't. My mistake."

He walked past her toward the road, and she turned to watch him go. Alice and Quinn stood near the car, watching them both, and when she saw them, she raised her hand to wave.

As she walked to greet them, she looked toward to the stranger. He had crossed to the opposite side of the road, headed back toward the city.

"Hey," she called out. "Are you okay?"

"No," he said, but did not stop. "I've been better, to tell you the truth."

"Do you need help? Do you need me to call someone?"

The man shook his head. "Not yet." He pointed toward the road and the countryside beyond. "This way to the city, right?"

She nodded. "Are you sure you don't need any help?"

"No," he said. "This time I need to walk on my own for a while."

Donna watched him walk on down the road until he disappeared in the late evening gloom. When he was gone, she drummed her fingers along her belly. "What do you think, kiddo? Should I go find my own way?"

Crickets in the field chirped in reply. Walking toward Alice and Quinn, Donna's thoughts drifted back to the stranger and what he'd said. *This time I need to walk on my own for a while.* She supposed that was true for everyone, sooner or later.

THE GHOSTS
OF WHO WE WERE

One year later

She was upstairs when the doorbell rang, standing over the sink as she washed the makeup from her face. Donna stared at her reflection and held her breath. Smudged mascara ringed her eyes like a raccoon. Toweling her face, she left the bathroom and peeked into the nursery.

Alexandra lay on her back with her head nuzzled against a mountain of plushy animals. The blanket was bunched around her feet, and Donna wanted to pull it back up—the room got so cold with the air conditioning—but the doorbell rang again, and the baby stirred.

Shit. Why won't this day just end?

That morning she had opted to take the bus into the city, but a traffic jam on the highway made her late for her interview at the courthouse. Who would want to hire a file clerk who can't be punctual? Not the local government, apparently.

But tomorrow was another day, right? With another job interview—this time at a law firm, on Quinn's recommendation—and another failed prospect, another wasted day she could have spent at home with her child instead of hiring Alice to watch after the baby on her day off. She had offered to stay and watch after Alexandra so Donna could have some quiet time, but that wasn't going to happen. Donna needed some time to herself, yes, but on her own terms. She needed time to think, to figure out a short-term plan, and to scour the job sites again. The generous inheritance from Michael's estate wouldn't last forever, no longer than another two months, in fact, not with all the doctor bills for herself and the baby.

The doorbell rang a third time when she reached the first floor. Her heart thudded in her chest, the symptom of a greater anxiety she couldn't place, a silly fear of answering the door she knew hadn't always been there, but for some reason she could not remember when or why it began. And, if she was being completely honest with herself, the last thing she wanted right now was to speak to another human being.

Especially another visitor.

She couldn't make sense of the people who had frequented her doorstep or had called her phone on occasion in recent months. And with this persistent stranger poised to ring the bell for a fourth time, she didn't have time to puzzle over it now.

As she raced toward the front door, Donna prepared herself for another strange conversation, another odd man or woman, apologetic, almost embarrassed to be there and yet compelled to be, too. To say thanks, they often said, but never offered to elaborate. They usually brought flowers to leave at her doorstep. Flowers in memoriam, perhaps, or maybe in tribute.

She cracked open the door and peered outside.

A young man and woman stood on the sidewalk. Both appeared to be college age, but only just, and if she had to guess, they both carried the weight of the world on their shoulders. That was a quality the others had possessed—a sort of world-weariness or fatigue, as though they had just suffered some unimaginable trauma. These two were the youngest yet, and she instantly regretted feeling the way she did. Something had happened to these kids. Their morose faces said as much.

"Can I help you?"

The young lady looked up, and a sign of life flickered across her face before dying in the evening light. She glanced at her companion before clearing her throat. "Are you Donna Candle?"

"This was a mistake," the boy whispered.

"Shut up," the girl said, and then: "I'm sorry, we…look, this is going to sound really strange, but…I heard about you. In a dream."

Donna stepped outside, crossed her arms. "In a dream?"

"Yeah," the girl said, her cheeks flushing red. "I know it's crazy, but a few months ago we—me 'n my brother here—took a tour of the old subway tunnels downtown, and…"

Her brother cut in. "Your phone number is painted on one of the walls down there. So's this address." He pulled out his phone and held out the screen. Donna hesitated, her gaze lingering on the young man in search of the joke, but all she saw was a stern, confused seriousness. "It's weird. All sorts of names and numbers down there on the wall, but yours goes the whole length of the terminal."

When she finally looked at the photo, a chill crawled across the back of her neck. "REMEMBER DONOVAN CANDLE?" was written in giant white letters, and sure enough, so was her phone number. Her address was scrawled in smaller letters below, almost as an afterthought.

"My husband," she whispered. "He's been…"

Forgotten. The word she couldn't bring herself to say, because who forgets their spouse? But the memories she once had of the man she had married and loved for most of her life were hazy, almost dream-like, and no matter how hard she tried she could not remember his face. Ever since that day of the earthquakes in the city, when he vanished and presumably died, she felt her grip on those memories slowly weakening.

Donna cleared her throat. "My husband has been dead for a year now. The quakes last year…"

No body. No trace.

The young man frowned, nodded in understanding. He turned to his sister and tried to usher her back to their car. "Come on, sis—"

"No," the girl said, "you don't understand, Mrs. Candle. He told us to find you." She pulled away from her brother and drew close to Donna. "After I was there, I started having these weird dreams, except they didn't feel like dreams at all. They felt like memories. I was down in the subway tunnels, living with a group of people, and everything was…I don't know how to explain it. Gray? Everything was gray, like an old movie, and there were these monsters, and…" She reached out and took Donna's hand. "There was a man there. He saved me. He took me out of there, brought me back here, and I think his name was Donovan Candle. I think seeing his name made me remember."

At any other time, this would have been the moment when Donna politely asked them to leave her property, only she didn't, and for reasons she could not bring herself to confess. Reasons sheathed in a haze of gray and lost somewhere along the empty streets of a dead city.

"See? I told you she wouldn't believe you. Come on, Brenda, let's go."

"No, Craig, I didn't tell her about the man in the tunnel."

Donna took a breath, confused. "What man? The one in your dream?"

Brenda shook her head. "A different man. A real man. He was down there. Homeless, I think, but I'm not sure. I thought he was a busker, but he didn't have an instrument or anything. He was just…there, you know? Like he was waiting for someone. And the weirdest thing is, I couldn't remember his face after the tour was over. It's like a weird gray spot in my head." She looked at her brother, who was frowning, embarrassed. "You couldn't either, Craig. Look, I've taken the tour twice since then, and he's always been there."

"Why did you go back?"

"I wasn't sure it had happened. Even Craig wasn't sure. Like the whole thing was a dream, and I couldn't get it out of my head. Like déjà vu but a hundred times stronger. Anyway, the next time I went, I figured the wall would be clean, and the man would be gone. They were both still there." She reached into her pocket. "This last time—yesterday—he gave me this. He said, 'If she's ready to remember, tell her I'm not afraid anymore.'"

She gave Donna a thin slip of paper. There were words, some of them faded with age, but the two which caught her eye sparked a surge of memories so intense she became lightheaded.

"Mrs. Candle?" Brenda put her hand on Donna's shoulder.

"Yeah," Donna whispered, "I'm okay. I'll be okay. Thank you for this—Brenda, right? Thank you."

"Sure," the girl said. "I thought you should know. He seems to be waiting for you, and…in my dreams, there was a story about the man who saved us. They said he was just trying to get home to you."

Donna forced a smile and thanked them again. She waited until they'd driven away before glancing at the row of flower bouquets left along her doorstep. Then she looked at the strange man's gift once again. A concert ticket stub from the old club downtown, closed now for a decade. The only legible text was "Admit One" printed across the top, and a date.

Their date.

I think I'm falling in love with you, Donnie Candle. She pocketed the stub and wiped the tears from her eyes.

———————•———————

That evening, she sat upright in bed with her laptop open. Alexandra sat next to her, babbling as she played with her toys. A cartoon played on the television, painting the room in a warm technicolor glow, but the baby was more occupied with the building blocks in her hands.

On her screen, Donna read about the city reopening the old subway station as a preservation effort. Local tourism revenue, job creation, and a push to clean up the long-derelict south side were cited as the primary reasons.

Job creation.

She looked down at Alexandra and smiled. "What do you think, baby girl? Do you think mama could be a tour guide?"

Alexandra cooed. She set down her blocks and pointed to the screen. "Da…"

Donna gasped. She'd tried coaxing words from the child every day for the last couple of months, basic nouns from bird to dog to mama. "Daddy" wasn't one of them. She couldn't bear to think about teaching the child a word for someone who wasn't there. She might as well have tried to teach Alexandra to say "gone" or "missing."

"What did you say, Alex?"

The infant grinned and cooed a mouthful of bubbles. She pointed again to the screen. "Da…da…dadadada."

"Okay," Donna whispered, turning to the nightstand where she'd placed the old ticket stub. She had fond memories of that night, even if she had nearly been injured in the crowd. For her it was the significance of the day as a whole, the day she realized she had fallen in love with him. He had suffered a broken nose to save her from that crowd, ditched the chance to see his favorite band perform so he could comfort her, and as they sat together in the park, she quietly realized she would marry him.

And yet those memories felt more like dreams with each passing day. His face had been erased somehow, a permanent blind spot in her mind's eye. Looking at old photographs hadn't helped either—his face was there and then gone again, the details slipping into a fog she could not penetrate.

Just like in her dreams. The real reason she hadn't kicked those kids off her property.

I heard about you in a dream.

She too had strange dreams in the last year. Dreams of a man she loved battling a bizarre creature that was killing the world. There was a labyrinth and there was a strange column stretching into the sky. There were monsters that twisted people into nightmarish mutations. Gaunt things that could eat men whole, and tiny things that could make others forget.

The stuff of nightmares, sure, maybe brought on by stress or hormones or literally anything else.

Or maybe they were memories. Ghosts of who she'd been, rising from their graves in an attempt to reach her.

If she's ready to remember, tell her I'm not afraid anymore.

Alexandra leaned her head against Donna's belly. "Mama."

Donna was overcome with a flood of emotion, bittersweet happiness and pride swirling in a stew of anxiety. But she had to be brave. This was about more than her now. "Good girl," she said, clapping her hands. "And your mama loves you."

After putting the baby to bed, Donna lay awake, staring at the empty space where Donovan used to be. She placed her hand there, and for the first time since giving birth, slipped into a deep and dreamless sleep.

"**A**nd here is the crown jewel of the city's former glory. Built in 1904…"

Donna followed the tour group into a cavernous room lined with colorful mosaic tile and archways. Chandeliers cast the station in a warm glow. One of the old subway cars had been relocated on the tracks and stood open at the end of the platform. She took it all in, breathing the stale air, feeling as though she had been here before. Or maybe not here, but somewhere nearby. Another dream, another hidden memory, one of those scenarios she was so certain had happened but did not feel real. It was like Brenda said: déjà vu, but a hundred times stronger.

Bright colors caught her eye. She broke away from the group, following the length of wall along the platform where a mural of words had been painted. Names and numbers and addresses. Business names. Messages scrawled as reminders. As expected, the message "REMEMBER DONOVAN CANDLE?" stretched across the entire wall, and her contact details followed below.

The tour guide, a fresh-faced college kid, noticed her interest. "Ah, this is the one part of the station we have decided not to renovate."

She turned to face him. "Why's that?"

"I'm not sure," he said, staring intently at the painted messages. "It's not the usual graffiti we find down here. It's almost like a place of reverence, I think. Too many people came here at some point to leave their memories in paint. Would seem wrong to wash it all away."

"Memories," she whispered, and reached out to trace her fingers along the words. "A wall full of memories."

"Yeah," the tour guide said. "That's what we heard some homeless folks call it, anyway. The Memory Wall." One of the other tourists called out to him. "If you'll excuse me… Yes, sir, what can I do for you?"

Donna looked at her fingertips. They were coated in white. The paint with her address was still fresh.

"Sorry about that. I thought it might've dried by now."

"It's okay, I—" She turned to find a man standing near the platform's edge. He carried a rolled sleeping bag beneath one arm, with a dusty backpack slung over one shoulder. His clothes were dirty, covered in stains, and hung loosely from his slender frame. She tried to make out the details of his face, but they were obscured somehow, hidden in shadow.

Only that wasn't right. It wasn't a shadow so much as a dark gray haze molded to the contours of his face. At a glance, she might have said he didn't have a face at all. She looked away to the others, but they were crowded around the tour guide, listening to a story he had to tell.

"I hope I didn't startle you."

"No, I..." She trailed off, felt foolish of her reluctance. "Just a weird sense of déjà vu, that's all. Did you paint this?"

The faceless man nodded. "I come here every day to wait. Ever have that feeling? Like you're waiting for something, but you don't know when it will arrive." He moved past her and placed his hand on the wall. "You spend all your time thinking about what you'll do when it gets here, and when it doesn't show, you start to think about all the things you've done. You start thinking maybe you did something wrong, or maybe you didn't do enough, and by the end you're a knotted ball of nerves. Just one big anxiety attack, living your life in a state of fear."

She listened, unsure what he was talking about, and afraid he might be unhinged. But some of his words resonated. Hadn't she spent countless nights wondering what she could have done differently? Hadn't she lost so much sleep wondering if her husband would return?

Hadn't she been driven from slumber by the absolute certainty he was still alive somewhere?

How much of her life had been dictated in fear these last several months? Fear of going on alone, fear of raising Alexandra alone, fear of losing her grip on the memories that meant so much to her—and fear of forgetting her partner in life and love. In her dreams, her memories, his face was already gone. His face—

"But you're not afraid anymore," she whispered. The faceless man turned toward her, and she thought she saw a hint of a smile, the blank contours turned upward slightly.

"No, I'm really not. Took me too long to figure that out. People close to me suffered because of it, and I had to put my life on pause for a while. To sort it all out up here, and then in here." He pointed to his head, and then to his heart. "You know what I discovered?"

He crossed the gap between them. Donna sucked in her breath, not quite afraid, but apprehensive. She wished she could see his face.

"I discovered that, despite everything I was afraid of, I am who I've always been meant to be. I am the only man I *can* be. And it took losing everything to find myself again, the man I always was, the man I always will be. The man I am."

A single tear slid down her cheek. She brushed it away, wished she could escape the cloying heat surrounding her face. The faceless man stared at her, waiting for the question he knew she wanted to ask. The question he needed her to ask.

"Who are you?"

"I know, but do you, Donna?"

She resisted the urge to walk away, resisted the fear dwelling in her heart, the nagging fear telling her this man was crazy, she needed to leave, she needed to run and never look back, forget this place and forget this job, she could find something else to pay the bills and support her daughter. This was all too strange, too dream-like, but like her so-called dreams of late, even being here with this man culled memories she thought were long forgotten. They were hazy, coated in the silt of unconsciousness, but as they rose from the murk of memory she saw herself a little younger, standing on the foot of a subway platform next to a man she loved more than any words would describe.

Heart pounding, her soul screaming, Donna Candle reached out and touched the man's face. The gray shadow slowly disintegrated beneath her fingertips, spreading outward across the man's features. Eyes. A nose. His mouth and chin framed in the shag of a coarse beard, streaked with the gray of age and experience, a coloration shared in his messy hair.

"I had to lose everything to find you again, just like I said I would." His eyes clouded with tears, and when he blinked them away, twin tributaries streaked down his dirty face. "I would for you," he whispered.

Donna swallowed the lump in her throat. She took his face in both her hands. "I know you," she said, her breath hot against his lips. "I'll always know you."

They kissed. A sensation of familiarity washed over her, a warmth in her chest like the sweetest of comforts, the relief of finding one's way back home.

She pulled back and smiled faintly. "I need to tell you a secret, and I'm not afraid to say it. I think I'm falling in love with you, Donovan Candle."

"That's okay, Donna Candle. I have a secret too. I fell for you a long time ago." He wrapped his arms around her and whispered in her ear. "And I am not afraid."

THE END

September 25th, 2006 - July 21st, 2021

IT'S A TRILOGY

T hose three words haunted me for nearly a decade.

I didn't set out to write a trilogy, but Amelia's insistence rang true: the ending I originally had in mind for the second novel just didn't work. It was rushed, a young writer's desperate effort to cross the finish line no matter what, and the story suffered. In that version, Sparrow was defeated, Donovan vanished into the Monochrome with Dullington, and other characters began receiving messages from Don over the ensuing weeks, ending with his reappearance and reunion with Donna.

That ending was too neat and tidy. Worse, it left a gaping hole in the plot: What, exactly, was Donovan doing in the Monochrome for those weeks? Amelia gave me an ultimatum: either I write a third book, or add another 70k words to the second. Naturally, I chose the path of least resistance—a cliffhanger ending with the promise of resolution in a third and final novel.

And that's where this story almost ended.

The second novel didn't sell very well, a fact that I didn't come to terms with until the following year among a dark period of depression and self-reflection. Why bother writing a third novel when no one bothered to read the second? I couldn't answer that question at the time. Pressure from readers about the whereabouts of the final novel didn't help, nor did the constant feelings of failure. Desperate for a change, I set the Monochrome aside and returned to short fiction, something I hadn't written since college.

Those stories became the building blocks of my first collection, *Ugly Little Things*, which was published five years after *The Liminal Man. Devil's*

Creek followed and took off in ways I didn't anticipate, and…well, if you're a fan of mine, you already know this story.

But somewhere between completing that monstrous tome and finding a home for it, I began thinking about the last Monochrome novel again. There had been several false starts along the way—about one every year, I think. The problem I ran into every time was that I couldn't connect the dots between plot events. Sure, I knew the Monochrome and Spectrum would collapse into one another, I knew there was a bigger villain, and that Donovan would have to go deeper into the Monochrome in order to escape. But connecting the dots in between proved elusive for reasons I still don't understand.

Maybe it was the pressure, or maybe I was just burned out from Donovan's story. I'd outgrown him in a lot of ways, both as a person and as a writer. Writing *Devil's Creek* unlocked something for me, though. Maybe it was a matter of confidence, or the simple realization of "Hey, I can actually do this," but I finally saw ways to connect those scenes.

Nonentity was the result. About 80k words, give or take. A smidge more than the 70k that Amelia suggested back in 2012.

The key to writing that book was revising the first two so that elements of the plot made better sense. Pontius Vile's presence had to be there from the start, even while we think Dullington is the real villain; Dullington's more menacing presence in the earlier drafts was softened as a result; and then there's Cosma, the Ungod and Great Weaver, with subtle references throughout as well.

Once the holes were patched up and I could view the plot as a single thread, everything else fell into place. Even as the world fell under the spell of Covid-19 in 2020, I found some comfort in returning to Donovan's story, and in doing so I realized I'd found the reason why I *should* bother—and why I couldn't write it sooner, despite all those failed attempts.

I bothered to complete the trilogy because it's what I wanted to do. And I couldn't write it sooner because I wasn't ready yet. Looking back on these books, I see myself and the growth I had to undergo as a person to tell each part of the story. I see a child, I see a young man, and I see an adult who's finally found his purpose.

Donovan's journey was my journey away from fear. The time I spent between books two and three was necessary because I had to find my own way out of the Monochrome first. It couldn't have happened any other way.

The Monochrome Trilogy is and has always been about self-discovery, identity, and purpose. It was a springboard earlier in my career when I was still trying to figure out what kind of writer I wanted to be. I began the story in 2006 when I was 23 years old, finished it in 2021 when I was 38, and now, at 42, I think the trilogy was my way of processing growth into adulthood. A way of processing my life and the many turns it took to get where I am today.

In closing, I'll share an anecdote: In 2013, I developed appendicitis, and had the good fortune of being an overnight guest at St. Joseph's. Somewhere in between drinking a gross vanilla-flavored contrast solution for my MRI and being shot full of morphine, I managed to send a message to loved ones about the impending surgery.

Amelia responded, "Don't die, Todd. Remember, it's a trilogy."

And goddammit, folks, she was right.

Thanks for reading.

Todd Keisling
Womesldorf, Pennyslvania
May 7th, 2025

ACKNOWLEDGMENTS

I can't count how many times I've said "thank you" over the last nineteen years regarding this series, nor can I recall all the names. Friends, family, some now estranged, some who've shuffled off this mortal coil, and some who are closer than ever—all of them had a hand in making this series what it is. And you all know who you are.

So, here's one more: Thank you. For taking the time to read these weird books; for being patient and keeping Donovan Candle's spirit alive over the years; for helping a kid with big dreams take his first step toward achieving them. Y'all didn't have to come along for the ride, but you did anyway, and it made this journey a lot less lonely. I've come a long way since that law firm copy room where Donovan Candle was born, and I owe it all to you, Readers. Thank you for everything.

I'll see you further down the road, somewhere in the Southland.

-TK

Photo Credit: Wayne Becker / Zerbe Photography

TODD KEISLING is the two-time Bram Stoker Award®-nominated author of *Devil's Creek, Scanlines, Cold, Black & Infinite,* and most recently, *The Sundowner's Dance,* among several others. A pair of his earlier works were recipients of the University of Kentucky's Oswald Research & Creativity Prize for Creative Writing (2002 and 2005), and his second novel, *The Liminal Man,* was an Indie Book Award finalist in Horror & Suspense (2013). He lives in Pennsylvania with his family.